Jonathan Franzen is also the author of the novels *The Twenty-Seventh City* and *The Corrections*. His fiction and non-fiction appear frequently in *The New Yorker* and *Harper's*, and he was named one of the best novelists under forty by *Granta* and *The New Yorker*. He lives in New York City.

$12
IZM

STRONG

MOTION

A Novel

Jonathan Franzen

FOURTH ESTATE • *London* and *New York*

First published in the United States by Farrar, Straus and Giroux
First published in Australia in 2003 by
Fourth Estate
A Division of HarperCollins*Publishers*
77–85 Fulham Palace Road
London W6 8JB
www.4thestate.com

10 9 8 7 6 5 4 3 2 1

Grateful acknowledgement is made for permission to reprint lyrics
from the following songs:
"Marie Provost" (N. Lowe) Copyright © 1977 Rock Music Company Limited;
"I Love the Sound of Breaking Glass" (N. Lowe, A. Bodner, S. Golding)
Copyright © 1978 Rock Music Company Limited; "See No Evil" (T. Verlaine)
Copyright © 1978 Double Exposure Music, Inc.

The characters in this novel, as well as the character of certain familiar
institutions that appear in it, are entirely imaginary.

A catalogue record for this book is available from the British Library

ISBN 1-84115-749-X

Printed and bound by Griffin Press, Netley, Australia

For Valerie

Grateful acknowledgment of support is made to the Mrs. Giles Whiting Foundation, the Corporation of Taddo, Sven-Erik and Marianne Ekström, and Dieter and Inge Rahtz. Thanks also to Lorrie Fürrer and Robert Franzen, and especially to Göran Ekström for his advice and seismograms. Parts of Chapter 13 draw heavily on William Cronon's *Changes in the Land* (Hill & Wang, 1983).

A rock was sticking out of the water, jagged and pointed, covered with moss—a remnant of the Ice Age and of the glacier that had once gouged out this basin in the earth. It had withstood the rains, the snows, the frost, the heat. It was afraid of no one. It did not need redemption, it had already been redeemed.

—I. B. SINGER

I

Default Gender

1

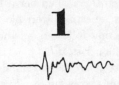

Sometimes when people asked Eileen Holland if she had any brothers or sisters, she had to think for a moment.

In grade school she and her friends had played foursquare during recess, and when fights broke out in far corners of the playground, it usually turned out that the person whose face was being smashed into the blacktop was her younger brother, Louis. She and her friends would continue to bounce their ball from square to square. They were skipping rope the day Louis fought a boy on the top tier of the old tetanus-infested jungle gym and damaged a different part of himself on each of the pipes he hit during his fall, breaking off his front teeth on level three, bruising his ribs on level two, getting a concussion by impact and whiplash on level one, and stunning his diaphragm on the asphalt. Eileen's friends ran to look at the possibly dead boy. She was left holding the jump rope and feeling as if she'd fallen and no one would help her.

Eileen was a faithful and pretty image of her mother, with astonished dark eyes and pencil-thin eyebrows, a high forehead and plump cheeks and straight dark hair. She had the limbs of a willow tree and sometimes she even swayed like one, with her eyes closed, when she was so happy to be among her friends that she forgot they were there.

Louis, like his father, was less ornamental. From the age of ten onward he wore aviator-style glasses whose metal frames vaguely matched his hair, which was curly and the color of old brass screws, and was thinning by the time he finished high school. His father had also donated a barrel chest to his genetics. In junior high and high school new friends of Eileen's expected to be told, "No, no relation," when they asked her if Louis Holland was her brother. To Eileen these questions were like vaccination shots. The soothing alcohol swab that followed was her friends' avowal that her brother was not like her *at all*.

"Yeah," she'd agree, "we're real different."

The young Hollands grew up in Evanston, Illinois, in the shadow of Northwestern University, which employed their father as a history professor. Once in a while, in the afternoon, Eileen caught sight of Louis in a booth at McDonald's surrounded by the misfits he hung out with, their snide menu selections, their cigarettes and pasty faces and military clothing. The negativity emanating from his booth made her feel like she couldn't wedge herself tightly enough between the elbows of her peers. She was, she told herself, very different from Louis. But she was never entirely safe from him. Even in the middle of a jammed and laughing back seat she would glance out a window just in time to see her brother striding along the trashy shoulder of some six-lane suburban thoroughfare, his white shirt gray with sweat, his glasses white with road glare. It always seemed that he was there for her alone to see, an apparition from that parallel private world which she herself had stopped living in when she started having friends but which Louis still obviously inhabited: the world where you were by yourself.

One day in the summer before she started college she suddenly needed to use the family car to see her boyfriend Judd, who lived farther up the Lake Michigan shore in Lake Forest. When Louis pointed out that he'd reserved the car a week earlier, she became furious with him, the way a person gets with an inanimate object that she keeps dropping and mishandling. Finally she made her mother go ask Louis to be selfless, just this once, and let her use the car to visit her boyfriend. When she got to Judd's house she was still so furious that she left the keys in the ignition. The car was promptly stolen.

The Lake Forest police were not particularly nice to her. Her mother was even less nice, on the telephone. And Louis, when she finally got home, came down the stairs in a diver's mask.

"Eileen," her mother said. "Honey. You let the car roll in the lake. Nobody stole the car. I just got a call from Mrs. Wolstetter. You didn't set the emergency brake and you didn't put the car in Park. It rolled across the Wolstetters' lawn into the lake."

"Park, Eileen?" Louis's voice was glassed-in and adenoidal. "The little 'P' on the far left? N for Neutral? P for Park?"

"Louis," their mother said.

"Or is it N for No and P for . . . Proceed? D for Desist?"

After this trauma Eileen could no longer retain information about where Louis was or what he was doing. She knew he went to school in Houston and was majoring in something like electrical engineering, but when her mother alluded to him on the telephone, perhaps to mention that he'd changed his major, the room Eileen was calling from suddenly got noisy. She couldn't remember what her mother had just said. She had to ask, "So he's majoring in—what now?" And the room got noisy again! She couldn't remember what her mother was saying even as she said it! And so she never did figure out what Louis was majoring in. When she saw him during Christmas vacation of her second year of graduate school —she was getting her MBA from Harvard—she had to make a wild guess about what he'd been doing since he graduated from Rice: "Mom tells me you're, like, designing microchips?"

He stared at her.

She shook her head no no no no, cancel that. "Tell me what you're doing," she said humbly.

"I'm staring at you in amazement."

Later her mother told her he was working for an FM radio station in Houston.

Eileen lived near Central Square in Cambridge. Her apartment was on the eighth floor of a modern high-rise, a tower of concrete that loomed above the ambient brick and clapboard like a thing that had failed to erode, with shops and a fish restaurant in the basement. She was at home making triple-fudge brownies one night at the end of March when Louis, whom she'd last seen reading a crime novel by the Christmas tree in Evanston, called her up and informed her that he'd moved from Houston to the town of Somerville, Cambridge's budget-class neighbor to the north. She asked what had brought him to Somerville. Microchips, he said.

The person who walked into her apartment a few days later, on a raw late-winter night, was effectively a stranger. At twenty-three, Louis was nearly bald on top, with just enough curls remaining to have captured sleet. His crude black oxfords squeaked on Eileen's linoleum as he walked around her kitchen in a star-shaped path, slowly ricocheting off the counters. His cheeks and nose were red and his glasses were white with fog.

"This is so contemporary," he said, meaning the apartment.

Eileen pressed her elbows to her sides and crossed her wrists on her chest. She had all four stove burners going full blast and a pot simmering on one of them. "Can't keep it *warm* enough," she said. She was wearing a bulky sweater, fluffy slippers, and a mini-skirt. "I think they turn the furnace off on April first."

Her doorbell rang. She buzzed. "It's Peter," she said.

"Peter."

"My boyfriend."

Soon there was a knock on the door, and she led the boyfriend, Peter Stoorhuys, into the kitchen. Peter's lips were blue with cold, and his skin, which was suntanned, was a leaden gray. He hopped up and down, his hands in the pockets of his twills, while Eileen made introductions that he was evidently too frozen to pay attention to. "Shit," he said, crouching by the stove. "It's cold out there."

There was a tiredness to Peter's face that no suntan could conceal. It was one of those urban faces that had been reconceived so many times that the skin, like a piece of paper smudged and abraded by multiple erasures, had lost its capacity to hold a clear image. Beneath the shadings of his current neo-Angeleno look were visible traces of a yuppie, a punk, a preppie, and a head. Repeated changes of style, like too much combing, had sapped his long blond hair of its resilience. For weather protection he was wearing a houndstooth jacket and a collarless shirt.

"Peter and I were in St. Kitts last month," Eileen explained to Louis. "We still haven't readjusted."

Peter put his white-knuckled hands over two burners on the stove and toasted them, investing this warming process with such importance that there was little Eileen and Louis could do but look at him.

"He looks like a total sillybird in hats," Eileen said.

"I find *coats* useful in this regard," Louis said, dropping his fiberfill jacket in a corner. He was dressed in his uniform of the last eight years, a white shirt and black jeans.

"You see, that's the thing," Eileen said. "His favorite coat is at the cleaner's. Is that a silly place for it to be?"

It was another five minutes before Peter was thawed enough to allow them all to retire to the living room. Eileen curled up on the sofa, pulling the hem of her sweater down over her bare knees and draping one arm over the back of the sofa just in time to receive the glass of whiskey Peter had poured her. Louis paced around the room, stopping to bring his face myopically close to books and other consumer goods. All of the apartment's furnishings were new and most were combinations of white planes, black cylinders, and cherry-red plastic hardware.

"So, Louis," Peter said, joining Eileen with a whiskey. "Tell us a little about yourself."

Louis was examining the VCR's remote-control box. In the big steamed windows the distant lights of Harvard Square formed halos the color of mother-of-pearl.

"You're in communications," Peter prompted.

"I work for a radio station," Louis said in a very slow and very level voice. "It's called WSNE . . . ? News with a Twist . . . ?"

"Sure," Peter said. "I'm familiar with it. Not that I ever listen, but I've dealt with them a couple times. In fact I understand they're in some doo-doo, financially. Not to say that's not the norm for a thousand-watt station. One thing I'd suggest is try to get paid at the end of every week, and whatever you do don't let 'em involve you in any kind of ownership scheme—"

"Oh I won't," Louis said, so earnestly it would have made an observant person wary.

"I mean, go ahead if you want," Peter continued. "But, uh— a word to the wise."

"Peter sells ad space for Boston magazine," Eileen said.

"Among other things," Peter said.

"He's thinking of applying to the business school in the fall. Not that he hardly even needs to. He knows so much stuff, Louis. He knows tons more than I do."

"Do you know how to listen?" Louis said suddenly.

Peter's eyes narrowed. "What do you mean?"

"Do you know how to listen when you've asked somebody a question about themself?"

Peter turned to Eileen to consult about this remark. He seemed to have some doubts concerning its purport. Eileen jumped to her feet. "He was just giving you some *advice*, Louis. We all have lots of time to listen to each other. We're all very interested in—each other! I'm going to get some breadsticks."

As soon as she was out of the room, Louis sat down on the sofa and put his hand on Peter's shoulder, his ruddy face right next to Peter's ear. "Hey, friend," he said. "I have some advice for you too."

Peter stared straight ahead, his eyes widening a little at the pressure of a swallowed smile. Louis leaned even closer. "Don't you want to hear my advice?"

"You've got some problem," Peter observed.

"Wear coats!"

"Louis?" Eileen called from the kitchen. "Are you being strange to Peter?"

Louis thumped Peter's knee and went around behind the sofa. On the floor, on a folded-out newspaper, was a cage in which a gerbil was availing itself of an exercise wheel. The gerbil ran haltingly, pausing to stumble with its microscopic toenails on a crossbar, then galloping onward with its head high and its neck turned to one side. It didn't seem to be enjoying itself.

"You silly bird." Eileen had returned from the kitchen with a faceted beer mug full of breadsticks. She handed them to Peter. "I keep telling Peter our whole family's wacko. I've been warning him since the day we met not to take it personally." With breathtaking suddenness and fluidity she dropped to her knees and, unlatching the door of the cage, extracted the gerbil by its tail. She raised it above her head and peered up at its twitching nose. Its front paws clawed the air ineffectually. "Isn't that right, Milton Friedman?" She opened her mouth like a wolf, as if to bite its head off. Then she lowered it onto her upturned palm and it ran up the sleeve of her sweater to her shoulder, where she recaptured it and boxed it in her hands so that only its whiskered, pointed face stuck out. "Say hi to my brother Louis?" She thrust the gerbil's face up close to Louis's. It looked like a furry penis with eyes.

"Hello, rodent," he said.

"What's that?" She brought the gerbil to her ear and listened closely. "He says hello, person. Hello to Uncle Louis." She popped the animal back in the cage and latched the door. Still anthropomorphized but free now, it seemed imbecilic or rude as it ran to the tube of its water bottle and nibbled on a droplet. For a moment longer Eileen remained kneeling, hands pressing on her knees, head tilted to one side as if she had water in her ear. Then with the fluid quickness at which Louis was visibly marveling she went and rejoined Peter on the sofa with a bounce. "Peter and Milton Friedman," she said. "Are not on the best of terms right now. Milton Friedman did number one on some poplin trousers that Peter was very attached to."

"How funny," Louis said. "How terribly, terribly funny."

"I think I'm going to take off," Peter said.

"Oh come on, be patient," Eileen said. "Louis is just protective. You're my boyfriend but he's my brother. You guys will just have to get along. Have to put-choo in the same cage together. You can have the wheel to walk on, Louis, and I'll put some Chivas in the bottle for my little sozzlebird. Ha ha ha!" Eileen laughed. "We'll get Milton Friedman some poplin trousers!"

Peter drained his glass and rose. "I'm going to get going."

"OK, I'm being a little hard to take," Eileen said in a completely different voice. "I'll stop. Let's loosen up. Let's be adults."

"You be adults," Peter said. "I've got work to do."

Without looking back, he left the room and the apartment.

"Oh great," Eileen said. "Thanks." She dropped her head back over the top of the sofa and looked at Louis with upside-down eyes. Her narrow eyebrows were like unbreathing lips, and without brows above them the eyes had an expression foreign to the human vocabulary, an oracular strangeness. "What'd you say to him?"

"I told him he should wear coats."

"Real cute, Louis." She stood up and put some boots on. "What's wrong with you?" She ran down the hall and out the door.

Louis observed her departure with little interest. He wiped a porthole in the condensation on the window and looked down at the taillight-pinkened sleet that was falling on Mass Ave. The telephone rang.

He went to the communications equipment, which sat on its own little table, and ran his eyes over it as if it were a buffet where nothing appealed to him. Finally, after the fifth ring, the machine not coming on, he picked up the receiver. "Hello?"

"Peter?" The speaker was an old woman with a tremor in her voice. "Peter, I've been trying and trying—"

"This isn't Peter."

There was an uneasy rustle. Muttering an apology, the woman asked for Eileen. Louis offered to take a message.

"Who's this?" the woman asked.

"This is Eileen's brother. Louis."

"*Louis?* Well, for goodness' sake. This is Grandmother."

He stared at the window for a long time. "Who?" he said.

"Rita Kernaghan. *Grandmother.*"

"Oh. Hey. Grandmother. Hey."

"I don't believe we've met but once."

Belatedly Louis recalled an image, the image of a potbellied woman with a painted kitty-cat face who was already seated at a table at the Berghoff, in Chicago on a snowy evening, when he and his parents and Eileen trooped in. This was some seven years ago—about a year after his mother had flown to Boston for her father's funeral. Of the Berghoff dinner he remembered nothing but a plate of braised rabbit with potato pancakes. And Rita Kernaghan touching Eileen's hair and calling her a doll? Or was this some other dinner, some other old woman, or maybe a dream?

Not grandmother: step-grandmother.

"Yes," he said. "I remember. You live around here."

"Just outside Ipswich, yes. You're visiting your sister?"

"No, I work here. I work for a radio station."

This information seemed to interest Rita Kernaghan. She pressed Louis for details. Was he an announcer? Did he know the programming director? She proposed they have a drink together. "You can get to know me a little. Shall we say after work on Friday? I'll be in the city in the evening."

"All right," Louis said.

No sooner had they set a time and place than Rita Kernaghan murmured goodbye and the line went dead. Moments later Eileen returned to the apartment, wet and angry, and disappeared into the kitchen. "No dinner till you apologize to me!" she said.

Louis frowned thoughtfully, consuming breadsticks.

"You were very childish and very bullyish," Eileen said. "I want you to apologize to me."

"I will not. He wouldn't even shake hands with me."

"He was *cold!*"

Louis rolled his eyes at his sister's sincerity. "All right," he said. "I'm sorry I messed up your dinner."

"Well, don't do it again. I happen to be very fond of Peter."

"Do you love him?"

The question brought Eileen out of the kitchen with a confounded look on her face. Louis had never asked her anything even remotely so personal. She sat down by him on the sofa and reached for her toes, in a leg-shaving posture, the tip of her nose resting lightly on one knee. "Sometimes I think I do," she said. "I'm not the real romantic type, though. Milton Friedman's more my speed. I mean, it's funny you should ask."

"Isn't it the obvious question?"

Still bent over, she closed one eye and studied him. "You seem different," she said.

"Different from what?"

She shook her head, unwilling to admit it had never occurred to her that her little brother might, at the age of twenty-three, be acquainted with the concept of love. She gave careful attention to her ankles, fingering the round protruding bones, pinching the tendons in back and rocking a little. Her face was already losing prettiness. Time and sun and business school had made her color more shallow, a conceivable middle-aged Eileen suddenly beginning to show through like old wallpaper beneath a coat of new paint. She looked up at Louis shyly. "It's nice we're in the same city again."

"Yeah."

She became even more tentative. "You like your job?"

"Too early to say."

"Would you give Peter a chance, Louis? He comes on a little arrogant but he's very vulnerable underneath."

"Which reminds me," Louis said. "He got a phone call while you were out. I was like, Grandmother? Grandmother who?"

"Oh. Rita. She tried to get me to call her Grandmother too."

"It slipped my mind that she existed."

"That's because she and Mom are like—agggggh." Eileen started strangling herself with both hands. "Do you know anything about this?"

"You know when the last time I had a real conversation with Mom was? Ferguson Jenkins was on the Cubs' roster."

"Well, but apparently Grandpa made a whole lot of money at some point, and when he died he didn't leave anything at all to Mom or Aunt Heidi, because he was married to Rita. Rita got everything."

"Definitely not the way to Mom's heart."

"Except Peter says Rita didn't really get anything either. It's all in a trust fund."

"What's Peter know about this?"

"He was Rita's publicist. That's how I met him." Eileen hopped up and went to her bookshelf. "Rita turned New Agey after Grandpa died. She's got a pyramid on the roof of the house. She keeps her wine in the barn because she thinks it won't mature under the pyramid. This is her new book." She handed Louis a thin, hot-pink volume. "She has them printed by some pretend publisher in Worcester, and they all come in one shipment, on these huge flats. Last time I was at her house she had them all in the barn, with the wine. Just this massive wall of books. That's what she needs a publicist for, and for her lectures too. But listen, do you want tortellini with red sauce or linguine with white clam sauce?"

"Whichever's easier."

"Well, they're both in bags."

"Tortellini," Louis said. The title of the hot-pink book was *Princess Itaray: An Atlantean Case History*. On the title page the author had written: *To Eileen, my little doll, with love from Grandmother*. Louis paged through the book, which was divided into

chapters and subchapters and sub-subchapters with boldface num-
bered headings:

**4.1.8   Implications of the Disappearance of the Dime-
sian Appendage: A Reversible Fall from Eden?**

He looked at the flap copy. *In this fanciful yet erudite work,
Dr. Kernaghan advances the hypothesis that the cornerstone of
Atlantean society was the universal gratification of sexual desire,
and proposes that the human appendix, now a vestigial organ,
was, among the Atlanteans, both external and highly functional.
With the hypnotic regression of a 14-year-old schoolgirl, Mary
M—— of Beverly, Massachusetts, Dr. Kernaghan embarks on a
compelling exploration of Atlantean deep psychology, the historical
origins of repressed sexuality, and the modern world's potential
for a return to a golden age . . .*

"She's written two other books too," Eileen said.

"She's a doctor?"

"Some honorary degree. Milton Friedman thinks it's the silliest
thing he's ever heard of, isn't that right, Milton Friedman? Peter
helped her a lot—got her on the radio and on TV a couple times.
He has all kinds of connections and he's only in it part-time. Eventually he had to tell her to get somebody else, though. For one
thing she drinks an awful lot. She also talks about Grandpa like
he's alive and talks to her all the time. You don't know whether
you're supposed to laugh or not."

Louis didn't mention that he'd made a date for drinks with
this woman.

"But anyway, that's how I met Peter. She's got a beautiful
estate, you probably don't remember it. We stayed there for a week
or something when we were little. You remember?"

Louis shook his head.

"Neither do I, really. Rita wasn't on the scene yet. I mean, she
was still Grandpa's secretary. Sometimes I wonder what we'd think
of him if he was still alive."

For the rest of the evening Louis sat in various chairs and
Eileen orbited. A plate of food was something towards which she

showed no particular sense of responsibility; she left the table and came back; her food was at her mercy. When Louis put his coat on to leave, she awkwardly patted his arm and, still more awkwardly, embraced him. "Take care of yourself, huh?"

He tore himself away. "What do you mean take care of myself? Where do you think I'm going? I'm going two and a half miles."

She kept her hand on his shoulder until he was out the door. Moments later, as she turned the news on, there was a knock. Louis was standing in the hall, businesslike, looking aside with a frown. "I just remembered something," he said. "I just remembered the place in Ipswich, Mom's father's place. We threw rocks—"

"Oh!" Eileen's face lit up. "At the horses."

"We threw rocks at the horses—"

"To save them!"

"To save them from dying. So you remember too. We thought they'd die if they stood still."

"Yes."

"That was all." His round shoulders turned away from her. "See you later."

In high school Louis had never become so disaffected that he apologized for loving radio. Radio was like a crippled pet or retarded sibling that he always made time for and didn't mind— didn't even notice—if people laughed at. When Eileen saw him out walking in distant wastelands he was generally in transit to or from an airconditioned and empty electronics-supply store in some weedy plaza where the only other going concern was a Chinese restaurant in the last of its nine lives, and maybe a depopulated pet store. From the wall of prepackaged ICs and RF connectors and micropots and gator clips and jumpers and variable capacitors he selected components from the top of his wish list and added up the prices in his head, guessing on the sales tax, and handed them to the sad mustached man who preferred to sell stereo systems, and paid for them with the small bills that neighbors had given him for doing low-caste work: wall-washing; brush-clearing; dog-related services. He was ten when he got a crystal diode set, twelve when he built his HeathKit shortwave radio, fourteen when he became WC9HDD, and sixteen when he got his general license. Radio was his thing, his interest. A kid derives a satisfaction that rivals sex or maybe instead connects with it along obscure mental byways when he puts together a few simple metal and ceramic objects—objects he knows to be simple because he has experimentally destroyed many of them with screwdriver and pliers—and connects them to a battery and hears distant voices in his bedroom. There were stray resistors on his bedspread, resistors whose color coding he'd known by heart a year before he learned about sperm and eggs, the afternoon he lost his virginity. "Ouch, what is this?" (It was a 220-ohm metal-film resistor with a gold tolerance band.) Louis also happened to be one of the few ham operators in greater Chicago willing to speak or encode in French, and so when the sunspots were heavy he could be kept busy half the night trading temperature readings and autobiographical data with operators in all the snowed-in corners of Quebec. Which didn't make him talkative in French class, only bored, since anything he did really well he kept hidden.

He entered Rice University as a prospective double-E major and left it with a degree in French, having in the meantime managed KTRU, the campus station, for three semesters. A week after graduation he went to work for a local C&W station, attending to relatively attractive duties for the abrupt abandoning of which after only eight months he would give no more satisfactory account to Eileen than the question: "Why does anybody quit a job?"

The studios of WSNE, his new employer, were in the western suburb of Waltham, in an office building overlooking one corner of the forty acres devoted to the intersection of Route 128 ("America's Technology Region") and the Mass Pike. Louis's job title was board operator, a peonic position that involved operating the cartridge player, cuing up records, and backtiming the AP network news, but he did this only from six to ten in the morning, because only the morning drive announcer, Dan Drexel, was considered irreplaceable enough to rate his own operator. Louis understood that the remainder of his workday, which ended at 3 p.m., was to be spent on exciting tasks like entering traffic data on a keyboard, transferring agency commercials from reel to cart, writing PSAs, and grading the contest entries with which the station's dwindling listenership sought to win various worthless gifts. He understood that he would be paid the federal minimum wage.

One reason he had had little competition for the job was that WSNE's bid for license renewal in June was expected not to be routine. Paychecks were issued with precise instructions about when and when not to attempt to cash them. The insatiable payroll had gotten into the main production studio and torn out the sound equipment and acoustical panels and everything else with resale value, leaving ragged empty rectangles with exposed particle board in the Formica consoles, and butterscotch-colored glue spots on the walls. A new FM college station had bought all of WSNE's record collection except the juvenile section (the Care Bears' entire LP oeuvre; the Muppets; the original Disney sound track of *Winnie-the-Pooh*; the Flintstones doing times tables) and the comedy recordings. The grooves of the latter were rapidly being worn smooth by WSNE's morning News with a Twist programming, which interlarded news and comment with "the funniest routines of all time."

A man named Alec Bressler owned and operated WSNE. Alec was a Russian émigré of German extraction who in the mid-sixties had allegedly paddled from Kaliningrad to Sweden in a rubber dinghy. The only official duty he gave himself was to tape the daily broadcast editorial, but he was always hovering in the studios, observing with immense satisfaction that electricity was flowing through all the necessary circuits, that this station that belonged to him was actually functioning and transmitting his chosen programs. He was a moderately paunchy fifty, with East-bloc hair, devalued somehow and slow to grow, and skin grayed by a cigarette habit he resisted only to the extent of addicting himself to nicotine lozenges as well. He dressed in thin sweaters and faded, thigh-hugging, too-short pants, each pair of which looked old enough to have come along with him in the legendary dinghy.

Louis soon realized that one of the functions he was expected to serve was to be a private audience for Alec Bressler. "Do you like expressing opinions?" the owner asked him on his second day of work, when he was printing out affidavits for commercial sponsors. "I just expressed a really good one. I commented on a current event. Can you guess which one?"

Louis's face became guarded, ready to be amused. "Tell me," he said.

Alec seated himself on the air and groped backwards to pull a chair over. "This horrible plane crash on the weekend. I forget which midwestern state, it starts with 'I.' Two hundred nineteen dead, no survivors. Complete dis-in-te-gration of the fuselage. I questioned the nooseworthiness of this event. With all respect to the families of the dead, why do we have to see this on television? We see it last month, why see it again? If people want to see crashes, why don't we look at Navy missiles and Air Force planes that crash any time we test them. If people want to see death, let's take the cameras to the hospitals, eh? See how most people die. I told what we can watch instead of network noose which should be boycotted. There's M*A*S*H, same time, also Cheers and Family Ties and Matt Houston. Better commercials too. Let's watch these programs. Or let's read a book, but I didn't stress that. I say read a book too much."

"Isn't this kind of a lost cause?" Louis said.

Alec pressed on the armrests of his chair and slid his butt farther back, the better to lean forward and claim whatever tiny portion of Louis's attention he hadn't claimed already. "I bought this station eight years ago," he said. "It had real strong local noose coverage, popular music, also Bruins games. For eight years I try to *remove politics* from WSNE. It's my 'American Dream'—a station where people talk all day long (no music—it's cheat-ting!) and not a WORD about politics. This is my American Dream. Radio with talk all day and *no ideology*. Let's talk about art, philosophy, humor, life. Let's talk about being a human being. And closer I come to my goal—you can plot this on the graph, Louis—closer I come to my goal, fewer people listen to me! Now we have one hour of current events all total in the morning, and people listen for that one hour of noose. We all know Jack Benny is more fun than Geneva arm talks. But take away Geneva and they stop listening to Jack Benny. This is the way people are. I know this. I have it plotted on a graph."

He grouped his fingers and tweezed a cigarette out of a Benson & Hedges pack. "Who's the girl?" he asked, inclining his head towards a snapshot in a half-open drawer. The young woman in the picture had dark rings beneath her eyes and a shaved head.

"A person I knew in Houston," Louis said.

Alec ducked, and ducked again as if to say: Fair enough. Then he ducked once more, very affirmatively, and left the office without another word.

After work on Friday Louis drove his six-year-old Civic down the Mass Pike into Boston and parked it on the top level of a garage with the dimensions and profile of an aircraft carrier. A wind from the east lent a forlorn sort of finality to his car-leaving procedure, which involved peering in through the driver-side window, slapping the keys in his pants pocket, lifting the handle of the locked driver-side door, slowly circling the car and checking the passenger-side door, slapping the keys again, and giving the machine a last, hard, worried look. He was due to meet Rita Kernaghan at the Ritz-Carlton in two hours.

An advancing warm front had begun to curdle the clear blue of the sky. In the North End, a slender neon boot named ITALIA kicked a monstrous neon boulder named SICILIA. It was impossible to escape the words MEAT MARKET. The Italians who lived here— old women who stalled on the sidewalks like irrationally pausing insects, their print dresses gaping at the neck; young car owners with hairstyles resembling sable pelts—seemed harried by a wind the tourists and moneyed intruders couldn't feel, a sociological wind laden with the dank dust of renovation, as cold as society's interest in heavy red sauces with oregano and Frank Sinatra, as keen as Boston's hunger for real estate in convenient white neighborhoods. MEAT MARKET. MEAT MARKET. Midwestern tourists surged up the hill. A pair of Japanese youths sprinted past Louis, their fingers in green Michelin guides, as he approached the Old North Church, whose actual cramped setting immediately and quietly obliterated the more wooded picture his mind had formed before he saw it. He skirted an ancient cemetery, thinking about Houston, where summer had already arrived, where the downtown streets smelled of cypress swamps and the live oaks shed green leaves, and remembering a conversation from a humid night there—*You'll be lucky next time. I swear you will.* In the buildings facing the cemetery he saw white interiors, entertainment equipment as blatant as ICU technology, large toys in primary colors in the middle of barren rooms.

On Commercial Street there were a thousand windows, bleak and square unornamented windows reaching up as high as the eye cared to wander. Pale green, opaque, unblinking and excluding. There was no trash on the ground for the wind to disturb, nothing for the eye to rest on but new brick walls, new concrete pavement, and new windows. It seemed as if the only glue that kept these walls and streets from collapsing, the only force preserving these clean and impenetrable and uninspired surfaces, was deeds and rents.

Out of Faneuil Hall, haven of meaning and purpose for weary sightseers, there blew a smell of fat: of hamburgers and fried shell-fish and fresh croissants and hot pizzas, and chocolate chip cookies and french fries and hot crab meat topped with melted cheese, and baked beans and stuffed peppers and quiches and crispy fried Oriental Nuggets with tamari. Louis slipped in and out of an arcade to appropriate a napkin and blow his nose. The walking and the cold air had numbed him to the point where the entire darkening city seemed like nothing but a hard projection of an individual's loneliness, a loneliness so deep it muted sounds—secretarial exclamations, truck engines, even the straining woofers outside appliance stores—till he could hardly hear them.

On Tremont Street, under the gaze of windows now transparent enough to reveal unpopulated rooms full of wealth's technology and wealth's furnishings, he found himself bucking a heavy flow of anti-abortion demonstrators. They were spilling over the curb into the street as they marched towards the State House. Everybody seemed to be on the verge of angry tears. The women, who were dressed like stewardesses and gym teachers, held the stakes of their placards rigidly vertical, as if to shame the lightness with which other kinds of protesters carried placards. The few men in the crowd shuffled along empty-handed and empty-eyed, their very hair disoriented by the wind. From the way both the men and the women huddled together as they marched, sullenly dodging other pedestrians, it was clear that they'd come to the Common expecting active persecution, the modern equivalent of hungry lions and a jaded crowd of heathen spectators. Interesting, then, that this valley of the shadow was lined with restaurants, deluxe hotels, luggage stores, cold windows.

Louis emerged from the rear of the parade with his necktie on. He'd tied it while avoiding STOP THE SLAUGHTER signs.

It took him more than an hour, at a much-bumped table in the dusky Ritz bar, to realize that Rita Kernaghan had stood him up. The gin and tonic he'd ordered automatically turned his face a stoplight red, and the one conversation that kept surfacing in the sea of vying voices concerned eunuchs. He soon figured out that the word was UNIX, but he kept hearing eunuchs, the great thing about eunuchs, with eunuchs you can-do, I hated eunuchs, I resisted eunuchs, eunuch's budding monopoly. "I feel very sick," he murmured aloud every few minutes. "I feel very sick." Finally he paid and went out through the lobby to find a telephone. He had to swerve around a trio of businessmen who might have been identical triplets. Their mouths moved like the mouths of latex dolls:

You feel it?

We couldn't, here.

Are you calling me a liar?

The time was 7:10. Louis called directory assistance and to the question of what city, said: Ipswich. The instrument he was using was drenched with a cologne to which he might have been allergic, so denaturing was its effect on his nasal membranes. He let Rita Kernaghan's number ring eight times and was about to hang up when a man answered and said in a dead, low, institutional voice: "Officer Dobbs."

Louis asked to speak with Mrs. Kernaghan.

Eunuchs, cologne, fetus. Dobbs. "Who's calling."

"This is her grandson."

Over the line came the wa-wa of palm on mouthpiece and a voice in the background, followed by silence. At length a different man spoke, one Sergeant Akins. "We're going to need some information from you," he said. "As you probably know, there's been an earthquake up here. And you're not going to be able to speak with Mrs. Kernaghan, because Mrs. Kernaghan was found dead a few hours ago."

At this point the synthetic operator began to insist on more coins, which Louis fumbled to supply.

2

Like Rome, Somerville was built on seven hills. The apartment in which Louis had found a share opportunity was on Clarendon Hill, the westernmost of the seven and, by default, the greenest. Elsewhere in the city, trees tended to be hidden behind houses or confined to square holes in the sidewalks, where children tore their limbs off.

Earlier in the century Somerville had been the most densely populated city in the country, a demographic feat achieved by spacing the streets narrowly and dispensing with parks and front lawns. Clapboard triple-deckers encrusted the topography. They had polygonal bays or rickety porches stacked three high, and they were painted in color combinations like blue and yellow, white and green, brown and brown.

The streets of Somerville were lined solidly with cars that were less like cars than like mateless shoes. They trudged off to work in the morning or shuffled back and forth across the pavement under the pressure of twice-monthly street sweeping. Even in the early 1980s, when the Massachusetts economy was experiencing a Miracle, with billions of dollars flowing from the Pentagon into former mill towns in the Commonwealth, Somerville continued to house mainly the lowlier members of the footwear hierarchy. There were salt-stained Hush Puppies and scuffed two-tone pumps in unfortunate colors parked near the doors of the Irish and Italian middle class; well-worn Adidases in the driveways of single women; bovver boots and Salvation Army specials near the spaces of those who found the town perversely chic; laceless Keds up on blocks in the back yards of the waning counterculture; wide untapering leisure shoes with soft crinkly uppers and soles of rubber foam marking the homes of realtors and retirees; battered student Wallabees under the eaves of battered student houses; a few tasseled Gucci loafers in the City Hall parking lot; and shiny stud boots and flimsy dancing slippers and Flash Gordon–style athletic footwear in the driveways of parents who still had eighteen- and twenty-year-olds in the house.

Towards the end of the eighties, just before the nation's arms buildup slowed and Massachusetts banks began to fail and the Miracle was shown to be not so much a Miracle as an irony and fraud, a new breed of car invaded Somerville. The new breed looked intrusion-molded. For just as Reebok and its imitators had finally succeeded in making real leather look wholly artificial, Detroit and its foreign counterparts had managed to make real metal and real glass indistinguishable from plastic. The interesting thing about the new breed, however, was its newness. In a town where for decades, when a car came home for the first time, its price had more often than not been written in yellow crayon on the windshield, one suddenly began to see the remains of stickers in rear left windows. Not being stupid, local landlords began to double rents between leases; and Somerville, too close to Boston and Cambridge to remain a renter's heaven forever, came of age.

Louis had a room in a two-bedroom apartment on Belknap Street that was leased by a graduate student of psychology at Tufts. The student, whose name was Toby, had promised Louis, "Our paths will never cross." Toby's bedroom door was open when Louis came home from work, still open when he went to bed, and closed when he left in the predawn darkness. The shelves in Toby's refrigerator were bisected vertically by slotted pinewood panels. The bathmat was also made of pinewood, good for fungus control and stubbing toes. The living room contained two broad-beamed armchairs and one sofa, all upholstered in beige, plus a beige wall unit that was empty except for phone books, a Scrabble set, a glossy beige bud vase made of GENUINE MOUNT ST. HELENS VOLCANIC ASH in a plastic suspension, and receipts for the wall unit and the furniture totaling $1,758.88.

Louis kept to his bedroom. The thirtyish couple in the apartment opposite his window owned a piano and often sang arpeggios while he ate his evening meal of sandwiches, carrots, apples, cookies, and milk. Later the arpeggios stopped and he read the *Globe* or *The Atlantic* laboriously, front to back, skipping nothing. Or he sat cross-legged in front of his television set and frowned as intently at baseball—even at the beer commercials—as he would have at war news. Or he stood in the harsh light of the overhead fixture and studied the beige walls and tiled ceiling and wood floor of his bedroom from every possible angle. Or he did the same in Toby's room.

On Friday night, once the Ipswich police had finished with him on the telephone and he'd driven back to Somerville, he called Eileen. "You won't believe what I just saw on the news," Eileen said. What she'd just seen via live minicam was the ambulance that held their step-grandmother's body. Eileen thought she'd felt the earthquake without knowing it while she was studying. She'd thought it was trucks. She said it was the second little earthquake she'd felt in Boston in two years.

Louis said he hadn't felt it.

Eileen said their parents were flying into town on Sunday, because of Rita's death, and staying in a hotel.

Louis said, "They're spending money on a hotel?"

In the morning he went to the corner drugstore to buy newspapers. It had been raining all night and the rain clouds looked unspent, but the sky had brightened for a moment and the fluorescent light inside the drugstore was the same color and intensity as the light outside. The Saturday *Herald* had printed on its cover:

EARTH-QUAKE!

DESTRUCTION AND DEATH IN IPSWICH

New Age Guru A Victim

The earthquake had also made the front page of the *Globe* (TREMOR ROCKS CAPE ANN; ONE DEAD), which Louis began to read as he headed home again. Absorbed, he was late in noticing a tall old man in a cardigan and unbuckled rubber boots who was rubbing his four-door American-made brogue with a hand towel. Spotting Louis, he stepped out to block the sidewalk. "Reading the paper, are ya?"

Louis did not deny it.

"John," the old man goggled. "John Mullins. I see you live next door here, I saw you movin' in. I live on the first floor right here, lived here twenty-three years. I was born in Somerville. John's the name. John Mullins."

"Louis Holland."

"Louis? Lou? You mind if I call you Lou? You reading about the earthquake there." Suddenly the old man might have bitten a lemon or a rotten egg; he made a face like the damned. "*Terrible* about that old woman. *Terrible*. I felt it, you know. I was at the Foodmaster, you know, round the corner here, it's a good store. You shop there? Good store, but what was I, what was I . . . I was sayin' I felt it. I thought it was me. I thought it was nerves, you know. But I was watching the news and wooncha know, it was a temblor. That's what they call it, you know, a temblor. Thank *God* it wasn't any worse. Thank *God*. What are you, a student?"

"No," Louis said slowly. "I'm in radio. I work for a radio station."

"Lot of students live around here. Tuff students mainly. It's right up the street. They're not bad kids. What do you think? You like it around here? You like Somerville? I think you'll like it. I tell you I felt that earthquake?"

John Mullins hit himself in the forehead. "Sure I did. *Sure* I did." The encounter was evidently becoming too much for him. "All right, Lou." He squeezed Louis's shoulder and stumbled towards his car.

As Louis went inside he heard his soprano neighbor's arpeggios commencing, the fundamentals being struck on the piano in a rising chromatic scale. He sat down on the bare floor of his room and opened the papers. "Drat it," he distinctly heard John Mullins say to some other neighbor. "They said it wasn't going to rain anymore."

Neither the *Globe* nor the *Herald* could quite hide its delight at having a death—Rita Kernaghan's—to justify big headlines for a small local temblor. The shock, with a magnitude of 4.7 and an epicenter just southeast of Ipswich, had occurred at 4:48 p.m. and lasted less than ten seconds. Property damage had been so insignificant that a photograph of an Ipswich man fingering a crack in his breakfast-room wall received a prominent enlargement in both papers. Being the higher-brow paper of the two, the *Globe* also ran boxed articles about the history of earthquakes in Boston, the history of earthquakes, and the history of Boston, including a special graphic time line revealing (among other things) that the last two significant tremors to shake the city had coincided with the end of Henry Cabot Lodge, Jr.'s second term as U.S. senator (1944) and the end of his third (1953).

Another box on page 16 contained an update on the doings of a Protestant minister by the name of Philip Stites, who according to the *Globe* had six months earlier moved his Church of Action in Christ up to Boston from Fayetteville, North Carolina, with the stated intention of "eliminating abortion in the Commonwealth." Stites's followers were attacking fetal murder by standing at the doors of clinics. On Friday evening people of conscience from thirty-one states and possessions had marched to the third in a series of protest rallies in downtown Boston; in a subsequent television interview Stites said the earthquake had come close to striking "the epicenter of butchery," by which he meant the Massachusetts State House. God (he let it be inferred) was angry with the Commonwealth. Like the Church of Action in Christ, He would not rest until the slaughter of the unborn had ceased. "Look for me everywhere," Stites said.

"I was at the Foodmaster," John Mullins said above the rain and arpeggios. "I thought it was the old nerves."

Victim Was a Writer

Rita Damiano Kernaghan, whose death was the only one reported in yesterday's earthquake in Ipswich, was a popular lecturer on the local New Age circuit and the author of three books on inspirational topics. She was 68 years old.

Kernaghan was perhaps best known for the battle she and the Town of Ipswich had waged since 1986 concerning the pyramidal structure she erected on the roof of her home, a farmhouse built within the town limits of Ipswich in 1765 and enlarged in 1623 under the direction of George Stonemarsh, a leading post–Revolutionary era architect.

In 1987 the Ipswich Town Meeting conceded that a clerical error had resulted in the granting of a building permit for the pyramid, and acted to retroactively enforce the local land-marks-preservation code and ordered the removal of the pyramid. Kernaghan sued the town in 1988 and later refused an out-of-court settlement under which the town would have paid the cost of removing the pyramid and restoring the house to its original 1823 design.

Kernaghan maintained that her right to build the pyramid —a geometrical form held by some to exert healing and pre-servative influences—is a First Amendment issue, rooted in the separation of church and state. The case, still unresolved, has become a cause celebre in the north-suburban New Age community.

Kernaghan, whose printed works include "Beginning Life at 60," "Star Children," and the recently published "Princess of Italy," was the widow of Boston attorney John Alfred Ker-naghan. She is survived by a step-daughter, Melanie Holland of Cleveland.

Higher and higher the soprano's fundamentals rose, a slow upward spiral of hysteria. Louis was frowning, his pinky on the bridge of his glasses, his fingertips on his hairline, his thumb on his jaw. The thing he couldn't stop looking at was his mother's name. Not because the *Globe* had stuck her in Cleveland but for the name's sheer personal resonant presence in print on paper. *Melanie Holland*: this was his mother, peculiarly reduced. Two words in a Boston paper.

Still frowning, and also beginning now to shiver, as if when the raindrops hit the windowpanes behind him their chill came right on through, he looked again at the boxed article about the Reverend Philip Stites. "*Up Tremont Street*," it said, "*and across the Common to the steps of the State House*." The facts were consistent with what Louis himself had seen of the march—consistent in a deep way, because the article, like memory, like dreams, reduced the event to an idea, illuminated not by twilight and street-light but by its own light, in the darkness of his head: he saw it because he knew that this was what had happened, because he knew that this was how things had been. And therefore it seemed to him that it could only be raining this morning. The rain had to be there to make this day different, to bar any return to yesterday afternoon and the particular conditions of atmosphere and light through which those marchers had been marching, the blue north-ern clarity of light in greater Boston when the earthquake struck. The rain made the morning real, so unshakably present that it was hard to believe there'd even *been* an earthquake; to believe the accidents had occurred anywhere but on paper.

Stacked against one wall of the bedroom were his cartons of radio equipment, which he'd faithfully shipped from Evanston to Houston and from Houston to Boston and never unpacked. He worked his fingernail under the duct tape holding the top carton closed. Strength failed him. He staggered to his futon, one foot slipping on the open *Globe*, crashed heavily and lay face down until long after the arpeggios had stopped.

Sunday night he had dinner with his family in a fish restaurant on the harbor. He was surprised to hear that his mother and Eileen took it for granted that Rita Kernaghan had fallen to her death less because an earthquake shoved her than because she was blind drunk at the time. Then again, they'd known her and he hadn't. The word was she'd fallen off a barstool, which sounded like a joke in bad taste but was apparently the literal truth. She was being cremated privately on Wednesday morning, her ashes hurled from a pier in Rockport on the afternoon of same, and her life celebrated the next day at a memorial service that Louis was expected to take time off from work to attend. His mother, obviously impatient with the whole deceased-disposal process, referred to the service as "the thing on Thursday."

It wasn't until shortly before "the thing" that he saw his par-ents again. He'd done Dan Drexel's board work until ten in the morning, and then, possibly a little hurt that his mother hadn't planned any other get-togethers or shown any interest in where he lived and worked ("hurt," however, maybe not the word for his feelings towards a family in which people rarely had the resources to take or fake a personal interest in anyone's life but their own, "regret" or "bitterness" or "general sadness" maybe being more like it), drove straight to their hotel, a newish medium-rise by the river in Cambridge, just off Harvard Square. It would later transpire that his mother had made his father spend two afternoons in Widener Library so they could write off his half of the trip. Outside their door, at the end of a hushed hallway, Louis raised his hand but didn't knock. He lowered it again.

"Eileen, that's not the point."

"Well, what is the point."

"The point is to show some consideration for my feelings and try to understand things from my side. This has been an extremely upsetting—Yes! Yes!—an extremely upsetting week! So you might at least have had the consideration to wait—"

"You're *happy* she's dead! You're *happy!*"

"That's a very muffle muffle muffle to any person, muffle your mother. A very un-Christian thing."

"It's *true.*"

"I have to get dressed now."

"It's true. You're *happy!*"

"I must get dressed. Although I can't help wondering—well, muffle muffle muffle a young man who would put his casual girlfriend—"

"His *what?!*" Eileen's high voice went twice as high.

"His casual girlfriend up to—"

"His—!? What are you *talking* about? This has nothing to do with Peter. And for your information—"

"Oh Eileen."

"For your information—"

Here Louis, with a gesture of disgust, threw his fist against the door a couple times. Eileen let him in. Tears had muddied her eyeliner.

"Who is it?" their mother said from behind the bathroom door.

"It's Louis," Eileen said grimly.

"Hi Louis, I'm dressing."

Eileen retreated towards the window, which looked out over the river at her business school. She was wearing the same bulky sweater she'd had on the last time Louis saw her. Today it looked as if she'd been sleeping in it.

"Where's Dad?" Louis said.

"He's at the pool. What are you doing here so early?"

Louis thought a moment. "What are *you* doing here so early?"

She made a ghastly teenaged face at him, tongue and gums showing, and turned to face the window. Louis scratched his ear thoughtfully. Then, shifting gears, he prowled, he snooped. On one of the hotel room's many luggage surfaces, lying like junk mail amid car keys and open Trident packages, he found a pair of official-looking documents, a police report and a medical examiner's report, the back sides of which his mother had been using to jot down names and phone numbers. He looked at the official sides while Eileen carefully rubbed the skin around her eyes and their mother punctuated long bathroom silences with dressing and grooming noises. The police report consisted principally of the testimony of Rita Kernaghan's live-in Haitian maid, Thérèse Mougère.

At 15:45 on April 6 Mougère completed her afternoon duties and placed inside her reticule three oranges and a ladies novel in French. She was scheduled to drive the deceased to downtown Boston at 17:00. She stated that the novel was for reading in the parking garage. As Mougère was granted from 16:00 to 17:00 every afternoon to watch television she retired at approximately 15:50 to her room which is down a short hall to the rear of the kitchen. The deceased was speaking on the kitchen telephone when Mougère last saw her alive. Shortly before the end of her program (it was established that the program was "Star Trek" which ends at 16:58) the house began to shake. The windows of Mougère's room rattled and one pane broke. Mougère heard "a booming." The lights flickered and the television faded for a moment. Mougère went to the kitchen where vases had fallen from the table and the cabinet doors were open. In the dining room a plate and vases had fallen from the breakfront. Mougère went to the parlor. Small articles had fallen from tables and there was a smell of whiskey from behind the bar. Mougère went upstairs calling the deceased's name. Hearing nothing she became alarmed and searched all the upstairs rooms. She searched the parlor again and encountered the body of the deceased behind the bar. Blood, broken glass and a large volume of whiskey were present. A barstool was on its side. Mougère called the police. Dobbs and Akins arrived at 17:35. It was established that Mougère had not disturbed the body. When it was surmised that the deceased had fallen from the barstool while taking down a bottle Mougère averred that she habitually placed the deceased's favorite labels of whiskey on a high shelf to discourage consumption. Mougère volunteered that a familiar spirit named Jack inhabited the house and had caused the death and destruction. This and other supernatural theories were discounted. The death appears to have been accidental in nature, in all probability occasioned by the moderate earthquake at 16:48. Questions regarding Mougère's illegal residence status and the manner in which she obtained a valid Mass. operator's license were referred to USINS. USINS was advised that the Coroner no longer required Mougère's presence in the Commonwealth.

More hurriedly, because his mother was now making pre-exit noises in the bathroom (cases snapping, the water tap turned briskly on and off), Louis read through the report of the Essex County medical examiner, which assigned "massive counter-coup trauma" as the cause of death and attributed this trauma to an accident wherein the deceased, who was 62″ tall, had fallen from a 38″ barstool, resulting in a total drop of 100 inches, a fall sufficient, in combination with the marble floor, to flatten the left frontal portion of the skull and immediately terminate all brain activity. Blood loss from lacerations caused by broken glass was dismissed as a factor. The blood-alcohol content of the deceased was 0.06 percent, equivalent to "moderate" intoxication.

Louis covered up the document with a paperback and turned around. His mother was emerging from the bathroom.

It was obvious that she'd been spending money. Spending

money and (so it seemed to Louis) sleeping, for she looked approximately fifteen years younger than she'd looked at dinner on Sunday. The skin of her face was golden and glowing and so tautly attached to her jawline it seemed to pull her dark eyes open wide. She'd had her hair set in a short pageboy—and colored also? What Louis remembered as an even dark gray had been resolved into black and silver. She was wearing a pale yellow linen dress with black velvet trim, the hem about an inch above the knee. The high collar was joined with a brooch that contained a nickel-sized pearl. At the mirror, nostrils flared in concentration, she touched invisible and possibly nonexistent hairs around her temples. Then she went to the closet and with the exact same fluidity of vertical motion that Eileen had inherited, dropped to her knees and drew a shoe box from a plastic Ferragamo bag.

"You're lookin' nice there, Mom."

"Thank you, Louis. Isn't your father back yet?"

With raised eyebrows he watched her remove a pair of shoes from a bed of crimson tissue paper. He turned to Eileen, wondering if she too might raise her eyebrows at this spectacle of a mom transformed by sudden spending power. But Eileen was no less transformed. With eyes pinkened by hurt and hate and a face in which every muscle had gone dead she watched their mother slip her small feet into a pair of shoes as sleek as Jaguars. No way Louis could catch her eye. She needed to have her sorrows noticed by their mother, not by him. So while she suffered by the window (cold rain falling between her and the business school) and their mother complacently fitted a pair of white roses into the black band of a floppy white hat, he sat down on the bed and opened the sports section of a handy *Globe*. It could almost as easily have been he and not his sister suffering by the window, but what is a pack dog thinking, what's going on behind its yellow eyes, when it sees one of its fellows taken aside by a polar explorer to have its throat slit and be made into supper for its siblings?

"Your father's going to have about three minutes to shower and dress," their mother said. "Maybe one of you could—"

"No," Eileen said.

"No," Louis said. Their father swam in earplugs and goggles and had to be physically prodded to leave a pool.

"Well." Their mother stood up with her hat on, flattened her dress across her hips, and spun around once on her toes. "How do I look?"

There was a silence, Eileen not even glancing.

"Like a million bucks," Louis said.

"Ha ha ha!" Eileen cawed mirthlessly.

Their mother, without expression, began to reload a new-looking black clutch. "Louis," she said. "I'm going to have to talk to you."

"Yeah, well, I already heard it," Eileen said, stamping across the room. "So I'll see you guys at the service." She pulled her raincoat from a hanger and opened the door and reeled back before their father, who, towel around his waist and goggles nestled in the sodden gray fluff below his throat, was advancing like an interested lobster, saying to Eileen, "Well, if it ain't the Infanta Elena! Dark star of Aragon! Keepress of the emerald scepter!" She swung back into clothes hangers, her fingers splayed and rigid near her ears, while the lobster gathered her waist in the crook of its stout claw. She shied writhingly. "Don't! Don't! Don't! Oh, you're still wet!" Color was returning to her cheeks. Her father kissed one and released her, saluted across the room to Louis, and disappeared into the bathroom. Their mother had witnessed none of this.

Fifteen minutes later the four Hollands were sitting in the parental rented two-door Mercury, Melanie at the wheel, the kids in back. The kids' cars had stayed behind in the hotel lot because Bob Holland considered automobiles an abomination and had threatened to walk if they took more than one. Louis was folded together like a card table and incipiently carsick, with his under-insulated head against a cold fogged window and the taste of heavy rain and diesel exhaust in his throat. On his shins he held his mother's hat. Someone who was not Louis and probably not Eileen was farting steadily. Bob, looking diminished in a thirty-year-old suit, was glaring out his window at overtaken drivers in the heavy midmorning traffic on Memorial Drive. He thought that driving a car was an act of personal immorality.

Louis pushed out the hinged rear window and put his nose and mouth against the flat surface of the cooler air outside. He was beginning to relate his carsickness to *flatten the left frontal portion of the skull and immediately terminate all brain activity*, the imagination of death having advanced covertly and autonomously, penetrating his consciousness only now. He managed to suck a fortifying breath of air in through the window. "Do you think she knew it was an earthquake?"

Eileen gave him an ugly, morose look and retreated within herself.

"Who?" Melanie said.

"You know. Rita. Do you think she knew the shaking was an earthquake?"

"It sounds," Melanie said, "as if she was far too inebriated to think much of anything."

"It's kind of sad," Louis said, "don't you think?"

"There are worse ways to go. Better this than cirrhosis in a hospital bed."

"She's left you all this money. Don't you think it's kind of sad?"

"She didn't leave me any money. She didn't leave me anything but a quarter of a million dollars in illegally secured debts, if you want to know the truth."

"Oh come on, Mel."

"Well, she did, Bob. She had a mortgage on a house that didn't belong to her. The bank in Ipswich was unaware of this little fact, which—"

"Your mother's father," Bob said, "left everything he had in a trust—"

"Bob, this doesn't interest Louis."

"Sure it does," Louis said.

"And it's not particularly his business either."

"Oh, well."

"But the basic point," Melanie continued, "is that by the time my father died he had a very clear idea of the kind of woman he'd taken for a second wife, and while he had a duty to leave her comfortable he also didn't want her to fritter away an estate that he eventually wanted to go to his children—"

Bob barked with delight. "Meaning he didn't leave your mother a cent! And not a cent to your Aunt Heidi either! He wrote exactly the kind of spiteful, arrogant, dead-handed, lawyer's-lawyer will you'd have expected from him. Everybody beggared, everybody bitter, and a committee of three lawyers from the Bank of Boston meeting twice a year to write themselves checks on the fund."

"I like the way you honor the dead."

"Could you open a window a little?"

"And Mel's going to right a few wrongs now, isn't she? See, Lou, after Heidi died it all came to devolve on your mother. It was supposed to go to the surviving daughters. Your mother's in exactly the same position your grandfather was ten years ago. Only the rich have gotten richer, haven't they? Your mother's in a position to build some schools and clinics, maybe give a gym to Wellesley. Or help the homeless, huh, Mel?"

Melanie tilted her head back, removing herself from the discussion. Eileen smiled bitterly. Louis asked again to have a window opened.

The memorial service, which was to have been held in a meadow in Essex County if the sun had shone, had been shifted to the ballroom of the Royal Sonesta, a luxury hotel overlooking the mouth of the Charles at the extreme northeast corner of Cambridge. For a moment, when Louis followed his parents through the doorway, he thought they'd entered the wrong room; milling in sad social lumps were, it seemed to him, the very people he'd seen marching against abortion on Tremont Street a week earlier —the same inflexible middle-aged female faces, the same smattering of vacant-eyed men, the same curtain-colored clothing and sensible shoes. But then, alerted by the beeline Eileen was making, he saw Peter Stoorhuys.

Peter was standing slightly apart from a group of three uneasy-looking men in nice suits, three obvious executives or professionals. With his legs spread and his shoulders thrown back and his hands shallowly in his pockets, he looked like a person to whom the world may come if it really must. Eileen, colliding with him, pressed her ear against one of his houndstooth lapels and rested one hand on his stomach, the other on his shoulder.

Louis stopped in his tracks and stared at the embrace with his hands on his hips. Then, altering his trajectory as though a repulsive field now surrounded Eileen, he caught up with Bob and the two of them shuffled after Melanie, whose approach was causing the three gentlemen in suits to break into smiles of relief. She brushed cheeks with two of them, shook hands with the third. Peter freed himself from Eileen and came over to Melanie with his arm outstretched, but suddenly she was keeping her hands to herself. She smiled glacially. "Hello Peter." Bob Holland, like a grateful second-stringer, claimed the unshaken hand and pumped it, but Melanie's snub had not escaped Eileen's attention; she glowered at Louis. Louis smiled back pleasantly. He was interested to see that at some point during the week his parents had made Peter's acquaintance.

"This is our son, Louis," Melanie said. "Louis, this is Mr. Aldren, Mr. Tabscott, Mr. Stoorhuys—"

Mr. Who, Mr. Who, Mr.—?

"Good to know you, Louis," they chorused, pressing his flesh. The same courtesies were then extended to Eileen.

"Peter's dad," Mr. Stoorhuys added for Louis's benefit, waving a hand at his son, to whom he bore a resemblance both unmistakable and unflattering to himself. Seen from close up, Mr. Stoorhuys did not actually match his two companions. Mr. Aldren and Mr. Tabscott appeared to be real Men, men with the beefy faces and inflamed-looking bull's nostrils of frequent beefeaters, men who were emphatically not "young men" and even more emphatically not "women." They had gold chains across their necktie knots and a hard red shrewdness in their eyes.

Mr. Stoorhuys was more nervous and lanky. Three inches of shirt cuff stuck out of his jacket sleeves on either wrist. His hair grew in half a dozen directions and half a dozen shades of gray; a long, seventies-style forelock rested on his dandruffy eyebrows. He had sunken pitted cheeks, teeth so large he seemed unable to keep his lips over them, and bright intelligent eyes that were engaged in looking over his shoulder even as he stood facing Louis, one hand raised to keep him on hold.

"Louis," Melanie said. He turned to see her standing on one leg, leaning through bodies. "Maybe you'd like to get me a cup of coffee."

"Actually—" Mr. Tabscott pinched the cuff of Louis's jacket. "I think the, uh, service is going to start here in a minute."

"Yes," Mr. Aldren said. "We're going to sit with your mother if you don't mind."

"Good to meet you, son."

"Good to meet you, uh, Louis."

Mr. Stoorhuys followed them, escaping his stillborn conversation with Louis the easy way: by just leaving.

The drab crowd was herding itself towards rows of function-room chairs set up facing a lectern and a grand piano on which a Japanese man with expressive shoulders and a ponytail had begun to play the Pachelbel Canon. Louis's father, with his academic's respect for lecterns, had already taken a seat. Eileen stood hugging Peter's chest. And a tableau presented itself: Mr. Aldren leading Melanie away, his elbow linked with hers, and Melanie not needing to be led but walking with him as naturally as if they were sweethearts on a boardwalk; Mr. Stoorhuys following with a grip on her other arm, smiling his smile that was not a smile, lagging behind for a moment to look over his shoulder through the rough tufts of hair in his eyes; and Mr. Tabscott like a rear guard with his back squarely to the three of them, unambiguously warning off anyone foolish enough to pursue. A white hat and a yellow linen dress—a lady as little a man as at least two of these men were ladies—fenced in by dark pinstripe.

Louis, staring, extended one finger and rammed the tip of it into the bridge of his glasses.

The Canon had grown deafening. Melanie sat down between Mr. Aldren and Mr. Tabscott with Mr. Stoorhuys crowding in from Mr. Aldren's side, his thin arm almost long enough to reach behind all three of them, five inches of white shirt cuff showing now. Louis roughed up the pastel broadloom with a heavy shoe. Asking Eileen who and what these men were was not an option; she had her cheek against Peter's necktie and was feeling around under the back of his jacket as if looking for the key one wound him up with. Their lips were moving: they were conversing inaudibly. They and Louis were now the only mourners not seated in the array of chairs. An ashen-faced woman in a caftan had stationed herself behind the lectern and was resting one elbow on it as she gravely watched the pianist. The pianist had begun to grapple visibly with the Canon, trying to enforce a ritardando while hurrying the ponderous chords to find a respectable point for breaking off. The Canon was showing its backbone and seemed far from surrendering.

Louis walked over to the young lovers in their invisible sphere of oblivion and stood, as it were, outside their door. "Hi, Peter," he said.

Peter seemed to have a reflex problem. It was three or four seconds before he turned and said, "Hey, how's it going."

"Fine, thanks. Wonder if I could talk to my sister for a second."

Eileen removed herself from Peter and gave some attention to her hair. By almost but not quite meeting Louis's eyes she managed to appear entirely absent.

"I didn't do anything to you," Louis said.

"Didn't say you did."

"Mom give you a hard time or what."

"Let's just not talk about it."

"Yeah. Well."

"I'm going to go sit with Peter, OK?"

She left him standing in the middle of the ballroom, ten paces behind the last row of chairs. The lights shone more brightly on him than on the fifty or so assembled mourners, more brightly even than on the ashen moderator, who, after a nod of appreciation to the sweating and victorious pianist, looked squarely at Louis and said, "We may be seated."

Louis held his ground, arms crossed. The woman closed her eyes with raised eyebrows. Then she put on a pair of glasses that were chained to her neck.

"We're assembled here today," she said, reading from the lectern, "to honor the memory of Rita Damiano Kernaghan, a mentor unto many of us and a friend unto all. Can you hear me in the back row?"

The only person in the back row, Bob Holland, gave the woman a captain's salute.

"My name is Geraldine Briggs. I was a friend of Rita Kernaghan. I knew her well. At times, we were as sisters unto one another. We laughed together, we wept together. We were as little girls, sometimes."

The pallid mourners were listening raptly, their heads like so many compass needles pointing at the lectern. The men with Melanie, Mr. Stoorhuys included, sat with their fingers pressed into their foreheads.

"When first I met Rita at the Empowerment Center in Danvers in 1983, she had just penned a book entitled *Beginning Life at 60*, familiar to many of you, I'm sure, and seemed, she did, a perfect embodiment of the principles limned therein. Rita had learned that the soul is eternal and youthful, gay and joyous, filled with glad melodies. Age is no impediment unto the soul. Nay, death itself be no impediment. She had been a simple peasant girl, a gatherer of flowers and scented herbs, in Napoleonic times. Why should she not then make glad melodies even now when, a careworn widow, there was nought to be wrought of life but, nay, begin it again? Why should not we all? In her workshop, we hearkened unto her message. We learned. We grew. We laughed. We became as young again. We were healed, healed not as the modern world would have us healed, but spiritually. Nay. A new world was opened up unto us by her."

Louis, standing rock-like, watched Mr. Tabscott bury his face in both hands. His jeweled watch gleamed.

"But nay, what is the new but that which is most ancient? And what. What is death but the beginning of new life? Another turn in the eternal cycle? A young babe born? Let us therefore tell glad stories today. Each one of us as so desires, let them stand and celebrate with glad stories the eternal life of Rita Damiano Kernaghan and, nay, of us all!"

Here Geraldine Briggs paused and a woman in the front row popped up from her seat. She immediately sat down again, withered by a look.

"I see among us," Geraldine Briggs continued, reading, "friends of Rita's. Family of Rita's. Friends from her years of labor as a secretary. Friends and loved ones from all walks of her life. And so, friends, the Empowerment Center, which I'm proud to direct, has in accordance with Rita's express wishes requested that in lieu of flowers donations be made in Rita's name to the Empowerment Center. The name of the fund is the Rita Damiano

Kernaghan Fund. This is fund number 1145. Envelopes for giving are still available by the coffee urn. But nay, nay, let us now. Let us now hear glad stories!"

The first glad story was delivered by Mr. Aldren, who rose halfway from his seat and spoke in a guarded monotone. "Rita Kernaghan was an employee with us at Sweeting-Aldren Industries for some twenty-four years and was the, uh, wife of the principal architect of what is known to be one of the Commonwealth's high-tech and high-finance success stories of the, uh, last couple decades, and I and some fellow officers are here to, uh, pay our respects. She was a fine—fine woman."

Mr. Aldren dropped back into his seat and Geraldine Briggs, eyes closed, slowly nodded. Then the eager woman in the front row popped up and faced the congregation. Once, she said, after a class at the Empowerment Center, Rita Kernaghan had given her a bronze amulet to wear on her neck. The amulet had cured a large wen that was on her chest. Out of gratitude the woman had sent Rita a box of Harry and David's pears. Six months later, at a festival of the vernal equinox held at Rita's estate, the woman was taken into Rita's living room. For six months the box of Harry and David's pears had been stored close to the focus of power of the Pyramid on Rita's house. Rita and the woman pried the staples—the staples were copper and heavy-duty—pried the staples out of the box. The pears were not rotten. The woman and Rita shared a pear, trading bites. It was good. The woman sat down.

Geraldine Briggs smiled uncomfortably and coughed a little.

A man with dentures like carp teeth stood up and unfolded a clipping. It was an editorial from the Ipswich *Chronicle*. The editorial was a thanksgiving that explicitly invoked the Judeo-Christian god and thanked him that property damage in the recent earthquake had been minor. The editorial noted that Rita's famous Pyramid, so much in the news in recent years, had not protected her when push came to shove; damage on the Kernaghan estate (still slight) had been among the most severe. The man folded up the clipping. He said that he had taken two of Rita's workshops. He said Rita had never maintained that the Pyramid offered eternal life in the present existence. That was not the point. It was this man's personal view that the Pyramid had in fact served to *concentrate* the earth forces in the neighborhood—

"Yes," said Geraldine Briggs. "Yes perhaps. Other stories?"

A woman rose to describe an occasion on which Rita had cried upon hearing of the death of a young person.

Another woman rose and told of Rita's refusal to accept money from a person ill able to afford a workshop.

Another woman rose and spoke of her friendship with Rita during the Ming Dynasty.

It was not clear what sort of story besides Mr. Aldren's would have pleased Geraldine Briggs; certainly few of these stories did. But having opened the door, she was powerless to close it. The anecdotes poured out, ranging from the sentimental to the borderline insane, and their accreting weight slowly unmanned Louis, uncrossing his arms and bowing his shoulders, until finally he went and sat down by his father. His father seemed to be having a grand time, tossing his head back in delight, feasting on the dismal confessions as though they were popcorn. He went so far as to frown at Geraldine Briggs when, for the third time, she said, "Well, if there are no more . . ." She paused. It finally seemed as if there really might be no more. "If there are no more stories I think we'll—" But yet again she was forced to stop, because Melanie had sprung to her feet.

Melanie smiled prettily, twisting her head around to meet as many eyes as possible, leaning back to catch a few more. The only ones she avoided were her family's.

"I knew Rita Kernaghan, too," she said. "And I wanted to tell you all that I *firmly believe* she's already reincarnated! I believe she's now . . . a parakeet! Isn't that marvelous?" She clasped her hands in front of her and swung them like a happy girl. "I just wanted to tell you all how marvelous I think it is that she's a parakeet now, how simply marvelous. That's all I have to say!"

With an unfortunate little wiggle of her bottom, and with one hand on her hat to keep it on, she dropped back down between her protectors, Mr. Aldren and Mr. Tabscott. The protectors traded smirks. The drab crowd, with dawning outrage, turned to Geraldine Briggs for guidance, but she appeared to have something urgent to say to the pianist. Eileen and Peter were whispering and nodding, maturely pretending not to have particularly noticed what Melanie said. The crowd began to murmur: Honor the dead! Honor the dead!

Louis was looking at his father, who in turn was looking at his wife. Once the surprise had faded there was nothing amused or affectionate or even angry in Bob's expression. It was pure disappointed disapproval. And, as such, an expression that only love could sponsor. He would have looked exactly the same if Melanie had said, "I'm being unfaithful. That's all I have to say!"

The pianist had struck up a New Age melody, cosmic and burbling. "PEOPLE!" Geraldine Briggs shouted. "People, people, people. We have now heard BOTH sides, the glad and the unenlightened. So let us now go forth into the world with GLADDENED HEARTS AND SOBERED MINDS. REMEMBER THE ENVELOPES. AMEN!"

The drab men and women rose. As they headed for the refreshments they slowed and walked in half circles around Melanie like sullen, beaten hounds. She smiled and nodded to them all as she chatted with Messrs. Tabscott and Aldren and Stoorhuys, these favored hounds crowding around her. Soon Louis and his father were the only people still sitting.

"Sweeting-Aldren?" Louis said.

"Nature's helpers. Herbicides, pigments, textiles."

"Mom has something to do with them now?"

"You could put it that way."

"She was so rude."

"Don't judge her, Lou. There's no reason for you to trust me on this, but please don't judge her. Will you do me that favor?"

Coquettish was the only word for the way in which Melanie was accepting an ordinary cup of coffee from Mr. Stoorhuys, pretending to be tempted against her better judgment. "I thought I was going to *scream*," she went on to Mr. Aldren. For one brief moment, in the unblinking intentness of the smile Mr. Aldren had trained on her, the smiling wolf behind the smiling dog showed through, the cruel and hungry animal biding its time. He said, "You're free for lunch, I assume." To which Melanie replied, "I think I can squeeze you in."

"Look at her," Bob said. "Have you ever seen her so happy? You don't know how long she's had to wait. Hard to begrudge her a couple happy hours."

"Yeah, although—"

Bob looked straight ahead at the empty lectern. "I'm asking you not to judge her."

3

From the memorial service Louis drove his father to a cheap hamburger restaurant in Harvard Square, a place with the air of a selfconscious institution, and it was there, in a booth near the door, that he was introduced to a figure that took away what little appetite he had. His father named the figure while holding the top half of his hamburger bun in his palm like a calculator and spreading mustard on it. The figure was 22 million dollars. It corresponded to Louis's mother's new approximate net worth.

Scarves and coat sleeves were brushing his head as various lunch hours were exhausted and the restaurant emptied out. Cold air blew in through the busy doors. He asked what his mother was going to do with so much money.

His father looked a little bum-like in his ancient suit, with its narrow lapels overlapping as he hunched over his hamburger. "I don't know," he said.

Louis asked if they were going to stay in the house in Evanston.

"Where else would we go?" his father said.

Was he thinking of retiring?

"When I'm sixty-five," his father said.

Unequal to the asking of more questions, Louis watched in silence as his father cleaned both their plates and paid the check with a ten-dollar bill, leaving a tip of dimes and quarters.

It was midafternoon when he got back to WSNE. The clouds were darkening further, deepening and collecting themselves for serious nighttime rain, and in the studios it might already have been midnight. All the lights were burning, the building's various circulatory systems humming audibly, the phones in the advertising department as silent as always. Through the Studio A window he could see the afternoon announcer, an alcoholic-looking veteran named Bud Evans whose few cobwebs of hair were painstakingly arranged over his chapped, bald scalp. He was gazing uneasily over the boom mike at his guest, a gentleman with golden shoulder-length locks and a Hawaiian shirt. For five or six seconds neither spoke. It was like a pensive lull in conversation, except that they were on the air and the lull was being broadcast. Still feeling carsick, Louis went to the men's room and leaned over the urinal with his forehead pressing into tile. His urine broke up a tarry wad of tobacco shreds. Moving like a person with a hangover, he sat down at the terminal in his cubicle and began to enter commercial logs. He did this for three hours, which at the wage he earned netted him somewhat under twelve dollars, assuming he eventually got paid. When he left Waltham, rain was dropping out of a sky the color of a TV set's afterglow. On Clarendon Hill he went straight to the bathroom and vomited a clear ropy liquid into the beige toilet.

Louis was, at twenty-three, a not entirely untroubled person. His relationship with money was particularly tortured. And yet what he realized, when the import of the figure began to sink in, was that up until the moment he'd sat down in the burger joint with his father, he'd basically been content with his life and its conditions. A person accustoms himself to what he is, after all, and if he's lucky he learns to hold in somewhat lower esteem all other ways of being, so as not to spend life envying them. Louis had been coming to appreciate the freedom a person gained by sacrificing money, and to pity or even outright despise the wealthy—a class represented in his mind, justly or not, by the various suntanned narrow-nosed boyfriends Eileen had sported over the years, up to and including Peter Stoorhuys. But now the joke was on Louis, because he was the son of a woman worth 22 million dollars.

That night he had a lucid and unpleasant dream. The setting was a paneled boardroom or club room furnished with red leather chairs. His mother had leaned back on one of them and, raising the hem of her yellow dress, allowed a fully clothed Mr. Aldren to stand between her legs and pump semen into her while Mr. Tabscott and Mr. Stoorhuys looked on. When Mr. Aldren was done, Mr. Stoorhuys mounted her, only Mr. Stoorhuys had become an Irish setter and had to strain and prance on his hind legs to maintain an effective mating position. Mr. Aldren and Mr. Tabscott stood watching as she reached around to steady the eager dog between her legs.

On Saturday Louis left two messages on Eileen's machine. When she didn't return them, he called his parents at their hotel and learned that they were driving to the Kernaghan estate the next morning, his mother to stay there for perhaps a week, his father only for the day, since classes at Northwestern resumed on Monday. "I'm going to be very busy," his mother said. "But if you want to do something for me, you could take your father to the airport. The flight's at seven."

Ignoring the hint, he set out for Ipswich at ten on Sunday morning. A humidity and stasis lay on Somerville. The rain had finally stopped in the night, but eaves and fenders and budding trees were still pregnant with it, there being not a breath of wind. Where sight lines opened, down streets and through the narrow prisms between houses, the humidity added up to a paling of the distance, a blurring of edges that affected even the tolling of a distant church bell, the separate strokes of which were almost lost in the intervening resonance. Louis steered awkwardly around a pair of Somerville patrol cars that had stopped in the middle of an intersection, driver's window to driver's window, as if they were insects and this was how they coupled and their need was urgent. Through the portal of an empty, lighted church he glimpsed banks of Easter lilies.

The highways were deserted. From stretches of elevated grade, up through Chelsea and Revere and Saugus, he looked down on crabbed patchwork neighborhoods in which streets and driveways had hegemony. Many were half underwater now, with cars parked crookedly at their margins as if they'd been deposited by a flood.

A different flood, a receding flood of dollars, had left countless new condominiums stranded in fields that were muddy and barren and rutted with Caterpillar tracks. The town house condos differed only in location; every one of them, without exception, was faced with pastel clapboard and had postmodern semicircles and triangles interrupting the roof lines. The high-rises, on the other hand, came in two varieties: the kind with plywood on their windows, and the kind with banners draped from the roof advertising incredible deals on 1 & 2 BRS.

Thorn bushes and stunted trees filled the flat, exhausted land north of Danvers. In the mist outside Ipswich, near Ipswich Ford, Louis braked to let a shaggy drunk no older than thirty reel across Route 1A. He left the town on Argilla Road, passing widely spaced houses with BMWs and Volvos and tremendous oak trees planted outside them. Soon he came to a stone gate marked KERNAGHAN. A driveway bordered with spruce trees wound up a hill through rolling unmown pastures. At the top of the hill was a gracious white house with symmetrical wings, a domed portico, and, squatting among its dormers, a pyramid made of white aluminum siding. It was easily fifteen feet tall. The effect was of a well-dressed woman wearing a plastic garbage pail on her head.

He stood for a moment on a hemp mat stenciled with a black yin and yang and peered in through a narrow window beside the front door. He saw a tiled entry hall and a living room that extended to the back of the house. In theory at least, since this house now belonged to his mother, it was a second home to him. He opened the door and walked in.

The dining-room table, to his left, was covered with folders and portfolios. A broad-shouldered man in a white shirt was seated with his back to the hall, and at the head of the table, reading a stapled document, sat Melanie.

"Hi Mom, how you doin'," Louis said.

She looked up at him severely. Only the white tip of her long nose held her half glasses on. She was wearing a crimson silk dress, crimson lipstick, and earrings with large black stones. Her dark hair was pulled tightly behind her ears. "Hello Louis," she said, returning her eyes to the document. "Happy Easter."

Her companion had swung around, capturing the back of his chair in an armpit, and revealed a flushed and amiable face with chalky blue eyes and a bushy reddish mustache. His collar was open, his necktie loosened. He seemed so delighted to see Louis that Louis immediately shook his hand.

"Henry Rudman," the man said. He almost but did not quite say *Henwy Wudman*. "You must be the son that lives in Sumvull. I think your mother said Belknap Street?"

"That's right."

Henry Rudman nodded vigorously. "Reason I ask is I grew up in Sumvull myself. You familiar with Vinal Avenue?"

"No, sorry," Louis said. He leaned over his mother's shoulder. "Whatcha reading there, Mom?"

Melanie turned a page in pointed silence.

"It's an old brief," Wudman answered, leaning back in his chair expansively. He waggled his pen like a drumstick. "We got a piece of architectural ornamentation upstairs that's worn out its welcome. The town of Ipswich agreed a few years back to pay for its removal. Now it's looking like they want to welsh."

"That's some ornament," Louis said.

"Hey, to each his own. I know what you mean, though. I understand you moved up here from Texas. What do you think of the weather?"

"It stinks!"

"Yeah, wait'll you see it do this in June. Tell me, you a Sox fan yet?"

"Not yet, no," Louis said. He was appreciating the attention. "Cubs fan."

With a big mitt the lawyer swatted his words back in his direction. "Same diff. You like the Cubs, you got everything it takes to be a Sox fan. I mean for instance, who lost us a Series in '86, Bill Buckner. Who did us the favor of trading us Bill Buckner, Chicago Cubs. Like some kinda conspiracy there. What two teams played the most years without winning the ultimate cigar, you got it, Sox and Cubs. Listen, you want to see a game? Let me send you a couple tickets, I'm a nineteen-year subscriber. Unlikely you'll get tickets like these through normal channels."

Louis drew his head back in surprise, thoroughly disarmed now. "That would be great."

Melanie cleared her throat like a starter motor.

"Hey, don't mention it," Rudman said. "I'm a corrupter o' youth. You gotta excuse us, though, we're looking at a snake's nest here."

Louis turned to his mother. "Where's Dad?"

"Outside. Why don't you look in the yard. As I told you on the phone, Mr. Rudman and I have a lot to discuss by ourselves."

"Don't let me . . . disturb you," he told her in his Nembutal voice.

In the kitchen he found coffee cake, a party-sized urn of coffee, and, on a long counter, other bakery products in white boxes with the name "Holland" in blue crayon. His eyes widened when he opened the refrigerator. There were pâtés and seafood salads in transparent plastic cartons, jumbo fruits in decorated tissue paper, a tin of Russian caviar, half a smoked ham, whole foreign cheeses, premium yogurt in unusual berry flavors, fresh artichokes and asparagus, kosher dill pickles, an intriguing stack of wrapped deli items, German and Dutch beers, name-brand soft drinks, juices in glass bottles, and thirty-dollar-a-pop champagne—

"Louis." His mother spoke from the dining room.

"Yeah, Mom."

"What are you doing in there?"

"I'm looking at the food."

Silence.

"No way you're liable," Henry Rudman said. "Guy pocks his Jag in the street, somebody else comes along secures a loan with it, no way on earth Guy A's responsible. It's straight fraud, doesn't involve you whatsoever. Can't really blame the bank either. She's living in the house and the title she shows 'em's a first-rate forgery, so good it makes you wonder if she did it all by herself, I bet not. It's a slick trick. She gets a home-equity loan for two hundred K, spends seventy-two on this pyramid that she's just gotta have, can't live without, and puts the difference in a different bank. It'll cover payments for another ten, fifteen years plus she can throw the occasional pahty on it. Slick trick. She dies, the bank's screwed. I mean assuming the trustees still have the real title. Your pop must've known what he was doing. Four thousand a month tax-free plus a free house with groundskeeping fully paid and she still can't quite make ends meet, not even paying the Haitian slave wages. I can't say I like this dead-hand business (you understand this is just a professional opinion), but if I'd been married to a woman like that I wouldn't let her near the capital myself. Next thing you know, we'd be looking at Mount Fuji in the back yod."

"Louis."

"Yeah, Mom."

"Would it be possible for you not to be in the kitchen?"

"Yeah, just a sec."

A dark, cold hall off the rear of the kitchen ended in three doors, one leading outside, the others into a bathroom and a bedroom. Louis sat down on the bed and slurped coffee and wolfed cake. All the hangers in the closet were bare. It was a while before he noticed that a pane was missing from the window. This was the only earthquake damage he saw all morning.

Out in the back yard he could find no sign of his father, although the air was so still and thick it almost seemed a person walking through it would leave a trail. He crossed a patio and tried one of the French doors at the rear end of the living room. It swung right open.

The living room was large enough to hold four separate clusters of furniture. Above the fireplace hung a large oil of Louis's grandfather, a formal portrait painted in 1976, when John Kernaghan was seventy-five or so. His eyebrows had still been dark. With his near-perfect baldness and firm skin and elegant, compact skull he looked ageless. He was, Louis realized, the man responsible for his loss of hair. The painted image drew further life from the living daughter sitting across the hall in the dining room, reading documents with her father's own glittering unapproachable dark eyes.

"When they meet on the thirtieth," Henry Rudman said quietly, "they have to distribute the entire corpus. The entire corpus, it's unambiguous, they have no choice. The full transfer may take another four to six weeks, but we're looking at June 15 absolute latest."

That the living room did not entirely belong to Melanie yet was clear from the New Age reading matter on the coffee tables, from the ugly phantasmagoric acrylics on the walls, and from the copies of *Princess Itaray* and *Beginning Life at 60* and *Star Children* that filled the only bookcase. To say nothing of the smell emanating from the bar, a smell of spilled alcohol and bubble-gum-scented disinfectant. The bar jutted out from the wall near the inner rear corner of the room and was made of the same blond wood as the two slender barstools in front of it. Shelves reaching nearly to the ceiling displayed several hundred different bottles—liqueurs and digestives with labels in foreign alphabets, a few with pictures of unlikely vegetables. Louis knelt by the gray marble floor behind the bar. There was plenty of room here for a small woman to lie dead, head smashed. It wasn't hard to see the faint brownish fingers and ridgelines of splashed liquor on the wall. Nor was it hard to see blood. There were traces of it in the sutures between the squares of marble, hardly browned, the nail-polish redness especially visible where the edges of the squares were chipped. Who had cleaned things up? The maid, before her deportation? With his fingertips he pressed on the cold, unyielding marble, putting his body's weight on it, hearing clearly the *whock!* of the splitting head.

"Louis. For God's sake. What are you doing?"

He jumped to his feet. His mother was approaching the bar. "Dropped a coin," he said.

"You have a morbid interest?"

"No, no, I just happened to come inside this way."

"You came in—?" Melanie shook her head at the French doors as if they were a grievous disappointment to her. "This house," she said, "has no security whatsoever. I suppose she expected the pyramid to protect against burglars too. That's very logical and rational, don't you think? That's par for the course."

Louis heard a faint tinkling in a toilet behind a wall.

"Well. You see where she died." His mother crossed her arms and gazed up at the liquor bottles with satisfaction. "Personally, I can't think of anything tackier than putting a full-sized bar like this in your living room. Or do you not agree. Maybe you think everyone should have a saloon in their living room. And a beer keg?"

She looked at Louis as if she actually expected him to reply. "The insult on the injury," she continued, "is that she probably had it installed with money that didn't belong to her. I don't suppose you missed what Mr. Rudman was saying. That she forged a title to this house to borrow money on. What do you think of that, Louis? Do you think that's proper? Do you think that's OK?"

With a beautifully shod toe she flipped up one end of a Chinese rug, tilted her head to read the label, and flipped the end down again. She sneered at a coffee table. "Harmonic Lifestyles. Phoenician Deities. Orgone Redux." She made a gagging, dismissive face. "What do you think of all this, Louis?"

"I think I'm going to scream if you ask me another question like that."

"Every single thing I see here makes me sick. *Sick*." She said this to the portrait above the fireplace.

"But it's all yours now, right?"

"Effectively. Yes."

"What are you going to do with it?"

"I have no idea. I came in here to tell you that you're making Mr. Rudman and me very nervous lurking around like this. You couldn't find your father?"

"No."

"Well, if you want to stay, you can be in the back room, there's a TV in there, maybe you can find a game on. There's lots of food in the refrigerator, you can help yourself. Or you could sweep the patio for me, and I have a few other little jobs for someone, but I do not just want you lurking around. This isn't your house, you know."

Louis looked at her with neutral expectancy, as if she were a chess opponent who'd made a move he wanted to be sure she wasn't going to change her mind about. Then, the arbitrary grace period expiring, he said, "You have a good lunch on Thursday?"

"It was a business lunch. I thought I explained that to you at the time."

"What did you eat?"

"I don't remember, Louis."

"You don't remember? That was three days ago! Piece of fish? Reuben sandwich?"

They could hear Mr. Rudman handling dishes in the kitchen now, whistling a show tune.

"What is it that you want?" Melanie asked levelly.

"I want to know what you had for lunch on Thursday."

She took a deep breath, trying to contain her annoyance. "I don't remember."

He scrunched up his face. "You serious?"

"Louis—" She waved a hand, trying to suggest some generic entrée, something not worth mentioning. "I don't remember, a piece of fish, yes. Filet of sole. I'm extremely busy."

"Filet of *sole*. Filet of *sole*." He nodded so emphatically, it was like bowing. Then he froze, not even letting breath out. "Broiled? Poached?"

"I'm going back to the dining room now," Melanie said, remaining rooted to the center of a Chinese rug. "I've had a very upsetting week—" She paused to let Louis challenge this. "A very upsetting week. I'm sure you understand that and can show some consideration."

"Yeah, well, we're all grieving in our own way, obviously. It's just I heard this crazy rumor about your having inherited twenty-two million dollars." He tried to meet her eyes, but she'd turned away, squeezing her thumbs, fists balled. "Crazy, huh? But getting back to this lunch, let's see, Mr. Aldren and whatever his name is, Tweedledum, they had steak, right? And Mr. Stoorhuys—" He snapped his fingers. "Rabbit. Half a rabbit, grilled. Or what do you call it? Braised."

"I'm going back to the dining room now."

"Just tell me, come on, is that what he had? Did he have rabbit?"

"I don't know, I didn't happen to notice—"

"You didn't notice *rabbit?* Sort of stretched out on the plate? Maybe a little cranberry sauce with it? Or red cabbage? Potato pancakes? What kind of restaurant was it? Help me picture this, Mom. Was it really *expensive?*"

Melanie took another deep breath. "We went to a restaurant called La Côte Américaine. I had filet of sole and Mr. Aldren and Mr. Tabscott and Mr. Stoorhuys had soup and grilled steaks or chops, I truly don't recall exactly what—"

"But not rabbit. You'd recall that."

"But no, not rabbit, Louis. You're being quite a bit less funny than you seem to think you are."

Louis's eyes narrowed. "All right," he said. "Let's get back to the twenty-two million, then. What are you going to do with it?"

"I have no idea."

"How about a yacht? They make nice gifts."

"This is not at all funny."

"So it's true?"

Melanie shook her head. "It's not true."

"Oh, it's not true. Meaning it's false. Meaning, what, twenty-one point nine? Twenty-two point one?"

"I mean it does not concern you."

"Oh, I see, it doesn't concern me. Let's forget it, then, let's drop it. Hey, people inherit twenty-two million dollars every day. What'd you do at work today? Oh, I inherited twenty-two million dollars, would you pass me the butter?"

"Please stop mentioning that figure."

"Twenty-two million dollars? You want me to stop mentioning twenty-two million dollars? All right, I'll stop mentioning twenty-two million dollars. Let's call it alpha." He began to pace around the rim of a rug. "Alpha equals twenty-two million dollars, twenty-two million dollars equals alpha, alpha being neither *greater* than twenty-two million dollars nor *less* than twenty-two million dollars." He drew up. "How'd your father get so rich?"

"Please, Louis, I asked you to stop mentioning the figure and I meant it. It's very painful to me."

"Yeah, so I see. That's why I suggested we call it alpha, although I'm afraid alpha doesn't quite capture the impact. What a terrible painful thing, to inherit that much money. You know Dad says he's not even going to quit teaching?"

"Why should he quit teaching?"

"Don't tell me you need his salary when you've got twenty-two, oops."

"I would be grateful if you did not try to tell me what I need and don't need."

"You'd be grateful if I just walked out of here and never mentioned this again."

Melanie's face lit up as if he were a student of hers who'd blurted truth. "Yes, as a matter of fact, that's exactly right. That is what I would *most* like from you."

Louis's eyes narrowed further. He said: "Twenty-two million dollars, twenty-two million dollars, twenty-two million dollars." He said it faster and faster, until it twisted his tongue, becoming *twollers, twollers.* "What a *huge* amount of money. It means you're *rich, rich, rich rich, rich.*"

His mother had turned to face the mantel and covered her ears with her palms, applying such strong isometric pressure to her head that her arms trembled. This was as close to fighting as she and Louis ever got; and it wasn't really fighting. It was like what a pair of bar magnets do when you try to force the north poles together. It had always been this way. Even when he was a boy of three or four and she had tried to smooth his hair or wipe food off his face, he had twisted his head away on his stout, stubborn neck. If he was sick in bed and she laid a cold hand on his forehead, he had tried to press himself into pillow and mattress with triple gravity, as blindly and determinedly resistant to her touch as the magnet to whose permanent invisible force field the relief of rupture or discharge can never come. Now she raised her head, her white fingers flat on her cheeks, her elbows on the mantel, and looked up at her father. From the rear of the house came the sound of television, amplified rumblings and collisions: bowling.

"I'm paying Mr. Rudman for his time, Louis."

"Right. What's a lawyer get, a couple hundred bucks an hour? Let's say 220 an hour into twenty-two million (oh, *I'm* sorry, there I go again), ten to the second into ten to the seventh, that's a hundred thousand hours, and assume ten-hour days, two hundred fifty days a year, my God, you're right. That's only forty years. I'll try to be quick."

"What is it that you want?"

"Well, let's see, I've got a job and a cheap apartment and a car that's paid for, I'm not married, I don't have expensive habits, and in case you haven't noticed, I haven't asked you and Dad for a single thing since I was sixteen years old, so it's probably not *money* I want, is it, Mom?"

"I appreciate all that."

"Don't even mention it."

"I will mention it. I never get to tell you how proud I am of your independence."

"I said *forget it*."

She turned around to face him. "I have an idea," she said. "I suggested something like this to Eileen and she seemed to feel it was a good idea. I hope your father will go along with it too. I think we should all just act as if this never happened."

"This twenty-two million dollars."

"Please. Please, please, *please*. I think we should all just go on with our lives as if nothing is different. Now, it may be that as time goes by a few things will change, in small ways and perhaps in large ways too. For example, I'll probably be able to make it very easy for you to go back to school if you should ever decide to. And I'm not promising anything, but it's possible that if you or Eileen ever want to make a down payment on a home I could be of some help there too. But all these things are in the future, and I think the best thing for the four of us to do now is just put it out of our minds."

Louis scratched his neck. "You say Eileen thought this was a good idea?"

"Oh yes."

"Then what was she crying for on Thursday."

"Because . . ." A faraway look came into his mother's eyes, and then they began to glisten, tears seeming to form directly on her dark brown irises, the way rock candy grows wet with itself. "Because, Louis, she had come to me to ask for money."

He laughed. This was the Eileen who let cars roll into lakes. "So? Write her a check. Or don't write her a check."

"Oh!" His mother's hands rose to her face again, her fingers bent hard at the knuckles. "Oh! I won't have you talk like this!"

"Like *what?*"

"I'm not going to discuss this a moment longer. We *must* put this out of our minds. I want you to leave now. Do you understand? I have asked you and asked you not to joke about these things, and you will not listen to me. You are *worse* than your father, who I know you think is very funny. But it is not the least bit funny, it is simply inconsiderate— *And don't you roll your eyes at me! DON'T YOU ROLL YOUR EYES AT ME!* Do you understand? I want you to leave the house this minute."

"All right, all right." Louis walked into the front hall. "Just drop us a postcard from Monaco, OK?"

Melanie pursued him. The volume of the television had tactfully been increased. "Take that back!"

"All right. Don't drop us a postcard from Monaco."

"You really don't understand how inconsiderate you're being. Do you?"

When Louis got mad, as opposed to merely feeling righteous, he stuck his chest out and raised his chin and looked down his nose like a sailor or an ugly asking for a fight. He was completely unaware of doing this; the look on his face was dead serious. And as he faced his mother, who after all wasn't likely to shove him or take a free swing, he looked so incongruously belligerent that her expression softened. "Are you going to punch me, Louis?"

He lowered his chin, angrier still to see he was only amusing her.

"Give me a hug," his mother said. She laid a hand on his arm and held it firmly when he tried to pull away. She said, "I'm not selfish. Do you understand?"

"Sure." His hand was on the doorknob. "You're just upset."

"That's right. And it will be some time before I even see the money."

"Sure."

"And when I do, I don't know how much it's going to be. The figure you mentioned, which you must have gotten from your father—could change a great deal. It's a very complicated and unfortunate situation. A very—very unfortunate situation."

"Sure."

"But no matter what, we'll all be able to do some nice things."

"Sure."

Her irritation flared. "Stop saying that!"

A bowling ball struck pins. A crowd cheered. "Sure," Louis said.

She dropped his arm. Without looking at her he walked out the door and closed it quietly behind him. Continuing to stare straight ahead, he marched past his car and down the drive, stiff-legged, letting gravity do the work, depressed the way he'd been when he read about the earthquake eight days earlier, depression an isotope of anger: slower and less fierce in its decay, but chemically identical. When his father came into view, at a bend near the bottom of the drive, he hardly noticed him.

"Howdy, Lou." Bob's head was aglow in a nest of Gore-Tex and plaid lining. He smelled like burnt marijuana.

"Hello," Louis said, not breaking stride. Bob smiled as he watched him go and immediately forgot that he'd seen him.

East of the Kernaghan house the land became even more park-like, the yards giving way to estates with hurdles in the pastures and horse trailers in the driveways. A sleek Japanese-made ski boot whooshed past Louis. Pasted to a window was the face of a young girl in a pink church dress. The boot braked and turned and faded a little in the white air as it drove up a hill. The girl jumped from the sliding door running, carrying something in her hand, a book maybe, a Bible.

Between the ages of six and fifteen, Louis himself had returned from church on approximately 350 Sunday mornings. He'd emerged from the back seat with a light head and the sense of a morning's worth of playtime lost, wasted in basement church-school rooms which had the accidental furniture arrangement and dank smell of places frequented only by transients. In the early years, of course, there were efforts made to cover up the swindle. There were jars of paste and rusty scissors, mimeographed leaves from a coloring book, and brown crayons with which to color the donkey on which Jesus sat. (These crayons were among the first contributors to his sense of the vastness of the past and the strangeness of history, their unfamiliar design and soiled and dried-out wrappers suggesting that this business of coloring donkeys had been going on significantly longer than his life had, longer than anything at real school, where supplies were always new.) There was music—in particular one song about how Jesus loved the little children of the world who came in crayon colors: red and yellow, black and white. There was cottage industry, the manufacture of styrofoam Advent wreaths, construction-paper palms, ceramic Mother's Day items, and (one morning when Louis dislodged the front tooth of a boy who was using his blue tempera paint, and miraculously wasn't punished for it) plaster crèche figurines. But he was no more fooled by this veneer of fun than he was fooled at the dentist by the sweetness of the tooth polish. And when he reached seventh grade, the veneer fell away entirely. He was issued a Bible with a red leatherette binding and his name in gilt capitals on the front: LOUIS FRANCIS HOLLAND, and spent the Sunday morning hour in an even smaller and more barren cubicle in a different wing of the church, the class size for some reason much diminished in the transfer, all his male friends having dropped out, able now to spend the morning watching the Sunday cartoons to which he himself had become attached during the summer, so that he occupied without challenge the very bottom of a mainly female class in which, there being no grades, he deduced his rank from the fact that unlike all the other Bibles, his had immediately and through no conscious fault of his own acquired a blackened and ragged spine and a back cover with a rip across one corner, to say nothing of the fact that he was called upon to read aloud from this Bible three times as often as anyone else and was forever being told, in a too-gentle voice by a parent named Mr. Hope, to speak up a little, to not be shy. On one occasion the class was asked to describe Jesus the man, and a girl offered that he had been frail and gentle—a characterization with which Mr. Hope took issue, reasoning that this carpenter's son must have been physically powerful in order to overturn the money changers' tables in the Temple; Louis thought that for once the frail and gentle Mr. Hope had a point.

Even though their own father used Sunday mornings for swimming rather than for worship, church school had never seemed optional to the Holland kids. Nine months a year Melanie herded them along in front of her, up the rear stairs of the church from the parking lot, and gave them a last push towards the classrooms while she proceeded into the sanctuary, there to occupy a pew close to the pulpit, not because such proximity made her a better Christian (that was for God to decide) but because she liked to have her clothing noticed. She kept going to church even after her children reached fifteen and proved unconfirmable—Eileen because girls with social lives needed to sleep late on Sunday, and Louis because he had a personality clash with every single person in the church. Despite ten years of Sunday school, the permanent escape from all further responsibility turned out to cost him no more than saying nope, I don't buy it. It was the final proof that the Church's authority could simply not be compared with the school district's.

The horse farms now behind him, he was walking between swampy fields and dense black loaves of bramble. Abandoned among dead rushes, looking severe and prophetic, stood an entirely rusted bailer; as if they'd just picked the last flesh off its skeleton, two sea gulls wheeled away from it. Louis watched them until their wings dissolved in the whiteness and their bodies dwindled to the status of floaters in his vision.

The road to the beach seemed to rise and vaporize. It stretched out so long and straight that he started jogging, working the stiffness out of his legs, running faster. Soon, as he heard his breathing grow heavy, and as he watched the cordgrass and rockweed of the marshes bob up and down with the motion of his head, it began to seem as if he were watching a scene from a movie, a scene of a psychopath closing in on a girl in underthings, where the killer's point of view is rendered with a moving handheld camera and heavy bronchial action on the sound track. This sensation became so powerful and disturbing and his breathing filled his ears so much that by and by, to reclaim himself, he began to chant aloud: "Ho! Ho! Hey! Me! Here! Here! Ho!" This did the trick, but something else must have been happening as he ran down this road, because when he passed a guardhouse and abruptly drew up and slowed to a walking pace, he felt as if he'd run not only out of the marshes but clear out of Sunday as well, ending up in the dunes of some eighth, nameless day of the week which he was the only person in the world to know about.

A siren was wailing in his head. The sky (if sky was the word for a thing commencing directly before his eyes) was still the same uniform white, but now it seemed as if the sun were hovering right beyond the threshold of visibility, an arrow's flight away and single-serving-sized, and as if, when the mists blew off, the proximate borders of a miniature world would likewise be revealed, an un-threatening brook-like void now lapping behind him in the direction he'd come from, the direction of Sunday and his mother and her wealth.

He entered a parking lot. Its perimeter was guarded by

a detachment of green barrels stenciled with a single word:
P L E A S E. Clumps of beach grass to the seaward side were sus-
pended in the air, the supporting dunes invisible. Through his feet
he thought he could feel the impact of waves, the faint shudder.
The siren left his head and localized itself in a lone, clog-like Le
Baron parked at the far end of the lot. Its theft alarm was ringing.
Then the ringing stopped, but it had stretched something inside
Louis's head, some muscle-like apparatus that continued to throb
after the sound was withdrawn from it.

He was still trying to figure out what kind of place he was in
when a black animal came charging up from behind a trash barrel.
It was a retriever, fully grown. She skidded past him and paused
in a playful attitude, head lower than her tail. Then she jumped
on him. He removed her paws from his chest but it was like dealing
with a rubber ball, the paws bouncing back into his hands as soon
as they'd hit the ground. One of her tags listed a 508 number and
the name JACKIE. There was no owner in sight. She followed him
companionably up a wooden walkway and onto the sand, sniffing
his footprints as they formed.

The beach was rain-soaked and unpeopled. Brown waves were
stopping in their tracks, each of them like a failed quarterback
sneak, the opposing forces meshing and falling to little purpose.
Well south of the parking lot, at a point where the beach widened
and a creek carried iron-rich mud out from behind the dunes, the
dog suddenly took off running. She turned her head hard to one
side as though she wanted to look back at Louis but also did not
want to slow down, and then without showing even this much regret
she ran harder, far, far up the beach, and disappeared.

He felt a stab of real loneliness then. He sat down on a rock
and propped his chin on one hand. The sea drew breath like a sick
person; time stretched long between the impact of one wave and
the reassurance of the next. The breakers were dark and rotten
with suspended sand and organic matter. All Louis could see in
the direction in which the dog had run was sand, water, mist.

Though he'd laughed, it hadn't really surprised him to hear
that Eileen had already tried to tap their mother's new resources.
Very early in her life Eileen had acquired the ability to beg from
Melanie and live with herself afterward. In the years of their com-

mon adolescence, Louis would often pass her on the stairs and see her folding up one or more twenties, and then in the dining room he'd find further evidence of a transaction, the maternal purse occupying a new place on the table and its owner visibly composing herself, a message for him in her eyes: The wallet has been put away now, so don't you be asking me, too. Which was interesting, because he never did ask, not even when he had a need more compelling than Eileen's need for another lightweight Benetton item or another concert ticket. He never asked because it somehow always seemed that Eileen had beaten him to it. And this must not have been a matter of timing, since whenever it did occur to him to ask, he always felt he had to hold off for a while because Eileen had asked so recently, and while he held off she would go and ask again and receive again. It was clear that if she really had beaten Louis to their mother's money, she'd done it long ago, once and for all.

The day was bound to come when they met in the hall and did not pass in silence. It came the same summer that Eileen put the car in the lake. Louis had returned from mowing grass, and in the hall upstairs he saw her with the usual twenties in her hand, twenties folded into quarters and held with the nonchalance of a victorious dog walking from a fray with a disputed scrap of pot roast in its teeth. Long-compounded resentment and the ugliness of the fingers clasping the twenties made Louis say, "How much do you have there?" She said, "How much do I have where?" He said, "In your hand. Maybe you'd like to give me twenty of that." She stared at him as though he'd suggested she take her shirt off. "No way! Go ask for yourself. I asked for this for me." He said, "Yeah, well, you just asked, so what am I supposed to do?" She said, "I asked for this for *me*. You can go ask for yourself." And he said: "I don't feel like asking. I like to *earn* my money."

It was as if she'd known all her life that this moment would come. Her face boiled and she threw the poisoned bills at his feet and slammed the door of her room behind her. Later, from his own room, Louis heard his mother say, "Eileen? Eileen, honey, you dropped your money out here."

In truth, Melanie might have preferred to be more evenhanded, especially if it hadn't involved increased outlays. Certainly she took

Eileen's requests as opportunities to upbraid her for her selfishness and to make an example of Louis and his independent spirit. But with one of her children making no demands at all, it became not only financially feasible but personally more convenient just to give the other child everything she wanted. Eileen could be supernaturally silent and evil when something had been denied her. She sat at the dinner table and stared at Melanie's clothes and her jewelry so long and so hard that she began to poison the simplest of her mother's pleasures. She would not relent until money or its equivalent in goods was offered. It was joyless, this conspiracy between mother and daughter, but it worked. The end of the conspiracy was to keep the money unpoisoned, and to achieve this end only Louis had to be tiptoed around, since his father could satisfy his few personal wants through direct withdrawals and otherwise left everything to Melanie. Only Louis—odd, grumpy Louis—had the power to poison money. The others' comfort depended on his restraint. And he exercised this restraint, and deliberately let Eileen be spoiled, and only once, when he confronted her in the upstairs hall, was there any hint of all the poison pooling up inside him.

Eileen went to Bennington College. It was the best school she'd gotten into and was the choice of Judd, her North Shore boyfriend. It was also the most expensive undergraduate institution in the country. She and Judd had broken up before they arrived for orientation.

Two years later Louis went off to Rice. Rice was cheap and had offered him a good aid package. He worked seventeen hours a week behind the circulation desk in the library, which had the strange effect of making his face widely recognized on campus. He also played poker avidly and kept records in a notebook; by the end of his junior year his three-year average weekly earnings were a very respectable $0.384. He was still accumulating debt, though, and so when an opportunity arose to cut expenses drastically during his senior year, he seized it first and questioned the wisdom of this only later, when his troubles had already begun.

His father had put him in touch with an old grad-school acquaintance of his, a man named Jerry Bowles who taught at Rice and lived with his wife in a house a few blocks west of campus, on Dryden Street, south of Shakespeare, north of Swift. Mr. Bowles had developed a heart condition and was looking for a student to do heavy yard work in the spring and fall in exchange for room and board. Louis appeared to be ideally suited for the job. When he returned to Houston in late August, the Bowleses picked him up at the airport.

During their interview with him the previous spring the Bowleses had been brisk and businesslike, but now that Louis had arrived, like a toy from a catalogue, they were like children scrambling to unwrap him and see if he worked the way they'd hoped he would. They had a toy of their own making, a daughter, an only child, but she was away at school and apparently no longer much fun to play with. Louis was their new enthusiasm. Over dinner the first night they kept editing each other:

"MaryAnn is more than happy to make lunch for you—"

"Jerry, there is no *question* of me not making lunch, we did offer him full—"

"Do you have some kind of tupperware container that you could—"

"Louis, I am *always* in the house. I am *always* in the house, so whenever you want to come home, it makes absolutely no difference—"

"We may be a trifle more particular about dinner—"

"Jerry, why, Jerry, *why* do you—"

Louis, between them at the table, ate his pork chop and minded his own business the way he used to on the El in Chicago, when a maniac had taken the floor. He'd made a mistake, he could see that. He'd stumbled into the wrong car. But he wasn't riding for pleasure, he was riding to save money.

Mr. Bowles had a trim white beard and a pipe that he often chewed on and still sometimes smoked. When he wasn't teaching linguistics, he patrolled his property for weeds and brown branches and crooked flagstones, for dripping faucets, squeaky floorboards, sticky doors, torn screens and dirty windows. His hammers and saws and clippers hung on pegboards with each tool outlined in black magic marker. He didn't seem to have any friends or hobbies. He liked to explain to Louis how things were done in his house. He rationalized in detail every aspect of his wife's cooking, relating how she had come to steam vegetables instead of boiling them, how a creamier mashed potato was achieved, and how, over the years, with his own input, she had reached the decision not to serve meat more than twice a day. He outlined ergonomic methods of stacking dishes and reading a newspaper. A recurrent theme was their water softener and its manifold virtues. Louis listened to these discourses with a compassion bordering on horror.

"Look at the look he's giving you," MaryAnn said. "Jerry. Look at the way Louis is looking at you."

"Is something wrong?" asked a potentially miffed Mr. Bowles.

"Maybe he's heard enough for now about soft water," said MaryAnn.

"*I'm* sorry," Louis said, shaking his head as if to clear it of cobwebs. "I was thinking about—something else."

MaryAnn twinkled. "Like maybe some blueberry pie à la mode?"

MaryAnn was younger than her husband. She wore shawls and sandals and floral print dresses cut low to highlight her large and blue-veined bosom. She could often be found, silent, silent, in the corner of the gleaming laundry room where she ironed shirts and pillowcases and underpants. The house was full of places where she sat and rested. She kept books near all these places and could sometimes be seen setting one aside (Sigrid Undset, Edith Wharton, D. H. Lawrence), but the bookmarks never seemed to advance. The lunches she packed for Louis were heartbreaking: sandwiches on stone-ground wheat bread, carrot sticks, watermelon pickles, Bartlett pears, slabs of homemade yellow cake. The lunches he'd made himself in Evanston generally consisted of baloney on white bread, a banana, Twinkies when in stock, and a package of Del-Mark potato chips. In his entire life he'd never seen Del-Mark potato chips anywhere but in his mother's kitchen.

He was tactful enough to wait four whole days before telling MaryAnn that he didn't plan to be eating his dinners on Dryden Street. He said it would be best if he packed both lunch and dinner in a bag to take to campus.

MaryAnn had clearly been expecting this. "I'll pack them," she said sadly. "Although I can't really feed you very well from a paper bag."

It wasn't, Louis said, that he wouldn't enjoy eating dinner at home. But he had his senior thesis and his duties as station manager at KTRU to consider.

"Well," said MaryAnn. "Maybe on Sundays you'll have dinner here with us? And any other day you feel like it."

This would not be the last time that he reviewed the logic: (1) he needed to be polite because (2) he was getting a good deal here and (3) thereby avoiding debt. "Sundays, sure," he said. "That's fine."

It had been fifteen years since anyone had regularly made breakfast for him, and he had never in his life seen anything like the breakfasts MaryAnn made. He got fresh biscuits, fresh oat-bran muffins, fresh corn muffins, slab bacon. He got berry pancakes, veal-and-fennel sausages, french toast and cheese soufflés and steak and eggs. He got eggs scrambled with chives and sour cream, eggs Benedict, whole-grain hot cereals with cream and brown sugar, broiled grapefruit, homemade cinnamon-raisin bread, winter peaches topped with vanilla ice cream, honeydew quarters with strawberries in their hollows. After she had served the food, MaryAnn sat down and quietly drank coffee, showing him her profile, her jutting breasts. The terms of the moral problem were vivid to him each time he came to the table: *It would be better not to accept this food. But he was hungry and the food looked very good.* He continued to eat the breakfasts even when his pity for MaryAnn began to give way to something closer to alarm. It was a bad moment when he discovered that she'd been darning his socks. It was an even worse moment when a DJ at KTRU opened Louis's sack dinner and found the tupperware pie-slice container which he'd repeatedly declined to carry, and a note from MaryAnn that read: *Maybe you can buy some ice cream for the pie?*

One Friday night in January he came home at midnight with a head full of tequila and found MaryAnn on her knees in the dining room, unpacking her collection of Wedgwood teacups and saucers from the breakfront. "How's my acolyte?" she said. She thought his eternal white shirt and black pants made him look like an acolyte. She told him to sit down. He did so, his body leaning in the direction he wanted to go: upstairs. She took out piece after piece of china, murmuring that she ought to get rid of it all, sell it, what a stupid lot of cups, she'd had no idea how many there were. Finally she was kneeling in the midst of the entire collection, the tassels of her shawl fanned around her. "Take some," she said angrily, dumping a cup and saucer on Louis's lap. "Take a couple, take four. Who on earth would want these? You don't want those."

"Sure I do." Louis was pale and perspiring. "They're handsome."

"You know," she said, "I used to be in love with England. The whole country. I used to think I'd be considered pretty there, or prettiness wouldn't matter. Like it was some wonderful old minor league I'd shine in."

"You are pretty," the tequila said.

MaryAnn shook her head. "When I got my master's in English I was in New York. I went to work for the Duncan McGriff Agency, it was a big literary agency. I suppose we had some famous clients, but the way we really earned our money was by charging reading fees. I wasn't a reader. I was the person who took the readers' reports on manuscripts and turned them into personalized letters from Duncan himself. I had a sheet with about twenty different ways to personalize them, to say how he'd read the manuscript while he was sitting at home by his swimming pool where his three dear children were frolicking. Or how he'd read the manuscript on a mountaintop while watching a glorious sunset. This is literally what I had to write. But the sad thing was, no matter how bad a manuscript was, I always had to say that the work showed great promise but was not yet in commercially salable form. And there were various degrees to this, because there were people out there —innocent people out in Nebraska—who would send in their manuscripts again and again, and pay the full fee every time, and we could *never say yes*, and *never say no*. Which was also how Duncan was with me, although that's a different story. I worked there for five years. I was still sitting there in my little chair at my little desk the day the Justice Department came and closed us down for an even worse thing we were doing. And Louis, I was twenty-eight then. It was like I'd been stabbed! It's funny, twenty-eight still seems an old age to me, like I was never an older maid than I was that year. I couldn't believe it, I mean, what had happened to those years. But so anyway, I married Jerry, and that's when I really started to panic, because the feeling didn't go away. The feeling that I'd missed my chance to have the life I wanted. Everything still eluded me, except now it was worse, because *now I was married*. It wasn't so much that Jerry—well, you know him. It wasn't his fault. I knew what he was like and I married him. It was my fault. And do you know, once you've started to think about something, once you've gotten it in your head that you have insomnia, it makes it all the harder to fall asleep?"

Louis was drifting in a slow spin towards the center of his empty teacup. MaryAnn gave him a glance full of hurt and worry, as though it were he, not she, whom she felt sorry for. "Well," she said in a lower voice, "when I saw how nothing changed when I got married, I got it in my head that nothing ever would. I made Jerry hate me and then I said to myself: I have a husband who hates me. Do you see? There's an aloneness you can catch like a disease and not get rid of. A wrongness—a wrongness you can never fix. And it was the same thing when we adopted Lauren. Like everything else, it was my idea. I wanted to stop the slide, and the one thing I knew was I'd never seen a woman who didn't love her baby. But Louis—" Tears rushed into her face and voice and then receded. "I didn't have faith! I didn't have faith! The whole time we were dealing with the agency, I felt cold and dead inside. I tried to rationalize it. I said to myself, everything will change the instant I get to hold her (or him, we didn't know). But in my heart, in my *heart*, all I thought was: Maybe this won't work either. Maybe I'm the woman who even motherhood won't change. This is what I *felt*, in my *heart*, and I still didn't stop the process. Even though I was sick to my stomach every time we communicated with the agency. Sick for a week, from guilt and the strain of pretending to feel something I didn't. And then when she came— well, it was already a bit of a disappointment that she was eight months old. You know, of course *I'm* the one who gets the eight-month-old baby."

She pressed her crossed arms into her breasts and rocked a little. Louis dimly wondered what was so wrong with a baby being eight months old, but—

"But it was either that or nothing at all, and you know Jerry and I don't discuss things, we just blame each other afterward. But

that wasn't the worst thing. The worst thing was that Lauren knew.
Even when she was tiny she could feel me doubting myself. She
could feel how I didn't really believe I was her mother. No matter
how hard I tried, I couldn't get us to believe in me. And how could
I blame her then for all the things she did to me? For biting me
like an animal? For the gutter language? For all the worry and the
dread when she wouldn't come home? How could I feel anything
but guilt? Guilt, Louis, was the biggest thing of all. That this was
our life, our only life, and this was what I'd done to it. *I was not
going to get another chance.* Do you see?"

She looked up at him beseechingly, leaning forward, seeming
to want to pour her breasts out at his feet. She must have forgotten
who she was talking to. She must somehow have been thinking
that when she looked up at him he would take her in his arms and
rescue her. But all she saw was a drunken college boy swallowing
a yawn. "Oh God." She turned away, furious with herself. "Why,
why, why do I ever speak?"

After that night, things were more straightforward between
them, more like they were between Louis and his own mother, more
realistic. MaryAnn didn't watch him eat his breakfast anymore;
having explained herself to him, she could afford to be anywhere
in the house. He was part of the family now—family meaning action
at a distance, invisible fields that pass through walls. He began to
count the weeks until he was free of Dryden Street.

During Easter vacation the Bowleses urged him to bring someone over to dinner to help finish up the rack of arctic caribou a
colleague of Mr. Bowles's had brought them back from Elsemere
Island. Louis invited a girl he was friends with, a DJ at KTRU from
whom he'd been learning about Wagner and Richard Strauss and
with whom, in a mutuality of opportunism, he'd been spending
some afternoons in a dormitory bed. MaryAnn seemed to have
intuited this circumstance. Over the braised caribou she patronized
his friend relentlessly, harping in particular on the beauty of her
hair, as if it were understood that lookswise her hair was all she
had going for her. Afterward, as he walked her home, the friend
said she didn't think Mrs. Bowles was very nice. "She's crazy,"
Louis said. "They're both crazy." Nevertheless, the idea had been

planted in his head that this friend wasn't necessarily worthy of him, and he soon began to patronize her himself and then avoided her entirely.

The next morning he woke up very late with a queasiness he associated with the questionable taste of the caribou. When he stepped into the hall, in his gym shorts and gray T-shirt, it took him a moment to notice the girl standing against one wall of the alcove beyond the stairwell. It was like the moment when you realize there's a bird inside your house which happens to be still now but could fly into your face at any second. The spot in the alcove where the girl stood was just the kind of meaningless random spot where a bird in its confusion lands, and where Louis himself, in Evanston, could frequently be found. The girl was wearing a tight black tank top and a gray-and-white plaid miniskirt; she had a bimboish cumulus of dark blond hair, long bare legs, green ankle socks, and shiny shoes. Her fists were clenched and her jaw was set. Her chest was heaving with what appeared to be rage. She gave Louis a white-hot look, and his heart jumped as violently as if suddenly wings were flapping along walls and claws and a beak veering past his eyes.

He escaped to the bathroom. He washed his hair in the shower but forgot to wash the rest of himself. He stood naked and stared at the Bowleses' Water Pik for several minutes and then mechanically began to take another shower. He washed his hair again and again forgot to wash anything else. It was as if he'd suddenly found himself on the brink of a deep, dark pool marked LAUREN and said What the hell, and let himself fall in.

An hour later, at the bottom of the stairs, he exchanged hellos with another new face, a Texan youth with open, honest features and a military haircut who was reading the paper in the living room.

"Your lunch is on the table, Louis," MaryAnn said quietly in the kitchen.

Louis stared at her. How could someone so irrelevant exist? Where was Lauren? Was he going to have to eat lunch with Lauren? He pointed vaguely east. "I need to get to the station," he said.

"You want me to wrap it up for you? We were about to sit down."

He felt a hand between his shoulder blades, Mr. Bowles propelling him towards the kitchen table. "You've got ten minutes, sit down a minute and prime that engine."

"Aren't you off the air this week?" said MaryAnn.

Cut in two diagonally, a caribou sandwich on a plate awaited him. The elder Bowleses attacked their own sandwiches with unusual appetite, ignoring the voices in the living room and the heavy footsteps on the stairs, gnawing at their food with tilted heads like starved and nervous animals driven into one corner of the house by a daughter who, with a loose gait and no apparent selfconsciousness, entered the kitchen just as a tough slab of gamey meat slid into the no man's land between Louis's sandwich and his mouth.

"Lauren, this is Louis. Louis, our daughter, Lauren."

"Mumph," Louis said.

"Hi nice to meet you," Lauren said in a monotone. She was nothing like the mess or terror that MaryAnn had led him to expect. Her all-season tan, her turquoise earrings, her Mickey Mouse watch and the lazy way she turned one hip out all marked her as a mainstream good-times disaffected Texas college girl. She had smooth skin, a wide mouth, and permanent-looking bruises the color of iodine beneath her eyes. She'd written something in pen on the back of her hand. She told her parents that she and Emmett were driving to the beach at Galveston for the afternoon. Before she left the room she paused to take in Louis fully—his aviator frames, his thinning curls, his gutted sandwich, his searing blush. Her face became simply empty.

"We have a very open relationship with Lauren," Mr. Bowles explained when she was gone.

"Emmett's her fiancé," Mr. Bowles added.

"We didn't think she was coming down," Mr. Bowles explained.

"She's a wayward sprite," Mr. Bowles said.

"God! Full of energy. Full of life," Mr. Bowles reflected.

MaryAnn sank her teeth into her last piece of sandwich.

"I hope Emmett doesn't let her drive," Mr. Bowles concluded.

When Louis came home that night, the three Bowleses and Emmett were eating ice cream in the dining room. MaryAnn headed silently for the kitchen to get him dinner. "I've eaten," he said, already on the stairs. At the top of them he stopped long enough to hear Lauren say:

"I guess he studies all the time, huh?"

"He's a good worker," Mr. Bowles affirmed.

"Gosh, that's great," Lauren said.

This was all he heard. Mouth wide open, eyes staring, he shut his door and dropped to the floor and stretched out on it. He didn't get tired of being there. In his fever he heard Lauren and Emmett go out to a movie and return at twelve. He heard a Hide-A-Bed being opened for Emmett in Mr. Bowles's study, and then a fever dream of voices, music, footsteps and opening and closing doors that seemed to last all night and involve dozens of people.

The next morning, at the Soundwaves branch on Main, he was rummaging through the Thelonious Monk LPs on station business when he became aware that Lauren Bowles was standing in the next aisle. She had her back to him. She was wearing a man's shirt and was faintly pushing her head forward to the drum-machine-driven beat of optimistic British pop on the store stereo. She dropped a pair of CDs in their longboxes among JAZZ ARTISTS —B—, and flipped through Coleman, Coltrane, Corea. Then she leaned into the B's again. Twice she made a short fierce movement with her shoulder, as if out of his sight she were wringing the necks of small animals, and then already she was leaving, glancing at crates of new releases near the cash registers.

Outside, Louis watched her drop to one knee and retie a sneaker between parked cars. Quarry seldom lets a hunter come as close as he came to her then. He was twenty feet behind her when she unbuttoned the lowest button of her shirt and gave birth to the pair of stolen CDs, which fell neatly into her purse. She flipped the flap down over them and crossed the street through traffic.

It was the Saturday before Easter. Everything at Rice was closed. Louis returned to Dryden Street with his purchases and found MaryAnn making toffee, a big soup pot of it that filled the house with a caustic smell of butter and sugar. Up in his room he opened Volume II of Flaubert's collected letters on his desk. He hadn't read a word of them when, some fifteen minutes later, the door behind him opened and closed.

Lauren was standing with one hand lingering on the doorknob, the lowest button of her shirt still unbuttoned, her eyes sweeping the room with a planning kind of thoughtfulness. After a moment she sat down on his desk and, shifting laterally, lowered herself onto Flaubert. The book's spine broke audibly. "It's Mister Dean's List," she said. "That's your name, isn't it?" For a moment she monitored Louis closely for a reaction.

"Where's Emmett?" he said.

She leaned back on outstretched arms and knocked a jar of pens over. "He's in Bay City visiting his grandfather. He asked me if I wanted to go, which was like real appealing when they keep talking about how his grandfather's as yellow as a carrot. He's got some disease."

"Jaundice."

"Wow. You must know everything."

Louis kept his eyes on hers and hers avoided his.

"See my ring?" She dangled her left hand in his face. "It cost three thousand dollars. It's a three-quarter-carat diamond. Do you like it?"

"No."

"You don't like it? What's wrong with it?"

"The ugly little prongs here, to begin with."

"Oh." She took her hand back and breezily inspected the ring from various unilluminating angles. She had small, even spaces between her teeth. "They are, kind of, aren't they. You're pretty observant, I guess."

Forgetting about the ring, she twisted around to take a book off a shelf, her knees rising for balance. "What's this book?" She opened a critical study so far that its front and back covers touched and a chunk of pages fell on Louis's lap. "Oops. *Sorry*. Hey, it's French! You read French? Can you say something to me in French?"

"No."

"Please?" The mockery in her voice had modulated into the tonal flatness of a girl who thinks a guy is being a jerk and who wants him to, like, stop? Please?

"Je ne veux pas parler français avec toi. Je veux commettre crimes avec toi."

"God," she said with deep sarcasm. "You're *good!*"

The smell of toffee made his eyes and nose burn. His tiredness caught up with him in a rush. He had nothing to say. Lauren raised a leg and hopped lightly off the desk. "Do you like it here?" she asked. "Do you like my parents?"

"I guess you think I do, don't you."

She didn't answer. Her shoulders had gone tense; she was looking at the door; she'd heard something in the hall. She touched Louis's bed as if she were going to sit on it, but she changed her mind and ran on tiptoe to the door. She sat down on the carpeting and leaned her head against the keyhole, listening.

"Lauren?"

MaryAnn had spoken from halfway up the stairs. Lauren made her face stupid and mouthed her own name.

"Lauren?"

MaryAnn had climbed the remainder of the stairs and was coming up the hall. She stopped outside the door. This was the point at which Lauren closed her eyes and cried out sharply. She repeated it: a physical cry, a cry of pleasant surprise. Then she began to pant, and produce half-moaning coughs of fake transport, and drag her heels across the carpeting. She was glaring at Louis's bed, and what she was doing with her feet was angry too.

Louis lowered his head over the broken Flaubert and laughed joylessly. MaryAnn was descending the stairs again. Lauren stood up and smiled cruelly at the floor, as if she had X-ray vision and could see her mother entering the dining room and slumping into one of the chairs along the wall. Then Louis's bed attracted her attention. She stepped up onto it and started bouncing. Soon the springs were groaning and the one slightly shorter leg of the bed was tapping on the floor.

"Up – pan – down, up – pan – down," she said. Her singsong words matched the rhythm of the springs. "In – nan – dout, in – nan – dout. Up – pan – down, up – pan – down. In – nan – dout, in – nan – dout—"

"Stop," Louis said, more irritated than anything else. "She gets the message already."

Lauren stopped. "Am I bothering you?"

"You're fucked up," he said without looking at her. "You're really fucked up. And you've got the wrong idea about me."

"But you like me, right?" she asked him from the doorway.

"Yeah, sure. I like you. I like you."

Her new Eurythmics album was playing on her father's audiophile-quality stereo when Louis slipped out and down the stairs and out the front door into air that didn't smell like toffee. When he returned in the evening, from a long walk nowhere, he circled the house twice and didn't see any sign of youth. Inside, Mr. Bowles told him that Lauren and Emmett had driven back to Beaumont to be with Emmett's family for Easter Sunday. It was a full week before MaryAnn would speak to him again.

The retriever had come back. Louis, cold and stiff, watched her run arcs across the sand in front of him, nimble tangents along the retreating and advancing foam lines. He could hear voices from the direction of the parking lot. After a while the white air released three young or youngish figures who were fanned out on the beach and seemed to be combing it methodically. The one who passed right in front of him was a tall Oriental male in a down jacket and loose white yachting pants. He glanced gloomily at Louis, said, "Hey," and scuffed on by, gouging divots in the sand out of disgust or some vandalistic impulse.

The person closest to the water was having a problem with the dog. He was a bearded Caucasian whose glasses were held on with a black elastic band. Jackie was snapping at his raised elbows. "Go! Go! Get away!" he commanded as she barked and tried to corner him between a pair of broken waves scissoring up onto the sand from two directions. He gave the air a vicious warning kick, and she retreated. Meanwhile the third person, a female with short black hair, had run on far ahead, her windbreaker and jeans fading into the whiteness. This was the person who, when the group returned in tighter formation a few minutes later, said, "I'm going to go ask this guy," in a voice not low enough to escape Louis's hearing. She came up the sand towards him. She had a small, pleasant face, with a short nose and pretty brown eyes. Her expression was fixed in an intense, frosty smileyness. "Sorry to bother you," she said. "We were wondering if you'd been here for a while."

The bearded Caucasian drew up behind her shoulder, and the thought went through Louis's head that these people were plain-clothes cops; they seemed so purposeful.

"Yeah," he said. "Are you looking for something?"

Before she could answer, Jackie jumped on the bearded Caucasian, hooking her front claws on his belt and getting dragged along on tiptoe as he tried to pull away. Hands high, he turned reproachfully to Louis.

"Not my dog," Louis said.

"We're looking for disturbances in the sand," the smiley woman said. She held her arm out to one side and snapped her fingers and snapped them again, just casually getting the dog's attention, her eyes not leaving Louis. She was a few inches shorter than he and at least a few years older; there was some gray in her dark hair. "We thought that if you were here during the earthquake you might have seen something."

He looked at her blankly.

"We're from Harvard Geophysics," the bearded Caucasian explained in a grating, impatient voice. "We felt the earthquake and got a rough location. It was big enough, we thought there might be some surface effects on the sand."

Louis frowned. "Which earthquake is this?"

The woman glanced at the Caucasian. The dog was licking her fingers. "The earthquake an hour and a half ago," she said.

"There was an earthquake an hour and a half ago?"

"Yes."

"Around here?"

"Yes."

"That you felt, wherever, down in Cambridge?"

"Yes!" Her smile had become one of genuine amusement at his confusion.

"Shit." Louis scrambled stiffly to his feet. "I missed it! Or but, wait a minute, maybe it was not that big?"

With a loud sigh the bearded Caucasian rolled his eyes and headed back up the beach.

"It wasn't small," the woman said. "The magnitude will probably be about 5.3. The city's not in ruins or anything, but a 5.3, that registers around the world. Our colleague Howard"—she aimed some smileyness at the Oriental, who was skipping stones between waves—"is quite happy about that, as you can see. It means a lot of information."

Louis thought of the car with its theft alarm ringing.

"And you didn't feel anything at all?" the woman said.

"Nothing."

"Too bad." She smiled strangely, looking him right in the eye. "It was a nice earthquake."

He looked around, still disoriented. "You expected the beach to be all torn up?"

"We were just curious. Sometimes the sand subsides and cracks. It can also liquefy and boil up to the surface. There was an event here about two hundred fifty years ago that did some serious damage. We were hoping we'd see something like that. But—" She clicked her tongue. "We didn't."

By the water's edge her colleague Howard was playing with the dog, tapping her behind the ears with alternating hands while her head thrashed back and forth. Louis still didn't believe there had really been an earthquake. "Would a house around here be wrecked?"

"Depends on what you mean by wrecked," the woman said. "You have a house?"

"It's my mother's house. My ex-grandmother's house, which you couldn't possibly care less about, but she was the person who died in the earthquake last week."

"No! Really?" Concern became the woman better than amusement did. "I'm very sorry."

"Yeah? I'm not. I hardly knew her."

"I'm really sorry."

"What you sorry about?" Howard asked her, coming up from the water.

The woman indicated Louis. "This . . . person's grandmother was the one who died in the April 6 event."

"Bad luck," Howard said. "Usually, small earthquake like that, nobody dies."

"Howard is an expert in shallow seismicity," the woman said.

Howard squinted into the white sky as though wishing this description of him weren't accurate. He had a hairstyle like half a coconut.

"What about you?" Louis asked the woman.

She looked away and didn't answer. Howard slapped the dog on the muzzle and fled, taking crazy evasive action as the dog pursued him. The woman backed away from Louis, her smileyness assuming a leave-taking chill. When she saw that he was following her, a flicker of alarm crossed her face and she began to walk very briskly. He buried his hands in his pockets and matched her footsteps with his own. He had a faint predatory interest in this small-boned female, but mainly he wanted information. "There really was an earthquake?"

"Yes, uh-huh. There really was."

"How'd you know it was up here?"

"Oh . . . instruments plus an educated guess."

"So, and what's causing these earthquakes?"

"Rupture of stressed rock along a fault a few miles underneath us."

"Can you be a little more specific?"

She became smiley and shook her head. "No."

"Are there going to be any more?"

She shrugged. "Definitely yes if you're willing to wait a hundred years. Probably yes if you wait ten years. Probably not if you leave here in a week."

"It doesn't mean anything to get two earthquakes in a row like this?"

"Nope. Not particularly. In California it might mean something, but not here. I mean, of course it means something; but we don't know what."

She spoke as though she wanted to be precise for precision's sake, not for his. "As a rule," she said, "if you feel an earthquake around here, it's happening on a fault that nobody even knew was there, at some peculiar depth, in the context of local stresses that are pretty much anybody's guess. You have to be a fundamentalist minister to make predictions right now."

The white hairs she had ran across the grain of the darker

hair, lying on top of it rather than blending in. Her skin was cream-colored.

"How old are you?" Louis asked.

A pair of startled and unamused eyes came to rest on him. "I'm thirty, how old are you?"

"Twenty-three," he said with a frown, as if a calculation had yielded an unexpected result. He asked her what her name was.

"Renée," she said grimly. "Seitchek. What about you?"

In the parking lot Howard was stepping on the belly of a delighted Jackie and the bearded Caucasian was leaning against a ridiculous automobile, a low-slung late-seventies sedan with a bleached and peeling vinyl roof and rippling white flanks, gray patches of reconstruction, and no hubcaps. It was an AMC Matador. The bearded Caucasian had a long face and red lips. The lenses of his glasses were shaped like TV screens, and the cuffs of his jeans were tucked into the tops of brown work boots. Simply because she had stopped by his side, the half-full glass of Renée's attractiveness became half-empty.

The Matador apparently belonged to Howard. "You need a ride someplace?" he said to Louis.

"Sure, maybe to my house."

"If I were you," the bearded Caucasian said, "I'd go back right away and make sure everything's OK."

Renée pointed at Louis. "That's what he's doing, Terry. He's going right back."

"That's what I'm saying," Terry said. "That's all I'm saying."

Renée looked away and made a face. Howard unlocked the car, and Louis and Terry got in the back seat, sinking ankle-deep into pizza cartons, Coke cans, and sportswear. The car radio came on with the engine. It was playing a Red Sox game.

"Where's the dog?" Renée said.

Howard shrugged and put the car in reverse.

"Howard, wait, you're going to run over it."

They peered out their respective windows, trying to locate the dog. Louis took it upon himself to get out and look behind the car, the exhaust pipe of which was putting out blue-black clouds of the foulest smoke he'd ever smelled a car produce. It coated his respiratory tract like some poison sugar. He got back in the car, reporting no dog.

"This is Louis, incidentally," Renée explained to Terry from the front seat. "Louis, this is Terry Snall and Howard Chun."

"You're all seismologists," Louis said.

Terry shook his head. "Renée and Howard are the seismologists. They're real high-powered." There seemed to be a backhanded message here, Terry either not really believing the other two to be high-powered or else implying that to be high-powered was not the same as to be a worthwhile person. "Renée told me your grandmother died in last week's earthquake," he said. "That's awful."

"She was old."

"Howard and Renée thought it was a nothing earthquake. They were saying it was no good. They wanted it to be bigger. That's how seismologists think. I think it's terrible about your grandmother."

"Yeah, we don't, Terry. We're glad she died."

"I'm not saying that."

"What do you think he *is* saying, Howard?"

Howard turned the steering wheel obliviously, the car chugging and rumbling like a ferry boat. Louis looked out the back window, expecting to see the dog, but the lot the trash barrels guarded was completely empty now.

. . . *Two balls and two strikes*, the baseball announcer said.

"Two balls and one strike," Renée said.

. . . *The two-two pitch* . . .

"The two-*one* pitch," Renée said.

Ball three, *three and two. Roger had him oh and two and now he's gone to a full count.*

"*One* strike, airbrain. Three balls and *one* strike."

. . . *Scoreboard has it as three balls and one strike.*

. . . *Bob*, the color man said, *I think it is three and one.*

Renée turned off the radio in disgust, and Terry remarked, ostensibly to Louis: "Nothing's ever quite good enough for Renée."

In the front seat Renée turned to Howard and made a gesture of utter bafflement.

"I wonder if they felt the earthquake at the ballpark," Terry said.

"Yeah, I wonder," Renée said. "They're playing in Minnesota."

"Left at the sign," Louis told Howard. He hardly recognized the road they were on as the one down which he'd jogged.

"Where you wanna go next?" Howard asked generally. "Try Plum Island?"

"We better head back," Terry said.

"What a drag," Renée said.

"No death and destruction," Terry said.

"No sand blows is all I meant. Although it's true," she said to Louis, "that we feel some ambivalence about destructive earthquakes. They're like cadavers, full of information."

Her articulateness was getting on Louis's nerves. He pointed out the stone Kernaghan gate, and Howard hardly slowed the car as he started to turn. Then he slammed on the brakes and wheeled hard to the right, the car skidding almost sideways back onto the road. A black Mercedes swung out of the gate and swerved around them and sped off towards Ipswich. It was driven by a man Louis recognized as Mr. Aldren. Very belatedly, Howard applied the horn.

"See if you can kill me," Renée said, pressing with one hand on the windshield and sliding back on the seat cushion she'd been thrown from.

A strange and new and not entirely unpleasant sensation came over Louis as they drove up the hill and he saw, as these students were seeing, the money the estate represented. It was a sensation of exposure but of satisfaction too. Money: it says: I'm not nobody. The awed silence in the car held until the house and its party hat came into view and Renée laughed. "Oh my God."

"You ought to come inside," Louis said on a wealthy man's impulse. "Have some food, see some damage."

Terry was quick to shake his head. "No thanks."

"No, no," Louis insisted. "Come in." He was thinking how unwelcome his mother would find these visitors. "I mean, if you're at all curious."

"Oh, we're curious," Renée said. "Aren't we, Howard? It's our business to be curious."

"I just hope no one's hurt," Terry said.

Not until Louis had opened the door and ushered everyone inside did he realize how little he'd believed there'd been an earthquake. And what he felt most strongly, as he stopped in the front hall, was that he was seeing the work of an angry hand. The minister who'd said that God was angry with the Commonwealth; the Haitian who'd believed there was an angry spirit in the house: he saw what they were getting at, for a force had entered the house while he was away and had attacked it, pulling a piece of plaster from the dining-room ceiling and flinging it onto the table, where water from broken vases had soaked the plaster brown. The force had thrown open the doors of the breakfront, toppled anything more upright than horizontal and scattered china polyhedra across the floor. It had yanked on paintings in the living room, trashed the bar and opened cracks across the walls and ceiling. The room smelled like a frat house on a Sunday morning.

"Do you really want us here?" Renée asked Louis.

"Of course." He had his duties as a host to consider. "Let me show you the kitchen."

Howard stood on one foot and leaned to look into the living room, his other leg hovering in the front hall for balance. Terry, very ill at ease, stuck close to Renée, who said quietly, "You see what living on the epicenter does."

There was less evident damage in the kitchen: some broken jars, some paint chips and plaster on the floor. Louis's father, standing by the sink, was delighted to meet the three students. He shook their hands and asked them to repeat their names.

"Where's Mom?" Louis asked.

"You didn't see her? She's taking pictures for Prudential. I recommend you don't try to clean anything up before she's done. In fact, Lou," Bob added in an undertone, "I don't think she was even conscious of doing it, but I found her helping some stuff off the shelves in the living room. Ugly things, you know."

"Of course," Louis said. "Good idea."

"But what a day!" his father continued in a louder voice. "What a day! You all felt it, right?" He addressed the four of them and all but Louis nodded. "I was in the back room, I thought it was the end of the WORLD. I clocked twelve seconds of strong shaking on my watch." He pointed at his watch. "When it started, I felt the whole house *tense*, like it had got *wind* of something." His hands flew and twisted in the air like wheeling pigeons. "Then I heard this booming, it felt like a freight train going by outside the windows. This feeling of *weight*, tremendous *weight*. I could hear all sorts of little things falling down inside the walls, and then while I sat there looking—in all modesty, I wasn't the least bit afraid, I mean because it felt so natural, so inevitable—I sat there and I saw a window just *shatter*. And just when I thought it was over, it all *intensified*, wonderful, wonderful, this final climax— like she was coming! Like the whole earth was coming!"

Bob Holland looked at the faces around him. The three students were listening to him seriously. Louis was like a white statue staring at the floor.

"I guess you people must know," Bob continued, "that there's a whole history of earthquakes in New England. Were you aware that the Native Americans thought they caused epidemics? That made a lot of sense to me today, that idea of dis-ease in the earth. They were scientists too, you know. Scientists in a very profound and different way. You want to hear about superstition, let me tell you there was a woman in these parts in 1755, her name was Elizabeth Burbage. Minister's daughter, a spinster. The God-fearing citizens of Marblehead—he-he! Marblehead!—tried her as a witch and drove her out of town because three neighbors claimed she'd had foreknowledge of the great Cambridge earthquake of November 18. Sixty-three years after the Salem trials! Regarding an act of God! Marblehead! Wonderful!"

Louis was too mortified to keep track of people during the next few minutes. He opened the refrigerator and persuaded Renée and Howard to accept apples. His father began to repeat his story, and just to get him out of sight Louis followed him back to the room where his adventure had occurred. Here Bob reconstructed the twelve seconds of shaking second by second, insight by insight. He was as high as he ever got. The shattering windowpane in particular had seemed to him a quintessential moment, encapsulating the entire story of man and nature.

When Louis finally broke away, he found that Terry and Howard had gone outside, Terry to sit in the back seat of the car and

Howard to sit on the hood, eating his apple smackingly. Renée? Howard shrugged. Still inside.

Louis found her in the living room, talking to his mother. She gave him her now familiar smiley smile, and his mother, who wore a camera on a strap, conveyed her now equally familiar unwillingness to be disturbed. "Maybe you can excuse us for a minute, Louis."

He executed an ostentatious about-face and went and sat down halfway up the stairs. His mother and Renée spoke for nearly five more minutes. All he caught was the cadences—long hushed utterances from his mother, briefer and brighter repetitious noises from Renée. When the latter finally appeared in the front hall, she looked up the stairs. Louis was hunched and motionless, like a spider waiting for a fly to hit his web. "I guess we're going now," she said. "Thanks for having us in."

She turned to leave, and Louis was down the stairs in a flash, homing in on the entangled fly. He put his hand on her arm and held it. "What did you just talk about with my mother?"

Renée's eyes moved from the hand on her arm to the person it belonged to. She didn't look happy about this hand.

"She's worried about the earthquakes," she said. "I told her what I know."

"I'm going to call you."

She gave him a ghost of a shrug. "OK."

When he came inside, having seen the great fuming car off down the drive, his mother was photographing the dining room. She briefly lowered the camera from her face. "That Renée Seitchek," she said. "Is an extremely impressive young woman." She focused the camera on the ceiling and pressed a button, and for a moment the room went white.

4

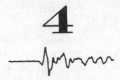

Louis's job at WSNE had come to him by way of a Rice friend of his, a woman named Beryl Slidowsky who'd had a popular show on KTRU playing music like the Dead Kennedys and Jane's Addiction. In February, at a point when the résumés and demo tapes he'd been sending to stations in a dozen northern cities had netted him all of two responses, both flatly negative, Louis called Beryl and asked about the radio scene in Boston. She had been at WSNE for about three months; it so happened that she was about to quit. The owner, she hastened to say, was great, but the person who managed the station was literally giving her an ulcer. She was happy to put in a good word for Louis, however, if he wanted. Wasn't he sort of, like, generally fairly tolerant? Hadn't he survived an entire year with those ghastly Bowleses?

The cause of Beryl's peptic distress turned out to be a female in her late thirties named Libby Quinn. Libby had come aboard as a receptionist eighteen years earlier, when the station was still located in Burlington, and although she'd never even finished high school she had made herself indispensable to WSNE. She did all the programming and much of the administration, wrote and recorded spots for local non-agency advertisers, and, with Alec Bressler, lined up guests for the talk shows. She had rosy Irish cheeks and dark blond hair that she wore in a braid or a bun. She favored the English Country look—heather-colored skirts and cardigans, knee socks, lace-up shoes—and was seldom seen without a mug of herbal tea. She seemed utterly innocuous to Louis.

At the beginning of his second week of work, Libby appeared at the door of his cubicle and beckoned to him with a single index finger. "Come to my office?"

He followed her up the corridor. In her office there were multiple photos of two blondes in their late teens; they were awfully old to be her daughters, but they looked just like her.

She handed Louis a dog-eared stack of printouts. "There's an uncollected ninety-five thousand here. It's only people who don't do business with us anymore. How would you feel about trying to collect some of it?"

"Love to."

"I'd do it myself, but it's really more of a man's job."

"Oh."

"It's easy. You just call them up and say, 'You owe us money, pay it.' Will you do that for me?"

He took the printouts, and Libby smiled. "Thanks, Louis. One other thing, if you don't mind—I'd like this to be our secret. Just you and me. All right?"

In radio, especially in a tough market like Boston, there is no such thing as an exciting or rewarding entry-level job. Even at a place like WSNE, Louis knew he'd have to do shit work for several years before he could hope to get any meaningful air time, and so he was grateful to Libby for asking him to do collections. The work was more fun by far than anything he'd done at KILT in Houston. It allowed him to be as obnoxious as he dared. He devoted every spare minute to it.

A few days after Easter, Alec Bressler dropped into his cubicle while he was generating threatening letters on his printer. The station owner frowned at the output through his generic eyeglasses. "What's this?"

"Delinquent accounts," Louis said.

Alec's curiosity deepened into concern. "You're trying to collect?"

"Trying, yes."

"You're not put-ting—*pressure* on them?"

"Actually, yes, I am."

"Oh, don't do that."

"Libby's orders."

"You mustn't do that."

"I tried to keep it from you."

Just then Libby herself passed by the cubicle. Alec arrested her. "Louis tells me he's doing collections using *pressure*. I thought we didn't do this."

Libby lowered her chin contritely. "I'm sorry, Alec."

"I thought we didn't do this. Really, am I wrong?"

"No, of course, you're right." She gave Louis a conspirator's wink. "We'll have to stop."

"If I can interject something," Louis said. "It's netted us like forty-five hundred dollars in the last ten days."

"You men discuss it," Libby said. "I'm on the air in ninety seconds."

"What's this? Where's Bud?"

"Bud has a little problem with his paycheck, Alec, if you'll excuse me."

"A little problem? What? What?" Alec followed her into the hall. "*What* problem? *What* problem?" The studio door at the far end of the corridor was heard closing. Alec pushed all his fingers into his hair, rapidly achieving frenzy. "I pay this woman! And she won't tell me what problem!"

He continued to stare down the empty corridor. Louis watched him locate and make sooty and finally ignite a Benson & Hedges entirely by feel. "So, yes," he went on, capturing wayward pennants of smoke with deft, sharp inhalations, "you don't do this with the pressure anymore. Why burn the bridges, eh? Put things away. Did you grade contest entries? Inez has hundreds. Think of it— hundreds!"

In Somerville, meanwhile, it was springtime. In one sunny day, while no one was looking, fully grown grass had appeared all over the seven hills, shaggy patches of it suddenly occupying every lawn and traffic island. It was like some garish chlorophyll-colored trash that had been dumped on top of the town's more indigenous ground cover, which, around the time the last snow melted, reached its peak of richness and variety. As always, there were black leaves, cigarette butts, and dog logs. But on any block-long stretch of parking strip even the casual hiker could also expect to spot fabric-softener squares; snow-emergency cinders; Christmas pine needles and tinsel; solo mittens; bluish glass dice from vandalized car windows; compacted flyers from Johnny's Foodmaster and the Assembly Square Mall; marvelously large wads of gum; non-returnable wine-cooler and premixed-cocktail bottles; sheets of gray ruled paper on which were copied crudely in pencil simple sentences containing backwards *P*'s and *h*'s; rotten Kleenexes resembling cottage cheese; rubber blades and choked filters; exhausted lighters; foody leakages from trash bags torn in transfer to garbage trucks, orange peels and tuna cans and ketchup-bottle lids set down on the ground by dwindling snowbanks; and maybe, if the hiker was lucky, some of Somerville's more singular specimens as well, such as the magnificent wall unit that for many months had been lying face down on an island in the Alewife Brook Parkway, or the supply of Monopoly money that was spreading up side streets from its release point on College Avenue—yellow tens, blue fifties. This was the kind of congenial and ever-changing profusion of objects which Nature, "the great litterer," had once again trashed up with stunted weeds and plasticky-looking daffodils and finally, in a moment when people's backs were turned, a thousand cells of alien green grass. No foreign power could have been more sly and zealous than spring in its overnight infiltration of the city. The new plants stood out with a brazenness akin to that of the agent who, when his life is at stake, acts even more native than his native interrogators.

When Louis got home he found his neighbor John Mullins swabbing his car with a large brown bath sponge. The car never seemed to get driven past the end of the driveway, where Mullins washed it. It also never seemed dirty. Fleshy tulips now filled the bed below the porch of the triple-decker the old man lived in; their heavy purple and yellow heads leaned aside at various casual angles, as if specifically avoiding Louis's eyes.

"Hey there, Louie boy," Mullins said, leaving the sponge on the windshield and intercepting him. "How are things? You likin' it here? You likin' Somerville? What do you think of this weather? I don't think it's gonna last. I just listened to the weather, always listen at 5:35. Tell me something. You feel the earthquake there on Sunday?"

Louis had been shaking his head to this question for several days.

"Golly it scared me. You think we're gonna get any more of these? I hope to God we don't. I've got a little heart condition—a little heart condition. Little heart condition." Mullins patted himself rapidly on the breast, calling Louis's attention to the heart in there. "I'm not supposed to get scared like that." He laughed hollowly, real fear in his eyes. "I tried to get outside and would you believe it I fell down right on my bum. I couldn't get up! God if I wasn't scared. Girl upstairs here, the one that sings—nice girl. She told me she didn't even feel it."

"If there's another earthquake," Louis said, "you should try to stand in a doorway."

The old man grimaced deafly. "What's that?"

"I said you should try to stand in an interior doorway, or get under a table. They say it's the safest place to be."

"Oh yeah, huh. All right, Louie boy." Mullins tottered back to his sponge. "Allll right, Louie boy."

There was an envelope in the mailbox from the law firm of Arger, Kummer & Rudman. It contained two Red Sox tickets and Henry Rudman's business card. In the rear window of Louis's room a flowering white bush had appeared and was startlingly ablaze with sunlight, the ecliptic having swung around far to the north since the sun's last appearance at dinnertime. He made a fried-egg sandwich and watched Hogan's Heroes. He made another fried-egg sandwich and watched the network news. Midway through this informative half hour, NBC took a trip to Boston and discovered, to its astonishment, that a pair of earthquakes had occurred outside the city. Footage was run of broken plate glass and of supermarket aisles where solitary employees mopped up juice and jelly from fallen bottles. The correspondent related facts that were actually consistent with what Louis had been hearing hourly at WSNE: the Easter earthquake, which had measured 5.2 on the Richter scale and had been followed by several small aftershocks, had caused an estimated $12 million damage in three counties and resulted in fourteen injuries. (Almost all the injuries, as Louis had noted in the *Globe*, were due to panic, a surprising number of people having seriously bruised or cut themselves while fleeing their shaking homes, and one angler on a causeway north of Ipswich having put a fishhook in his eyelid during a dash to solid ground, and one motorist having steered his car into a ditch.) NBC viewers were then treated to a taste of history ("earthquakes are not *unheard* of in New England") and an aerial glimpse of the nuclear power plant in Seabrook, followed by reassuring words from a power-company spokesman, an angry statement from a wine merchant (for him, apparently, nature was just another local with no appreciation of fine vintages), and finally a heartwarmingly inarticulate account of the earthquake from an Ipswich teenager, delivered with much incredulous head-shaking: "It started slow. Then bam!" The correspondent earned the right to say his own name in a low and earnest voice by first saying, in a low and earnest voice, that this earthquake "may not have been the last." There was a brief, medium-distance shot of the NBC anchorman wearing a wry smirk (he was paid $34,000 a week not to yawn during these shots) before the scene changed to an old-time drugstore with an avuncular pharmacist behind the counter. America watched helplessly as the promotional drama unfolded. Not long ago, on late-night TV, Louis had seen this variety of commercial made fun of. The worried consumer returned to the drugstore and, instead of thanking the avuncular pharmacist for his advice, listed the grotesque disorders and hormonal imbalances induced by the recommended preparation, and ended up (a bit predictably maybe?) murdering him with a gun. This hard-hitting NBC satire had been followed by a real ad, for condoms.

After the news there was baseball, which Louis had been watching between nine and eighteen innings of per evening. While the Red Sox piled up an early 8–0 lead, he paged through the *Globe*, and for the second time in two weeks the paper gave him an uncanny feeling. It might have been a prank birthday issue with familiar names in it. The lead story in the business section was headlined *Sweeting-Aldren Shares Take Another Beating*. The woes suddenly besetting New England's second-largest chemical producer were so numerous that a jump was required to page 67. The company's latest quarterly report, released this morning, showed a sharp decline in profits, as sales remained flat and rising energy prices and a cyclical shortage of several key raw materials increased production costs. In light of this report, investors on Wall Street continued to react highly negatively to the news on Tuesday that Sweeting-Aldren's facilities in Peabody might have suffered significant damage in Sunday's earthquake; the company's price per share had already fallen by 4.875 to 64.5—the largest two-day point drop in the company's 48-year history, and the largest two-day percentage drop since August 11, 1972. Sweeting-Aldren press officer Ridgely Holbine emphatically denied that any production lines had been damaged in the earthquake, but speculation continued to be fueled by the discovery late Monday of large quantities of a greenish effluent in a culvert running through a residential development four hundred yards from a Sweeting-Aldren installation. Holbine said the company was investigating the "extremely remote possibility" of a connection between the facility and the effluent; according to one analyst, these remarks were immediately interpreted on Wall Street as a "virtual mea culpa." Holbine stressed that Sweeting-Aldren was known to have "perhaps the best environmental record of any player in the industry." He explained that its energy costs were high because of its commitment to "recycling, not dumping, toxic waste," and noted that as recently as January, *Forbes* magazine had cited Sweeting-Aldren's "established track record as the most profitable chem concern in America." Nevertheless, the price of a share of the company's stock had yesterday fallen by more than a point in the last thirty minutes of trading on the NYSE. The fear of further damaging earthquake activity north of Boston, and no less important, the specter of lawsuits raised by the discovery of the effluent, were combining to—

Louis looked up at the TV screen to see a baseball sailing into the visitors' bullpen at Fenway. The Sox lead had been cut in half. In the kitchen, the telephone rang.

It was Eileen. Nearly a week had passed since Louis had left a string of increasingly sarcastic messages on her machine, but she was not apologetic. *She just wanted to say* that she and Peter were having a big party at Peter's on the twenty-eighth. "It's a *disaster-*

theme party," she said. "You have to wear a costume to get in, OK? You *have* to. And it has to have something to do with disasters. It won't be any fun if people don't dress up, so you really have to."

Louis was looking down at yesterday's *Globe,* which he'd dropped on the outgoing stack after relieving it of its comics. Plain as day the headline on page one: *Quake Aftermath: Large Chemical Spill in Peabody.*

"Just come, all right?" Eileen said. "You can bring people if you want to, but they have to have a costume too. Let me give you the address."

Louis took the address. "Why do you want me at this party?"

"Don't you want to come?"

"Oh, definitely maybe. Just I'm not sure why you happened to invite me."

" 'Cause it's going to be a lot of fun and lots of people are coming."

"Are you saying you enjoy my company?"

"Look, if you don't want to come, don't come. But I have to get off now, OK? So I'll see you on the twenty-eighth, maybe."

According to the *Globe,* the greenish effluent had first been noticed by residents of a Peabody subdivision on Monday morning, eighteen hours after Sunday's earthquake fourteen miles to the northeast. A four-year-old boy and his two-year-old sister were playing by a swale adjacent to the subdivision and returned home with "a substance resembling Prestone antifreeze" on their clothing. In the course of the afternoon, homeowners observed that the swale, still filled with runoff from recent heavy rains, was turning green. A cloying organic odor, "like magic marker," was noticed. As of Wednesday evening the odor had largely dissipated. State environmental officials had so far not succeeded in isolating the source of the effluent but were focusing their investigation on a fenced and wooded property owned by Sweeting-Aldren Industries, and an adjacent five-acre wetland drained by the polluted swale. Ridgely Holbine of Sweeting-Aldren repeated his claim that the company had not discharged significant quantities of industrial waste in Peabody for nearly twenty years. He said the property in question housed a milling facility and a number of small holding tanks for "intermediate processes," none of which showed any signs of earthquake damage. Meanwhile one Peabody resident, Doris Mulcahey, told reporters that her husband and eldest daughter had both died of leukemia within the last seven years, and that she had not been aware until now that the wooded property four hundred yards from her home belonged to Sweeting-Aldren. "I'm not saying they caused it," Mulcahey said. "But I sure as heck don't rule it out."

The ball game ended sadly for Sox fans.

Early the next morning, moments before his alarm would have rung, Louis had his dream again. A door in the Bowleses' house on Dryden Street had led him back into the room with the red leather chairs, and here he found that in all these days his mother had not gone anywhere. She was still perched on a chair, the hem of her yellow dress still raised almost to her hips. But now there was only one man in the room. Louis recognized him from the painting above the fireplace. The neat, bald skull, the lusting black eyes. Catching sight of Louis, he at once turned away and did something to his pants, adjusted something in front. This was when Louis realized that the entire room was slick with semen, greenish white semen deep enough to cover the soles of his shoes, and he woke up quaking violently. He succeeded in not examining this dream later on, though he did not quite forget it either.

Birds were awakening while he ate his Cheerios. As happened every morning, when he passed by his roommate Toby's beige furniture ensembles—the big sofa and chairs emerging from the unpeopled night into another day of being stationary, of being big, of weighing a lot and occupying volume—his sense of the unreality of life hit a sharp peak.

The time it took him to drive to work, down the Alewife Brook Parkway and onto Route 2 past the Haiku Palace Chinese Restaurant and the Susse Chalet motel, up the mile-long grade which every day two or three unfit automobiles failed to make, and out through historical suburbs where the strengthening light made the headlights of eastbound cars and semis seem funereal, was the same amount of time his juice and coffee needed to percolate down through kidneys and bladder and send him straight to the men's room at WSNE. Alec Bressler was shaving at the mirror, his decrepit kit bag balanced on the sink. "You spent the night here again," Louis observed, peeing.

Alec palpated his blue neck. "Mm—hm!"

At the studio board Louis sat down with a chocolate cruller purchased from Dan Drexel and glanced over the log printout for the six-to-seven slot. Drexel, using his palm to ram a 150-degree arc of doughnut into his mouth, changed places in the booth with the night announcer and read through his copy of the printout. There would be powdered sugar in Drexel's lumberjack beard until his bathroom break at eight. (To the listener, few radio announcers sound bearded. But many radio announcers are.) Louis loaded Cart 1 with a 30-second Cumberland Farms spot, let it roll at 5:59:30, and cued Drexel. Morning Rush Hour News with a Twist began.

They were in the midst of a Bob Newhart Festival. "We're playing every comedy recording," Drexel reminded the audience, "that the Button-Down Mind ever made and WSNE ever purchased. In just one moment we'll hear what must be an all-time favorite Newhart act, but first a roundup of world news."

Louis cued up the fourth cut on Side Two of *Behind the Button-Down Mind* while Davidson Chevy-Geo talked financing.

"You have sugar in your beard," he told Drexel.

As always, Drexel brushed at the wrong spot. The ad was ending, and he cozied up to the boom mike with a lusting cat's unconscious simper. "Nineteen sixty-three," he crooned. "And the Button-Down Mind takes on the sur*prising* world of children's TV." On the word "TV" his pointing finger came to rest on Louis, who removed his thumb from the turntable and let it spin.

Four hours later the talk-show announcer Kim Alexander took over the studio board. Outside in the midmorning sun, Louis sat down by a willow tree on part of the grassy expanse that made the Crossroads Office Park a park. The lawn was one of those familiar suburban places where the concrete of the enclosing curbs hasn't lost its white film of lime yet, and the agreeably nose-curdling smell of junipers hangs heavy, and there's no litter, not even cigarette filters (or maybe one single piece of artful litter, in the Japanese style), and no one, but no one, ever picnics. Louis didn't understand these spaces. Why astroturf and plastic trees weren't used instead.

He watched a new Lincoln Town Car with smoked side windows round the cul-de-sac and ease to a stop opposite the WSNE entrance to Building III. Its vanity plate read: PROLIFE 7. Libby Quinn debouched from the passenger side and hurried into the studios. The Lincoln's engine surged like a powerful man sighing: PROLIFE 7. Louis shrugged and lay back on the warm new grass, letting the sun saturate his optic nerves with orangeness.

It can make a person dizzy to lie in hot sun. For several seconds he thought the funny thing happening to him was due to a loose wire in his nervous system, some spazzing synapse, and not, as the chorus of car alarms from the parking lot suddenly indicated was the case, to an earthquake.

He lost several seconds scrambling to his feet. By the time he was upright the event was ending, the ground now moving almost imperceptibly, like a diving board when a person stands motionless at the very end of it, above a swimming pool.

Traffic on 128 was unruffled. Louis looked challengingly at the air around him, as though daring the physical world to *do that again* when his back wasn't turned, just daring it. But the only disturbance remaining was the marginal instability of his own body, the swaying of legs through which blood was being pumped with less than perfect smoothness (even great mimes and palace guards can't be statues). The ground itself was still.

Inside, as he approached Alec's office, he heard the owner quarreling with Libby in the inner sanctum. Someone less attracted to fights might have retreated, but Louis stationed himself on the threshold of the outer office, which contained a ten-inch black-and-white Zenith and a sofa with folded bedding and unironed shirts on the armrest.

"I won't return this man's calls," Alec said. "I refuse to know this man. But my station manager has breakfast with him? My station manager who I told, no, we don't deal with this type person? I understand he's a very good-looking young man. Very moral, very char-is-ma-tic. It compromises you to have lunch, yes, or cocktails, or *dinner*. But breakfast—is a very moral meal!"

"Closing your eyes won't make him go away, Alec. Not unless

you can also find a couple hundred thousand dollars to buy him off with. He's already filed the challenge."

"So? Last time we renewed—"

"The last time we renewed, nobody challenged it and the station wasn't gutted."

"They don't take away licenses so easily."

"Plus Philip Stites hadn't paid Ford & Rothman to study our audience."

"So—blackmail! A very moral sing!"

"Face it. He wants a station."

"And you're going to work for this man? You're going to be his station manager?"

"When you won't let me collect on dead accounts? When all you can broadcast during drive hours is Somalian war news and Phyllis Diller?"

"People love Phyllis Diller!"

"One point seven percent at 8 a.m. That's the March figure. I think it speaks for itself."

"OK, we do some local noose. We do the war on drugs. We do airplane crashes. OK. All-new programming, as of today. We tell FCC, new programming, very noose-oriented—"

"Alec, there's nobody to *do* the news, besides me."

"Maybe we get Slidowsky back—"

"You know very well what I think of that girl."

"I can do it. Louis can do it. We listen to the other stations and copy it down. We can hire a student, I can sell—"

"What can you sell?"

"I sell my car. When do I use this car? I don't need this car."

"I don't know whether to laugh or cry."

"But sink about it. Libby. Sink about it. I sell my station to Philip Stites, against my principles. Do you respect me for this?"

"I respect a man who does the responsible thing. And I think the responsible thing to do here is sell the station while you still might come out in the black."

Alec muttered something vaguely, something about sinking.

"Do you need me?" Libby said to Louis, coming through the outer office.

Louis assumed a preoccupied air. "You feel the earthquake?"

She patted her bun and smiled demurely. "I guess I didn't."

"Ersequake?" Alec wore the expression of metaphysical amusement that came from sucking a nicotine lozenge. "Just now?"

"Yes. You feel it?"

"No . . . I was busy." He beckoned Louis into his sanctum, where two cigarettes of different lengths were burning in a heaping ashtray. His shortwave was set up by the window, and along the wall were piled packing cartons. It was beginning to appear that these rooms were the only place he had to live.

"Two things," he said. "Sit please. First thing, I thought again—is maybe not so bad to do those collections. If they won't pay immediately, say we settle for half if they pay right away. It must be right away." He selected the shorter of the burning cigarettes, killed it, and drew on the longer one, still rotating the lozenge in his mouth. "Other thing: honest answer. Do employees respect a boss who smokes?"

"Sure. Why not?"

"They appear weak. Smokers."

"Are you talking about me or about Libby?"

Alec did a foreign thing with his upper lip, curling it like a vampire about to bite, behind a veil of smoke. "Libby."

"I'm sure she respects you. Why wouldn't she?"

Alec nodded very slowly, lip still drawn, eyes on an odd corner of the room. "Do those collections," he said.

Louis returned to his cubicle and reopened the files, but his first call was to the Harvard University switchboard. After one ring he was speaking to Howard Chun, who with an unpromising grunt went to try to find Renée Seitchek. When her voice came over the line she sounded neither surprised nor pleased.

"I felt the earthquake," Louis said.

"Uh-huh. So did we."

"Where was it? How big?"

"Outside Peabody, smaller than Sunday's. This we get from the radio, incidentally."

"The reason I'm calling is to see if you want to go to a party my sister is giving on the twenty-eighth. Not that this is an idea I personally endorse, but supposedly it's an earthquake-oriented party. A costume party. Will it be fun, I have no idea. But that's what I'm calling for."

He bent his head and listened extra-closely to what came out of the receiver.

"The twenty-eighth."

"Yes."

"Well—OK. But I'm not going to wear any costume."

He released his breath, which he'd been holding. "Let me suggest that you wear some token costume. Like maybe a Band-Aid. Not that I personally—"

"All right. I'll wear a token costume. Where's this party going to be?"

He arranged to pick her up in his car. It turned out that she lived in Somerville herself. She gave him her home telephone number and said it was better not to call her at work. He hung up with a bad taste in his mouth, feeling unwanted.

A week of uneasiness ensued. After a couple of lucky collections Louis had begun to run into stonewalling receptionists, dilatory assistants, and a few outright ogres. He was also having trouble finding funds for postage. Once he'd exhausted the little caches of one- and two- and five-cent stamps from various abandoned desks, he had to draw on petty cash, which was kept in the owner's wallet.

More and more often Alec could be found watching the little Zenith in his office. At dinnertime, alone or not, he provided running oral glosses on TV news and advertising; otherwise he liked to watch Westerns and war films.

"TV noose and noosepapers," he told Louis, "are the enemy. For eight years we had a U.S. President with subnormal intelligence. Every day he does horrible harm to language, the future, the truth. Every single sinking person in the country knows this, except not the networks and noosepapers. Is suspicious, no? Or is maybe Stupid People now also minority group we don't say bad things about? Let's go all the way, let's have a retarded President. And noose conference, and President is bellowing and drooling, and his advisers say, he has interesting new program, and CBS says, the President drooled tonight, and we have five analysts here to talk about his interesting new program and also perhaps about is he drooling less than last time? And New York Times prints a transcript of noose conference, is all drool drool bellow bellow, also one coherent sentence, *and on page one they print the one coherent sentence!* I guess they don't want to offend retarded people by saying is bad to have a retarded President.

"Still, OK, fine, is their prerogative. But isn't it the responsibility also of every sinking person in the country to say to networks and noosepapers: You are my enemy now. You betrayed me. You are not really on my side. You are on side of money and I see through you now and is the end. No more! You are out! I'll find a good magazine and radio station, sank you!

"But it's a horrible venal world. Sinking people—artists and intellectuals, the good reporters—must write for Times and talk to CBS, otherwise their enemies will. And so with *blackmail* the big noose media buy writers and intellectuals. Personally the media don't give a *fuck*, Louis, they don't give a *fuck* about truth. They're just businesses that must always be making money, never stop making money and never offend any group.

"Now Mr. Pro-Life wants to buy my station because not enough people listen. Am I angry? Yes I am angry. But not politically angry. I will not say, 'I disagree with these people's politics.' Because all politics is the same. Left, right, is the same! Exactly the same! But noosepapers must have readers and networks must have viewers, and without politics everyone could see this emperor of culture has no clothes on, so everything is politics! The far right gets nowhere if the media talk about what is beautiful and what is true and what is just, instead of what is politically feasible. The far right is not beautiful and not true and not just. Is their very good fortune only to be looked at politically . . ."

Though he was paid for only eight hours, Louis seldom left Waltham before six in the evening. He was surprised, one night at the end of the week, to find Libby Quinn sitting on the sofa in the TV room, breathing Alec's smoke. Usually at this hour Libby was home with her daughters.

"Louis," Alec said in greeting. "We have special programming tonight. A portrait of the man who—"

"Sh, sh, sh, sh, sh," Libby said.

"I was just going to tell Louis—"

Louis ignored him. He was transfixed by the television. It drew him closer. He turned it up loud.

"We're talking about a building," the image of DR. RENEE SEITCHEK said, "that was condemned three years ago by the Chelsea city manager and that's sitting on completely unconsolidated landfill. It's hard to imagine a building more prone to damage in an earthquake, and to me it's just insanity to allow 250 church members to be living in it, even if every one of them signed a waiver."

"So you believe there could be further earthquakes," an unseen male interviewer said.

"You can't rule it out. Not after what happened in Peabody on Friday."

"Dr. Axelrod at MIT told me he thinks the odds of a damaging earthquake in central Boston in the next twelve months are still less than one in a thousand."

"They could be one in a million, there still shouldn't be people living in that building."

"I take it you're not in agreement with Reverend Stites on the issue of abortion."

AS DR. RENEE SEITCHEK struggled to reply to this irrelevant question, the camera zoomed in on her until the tiny freckles around her eyelids could be seen. In her right ear she wore three small silver hoops in separate holes. Out-of-focus leaves and sunshine played in the window behind her.

"I don't think a woman who terminates a pregnancy needs Philip Stites to tell her the significance of what she's done."

"Think again," Libby murmured. "Think again."

DR. RENEE SEITCHEK blinked in the bright lights, her face still filling the screen, while the interviewer asked a final question: "If it's not OK for the state to interfere in a woman's decision about abortion, why is it OK to interfere with the church members' decision to live in the Central Avenue apartment block?"

"Because Philip Stites made that decision for them."

DR. RENEE SEITCHEK's reply had apparently continued from here, but the sound was cut off as the reporter brought viewers back to Central Avenue in Chelsea, where a female member of Stites's Church of Action in Christ was leaving a bleak yellow-brick apartment complex that had sheets of weather-bleached plywood on its windows.

"The reason I live in this yere building," the woman said. "Is that I trust in God more than I trust in scientists and engineers. This yere's a building with NO PROTECTION. The unborn have NO PROTECTION. But if God will protect me here, I've got the power to protect the unborn."

"One scientist I spoke to," the reporter said, "claimed it was Reverend Stites's persuasion that made you sign the waiver, rather than your own free will."

The woman held up a placard reading THANKS MOM I ♥ LIFE. "The will that moves me," she told the camera, "is the same will as moves the Reverend Stites, and that is the will of God."

"How does it feel to go to bed at night knowing that even a small earthquake could send all these bricks down on top of you?"

"There's no man in this world that wakes up in the morning but by the grace of our Lord."

The television's response to this avowal was a perfume ad. Libby Quinn shifted on the sofa, looking around the room self-consciously, as if she thought Louis and Alec expected her to justify herself. She stood up suddenly. "I'm a mother, Louis. You know I have two girls in high school. And what that little Harvard girl doesn't understand is that to a lot of these teenagers, an abortion's like a trip to the dentist. I know for a fact that there's no one out there telling kids that what they're flushing into Boston Harbor is tiny babies."

"Ah, yeah," Louis said. "Although these pro-lifers aren't just trying to educate some teenagers."

"*These* pro-lifers," Libby said pointedly, "think it's important to take responsibility for your sexual behavior."

"What do you sink, Louis?" Alec said. Libby might have been a controversial film they'd been watching. "You agree with her? Take your time! Your future at this station may be at stake."

"Let me ask you this, Louis," Libby said. "Why do you think the people who hate economic greed always want to be excusing *sexual* greed? Why do you think that is?"

Alec turned expectantly to Louis, sucking his lozenge of amuse-ment, his eyebrows raised.

"Economic greed hurts other people," Louis said.

Alec's eyes followed the ball back into Libby's court.

"Right," she said with an unhappy smile. "Sexual greed doesn't hurt anybody. Unless you happen to consider a fetus a victim."

It was an exit line; she left the room.

"And what does Vanna have to say to that?" Alec asked, changing channels. "No, no, Vanna stands higher than such concerns."

Louis was trembling. He didn't understand what he'd done to make Libby turn against him.

Alec leaned back comfortably on the sofa to soak up Wheel-of-Fortune rays. "Libby," he said, "is an unhappy person. You forgive her, eh? She raised two girls without a husband. The man was no good. He came back and married her when the older girl was two, then left again. Is a hard life for her, Louis. She made a mistake twice. One time, OK, but twice, is hard to live with."

"She's selling you out," Louis said.

Alec shrugged. "I owe her back pay, she's ambitious. She should have gone to college, but she had her babies. Is hard for her to see girls have abortions now. You forgive her."

Louis shook his head. He went outside into the twilit parking lot. "Hey, Libby," he said. She was getting in her car. "Libby!" he said again, but she had closed the door. He watched her drive away.

It may be that to understand is to forgive; but Louis was tired of understanding. Almost everyone he knew seemed to have good reasons for not being kind and polite to him, and he could see these reasons, and yet it didn't seem fair that it was always him who had to understand and forgive and never them. It seemed like the world was set up so that the unhappy people who did rotten things—the abused child who became a child abuser, the injured Libby who injured Louis and Alec—could always be forgiven because they couldn't help what they did, while the unhappy people who still refused to do rotten things got more and more hurt by the other people's rottenness, until they'd been hurt so many times that they too stopped caring what they did to other people, and there was no way out.

"Why aren't you speaking to me?" he'd asked MaryAnn Bowles, a week after the previous Easter. She was making pickled beets in a haze of vinegar.

"I'm surprised you have to ask that," she said.

"Oh, I've got a theory. But I wanted to check."

She stuck a fork into a purple chunk of beet. "Well, Louis," she said. "I'm not blaming you. But I guess you must know that I am very, very hurt by what's happened. I am very, very, very hurt." The sound of her own words made her throat tighten and her face crumple up. "All I can say is this has nothing to do with you. She was only trying to hurt *me*. And I guess you can see"—her words continued to affect her violently—"that she succeeded very well indeed."

Louis despised the woman. He loathed her powdered face, her heavy breasts, her naked misery. And the more he loathed her, the more he had the feeling—a caffeinated, weightless feeling—that Lauren really had seduced him on the floor of his bedroom. He had no desire to set the record straight. He became a bad son, subsisting on peanut-butter sandwiches and party food, crashing in people's off-campus apartments and returning to Dryden Street only when he needed to sleep twelve hours. The Bowleses raised no objections; they didn't like him anymore.

After his final exams he moved into a two-room apartment in a poor black neighborhood off Holman Street and started work at KILT-FM, doing the board during drive hours and otherwise punching keys. On the day after Commencement he returned to Dryden Street one final time, to collect his books. It was a trip he'd delayed in the hope of running into Lauren, and he was rewarded by the sight of a white VW Beetle in the driveway, with a U of Texas parking sticker on the windshield.

He went into the silent, airconditioned, sun-filled house. The door to the laundry room was ajar, MaryAnn probably ironing underwear in there. Upstairs he almost passed Lauren's bedroom by, it seemed so much the way he'd seen it last. But today there was an extra element, a woman in a white sundress sitting cross-legged on the bed and reading. She looked up from her book, squinting because the sun was in her eyes. He braced himself for a blast of mockery, but as soon as Lauren recognized him she dropped her head again, biting her lip and scowling at the book.

"Yeah, surprise surprise," he said.

The book on her lap was a Bible. She hunched over it deter-minedly and pretended to read it, evidently hoping he would leave. He remained in the doorway.

"I didn't think you were still living here," she murmured.

"On my way out right now."

"Oh. Uh-huh. Lucky you."

Someone seemed to have pulled the plug on the electrified woman he'd met two months ago. Without makeup and without malice her face looked like an empty page. Her hair was pinned up with a barrette, in the style of a ten-year-old groomed for church. She said, "Is there something you want?"

He stepped inside the room and shut the door. "Can I talk to you?"

"You're not mad at me?"

"No."

Her head drooped several inches lower. "I thought you'd be mad at me. I guess you must be a nice person." She extended her left arm, spreading her fingers as though admiring them. She'd tied a piece of thin white string around her wrist. "You see I gave Emmett his ring back. Emmett's been thinking about you all the time. I think he wants to kill you."

Louis looked at her steadily.

"Actually that's a lie," she conceded, her eyes still cast down. "But he didn't seem to think too highly of you. He didn't think too highly of me either. I thought the whole thing was pretty funny. You know what MaryAnn did? She told me she thought I needed counseling. I just told her she was jealous. She acted like she didn't know what I meant." Lauren's lip curled evilly.

"What are you doing this summer?" Louis said.

"I don't know yet. Staying at home. Trying to be nice."

"Can I see you?"

She looked up at him with something like terror. "What do you want to see me for?"

"Why does anybody want to see anybody?"

"I can't."

"Why not?"

" 'Cause I told Emmett I wasn't going to see anybody. He's working for his dad in Beaumont."

"So you're like engaged but not engaged. Fun arrangement."

She shook her head. "It's just I already made him so sick. He's *really* a nice person, you know, not as smart as you."

"Yeah, this is another thing. Where do you get the idea I'm so smart?"

"Well I only spent a whole vacation here at Christmas. I only heard how smart you are a couple hundred times. And you see how well I turned the other cheek." She paused, appearing to consider her own history. "You know what, though? This semester, I got at least a B in every class. And I went swimming every day and I studied on Saturday night. I was on academic probation my whole sophomore year. It was like I'd go into the classroom and lie for an hour. Lie, lie, lie." She looked up at Louis again and saw his skepticism; her eyes fell. "So anyway. I'm trying to read the Bible."

"Congratulations?"

"I'm still more at the point where I like how I feel sitting here reading than where I'm actually reading. I go through the laws till I get to the sex laws. The punishment's always stoning the person until they're dead. That's what you get for sodomy. Sodomy's nice! But it's an abomination unto the Lord."

Louis sighed. "What's with the new costume?"

"What do you mean?"

"The white dress. The, uh, Shirley Temple thing in your hair."

"What's wrong with it?"

"What's wrong with it, nothing's wrong with it. It's just, like, no offense, but are you on some kind of medication?"

She shook her head and smiled lamely. "No."

"Lithium? Valium?"

His words sank in. Her eyes grew dark and she straightened her back. "What kind of question is that?"

"You're just very different," he said.

"I'm the way I want to *be*. So you can leave me alone, all right? Get out of my room!"

Louis, gratified by her response, was about to apologize when he was struck in the ear by the spine of a flying Bible. He leaned his head on the door and held his hurt ear. Lauren hopped off the bed and picked up the floppy Bible by one corner, as if it were a pelt, and sat down with it again. "Are you OK?"

"Yeah."

"I haven't been very nice to you, have I? I guess I must have a problem with you. I must not like you or something."

He laughed sadly.

"It's not personal. You're obviously a nice person. But it's better if you just keep away from me, don't you think? So goodbye, OK?"

Louis felt exactly like a casual lover being discarded.

Later, though, after he'd driven home with his books and drunk a beer, he decided that the only explanation for how she'd acted was that she recognized his existence and had strong feelings about him. His logic was confirmed empirically the following week, when she called him on the telephone. Again there was a curious lack of connection between present and immediate past. She just started telling him what she was doing, which was mainly that she'd enrolled in a couple of summer-session courses at U of Houston. She wanted to graduate after one more semester in Austin and so she was taking a course about the Incas and the Mayas and also Introductory Chemistry, the latter because she'd gotten an F in high-school chemistry and she wanted to try to do something really hard now, as penance. She didn't ask Louis about his own life, but at one point she did stop talking long enough for him to suggest they get together sometime. There was a silence. "Sure," she said. "I don't care. Just not at my house."

He was waiting outside the physical sciences building at the U of H after her first chemistry lecture. A thousand grackles were conversing in the quadrangle, and there was an alien, a freak, among the students leaving the building. It was Lauren. She'd cut her hair off and shaved her head.

She was glaring at every student who looked at her. Her head was small and very white, almost as white as her dress, and the half-moons of bruise-colored pigment beneath her eyes seemed darker. She asked Louis, in a nasty voice, how she looked.

"Like a pretty girl who shaved her head."

She turned away, disgusted. "You think I care what you think?"

As they walked to the parking lot he almost hoped some man passing by would be rude to her so he could knock him down. When they got inside her Beetle she didn't start it right away. She twisted her head around as if she needed to feel its bareness. Her knuckles, on the steering wheel, were white. "Do you still want to sleep with me?"

"When you put it like that?"

"It's what you wanted, right? I'll do it if you want me to. But it has to be now."

"I only want to if you want to."

"Well I'm never going to want to, ever. So this is your chance."

"Well so I guess that means no."

She nodded, not taking her eyes off the windshield. "Don't forget, OK? You had your chance."

On the stoops in the neighborhood north of U of H, not much more than a mile from downtown, middle-aged men drank beer from quart bottles and listened to low-volume hip-hop on twenty-year-old transistors. The hoods of rusted yellow, orange, green wingtips were raised in the driveways of shotgun shacks that squatted in the sandy mud. The early evening air was still and smelled like the black hamlets at the end of gravel roads in backwoods Mississippi.

At a Vietnamese restaurant up the street from the King of Glory HOLINESS CHURCH, Louis ordered pork with lemon grass. It came with sticky, translucent rice pancakes which when wrapped around the meat and lettuce and mint and bean sprouts bore an uncanny resemblance to condoms. Lauren looked at them with grim amusement. She'd ordered coffee that she wasn't drinking. She tore the tops off sugar packets and made them wink at her. Finally, reluctantly, miserably, she said, "What's an electron?"

"An electron?" It was as if she'd mentioned the name of Louis's best friend. "A subatomic particle. It's the smallest unit of negative electric charge."

"Oh thanks." She was disgusted again. "That really helps me. I *have* a dictionary."

"You can also think of it as kind of an imaginary construct—"

"I'm sorry I asked. I am *very sorry*." She looked around wildly, as if she wanted to walk out on him. "What *is* it about this stuff?

It's like the smart people aren't really learning about science, they're just learning how to sound like assholes."

"What don't you understand?" said Louis quietly.

"I don't understand what the thing *is*. I don't understand what it *looks like*. What's it *for?*" Coffee sloshed from her cup as she shoved it away. "I can't even explain this. I just thought you might be able to help me a little. It's very hard for me and it's not because I'm so stupid. I just can't sit there and nod intelligently like everybody else when the professor goes on about electrons and protons. I want to *understand* it."

"I can help you understand it."

She sneered. "I bet you can."

"We can get together and talk about it, if you want."

She rifled her purse for a cigarette, shaking her head all the while. "It was just going to be me," she said. "I was going to read and I was going to study something really hard for me. And now you want to come in and bullshit everything up."

"Yeah, but . . . who called who? Who just asked what an electron is?"

"I was happy. I thought you cared about me. I'd had this idea and I wanted to tell somebody. But you're just in it for yourself. You're going to think I'm going to owe you something. You're going to think you can put your arm around me, when I already said."

"I just want to see you. That's all I want."

She'd inhaled a fifth of the cigarette, and now it seemed the exodus of smoke from her nostrils would never stop.

"Right," she said. "You're nice, I keep forgetting. But don't forget, all right? I'm not going to owe you *anything*."

As the days got hotter and the nights got longer, Louis watched Lauren's hair grow back and saw the string on her wrist turn gray and shiny. She wasn't shy about asking him for help. One night she spent almost four hours in his kitchen refusing to understand gram-molecular weights. Every statement in her chemistry book was like a nerd she specifically despised, and it wounded her pride to have to consort with it as a true and accurate reflection of physical reality. What she hated most of all, though, was Louis's explanations. She didn't want to hear about page 61 or page 59 if the problem she was having was on page 60. She claimed to understand everything except the one thing she wasn't understanding right then. She just wanted him to tell her the *answer*. When she was especially provoked, she accused him of sounding like her father. But she always ended up thanking him for his help, and as the summer aged he believed he could see it getting harder for her to leave his apartment without touching his hand or kissing him good-bye. She had to bite her lip and bolt.

One night in late July he met her outside the chemistry lab, which smelled strongly of pickles, and he almost had to run to keep up with her as she marched to her car and yanked the door open. When they got to his apartment she ransacked his impoverished cabinets and opened his bottle of gin.

"You're upset," he hazarded from the kitchen doorway.

She burped rippingly and drank a glass of water. "We were supposed to make aspirin today."

"I remember making aspirin."

"I bet you do. But the Clown decided to have a little contest." She wiped her mouth. "We all got certain amounts of chemicals and we were all going to weigh our yields at the end and whoever had the biggest yield would win. Just *win*, you know, whatever that means. These teachers, Louis, they set things up to be so good for people like you and so shitty for everybody else. The best person *wins*, and the people in the middle don't, and the worst person *loses*. Well, Jorryn and me, we always finish last anyway. But we're real careful to follow the recipe, even though we already know we're going to be the worst because that's what we're there for. Meanwhile everybody else is bringing their aspirin up on filter paper—it's this clump, like a potato after you chew it? And it gets weighed, and the Clown writes the names and percentages on his chalkboard, and things get louder and louder. The guys are all *roaring*, about, you know, a difference of half a percent: WO-HO! WO-HO!" Lauren savagely mocked the guys. "And there comes this point where you're supposed to cool the stuff down and filter it, and there you have your aspirin. Well, we do this, Louis. We follow the instructions. And what happens is it all goes through the filter paper. There's nothing there at all. And so then comes the Inquisition, like what did we do Wrong this time? Everybody's staring at us, they're standing there while the Clown reads my notebook. And he can't figure it out! He goes, Did we observe this temperature rise? And we go, Yes! Yes! And did we scratch the flask to make it crystallize? And we go, Yes! Yes! And I'm thinking he's going to say it's all right, he's going to tell us not to feel too bad. I'm feeling pretty bad already, although Jorryn's standing there with her hand like this, you know, not *my* problem, man." Lauren laughed at the thought of Jorryn. "But you know what he did? He got totally pissed off. He said we must have done *something* wrong. Because you cannot put these three things together and heat them up and cool them down and *not, get, aspirin*. And Jorryn and me throw our hands up in the air and we're going, We did! We did! And there's no aspirin! It just didn't work this time! But the Clown he's getting totally worked up and he goes, You're going to get an *F* in this lab unless you redo the experiment and show me at least three grams of aspirin. He says he's going to keep the lab open till midnight if that's how long it takes us. Well, Jorryn starts shaking her head, like, fuck *this* shit—and she walks out. But I didn't even have the heart to leave. I just sat there while everybody was writing up their final reports at the front, I sat there at the lab table all by myself, just sitting there *all by myself* being *punished* because I didn't get any *aspirin*. And I followed the instructions. And there was NOTHING THERE."

Lauren, leaning with both hands on Louis's kitchen card table, began to cry more loudly than he'd known a person could. Fat staves of grief shuddered up through her chest and left her mouth. The voice was her own, voice the way it is before it becomes words: a bath of red sound. Louis put his arms around her and held her head against his shoulder. It fit in his hands. It was as if this were all there was to her, this crying head. He didn't know why he loved her so much, he only knew he wanted admittance to her grief, to her whole damaged self, as he'd wanted it since the first time he saw her. He kissed her bristly hair and kissed behind her ear. For this liberty, she slapped him so hard that his glasses were bent and the plastic pad cut his nose and bruised the bone.

He stood there for a while trying to straighten the frames.

"I'm sorry I hit you," she announced when she came back from his bathroom, her fist full of toilet paper. "But you said you weren't going to do that. It's not fair of you."

She blew her nose.

At midnight they were still watching TV in his kitchen. When Lauren finally turned it off there was a delicious moment when he didn't know what was going to happen next. What happened was she raised a window and said, "It's cooled off."

They went for a walk. Somehow a mild, damp Gulf breeze had banished summer to the north, restoring April. It seemed as if it were the breeze, not the hour, that had emptied the streets and sidewalks of everything but skidding leaves. The cars that did pass were less like cars than like waves breaking gently, like gusts of wind; the humidity sucked them back into itself as soon as they went by. In Houston, a city that accommodated nature, every patch of dirt could smell like beach or bayou. Louis loved the dense live oaks, where purple male grackles and tan female grackles sang irresponsible songs and mewed and moaned and laughed. He loved the squirrels, which were like Evanston squirrels wearing fake long ears; it was an insultingly transparent disguise.

In Hermann Park, he and Lauren climbed the man-made hill and circled the man-made lake with a railing around it. They sat down on some miniature railroad tracks running through a meadow. Lauren lit a cigarette, awakening a grackle that began to speak in tongues.

"Louis," she said. "Do you really love me?"

"Is this a trick question?"

"Just answer."

"Yes, I really do."

She bowed her head. "Is it that thing I did?"

"No. It's just the way you are."

"You mean the way I supposedly am. You think I'm some way that's like you. But I'm not. I'm *stupid*."

"That's bullshit."

"You go to Rice and get A's and I go to Austin and get D's, but I'm not stupid. I'm exactly like you."

"Yep."

She shook her head. " 'Cause I'm smarter than you are too. I've never really loved anybody, so I can't put a whole lot of weight on love. What if it doesn't let you see what's best for me? Emmett loves me too, is one thing, and he doesn't think I should see you at all. So it's like love doesn't necessarily tell the truth. I can't trust anybody but myself. And the thing is, there are two ways to be."

She stood up. "I've been trying to figure out how to explain this without sounding like a total dipshit even to myself. I want to try real hard to explain this, Louis. Let's say you had to study for a test, but you said before I study I'll watch an inning of Cubs."

He smiled. This was apt.

"Well, there are two ways. You either turn it off after an inning and a half, or you watch the whole game and feel terrible. But say you're just very unhappy and you really love baseball. That means the two ways are either to watch the whole game, or none of it at all. Because you know you're so unhappy you'll watch it all if you watch any. And it's *very hard* not to turn it on at all. Because you're *so* unhappy, why shouldn't you at least be allowed to watch baseball? But don't you know, if you try hard even for five minutes not to watch it, you feel something good in you? And you can imagine, I'd feel *really* good if I could always say no. But you never can because you're so unhappy you always end up saying what the hell. Or, I'll stop watching baseball tomorrow. And the same thing happens the next day? Why can't I explain this right?"

With rigid fingers she tried to wrench substance out of the air in front of her.

"Because, see, it seems so *uncool* to give something up. Other people don't, so why should you? Or the people who do are disgusting and seem like they've only given something up because they didn't like it to begin with. It seems like all the really interesting and attractive people in the world just go on doing whatever they want. It seems like this is how the world works. Plus, remember, it's *so hard* to give something up. And that's why you go all around today and it seems like there aren't really two ways, there's only one way. Maybe sometimes you still get little glimmering feelings of what it's like to be a good person. But the BIG GLOWING THING just doesn't seem like a real option. I used to do something good because I liked how it felt, but then the rest of me just wanted to *use* that good feeling as a ticket for getting wasted. It started feeling like feeling clean was just another useful feeling, the same as being drunk, or having money. But you know what? You know what I thought of one day? It was before Christmas, I was with these guys in Austin that I'd met, and I was noticing how instead of not drinking at all that day, like I'd promised myself the night before, I was having some Seagram's for lunch. And it came to me: it was *literally possible* not to drink today. Or fuck, or even smoke."

"Like Nancy Reagan," Louis said. "Just say no."

Lauren shook her head. "That's just bullshit. That makes it sound easy, and it's the hardest thing in the world. But that's not the thing I figured out. What I figured out is: you have to have faith. That's what I'd never understood before. That faith isn't stupid buddhas, or stupid stained glass, or stupid Psalms. Faith is inside you! It's white, and thin, it's this *thing*—this *thing*—" She clutched the air. "That the miracle of doing something so impossible . . . would be so beautiful . . . would be so beautiful. The reason I can't describe this, Louis, is because it's so thin I keep losing sight of it. It's that there's no *trick* to giving up bad things. No *method*. You can't use willpower, because not everybody has that, which means that if you do have some of it, you can't really take credit for it, it's just luck. The only way to *truly* give something up is to feel how totally impossible it is, and then hope. To feel how beautiful it would be, how much you could love *God*—if the miracle happened. But so you can guess how popular I was last semester, which is when— Hey! *Hey!* Oh shit, Louis, don't walk away from me. Oh shit . . . ."

Walking is broken falls, the body leaning, the legs advancing to catch it. Lauren caught up with Louis in a rush of slapping soles and heavy breaths, stopped, then ran some more because he wouldn't stop. "Louis, just let me finish—"

"I already get the idea."

"Oh, this is the thing, this is the thing. People hate you if you try to be good—"

"Yeah, hate, that's the problem here."

"I didn't know it would turn out this way. I thought we could be friends. Louis. I thought we could be friends! And you said I wasn't going to owe you anything! Why am I so stupid? Why did I do this to you? I shouldn't have ever called you, I made everything so much worse. I'm so *stupid*, so *stupid*."

"Not half as stupid as me."

"And but you're not being very nice either. You're trying to make me feel guilty so I'll do something I *don't want to do* because I am *trying to stop feeling like such shit.* Can't we just decide you were unlucky?"

"Yeah, great."

"You'll be lucky next time. I swear you will. Nobody's such a mess like I am." She was crying. "I am such *garbage.* I am not *worth it.*"

It did seem unfair that Louis, who wanted nothing more than to stay with her, was the one who had to shut up and walk away; that she was so neutral towards him that even the job of getting rid of him had to be done by him. But as a final act of kindness, and knowing he'd never get any thanks for it, he let her have the last word. He let her say she wasn't worth it. They walked out of the park and into summer, which was regrouping as suddenly as it had retreated two hours earlier, and again bound together in its humid matrix the million voices of its airconditioners. Lauren got in her car and drove away. In the predawn silence Louis could hear the Beetle's tweeting engine and the shifting gears for maybe twenty seconds before he lost it, and already in those twenty seconds he had difficulty comprehending that she was doing without him, that she was shifting the gears and working the pedals of a car and a life that didn't include him; that she didn't just stop existing when she drove out of sight.

As the days passed and he went to work at KILT and came home to baseball, he was conscious that every hour that passed for him was passing for her too somewhere; and as the days became weeks and he remained just as conscious of how the hours were mounting up, it began to seem more and more incredible that never in all these hundreds of hours, these millions of seconds, did she call him.

October came, November came, and he was still waking up in the morning looking for some loophole in the logic of his self-restraint that could justify his calling her. He wanted her terribly; he'd been good to her; how could she not want him? He felt like there was a rip in the fabric of the universe which it had been his misfortune to blunder through without possibility of return, as though even if he wanted to love somebody else now he wouldn't be able to; as though love, like electricity, flowed in the direction of diminishing potential, and by coming into contact with Lauren's deep neutrality he'd grounded himself permanently.

Christmas in Evanston was ridiculous. Eileen thought he was a computer scientist. As soon as he returned to Houston, he made a demo tape and began to send out query letters. This was the only thing he'd been able to think of doing when, among the mail that had accumulated in his absence, he'd found an announcement of a wedding, Jerome and MaryAnn Bowles formally sharing the news that on the Friday after Thanksgiving their daughter Lauren had married Emmett Andrew Osterlitz of Beaumont, and the sender appending a note in blue ink on the back of the card: *Merry Christmas! Don't make yourself a stranger. —MaryAnn B.*

To reach Renée Seitchek's apartment, he had to drive the entire length of Somerville's east–west axis. In failing light he passed a bank that looked like a mausoleum, a hospital that looked like a bank, an armory that looked like a castle, and a high school that looked like a prison. He also passed the Panaché beauty salon and the Somerville City Hall. The most prominent breed of teenaged girl on the sidewalks had frizzed blond hair, a huge forehead, and a sixteen-inch waist; the other prominent breed was overweight and wore pastel or black knitwear resembling children's pajamas. Twice Louis was honked at from behind for stopping to allow surprised and suspicious pedestrians to cross in front of him.

With the help of some recent *Globes*, he had brought himself up to date on the doings and sayings of the Reverend Philip Stites. Stites's "actions" in Boston were attracting hundreds of concerned citizens from around the country, and to house those citizens who wished to participate in further "actions," he had acquired (for the sum of $146,001.75) a forty-year-old apartment block in the town of Chelsea, directly north across the water from downtown Boston, on the Wonderland subway line. The building, which Stites immediately christened as world headquarters of his Church of Action in Christ, happened to have been condemned three years earlier, and soon after Stites's flock had moved in and hung ABORTION IS MURDER banners from the windows, the Chelsea police paid a visit. Stites claimed to have converted the officers on the spot;

this was later disputed. Under murky circumstances, a compromise was reached whereby every church member who entered the building had to sign a three-page waiver to protect the town from lawsuits. (A *Globe* editorial suggested that the mayor of Chelsea was in fundamental(ist) sympathy with Stites.) The condemned building apparently had almost no lateral stability and was liable to collapse even without the help of an earthquake.

"What the state condemns," Stites said, "the Lord will save."

A *Globe* cartoon showed a newsstand where nothing but dubious waivers were on sale.

Renée lived on a narrow street called Pleasant Avenue, on the easternmost of Somerville's hills. Her house was a shingled triple-decker with a slate-covered mansard roof. The branches of what appeared to be honeysuckle had engulfed the chain link fence in front of it, and Louis was almost through the gate before he saw Renée. She was sitting on the concrete stoop, leaning forward with her hands clasped, hugging to her shins the hem of an antique black dress. Its scooped lace neckline was half covered by the black cardigan she was wearing.

"Hi," Louis said.

She tilted her head. "Listen."

"What?"

"The wind. Listen."

Louis didn't hear any wind at all. A Camaro spewing music approached and pushed its sonic fist into his face and turned a corner. He looked up the parked-up street, at the end of which, above the broken branches of lopsided trees, there was still some turquoise in the sky and a bright star, maybe Venus. Night had already settled on the intervening yards, which were small and filled with plastic toys and more cars and dark piles of things. This part of Somerville seemed both farther from the suburbs and closer to nature than Louis's neighborhood. The trees were taller here, the houses in worse repair, and the stillness less neighborly and more wary and forbidding.

"Oh, come on," Renée said to the reluctant wind.

It did come. Louis heard it first at the far end of the street and saw the branches there suddenly buck, and then he heard it glancing off the nearer roofs and whistling on the nearer eaves and aerials, approaching like some specific and discrete messenger or angel. Then it reached him, an invisible hand that spread his collar and set the honeysuckle heaving before the trees took it up and made it general. When it died away it left the street seeming closer to the sky.

"Well. That was it." Renée stood up and spanked the seat of her dress. "Where's your costume?"

"It's in my pocket," Louis said. He was wearing a loud tweed jacket over a plaid flannel shirt; from the neck down, he looked Sicilian. "Where's yours?"

"This is it."

"You're in mourning."

"Yes, that's right."

Another quantum of wind came whistling down the street and flattened her hair, parting it above her ear. There was something bare about her, something she wasn't wearing. A purse, Louis thought; but it was more than this. In his car, she pulled slack into her shoulder belt and moved away from him, leaning into the crook between seat and window. She rested her palms on the upholstery to either side of her legs, and it seemed to cost her an effort of will to hold her shoulders back, as if she were fighting the inclination to hunch over and cross her arms across her chest, as if she were in a doctor's office, sitting naked on the paper-covered table and fighting that inclination. But of course she was fully clothed now. Louis said he'd seen her on TV.

"Oh yeah?" She raised her arm slowly, trying to rest her elbow on top of the bucket seat, but the seat was too high. More slowly yet, she lowered her hand to the cushion again. "Was it awful?"

"You didn't watch it?"

"I don't have a TV."

"What makes you think it was awful?"

"Well, only that this jerk of a reporter started asking me questions about Philip Stites. Which I understand is what they put on the show."

Her voice, which was strangely bright to begin with, became downright merry at words like "jerk" and "awful."

"The regular department chairman where I work's on leave in California, and of the other two seismologists you can talk to, one's been in the hospital since February and the other's kind of an amazing person, because he's never available although he lives right in Cambridge and works all the time. But so when Channel 4 called up to arrange to get the *Harvard view of things*"—this with a merry stress—"I was the person to be talked to. They obviously had this angle which was going to be science versus religion, only it wasn't so obvious at the time. Plus I was a woman, so it was a perfect setup. I'd never been in front of a camera before. It just didn't occur to me that I didn't have to answer. The other seismologists he talked to not only actually know something about New England seismicity (which I don't) but from what I hear were smart enough not to take the bait on Stites."

"Somebody has to say these things," Louis said, piloting the car onto I-93.

"It's so disgusting. This idea of a single-purpose church, the Church of Hating Women, which typically it's mostly women who've been joining. And they're all nesting in that slime pit of a building in Chelsea, which as you probably know is kind of a slime pit itself." She lowered her head and with a pensive sneer followed the movements of other cars changing lanes, eyeing them like enemies. A strong gust of wind made the Civic shy and a line of winter sand slide sideways through the headlight beams.

"I talked to your mother again," Renée said, as if to change the subject.

Louis concentrated on the road. A pack of headlights had filled the rearview mirror and begun to pass him on the right; the car shied again in the wind. It took Renée a while to realize that he was ignoring what she'd said. Slowly, with one finger, she pulled a dark, pointed tongue of hair off her temple. "I said I talked to your mother again."

"Yeah, I have no comment."

"Oh. I see." She made a face. "She called *me*, you know."

"For professional advice."

"Yes."

"You should bill her." He looked over his shoulder, pushing on the brake pedal. There was a car in his right-side blind spot, cars passing him on the left and swerving in front of him, cars crowding and plunging like lemmings down a curved ramp. He played essentially no part in bringing the Civic through a rotary and onto Storrow Drive.

Renée asked him if he was a student or what. It transpired that she'd actually heard of WSNE and had even, on occasion, listened to it. She said it was like a college station that had gotten lost in the AM band. "That's us," he said.

"Do you like living in Boston?"

"I have a neighbor who keeps asking me that. Kind of a pathetic old guy. He's very concerned about whether I like Somerville. Keeps asking me if I think I'm gonna like it here."

"What do you tell him?"

"I tell him, Aw fuck you, old man. Ha-ha."

"Ha-ha."

"But what about you?" Louis said. "You like it? You like it here in Boston?"

"Sure." Renée smiled at some hidden irony. "It's where I always wanted to live. The east coast in general, Boston in particular."

"This was during your childhood in Waco?"

"My childhood in Chicago. My childhood and adolescence."

"Where in Chicago?"

"Lake Forest."

"Ah, Lake *Forest*, Lake *Forest*." The words had a Pavlovian effect on his blood pressure. "That's where *I* wanted to live when I was a kid in Evanston. You have one of those places right on the lake?"

"You're from Evanston?"

"Whether you had one of those places right on the lake, is what I asked."

"No. We did not."

"That's what I call easy livin'. One of those places right on the lake. Did you have a boat?"

Renée crossed her arms and kept her mouth closed. She was clearly not enjoying Louis's company.

"We were talking about Boston," he said.

She looked out her window tiredly. It didn't seem to be sociability that made her go on and say: "Squantum. Mashpee. Peebiddy. Athol. Braintree. Swumpscutt. Quinzee."

"I'm hearing an issue with the place-names."

"It's cheap, I know. But there's something about the place . . . a coldness, an ugliness. I mean every week there's some incredibly twisted crime here. And somehow all the people who think Boston's a center of culture and education manage to ignore it. They see this cute, manageable, safe city, you know, that's not as scary as New York. It's like New York, only better. But I look and I see overt racism and a rotten climate and elevated cancer rates and bad drivers and a harbor full of sewage, and I see all these young mothers with their Saabs in Cambridge blissing out on being in Cambridge, and who wouldn't be revolted?"

Louis was laughing.

"You laugh," Renée said. "It's obviously a problem I have. I always wanted to live here. But then I found out that the part of me that made this place attractive, the part of me I shared with the other people who actively wanted to be here, was not a part of me that I liked anymore. And the fact that I'm still here after six years is this ghastly reminder of something about myself I wish I'd forgotten six years ago. I feel so implicated. People come here and soak up the experience for a few years and then they move away to real places, and all their lives they talk about this romantic time they had in a city they were too young to notice wasn't much, and the whole country buys this image of Boston as a fun town, and what's sickening is that Boston itself buys it more than anybody. And after six years it's assumed that I buy it too."

"Why don't you get out of here?"

"I am, in September. First I had to get a degree, though."

Louis was looking up at house numbers on a street called Marlborough.

"Besides, I hate the idea of the place more than the place itself. And I don't hate Somerville at all. Perversely. What's the number we're looking for?"

"This one here," he said, pointing at a brick town house. He had only this moment realized that parking might be a problem. In the next twenty-five minutes he and Renée passed the Peter Stoorhuys residence eight times. Traffic was heavy and abnormal, the cars creeping through the gentrified grid in an inverse cakewalk, everyone waiting for a space to open up. Louis spiraled farther and farther away from Peter's house. He ignored spaces that seemed too distant, and then when he returned to them with a more informed idea of their value, they were filled. (It was like learning the hard way how to time stock purchases.) He tried backing into spaces that he knew were too small. He slammed on the brakes for hydrants and then floored the gas pedal. He ran red lights. And when, closer to ten o'clock than to nine, he found an empty spot one block from Peter's house, he was almost too suspicious to take it. Three cars ahead of him had passed it with the blitheness of insiders. There didn't seem to be a hydrant or a driveway or a RESIDENT PERMIT ONLY sign, and the space must just have opened up, but somehow it didn't seem *fresh*. He backed in, frowning warily, as a tiger in the forest might if it ran across a raw beef roast on a sheet of waxed paper. His hips were wet with runoff from his armpits.

"Looked like a nice party in there."

"This sucks. This sucks."

At the door of the first-floor apartment he put his costume on. It was the dust mask he'd worn in high school for cutting grass in dry weather. It had two protruding snout-like vents that he still had some paper filters for. "That's very . . . off-putting," Renée said.

"Thank you."

Eileen came to the door with a bottle of beer. She had her hair pinned up and was wearing a man's double-knit plaid suit and a fat pumpkin-colored necktie. Her cheeks were flushed. "Is that *you*, Louis?" From her tone you might have gathered he was six years old. She smiled tentatively at Renée.

"This is my sister, Eileen," Louis huffed, pointing at her with his left-side snout. Renée finished the introduction herself, and Eileen turned on a frantic superficiality worthy of a woman twice her age. She hovered by the newcomers, explaining the party and pointing out the available pleasures. Louis noticed that Peter owned a sofa and a coffee table identical to the ones in her apartment. In the high-ceilinged living room, which had the stark soffits and smooth walls of a recent rehab, about half the guests were in costume. The prizewinner was an individual in a Mylar suit complete with a reflector visor, a hard hat, and a pendular air-filtration system that put Louis's to shame. Surrounding this figure was a group of young men in weekend-wear. From the basking movements of its head it appeared to be receiving their ongoing congratulations. Good friends of hers from school, Eileen explained. Another good friend of hers sat by the stereo equipment with his arm draped over the top component, his fingers on a control knob, his head nodding to the beat of tinny reggae in a major key. His other arm was in a sling. In the center of the room, a herd of young women with execu-clipped hair were raising and lowering their feet in the kind of semiconscious dancing a person does on too-hot sand. Some wore bandages on various body parts; all wore drop-waisted dresses. "What's your costume?" Louis asked Eileen.

"Can't you *guess?*"

"Small businessman with heavy losses."

She gave him an anguished look. "I'm an *insurance* adjusterrr-*rrr!* You see my tape measure, my notepad, my calculator—" She stopped. She looked just like a cat that had suddenly become aware of being watched. She retracted her head a little and her eyes moved back and forth between Louis and Renée, who were standing two feet apart and paying careful attention to her. One thing was she'd never seen her brother with a female escort.

There was an oddly compassionate note in Renée's voice. "What were you going to say?"

"Nothing, nothing," Eileen becoming flustered. "Just an adjuster, 'surance injuster. There's lots and lots of food, so. Help yourself."

Renée looked on with even more noticeable compassion as Eileen burrowed through the group of dancing women, who two by two glanced over their shoulders at the newcomers. Before they could venture further into the party, an ugly thing happened.

The figure in the Mylar suit was approaching them, doing a lunar-gravity thing. They tried to ignore it, but it stepped between them and peered up through its shiny visor into Louis's face. He saw a masked, bronze-toned image of unamusement. The figure's retinue of friends looked on in suspense and delight as it contorted its limbs in elaborate slow motion and peered up into Renée's face. It touched Louis's head with kinked rubber fingers. It touched

Renée's ear, robotic squeaks and clicks emerging from its vents. Its friends were cracking up. Louis was afraid Renée was going to joke along with it, be "weird" in return, but she remained stone-faced. When the figure again made so bold as to touch Louis's head, he caught hold of its wrist and looked down his nose and squeezed through the rubber glove until he heard a squeal of pain inside the headgear.

"Shit!" the figure accused in a muted voice, retreating towards its friends. The friends weren't laughing anymore. One forty-year-old twenty-two-year-old in green pants detached himself from the group. With terrible, paternal maturity he said to Louis, "We're dealing with a rented suit here, dude."

"We're dealing with an asshole. Dude."

"Yeah, and I kinda think it's you."

Louis smiled inside his mask, pleasantly out of control. "Wooo-ee."

"Let's not be stupid," Renée interposed. "Your man in the suit here started this."

The enemy had enough control of himself to generalize. "I guess some people can't take a joke."

I'm going to kill you, Louis thought. I'm going to smash your fucking nose.

"That's right," Renée said sweetly. "We have no sense of humor."

The enemy looked at Louis, who thrust his head out invitingly. "I'm not going to fight with you," he said.

Louis understood then that he was losing, had lost, in fact. "Love your pants," he said futilely as the enemy walked away.

It appeared that Eileen hadn't seen any of this. She was doing a little dance by one of the stereo speakers, her beer bottle swaying back and forth, her bottom wagging at the rest of the room. It was like a worker bee's coded dance of good tidings, very self-absorbed and yet very public: significant honeysuckle to the north-northwest. Louis had the thought, as he and Renée passed by the bandaged females, that in her own circle Eileen was probably considered a free and quirky spirit.

"Charming fellow," Renée said.

Louis lowered his shoulder and bumped her so hard that she had to take a step sideways for balance. She didn't seem to appreciate this.

The apartment was huge. The only people in the room behind the living room were three extremely pretty girls, three jumbo girls, the kind with long legs and long arms and long hair. (In Homer's world, a god among strangers could be recognized by its unusual beauty and unusual height.) Renée suddenly began to act as if she didn't know where she was going; she almost went back into the living room. Evidently it hadn't escaped her attention that one of the jumbos was in exquisite mourning, an ensemble that included a silk shawl, a pert little hat, and a sheer black veil. The girl looked Renée over with negligible interest and then buried her head in the consultations of her companions, who were methodically taking food from a well-stocked table and putting it in their perfect mouths.

The people in the kitchen were pretty clearly Peter's friends. Pale nightclub arms were aiming cigarette ashes at various receptacles. Drinks were being raised to urban palimpsest faces— punk-yuppie hybrids, pixyish women in thematic costumes, a tank-topped *Homo nautilus* with slicked-back hair. Three middle-aged New Englanders with mustaches sat at the table drinking Jack Daniel's, and Peter himself, in a faded Blondie T-shirt and the billed cap of a Boston city cop, was seated on the rim of the sink. His head had nodded onto his chest.

"Case in point," he said, raising it with effort, "is my old man's company, old Sweet-Ass Incorporated." He glanced at the doorway. Seeing Louis in his dust mask, he rolled his eyes.

Louis blinked innocently. Renée offered him a dripping bottle of Popular Import, which he declined. He was pretty sure the table and chairs here were Eileen's.

"For fifty years," Peter went on, to an apparently appreciative audience, "they've been making their little contribution to the GNP and not incidentally doing some very dubious shit indeed to the environment. I could tell you a fact or two that you would not believe, repeat, not believe. And then suddenly it's the nineties, and that environment which they'd always thought was this nice soft thing they could screw over any way they felt like turns around and does a little damage to their property in Lynn and also keeps the heat on so their stock price falls and they aren't sure if they really ought to be operating that plant with all its nasty by-products because what are they gonna do if one day it cracks wide open—" Peter gasped for breath. "And then it's: Incredible outrage! Mother Nature, dearest Mother Nature dear, what'd we ever do to you to deserve a thing like this? I told my old man, Hey, maybe you had it coming, and he did not take kindly to that point of view. He told me: We are an asset to the Commonwealth. No lie, I'm telling you: an asset to the Commonwealth."

There were joyful noises in the living room as the reggae gave way to a fifteen-year-old Bruce Springsteen recording. From behind Louis someone asked Peter in a loud, clear voice: "What are you talking about?"

It was Renée. Peter swung his head drunkenly and smiled as if to say, What have we here?

"Sweeting-Aldren," a woman in a hard hat and a see-through chemise answered for him.

Renée's mouth formed the word "oh."

"That's right," Peter said. "The company from which all blessings flow. We are blessed with fruits and vegetables that don't have brown spots. We're blessed with Warning Orange price stickers, Warning Orange road cones, Warning Orange gym socks. We're blessed with Asian jungles that don't have foliage." He snapped his fingers. "You—what's your name?"

"Renée. What's yours?"

"Renée." Peter turned the name over in a toying tone. "Tell me, Renée. You buy a swimsuit in the last ten years? Be cool, I'm serious. You must have bought one. And right, you're offended, OK, but chances are it was made of the miracle fabric, the one that doesn't sag or pinch. Stuff called Silcra."

"Spandex," an apocalyptic horseman said.

"Silcra spandex," Peter said. "The miracle bathing-suit fabric. It's another of those Sweeting-Aldren blessings. You see, that's what my dad means about their being an asset to the Commonwealth. No sag, no creep. And hey, really, I'm a little drunk, OK? It's cool?"

Renée stared at him with no expression at all.

"But listen," Peter continued generally, "I'm telling you what

I can't wait for is the total blast, Richter magnitude nine point oh, that makes the whole company go belly up. And oh shit—I just had this flash—let me—" His aged face was lit by the brightness of the idea before his eyes. "I just had this flash of nude beaches, after the cruncher. No more Silcra, no more swimsuits, no more buildings. Naked nature—can you feel it? Can anybody get at that?"

"I feel it," said the horseman.

"Oh yeah. Yes indeed," Peter said.

"They've gotta be insured to the gills, though, Peter," one of the whiskey drinkers pointed out.

"What?" Peter suddenly became more reasonable. "No, that's not what I'm talking about. I'm not talking about money. All these execs like my dad, they're totally protected, they'd hardly feel it. And the stockholders, they lose a little, but it's just a part of their portfolios, a good risk that didn't pay, I mean everybody's ass is double-covered. I'm talking about poetic justice. I'm talking about how pious these people are. You've got to believe me, there is nobody more pious than somebody in the chemical industry. Sure they're rich as pigs, but that's not what they're in the business for. They're in it as a public service. They're making the world a better place to live. They're doing all the nifty things that nature can't do by herself. And who cares about a million gallons of toxic effluents annually if you never find a worm in your Boston lettuce? That's what I'm talking about. That's why I'm just waiting for the cruncher, just to shove all that shit back up their ass." Peter turned to Louis, who had discovered Eileen's dishes in a cupboard by the refrigerator. "You looking for something?"

"Found it," Louis said. He took Renée by the shoulders and moved her out of his path. As he left the kitchen he heard Peter say, "Renée, yo. You're not mad at me, are you? You understand."

"Why should I be mad at you?"

"Hey, absolutely. What's to be mad about. Absolutely."

The jumbo girls had vanished, off to greener pastures. The bathroom door was closed, and when Louis failed to find Eileen in the living room he stationed himself by the food table to wait for her. The wall above the table was festooned with yellow-and-black NOT CROSS POLICE LINE DO tape. Some of the food didn't seem intended for consumption. There was a map of greater Boston attached to a piece of cardboard and decorated with whole, white, upright mushrooms, the biggest ones—a Siamese-twin pair—rising from downtown. There was also a plate of raw vegetables selected for their deformities, tomatoes with lingual protuberances, cleft carrots, gnarled peppers. Also an iced flat cake with stylized barbed wire dribbled on in mocha. Also a crystal bowl full of punch the color of old radiator water, with an iridescent film on top and a sheet of self-adhesive notepaper saying *love canal punch try some!!* Also a bowl of chocolate-chip cookies broken and piled up like rubble, with a toy bulldozer on top and the arms and heads of plastic men sticking up through the crumbs. Also a dish of cinnamon ATOMIC FIREBALLS.

When the bathroom door began to open, Louis stepped over quickly to block Eileen's escape. He found himself face to face with the person in the Mylar suit.

The door closed defensively. Louis turned a corner and found two bedrooms and another closed bathroom door. Suitcases were opened up like sandwiches on the floor of the larger bedroom. Perched on a rattan hamper, glittering in the streetlight the Levolors let in, was Milton Friedman's cage.

Louis knocked on the bathroom door, air rasping hard in the vents of his mask. The door opened a crack and Eileen peered out anxiously. "Maybe you can help me?" She let him in and locked the door. "I can't get the toilet unplugged."

"You have a plunger?"

She pushed one eagerly into his hands. The tip of her necktie was wet. "You have to get a good seal," he said, bearing down through the cloudy, pinkened water. It appeared to be a matter of a tampon. Eileen looked on with her fingers knit together, and when the water suddenly dropped and made the familiar flushing sound, she said, "Thank you *so* much," and unlocked the door. He grabbed the knob.

"What?" she said, retreating from him.

"Talk time."

It was interesting to see how her superficiality fell away, like a shell of dry Elmer's glue coming loose, and exposed a tired, vacant face. She tried a smile. "You having a nice time?"

"Do you know what I just figured out?" He crossed his arms and put his back against the door. "I just figured out why you didn't return my calls. You didn't return my calls because you're not living in your apartment. You're living here."

"Yeah, Louis," she said in a different voice, "I don't even have that apartment anymore. My machine's right here. When was the last time you tried to call?"

"And you didn't bother to tell me."

"I knew you were coming tonight, I thought I'd tell you now."

"But you didn't tell me now. I had to come and ask."

"Yeah, you had to come and ask."

"So the idea is you're living with him now."

She laughed. "I guess so."

"You guess so. You're only sleeping in the same bed with him."

"Is this what you wanted to talk to me about? What bed I'm sleeping in?" She took a twisted towel off a rack and began to fold it and pet it. "My little brother wants to talk to me about who I'm sleeping with. I guess he thinks that's what brothers are for." She put the towel back on the rack. "Will you let me out now, please?"

"Eileen, the guy's a snake."

"Oh, is that so?" The pitch of her voice neared the upper range of human hearing. "My fiancé is a snake? That's very nice of you, Louis. That's very thoughtful."

"Ah, *fiancé, fiancé*." He couldn't figure out these women and their "fiancés." They wielded the word like a weapon; it didn't seem natural. "You should have said so sooner. I meant to say, he is a prince!"

She reached and yanked the mask down below his chin. "You are so hateful. You never gave him a chance! You are so so hateful."

"That's what Mom tells me too."

"And so cool too. You've always got an answer."

"Can I help it if he's a snake?"

"*He is not a snake*. He is a very, very vulnerable and sensitive person."

"Who when I last saw him was making suggestive remarks to my—to the person I brought to your party."

"Well, maybe he has less inhibitions than you do. Maybe he has less inhibitions than anybody in our family. I mean it, Louis,

I know Peter and you don't. I don't see why you think you can just
go calling somebody I care for a—a—a snake!"

"Ah, 'care for.' You 'care for' him and you're—"

"YOU'RE a snake! YOU'RE a snake!"

"You 'care for' him and you're going to marry him. Makes
sense, I'm sure he cares for you too, Eileen. But I wonder if maybe
you're not being taken for a ride. Let me ask you a question, this
little property here, do you guys rent or own?"

"That is none of your business."

Louis threw his head back into the door. "Meaning you actually managed to do it. You actually kept after her until she
couldn't stand it anymore and she broke down and gave you whatever you needed to buy this place. Isn't that right? *Isn't that right?*
You were so ruthless you actually got her to cough up money she
says she doesn't even have yet. *Isn't that right?*"

Eileen looked at him so furiously he was sure she was going
to hit him. But instead she opened the glass shower door, stepped
in, and shut the door behind her. Her voice echoed dully in the
stall. "I'm not coming out till you're gone."

He was too close to tears to say anything for a moment. It was
the money, the money. He thought of the transfer of those funds
and felt a column of tears pushing on the inside of his head, from
his throat to his eyes. Behind the shower door the shadowy outline
of his sister had sunk to its knees. The wet, hollow sound of her
crying was like something in the pipes. He wished he'd never left
Houston.

"What do you think about when you think about me?" he
asked her, looking into his eyes in the mirror. "Do you think of an
enemy? Do you think of a person, who knows you and used to play
with you? Or do you ever even think about me at all?"

Eileen sniffled and gasped. "He is not a snake."

"Yeah, I don't even have anything against him anymore. I
mean, you're right, I don't know him. And it doesn't matter anyway.
I'm not going to bother you anymore."

In reply she only cried. Louis started to leave the bathroom,
but something he'd seen in the mirror without seeing it now registered. He unfastened his fallen mask and put it in his pocket.
The face he was looking at was both softer and older, more sensual,

than the face he considered his own. He thought: *I'm not such a bad-looking guy*. For some reason the thought brought a rush of fear to his head and heart, the fear you feel when you fall in love; when you swing out to pass a car on a narrow road; when someone catches you in a lie.

Renée was standing in the kitchen doorway, her back arched a little so that her neck and shoulders rested against the jamb. Her beer bottle was empty. When Louis appeared, she gave him a weak, ironic smile, as if to indicate both boredom and a diminished faith in his ability to relieve it. He asked her: "Do you want to be here?"

She shrugged. "Sure. Do you not?"

"No, but you can stay if you want. Or we can go get something to eat or something."

Neither alternative seemed to appeal to her much. "Let's go," she said.

The last they saw of the party was the man in the Mylar suit doing a gorilla dance for the amusement of the other guests.

Outside, there was a moon. The silver smoothness of the street was broken here and there by manhole covers and the furry remains of squirrels. "Is something wrong?" Renée said.

"Yeah, a bunch of stuff. Mainly I'm sorry I dragged you to this party."

"Don't be. It was interesting. Although . . ."

"Although what a waste of a parking space."

In the car he divided his attention equally between the road and his silent passenger. The more she didn't look at him, the more he turned to look at her. Her upturned nose, her pale cheeks, her whole thirty-year-old head, of which the plain wedge of dark hair, with its overlay of individual and meandering white strands, seemed the truest part. Spillages of orange street light ran over and over down the front of her dress, turning it an orange that was black in the orange context.

"You have pretty hair," he essayed.

She shifted sharply in the bucket seat, repositioning her legs and shoulders like a person with a stomach cramp.

"Fuck," he said, "never mind. But I do like it."

"So do I," she said flatly, throwing him a quick, smiley glance. When they reached Pleasant Avenue he set the brake and turned the engine off. Renée stared penetratingly at the rear window of the car in front of them, its corroded chrome frame and Celtics decal. On the sidewalk to the left of Louis lay a copper-tone range, the oven door uppermost and asterisked with guano. "This party totally depressed you, didn't it."

A gust of wind rocked the car.

"I was going to ask you," she said, ignoring his question, "if you thought it was true what that person was saying about Sweeting-Aldren. The thing about a million gallons of effluent every year."

"I was hardly listening."

"Because that's definitely not what they're saying in the paper. In the paper they're talking about zero gallons."

"My sister wants to marry this guy."

"He's the boyfriend?" Another gust rocked the car. "I didn't realize."

"For richer and for poorer."

"But I actually kind of liked him. He wouldn't be my first choice as a brother-in-law, but he's not stupid. Just a type."

Louis leaned over the hand brake and kissed her.

She let him walk right into the warm vestibule of her mouth. It might have been a minute's journey from the enamel rill between her front teeth to either of the elastic dead ends to which her lips came; an hour's journey down her throat. He took her hair in his fists, pressing her head into the seatback with his lips.

Headlights turned up the street. She pulled away, flattening her offended hair with one hand. "I was just about to say I can't stand sitting around in cars."

Inside the house they were greeted by a baying from the large lungs of several dogs in the ground-floor apartment. "Dobermans," Renée said. The air was hot and canine. It was fresher on the second-floor landing, and when she stopped to take a key down from a ledge, Louis kissed her again, backing her into a wall covered with paper that smelled like a used-book store. The baying downstairs subsided into frustrated gnashings, and she tried to pull away even as her mouth kept pressing into his. Suddenly a baby started crying, it seemed like right behind the door beside them. They went up a set of steeper stairs to her apartment.

It was a bare, clean place. There was nothing on the kitchen counter but a radio/cassette player, nothing in the dish rack but a plate, a glass, a knife, and a fork. That the light was warm and the four chairs around the table looked comfortable somehow made the kitchen all the more unwelcoming. It was like the kitchen of the kind of man who was careful to wash the dinner dishes and wipe the counters before he went into the bedroom and put a bullet in his brain.

A large room opposite the bathroom contained a bed and a desk. Another large room contained an armchair and bookshelves and many square yards of blond floorboards. When Renée came out of the bathroom she stood with her back to the woodwork between the doors to these two rooms and faced the kitchen, her hands clasped behind her. "Do you want something to eat, or drink?"

"Nice place," Louis said simultaneously.

"I used to share it with a friend."

She didn't move, didn't lean aside even a little bit, as he went into the bedroom. He put his feet down as quietly as he could. Everything about the place made him feel intrusive, as though even loud footsteps might disturb things. (When police detectives arrive at the scene of a crime, aren't there often some respectful, meditative moments before attention is turned to the body on the floor?) The desk lamp had been left burning over a stack of 11 x 17 fanfold computer paper, on the top sheet of which a program in Fortran was being revised in black ink. (Until the moment of the crime, yes, work had been in progress, it had been an ordinary evening . . .) Above the desk hung a bathymetric map of the southwestern Pacific Ocean. It was spattered with thousands of dots in different colors, many grouped in dense elongated swarms like army-ant columns; beneath them, barbed line-segments were applied like war paint to the ocean. Continuing to tread carefully, as he had when he first entered Rita Kernaghan's living room, Louis returned to the kitchen. Renée was still standing with her hands behind her back. She might have been a missionary at a stake, with her hands tied, unable to cover her nakedness, unable to cross herself or shield her face from the flames that would soon be leaping up, but like

that missionary she stared straight ahead. She did flinch discernibly
when Louis touched her shoulders (even the greatest saints must
have flinched when the first flames licked their skin), and despite
the way she'd kissed him on the landing he was surprised by her
unhidden look of need.

The wind whistled on the dormers in the bedroom. It rose
without falling, consuming more and more of the roof, finding
further timbers in the house to bend and further panes to rattle,
further expanses of wall to lean on. It seemed to be doing the work
for Louis as he parted and lifted the two sides of Renée's cardigan,
which slid easily off her shoulders and, falling to the floor, unbound
her hands. She put her wrists around his neck.

It was still dark when he woke up. DR. RENEE SEITCHEK, whose
internal anatomy he imagined had been rearranged in the escalating
violence of their union, and whose hands had proved no less ar-
ticulate than the rest of her in showing his own hands how best to
bring her the releases he couldn't deliver otherwise (he liked and
admired the silent and perspiring and possessed way she came),
now lay next to him and slept so heavily that she looked like she'd
been struck unconscious by a blow to the head. There were sparse
flocks of freckles on her shoulders. Through a crack between a
shade and a window frame Louis could see tree boughs, lit by
streetlight from below and blanketed with blackness, rocking in
the wind. This wind tonight, she'd told him during a lull, had
reminded her of an earthquake she'd seen in the mountains once.
She'd been hiking in the Sierra Nevada with a high-school group.
"And all of a sudden there was something happening in the country
to the east. We could see for forty or fifty miles, and what it was
like was when you're by a perfectly calm lake, and you can see the
wind coming the way you could hear it on the street tonight, the
way the leading edge roughs up the water when it comes. That's
exactly what this event was like. It was this *thing* coming across
the mountains, this visible rolling wave, and then suddenly we were
in it. We definitely knew we were in it because there were little
rockslides and the ground shook. But it wasn't like the other events
I've felt, because there was this visual connection." She had actually
seen the wave they were feeling. It hadn't come out of nowhere. It

had looked like nothing on God's earth. And he wanted then, again, to *take possess have take possess possess* the body in which this memory resided.

The alarm clock showed twenty to four. He slipped out of bed and went to the bathroom. When he returned, Renée was kneeling in the center of the bed. He said, "Hi," and she backed towards the bottom of the bed, dragging the sheet along with her. She looked terrified.

"What's wrong?"

She backed off the bed and fled to the far corner of the room, one hand raised vaguely to ward him off. Standing up showed the complexity of her nakedness, how the legs had to connect with the torso, how peculiarly narrow the female waist, how much more delicate the shoulders than the hips, how detached and attention-demanding a woman's breasts. "I don't have it," she said to him in a loud voice that wasn't bright or merry.

He hardly noticed the erection he was rapidly and in full view of her reacquiring. "You're dreaming," he said.

"Leave me ALONE. Leave me ALONE."

"Sh-sh-sh." He sat down on the bed, showing her his empty palms. This seemed to scare her all the more. Without taking her eyes off him, she edged along the wall. Then she made a break for the door but curved towards him as she ran, her hands outstretched as if she were falling, and he saw how just before she reached him she seemed to crash through a sheet of glass or some similar planar discontinuity. She took hold of his shoulders and said, "Oh, I was having such a bad dream."

The house swayed in the wind. She sat on his thighs and let herself be held. Strong, low-pH fumes rose from between them. Experimentally, he tried to put his penis back inside her.

She clutched his shoulders, pain cutting streaks into her face. "This is a little much."

"I'm sorry."

"You're not sore?"

"What do you think?"

"Oh, well, in that case." She used her whole weight to impale herself on him. His nerves were screaming *harmful! harmful!* She rolled her hips angrily. "Hurt?"

"Yes!"

After a while the pain diffused into a large zone of ache, a pool of melted sulfur with little blue flames of pleasure flickering across the surface. Then the flames became scarcer and then disappeared altogether, and the sulfur began to crystallize into a column of hard, dry, sharp chunks. He might have been rubbing against broken bone. Renée's eyes and cheeks were wet, but she didn't make any sound.

When they stopped he was bleeding enough to leave marks on the sheets. Renée sat on the edge of the bed and rocked with her knees pressed together. He just assumed he wouldn't die because of this, a few years down the line.

5

He went to the house with the pyramid on top. The front lawn was a metallic green now and the grass lay down and shivered as if under a running tide, some large-scale flow of invisible matter related to the brilliant wrongness of the light, which was messing up the colors, throwing some of the black of the tree trunks into the blue heaven and some of the white of the clouds into the trees. For the person who hasn't slept, what makes the new day strange and fills it with foreboding is that the setting sun is in the east and not setting; all day the light is like the light in dreams, which comes from no direction.

"Louis, my God," Melanie said, clutching the lapels of her dressing gown and peering out over a new brass door chain. "It's nine in the morning, I'm not even up. I have to catch a plane."

"Unchain the door?"

"You didn't call! If you'd come two hours later—"

"Unchain the door?"

An alarm-system number pad had been installed in the entryway. In the living and dining rooms the broken plaster had been repaired, and Rita Kernaghan's books and decorative objects, including the portrait of Melanie's father, had given way to a more standard opulence, suitable for a luxury hotel suite—Japanese lithographs, sheer curtains, gold brocade.

"I meant to call you," Melanie said. "I just flew in on Thursday and there's been so much to do."

"I bet," Louis said. He walked into the living room and stepped onto a silk-upholstered sofa and stamped from one end to the other, listening to the twangs of its internal injuries.

"Louis! For God's sake!"

He crossed to the coffee table. In good soccer style, using his instep, he penalty-kicked a cut-glass bowl into the fireplace. "I understand you're handing out money to your children," he said, stepping back onto the sofa. "I'm here for my share."

"Get down off the sofa. That is not your sofa."

"You think I'd do this to a sofa that was mine?"

"I told you. I'm not going to talk about money. If you want to talk about something else, all right, but—"

"Two million."

"But not money. I never expected I would have to—"

"Two million."

Melanie placed her hand on the side of her head she got her headaches on.

"How much did you give Eileen?"

"Nothing, Louis. I gave her nothing."

"So where'd she get the condo?"

"It's a matter of a loan."

"Oh, I see. How about you *lend* me two million?"

Melanie's hand slid forward to cover her face, two fingertips pressing on her eyelids.

"I'll never bother you again, Mom. Promise. Two million and we're quits. I'd say that sounds like quite a deal. You know, maybe I'll even pay you back."

"I can no longer consider this a joke."

"Who's joking? I need the money. There's this radio station I have to buy. Two million's the figure I had in mind, but I could do a fair amount of good with two hundred thousand. That would stabilize things till you come through with the rest."

"What are you talking about?"

"I'm talking about Philip Stites. You've heard of him, the anti-abortion guy. I want to make him a present of two hundred thousand dollars. Just to aid his cause, you know. Ever since we all got so rich I've become a very Christian person, Mom, you're not aware of this, of course, because you never call me or—"

"And you never call me!"

"Oh, and Eileen does, and that's why she gets rewarded with cash gifts?" Louis stepped up onto the shoulders of the sofa and tipped it over backwards, alighting just before the thud. "Why is it that everybody but you can see she only calls you to get money out of you? You think she cares about you? She hates you till you give her money and then she rewards you by not hating you until she needs some more. Haven't you ever noticed this? It's called being spoiled."

His mother turned away as if the conversation didn't interest her. The sudden sharp tremor that made her whole body jerk and brought tears to her face seemed to take even her by surprise. She made a coughing, gulping noise. Louis might have had more sympathy if he hadn't felt that her tears and Eileen's tears always came at his expense, and if he hadn't suspected that in his absence they were basically happy.

"I'm trying to do you a real favor here," he said. "I mean, just think. You give me two million, and for the rest of your life you can consider me a selfish jerk. You'll never have to feel guilty again. No more tears, no more evasions. Plus you'll still have your twenty million to play games with Eileen with."

His mother was shaking her head. "You don't understand. You don't understand. I've lost—" A strong aftershock rocked her shoulders. "I've lost—" Another aftershock. "I've lost—"

"Money?"

She nodded.

"How much?"

She shook her head; she couldn't say.

"So you've lost money. Amazing. Eileen gets to you in time to get an apartment out of this, but I'm a little late. Amazing the way these things work out."

Still trembling, Melanie parted a sheer curtain and looked out at the false-color daylight, the fair-weather clouds grazing the top of the last hill before the ocean. "Your request is not reasonable."

He tested the heft of a crystal objet from an end table. "You're saying this place of hers cost substantially less than two hundred thousand dollars?"

"Your request," she repeated, "is not reasonable. Eileen will be starting a very fine job at the Bank of Boston when she graduates in June. She'll have an excellent income and she'll pay me interest on the loan. This is not particularly your business, I'm only telling you so you understand. The condominium was a reasonable investment for both of us. There is simply no equating her financial position with yours."

"Sure, if you're a bank. But what about the social value of what she's doing as opposed to what I'm doing? She's going to help the grotesquely rich get grotesquely richer. You think she really needs your help? I'm trying to save a good radio station from some fanatics."

"And what a polite way you have of asking. Walking on my sofa."

"Oh, I get it. You would have come across if only I hadn't walked on your sofa."

Melanie spun around to face him. Her uncombed hair hung in the shape of a kaffiyeh. "The answer is no, Louis. No. I am not giving any more money to anyone, including Eileen. You can hate me, but I *can't*. I am incapable of it. Do you understand? Please don't make it any worse."

She left him standing beneath the spot where his grandfather's portrait had hung. He heard a door close upstairs. He covered his face with his hands and breathed in the smell of Renée Seitchek's vagina.

On Monday morning Alec Bressler sold WSNE-AM to the Reverend Philip Stites's Church of Action in Christ for a sum undisclosed by either party but rumored, in light of the station's crippling debts, to be in the neighborhood of forty thousand dollars.

Louis was emptying his desk when Stites and his lawyers, a leather-faced duo with nice manicures, stopped in the doorway to assess his cubicle. Stites was roughly Louis's height and no more than a couple of years older. He had one of those handsome, chubby Southern faces, round tortoiseshell glasses, and the lank, ultra-fine blond hair of a young child. He was wearing khaki slacks, a blue blazer, and a striped tie knotted in a four-in-hand. "How're you doin'?" he said to Louis in a warm Carolinian accent.

"Not bad, for the Antichrist."

The young minister chuckled affably. "You already quit, did you." He returned to the hallway. "Hi there, Libby, you got a second to show us around here? You met Mr. Hambree already. This here's Mr. Niebling. This pretty lady's name is Libby Quinn."

Louis would sooner have not been paid for his last two weeks of work than go and bother Alec this morning. Fortunately for his finances, the ex-owner came to him. He had a sheaf of twenties and briskly counted out twenty-five of them.

"This is more than you owe me."

"Is a gift from Social Security. You need a recommendation? I send it to you."

"I can't believe this happened."

"Yes, I know, is a bad sing for you. You need a job. But the free market decides: not enough listeners. Meanwhile I broadcast 425 editorials. I have letters to show people listened. Maybe one person changes his mind because of me. Eight years to change one mind. But you can't sink about results. You do what you have to do, regardless of results. Is a matter of faith."

"Stites has the faith," Louis said in an ugly voice.

"So other people live with nasty faith. This means you live without faith yourself? No hope for any sing? If everyone's faith is same as yours, you don't need faith."

Louis drummed his fingers on his desk. "What are you going to do now?"

"Same as twenty years ago," Alec said. "Make lots of money."

Sometime between one and two in the afternoon he began to wait for an earthquake. He'd been sitting in his room doing nothing anyway; waiting didn't take much extra effort. He tried to make himself as ready to feel the next tremor, should it come, as he was to hear thunder when he'd seen a flash of lightning: to be on the edge, to have his consciousness flush with the instant. Unfortunately this involved keeping his eyes open, and his eyes kept sliding off smooth surfaces and catching on irregularities, for example the sheet of wallpaper whose edges had lifted away from the plaster, exposing some of the underlying streaks of glue. Eventually this glue gave his optic nerve a kind of blister, and the blister tore open and began to bleed, and yet there was nothing else on the wall for his eyes to hold on to.

Just looking at his unopened cartons of radio equipment exhausted him. The cartons might all have been stacked on his chest, raising his gorge and stifling his breath.

The ceiling was covered with off-white tiles made of some sad paper product. He ascertained that all the tiles bore the identical pattern of little holes, the seeming differences due only to differing orientations. From five to roughly six in the afternoon he made perfectly sure that the offset between the rows of squares at one end of each row was the same as the offset at the other end. It occurred to him that if a team of people in the Boston area would do what he was doing, at all hours of the day and night, that is, if there were always at least one good guy waiting in full consciousness for the ground to shake, then there might never be another earthquake, so shy of human consciousness are the random events of nature. (This is the fundamental axiom of superstition.) But maybe nature, in her great need to relieve those underground stresses, would be driven to the radical, Old Testament–style expedient of bringing a supernatural sleep to the particular consciousness on duty when the moment came and the rupture could no longer be postponed. The boy whose finger had been in the dike later speaking of a golden and irresistible drowsiness? Obviously this fatal moment had not arrived yet, because Louis held off the seisms in perfect wakefulness until the Red Sox came on the air.

Tuesday was hot, the solar and convective furnaces already stoked and roaring at nine o'clock. The duct tape made a sound like tearing clothes as Louis unpacked his boxes. He handled everything. He took the top off the twelve-band receiver he'd built at fifteen and could hardly believe how well he'd soldered then. He had to look hard to find those spatters and botched cuts and crooked screws that at the time had caused him such self-hatred.

In the afternoon he listened to music on the FM band, spinning the dial to dodge commercials. When night fell on all the spectrums, visible and radio, he switched to shortwave. He heard the chirping of radio-teletype, rapid and cool and neutral in tone, as unstressed as spoken Swedish. The code sent by hand he got most of—in high school he'd been a twenty-four-word-a-minute man—but it was mainly numbers and abbreviations, more pleasing as noise than as communication. There was emphatic and tireless tooting from freighters and beacons in the Atlantic night. Birdies and blaring mystery tones the color of back pain. An inflamed Slavic commentator inveighing above heavy sonic surf and going under, seeming to protest more stridently that he was not going under, and going under for good.

The Voice of South Africa, calling from Johannesburg. Radio Habana. Radio Korea, the overseas service of the Korean Broadcast System, coming to you in English from Seoul, the capital of the Republic of Korea. Deutsche Welle, Radio France Internationale. Adventist World Radio offering program notes to far-flung believers, whistles faintly modulating through, like flies circling the pulpit. Injā Tehrān ast, sedā-ye jomhūri-ye eslāmi-ye Irān. The East is Red, the East is Red . . . Radio Baghdad reported that Zionist occupying forces had today murdered three Palestinian youths in south Lebanon; despite her Kensingtonian phonetics, this Voice of the Iraqi People's Republic seemed not to understand what she was saying. "Reuters reported that on Sun. Day in the aftermath of the abor. Tive coup. Attempt in Mali three senior officers of the national air. Force had been executed in the square outside the." But then the strings began to wail, and in her own tongue now the Voice, the same apprised female Voice, sang a ballad with a sexy and ironic slackness to the chorus, as though we all Know-ho-ho-ho ho-ho-ho this story well and have heard it many tiyee-yimes, and the strings agreed. Already the sun was rising on Islam. Jeeps and bundled women in the streets, another day's devotions and atrocities under way. In Somerville, a night wind broke the dark shadow of a branch into several less dark shadows that bowed and crossed and canceled in the rhomboids of streetlight on the wallpaper.

"Hey there, Louie boy. Taking the day off?"
"Yes."

"Hall right. Good for you."

"I was fired from my job."

John Mullins was aghast. "They fired you? What for?"

"I'm not sufficiently Christian."

"You know for a second there I believed you."

"It's the truth."

"Ha. You had me fooled there for a second."

By the time the post office closed, Louis was ready with eleven query letters. He had only two copies of his demo tape and he hoped he wouldn't have to pay for more. His monthly expenses came to about $720, which included rent, food, utilities, car expenses, and payments on a college loan. With the $500 Alec had given him, his life savings came to $1,535.

In the evening he stood to one side of his window and looked out of it over his shoulder, like a man under siege. Couples in their early thirties were ringing the doorbell next door and emerging in the yellowly lit living room opposite his window. The soprano carried a frosty pitcher of water and wore a jumper with wide shoulder straps. She had auburn hair and matching freckles and fleshy white upper arms. Louis imagined he could see her vaccination mark, deep and annular, unpigmented. At the piano sat her husband, a blond, athletic frog with a crooning mouth. All the male visitors wore short-sleeved shirts with collars; all the females had bare calves and wore sandals or hard shoes. They began to sing hymns. It was like an old-time sing-along except that every voice was trained. They smiled as they sweated, eyes meeting across the room and glinting at each meeting like a distant photo flash or a diamond catching sunlight. Louis shut his window to keep the heat of all these bodies out.

Thursday night a serious amateur who'd advertised in the *Globe* came and took away all the radio equipment in a station wagon for $380 cash. Louis had initially asked six hundred.

On Saturday and Sunday, roughly every two hours, he dialed Renée's home number and work number. There was no answer at either. He decided that she had no interest in seeing him again. The thought maddened him and he began to dislike her, because he wanted to use her body and was fully prepared to like her, if that was what using it required.

In the studios of WOLO-AM in downtown Boston, in a glass tower across the tracks from North Station, a sea-captain type wearing white dungarees and red kerchief was being ushered from the vestibule. Moments later the man was heard speaking on the house monitor, extolling a balloon race scheduled for the weekend.

WOLO's receptionist returned to her desk behind the counter, warded Louis off with one arm, and pounded on her keyboard. She was a dark-haired jumbo girl, about the same age as he and ridiculously pretty. Her thighs were crossed and her tight skirt was bunched into exciting rills. At length she stopped typing, squinted at her screen, and delicately touched a function key. The screen went blank. She clapped her hands to her cheeks in horror and stared. She turned to Louis, eyes and mouth round. "I don't know where it went! I don't know where it went!"

"I'm supposed to see a Mr. Pincus?"

"He was in." She put a finger on a new key and pulled it away as if stung. "But he went out."

"Is he coming back?"

"You're Holland, Louis, right? Why don't you leave your name. I can't deal with you. The manual for this printer was generated on the same printer for quote heuristic reasons unquote and the one sentence I could care less about ends with the phrase, I've got this memorized, 'not to the not to.' *Ends* with it."

"I thought I had an eleven o'clock appointment."

"Definitely not looking good in terms of seeing Mr. Pincus."

"Do you know when he'll be back?"

"Why don't we start with where did he go? Hey? He went to the airport. Unlikely thing that's his final destination. What's his final destination? 'Not to the not to.' You follow me?"

"Maybe I could make a new appointment."

"I'd love to reschedule you, but for reasons of blankness of screen and total unresponsiveness to keyed commands that's not possible. Why don't you write your name and number down, and I'll give him the message, Holland, Louis. I'll tape it to his screen."

She unrolled eight or ten inches of Scotch tape and stuck one end to Louis's memo and the other to the doorway leading from her cubicle. From a drawer in her work station she removed a cantaloupe-sized red apple and made a tiny white notch in it with her teeth.

"Do you want to have lunch with me?" Louis said.

She held the apple up and wiggled it. "Not to the not to!"

"How about a drink after work?"

She shook her head and took a larger bite of apple and munched in a glum, blank-minded way, staring at an electrical outlet. Jackhammers rattled in the distance, at some unguessable compass point; cars honked plaintively, as though calling to their young. With a whack the girl bit a slab off the apple. Clearly it would take her another five minutes to reach the core (each bite reinforcing the superfluity of lunch) and another three minutes after that to suck her teeth clean and readjust her mouth, checking its perimeter with the tip of her tongue and then patting it with the back of her wrist. Her screen was still blank.

"Are you free on the weekend?" Louis said.

"This person," she complained.

"We could have dinner."

"Do I know this person? Why am I talking to this person?"

In the help-wanteds there were thousands of boring jobs and no interesting jobs. Until you opened the help-wanteds it was possible to forget the essence of the average person's job, which was: you perform this soul-killing "data entry" or "telemarketing" or "word-processing" function and we will reluctantly give you money.

The help-wanteds were even sadder than the personals. "Very attractive benefits package," some promised. (STUNNING BLUE-EYED SWF, fortyish but looks 25, seeks . . .) Was there anyone in the world who was independent, highly motivated, creative, and possessed of a minimum five yrs exp w/ T-1s, SDLC, HDLC and 3270 BISYNC? And if such a dream candidate did exist, would it not be suspicious in the extreme if he or she were looking for a job? Ads like these seemed to have been placed as bitter ceremonial reminders, lest anybody think that corporations did not, like everyone else, have needs and desires that could not be satisfied.

At the other end of the scale were the laconic one-liners seeking watchmen or receptionists and mentioning no benefits or wages; ads like ugly prostitutes who, on the plus side, didn't ask much.

Running a business was clearly nothing but unpleasant trouble. Companies wanted good employees and did not want bad employees. But the bad employees were eager to stay and take the companies' money, while the good employees were eager to leave and work for competitors. To Louis all the thousands of jobs listed in the paper seemed like noxious effluents that the companies were trying to pay people to take off their hands. How they hated to have to pay so much and offer such juicy "benefits" to be rid of these noxious duties! How they wished it weren't so! He could feel their anger at the expense of disposing of all this garbage. The top executives dumped the problem on the personnel department, and the people in personnel wore plastic suits easily mistaken for faces and personalities. Their job was to handle the poisonous but inevitable employment by-products without letting them come in contact with their skin. Their cordiality was guaranteed non-stick. It was 100 percent impermeable.

"What are you, on vacation, Lou?"

"No, I told you. I was fired."

"You didn't tell me you were *fired*."

"Actually, I did."

"Gee that's tough, I can't believe it. Seems like everybody's getting laid off these days."

"Yeah, although that obviously can't be the case."

"What I don't understand is why would anybody want to fire a nice kid like you."

"Well, because I don't believe that Jesus Christ is my personal savior. I don't believe in the literal truth of the Bible."

Mullins frowned. "What's that got to do with it?"

"The place where I worked was taken over by fundamentalist anti-abortionists and all non-Christians had to go."

"Aw Lou. Aw *Lou*. You shouldn't of done that." Mullins shook his head. "Now you're, whataya, whataya, lookin' for a new job?"

"Right now I'm looking for a woman I saw ten days ago and want to see again."

"You're not married, are you."

"No."

"You gotta have a job, Lou."

On Pleasant Avenue a ten-speed chained to a parking sign had been wrestled to the ground without relinquishing its hold on the signpost. The bumblebees bouncing off the honeysuckle were like coalescences of the day's yellow, angry heat. The noise of hard-winged insects like the buzz of high-voltage transformers damaged, overloaded, by this heat; like the monotonous, depersonalized spir-its of exterminated Indians made volatile by this heat.

Inside the front door, in a chamber filled with incredibly pow-erful and hot canine body odor and dog-food breath, Louis saw orange flowers bloom and had to fight his way up the stairs like a diver close to not making it. His glasses slid off his sweating head. No one answered his knocking, although Renée's apartment was traitorous and welcomed his mind's eye.

It was a twenty-five-minute walk to Harvard. With the help of some friendly strangers he managed to locate the Hoffman Lab-oratory of Geological Sciences, which was a quintuple-decker sand-wich of brick and window on white concrete slabs. The interior was airconditioned and smelled like the sterile insides of computers. The office of Dr. Seitchek was situated on the ground floor, across from a computer room, and contained two desks. Howard Chun was sitting with his feet up on the one closer to the door, energet-ically firing a rubber band at the wall in front of him and shagging it on the fly. The other desk, by the window, was bare except for a stack of unopened mail.

"She's not here."

"Do you know where she is?"

Howard lurched forward to catch the rubber band before it fell between his sneakers. "What you want her for?"

"She's a friend of mine."

"Oh yeah."

"Do you know where she is?"

"Think she's at home."

"I was just there."

Howard began to snap the rubber band viciously against his own fingers, frowning at the reddening skin. Suddenly he peered over an armrest at the floor. "Wanna see something?" He shot the rubber band at a piece of paper on the wall. "That's the earthquakes we got since March."

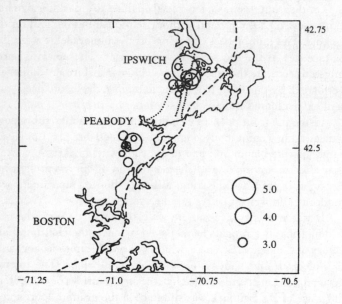

The circles appeared to be epicenters, scaled linearly to magnitude. "What are the dotted lines?" Louis said.

"Mapped faults near Ipswich. Dashed line, big aeromagnetic feature, may be old suture, may be nothing. Six miles deep, maybe four or five. Mapped faults are shallow. Only problem is, Ipswich cluster's deep, more like five, six miles."

"Meaning what?"

"Probably there's other faults. Or faults aren't mapped right. Doesn't look right. Two unrelated swarms, so close in time and space. That's low probability."

"Like how low?"

Howard crossed his arms and wrinkled his nose. "Like really low. Never see it."

"Huh." Louis looked again at the pile of mail on Renée's desk. Outside the window Japanese tourists were filing up an asphalt-topped path between oak trees.

Howard leaned dangerously far back in his swivel chair and retrieved his rubber band with outstretched fingers. "Wanna see something else?" Feet still on his desk, he rolled back and opened his top drawer and handed Louis a photograph, a 5 × 7 on yellowing, once-glossy paper. It was a picture of an adolescent girl in a marching-band uniform. She was clutching a clarinet to her chest. The jacket was Prussian blue with cream-colored trim and gold buttons; the cap had a black plastic bill and gold braid on the band. Long limp hair, mid-seventies hair, framed her face and did its best to conceal (but actually in effect extended and accentuated) the zones of acne on her cheeks and forehead. She was wearing the rigid, self-defeating smirk of teens who hate their face and for whom being photographed is an unspeakable cruelty, and was staring at an infinity somewhere to her left, as if by not meeting the camera's eye she could make it overlook her. Pentagonal yellow leaves lay on the lawn between her and an out-of-focus station wagon and a double-door garage.

"You know who it is?"

"Where'd you get this?"

"It's Renée."

"Where'd you get it?"

Howard slammed his back into the vinyl backrest of his chair several times. Then he shoved off the desk with his feet and rolled halfway across the room. "Found it."

"Where?"

"Just got it."

Louis tried to give it back.

"Take it," Howard said. "You want it?"

"Why are you giving it to me?"

Howard shrugged. He'd made his last offer.

"Did you steal it?"

"Just got it. You want it, take it. I don't want it."

In the twilight, through his open window, he heard John Mullins tell the soprano and her husband that that nice-looking fella next door here—just moved in, nice-looking kid—had gotten fired from his job. He told 'em he didn't believe in Jesus, and they fired him.

"I've been trying to call you," Louis said.

Renée was eating seedless red grapes at her kitchen table. She held the glass bowl at chest level and used only her wrist, bending it back and forth efficiently, to convey them to her mouth. "Very bad week for that."

"I got what's-his-face, Terry, once, and he hung up on me."

"People are a little angry with me, through no fault of my own." Quiet in bare feet, she got up and put the grape bones in the sink. Sweat stuck her hair to her neck and forehead in narrow, curving blades. In the window behind Louis, a box fan hummed on Lo, dispensing comfort with its sound, not its draft. (While their dressings are being changed, burn patients would rather listen to white noise than to music.)

"I'll just give you an idea of what things have been like." She showed him the jack of her disconnected telephone, then plugged it in and upended a paper shopping bag from DeMoula's Market Basket, dumping maybe sixty or eighty envelopes onto the kitchen table. "Here's a nice one." She handed him an envelope without a return address. It contained a typewritten note:

> *Dear Bitch,*
> *I hope you die of aids.*
> *Sincerely,*
> *An enemy.*

"Gets right to the point," she said brightly. "Here's another nice one."

Dear "Ms" Seichek,

I saw you on TV and your attitude makes me sick. Your attitude is have sex then kill the baby. What's the difference between abortion and infancitide? One. Abortion is legal in Mass and infancitide is murder. You explain it to me. You said abortion on demand is o.k. for 14-years-olds. What about the parents. Another thing is you never mention adoption or homes. In this poor world there is no such thing as an unwanted baby. Maybe you want to have babies someday but your sterile. I think abortion stance should be taken into account for adoption. You don't get any. Have you ever held a baby in your arms? Maybe you won't have a chance now because of what you said. Maybe God is Merciful if you pray. Do you know how to pray? I can not pray for you.

Mrs. Axel Hardy
68 Frond Drive
Hingham, Mass.

"That's the one about adoption, right? Check this one out. This guy put part of the chain letter in too."

Dr. Renee Scheik
Hoffmann Laboratories
20 Oxford Street
Cambridge, Mass. 02138

Dear Dr. Scheik,

Next to convicted drug kinpins there is nothing more dispicable in the world than abortionists. Half the people entering abortion clinics never come out alive. How can you sleep at night knowing all the lives you took at work? Or do you take drugs to sleep (ha ha). I hope they shut you down and you go to jail. The keep men and women apart in jails, good thing. May they do the worst to you.

Signed,
John Doe

This had been typed on the back of an nth-generation Xerox reading:

-2-

has IMPACT but sometimes you cannot get through. Sometimes the number will be changed temporarily to an unlisted number. Sometimes you will get a busy signal or a no-answer or a machine. If a work number has been changed, get the new one from directory assistance (555-1212). *Remember that clinics and private doctors cannot afford to be unlisted.* Persistence is important—for a week, two weeks, even three. However it is also important to match EACH CALL with a first class letter. If the chain is not broken, it has been estimated that each pro-abortionist on the list will receive UPWARDS OF 1600 LETTERS by the time all nine boxes on page 1 are full. There is power in numbers! Imagine the impact of 1600 impassioned personal pleas! And 1600 telephone calls! But if you break the chain this number will be cut in half, and if another friend breaks the chain, it will be cut in half again.

Jesus fed 5000 with five loaves and two fishes. You can have the SAME POWER if you send out six copies of this letter. If this copy is too blurry, *retype before sending.*

Note: Long distance dialing is cheaper between 5pm and 8am (local time), but keep in mind most clinics keep regular working hours in their time zone (i.e. 9 to 5).

HOW TO CHOOSE

DO NOT choose names from the list at random. Start with the DAY OF THE MONTH you were born on—you will see there are 31 names on the list—and work *forwards* through the list if you were born in an odd-numbered month (e.g. January = 1, February = 2 etc.), and *backwards* if you were born

"I'm going to eat some more grapes," Renée said. "Do you want some?" Her refrigerator had round shoulders and a handle that latched. The chrome trademark on the door said FIAT.

Louis was shaking his head in wonder. "This is so much worse than what happened to me."

"You sure you don't want any? Grapes?"

"Who put you on the list?"

"Stites or somebody else in his organization, I'm 95 percent sure. It's all Boston-area addresses. The thing about 'Hoffmann Laboratories' is a nice touch. These people aren't stupid."

"You ought to complain to somebody."

"I talked on the phone to this guy at the Globe. He asked me to send him some copies of the letters, which I did. I guess they want to see who else is getting them before they run anything. He said he'd call me back through the department office, but he hasn't yet."

"What about the post office. The phone company."

"That just seemed hopeless somehow. I don't care about getting these people prosecuted, I only care about the world knowing what incredible jerks they are."

The telephone on the table began to ring. Louis put his hand on it and looked at Renée, who shrugged.

"Is, ah, Dr. Seechek there?"

"Speaking."

"Oh, you're a man, I didn't—"

"No, sir," Louis said. "I have a deep voice."

Renée threw him a very doubtful look.

"My name is Joe. Uh, Doe. John Doe. I understand you're employed at the Hoffman Laboratories and"—Mr. Doe's voice became high and strangled—"that abortions are performed there?"

"Yeah, I understand you understand that."

"I'd kinda like to talk to you about your work for a second, if I can, Dr. Seechek. Do you have a second?"

Louis was enjoying himself, but Renée unplugged the phone, took the handset from him, and said to the dead line, "Fuck off, fuck off, fuck off." The DeMoula's bag tore as she began to stuff her hate mail back inside it, faint shadows of words playing on her lips. He was surprised to notice areas of redness and roughness encroaching on her pale complexion. He wondered whether this was a recent development or whether, clued in by the old photograph, he was seeing things about her that until now her manner had concealed. Her pores had become evident. There was a patch of subdued but not eradicated acne high on one cheek, also blemishes around her mouth that made it seem to run. She struck him as younger and a little dirtier, more like the kind of girl it was easy to do whatever you wanted with—the kind with more passion than self-esteem.

"I hate it when women swear," she said.

"Why?"

She stood at the head of the table. "I guess because there's this idea that it's sexy, in the popular imagination. The approved male popular imagination. Even when a woman says fuck in anger, even a radical feminist saying fuck, that's a turn-on. Every time *I* hear a woman do it I get carried—" She addressed Louis directly. "I get carried to the subway station at Central Square. There's an angry woman there, with her bags and her papers. It's like her face is the face of All Women Saying Fuck. This insane anger towards everybody, which to me is especially ugly in a woman, although this is not politically correct of me and therefore makes me wonder what exactly my problem is. And I can't help mentioning," she went on, entirely to herself, "something else I forgot the other night, when you asked me what my problem is with Boston, I forgot to mention the way people call the subway the T. The people, I mean the implicating people, don't say 'I'm going to take the subway,' they say 'I'll take the T.' What's sick—to me; what I consider sick—is that it's like this code word, which every time I hear I become angry because I can hear the whole history, all these kids learning to say 'T' instead of 'subway.' They write home to their parents about taking the T. They explain that it's called the T, which is kind of cute. Oh, listen to me." She walked away, hitting herself in the head. "You wonder why I didn't call you."

Louis karate-chopped the tabletop impatiently. "Is there any beer or something?"

"It's because I can't control myself."

"Or any kind of liquor or drug that we could do together here."

The hum of the fan in the window, its quiet, oiled grinding, was the sound of all night hours in a heat wave. The hour of conversation wearing thin. The hour when a reflected piece of streetlight hovers at a certain point the blades pass through. The hour when dawn forces itself through the weary curtains. The hum and the hours all the same, the monotone of humid heat, and the burn patients say Don't turn it up. Don't turn it down. Let it stay right like it is.

"Do you have friends?" Louis asked, opening bottles. "People you can call up?"

"Sure. I mean, I used to." Renée, across the table from him, showed no intention of drinking the beer he handed her. "I had a roommate, who I really liked, although she's married now. I guess I was an improvident gardener. I made friends with people a couple of years older than me at work, people from the tail end of the sixties who didn't like the front end of the eighties, which I didn't either. I guess what I have now is an interesting correspondence, and some places to stay in Colorado and California." With her thumbnails, she bunched up her sweating bottle's neck wrapper like a cuticle, trying belatedly to gauge the angle of his question. "I see people, if that's what you mean." Her eyes followed her right index finger as she ran it along the edge of the table. She called her hand back and placed it palm-down to one side of her full bottle, and placed her other hand palm-down to the other side of the bottle. She sat perfectly still for a moment, staring at the bottle. Then, with violent decision, as though sitting like this had been a physical torment all along, she stood up without even pushing the chair away from the table. She had to stagger for balance on one leg and slide the chair back to extricate herself, and the chair stuck on the humid floor and tipped over.

She returned from her bedroom with several manila folders.

"I've been staying in the library," she said, righting the chair. "Two people came to my office last Friday to be nasty in person. I haven't gone back since."

"That's what Howard said."

She nodded, yawning. "I was thinking about what that boyfriend of your sister's was saying. I remembered something, or I thought I did. I remembered it was on a right-hand page facing something else I'd looked at. And . . . I was right." From the top folder she took a stapled sheaf of photocopies. "This is an article from the Bulletin of the Geological Society of America, July '69. You can just read the abstract and what I've underlined."

"What for?" Louis said.

"Because it's interesting."

A Theory of Subcrustal Petroleogenesis

A. F. Krasner

Research Chemist, Sweeting-Aldren Industries

Abstract: Significant releases of methane and petroleum in non-fossiliferous regimes (Siljan, Wellingby Hills, Taylorsville) have called into question the assumption that subterranean hydrocarbon deposits derive principally from breakdown of trapped organic matter. Improved estimates of the chemical composition of comets and the major planets suggest levels of carbon within the Earth 10^2–10^5 times larger than earlier estimates. A laboratory study demonstrates the possibility of synthesizing petroleum from elementary hydrocarbons under pressures approaching those in the Earth's interior. A model of hydrocarbon capture during planetogenesis predicts the formation and accumulation of methane and more complex hydrocarbons at the upper boundary of the asthenosphere and explains the releases observed at Wellingby Hills. A program of deep drilling to further test the model is proposed.

The only underlined words Louis could find in the article were in the last paragraph. Renée had done her underlining with a straightedge, a work habit that had always given him the creeps. *Advances in deep-well technology have for the first time made feasible narrow-bore holes to depths in excess of 25,000 feet. Two sites in the Berkshire Mountains Synclinorium, including the Brixwold Pluton (in the vicinity of which there is some evidence of slow methane release),*[31] *have been chosen for a drilling program, initiated by Sweeting-Aldren Industries, which pending final funding will commence in December 1969 and, it is hoped, attain the critical depth of 25,000 feet in Spring of 1971. Significant quantities of methane or petroleum found at this depth, under a heavily metamorphosed granitic pluton overlaying pre-Cambrian schists, would provide strong confirmation of the trapped-layer model.*

"Lot of big words here," Louis said.

"Actually a seminal article in its way." Renée, with unseemly possessiveness, kept a hand extended until he gave her back the article. "The evidence back then was so flimsy the paper should never have been published, but this is an idea that's still around.

That there's this huge ocean of crude oil and natural gas pooling right below the earth's crust, and that all this fuel is from the primordial gunk that went into making the planet, and that the total reserves of so-called fossil fuels are just a drop in the bucket compared to all this stuff farther down. The Swedish government fairly recently spent ten million dollars drilling an inconclusive well in this Siljan basin. The idea's not dead. Not many people take it seriously, though."

"Uh huh."

"So then there's this thing from *Nature*. January '70."

She'd neatly boxed in red ink a one-paragraph note in the News section to the effect that the American chemical concern Sweeting-Aldren had begun to sink a deep well at an undisclosed site in eastern Massachusetts, with a view to testing the hypothesis of chemist A. F. Krasner regarding the non-fossil origin of much of the world's oil and natural gas. The drilling was proceeding at a rate of 100 feet per day and, allowing for the usual delays and equipment failures, was expected to reach 25,000 feet—"the critical depth, in Krasner's view"—late the next spring.

"Do you notice anything there?"

Louis waved a hand tiredly. "These brain-teaser kind of things—"

"The Berkshires aren't in eastern Massachusetts."

"Oh." He nodded. "I didn't know that. So I wouldn't have gotten it anyway. So it's good you told me."

Renée closed one folder and opened another. The handwriting on the tabs of the folders was as regimented as a draftsman's. "February 25, 1987," she said. "Boston Globe: 'Tremors in Essex County Persist.' " She handed Louis a photocopied clipping. "April 12, 1987. Boston Globe, again. 'Scientists Puzzled by Peabody Earthquake Swarm.' " She took out a third article. "Earthquake Notes, 1988, number 2, 'The Peabody Microseisms of January–April 1987 and Their Tectonic Environment.' Penultimate paragraph: 'The spatial and temporal distribution of the microseisms bears a marked similarity to known instances of induced seismicity in the vicinity of *injection wells*.' Emphasis added. 'However, the relatively great depth of the Peabody tremors (i.e., on average 3 kilometers deeper than the deepest commercial waste-disposal wells) would appear to rule out such a mechanism. Furthermore there are no licensed injection wells operating within a 20-kilometer radius surrounding the site of activity.' "

She looked her beer bottle in the face for a second, and then took a long pull. She was definitely able to control herself now.

"I remember when this swarm started up in Peabody. It happens in a couple other places in New England with some regularity. You get these tiny earthquakes, for the most part too small to feel. Anywhere from one to several hundred per day for days or weeks or months. Nobody really knows what causes them. The Peabody series was of interest because there'd never been anything like it there before."

"Did I understand this right that injection wells cause earthquakes?"

"Yeah, it's called induced seismicity. It happens after you've been pumping lots of liquid underground, and basically it's as if the rock down there gets slippery from all the extra liquid. The classic example was in the early sixties, at the Rocky Mountain Arsenal, outside Denver. The Army was making chemical weapons and generating millions of gallons of toxic liquid waste and pumping it down a 12,000-foot well. Denver had always been pretty quiet seismically, but about a month after the pumping started they started recording all these earthquakes. On average about one a day, none of them bigger than 4.5 or so. Whenever they stopped pumping, the earthquakes stopped too, and when they started again, so did the earthquakes. It was pretty open and shut. The GS did a study—"

"The what?"

Renée blinked. "Geological Survey. They pumped water into dry oil wells in western Colorado. Whenever the water pressure in the bedrock got above 3,700 pounds per square inch the earthquakes started up. If you have some kind of pre-existing strain underground, the water in the cracks lubricates things and disturbs the balance of forces. The same thing also happens when you build a dam and form a reservoir. The weight of the new lake forces water into the underlying rock. There was a long series of events in Nevada, behind the Hoover Dam, after it filled up. Same thing in Egypt, behind the Aswan Dam. Same thing in Zambia, and

China, and India. I think the one in India was very good-sized. Killed a couple hundred people."

"I get the feeling you don't spend your nights watching baseball on TV."

She opened a third folder, disregarding him. "Krasner disappears from the literature after one article. He's not in any chemistry journal, not in any geophysics journal, and he was never in American Men and Women of Science. One full-length paper, one paragraph in *Nature*, and that's it. His theory got reinvented independently in the late seventies by a guy named Gold, at Cornell. Gold cites Krasner once, calls him 'prescient,' in the papers I could find. And that's it."

"You've read all these things."

"I've been stuck in the library."

"And you underline them and put them in folders even when you're not going to get graded on them."

"That's right."

"Why do you do this?"

"Why?" The question seemed almost to offend her. "Because I'm curious."

"You're curious. You do all this stuff because you're curious."

"Yes."

"There's nothing else in it for you."

"Not that I know of."

"Just simple curiosity."

"How many times do I have to say it?"

Louis blew out air. He tapped on the tabletop. Blew out more air. "You've been talking to my mother again."

"What makes you think that?"

"Only that she has a large financial interest in Sweeting-Aldren."

"I didn't know that. That's actually very interesting. But I haven't been talking to her, and I definitely did not know that." She shuddered a little, trying to rid herself of his vague imputations.

"So go on," he said.

"There's nothing else, really. It's just—You know. It's just like you say. My little presentation."

"I'm *sorry*. I want to hear the rest. Drink some beer. Tell me the rest."

She took a deep breath and started speaking to the tabletop, full of body English, as though engaging him directly; but it was clearly beyond her power to sustain both articulateness and eye contact.

"In 1969 Sweeting-Aldren's swimming in cash, mainly because of Vietnam. They have a bunch of scientists on the payroll, and this person Krasner comes up with a theory that Massachusetts is sitting on an ocean of crude oil. The company decides to fund a hole to see if he's right, except something happens to make them change their mind about where to put it. Who knows what. Maybe they figure that if there's a huge pool of crude oil under western Mass, it must be under eastern Mass too, where they own property. The only reason to drill at the site in western Mass is because the site's geology is supposedly incompatible with petroleum deposits. But what do they care about Krasner's theory? They're worried about getting some money out of the hole, if it happens not to be a gusher. And one thing is in 1969 people are also starting to get nervous about the environment, especially water pollution, and what I think they decide is that if the deep well comes up dry, they're going to pump industrial waste down it. And meanwhile Krasner retires, or dies, or opens an antiques store. Or was just a pseudonym to begin with."

"And pump industrial waste down it . . ."

"And then what your sister's boyfriend was saying"—the sound of Louis's voice caused her to concentrate all the more on the tabletop—"is that *even now* the company is dumping a million gallons of effluents every year. But in the paper, basically every day for the last two weeks"—she opened another folder, which he could see was full of clippings from the *Globe*—"both the company *and* the EPA say the company puts nothing in the Danvers River except clean, slightly oily hot water. The plant's a model nonpolluter."

He thought: And pump industrial waste down it . . .

"So where did they drill? Obviously they drilled within a couple miles of the plant in Peabody. And the thing is you can pump liquid into a hole for a long time before anything happens. It takes a lot of liquid to bring what's called the pore pressure to the critical level where the rock starts to relieve its internal stresses by rupturing seismically. It's not implausible that Sweeting-Aldren was injecting effluents from the early seventies all the way into the mid-eighties without anything happening. But suddenly they reach the critical level, say in January '87, and they start having little earthquakes. The swarm goes on for four months and then stops, which to me suggests the company got scared and stopped pumping. And for a couple of years everything's quiet, and then about two weeks after the first Ipswich event there suddenly start being these earthquakes in Peabody again—the papers talk about Lynn too, but the epicentral area is the same as in the '87 series—which nobody can relate to the Ipswich events as anything but a low-probability coincidence. But what's been happening to all these wastes that the company normally would have been pumping underground? They had to stop pumping in '87, and so presumably they've had to store the liquid somewhere, which I'm sure they're not happy about. And maybe what they've been waiting for is some good-sized local earthquake, so they could start pumping in Peabody again, full speed ahead, with the idea that any new earthquakes would be associated with the Ipswich events. Maybe what spilled on Easter was some of the backlog they'd been storing up since '87. Maybe they decided they had to try to get as much of that stuff underground as soon as possible, no matter what happened. And sure enough, within a week or two, we start getting more tremors in Peabody."

Finished at last, Renée pushed her hair off her forehead and took another long pull on her beer, withdrawing into herself, taking care not to expect any response. Louis was staring at the bottle of Joy by the faucet of her deep, white sink. The kitchen had grown brighter and smaller. He leaned back in his chair, filling the sweet spot of his field of vision with her image. "The thing about the stuff in 1987, how it can't be from a well. Can you read that again?"

Obediently she opened the proper folder. " 'However, the relatively great depth'?"

"Yes! Yes! That proves it, doesn't it?"

" '. . . (i.e., on average 3 kilometers deeper than the deepest commercial waste-disposal wells) would appear to rule out such a mechanism. Furthermore there are no licensed injection wells operating—' "

"Those slimes! Those slimes! This is *great*." Louis leaned over the table and put his hands on her ears and kissed her on the mouth. Then he started pacing the room, socking the palm of his hand.

"Do you know something about these people?" she said.

"They're slimes!"

"You've met them."

"I told you, my mom's like this major stockholder all of a sudden. I met them at my grandmother's funeral. They're these totally classic corporate pigs." He lifted Renée out of her chair by the armpits so he could squeeze her and kiss her again. "You're amazing. I can't believe you just sat down and figured this all out. You're terrific."

He lifted her off the floor and set her down. She looked at him as if she hoped he wouldn't do this again.

"It's illegal, right?" He pushed his glasses back up his sweaty nose. "To pump waste underground without a license?"

"I assume. Otherwise why have licenses?"

"Ha! And if these earthquakes cause damage, the company's liable, right?"

"I don't know. In theory, yes. At least for any damage near Peabody. It's pretty gross negligence on their part. It would be a harder thing to prove, though, if it's a matter of a large earthquake some distance away and you had to speculate about whether what they'd done in Peabody had triggered a more general release of strain."

"You mean that's possible? That can happen? You can trigger things like that? Boston gets wiped out and the company has to pay for it?" Louis was getting more euphoric by the second.

"It's very unlikely that Boston's going to get wiped out," Renée said. "And although there's a lot of talk about trigger events, it's very hard to demonstrate strict causality. You can talk about the April 6 event in Ipswich having 'triggered' the Easter event, but if you don't know what causes earthquakes to occur at the particular times they do, and we don't know this, you might as well say 'precede' instead of 'trigger.' "

"But if the first earthquake is caused by pumping, and then you have a major one . . ."

"There'd be a case, yes. But not an airtight case."

"But anything that happens right where they're pumping, you'd have a good case there."

"I think so. For a civil suit. Probably by insurance companies."

"So the only question is, Do we stick it to 'em right now for breaking the law all these years, or do we maybe *wait*, and see if something worse happens, and then stick it to 'em for that too."

"You mean wait and see if some people get killed?"

"Yeah!"

"Well." Renée gathered up her folders and hugged them to her chest. "You seem to have a grudge against these people, which I of course don't, although if I'm right about this I agree it's pretty disgusting. But I still haven't decided what I'm going to do about it." The first-person singular spoke for itself. "The Peabody earthquakes are of general interest to the scientific community. I might do some more research and then talk to people at MIT and Boston College. The EPA should also be talked to, maybe the press too. If the company does induce a destructive earthquake I'd just as soon not have it on my conscience."

"Why would it be on your conscience?"

"Because I might have been able to prevent it."

Louis's surprise was genuine. "You actually believe in this stuff? Service to mankind and all that?"

In the calm upper stories of Renée's face a powerful furnace kicked on suddenly, a bank of white jets of anger. "I wouldn't have *said* it if I didn't believe it."

"Yeah, but, like, who's to say what's a service to mankind? If we let the company off the hook before anything worse happens, maybe we save a few lives. But if we wait and something worse does happen and *then* we blow the whistle, then it becomes a *message*. Then maybe people finally see what kind of sharks we have running the country. Which might really be a service to mankind."

"All right, Louis." Her use of his name and her sudden smileyness sent a chill down his spine. This was a person whose disapproval he feared. She was pushing the stack of folders into his hands. "It's all yours. I think you should show this to a man named Larry Axelrod at MIT; I think you should show it to the EPA. Are you listening? I'm telling you what the right thing to do is, and if you don't want to do it, that's your problem, not mine. All right?"

"Wait a minute, wait a minute." He laughed defusingly. "We're friends, aren't we?"

"I slept with you, once."

"And if we go broadcasting the news, what's the company going to do? It's going to deny everything. It'll bulldoze everything over, and probably start doing something even worse with all this waste, and then you won't have anything, not even the satisfaction of being right."

"It's your decision."

"We make some inquiries. We talk to my good friend Peter. Drive up to Peabody and look around. Take some pictures maybe. Then we've got some hard proof to go to whoever with."

"I did this work myself, you know. I didn't necessarily mean for you to come over and make yourself an equal partner."

"I tell you how terrific you are—?"

"Like a dog that's been good? I can fetch?"

"Oh, all right, well." He tossed the files into the space between the refrigerator and the wall, where Renée's extra paper bags were carefully folded. "Keep it. And keep your little haircut too. And your little earrings, and your little smiles, and your neat little apartment. Your little folders. And your theories, and your scruples, and your old roommate, and your former friends. You know, this whole neat little perfect life. Just keep it."

The hum of the fan in the window was the sound of unhappiness in its rotary progress, always developing and yet always the same, a sound that marked every second of the minutes and hours in which improvement was failing to occur. Time flowed along an axis through the center of the fan, and the tips of the blades traced unending spirals around this axis.

"I don't even know you," Renée said. "And you just hurt me. There was no reason to hurt me. I didn't do a single thing to you, except not call you."

"And tell me to get lost."

"And tell you to get lost. That's true. I did tell you to get lost. Everything you said is true. But it doesn't mean you're any better than I am. You're just less exposed. And I'm so embarrassed." She kept her shoulders rigid as she walked from the room, tottering slightly and repeating, "I'm so embarrassed."

Louis drank another beer and listened to the fan. After about half an hour he knocked on the bedroom door. When she didn't answer, he opened it and followed the wedge of light into the dark, stuffy room. She was nowhere in sight. Only after he'd looked behind her bed and desk and behind the drawn window shades did he see the light behind the closet door, powered by a cord leading over from a socket. He knocked.

"Yeah?"

She was cross-legged on the closet floor, bending over a lamp. The pages of *The New York Times Magazine* she was reading were strewn with big puckered dots of perspiration from her head. Her eyes rolled up and looked at him. "What do you want?"

Crouching, he took her hot, limp hands in his own. Birds were chirping angrily outside. "I don't want to go," he said. His stomach plummeted; he attributed this to the sick-making effort of sincerity. However, the real problem was the floor, which was moving. The panic that flashed through Renée's face was so cartoonishly pure he almost laughed. Then the left side of the doorframe lurched closer to him, and he tried to rise out of his crouch, like a surfer who'd caught a wave, and the frame abandoned him on the left and the right side body-checked him and knocked him onto his butt. Renée was fighting with the clothes and hangers she'd stood up into. She stepped on Louis, who was not good footing, and stumbled free of the closet. Things had been falling during the interval, and now pencils and pens were rolling across the floor, roaming and vibrating and bouncing like drops of water in hot oil. There was also a deep sound that was less sound than an idea of sound, a drowning of the human in the physical. And then only the miniature rumble, clear and strangely personal, of a beer bottle crossing the kitchen floor.

"I'm sorry I stepped on you," Renée said.

"Did you step on me?"

They wandered around the disturbed apartment, oblivious to

each other. The baby downstairs was crying, but the Dobermans on the first floor were either silent or out for the evening, eating prime rib somewhere. Louis picked up two beer bottles and, forgetting he'd meant to set them on the kitchen table, carried them from room to room and finally left them on the cushion of an armchair. He was dazed and without dignity, as if in the wake of a first kiss. Renée had a jar of pencils in her hand when he bumped into her in the hallway. "It's like I've been tickled," she said, dodging his encircling arm, "to the point where if you touch me—" she fought him off with her elbow—

The jar sailed down the hallway and the glass popped and the pencils bounced tunefully. Louis tickled her convulsing belly, and she slugged away at his arms and ribs, not hurting him at all and shouting pretty much constantly. Clothes were partially removed, body parts exposed, necks bent, the hard floor cursed. They kissed with their entire heads, like mountain goats. What was happening wasn't so much sex as a kind of banging together, a clapping and clenching of hands the size of bodies, a re-creation of strong motion; something other than satisfaction wanted out. Louis came violently and hardly noticed, he was so intent on the way she pitched beneath him. It seemed like she was trying to shed him even as they kept colliding, and finally they collided so hard they did separate and, still vibrating like bells, sat up against opposing walls in obscene disarray, shackled at the ankles by twisted jeans and underpants. Farther up the hallway there was broken glass and a swollen tampon at the end of a bloody skid mark.

Renée frowned. "I cut my hand."

Louis found his glasses and crawled over to look. On her palm was a semicircle of loosened skin, a bluish fish scale surrounded by crimson trickles and orange smears. "Does it hurt?"

"No."

"Are you OK otherwise?"

She looked down at her ankles. "I can't imagine a more degrading position to be caught in. But otherwise."

They took turns washing in the bathroom, which was in antiseptic condition apart from the fact that in patching her hand Renée had unaccountably left a Curad wrapper in the sink. Louis opened her medicine chest and found expensive facial cleansers, the basic drugs, nonoxynol jelly, some dental floss.

She was opening beers in the kitchen. The fan had fallen from the window, unplugging itself; it was still on the floor. Louis started to turn on the radio. "Don't," she said.

"What do you have for music?"

"The radio. But I don't want to hear about the earthquake. Not even—not even anything."

"You don't have any tapes?"

She leaned against the table and drank. "I have . . . no tapes."

"What's this?" He held up a tape.

She regarded it soberly. "That's a tape."

"But it's not music?"

She tried several times to say something, and stopped each time. "You're kind of nosy."

"Forget I asked."

"It's one song. Which I never listen to. There's no significance to this, it's just a song. Do you want me to embarrass myself?"

"Yes. Yes. More than anything."

She sat cross-legged on a chair and hugged herself, covering the nakedness that went through clothes. "It's only that when I was seventeen . . ."

"I was ten!"

"Thank you for pointing that out."

Louis wondered what the awful confession would be.

"I was a punk fan," she said. "Or should I say new wave? These words." She hugged herself more tightly. "I can hardly make myself say them. But I was very happy at the time. And I still want people to know I saw Elvis Costello four times in '78 and '79. But there's so much to explain about how he was different and I was different. I want people to be impressed but it's just not impressive. I was sprayed by David Byrne's saliva before he got blissy. I was right up against the stage. I got a pick from Graham Parker, I took it right from his hand."

"Are you serious? Can I see it?"

"Exciting. It really was. I saw the Clash and the Buzzcocks and the Gang Of Four. It embarrasses me to even say the names now, but I saw them and I knew their lyrics, and they were all so good until eventually they all got so bad."

"They were great," Louis said. "I was kind of a ham operator, in high school? I used to trade Nick Lowe lyrics with this person in Eau Claire, Wisconsin, in Morse code. 'She was a winner / That became the doggie's dinner'? Di-di-dit, di-di-di-dit . . . ?"

Renée seemed to assume he was joking. "I liked the attitude," she said. "But I wasn't really a punk. The real punks scared the hell out of me. They were violent and sexist, and they hardly even listened to the music."

"Did you have a biker's jacket?"

"Suede," she said bitterly. "Which I was very happy with then and which is now a source of shame that will never die. A suede jacket sums me up completely. There were a lot of people like me at the concerts, although I think a difference between me and the others was that I thought this was *it*. I *loved* the music. I applied it to my *life*, but in a, what's the word, hermetic way. The place where it all happened was in dorm rooms, where I had the lyric sheets. It kills me to think about how innocent and happy I was, even though at the time what I thought the whole message was was black humor and anger and apocalypse. You can be very innocent and happy about that stuff too. And it seemed so much safer than sixties and seventies music, because it wasn't really happy or innocent or hopeful at all. It was tough and simple. I kept all the records, and I liked the records *better and better*. I kept on dressing the way bands dressed in '78. The same way I dress now, which is like nothing, you know, jeans and T-shirts. But it got to be 1985, and it started to seem pathetic that the only records I listened to were these old records. But I didn't like the new music or at least I wasn't finding out about the good things, because I wasn't in college anymore."

She took the last two beers from the refrigerator. Louis had been observing that every time he drank from his bottle, she drank from hers.

"Meanwhile I stopped listening to more than a song or two at a time. I guess partly I was trying not to get tired of the things I loved, and partly I was so affected that it was too distracting to play a whole album, I couldn't do any work, I mean, because the music was *designed* to rev you up, to make you anxious and angry and excited, and so it was very bad music to move on in life with, because it's one kind of music that simply won't function as background. But the biggest thing was just how embarrassed I was to see myself still listening to it."

"You like the Kinks?"

"Never much."

"Lou Reed? Roxy Music? Waitresses? XTC? Banshees? Early Bowie? Warren Zevon?"

"Some of them, yeah. I never really bought that many records, because I stopped taking money from my parents. But—"

"But so."

"I started to pare down. I got rid of the really old stuff, the stuff I had from high school, and I got rid of the records that only had one or two good songs on them. Then I started taping the medium-good records, and keeping the good part. Then I decided it was stupid to have a big stereo, because I could get the same effect from the little tape player—you know, you're the first person I've ever really talked about this with. I just wanted to say that."

They looked at each other. The refrigerator shuddered and fell silent. "I like you too," Louis said.

She pushed her hair around, doing a good job of seeming not to care. "But so I was left with about twenty tapes which I listened to less and less, just one or two songs every once in a while, when I needed to feel better. It used to make me feel better because it made me feel tough, and angry and lonely in a good way. But then without my even really noticing, it started to make me feel better because it made me feel *young*, the way 'Alice's Restaurant' makes forty-year-olds feel young. When I finally noticed this I was even less inclined to play the tapes. And did I really ever need to hear 'Red Shoes' again?"

"No argument on that one."

"Or any of *Give 'Em Enough Rope?* Or even any Pretenders?"

"Fine records. Keep 'em."

"I got rid of everything. I pared it down to one song, one more or less arbitrary song, which I haven't listened to in at least six months, if not more like a year. I don't listen to it. But I also can't bring myself to throw it away."

"Can I play it?"

She shook her head. "Sure. Just be decent to me. I know you're a radio person."

Out of the little tape machine came the opening guitar line on Television's first record.

"Oh," Louis said, increasing the volume. "Fine song. You dance?"

"Are you kidding?"

"Me neither."

"I could when I was twenty."

> Iunderstandall . . . ISEENO . . .
> destructiveurges . . . ISEENO . . .
> Itseemssoperfect . . . ISEENO . . .
> I SEE . . . I SEE NO . . . I SEE NO EVIL

"You can turn it off."

"Wait, doesn't Verlaine have like a perfect riff in here? It would have been good to hear these people before they broke up. Or did you?"

"No."

"I hear they were very fine."

"Everything became a competition. I stopped trying to get to concerts because it seemed like I was only trying to build credentials as a concertgoer. Which wasn't working anyway. I ran into people who went to clubs every weekend. People who'd seen the Clash before I had. People who were friends with Tina Weymouth's siblings. People who hung around at CBGB and could invest so much more time in being cool. Maybe it was just self-protection, but I started despising these people, and the way they all had to constantly be scrambling to discover something new. I decided this was just pathetic. But I was still afraid of these people. I was afraid they'd find out how much I loved the music I'd grown up with. It seemed like the only way to compete with all their originality, the only way to keep my love safe, was to hate music. Which wasn't a particularly original solution either, but at least I was protected. And it really is pretty easy to hate rock and roll."

"Less so jazz and classical."

"No problem, for me. I just think about the personalities of the people who play it for brunch, and even worse the people who really love it. How good it makes them feel about themselves to know who played drums for Charlie Parker in nineteen-whatever, and how the songs in The Magic Flute go. I find it a huge strain to be responsible for my tastes, and be known and defined by them. If you're not artistic, which I'm not, at all, and you still have to make these aesthetic decisions . . . That's why punk was so good for me. It was this style I picked up before I got too selfconscious about style. I didn't have to apologize, in my own mind. But then I got older, and suddenly it started to define me anyway, in a very pathetic way. Plus suddenly everybody under the age of forty had a leather jacket and fifties sunglasses and punky clothes, and they all felt really cool. At which point jazz might have been a good thing to turn to, except it was art, and as soon as something becomes art, you get experts, and do I want to be one of these experts who're all trying to be more knowledgeable than each other? But if you don't become an expert, you might play something and like it and then find out it's considered sentimental or unoriginal or something. And I know from experience that people are so insecure that they never hesitate to let you know that what they like is more original and better than what you like, or that they liked what you like years before you liked it . . . I don't even have *time*. And it's the same with African music, and Latin music. I'm terrified of being implicated by all the smarmy experts. Either that or finding out my tastes aren't good, or aren't original. Radio would be the perfect solution, except so much of what they play is bad."

> I'm running wild with the one I love
> *I see no evil*—
> I'm running wild with the one-eyed ones
> *I see no evil*—
> Pull down the future with the one you love

Louis turned off the tape player. "Let's go get some stuff from my apartment."

"Can you drive?"

"Spoken like a true punk."

On the stairs Renée said, "The time to be a punk was fifteen years ago. It's just utterly embarrassing to try to be one now."

"Anarchy's a very old idea," he said, breathing through his mouth in the dog zone.

Outside, on Pleasant Avenue, it was no longer a holiday but a dead Thursday night. The night was cool, with a foretaste of dew in the air. Louis drove as fast as he dared and in his drunkenness caught only about one out of every three or four seconds as they passed. Distant, ghostly sirens in the night formed a cushion of noise on which the tires seemed to glide and bounce like water skis. Just east of Davis Square, the Civic plunged into a tunnel of power-lessness, deep inside which was visible the turning of blue flashers. Two figures lit only by glowing urban clouds were straining to hustle what appeared to be cartons of liquor up a side street.

"Looters! Were those looters? They were looters!"

Lights were burning in his apartment. The bigger pieces of furniture hadn't budged, but the vase made of Mount St. Helens ash had fallen from the wall unit and broken in two, and some of the dining-room chairs had edged away from the table. Behind the closed door of Toby's room a dot-matrix printer gulped and stridulated. Renée flopped in a U-shape on Louis's futon. He had to set down the beer and gin and tapes he'd collected and pull her to her feet.

When they returned to her apartment she opened beer bottles briskly. "What's your favorite kind of music?" she said.

"I don't believe in favorites. I don't have any. This is my favorite, just a second here." He turned the machine up loud.

> I love the sound of breaking glass.
> Especially when I'm lonely.
> I need the noises of destruction.
> When there's nothing new.

"This is good. Who is it?"

"This? My God. The great Nick Lowe? It's a classic."

"How old?"

"Bronze Age. Here." Louis interrupted the song. "We'll put

in something almost as old as me. Everybody likes this record. It's a classic. It never gets old. Isn't that what a classic is?"

"I can't think of anything more pathetic than radio stations that play 'classic rock.' "

"Is this pathetic?"

It was *Exile on Main Street*.

"No," Renée said. "But I don't think you understand me."

"I could play you stuff from now until next Thursday that's old but not pathetic."

"That's right. Because you're one of those people. I mean, you're in radio. It's your business."

"So don't complain. I'll take care of your music for you. Do I feel like an old fart when I listen to this? This is not James Taylor here. It's sloppy, it's basic, it's good."

"Good for you, maybe. For me it's just retro. Which feels very sweet right now, but it won't last. None of these feelings last."

She continued to match him beer for beer. It was a little before three when "Soul Survivor" played and the tape finally ended. They drank gin and passed a mouthful back and forth until Louis lost it down his neck. A raccoon came to the window and pressed its rubber nose against the screen and stuck a paw through a hole in the screen. "My raccoon!" Renée exclaimed, stumbling towards the window. "It's my raccoon, that comes and visits me. It comes . . . sometimes. Oh!" She cried out tragically. "It's hurt! Look, it's hurt. I'm saying look. It's hurt. You can see, it cut its face. It comes up a drainpipe and comes to the window. It likes potatoes but I don't have any. And it's cute, but oh boy am I spinning."

For five minutes Louis had been sitting at the table with his mouth open and his brow furrowed.

"It's not my raccoon but it comes . . . frequently. It must live around here. I have an apple," she told the animal, which had grabbed the top of the screen and was gingerly putting a hind-foot through the hole in the mesh, its head wandering and sniffing, daunted by the sheerness of the wall above the window. "I'm coming with the apple," Renée said, surging over with two quarters of a golden delicious on a saucer and raising the screen an inch. "It's gone!" she said. "It's gone. It's gone. It's . . ."

Her face was gray. She threw herself against the sink and

emptied her stomach into it and dropped to her knees, hands still hanging on the rim. Louis was similarly occupied in the bathroom. Sometime after this she was lying on the kitchen table and he was chasing an unrolling roll of paper towels towards a corner of the bedroom where he'd thrown up again. Sometime after this he was sleeping in the hallway, pillowing his head on the mud rug, and she was under her desk with her face against the wall and her legs sticking out. The reflector strips on her sneakers shone in the light from bulbs burning in the bathroom and kitchen. The toilet was motionless. The sink was motionless. The walls were motionless. The refrigerator fell silent, and the sphere of ambient sound swelled enormously, encompassing expressways from which a few low-frequency waves managed just barely to reach Pleasant Avenue before expiring, a stretch of train track in some northern suburb made to clack by passing tank cars, and the tiny aural remnant of a hot rod's buzz in far eastern Somerville, on the McGrath Highway, heading out of Boston. The stove ticked, once. The lights dimmed by forty lumens, once. East wall stared at west wall and north at south, unblinking in the light. One manila folder had slipped down between paper bags and the others yawned; there was not a breath to stir the photocopies or the blade of the fan where it lay by the window. The table stood on the floor. A wineglass had shattered on the countertop. All the pieces still lay exactly where they'd first come to rest, as if the glass were still whole and could be seen whole again if only the break in time could be repaired. Books were scattered on the floor of the extra room. Two beer bottles nestled in the armchair. The armchair motionless. The motionless bookshelves silently bearing their load. The walls bearing the load of the ceiling. The ceiling motionless. Eleven beer bottles on the kitchen windowsill, green in the unsegmented incandescent light. Eleven bottles jiggling, clinking. They tumbled off the windowsill in a green shiny wave, some landing on the fan, some breaking. Thuds in the cabinets, the table rocking, a door turning on its hinge. A tower of cassettes collapsed. Crumbs danced behind the stove. Water in the toilet sloshed, panes buzzed.

The body in the hallway motionless. The body under the desk motionless. Everything motionless.

For fifteen days after the night of two earthquakes the files on Sweeting-Aldren and the Peabody microseisms lay untouched in the space by the refrigerator. It was something like superstition that prevented the otherwise orderly Renée from putting them away when she cleaned the apartment—superstition and maybe also a loathing like the one Louis felt when his eyes happened to fall on them, and the one he'd felt towards his radio equipment during those weeks before he sold it, and the one induced by the very thought of alcohol for several days after they got so drunk.

Renée set great store by the "fact" that although he recovered quickly and spent the next morning straightening the apartment, he'd thrown up before she had. He had doubts about this chronology and was surprised by the vehemence with which, still pale and unable to stay on her feet for long, she stuck to her version. It seemed like she was being rather mean about this.

On Saturday, awakened by the smell of toasted English muffins, he found an apartment key on the kitchen table. He twirled it and twirled it on its ring. He drove to his apartment and collected some supplies and appliances. In the afternoon he walked to the East Cambridge apartment of his friend Beryl Slidowsky and hung out with her. When the conversation turned to Thursday's earthquakes, which he knew from the *Globe* had occurred in the neighborhood of Peabody, he not only managed to keep silent about Renée's theory but also denied, absurdly, that he'd felt anything. Beryl was volunteering at WGBH now. She had no help to offer him employment-wise but was suitably outraged by Stites's acquisition of WSNE. She blamed it on Libby Quinn. Libby—or someone—really had given Beryl an ulcer; she showed Louis her bottle of Tagamet.

He had a Sugar Cubes recording playing loudly when Renée came home from work with a bag of groceries. "Is that dinner?" he said.

She tossed him a fishy-looking package from DeMoula's.

"Fish! Do I ever eat fish?" He watched her stock a cabinet. "I had some coquilles Saint-Jacques in mashed potatoes when my parents were here. I ordered them to impress my mother with my French skills. The place used insto-spuds, sort of summer-camp quality. It's very famous."

She broke her silence. "Do you want me to talk about well-known fish restaurants in Boston? I can do it if you'd like. I have a lot to say."

"What kind of fish is this?"

"This is cod."

"You bought this yourself?" He put his finger on one of the coarse-grained filets. "No one made you buy it? You decided, I'm going to eat cod tonight?"

"That's right."

"You felt like cod. You saw cod and were inclined to buy." She sniffed.

"Did you get us some liver for tomorrow?"

"Actually, I thought you might buy the food tomorrow."

"Shit," he apologized. "Of course. I will. I would have bought it today, but there was no way to reach you."

"I said. You can buy it tomorrow. Did I complain?"

"No, you didn't complain."

She crouched to file vegetables in the yellowed plastic drawers of the Fiat refrigerator. "I'm not at all positive it's a good idea for you to move in like this. At least not before we discuss a few things."

"The age aspect. Our, uh, Memorial Day–Flag Day relationship."

She laughed.

"You find me twerpy," he said. "I don't apply."

"No, as a matter of fact, I find you very attractive and fun to be with. This is not what I'm talking about at all." She frowned. "Is that how you see yourself? Why do you see yourself that way?"

Louis didn't answer; he'd retreated up the hallway, swatting the air with his fist. No one as reliable as Dr. Seitchek had ever told him he was very attractive. He returned to the kitchen with a swagger in his step.

"So what's to discuss?"

"Nothing. Everything. I feel like things are—out of control."

She looked him in the eye as though she wanted him to help

her speak. Then she got scared and seemed to realize there was no
one in the room but him and her. She vented her helplessness on
the tape player, turning it off, unplugging it, and removing the
cassette.

"If you want me to leave," he said, "say leave."

"I *don't* want you to leave. That's what I'm saying."

He assumed the abstracted expression of a Frenchman listening to an American fail to express herself in French.

"I just want to have things clear," she said.

"You don't want me to leave; I don't want me to leave; what
could be clearer?"

"You're right." A smiley smile. She began to peel an onion.
"It's all very clear."

Louis looked sadly at the silenced tape player. "What are you
doing to that cod?"

"I'm cooking garlic and onion in olive oil and wine and saffron
and tomatoes and olives and then putting the fish in and simmering
it briefly."

"Is there something I can do?"

"Do you know how to make rice?"

"No."

"Maybe you could make a salad."

"You could show me how to make rice."

"Why don't you just make a salad."

"You mean, so I don't fuck up the rice?"

"That's right." With slashing strokes she began to slice flesh
from the pits of brown olives. He was sure she was going to cut
herself, and when she suddenly dropped the knife he thought she'd
done it, but she was only angry.

"Do I want you watching me make dinner? Older woman
mothers younger man? Adorably inept younger man? Feeds him
first good meal he's had in months? Shows him how to make rice
for himself? If you want to know how to make rice, look on the
package, same as I did ten years ago."

She attacked the olives again. He watched muscles and tendons
come and go beneath the skin of her pale, thin arms.

"So where's this package?"

"Where do most people keep their food?"

He sighed. In the third of her three cabinets he found a bag of Star Market rice. "No instructions here," he said.

"Boil a cup and a half of water and half a teaspoon salt stir in one level cup rice cover and reduce to low flame check in seventeen minutes."

She watched him spend nearly a minute trying to measure exactly half a cup of water, taking too much, pouring out too much, taking too much, pouring out too much. "Oh, come *on*."

"I'm trying to follow your instructions."

"You're not making a bomb, you're making rice."

"I'm trying to do it right."

"You're trying to goad me. You're trying to be cute."

"I am not!"

Later they lay on her bed and watched the Red Sox play the Rangers on Channel 38 and looked at the *Globe*. For a long time Louis studied a full-page ad that showed a businessman using IBM equipment in his office at home. "The books on the shelves in the background of these things. Like this one here. Is that Mein Kampf?" He turned his head. "It's Mein Kampf! The guy's got Mein Kampf on his shelf! With his ten-thousand-dollar computer. And these, I bet these are Hustler magazines."

"Let me see that." Renée scrutinized the photograph. "It's Main Street."

"It's Mein Kampf!"

"This is an S. It's Sinclair Lewis. It's Main Street."

"I bet he keeps his Hitler stuff in the file cabinet."

"I noticed you reading about Sweeting-Aldren."

"Hence my attitude? Yeah. It's a probing news analysis. They're comparing the company to an ant." Louis paged back. " 'Wall Street looks on as the injured insect crawls slowly in a circle, trying to get its legs to work again. It is obviously injured, and yet it may be able to absorb the damage and begin moving again. Long minutes go by; it might be dead; it might be about to continue on its mission. No one knows what kind of pain it might be feeling. If too much time passes and Sweeting-Aldren still doesn't move, it will be presumed dead. But Wall Street has seen a lot of injured ants over the years, and it knows not to give up on this one quite yet.' Blah blah blah. Blah blah blah . . . Analyst David Blah of Blah-Blah Emerson attributes much of 17 percent drop in stock price since March blah to recognition that it was overvalued. Price-earnings blah blah. However, investors not encouraged by Dr. Axelrod's statements on Friday that in light of continuing signifi-cant earthquake activity in neighborhood of Peabody 'we just don't know what to expect in the way of future earthquakes'— Who's this Dr. Axelrod?"

"Seismologist at MIT. He's good. He's—fine."

"Concern focusing on disruption of production lines. Company operating near capacity, blah blah . . . If all production shut down more than three weeks, losses in neighborhood of million dollars a day. Further worry regarding lawsuits arising from release of greenish effluent containing biphenyls and other halogenated hydrocarbons . . . suspicion that hazardous wastes are being stock-piled rather than incinerated as company claims. (Ha.) Fear also of spillage in event of large earthquake, includes chlorine, ben-zene, trichlorophenol, and other highly volatile and poisonous or carcinogenic substances. Company insured against damage to capital investments, is 'looking into the details' of its liability coverage, undoubtedly meaning coverage is insufficient. How-ever, considering strong revenue history, moderate long-term debt burden, and relatively low risk of a major earthquake, three out of four analysts polled on Friday considered Sweeting-Aldren a good buy at Thursday's closing price."

Renée took his glasses off and joined him on the business section. As they kissed, he began to scratch the thick denim seam between her legs, below the zipper.

Two quick outs here in the seventh inning.

"I don't know where you came from. You just crashed in."

"I thought you were interesting. I pursued you."

"Is that what happened?" She raised her head from his chest, a god's face appearing in a cloud above the horizon of his rib cage. "What we did in the hall, after the earthquake. It was just like it's supposed to be."

"Lucky thing I came over, huh?"

"I love sex. It's almost the only thing I'm not embarrassed to like."

Good effort by Greenwell to hold him to a single.

"You make me want to be a woman," Louis said.

After the weekend the heat gave way to weather from Canada. The air smelled washed and sweet and full of oxygen, and the trees on Pleasant Avenue drooped pregnantly in the sudden overfullness of their foliage. The public library, on the last hill of Somerville, was like the bridge of a sailing ship, the emptiness of ocean sky commencing directly beyond the parking lot; air flavored with the sound of hammers and forklifts flowed up and over Louis's face as he and his girlfriend looked out over flat roofs and brick warehouses at the sky-blue span of the Tobin Bridge, and beyond it to the dusk-colored haze over Lynn and Peabody, and the prow of Cape Ann.

The music he'd been happy to eat sandwiches with and the TV he'd been happy to bury evenings under both began to seem shrill and irrelevant. There was a silence on Pleasant Avenue that belonged to Renée, and he wanted to be in it. One morning he borrowed her Harvard ID and for two hours assumed the identity of René Seitchek, visiting Frenchman. He returned from Widener Library with a backpack of Balzac and Gide. He felt like he'd been flung seismically out of a career in radio, a career he might very well have enjoyed and derived a sense of purpose or safety from, into a state where he not only didn't know what to do with himself but also doubted that it mattered much. Similar upheavals and subsidences were occurring in the landscape of his memory, familiar landmarks dropping out of sight, replaced by remembered scenes of a nature so radically different that he was almost surprised to realize that these things, too, had had a place in his life. A kind, wry Rice alumnus delivering a Commencement address that Louis no less than the other graduates had had to sit through, and reminding the graduates of a thing called social justice. The entire semester he'd spent in Nantes, the couscous he'd eaten with a group of Algerian students there, the students telling him: things are really bad in the country we were born in, and we as French citizens feel torn. His fourteenth birthday, the buck knife in a sheath Eileen had bought and given him. Also Marcel Proust, for whom he'd held a mental door open long enough to be overjoyed by the discovery that Swann was married to Odette and that the wretched painter

at the Verdurins' had grown into the great artist Elstir; the door
had fallen shut under the pressure of four five-page papers, each
to be written in French, but not before a splinter of joy had slipped
through, a splinter that it was evident now was still inside him,
like a self-contained and frightening djinn.

Every evening as he listened to the real Seitchek's footsteps
on the stairs he felt a mounting anticipation and curiosity that were
not, however, in any way satisfied by the person who after making
some noises in the kitchen came into the room where he'd been
reading. He saw her with a dreamlike clarity that was the same as
a dreamlike inability to really see her. Instead of a face he saw a
mask, a sign grasped directly: the image of the woman he slept
with. She looked much the same whether his eyes were closed or
open. Strangely or not, his presence in her apartment seemed to
disturb her less and less. She listened to his tapes while she made
dinner and hypnotized him with the precision and methodicality
of her cooking, and afterward, while he washed the dishes, she
watched his TV and read the paper and didn't appear to notice
any change in him, not even the way he dried all the dishes and
put them away and swept the floor and then for another fifteen or
twenty minutes stood in the kitchen doing absolutely nothing but
avoiding going in to join her on the bed. It was as if, in nuclear
terms, the configuration of forces had changed and he was no longer
an oppositely charged particle attracted to her from a great distance
but a particle with like charge, a proton repelled by this other
proton until they were right next to each other and the strong
nuclear force came into its own and bound them together.

"You can hurt me a little."

"What?"

"You can slap me, or bite me. A little. You can pinch me. It's
something you could do, if you want."

She lay on top of him, the field emanating from the large-eyed
steadiness of her gaze bearing down. "Would you do it?"

He twisted his head away. "No!"

"Why not?"

"I don't think a man should hit a woman."

"Not even in bed, if the woman asks?"

"Better not to."

"OK."

Her voice was so small only the *K* was audible. She rolled away and stared at the wall; her shoulder threw his hand back when he touched it. There were silences. Demurrals and qualifications, silences. It took hours to turn the clock back thirty seconds. Long after the last car had driven down Pleasant Avenue, at a time of night when actions and sensations had the moral weightlessness of dreams, he finally let her have her way with him.

The next night, for the first time, she returned to work after dinner. He was allowed to come along. In the computer room, consoles with bubble-shaped chassis like the busts of moon walkers were arrayed in a double row on a Formica-topped bench swamped by equipment manuals and used paper. A plate-glass window gave into a bright room filled with dryer-sized pieces of hardware and a throbbing, all-night white noise of NORAD-style vigilance. Ocean maps like the one in Renée's apartment hung on the walls, some with drooping corners tipped with squares of sticky stuff. The telephone, which sat on a radiator, had been unplugged, and the room's atmosphere of transience or abandonment was heightened by a lack of things to sit on. Renée said she hadn't been on hand when a shipment of new chairs arrived, and that students and assistant professors from the rest of the building had dropped in and helped themselves, and thrown their old chairs in a dumpster, because she hadn't been on hand.

"I did most of my work in this room. The computer's a Data General. We have a lot of Suns now too. They speak UNIX."

Louis stood by a map of the South Atlantic Ocean. "All these dots, all these lines."

"The dots are earthquakes."

"There are millions."

"Thousands every month, yes. The majority at sea."

He found a map showing most of North America, a ponderous beige mass between seas teeming colorfully with geological life. Red dots were scattered sparsely down the eastern seaboard, sparsely across the northern Ozarks, more thickly in the Western mountains. There was a red-alert mass of them in California.

"The crust of the earth," Renée said, "is broken into a dozen or so gigantic plates which for fairly well understood reasons related to the convection of molten rock beneath the crust are in constant motion. They bump and grind together, they spread apart. In some cases one plunges way down underneath another. Some of them move as much as a couple inches a year, which over the ages adds up. Ninety-five or so percent of all earthquakes happen near plate boundaries. You can see on the maps."

"But in Arkansas, and what's this, Wyoming? And New England . . . ?"

"And New York and Quebec and the whole eastern seaboard and out in the middle of the ocean nowhere near plate boundaries? Partly, around here, it's related to the fact that the Atlantic is getting wider, which puts a strain on the plates to either side of the central ridge. The rock in New England is very old and has a tortured history. There are faults running at all kinds of depths and in all different directions. But if you analyze the earthquakes that occur here—"

She rooted in the papers between a pair of consoles and found a map like the one Howard had shown Louis, with the addition of more epicenters and four balloons:

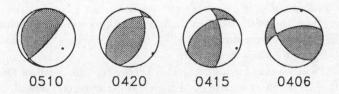

0510   0420   0415   0406

"Beach balls," she said. "They represent what's called the focal mechanism of the earthquake, which basically reflects the orientation of the faults and the direction of movement along them when they ruptured. You draw an imaginary sphere around the hypocenter. It's black in the directions where the earth has been compressed toward an observer on the sphere. It's white where the earth has been pulled away from an observer. And you can see here, all four of the events big enough to analyze had more or less the same mechanism."

"You mean, they're all black down the middle."

"Right. And they're reasonably consistent with a compressional stress on a fault running southwest to northeast, which is also true of most of the other events that have been analyzed in New England. Which indicates that the plate is being compressed by the spreading of the ocean."

"H.C. That's Howard."

She yawned. "Right."

"Is he good?"

"He's fine. He doesn't work enough. He also wasted a year playing around with strong motion."

"What's that?"

"That's what you felt on Thursday night. It's a term for the ground shaking felt near an epicenter. As opposed to the very weak signals normally recorded by seismic instruments. You can make recordings of strong motion, though unfortunately everything's so complicated by the local geological context that it's hard to extract much information about the earthquake itself." She yawned again. "Howard tried nobly."

In the periphery of Louis's vision, teeth sparkled in a beard; Terry Snall, quiet as a hunting brave, had appeared in the doorway and halted in his tracks. He looked at Louis. He looked at Renée. He looked at Louis.

"Oh," he said loudly, as though everything were clear to him now. "Don't let me disturb you."

"No problem," Renée said.

"I'm waiting for a print job." Terry shook his head in total and radical self-exculpation. "I'm just going to be one second."

"You can be five hours for all I care."

"Just one second," patting the top of the laser printer impatiently. "I'll be right out of here."

He waited pointedly for the printer to divulge his job. He inspected the feed end, inspected the excretory end, tapped on the feed tray, sighed hugely, put his hands on his hips, sighed hugely again, and surveyed the entire machine and shook his head. "Just one second," he said. "Don't want to disturb you guys."

Louis had to catch up with Renée as she stalked up a ramp into the sanctum of the heavy machinery. It was refrigerated and was tiled with off-white squares, the absence of one of which, near the main unit, revealed a snake's nest of cables underneath. On the long wall were racks holding thousands of rolls of magnetic tape. There were red-eyed modems, big tape drives loaded with tapes twitching anxiously, and several graphics screens.

"He is such a jerk," Renée said, taking a pair of wire-frame glasses from her shirt pocket and sitting down at a console.

"He's jealous," Louis said.

"Maybe."

"No, it's obvious."

"Well. If it's true, it's incredibly humiliating to me. It's also a little strange, considering he seems to have decided it's his mission in life to inform me that I'm full of myself." She frowned at the screen and typed rapidly, by touch. Louis thought her glasses were very poignant and pretty-making. "He's been involved with this local girl for about four years. You saw the window by the door? This woman is constantly appearing there and knocking on it, and if Terry's around, he *runs* into the hall and out the outside door. He's afraid somebody's going to let her inside. He thinks we can't see this." On the graphics screen to her right a color image was forming. She glanced through the picture window to make sure Terry wasn't somehow eavesdropping despite the noise. "Two years ago he got a new car and totaled it almost immediately. He wouldn't talk about how it happened. His girlfriend came by here one night and Howard let her in. He asked her how the accident happened, and apparently what it was was Terry was driving by this store that had sold him a window airconditioner that he didn't like and they'd been bad about, and he leaned across the passenger seat to give the store—the *building*—the finger, and while he was doing this he ran up over the curb and hit a tree. The girlfriend was amused, as were we—she's actually kind of sweet. And ever since then Terry won't let her anywhere near the computer room. Which makes you wonder what else she has to say about him."

"Who takes care of all this equipment?"

"It's supposed to be shared among everybody using it, but in practice—" Renée didn't like what she saw on the color screen. Her fingers flew across the keyboard and a new color image began to form. "We're missing two professors this semester, to begin with. And some people, like Terry, are conscientious objectors. He did a lot of work on the system in '88, which he thinks absolves him from all further responsibility; he gets very righteous about this although as far as I can tell, all the work he was doing was to install things that would help him with his own projects. And then there are the people who strategically absent themselves when it becomes absolutely necessary to do something like a system dump, which takes all night, and finally also I guess some people I simply don't trust—"

"Not to fuck it up."

"That's right."

"People must dislike you."

"Almost everybody, yes, to some extent. But I make up for it with self-love. Why don't you pull a chair over."

She loaded a camera on a tripod, turned out the lights, and began to shoot images while Terry's few seconds with the laser printer stretched into an hour at a console just outside the picture window. Like any good chaperon, he pretended to mind his own business. Louis listened gamely to Renée's explanations of the images, which were in rainbow colors and consisted mainly of reconstructed cross sections of a "slab" of rock 3,000 kilometers long and 650 kilometers wide and maybe 50 kilometers thick that was descending into the earth beneath a chain of islands running south from the Fijis through Tonga and the Kermadecs to a point not far above New Zealand. Earthquakes of all sizes and fault orientations accompanied the slab's descent at every depth, and her thesis, she told Louis, had "advanced the study" of what happened to the brittle rock as it fell deeper and deeper into the molten, pressurized goo of the mantle, and what finally became of it at the depth of 670 kilometers, below which depth no earthquake had ever been recorded anywhere.

"Did you get to go to these islands?"

"I thought geophysics would get me outdoors, compared to math or something. Six years later I've hardly left this room."

"You're very lucky."

"You think so." She squeezed the cable release.

"You've got something you're really good at, and it's really interesting, and it doesn't hurt anybody."

"When you look at it that way. I guess. It has its frustrations."

"I wish I could be an academic."

"Who said you can't?"

"I wish I could be *anything.*"

"Who said you can't?"

"I hate this country. I hate the piggishness. Everywhere I look I see pigs."

The glance Renée gave Louis in the blue light was tentative, or sad; distanced, like a mother's. "They're not all pigs," she said. "Think about the people who make the subways run. Think about nurses. Mailmen. Lobbyists for good causes. They're not all pigs."

"But I can't be those people. They just seem pitiful to me. They seem like dupes. Things are so fucked up it seems pathetic to try to be a useful citizen. Like if you're going to play the game why not go all the way and sell out completely. But if you're too disgusted to sell out, the only other options are to escape or try to tear things down. And I can't even escape into academics, because I had to watch my father be a professor. Every marxist I know has a life where it's think by day and drink by night. How could I choose a thing like that? I watch your fingers and your eyes and I feel so envious. You're in this position where you're really good at what you do. But I'm here and I can't imagine moving."

"We're going to have to do something about you."

"An island. An island."

Strong golden light lit the rooftops of Boston and formed a clear, free space in the air above them, an arena enclosed in the east by a shell of evening maritime mist and within which, to a distance of miles, were visible with perfect clarity billboards and green trees and overpasses on fire with the hour, and minor clouds the color and shape of moles. Jets above Nahant hung with no discernible movement in the blue-gray firmament to which their own engines bled contributions. On Lansdowne Street the faithful were entering the shadow of the temple, marching in a hush past carts selling icons and inspirational literature, past the worn façades of the shrines along the way, with their pre-game specials, their big dollar signs and tiny .95s.

Inside the gate Renée made a small green offering to the Jimmy Fund and its fight against cancer in children and showed no embarrassment when her more cynical companion reacted with a double take. A white charge of light was visible through the portal above them, and as they walked up the stairs the whiteness grew into a green field and thirty thousand fans, all with the skin tones of actors. Suited men were raking dirt. Royals and Red Sox in their dugouts. Keen smells of cigarettes and mustard. Henry Rudman's seats, halfway up the third-base line and ten rows back, were more than adequate. On either side of them, Rudmanesque individuals exuding pleasure were folding back their scorecards. At seven-thirty, when everyone in Fenway stood, Renée's eyes darted warily, and Louis, unable for once to change the channel, gritted his teeth and suffered through the hymn.

Few things bring happiness like good seats do. The Somervillians sat with their arms around each other's shoulders, Renée as rapt and radiant as Louis had ever seen her. She'd brought her baseball glove and she kept her hand in it. Earlier in the day they'd played catch, and he'd learned that she could sting his fingers, right through leather, with her throws.

For five innings the score remained 1–1. There was a fatness, a fullness, a pleasing lack of abstractness to the motion of the ball as it sprang off a bat and hissed through the infield grass, found the center of the third baseman's glove and received fresh kinetic energy and overtook the runner at first base. Louis later had no trouble understanding why he'd been so slow to see the other thing going on in front of him, the thing three rows down and a few seats to his left.

It was the hand he noticed first. A large, red male hand. With an intentness verging on urgency it was kneading a bare female shoulder, and the tanned neck above it, and the area behind her ear, and the ear itself, taking the skin and flesh in its fingers, taking for the purpose of having. Returning to the shoulder. Advancing in snake-like contractions under the narrow strap of her black dress, knuckles nudging the strap slowly out over the smooth globe of the shoulder and down the arm a little, palps of fingers indenting the skin there, palm molding and squeezing and possessing. Idly, with the hand she wasn't using to hold her beer, the girl pulled the strap back onto her shoulder. She shook her dark mane back and twisted around in her seat, chancing to look straight at Louis. She

was twenty and soft and tough, the kind of equine and unintro-
spective beauty that star outfielders go for. The hand gathered her
in again, her hair and shoulders and attention, and dipped under
the back of her dress and stayed there. Only then did Louis realize
the hand belonged to a fifty-year-old man whose face he knew.

Renée was hunched forward, chewing a nail. The tag of her
T-shirt stood up on her freckled neck. Apparently things were
happening on the field, things good for the Royals and bad for the
Sox. Louis followed the hand's creeping progress under the black
fabric and around under bimbo's arm and saw the fingertips halt
as close to her breast as propriety allowed, maybe even a centimeter
closer. Bimbo whispered into her companion's ear, mouth lingering,
lips dragging across his cheek and meeting his. The obscene red
hand squeezed her and released her. The plate umpire roared and
punched a batter out. The pigs cheered. The organist noodled.
Dimly Louis saw his graying girlfriend's smile fade and her mouth
open: "What's wrong?

"Is something wrong?

"Won't you tell me what's wrong?"

He made his hand a pistol, braced his wrist and took a bead
on the man's head. "CEO of Sweeting-Aldren. Right there."

Conceivably despite the cheering these words had carried into
Mr. Aldren's ears; he swung around and briefly scanned all the
seats less good than his own, allowing his pouchy and inflamed
face and narrow eyes to make their impression on Renée.

"Slime ball," Louis said, his arm recoiling from the shot he'd
let fly.

"I guess I see what you mean."

"Check out his pinky ring."

His own hands were cold and white, all his blood boxed up in
his heart and temples. Not even a Sox rally and a screaming eighth
inning could pry his eyes from the spectacle of fondlement unfolding
three rows down. Maybe to her credit, maybe from dim-wittedness,
the girl seemed oblivious to the liberties the hand was taking and
to the confident, possessing leer that Aldren trained alternately on
her and on the players at their feet. She was following the game.
And it was not implausible, Louis thought, that she would retain
partial possession of herself later on as well, when Aldren took her

off to some overfurnished room to penetrate her warm orifices in privacy, the same privacy in which even now, in all probability, his other effluents were being pumped into the yielding earth.

"He sure can't keep his hands off her," Renée observed.

"It's more like *she* can't keep his hands off her."

"But listen." She touched Louis's face and made him look at her. "Don't be so angry. I don't like it when you're angry."

"I can't help it."

"I wish you'd try, if only for my sake."

It was a declaration. Louis looked at the face of the person who had made it, the face with the pretty eyes and upturned nose and acne, and realized that this person had somehow become literally the only thing in the world he could even marginally count on.

"I love you," he said unexpectedly, but meaning it. He didn't see the fan behind him grin and wink at Renée and so didn't entirely understand why she bounced back in her seat so abruptly and gave her attention to the game, which was ending.

6

There's a specific damp and melancholy ancient smell that comes out in Boston after sunset, when the weather is cool and windless. Convection skims it off the ecologically disrupted water of the Mystic and the Charles and the lakes. The shuttered mills and mothballed plants in Waltham leak it. It's the breath from the mouths of old tunnels, the spirit rising from piles of soot-dulled glass and the ballast of old railbeds, from all the silent places where cast iron has been rusting, concrete turning friable and rotten like inorganic Roquefort, petroleum distillates seeping back into the earth. In a city where there is no land that has not been changed, this is the smell that has come to be primordial, the smell of the nature that has taken nature's place. Flowers still bloom, mown grass and falling leaves and fresh snow still alter the air periodically. But their smells are superimposed; sentimental; younger than those patiently outlasting emanations from the undersides of bridges and the rubble of a thousand embankments, the creosoted piers in oil-slicked waterways, the sheets of *Globe* and *Herald* wrapped around furry rocks in drainage creeks, and the inside of every blackened metal box still extant on deserted right-of-way, purpose and tokens of ownership effaced by weather, keyhole plugged by corrosion: the smell of infrastructure.

It was out in force when Louis and Renée came up Dartmouth Street from the Green Line stop at Copley Square. They walked in silence. The windy brake-lit night when they'd driven these streets searching for a parking place seemed buried in the past by much more than the month it actually had been. Again it was a weekend night, but this time the neighborhood was peaceful and sober and untrafficked, as though by some circadian coincidence all the residents had left town or were staying home with family. The twilight sky was like a painted blue backdrop hanging directly behind the row houses and their domestic yellow lights.

Eileen had been suspicious when Louis called. He'd found it necessary to fire a salvo of apologies at her, attributing his recent meanness to the fact that he'd lost his job. His remorse was just authentic enough to make her sentimental. She said it was "really tough luck" that he was unemployed. She expressed a vague interest in having him over sometime, to which non-invitation he instantly responded: "Great! How about Friday night?" She said she'd check with Peter. He said he and Renée would plan to come around eight. She said, but she had to check with Peter. He said one thing he should mention was that Renée didn't eat red meat or poultry. "Oh, that's OK," Eileen said, her voice brightening. "I'll just make some vegetarian thing."

Once the date had been set, the difficult task turned out to be persuading Renée to lie.

"A mathematician?" She'd gaped at him. "That's the stupidest thing you've ever said to me."

"Yeah," he said, "but what's Peter going to think when a seismologist starts asking him about waste disposal? He's going to think earthquakes. Do we want him thinking earthquakes? Mentioning to his dad that there's this seismologist who's curious about the company? You told *me* you were a math person, before you went into geophysics."

"I'm not even going to discuss this with you."

"Why? Why? All you have to do is say it. I mean assuming anyone's polite enough to ask about your work, which I doubt they will. You just say, whatever, applied mathematics. Isn't that what seismology is anyway?"

"It's a lie. I blush when I lie."

"Uh! You're so exemplary I can't believe it."

"Yeah, and I wonder if you appreciate that. I'm really beginning to wonder."

"Lying is a social skill," he said patiently. "Everybody has to lie. And this particular lie is like totally benign."

"Misrepresenting myself, manipulating two people who've invited us to dinner in good faith, trying to get some time alone with one of them so I can extract information on the pretext of idle curiosity? This is a benign lie?"

It was in moments of frustration like this one that Louis thought of Lauren. He was convinced that Lauren would have lied for him. Lauren would have known what to do.

"Look," Renée said. "If the subject comes up naturally, in the course of a conversation, and I don't have to lie, fine. Otherwise, I know you're angry at these people, I know you feel like you've been stepped on. But they're still people, and to go there in total cynicism, which is what you're doing—I find it very worrisome that you'd consider doing this."

"Oh, come on," he said. She was getting on his nerves. "Things aren't so black-and-white. For one thing, I actually had a not-bad talk with Eileen. It's not like I'm blaming her the way I blame my mother. You know, she's a victim too. You think I'd go there in total cynicism?"

"I'm saying I can see you beginning to think you can treat people whatever way you want to, because you're so angry. And the reason this matters to me is that I care about you."

He filled his lungs with air. He let it out slowly. The idea that Renée so fully understood his shortcomings was almost more than he could stand.

"OK, OK, you're right," he said, more temperately. "But it's like you're killing everything by thinking too much. I'm not asking you to be diabolical. I'm just saying let's go and have a good time and try to get what we want. It's like you do so much thinking that it's impossible for you to have dinner with people under *any* circumstances. The only way you can stay exemplary is to stay by yourself. Because you're never going to really respect the people you're with, and the music they like, and the food they eat, and the clothes they wear, and the less than totally intense thoughts they have—"

"I said I would go."

"And that's *morally wrong*, right? It's *deceptive*. To act like you're on the same level they are, when inside you feel more exemplary and aware and everything. It turns you into a false person, with a false smile and no friends, which is ultimately—"

"Fuck you, Louis. You really do abuse me."

"Which is ultimately very sad. Because underneath you're a very lovable person, and you want to be liked and have fun."

He was perplexed by her stubbornness. He honestly believed that she'd be a happier person if she could loosen up a little; but all he got for his pains was the feeling that he was an odious Male. Of course, maybe he *was* an odious Male. The odious Male seeking control over a virtuous and difficult woman won't scruple to exploit whatever weakness he can find in her—her age, her mannerisms, her insecurity, and her loneliness above all. He can be as cowardly and cruel as he wants to as long as logic is on his side. And the woman, yielding to his logic, can do no more to save her pride than demand his fidelity. She says, "You've humiliated me and won me now, so you'd better not hurt me." But hurting her is precisely what the man is tempted to do, because now that she has yielded he feels contempt for her, and he also knows that if he hurts her she'll become virtuous and difficult again . . . These archetypes forced entry to the apartment on Pleasant Avenue like vulgar relatives. Louis wanted to turn them away, but it's not so easy to slam the door in your relatives' faces.

In the brick house on Marlborough Street, at the door of the Stoorhuys-Holland residence, he watched stress do extreme and painful things to Eileen's face and Renée's face as they squeezed through the moment of hellos. Then he handed over a bag of beer. Eileen was wearing an oversized black karate outfit, with her hair fanned on her back and shoulders. The effect was stylish and reminded him of borzois, dogs which when he passed them on the street always seemed like they'd be happier running around in jeans and sneakers but couldn't, because their owners were rich.

He figured Eileen was entertaining them tonight because she'd lacked the skills to escape his self-invitation, but it was possible that she was also curious about Renée. She led them into the living room—empty of partygoers, it had some dignity now, was less of a station, more of a room—and explained that Peter had been helping one of his little sisters set up a new computer and was due home at any minute. She asked "you guys" if they'd had trouble parking. She hoped "you guys" didn't mind eating so late. She offered "you guys" beer or wine or beer or . . . whatever. She hoped "you guys" liked moussaka. Having thus exhausted the possibilities for addressing them collectively, she jumped out of her chair and said, "Where is my *boy?*"

They listened to her phoning in the kitchen, her voice getting higher, its girlish tone stretching thin as the irritation underneath it swelled. When she returned to the living room she slipped into her chair as though she didn't want to interrupt the conversation. However, there was no conversation. Her guests merely looked at her, and at length she pretended to wake out of a trance. "He's coming," she averred.

Renée spoke. "You— You're in business school?"

Eileen nodded rockingly, not looking at her. "Uh-huh. Uh-huh."

"You must be about done, though," Louis said.

"Oh, yeah." She nodded and rocked, some aspect of the stereo holding her attention. "I'm all done, actually."

"Where will you be working?" Renée asked.

"Um." She rocked. "Bank of Boston?"

There was a long silence. Shyness had paralyzed Eileen, shyness of the kind that makes a five-year-old bury her face in her mother's arms when a stranger asks too many questions.

"What kind of thing will you be doing there?" Renée said gently.

"Um . . . commercial loans?"

"And . . . what kind of thing does that entail?"

Blank-eyed, Eileen turned to Louis, who frantically indicated that it was her question to answer, not his.

"Commercial lending," she said. "It's, you know, helping corporations finance things. Capital improvements. Acquisitions, takeovers. Development. It's—really not very interesting."

"It sounds like it would be very interesting," Renée said.

"Oh, well, it is interesting. To me, it's very interesting. But I think Louis said that you're a scientist?"

"Yes."

"Oh, yeah, well. It's not interesting in that way. It's more of a people kind of job, you know, where you have to deal with different kinds of people. That's sort of where the interest is."

Here Eileen ran out of gas. No matter how Renée tried to draw her out, she could think of nothing else to say about the work she would be doing. What puzzled Louis was that she didn't take the obvious escape route, which would have been to ask Renée about *her* work, or him about his lack of it. She just squirmed and let the gruesome silences accrete.

It was almost nine when Peter breezed into the apartment, wearing a Harvard sweatshirt and carrying two boxes of floppies. Instantly Eileen became voluble again and launched into a more detailed account of Peter's day, beginning with his little sister's visit to the Computer Factory. When he returned from the kitchen, a tumbler of amber liquid in his hand, she tried to rope him into the narrative by smiling up at him, this her boyfriend, the topic of her conversation, her very words made flesh. "Did you get everything set up?" she asked.

Peter let the question lie on the floor a few seconds before he squashed it with an impatient "Yeah." To Louis he doled out a small and hollow "how's it going." Renée, however, he joined on the sofa and regaled with a long and thorough inspection of her head and arms and lap and head, smiling slyly all the while, as if they shared some secret. He dangled his whiskey glass between his knees and hunched over it like an ice fisherman peering through his hole. He said it was good to see her here again. He remembered she'd come to the party in mourning, very cool. He lamented that they hadn't had a chance to talk more at the party. He focused on Renée, saying one thing after another to her, as if Louis and Eileen were conversing separately and not listening. Or as if he were the host of the Tonight Show, forgetting the audience in his fascination with this special guest, appropriating our fantasies of leaning close to her. Renée, thoroughly confused, began to smile at her knees the way you smile at a pretty good joke told by a person you're not sure about. She gave no reply at all when Peter asked her if she'd seen yesterday's *Globe*.

"You're kidding," he said, "you didn't see it?"

She shook her head, still smiling. Peter looked over his shoulder at Eileen. "We still have that paper, don't we?"

Eileen shrugged crossly.

"It's gotta be in the kitchen," he said. "You want to get it?"

Louis was very sorry to see his sister unfold herself from her chair and silently obey the order. When she returned, Peter took the newspaper from her hands without looking at her.

"See this?" Peter let everything but the Metro/Region section slide to the floor. "Right here? Lead story? 'Pro-Choice Advocates Decry Mail and Phone Harassment.' And a fetching little picture of you? Courtesy of Channel 4 news. And here and here and here?" Inevitably, condescension had crept into his voice. "How about that? You're all over the place."

"We didn't get a paper," Renée vaguely said to Louis, as if this were his fault.

"Dr. Renée Seitchek, Harvard University seismologist—"

She turned again to Louis, with a dark and vindicated look.

"This TV show, I didn't see that. Sounds pretty wild."

"It wasn't wild. It was stupid."

"Right." Peter nodded as if he'd said it himself. "Like even worse than stupid. You express an opinion and next thing you know you're getting hate mail and you can't even use your own telephone. You know what?" He put his hand on his hip and leaned away so he could see her better. "I think you're being very brave. To speak up like this. I think that's awfully damn brave. Private citizen branded an abortionist for expressing an opinion on TV? It's like the ultimate nightmare."

She leaned over his lap and squinted at the paper. Louis was dismayed to see how readily she tolerated Peter's attention, and how pretty her flushing cheeks had made her, and how close her neck and shoulders were to Peter's face. Peter, for all his faults, appreciated what an interesting and sexy and brave person Renée was; odious, immature Louis only said unpleasant things to her and criticized her. How could she fail to notice the contrast? The worst of it was that Louis didn't know himself which way he wanted things, whether it was better to have a sad and twisted girlfriend who needed him so much that he could say whatever he wanted to her, or to be involved with a real woman who could attract other men and fill him with anxiety and forget him.

Eileen looked even less pleased than Louis. While the two

thirty-year-olds huddled on the sofa in their faded jeans, she sat in her goofy silk pajamas and leveled on Renée the same evil stare she'd been using for twenty years whenever something she felt was rightfully hers was being denied her, even momentarily.

"Need some help with dinner?" Louis asked her in a cartoon voice.

He followed her to the kitchen, where she continued to glance balefully in the direction of Renée and Peter.

"So," he said. "You're all done. You passed all your exams."

"Yeah." From the refrigerator she took Russian dressing and a green salad big enough for twelve. "You want to toss this?"

She put her head in the oven. Hearing nothing from the other room but a rustling paper, Louis imagined that Peter and Renée's mouths had already found each other, Peter squeezing her breasts and stifling her cries . . . His feelings had acquired such a physical bite that he could hardly believe he'd ever been in bed with her before, had ever tasted or touched any more of her than the mere idea: a voice, a willingness, a head, an older person—anything but the woman he now imagined in the other room. And it was a great thing, jealousy. It was a drug that charged up the nerve endings and delivered a first-class rush. On the minus side, it damaged his control over the salad he was tossing, which goaded by fork and spoon was surging from the bowl, cucumber disks splatting on the counter; and underneath the rush (which was great) he suspected he did not feel well at all.

Hands in thermal mitts, Eileen gazed dispassionately at the mess he was making. "Did I tell you what happened the night we had our finals party?"

"No."

She pulled her hair behind her ears with quilted paws. "It was so funny. It was *so, so* funny. My friend Sandi's dad owns this limousine company, and he was supposed to let us use three stretch limos, as a graduation present, and we were going to have this road party and end up in Manhattan and have dinner and go dancing at the Rainbow Room?"

"Uh huh."

"But so these limos come to pick us up, and we're all dressed and it's raining, but there are only *two* of them? And there are eighteen of us?" Briefly she doubled over with the funniness of her memories. "But we all pile into these two limos and we start having champagne and caviar, and we're watching this video that this other friend found in the library which what it's about is management training in the *dairy industry?* It's all these cows and milking machines and guys with clipboards and crew cuts talking to the guys who work the machines. And slapping the cows and looking at cheeses and lobbying in Washington? It's totally fifties, there's this long shot of the Capitol Building, where they're going to be lobbying for *milk subsidies?*"

"Uh huh."

"Hoo ha ha," she laughed. "But so we're somewhere in Connecticut, out in the middle of nowhere, and this horrible thing happens to the other limo—not the one I'm in, the other one— somehow all the radiator fluid ends up on the highway and none of it's in the radiator, and the driver won't drive it anymore? And there are eighteen of us and it's pouring rain and we only have one limousine to get to New York in, and the driver says he won't take more than ten, and of course nobody wants to volunteer not to go."

"Of course."

"But we can just barely see this truck stop, down in the valley, it's this *huge* truck stop, with about a million trucks out in front of it and nothing else around, just woods. So we all decide, who needs Manhattan, we're just going to have our party right here. So we all go in, and there are about a thousand of these big red-faced *truckers*, they've all got tattoos and they're smoking and eating this greasy food. And we're totally dressed up, the guys are all in black tie, and Sandi's in this Oscar de la Renta dress that's cut like—!" The neckline Eileen drew across her chest indicated nipple exposure on Sandi's part. "But we all walk right in anyway, and of course everybody's staring at us, we're carrying our champagne glasses, the tall kind, and the guys are carrying the bottles—"

"Was Peter there?"

"No, this was just from our class, we had to limit it. But we went to this room that had a jukebox, and, well. It was so much fun. We were surrounded by all these truckers and making all these jokes and listening to all these oldies and country music. Sandi called her dad and had him send an extra limo, but it was like midnight before it came and by that point the other limo driver had gone to Hartford for more champagne. Sandi was dancing with this trucker that she linked arms with and drank champagne? Everybody was really getting into it. But it was so much fun. We got back about six in the morning, we were all totally plotzed. Everybody asked us how New York was, and when we said where we'd been, nobody would believe us. They just *couldn't believe* we'd spent the night in a truck stop."

"It is amazing," Louis said.

She nodded, removing garlic bread from the oven. "You want to tell them we're going to eat?"

He went to the living room. The look Renée gave him as she headed for the dining room was neither friendly nor unfriendly; it was just miles away.

"Something smells very good," she said to Eileen, encouragingly, when they'd all sat down. Louis grunted in agreement. This was right before he realized that the sauce oozing from his slab of moussaka was full of ground beef. Appalled, he looked across the table at Renée, but she was now leagues away and filling her plate with salad. Raising a slice of eggplant with his fork, he uncovered a veritable ants' nest of beef granules.

"Did I tell you what happened the night of the last earthquake?" Eileen paused and with her eyes made an approval-seeking connection between Renée's plate and Renée herself. Renée, however, was occupied with raising fortifications, handling her hands and flatware with such absorption and willed inconspicuousness that although she was as nakedly in view as the other three, Louis could look straight at her and still not see what was happening to her moussaka or how she felt about it. He understood this to mean he shouldn't make an issue of it.

"It was so funny," Eileen said. "Last year's Nobel Prize winner in economics gave a talk at school, and afterward this professor of mine had him over to dinner with some of his students. He's got this gr-r-reat house in Nahant, with about three acres overlooking the water—"

"Nahant," Peter said. "Major Mafia neighborhood."

Renée nodded and smiled, her eyes on her napkin.

"It's not all Mafia, Peter. Because Seton lives there, and he's not Mafia."

"You got some kind of proof of that?"

"He's not! He's not Mafia. He's a—a Harvard professor!"

"Ohhhh," Peter said, smirking for Renée's benefit. "I see."

"He's not Mafia," Eileen assured Louis. "He's an adjunct professor. But the Nobel guy, he's Japanese. I can never get his name right. I know it when I hear it but I can't remember it. Do—you remember?"

Louis's jaw dropped. "You're asking me if I remember the name of last year's Nobel Prize winner in economics?"

"See, neither do I. But anyway, he's this funny little guy with round glasses, and we were having cognac after dinner in Seton's living room, and people were starting to leave, and suddenly there was this earthquake. I was standing by the fireplace and I started screaming, because it was really an earthquake, I mean it was really strong." She blushed a little, realizing she had everyone's attention now, even Peter's. "Stuff was falling off the mantel, and the floor was—it was like being on the T. Peter, that's what it was like. It was like standing up on the T, you had to hold on to something or you'd lose your balance. It only lasted a couple seconds, but everyone was shouting and glasses were breaking and the lights were flickering. But then it stopped, and like one after another we all started noticing—Hakasura? Haka—? Hakanaka? Shoot. But anyway, we started noticing that he was still sitting in his corner of the sofa and *talking about econometric inversions*. He hadn't even noticed the earthquake! Or he'd noticed it but he'd kept right on talking. He was holding on to the girl's arm to keep her from standing up, the girl he was talking to, and finally he sees that we're all standing there looking at him. He finishes his sentence and he looks up and he asks, 'Is someone hurt?' (but in his accent which I can't do), and we say, 'No,' and he goes, 'Well then. We have a saying in Japan—' "

She frowned. "Shoot. *Shoot.*" She looked at Peter. "Do you remember what it was?"

"You couldn't remember when you told me either."

"It was like, 'If you— If you—' " She looked around the table sheepishly. "I can't remember. I thought I did but I don't. It was something like—"

"They get the idea," Peter said.

It began to seem to Louis that he was the only person at the table who did not belong. By and by Renée rose from behind her fortifications to answer questions about earthquakes, as usual sounding like a seminar leader; and it was Peter, not Louis, who seemed to possess what she said; it was Peter whose face shone with the reflected radiance of her expertise.

After ritual consumption of Häagen-Dazs, Louis selflessly left the thirty-year-olds alone in the living room in case Renée needed more time to pry facts out of Peter.

"You seem kinda down," Eileen told him in the kitchen, as he watched her load the dishwasher. "Is it your job?"

"What job? I don't have a job."

"So you haven't found anything."

"I'm not even looking."

"But weren't you like real interested in radio?"

He duly noted that she'd scored a point by "showing concern" for him like this. He laughed, briefly, at the idea he was interested in radio.

"Do you have money to pay your rent and stuff?" she said.

"Nah. But I'm moving in with Renée this week, so."

Surprise muted her voice. "You are?"

"Yes."

"Oh. I didn't know that." She turned up the corners of her mouth. "That's nice."

"Yes."

She made a strong second effort. "She's r e a l l y smart, isn't she? She is so smart. And she's like—your age?"

Louis stared at his sister. "Yeah. My age."

"How'd you meet her?"

"I met her at the beach. She had a beach ball."

"Uh huh. Be sure and give me your new address, OK?" She scraped Renée's uneaten beef into the trash, where there were two Stouffer's frozen moussaka boxes, and put the plate in the dishwasher. "And you know, if you're really low on cash, you could probably ask Mom—"

"Hey. There's a thought."

"Well although she's kind of upset right now. I don't know if you heard, it's this really terrible thing. She's getting all this money, but about 90 percent of it's in stock in Grandpa's company, Sweeting-Aldren, you know, where Peter's dad works?"

"Oh, yeah. Chemical company?"

"Right. Except she doesn't get control of it until next month, and you probably haven't been reading in the paper, but the company's in really awful shape, because of the earthquakes and this chemical spill near their plant. Peter's dad's the operations vice president and he's in charge of all this stuff. But so for a while the stock price was falling like a point a day, which is really terrible, and Mom's sitting there with all this stock and she has to watch it fall like two million dollars in value without being able to do anything about it. Can you believe that? I mean, two million dollars? And she can't do a thing about it. Plus most of the other stuff she has is real estate, I guess mainly Rita's property, and there's suddenly this depression in real estate up there, because of the earthquakes. So she's *really* upset. She flies out here and then she can't do anything, so she goes home but then she just sits around and worries, so she keeps flying back. She doesn't even call me anymore, when she's here, which is fine with me; she's not herself. Does she call you?"

"I'm seldom near a phone, so I wouldn't know."

"I really feel sorry for her. I mean, sheesh! Two million dollars."

"It's a hard, cruel world," Louis said.

Eileen activated the dishwasher and looked around to see what dishes hadn't made the final cut. "Peter's family was really lucky," she said. "The last earthquake did a lot of damage to their house. We were out there and we saw. Part of the house sort of settled? They have this new addition which they're going to have to tear it down, and put a new foundation in, and their doors don't close anymore. They live in Lynnfield, they have this wonderful house, and it turns out they had earthquake insurance? It was just really lucky. You could get it as a rider, but nobody used to want it until this year. But I guess the Stoorhuyses just wanted to be completely insured, and so now they're not going to have to pay anything.

One of their neighbors, it's going to cost like twenty thousand dollars to fix their house. And you can't get the rider anymore unless you wait a year before it takes effect."

Louis thought of Mr. Stoorhuys, his forelock, his too-short jacket sleeves. His bushy, wagging tail. "Do you see them a lot? Peter's family?"

Eileen's face darkened. "Peter and his dad don't get along too well. His mom's real nice, though, so we see them a little. He's got four sisters and a brother. He's the oldest." She looked at Louis sideways; there was a clump of suds on her silk lapel. "You know, he's really a nice person. He's a great older brother. He's always doing stuff for his sisters."

Louis was at a loss. "I'll make an effort."

He was called upon to make that effort almost immediately. Eileen took him into the living room and asked Peter if he had any ideas for a job Louis could get. Peter scrutinized him as though his job qualifications were written on his body. Renée was also looking at him, flashing LET'S LEAVE signals. Peter asked what kind of minimum salary requirements we were looking at.

Louis spoke in his zombie voice. "I wouldn't say no to five thousand a month plus benefits and paid sick leave. I type thirty-five words per minute."

"Frankly," Peter said, "with requirements like those I think you're going to be looking for a lo-o-o-ng time. Now, what I was going to suggest is you look for the kind of arrangement I got into with Boston magazine a few years back. We're probably the best publication you could be with at this stage. We're a little labor-rich right now, so I would *not* get my hopes up, but, uh, I could put in a word for you, if you want."

Eileen gave Louis a huge smile: here was a really good possibility for him! Peter might be able to do something for him right away!

Peter swirled the ruddy liquid in his snifter. "What they may do," he said, "is start you off on a one hundred percent commission basis. Doesn't sound so great, huh. But if you don't let 'em set a ceiling, it can work in your favor. I started out that way myself, and you know what I made my first month?"

During the moment Louis was given to guess the figure, Renée listed illy on the sofa, overcome by the high voltage of misunderstanding in the room.

"Twenty-one hundred dollars," Peter said. "And that was three years ago. Granted, I had some experience at that point, so these may not be equivalent situations. You may have to bust your butt for a couple of months. But if you can hack it, you'll be pretty close to where I am now in two years max."

"Thanks for the advice," Louis said. "I'll think it over and get back to you. Do you have a *fax number?*"

"Just give me a call," Peter said.

"Think it over, huh, Louis?" Eileen earnestly touched his arm. "He can really help you."

Renée had teletransported herself to the door. Again the grotesque distortion of faces as she and Eileen exchanged thanks and good wishes, squeezing through the moment of departure.

"Yo, Renée," Peter said across the room. "Take care of yourself."

Outside, the city made its rustling noises, its sighs and murmurs, its auditory offerings to the indifferent sky above it. Somewhere a subway wheel screeched on a rail, so far away the sound was dime-sized. The avengers walked up the street without speaking, doing three-on-two rhythms with their feet, Louis's stride long, Renée's more rapid. She was biting her lip and blinking as if resisting tears.

"You had a bad time," Louis said.

"Yeah. I had a bad time. I had a very bad time, but it was my fault."

"It's your fault my sister gives you a plate of beef?"

"I can eat a little beef. It doesn't kill me. I mean, yes it does kill me: *I can't eat it.* But it's not like it makes me sick. It's only me. It's only my problem with it."

"I was the one," he objected slowly, "who made you go. The whole thing was my idea."

"Do you know why I stopped eating meat?" She was staring straight ahead. A damp breeze full of infrastructure dragged sickles of her hair across her forehead. "It's not for—moral superiority.

Just so you know that. It's only because I don't want to forget. I refuse to say OK, I'll forget this is a cow. It's nothing noble, it's nothing compassionate. It's only me and my problems."

Across the street a Camry had found a parking place and was swinging in happily, rump first. Louis decided this was a good time to say nothing.

The trolley snaked and groaned beneath the center of the city. Riders spoke quietly, and flattered by their deference the enveloping silence grew glutted and despotic. They were nearly at Lechmere before Louis dared ask if Renée had gotten anything out of Peter.

She shook her head. "He was very cautious, when I brought it up. He seemed surprised when I told him what he'd said at the party. He said he must have been very drunk. I said it must be true, though, what he'd said. And he said, yeah, his dad says the company doesn't do any dumping, but he's pretty sure they do. I asked him why he thought so, and he said he'd heard some things, but it wasn't anything he could prove. That was all I could get him to say, without seeming like I really cared."

"Did he ask you what's causing the earthquakes? I was noticing you—"

"Yes. I lied, exactly the way you wanted me to. I sat there and told him a lie."

Louis collared her and pulled on her ear, but she was very unhappy. He waited until they'd crossed Cambridge Street and were in his car before he said, "Aren't you going to ask what I found out from Eileen?"

"Did you find something out?"

"Nah. Only that Peter's parents had earthquake insurance for their house. A special rider."

He watched his words sink in. "You're kidding," she said.

"She volunteered it. I didn't even ask."

"Nobody. Nobody around here buys earthquake coverage."

"So I gather."

"Oh wow." She pressed her head into the headrest. "Wow." She took his hand and squeezed it hard, hitting her thigh with it. He gave her a kiss and she snapped it off like a grape from its stem.

"Are you mine?" he said.

"Yes!"

They drove home to Pleasant Avenue. On the kitchen table were the United Airlines tickets that had come in the mail that morning. Apparently Louis's father had purchased a Boston–Chicago round trip in Louis's name, without telling him, after a bad conversation they'd had on the previous weekend.

"These," he said tiredly.

"I still don't understand why he sent them."

He drank a glass of water. "It's this von Clausewitz side of him. We have this conversation where I basically hang up on him, and he turns around and buys me plane tickets. Because now it's *my* fault if he loses three hundred bucks because I don't go."

"You could just say you have to work."

"You mean, tell a lie? Funny you suggest it. Unfortunately, I already told him I'm unemployed. And the thing is, it's a *nice* thing. I was totally rude to him, and he turns the other cheek and gives me three hundred bucks' worth of tickets, because in his own pot-headed way he's trying to hold the family together. I told you he called me because he'd found out about my little run-in with my mother, up in Ipswich. He's like, You want to trash her sofa? That's cool, Lou, but you should consider *her* feelings too. Which has only been his refrain for about twenty years, you know, that I should consider *her* feelings too. Which is exactly what he's going to tell me if I go out there. And so, like, why go? I've already heard it."

Renée put her chin on his shoulder and her hand on his crotch and squeezed him. "*I* won't object if you don't go."

"The person who should go is you, not me. You and him would really hit it off." He dropped into a chair, and she sat down on his lap. He slid his hands up under her T-shirt. "I guess we'll just see how we feel next Sunday."

"When are we going to move you in?"

"I don't know. Sometime before then. Wednesday?"

"And in the meantime?"

"In the meantime . ." He pulled her shirt up slowly, bunching it above her black bra.

"I have to do some work. Plus the system backup on Monday, which will take all night."

He unhooked her bra and freed her breasts, these female things that it had seemed, tonight, that he had never seen before. They were soft and animate little scones. He was just beginning to take a good, hard look at them when—

"Mm!"

She jumped to her feet, pulling down her shirt, and crossed her arms and faced the wall. He thought she'd gotten tangled up in her selfconsciousness again. Once she'd fixed her bra, though, she apologized and said it was only the raccoon, the raccoon at the window, it had been looking straight at her.

He hadn't seen this raccoon yet. He went to the window, but with the kitchen lights on, all he could make out through the screen was some rear porch lights in the trees, and a length of white gutter at the bottom of the piece of roof outside the window.

"Listen," Renée said.

There was a strange huffing, almost too faint to credit.

"He's right around the corner," she said. "He gets nervous and goes around the corner, but then he gets more interested and comes back. I say he, but I'm not sure about that. Which is interesting, how an animal without gender, I always say he. Default gender: male. We should get away from the window, though. It—"

"I know what you're going to say."

"What?"

"It's like an earthquake. It only comes if you're not looking."

"That's right."

"But it does come. I mean, there really is a raccoon."

"Yes! You think I'm lying to you?"

They sat down at the table. Louis cheated, pretending not to watch the window but continually stealing peeks, and still it came as a complete surprise when he realized that the screen had stopped being blank. At what moment, exactly, had the dun-colored snout and perspicacious leather nose and shiny eyes appeared?

This time when he went to the window the raccoon retreated only as far as the gutter. From there it gave him a hurt look, over its shoulder, like a doubtful suicide on a ledge. It was a big animal, ring-tailed and bandit-eyed, larger than a cat. The moment Louis turned to glance at Renée, the raccoon returned to the window. It paced back and forth, a dark blur of fur for the most part, but now and again (and each time surprisingly) it pushed its nose against the screen and looked at Renée.

"Oh, it still has its sore," she said, concerned.

"This is great. Do you feed it?"

"Sometimes I put stuff out. It usually doesn't eat much. I don't see it very often. Sometimes it comes two or three nights in a row, and then I won't see it for a month. Three months, once. I thought it was gone. A dog got it, a car got it. Rabies."

Louis watched it climb up a drainpipe, hunching its furry and powerful shoulders like a cat, extending an arm like a monkey and then, as it put its chin on the gutter and heaved itself onto the roof, looking more like a person than anything else. The ceiling creaked, once, under its weight. With a smile, he turned to make a comment to Renée; but the room was empty.

He found her naked in the sheets. Full of desire, he stripped and came to her, but even in the midst of his anticipation, even as he clambered into her arms and rested his weight on her volume and felt the uniform warmth of her skin and took her head in his hands, he wondered how she always worked it so he came to her, rather than vice versa. He wondered why he had to feel so alone when they made love, so alone with her pleasure as he propelled the long wave train that led to her satisfaction (on the green plotting screen in the computer room she'd shown him what a large and distant earthquake looked like as it registered on the department's digital seismograph: a flat, bright line faintly rippled by the primary wave, settling down for a moment and then swinging more violently as the secondary wave arrived, and more violently still as more and more shock waves bounced off the earth's outer core and inner core and crust, the sS and ScS and SS and PP and PKiKP, until finally the line went totally haywire in the grip of tremendous, rolling surface waves, the Love waves and Rayleigh waves that demolished bridges and leveled buildings and tore the earth up everywhere). It wasn't that they didn't fit together or come enough; it just seemed as if at no point, not even in this most typical of acts between sexes, did she ever present herself or give herself or even let him see her as a woman. Even before jealousy had sharpened his interest, he'd been telling himself to stop and *look* at this woman the next time they made love, and each time they made love he forgot, and remembered only afterward. There was something like an earthquake's own shyness in the way she tricked his eye, so that he could be with her and feel the presence of everything but those very qualities his imagination called up when he was alone and pictured a Woman. Always it seemed to suit some obscure purpose of hers to have the two of them be the same sex, excitable through matching nerves and satiable through matching stimulation. Some principle of seduction, some acknowledgment of difference, was missing. And it seemed as if whenever she sensed that he felt an absence she started talking, in a voice orgasm-drunk and lulling —pro-him, pro-them, pro-sex.

So he turned the lights on. It was two in the morning. "I want to look at you," he said.

She squinted in the brightness. "We don't need all these on."

He turned on one further light and stood by the bed looking down, intending, once and for all, to really see this woman. The game was up; she couldn't hide; she didn't try. In the glare of the lights, he saw: the blackness of hair and eyelids. The red smudge of mouth and nipples. Wry labia distended and flecked with foam. An ear with metal in it. The loll of untensed muscles beneath grayish skin. Dull, puckered areas of dried or drying semen. Dark fuzz on upper lip and wrists. The fetal mashedness of a tired face. All the qualities laid out like organs for sale in a French butcher's meat case. This was the warm body he'd been holding? This was his girlfriend, Renée?

He'd been tricked yet again. He'd seen an angel floating on thermals high above him, and not believing in it had shot it down and found it to be nothing but a feathered and lumpy piece of meat. The report of the gun echoed off into space like the laughter of the angel that had escaped.

Suspiciously uncurious about what he was standing there for, Renée pulled the sheet over her shoulders. He supposed it was possible that she was just very sleepy. He crawled into bed, craving her desperately.

On Sunday the *Globe* ran an endless article on the recent earthquakes, the long columns flanked by the usual escort of photos and graphics and boxes. Renée wasn't mentioned in the main text, but she did get quoted in a box headlined EARTHQUAKES: GOD'S WILL, EARTH SPIRITS, OR CHANCE PHENOMENA?

> For Harvard University seismologist Renee Seitchek, the line between science and religion has proved particularly tortuous. Seitchek, who in the April 27 broadcast denounced efforts by Stites to link the abortion issue to the temblors, has become a target of illegal telephone and mail harassment directed at clinics and physicians who perform abortions and other pro-choice advocates in greater Boston.
>
> Stites and other COAIC leaders deny responsibility for the harassment, but Seitchek believes the barrage of hate mail she has received constitutes an attempt by the religious right to stifle free and accurate expression of scientific views.
>
> "The science of earthquakes is a science of uncertainties," Seitchek said. "By admitting this uncertainty we run the risk of appearing to allow room for superstition, and yet if a scientist tries to forestall this and draw a sharp line between scientific debate and moral debate, she apparently is running the risk of being harassed by Philip Stites."

According to the box, Stites's "successful prediction" of the recent earthquakes had attracted dozens of new followers to his church, which was still housed in the shaky tenement in Chelsea. The church claimed to have suffered "no real damage" since moving in, though by now nearly every home north of Cambridge had had a few dishes broken or walls cracked.

Cumulative property damage, in fact, had reached an estimated $100 million, with more than 80 percent of it due to the most recent pair of quakes near Peabody. On a sheet of paper marked THEIR FAULT, Louis wrote:

April 20, Peabody	$3,400,000
May 10–11, Peabody	$80,000,000+

It gave him great satisfaction to carry all the zeroes out.

In her spare moments, Renée was continuing to develop the

scientific case against Sweeting-Aldren, studying every documented instance of induced seismicity. Louis was glad to see her working, but he was in no hurry for her to finish. The longer they delayed taking action against the company, the more time the earth had to shudder again under Peabody and cause further damage and run the company's tab to still more satisfying heights. In his view, Sweeting-Aldren's management were slimes and enemies of nature, and he wanted to see them bankrupt, if not in jail. He felt a suspense almost erotic in intensity as he waited, day after day, for the next large earthquake. To occupy himself, he began to read basic seismology texts while Renée was away at work.

Late in the afternoon on Wednesday she came back to the apartment with a new manila folder filled with photocopies. She'd been at Widener reading old newspapers.

"Some interesting things here," she said.

He opened the folder greedily, but she stopped him. "Let's get your stuff. I'll tell you later."

It was summer again. Heat coiled off car roofs in the no man's land of Davis Square, the marquee of the Somerville Theater trembling in the giddy swirl of gas fumes. Louis and Renée had been going to the theater at night for cheap double features and free airconditioning.

On Belknap Street the soprano had her windows open and sounded near death. The voice seemed to come from everywhere. It was a sound so wide that it didn't seem capable of having issued from as narrow a thing as a human mouth. "I would like to make this person selfconscious," Renée said. Louis put her to work in the kitchen, the room farthest from the hell of melodious torments. The soprano screamed and screamed. The tortured ear could not believe that no person of authority was coming with a needle or a gun to stop the misery, for humanity's sake. Louis slid the catch down the front storm door's piston and got some rope out of the Civic. The futon was going to ride on top.

"Hey, Lou. Lou! Where you been?" John Mullins came down his porch stairs angrily. He planted his feet in the driveway with his head thrust forward like a desert prophet's. A cyst-like glob of sweat was hanging on his chin. "People been *lookin'* for you, Lou," he said, all opprobrium. "Where you *been?* Where you *been?* Oh my God, you're not movin' out, are you? Lou? You're not movin' out? Whatsa matter, don't you, don't you, don't you like it around here?"

"I love it here," Louis said above the aria. "I'm just making sure all my things fit in the car."

"Heh, little Hondacivic. You like this car? Oh, hey, Lou, that girl that was here looking for you, she ever find you? You know who I'm talking about? Pretty girl."

The instinctive part of Louis, the part connected to blood pressure and stomach, not the cognitive part, asked Mullins, "When was this?"

"This morning. About nine, nine-thirty. I was readin' the paper. I told her you're not around much in the day."

"What did she look like?"

"Big girl. Said she was looking for you."

"Fat girl with glasses?"

"No, no. Pretty girl. She had a suitcase."

Louis went inside. Almost immediately he came back out and looked at the car, trying to remember what he had to do. He touched the car once, on the hood, and went inside directly to his room and walked in circles. Renée packed plangently in the kitchen, flatware hitting skillet, the carton grunting as its flaps were folded under one another. He was supposed to pick things up and carry them to the car. However, everything he looked at with a view to carrying it seemed to be the wrong thing to carry at that particular moment. He kept walking around the room. He was like the person whose house is on fire who can't decide what possession is most precious and so can rescue nothing. The only thing he knew for sure he wanted was to murder the soprano voice, which had begun to hold long, high notes and exaggerate the tremolo. But this voice, its incessancy, now seemed to him a fundamental property of the world that he was powerless to alter. He stood by his window facing the soprano where she sang behind her opaque screens. He was not unhappy or happy. The wave front advanced across the mountains, changing the landscape as it came, and then he was in it, he was in it. That was all.

Sooner than he'd expected, he heard voices in the front of the apartment. Female voices. Footsteps. Renée appeared, the carton in her arms. She spoke like a fugitive's imperfectly deceived mother, when the police are at the door.

"There's somebody here to see you."

She stepped aside, opening the way past her, pointedly recusing herself from the difficulty. When instead of leaving he looked at her and tried to say something, she was compelled to add: "It's your friend Lauren."

"Oh," he said. "Oh."

He felt her eyes on him as he walked up the hall, felt the whole weight of her possession of him, and so it was not entirely a surprise that the girl standing just inside the front door, by a small straw-colored suitcase with a black leather jacket draped over it, should strike him as a vision of liberation. Lauren was tan and fair-haired and taller than he remembered her. One glance made clear how busily his mind had been training itself to appreciate Renée—to see those parts of her that were cute and fresh and to overlook the larger fact, which was that she was thirty years old and not beautiful. He could recognize a bill of large denomination without reading the numbers on it, and he could recognize Lauren's beauty without referring to her long, muscled twenty-two-year-old's legs, her golden twenty-two-year-old's skin, her silky twenty-two-year-old's hair, now grown out nearly to her shoulders. She was wearing the same plaid ruffled miniskirt she'd had on the first time he saw her, similar black shoes and ankle socks, and a white tank top damp with sweat between her breasts.

The soprano, breaking off, had left an unwelcome stillness.

"Hi Louis," Lauren said in a flat, unsteady voice, not looking at him.

"Hi, uh. What's up?"

"Nothing. I just came to see you."

"Where's Emmett?"

She gave no sign of having heard him.

"Not here, obviously," Louis said.

She bit her lips, still not looking at him.

"Where is he, Lauren?"

She raised her chin and said, "We're not together anymore."

"Oh, I see. You left him. He left you. You're separated. You're divorced."

These words caused her great discomfort. She looked at her shoes, inspecting either side of one of them. "I don't know. Can I come in?"

"Maybe not."

"I made a terrible mistake, Louis, a *terrible mistake*. Can I come in?"

"What do you want?"

"I want to know if I'm too late. If I'm too late I won't come in. Can I come in?"

Renée was now standing in the doorway between the dining room and kitchen. She and Lauren couldn't see each other, but Louis could see them both.

"That was your girlfriend, wasn't it," Lauren said.

He turned to Renée as if he had to check about this. Renée's face made it clear that she thought he ought to have been rid of the visitor by now. She gestured impatiently: Well? What are you waiting for! But as he continued not to speak, her impatience gave way to alarm, and then the alarm gave way to pain, and finally the pain gave way to an overwhelming disbelief, each of these stages visible and distinct.

"Oh, is she right there?" Lauren said with mock stupidity.

You can hurt me. A little. You can bite me, or—

He was aware of making a mistake, but he had no control. He was fascinated by the pain in Renée's face. He was finally seeing her. She was finally naked, and he kept looking at her, thinking *I am a rapist too. I am a sadist too* as he hurt her for his pleasure, doing it with his silence and understanding now what people meant when they talked about how a penis can rule a man, because that was exactly how it felt. But she was a person, just a decent person, and not interested in taking this. With terrible dignity she walked through the dining room and living room. She stepped around Lauren, who leaned aside as if avoiding a stranger on the sidewalk. Renée knocked the leather jacket off the suitcase, barely managing not to trip on it as she hurried out the door.

"Oh boy," Louis murmured, to the empty space she left behind. He couldn't believe all the blood on his hands.

Lauren closed the door and hung her jacket on the knob. "She was your girlfriend, wasn't she. You can tell me."

"Oh boy," he murmured again. He hadn't quite been sober enough to realize that what he was doing to Renée was the worst thing anyone could do to her. But he knew her and he knew this was the worst thing. It was the very worst thing. And though he hadn't "realized" this, he'd known it perfectly well.

"I figured you might have one," Lauren said, slouching almost horizontal on the beige sofa. "It was a risk I was taking. But I knew I could always turn around and go right back."

The fact that she would have to walk to her apartment now. The pride with which she'd walk the two and a half miles. And the dogs wouldn't howl, and she'd take the stairs two at a time in her sneakers and jeans and T-shirt, and lock the door behind her, and would she cry? Only once had he seen her cry, and that was from physical pain, and as soon as she'd locked the door, in his mind's eye, it became difficult to see her.

"You want me to go?" Lauren said. "She'll forgive you if you explain things. Just tell her the truth and she'll forgive you." She spread her fingers and studied her nails. "You know, because I don't want to butt in, if she's your girlfriend. She is your girlfriend, isn't she. I could tell by the way she looked at me. She's your girlfriend."

"Yeah."

"So do you love her?" Lauren swung her head nervously, not wanting to hear the answer. "I can leave right now."

"No! No. Just . . . let me lock my car."

Renée wasn't waiting by the car or anywhere close to it. He looked at the empty air above the sidewalk down which she necessarily had walked, since she was no longer in sight. Logic insisted that she'd traversed this distance even if no one had seen her do it. It further insisted that at this very moment she was somewhere between here and her apartment, not on just any block but on some particular block, walking forward, visible to all. It insisted that an observer in a balloon could have followed every step she took between leaving here and arriving on Pleasant Avenue and climbing the four crumbling concrete stairs to the door of her house and disappearing inside it.

Louis thought: I hate her.

As soon as he was inside again, Lauren stood up, stretched

her arms luxuriantly, and smiled as if it were morning and she'd
slept divinely and she knew that he, of all people, would be happy
to know this. Freed of the burden of seeing her through Renée's
eyes, he was now properly amazed to have in Toby's beige apartment this pretty and complicated girl he'd loved so much. She came
to him and put her face against his, bending back for a moment
to snatch his glasses off. Not kissing him, but with her eyes staring
into his with the astonishment and goofy emptiness that eyes take
on at point-blank range, and with her nose pressed against his and
her words making his lips vibrate, she said, "I am in love with you,
I am in love with you, Louis, I've been thinking about you every
minute of the day, I am in *love* with you, I love you I love you I
love you I love you I love you."

She caught her breath, her pupils and milky gray-green irises
still centered in his vision. She kissed him, placed his hands on
various parts of herself, curled up her own hands and pressed her
knuckles on his chest. She twisted her head back and forth beneath
his mouth, as if he were a shower she was taking. Her perfume
was so integrated with her sweaty face-smell that his nose couldn't
find the border between them, it was all one nice Laureny smell.

"I promise you," she said. "I'll do *anything* for you. I'll stay,
I'll go away, I'll stay with Emmett, I'll leave Emmett, I'll marry
you, I'll have babies for you, I'll work for you, I'll marry you, I'll
live with you without being married to you. I'll do anything. I'll
stay for as long as you want me to and I'll leave whenever you say,
you can own me, you can throw me away or keep me, you can do
anything but sell me, anything, anything, anything."

He held her, remembering her specific dimensions and how
her back had felt when she'd cried in his kitchen in Houston and
he'd put his arms around her.

"Oh Louis," she said, crying and smiling. "You were so good
to me, and I was so bad to you. But I'm going to make it up to
you. If you let me, I'll make it up to you."

"Although of course you're married now."

"Oh, that." A familiar guilty, sullen look crossed her face.
"You know, I'm still trying to be a good person. I'm trying to love
God and be a Christian, and I'm here in Boston seeing you. Marriage
is a holy sacrament and I'm here seeing you. It's like I'm the same

old person, right? Everything I touch turns into garbage. And the thing is you're the only person I've ever met who thinks I'm worth something. The only person. Remember when I told you I'd never really loved anybody?"

"Yes."

"Well, it was true. It was true. But it's not true now, because as soon as I couldn't see you anymore, I felt this thing. I guess I thought it was guilt or something, but I wanted to see you and talk to you, just to hear your voice a little, but I'd already told you we couldn't, and I thought you must hate me, or that you wouldn't believe me anyway."

She sat on the sofa and frowned as if something didn't quite make sense. "You see," she said, "but there was Emmett too, and I felt sorry for him because he'd always been so incredibly patient with me, plus his family really seemed to like me. They gave me all this stuff when we got engaged, his grandmother gave me these beautiful pearls and his mother gave this inlaid box that was like a hundred and fifty years old and had been in the family forever. But then I slept with some other guys and I also said I'd slept with you that time, right under his nose, and I gave him his ring back but I never even had the courage to give the other stuff back. And then when we started to get back together they were all still incredibly nice to me. They treated me like I'd been sick but now I was well, and I just felt so sorry for them, and really grateful too, and I thought, you know, This is the sacrifice I'm going to make. Because all I wanted was to be a *good person*. And it's so clear that if you want to be good you have to sacrifice things. Plus I thought, they're all so nice to me, it's not even that much of a sacrifice. And my parents wanted me to get married because they think Emmett's really great, which he is, I guess, except I don't love him. I only love you."

Louis closed his eyes.

"But so. We got married." Lauren chewed her lip, her eyes on some remembered scene or ceremony. He thought she was going to go on, but apparently this was all she had to say.

"So then what. It turns out he's a brute."

She shook her head.

"Yes? No?"

Perched on the edge of the sofa, she stared sullenly at a silver radiator. She tossed her head, flipping her hair off her shoulders. Her face was tough and uncaring. "I was unfaithful to him."

"Right. Of course."

"Aren't I a great person, Louis? Aren't I just the greatest? But there was this guy I knew from before, and it was like I had so much more in common with him than with Emmett, you know, he'd fuck anybody, you know that kind of person, and I just didn't care. I could tell I'd made too big a sacrifice, and it was like I needed to do some rotten stuff to make up, you know, and balance things. I don't know. I don't know what I was thinking. I guess what I finally realized was that I wanted him to throw me out again because there was this thing in me. And what the thing was, was that I was in love with another person who used to be in love with me until I hurt him, and I loved him so much, and I missed him." Tears came to her eyes again and she lowered her chin, as though trying to burp, still staring at the radiator. "I mean, Emmett's real nice and all. But he treats me like this sick baby, and after a while I can't stand it, so I go and do this horrible shit to him, but that just makes it all the more clear that I'm this sick baby, you know. And finally I just don't believe anymore that somewhere inside him behind all his niceness he doesn't really just hate my guts and wish I was dead."

There was a long silence. Louis felt panic at the thought of Renée, who during these minutes when he hadn't been thinking about her had doubtless made it all the way back to her apartment. Time was passing in her life even as it was standing still in his. She was getting all this time to think while he was not.

A question in a low voice crossed the room: "What's her name?"

"Who? Oh. Renée."

"That's a pretty name."

"She hates it."

"She does?"

"So she says."

"Is she in love with you?"

"I don't know."

"Are you guys really boy- and girlfriend?"

"I don't know."

"Do you think you might want to go out with me? I mean, right now?"

"Aren't you tired?"

"Yeah, but I want to go out with you. That's what I've wanted all day. I just have to go to the bathroom."

They were getting in his car when John Mullins came lurching and paddling down the driveway from behind his house. He aimed his ghastly face at Louis, his mouth like a gunshot wound, and stared without a trace of recognition.

"Have you ever been up here?" Louis said.

Lauren shook her head. "It's nice. It's so different. We've been hearing about all the earthquakes. Were you in them? Were you scared?"

"Nah."

The polygons of dirt between the footpaths in Harvard Yard had been seeded and roped off to fatten up the grass for the trampling pleasure of graduates and parents and alumni, later in June. For some reason a handful of women from the Church of Action in Christ were picketing the Holyoke Center, carrying large photographs of aborted fetuses. The colors were garish and oily, like Korean pickles. The messages were topical: QUAKES ARE GOD'S WRATH. CAMBRIDGE = EPICENTER OF BUTCHERY. PSALM 139.

By the Red Line escalators, young punks were drinking vodka and kicking beanbags. Hare Krishnas in robes the color of orange sherbet drummed and juggled in front of the Coop. Lauren swung her shoulders as she walked, undaunted by the scene. The pedestrians in the side streets, the men with scrubbed faces and narrow little shoes, the women with thin hair and small mouths and ultra-sexy shades, posed no threat to her confidence. She put her hand in Louis's back pocket. A year ago this had been all he wanted, just to walk down the street with her and be her man.

They stopped outside a slightly worn Tex-Mex establishment. He shied from the door—the clientele was what Renée would have called "the implicating people" and what he considered "the Eileen's-friends kind of people"—but Lauren towed him in. She had them seated in the smoking section, explaining in a low voice that she still smoked and drank a little, because she'd realized that it was impossible to make yourself perfect all at once. "The only time I haven't been a mess was last summer, when I was seeing you. That's the only time in my whole life I haven't felt like a mess. You helped me so much. And I was so bad to you."

She leaned back to allow room on her lap for a menu. Louis asked what she was doing for money. She said she was using her American Express card, which Emmett's parents paid the bills for. "It's pretty rotten of me, isn't it? To fly up here like that."

"Are you going to pay them back?"

She shrugged. "They're real well off."

"You should pay them back as soon as you can."

She nodded obediently. "OK."

He cast a benign smile on the loud students at neighboring tables. What a convivial and pleasant thing it could be to be normal and eat in a cheerful restaurant surrounded by other young people doing the same, and how especially pleasant to do it in the company of a pretty girl who had just declared her love. His towering resentment of the likes of the all-befouling Mr. Aldren dwindled to an irritation he could take or leave. It was true that when Lauren left him and their fajita dinners alone even for one minute, while she went to the bathroom, the fires in him reignited, and he began to burn holes in the heads of a table of male and female law students who kept making their harried waitress banter with them. A cake with candles came, and, being very original, four of the five men sang harmony instead of melody. By the time they were singing *Dear Nico-ole*, the fifth man had decided to be creative and original too, and so only the females were left to do the melody. But when Lauren returned and said maybe they could go dancing, Louis calmed down immediately. He gave her credit card a wistful look. He was pretty close to broke.

Cool lawns and cigarette smoke, a warm June night. It had now been five hours since Renée walked away; she'd now had five hours to be thinking by herself. Louis bought a *Phoenix* and Lauren picked out a club across the river which, when they got there, he was amazed to think had been operating probably every night he'd been in Boston, providing fun for a crowd whose median age was roughly his own. They put their hands out to get them stamped, the buckles and wrist strap on Lauren's jacket dangling. He didn't mention that the only time in his life he'd ever consented to dance was at a May Day party in Nantes, among Algerians. Fortunately the club was already crowded and it was mostly a matter of bumping and clutching anyway, and except for some rap cuts the music was abhorrent and difficult to move to, the rhythm "shallow," as restaurant reviewers sometimes say of spice in chili, it had a "searing, superficial heat" rather than the "deep burning heat" that comes from careful cooking and good ingredients. But with Lauren in his arms he could taste the joys of being uncritical.

They drove up Soldiers Field Road with the windows down and her hair billowing and migrating towards her inside shoulder, the river moving against the lights of MIT and Harvard, the lights moving against the six northern stars visible in the muggy night. That it was one-thirty meant Renée had now had nearly eight hours to be alone and think, but he computed the figure only out of habit, because he could no longer imagine her so well.

In his apartment they lay down in their clothes on his futon and Lauren tried his glasses on. "This is what you're like," she said, crawling over him, the glasses sliding down her nose and her hair hanging on his ears. It had been a long time since he'd seen anyone as happy as she was. She was full of sport and it suited both their needs to be like teenagers, enjoying the clothes that kept them separate, taking very small steps down the carnal road, enjoying the countryside along the road, its season and smells, and remembering when a season was so long that you forgot that other seasons followed it, and a smell was a smell and a sound was a sound, sensations not yet clogged with memories. At length, when they heard his roommate Toby's printer starting up, they took some clothes off. Lauren handed her breasts over casually, like surplus charms she was glad to donate to the needy. But when he put his hand in her underpants she stopped him, saying,

"Don't."

"Don't you—?"

"I don't need it," she said, very hoarse.

He lay on his back, needing it very much.

"If we did that now," she said, bending over him and tickling his chest with hers. "We'd just be pigs."

He pictured Renée alone in her apartment and thought he might as well have been a pig already.

"Don't you think?" Lauren whispered. "Don't you think we should just start right now trying to be strong and do the right thing? Don't you think there are certain things we shouldn't do if we're not going to stay together? Can't we just be happy like this?"

Louis seriously doubted there was any way at all for him to be happy. He knew that if he promised to love her, she'd take off her underpants and let him come inside her, and that somehow it would be easy then for him to dump her and go back to Renée. What stopped him wasn't the fear of hurting her. It was that he had always been good to her, and he believed she really loved him now, and he couldn't stand the idea of killing her precarious faith in a human being's goodness. All he could do was lie still and hope she'd fuck him anyway, faithlessly, out of a pity he didn't deserve. Then he could be rid of her.

"Don't you believe I love you?" She rested her chin on his thigh. "You have to. You have to give me time to show you how much I love you. You have to give me chances, because I do love you, Louis. I adore you. I adore you." She kissed his penis through fabric; it rocked stormily. "I'll do anything for you, if you just give me a chance. But if you really think you might still love me, but you're not sure, you won't ask me to do certain things yet."

"Your ticket," he said. "Do you have an open date of return?"

"I flew one-way."

"God, the Osterlitzes will really love you for that."

"No, I flew standby. I flew standby."

"Well, I think you should try to get a flight back on Sunday."

"And stay where?"

"You've got to have some friends you could stay with."

"Can't I go to Chicago with you?"

"No. I have to think."

"But you'll come back here, and she'll be here. And even if you see her just to tell her you want to break up with her you'll forget me and you'll want to stay with her. And I'll be hanging around in Austin waiting to hear from you, and then I'll have to come up here again, but you'll already have decided you love her more."

He didn't know what to say to this.

"But you're right," Lauren said. "You're right, but you have to look me in the eye and swear to God you won't forget about me. You have to promise you're going to think about me."

"Not a problem."

"Because I don't want you if you don't really want me. I don't want you to always be thinking you made the wrong decision, like I had to. I don't want you to be unhappy. I'll go, Louis. I'll go to Austin, because I love you so much. But you have to promise me you'll think about me."

"That's not going to be a problem."

"I love you so much. I love you so much. I love you so much . . ."

Over and over he dreamed that he was missing his flight. He was in waiting rooms with Lauren and she was cold to him; he had to beg her for a smile and a kind word. Over and over he realized that it was a day earlier than he'd thought and that he hadn't missed the flight at all. But this proved to be a delusion every time. It was Sunday and he saw a wall clock and realized he had three seconds to get to the other end of the airport. He could already see the plane being pushed back from its gate.

They were awakened by the buzzing of afternoon insects. Summer days that you wake into the middle of are angry with you, branches and dusty leaves tossing in a hot southern wind, air-conditioners working hard. Louis was speaking to Toby on the phone when Lauren emerged from her shower. "It's like Houston," she said. "I thought it was supposed to be cold up here."

Late in the evening they drove to Pleasant Avenue. Although he knew it was an evil thing, he let her brush aside his objections and come along with him. She waited in the car while he went inside. The Dobermans threw themselves against their door, but the lock held. Upstairs, taped to Renée's door, he found an envelope with his first name written on it in her principled hand. It contained his plane tickets and nothing else. Two DeMoula's bags were standing on the landing, his dirty clothes in one of them. The clean clothes had been folded and bagged with his tapes and miscellany. His TV set stood to one side.

Through the landing window he saw an immense white

Matador parked across the street. It was Howard Chun's. Cigarette smoke, ghostly in the cigarette-smoke-colored streetlight, was rising from Louis's Civic.

He put his eye to the keyhole; the kitchen light was on. He put his ear against the door; there was no sound but the ear itself rustling against wood. Then the Civic's horn honked, and he gathered up the bags and television and ran down the stairs, almost forgetting to drop his key into the mailbox.

II

I ♥ Life

7

The anglicizing of Howard Chun began when he was nine years old and his family enrolled him at the Queen Victoria Academy in suburban Taipei, an outpost of the Anglican Church where the letters of the English alphabet, each holding the hand of its lower-case daughter, paraded around the third-grade classroom between the chalkboards and the color head shots of Jesus, and instruction in Chinese was elective in the upper forms. By rights Howard ought to have become his class's Henry, since his given name was Hsing-hai, but there was a rival boy named Ho-kwang whose parents had done a better job than Howard's mother of pre-programming their son to demand what was due him for the 30,000 Taiwanese dollars that a year in Queen Victoria's lower school then cost. Ho-kwang grabbed Henry when the English names were being apportioned, and Hsing-hai, blinking back tears as he glared at the hoggish Henry né Ho-kwang, was given the less pleasing and regal Howard, his dispossession ordained and sealed by the Church of England before he'd even grasped what was happening.

Howard's mother was a screen actress. She'd lived one of those colorful lives engendered by the union of war and money. She had no great acting talent, but as a girl she'd made a medium-sized splash in Beijing's bourgeois cinema, most notably in the title role in *Maple-Tree Girl*, an otherwise forgettable film containing one immortal sequence in which Maple-Tree Girl is pursued by a rug merchant with immoral aims through the great Wuhan flood of

1931, eleven stupendous minutes of this chaste beauty staggering through ever deeper and dirtier water and more menacing locales, clutching her rent garment to her throat, her round eyes radiating unmodulated terror and anguish for the entire fifteen thousand frames. In the mid-forties, Miss Chun and a director old enough to be her father lived in fashionable exile in Singapore and ate up the pretty nest egg she'd set aside, making it necessary for her and her three young children to join her relatives in Taipei as soon as the Nationalists were back in the movie business. For a while she was prized by casting directors in need of "the less pretty older sister," and she subsequently spent many lucrative years playing a wicked stepmother on a soap opera called "Hostages of Love." At least once in every installment of "Hostages" the camera caught her baring her teeth and rolling her eyes, to remind viewers of her evil, scheming nature. In real life she was vague and good-natured and selfish, and mainly lived for eating sweets. When Howard came home from Queen Victoria on days when she wasn't filming, he would find her sitting up in bed, chewing in slow motion on some piece of candied fruit, frowning as though the flavor were a message trickling into her head by telegraph, which she had to strain to catch each word of.

Howard was her fifth and youngest child and the only one she'd had by a man of whom nobody in the family, including her, could furnish a satisfactory account. She indicated in a general way that the man was a war hero, "a noble spirit commanding troops in the struggle for freedom," though by the time Howard heard this, the Nationalists had been out of combat for twenty years. Occasionally he tried to picture his male parent up in the sky someplace, a marshal in the mile-thick tropical clouds above the Yellow Sea, at an altitude where hostilities hadn't ceased, but the picture was ridiculous and he made himself think about other things.

Howard's aunts and great-aunts were a philosophical bunch, willing to wink at the lapses in his mother's personal morality for the sake of the income she provided. They huddled and rustled in hallways, managing income; one was never sure in whose canvas neckbag her savings passbook could be found. Howard much preferred his aunts' realism to his mother's reveries, and consequently grew up feeling more like a pampered houseguest than a child. He never really adolesced. After his mother died, he adopted an easy, overfamiliar manner with his elders, hanging around the kitchen with them like a middle-aged man between jobs, the kind of family friend or much-removed relative who dropped in for dinner every day for a year and then was never heard from again. Altogether, though he was the brightest child in the house and no reasonable expense was spared in educating him, he wasted vast amounts of time; and whenever an aunt descanted on the brightness of his future he would leer at her strangely, as if this Hsing-hai of whom she spoke were a pathetic figment who only he, Howard, was privileged to know had no intention of inhabiting the future she foresaw.

One day he announced that he was going to college in America. His eldest half brother was a wing captain in the Nationalist Air Force and could have opened doors for him there, but he saw no reason to donate three years of his life to the military if it could possibly be avoided. He had long legs, and his visions of manned flight focused on nip-sized whiskey bottles, swizzle sticks shaped like propellers, and roomy first-class seats.

As a matter of law, his pacifism required that when he left Taipei, at the age of eighteen, he not return for at least seventeen years. Any regrets he had about this did not survive his first bus ride in America. One glimpse of girls in cowboy boots, one glance at a billboard-freckled hillside, one eyeful of U.S. 36 north of Denver—the Denny'ses and Arby'ses and Wendy'ses, the tall man's cars in the big man's lanes—sufficed to set his mind at rest: This was the place for him. He reclined in his seat to the maximum degree permitted and dozed until the bus arrived in Boulder.

Nobody could have loved life in America more than Howard Chun. Within a month of his arrival he had a MasterCard; within a semester he had a car. Everywhere he went his freshman year the Bee Gees were in the air, and he was among the first to catch the fever and the last to sweat it out. He loved to say "disco." He loved to dance it. He loved to freeze in a strobe and stretch his arm out with his fist clenched. With regard to dating, he was a fair success; certainly he wasn't so choosy as to often have to do without a girl. He liked fast food not because it was fast but because it tasted good. Various governments funded his education, and whatever else he needed to keep his charge accounts in trim came his way by serendipity, which often took the form of an export or an import or a trade, since he was always traveling and there were always friends and relatives willing to pay a premium on portable commodities. He regularly took $300 worth of new records and cassette tapes to the post office, wrote "records, tapes" on the customs slip, and six weeks later received a cashier's check for $600 U.S. from an older cousin in Taipei. Nightlifewise, these checks were enabling and sustaining. What he was doing was perhaps not very legal, but he never got caught and so never knew for sure.

All in all he had so much fun in Colorado that it took him five years and constant threats from the financial aid office to get his B.A. But just as his financial debts never stopped him from being a sharer of pizzas and stander-to of beers and offerer of rides, so his stints in the academic doghouse in no way interfered with his role as a selfless helper of younger students (especially blond female students) and as a central cog in the geology department's social life. In the spring of his fourth year, he had the good fortune to break both his legs on a ski slope. The senior thesis he wrote while he was on his back was fine enough to win him an aid package from Harvard.

At Harvard he decided to protect himself academically by mastering the ins and outs of the departmental computer. This way, the machine could do his work for him and he would only have to drop by the lab once a day, on his way to the squash courts or after a movie in the Square, and pick up the completed work and give the computer fresh instructions. Being a computer expert entitled him to skip the occasional class or seminar and discuss the material with his professors at times that didn't interfere with his sleep or social schedule. The only professor who objected to this mode of operation was Howard's adviser, who, in the spring of Howard's third year in Cambridge, raised his voice to new heights and said he considered it improbable that Howard would pass his orals. He was also tactless enough to wonder aloud how Howard could have accomplished so much less in three years than Renée Seitchek, for example, had accomplished in two. Renée Seitchek had effortlessly passed her own orals and was expanding her second-year project into a dissertation.

Though officially a year behind him, Seitchek was Howard's age or slightly older. Unlike him, she worked all summer and attended just one convention a year. When scientists from other institutions called the lab, they asked to speak to her even when their questions pertained to Howard's field. She went to dinners and parties thrown by faculty and other students; she only refused to go to the dinners and parties Howard threw. During her first year, he'd frequently proposed that she play squash or have a meal with him, and she was so polite and smiling in her refusals that it had taken him a whole semester to get the message.

Whenever he stopped by the lab to check on his work (he did this standing up, leaning over a keyboard, without removing his coat or unwinding his scarf), he could see Seitchek working implacably on her projects, her arm muscles losing their youthful tone from month to month, white strands appearing in her hair, her complexion picking up the gray of the fluorescent lighting while he, who played lots of squash and frequently vacationed, remained fit and rosy-cheeked. It was Seitchek who noticed that his programs were consuming too much CPU time and swamping the array processor every morning (while he was sleeping). She raised her voice and took the same Howard-you-have-been-told-and-told-and-told tone with him as his adviser did. When further funding proved unavailable, he had to abandon his work on strong motion, though everyone agreed that his inversions of acceleration records might eventually have shown interesting results if he'd had his own private supercomputer. He was forced to beat the bushes for a new project even as Seitchek homed in on her Ph.D.

Then one summer—it was the summer before the local earthquakes started—everyone stopped liking her. Maybe it was because the last of her older friends had left the department, or maybe because her new thesis adviser, the department chairman, had gone on leave for a year, but in a matter of weeks she managed to alienate practically every student and post-doc who remained. Terry Snall reported that he'd overheard her using an offensive word in reference to his manner; the word was rumored to be "faggy." One morning computer users found that valuable documents of theirs had been dumped in the trash for no worse sin than being part of the foot-deep drifts of paper engulfing the consoles in the system rooms. There soon followed an ugly scene when various students discovered that Seitchek was lowering the priorities of their jobs so that her programs would run fast while theirs stalled. She made one young woman cry and one immature petrologist so angry that he threw a wastebasket at the telephone and broke a table lamp. When Terry Snall stuck up for the petrologist, she became a pillar of rage. She said that 70 percent of the computer's funding came from her adviser's grants. She said that for three years she had personally done more than half the daily maintenance of the system, and if anyone wanted to argue with her they should begin by calling the chairman in California and see whose judgment *he* trusted, and ask him what *he* thought, whether *he* thought she had no right to lower the priorities, whether *he* thought that the petrologists who contributed nothing to the system or its upkeep had any rights here whatsoever. Howard strolled into the lab to check on his programs just as Seitchek was storming up the hall. He found Snall inciting the petrologist to lower her priority, now that she was out of the room.

His own turn came a few days later, right before he flew to London for a cousin's wedding and a week's vacation in Ireland. He'd stopped by the lab to set in motion a few hundred twenty-minute batch jobs to run while he was gone, and to collect his messages. Without really meaning to, he'd gotten involved with a Chinese-American engineer named Sally Go, who seemed to think he'd promised her something and burst into tears whenever he tried to find out what. He was pretty sure she thought he'd promised to marry her the following spring, but since she refused to say so, insisting instead on weeping and repeating, "You *know* what you promised," he in turn felt justified in barking, "What? What? What I promise? What?" He had now managed not to see Sally for some three and a half weeks, and the daily notes she left on his desk had begun to treat themes like "cowardice" and "skunkiness" and "disgrace." He was reading her latest, his nose scrunched up in displeasure, when he heard Seitchek across the hall in the system rooms.

"You'd think," she said, "that in ten years he might have learned to make an *r* sound. I'm going to have a *stroke* if I hear him say 'compyu pogam' one more time. Compyu pogam. Compyu pogam." Her voice was rushed and squeaky with malice. "I'm write me a compyu pogam cacawate weast squares."

Howard's eyes filled. He reeled out of his office blinking violently, scowling and jerking his head as if to clear it of an unwelcome hallucination. But it was no hallucination, and he knew it. Ten-plus years in America had done little to correct the crippling his language skills had suffered at the Queen Victoria Academy. The English instructor for the upper forms, Mrs. Hennahant, had taught phonetics on the principle that it was contagious, and she was curiously deaf to the immunity her students displayed. Day after day she repeated sentences like "*Hilary* plays the *clarinet,*" and then nodded sagely to the rhythm of the students' voices as each in turn reproduced this as "Hirry prays crarenet." After they'd all spoken she would nod and strut and try once again to hammer the hopelessly bent nail into their heads: "*Hilary* plays the *clarinet. Hilary* plays the *clarinet.* The alimentary—*canal.* The *alimentary—canal.* Henry?"

Back from London ten days later, Howard had just enough time to stop by the lab before flying on to San Francisco, where a different cousin was getting married. He removed several cubic feet of printouts from the line-printer basket and the counter next to it. Science had grown fifty kilos richer while he was touring Dublin and County Cork, and he added another hundred jobs to the batch queue to ensure that his time in California would be similarly productive.

Seitchek was sitting in their office with her feet up on a suitcase. He asked her if there had been any phone calls for him. Her "no" didn't faze him. Sometimes she answered no and then, when she'd reconciled herself to being interrupted, changed her mind and reeled off several interesting phone messages.

"Edward's looking for you," she said at length. "He heard you were back from London."

Edward was the name of Howard's ultra-picky adviser.

"Oh yeah," he said. The uppermost note from Sally on his desktop said *FORGET IT!!*

"He wants to see you on Monday," Seitchek said. "First thing in the morning. Something new on Alan Grubb, I think."

He beamed. "Can't come on Monday. Going to San Francisco." He nodded at Seitchek's suitcase. "What about you?"

"L.A.," she said. "I mean Orange County. I'm going to see my parents and my little . . . nieces. It's my every-third-year visit."

"Oh yeah." He had an uneasy feeling that this meant she'd finished her thesis while he was in Ireland. "Three years a long time," he croaked politely.

"Not long enough."

"You wanna ride to the airport?"

"No thanks," she said.

"You wanna ride to the Square?"

"You're very eager to have me ride in your car, aren't you?"

He shrugged. "I'm double-parked."

In California, large lesions of greasy orange flame were eating up the ranges from Eureka to the San Gabriels. Even in the city the air smelled like burning houses. For the first time in the longest time, Howard was sorry to be traveling. Neither the wedding on Saturday afternoon nor the banquet the same night in Chinatown measured up to the nuptial festivities in London. For one thing, the median age of the wedding guests was less than twelve. Howard wore a zootish pinstripe suit and Dock-Sides, without socks; he was the tallest person present. Since his more important relatives had already cornered him in London and updated themselves on his brilliant career, he spent many minutes by himself, drinking beer from a can and wearing an expression of dignity and moderate discomfort as he gazed down on the wizened heads of great-great-aunts and the high-fashion hairstyles of the pre-adolescents. He was getting sick of weddings.

On Sunday morning he steered his rented car east towards the hills in which he planned to do some camping and casual inspection of fault scarps. There was a bromine-colored pall above the country he was entering, and soon he began to pass blackened fire fighters who had thrown themselves on the road embankment and were sleeping. Already the fires surrounded him on all sides. Changing his mind, he headed for the coast again, wondering if maybe the time hadn't come to confront Alan Grubb. Grubb was a student at

Scripps Institution in San Diego whose thesis was rumored to be identical in content to Howard's own and two years closer to completion. Howard been told and told and told, by Edward and Seitchek and other stand-ins for his conscience, that he ought to give Grubb a call or try to see him at a convention, but until now he'd only blinked at their suggestions.

At a supermarket north of Santa Barbara he bought a three-pack of Latin disco tapes, and by midnight he was sleeping in his bucket seat on a side street in central San Diego. At nine the next morning he drove to Scripps. It was dead in the Labor Day sun. A watchman led him to a laboratory where, from a beachfront window, a dour post-doc told him that Alan Grubb would not be back from Italy until September 23. The moral was so plain that it might have been posted in institutional ceramic letters over the entrance to the lab: IT PAYS TO PHONE AHEAD.

Later in the day, after a productive tanning session, Howard invited himself to visit some friends of his oldest half sister who lived nearby in Linda Vista. He had decent barbecue there. As the afternoon aged, he slouched in his plastic chair and watched the ponderous plate-like migrations of the ice blocks his hosts cooled their pool with, his face almost purple from the martinis he'd been given, his spirits sinking at the thought of spending one more minute in a rented car or entering one more Wendy's or logging one more frequent-flyer bonus mile. Burnt sesame seeds were falling from the chins of the hosts' children. His own Mandarin small talk sounded whiny and bitchy to his Americanized ear. Compyu pogam, compyu pogam. He asked to use the telephone, and his hosts led him to it, urging him to stay in Linda Vista for as long as he liked; they hoped (indeed already planned) to take him deep-sea fishing and to Sea World.

Directory assistance had a single Seitchek listed in Newport Beach. As soon as he heard her voice, Howard began to shake his head emphatically. Seitchek, however, sounded happy to hear from him. She asked him how he was.

"Not bad," he said. "See some friends, got some friends in Los Angeles, rent a car, not bad. It's a vacation."

"Are you going to come and see me?"

The invitation in her voice was so warm that he assumed there was a catch somewhere. He lunged at the curtains facing the street and looked out at a car driving by. It was just an ordinary car without any relation to him.

"No, really," Seitchek said. "Did you call because you wanted to get together or something?"

"Sure, why not," Howard said, as if it were entirely her idea.

The sky above Newport Beach the next afternoon was a brutal white the mere sight of which, in the single wide window of Seit-chek's bedroom, negated the effect of the airconditioning and brought into the room the torpor of the young, full-bodied palms outside the window, and the white fire on the terra-cotta roofs beyond them, and the blazing monotony of the beaches in the distance. The walls of the room were bare except for a poster of Magic Johnson slam-dunking and a large acrylic seascape in the muted colors of upholstery. The closet door was open and on either side of it were Hefty trash bags and stacks of cardboard cartons, yellow ones, from Mayflower moving.

From the hallway Howard gave the room a courteous once-over, leaning in as if there were a velvet rope in the doorway. His neck was covered with shaving cuts and areas of abrasion whose cumulative redness gave him a guilty, crabby, immature expression. Before leaving San Diego he'd scraped himself mercilessly, Seit-chek's cordial invitation having led him to expect an introduction to her family and perhaps a sit-down lunch. When he arrived, though, the house was empty, and she did not even offer him a glass of water. She went back up the staircase which from outside the door he'd heard her descending, and let him follow. She ap-peared not to really recognize any of the things her eyes fell on, including Howard. She was hollow-cheeked and waif-like, as pale as a person with the flu.

"You feeling OK?" he said.

She didn't answer. On a desk by the window stood a bottle of Nexxus shampoo and a dozen or so Hummel figurines. She pushed on the figurines until they were flush with the wall.

"I was amazed when you called," she said suddenly, her back to him. "I was amazed because I'd been lying on the floor here," she nodded at a space between a twin bed and a wall, "for about five hours, and I was wondering what could possibly ever make me stand up again ever in my life, and obviously the answer was, my mother knocking on the door and saying there was somebody on the phone for me. I was amazed when she told me who it was."

She pushed on the figurines again, making sure they could not be straightened more. She turned to Howard and spoke dully. "Did you get to Scripps? Did you see Alan Grubb?"

"Yeah, no. He wasn't there. You got a bathroom?"

"A bathroom? Do we have one?" She waited for him to leave.

At the bathroom mirror he tugged on his shirt, trying to get it to hang right, and scraped some of the dried blood off his neck. He looked out the window at the swimming pool. When he returned to the bedroom, Seitchek was kneeling near the closet, tossing paperbacks from a full carton into a less full carton. A bit of gum that had once been bright green was lodged in the tread of her left sneaker. Between the waist of her jeans and the white skin of her lower back was a space wide enough to stick an arm down. "Is it OK I parked my car in your driveway?" Howard asked.

"Sure." She looked up from her books very briefly. "You can poke your cow anywhere you feel like."

Poke his cow? Poke his cow? She'd said it so casually, and yet . . . He sat down on a twin bed and pounded on the mattress until the pounding became stylized and irrelevant. "You want to go out? Get something to eat?"

"No," she said. "Do you?"

"Maybe. Maybe get some fish and chips. Saw a fish and chips place. You wanna go there?"

Ignoring him, she flipped books into the carton, *A Separate Peace, Franny and Zooey, Zen and the Art of Motorcycle Maintenance, The Women's Room. The Glass Bead Game, The Sot-Weed Factor*, a stack of Vonnegut, some Frank Herbert and Robert Heinlein, *Watership Down, Fear of Flying, The Sunlight Dialogues*, a boxed set of Tolkien, more Salinger, some P. D. James, *The Bell Jar, 1984*. She straightened her back and reported:

"My mother went out specially to buy cold cuts and hard rolls and Heineken Dark before she went golfing. I told her you were coming by."

Bending over the boxes again, she riffled the pages of *The Bell Jar* and then put it back in with the discards. D. T. Suzuki, *The*

World According to Garp and *Ragtime* followed. She turned to Howard. "You want some books?" With a tremendous shove she slid the box across the carpeting.

He selected two Heinleins. "These OK?"

"Anything you want. Really. It's all going out. How about some shoes? Do you have any little sisters?" She held up a pair of sandals with four-inch cork platforms, a pair of Earth Shoes, a pair of clogs with daisies tooled on the brown leather, a child-sized pair of white plastic go-go boots. She unfolded a pair of polyester bell-bottoms with giant green-and-white checks. "I'm supposed to go through life feeling good about myself, knowing there was a time I was seen in public in these?" She rooted further in a box. "My Nehru jacket. Any interest in Nehru jackets in Taiwan these days?" She stuffed the jacket into a garbage bag.

"Cold cuts," Howard hinted.

"Yeah, pork, beef. My favorite foods."

He made an encouraging noise, but it was clear that she'd only been toying with this lunch idea. She pushed her bangs out of her eyes and opened a new carton. "See my first-grade class?" She handed him a sheet of photos. "Here, you want these? You want about five hundred pictures of me?" She slid the whole box over to him. While he peered into it, lifting the corners of a few photographs, she unearthed further treasures—a felt Peanuts banner stating that happiness is a warm puppy; Walter Carlos albums, Three Dog Night albums, Cat Stevens albums, Janis Ian albums, Moody Blues albums, Paul Simon albums; posters by Peter Max; the Game of Life; collections of *Doonesbury* strips; a throw pillow upholstered with artificial zebra fur; a lamp made out of a 7UP can. She unrolled a full-length poster of Mark Spitz. "I won this," she said. "I won this at dancing school. The thing is I actually put it up. I put it on my closet door and he looked at me for an entire year, with his seven gold medals. His eyes would *follow* me."

Howard was trying to show an interest in the poster when she let it roll back up and pushed it deep into a trash bag. She released a breath and slumped, generally, staring at the floor. "I had nothing to do with any of these things coming out here. The last time I was here I spent about two days looking at all the pictures and going through my old papers and notebooks. Every single band concert program that had my name in it. All my blue ribbons and acceptance letters and every quiz I ever took and every little paper I ever wrote. Even if I throw it away, it's like this tremendous weight of implication, which how can I ever, ever, *ever* escape?"

Her eyes alighted on a pale blue college exam book lying near her on the floor. She stuffed it in the trash bag. "My parents moved out here the year I went to college. They got this nice four-bedroom house, one bedroom for each of us kids and a big one for themselves. Mine's also the guest room, isn't it great? The decor? It's really me. That's the thing: it really is me. This is what I try to forget."

Howard looked at the poster of Magic Johnson and the Hummel figurines. He bounced a little on the bed. "What you come here for if you don't like it?"

"To throw things away."

An insight made his eyes glitter evilly. "Thought you came to see your nieces."

"Oh, my nieces, yes." She aimed a sneer through the open door. "You know I'd never seen them before? Not any of them?"

"Sure."

"Although the last time I was here I did have the pleasure of seeing a sister-in-law pregnant. You can see we're not living in poverty. We could have afforded to bring me home. Obviously I chose not to come."

"I don't go home," Howard said.

This interested her. "What, to Taiwan?"

"Can't go. Don't wanna go."

She shook her head, forgetting him again. "I start thinking there's something here for me. That I can come home, I can drink, I can eat, I can sleep, I can come here and be rich like they are, drive the BMW, see the babies, and just *be it*, you know, for a week. I actually start looking forward to it. I kill myself trying to finish the thesis and get on the plane, and it's just so dumb of me to set myself up like that. My whole family's in the living room when I get here, both my little brothers, both my little sisters-in-law, all my little nieces. I've finally come to view the babies. I'm very late. But not too late. The suspense must be unbearable for me. Unthinkable that I could be anything but dying to have my nieces crawling on me. And the simple fact that it's unthinkable is enough to kill my interest on the spot."

She smiled, seeing that Howard was flipping through her pictures. "The thing is I can't just show pleasure and interest in the abstract. I have to *talk* to these girls. I have to have a relationship with them. With this two-and-a-half-year-old girl and these two babies who don't speak a word yet. I start to say some clever thing, like I'm talking to a dog or something, but then I hear them all listening, and so I try to think of something sweet to say, and that's even worse, I mean, it's just a *child*, what do you say, what do you say?——"

She paused, staring at the back wall of the closet, and Howard leaned to look inside it, almost believing there was someone in there listening to what she said.

"All I can hear is the incredible stupidity and lameness of the things I'm saying. And the girls know it. At least, the oldest one definitely knows it. She knows I'm not one of those women who think there's nothing better in the world than having a child like her, and so of course she doesn't like me, why should she. And there's this little scene where she won't come near me, and I hate her and she hates me, and the reason is that I'm more like her than I'm like any of the four parents, and she knows it." She nodded positively. "I'm almost thirty years old, and I'm more like her than I am like them. And it's one thing to be three years old and be a child, but to be me and still be so selfconscious—— I could still stand it if they didn't all so obviously pity me. They give me these pitying looks, and they actually have the gall to tell me that I can't imagine what a grownup life is like—I can't imagine how *busy* you are, and how *little time to read the newspaper* you have—because I don't have children myself. As soon as I have children, I'll understand. And what I want to say is, Let me tell *you* some of the things *you* don't know about life and *never will*. But these women, it's like they've been waiting all their lives for a chance to ignore a person like me, and now that they have their babies they're allowed to. They're allowed to be totally self-absorbed and totally rude to me, because they have *children*. As soon as you have children you're allowed to close your mind. And no one can say you're not grownup. And any kind of life that *I* might have, any different kind of life, any kind of life that could be envied—it's obviously not working, because I'm still just this incredibly embarrassing adolescent. I can't possibly compete with these twenty-four-year-old parents, all their narcissism and basic human decency. There's just no contest."

She fell silent, shaking her head and staring into the closet. Howard had begun to bounce on his toes with his hands in his pockets and elbows flapping. He raised a leg for balance and peered into the hall, as if he'd heard a sound. There had been no sound. When he turned back, Seitchek's eyes were on him.

"And this is what I see," she said bitterly. "In my free, exciting East Coast life. This is what I look up from the screen and see. This is the great alternative."

He bounced on his toes. "Think I gotta go now," he said. "Gotta see some people, think I better go."

She smiled at him horribly. "What about your core cuts? Don't you want your core cuts? Don't you want to go poke your cow in the diveway?" She turned away in disgust. "See, I don't even care what I say anymore. I don't even care who's listening."

Howard continued to bounce, wandering and tilting like a top in the latter stages of its revolution, his vibrations jarring his hands out of his pockets. He veered close to Seitchek. When she looked up at him, he slapped her so hard that she fell back on her elbows.

They stared at each other. There was an odd, silent moment of discovery. It was as if the time of day had changed. Then Seitchek's face twisted and she covered it with her hands. "Oh God. Oh God, I am so embarrassed."

Already Howard was bending down, his hands in the neighborhood of her head. He patted her cheek and touched her ears and then patted her shoulders with both hands, not remorsefully but impatiently, as if he'd bumped a table and was rushing to right the stupid vases that had fallen. "Sorry," he said. "Sorry, sorry, sorry."

She hit him on the jaw with her fingernails. "Get away from me! Get away from me! Go dive your cow, get away from me." She struck at his eyes, and he had to grab her wrists and pin them cruelly as she fought to break free. She struggled beneath him, gulping air and breaking into what he thought was sobs but turned out to be something more like laughter, because things were not at all the way he'd thought they were. Her fingers were in his hair. She was pressing his face into hers, and he squeezed his eyes shut, the short lashes interlocking like the stitches a rag doll has to see with, because he was not yet ready to look at the person underneath him and believe his luck in obtaining a girl like this, in a house like this, with four large bedrooms and a thirty-foot pool and a wet bar in the living room.

8

Earthquakes aren't a man's murder of his pregnant wife. They're not court-ordered desegregation. They're not Kennedys. For several weeks after the last network news crew packed up and left Boston, you could feel the city's disappointment with the earth. Obviously, no one had been eager to be personally crushed by falling timbers or to see their possessions go up in flames, but for a few days in the spring Nature had toyed with the city's expectations, and people had rapidly developed covert appetites for televised images of bodies under sheets of polyethylene, for the carnival-ride sensation of being tossed around the living room, for a Californian experience, for major numbers. A hundred dead would really have been something. A thousand dead: historic. But the earth had reneged on its promises, mutely refusing to reduce buildings to exciting, photogenic messes; and the death count never made it off the ground. For all the impact the numbers had on local viscera, the thirty-seven earthquake-related injuries could have been caused by boring car accidents, the $100 million of property loss by neglected maintenance, and Rita Kernaghan's death by a boring heart attack. Journalistic aftershocks dwindled to an article or two per week. Local reporters still scoured Essex County in search of lives ruined by the disaster, but, to their dismay, they couldn't find a single one. Homeowners were repairing walls and ceilings. Questionable structures were being inspected and reopened. It was all so morally neutral, so sensible.

Fortunately for everyone, the Red Sox began June by sweeping a series with the Yankees at Fenway and carrying a streak of seven wins on a trip to the American League West. No sane person believed the Sox would actually end up winning their division, but at the moment they could hardly be said to be losing ground, and what was one supposed to do? Boo in advance? Later in the summer there would be plenty of opportunities to revive the old hatred and envy—Bostonians' hearts would pound and their throats would tighten at the very thought of baseball's winners, their soporifically effective pitching staffs, the arrogant baby-cheeked sluggers whom God unbelievably permitted to hit homer after homer, and the horrible fair-weather fans, cheap euphoria smeared across their faces like the juice of sex and peaches, who thought that this was what baseball was about, that it was about winning and winning handily— but as long as the streak lasted, the city was full of heathen haves blissfully oblivious to the have-nots of the sports world, and in the absence of further tremors, the fear of death and personal injury had retreated to its rightful place, far to the rear of people's minds.

This wasn't to say that Essex County had entirely stopped shivering. Portable seismographs installed cooperatively by Boston College, the USGS, and Weston Geophysical were registering as many as twenty shocks per day in the vicinity of Peabody, and the occasional blip near Ipswich. The Richter magnitudes seldom exceeded 3.0, however, and although no two scientists agreed about exactly what was going on, the activity was generally taken to represent aftershocks to the events of April and May. Granted, aftershocks to moderate earthquakes usually tail off quickly, and granted, the aftershocks in Peabody weren't doing this, but in view of the unusually strong foreshocks to the May 10 events, Larry Axelrod and other seismologists theorized that the rupture of rock beneath Peabody had for some reason been "unclean." As Axelrod explained it to the *Globe*, the chicken with its head neatly lopped off convulses for a moment but soon lies still, while the chicken with a mangled neck can go on thrashing for an hour, though ever more feebly.

Almost no one in seismology would absolutely guarantee that Boston had seen the last of strong motion. The sole exception was

Mass Geostudy, a private research venture sponsored by the Army Corps of Engineers and the nuclear power industry. Overlooked in news articles, Mass Geostudy wrote a testy letter to the *Globe* and informed readers that "there is zero probability of greater Boston experiencing an earthquake as severe as the May 10 temblors in the next 85–120 years." Many other scientists agreed that the stress release on May 10 had indeed diminished the risk of further major earthquakes, but a substantial minority, including the venerable Axelrod, continued to warn that "it ain't over till it's over." They pointed to the unusual aftershock pattern and to evidence of deep, fault-like structures in the dozen miles separating Ipswich and Peabody. While there was no reason to expect a rupture over the entire twelve miles (this would be a major earthquake), a smaller rupture couldn't be ruled out either.

The phrase of the hour, applied willy-nilly to all things geophysical in the eastern United States, was "not well understood."

Rather than spend a billion dollars making Massachusetts as catastrophe-resistant as California, the state legislature chose to allocate a million dollars for immediate seismological research. (Even a million seemed like a lot to a state with serious budget troubles.) Much of the money went to Boston College to fund a full-scale seismic mapping of Essex County. Exposed faults were inspected for fresh offsets (none was found), and Vibroseis equipment was put to work. Students drove a truck-mounted machine to selected sites and surrounded it with a grid of listening devices called Geophones. At carefully timed moments, the machine chirped into the earth, and from the underground refractions and reflections and dilations of the chirps, as recorded on the Geophones, buried structures could be mapped in much the same way as a fetus is mapped by ultrasound.

Early results of Vibroseis mapping revealed a tangle of discontinuities crisscrossing Essex County and extending to greater depths than had previously been supposed. Ambiguity escalated as seismologists tried to correlate earthquake hypocenters with mapped structures. The new data lent support to a variety of competing models. It also gave rise to new models that contradicted not only each other but all the earlier models.

On June 7, a BC student planting a Geophone in a wooded lot

in Topsfield discovered the naked body of a Danvers teenager who had been missing for a month, and the Red Sox edged Seattle in ten innings.

The rest of the state money was being spent on studies in short-term earthquake prediction, organized by scholars from as far away as California. One group planted sensors in the bedrock to measure changes in its electrical conductivity. Another was monitoring magnetic fields and listening for extremely low-frequency radio waves. Four independent groups were studying less glamorous but equally well established indicators: changes in the depth and clarity of water in wells, release of methane and other gases from deep holes, oddities in animal behavior, and foreshock-like clusters of tremors.

A mini-scandal broke when Channel 4 learned that the state had given a Michigan post-doc $15,000 to import a tank of Japanese catfish and observe them in a darkened motel room outside Salem. Several studies had indicated that this species of catfish became upset on the eve of earthquakes, but the Michigan post-doc was shy and made a poor impression on camera. The Channel 4 reporter, Penny Spanghorn, called the experiment "perhaps the ultimate rip-off."

By and large, the media and the public assumed that the research groups would issue urgent warnings if a cruncher appeared imminent; that this was what they'd come to Boston for. The groups themselves had no such plans. They were scientists and had come to gather information and advance their understanding of the earth. They knew, in any case, that the governor would never take the economically disruptive step of issuing an all-out warning unless most of the prediction methods agreed that a major shock was due. In the past, the methods had specifically not agreed about the timing, severity, and location of major earthquakes. This was why the methods were still being tested. When the groups said so, however, the public took it as modesty and continued to assume that somehow, should a disaster loom, a warning would be issued.

Aside from the catfish story, press coverage of the prediction efforts was enthusiastic, and the experimental installations became highly sought after by local young people. A report of muddied water in a pair of wells in Beverly was later retracted when a teenager confessed to having dumped dirt and gravel into them "as a prank." Soon after this, a far-flung carful of Somerville youth was arrested by Salem police while "box-bashing" in a lonely place. The youths had thought it would be fun to confuse a portable seismograph by jumping on the ground and simulating tremors, but it was not much fun, and so they attacked the seismograph with baseball bats.

In the first week of June every household in eastern Massachusetts received a brochure called TREMOR TIPS. The brochure, which had been printed in California, was illustrated with palm trees and Mission Style houses and recommended that children crouch under their desks at school, that downed electrical wires be avoided, that gas leaks be reported pronto, and that supplies of canned food and bottled water have been purchased well in advance. Supermarkets and discount stores responded with special Quake Survival displays, and gun dealers throughout the region reported a jump in sales.

Insurance companies had resumed sales of earthquake insurance, although they freely admitted that with rates beginning at $30 per $1,000 of coverage, almost no one was buying. Con artists working door-to-door did brisk business in bogus discount policies, however. The stock of companies and banks with large capital investments in the Boston area remained depressed, as did the market for real estate in Essex County and in low-lying areas farther south, including Back Bay and much of Cambridge. (Buildings on filled marshes and other reclaimed land were particularly susceptible to seismic shaking.) Wealthy municipalities were afraid of sparking an all-out panic by sponsoring earthquake drills; poor communities had other worries; and so no drills were held.

The Reverend Philip Stites quietly observed in a broadcast editorial on WSNE that he didn't think God was done with the Commonwealth, nor would He be until the last abortion clinic in the state had closed its doors. Stites went on to condemn as un-Christian the recent bombings of facilities in Lowell, saying that it was for God, not man, to mete out punishment. As of June 8, fifty-eight members of Stites's Church of Action in Christ were sitting in Boston and Cambridge jail cells. They had declined to post bail after their arrest for blocking entrances to various clinics. Car-

toonists and columnists portrayed Stites as a wealthy dandy unwilling to soil his hands by getting himself arrested with his troops;
they made fun of his highly visible wooings of local conservatives;
they detected "an odor of hypocrisy" in everything he did.

On the other side of the fence, a coalition of local pro-choice
groups was promising to flood Boston Common with a hundred
thousand protesters during a rally on July 14. One of the organizers
had written to Renée for permission to include her in a list of public
figures supporting the rally. Renée had called the organizer and
asked her, "Why do you want me on your list?"

"You're the geologist. You were on TV."

"A lot of people were on TV."

"Are you saying you don't want to be on the list?"

"No, no, go ahead. Put me on it."

"All right." The organizer had sounded annoyed. "We'll put
you on it."

The regional administrative offices of the Environmental Protection Agency were on the eighth floor of a prewar granite block
across from the Federal Courthouse, in the old part of downtown
where if you studied the tops of the buildings and then looked at
the street again you expected to see all the men wearing fedoras
and dark narrow ties and Buddy Holly–style glasses.

Outside the courthouse, six female protesters in knitted mittens
had wound Saran Wrap around their photographs of fetuses. Sheets
of cold water were sliding over themselves on the slopes leading
down into the combat zone, rain streaking the city's gray-green
windows and soaking the handcards advertising sex by telephone
that were lodged under every wiper blade that wasn't moving. It
was a trick Renée had seen New England summers play many times
before: a high of 53° today and more of the same expected on the
weekend.

The hard plastic chairs in the vestibule of the EPA offices
discouraged sitting. Some were grouped in a half circle that suggested clubbiness even though they were empty; the rest stood
isolated at odd angles to the walls. When the deputy regional administrator, Susan Carver, came out to meet her, Renée left rain

marks on the floor by the notice of equal employment opportunity she'd been reading.

Carver was a tall and heavy person with fleshy white cheeks and thick eyebrows. Her glasses had round cranberry-colored rims and lenses soaped by the federal lighting. She was like a brainy white rabbit stuffed into a size 14 suit. She was leading Renée back to her office when a balled-up piece of paper sailed out of an open door and glanced off her massive shoulder. She caught it on the fly, with surprising deftness, and stopped in the doorway. Four middle-aged male administrators wearing colors such as rust brown and silver-blue looked up from their desks with a guilt that was more like a bated delight. Wordlessly, Carver tossed the ball of paper through an orange hoop attached to the wall and returned to Renée while the men cheered.

"You wanted to talk to me about Sweeting-Aldren."

"Yes."

"This is in regard to the earthquakes in Peabody."

"Yes."

Obviously pleased with herself for making the basket, Carver sat down behind her desk and joined her white paws on the desk top, stretching the pinstripes at her elbows and shoulders. On the windowsill behind her stood framed photographs of her family: a chunky teenaged girl with a small nose and a flat, eager face who looked like she was good at computers, a doughy boy of eight or ten, and a skinny, grinning husband. There was a water pistol, a .38 revolver, by her Rolodex. With an amused maternal wariness, as if the company were another of her children, she said, "What has Sweeting-Aldren done, in your opinion?"

Renée reached for the shoulder bag that held her documents but slowly drew her hand back without having touched it. "There's some evidence," she said, "that they've been pumping liquids down a very deep well for a number of years, if not decades, and that they may have induced the earthquakes we've seen in Peabody."

Carver's eyebrows rose and fell almost imperceptibly. "Go on."

Renée opened her bag and gave a poised and cautious presentation. She didn't look up from her documents until she'd finished. Carver was wearing a faint, abstracted smile, as if continuing to savor the basket she'd made.

"Let me see if I've understood your chronology," she said. "First Sweeting-Aldren begins to drill a deep well somewhere, in the late sixties. Then in 1987 there's a swarm of small earthquakes near Peabody that lasts three months—"

"And tails off with unusual abruptness."

"And tails off rapidly. Then there's a spill in Peabody, not particularly large—at most a couple of years' worth of undumpable effluents. And finally, not long after the spill is discovered, the Peabody earthquakes start up again, apparently in connection with the Ipswich earthquakes but actually not, according to you."

"Not just me. Nobody in seismology has a persuasive model for linking Ipswich and Peabody."

Carver nodded. She'd picked up her water pistol and was nibbling on the sight blade. "I understand. Although the impression I get is that there's a lot that seismologists don't know about what makes earthquakes happen when and where they do, especially earthquakes on the east coast."

"A model of induced seismicity explains the Peabody swarm perfectly."

"Yes, I understand. Although again it all depends on your assumption that a hole was actually drilled and drilled near Peabody. Since there may be other 'models' that are equally persuasive."

"Such as?"

Carver shrugged. "Maybe a natural source of earthquakes in Peabody, and then a 'model' of cyclical demand that explains April's spill there. You see, I'm not sure how well you understand the chemical industry. Short-term stockpiling of both raw materials and unprocessed wastes is very commonplace. Sweeting-Aldren stores incinerable wastes until demand improves for the products they make in their high-temperature reactors. And in the meantime, last month, an earthquake ruptured one of their storage tanks."

Renée nodded. She'd expected—in fact, hoped—that Carver would play devil's advocate. "Can I ask if you guys, the EPA, have actually been inside the Peabody plant to make sure they're treating all these wastes the way they say they are?"

"Certainly you may ask. The answer is no. We have not been lowering probes into their tanks. We have not been watchdogging their internal processes. We have neither the staff nor the legal right to go checking every pipe and every valve in every factory in America."

"Although of course this is kind of a suspicious case."

"Ah, yes. A suspicious case." Carver pushed on the arms of her chair and with considerable exertion repositioned herself. "Let me explain something to you, Renée. As a survivor of the eighties who's still working for EPA. The reason we're doing a minimally acceptable job of protecting this country's environment is that we're realistic, and we have priorities. This is the real world we're dealing with, and in the real world you can't acid-test every conceivable hypothesis. You have to focus on what's coming out of the drain-pipes and the smokestacks, and that means taking some things on faith occasionally. If a company like Sweeting-Aldren isn't polluting the air or water—"

"Until the spill last month."

Carver smiled. The smile meant: Will you let me finish? "Sweeting-Aldren is a responsibly managed company. Maybe if I had nobody else to worry about, I might go in there and double-check all this stuff. But I'm dealing with companies pouring half a ton of cadmium and mercury salts per hour into estuaries. I'm dealing with waste-management contractors taking oil with PCB levels in the parts per thousand and toluene and vinyl chloride levels in the parts per ten and dumping them in fifty-year-old tanks beneath abandoned gas stations. I'm dealing with landfills that are on the brink of contaminating groundwater pretty much statewide from here to Springfield. I'm dealing with companies who"— Carver counted the strikes on her fingertips—"ignore our regula-tions, ignore the fines we levy, ignore court orders, and finally go bankrupt and leave behind hundred-acre sites contaminated for eternity. On the other side we have a public prone to panic, and presidents who make it a point of pride every couple of years not to *cut* our funding any further."

"But the spill in Peabody."

"There were PCBs in it. I can hear you. And the company misled the public for a couple of days, not that Wall Street didn't see right through it. Then again, it's an extremely human response to deny something when you're embarrassed. Hi, Stan." Carver aimed her pistol at the doorway, where a man in a pea-green blazer was holding a manila folder. "I'll be with you in a few minutes."

Renée frowned. A few minutes?

"This hole of yours," Carver said. "If it was drilled at all, it was supposedly drilled outside Hereford, Massachusetts. In order to make your 'model' fit, haven't you more or less arbitrarily moved a five-mile-deep hole a hundred fifty miles east?"

"Eastern Massachusetts is what it says in *Nature*. Eastern Massachusetts."

"Do you have any other references on that?"

"Not—yet."

"And *Nature* is a . . . British publication. You know, I hate to say this, but I'm not particularly comfortable with a theory that depends on a British magazine editor's grasp of American geography."

Renée's eyes narrowed.

"Other objections, off the top of my head. Why spend umpteen million dollars on a deep oil well in 1969? Do you know what a barrel of oil cost back then?"

"Yes. I do know. But I can't believe there wasn't anybody in America able to see 1973 coming. They had huge profits. They were probably glad to take the write-off."

"You don't make money on a write-off. And wouldn't a company with so much foresight know about induced seismicity too? Anybody who opens an elementary seismology textbook must know about it. But according to you, the earthquakes in 1987 took them by surprise."

"I assume they'd looked at the Denver study," Renée said. "In Denver there was some history of earthquakes and the largest induced event was a magnitude 4.6. In Peabody there was no history of earthquakes and no reason to expect any. Plus they were pumping at a small fraction of the rate the Army pumped in Denver. And there's something else, actually, that I forgot to mention, which is that the operations vice president of Sweeting-Aldren has his house insured against earthquake damage."

Carver touched the muzzle of her pistol to her lips, as if blowing smoke off it. She smiled at Renée serenely. Was it possible she'd been corrupted by Sweeting-Aldren? Renée dismissed the idea. She could see that the problem here was that Carver simply didn't like her.

"I take it you're not a homeowner," Carver said.

"That's right. I'm not a homeowner."

"Nothing wrong with that, of course. However, it may be that you don't quite understand how much the people who do own homes are concerned about losing them. And that people who've been in Boston all their lives might remember the earthquakes in the forties and fifties. Who is that—Dave Stoorhuys?"

She made him sound like somebody she drank beer with.

"Yes."

Carver nodded. "Caution. Caution is the only word for him. Have you met him?"

"I know his son."

"Yes, but you see I actually deal with these companies on a daily basis. And strange as it may sound, there happen to be some very decent and well-intentioned people in the industry. In fact I've seen as much or more self-interest and self-promotion on the academic side of the fence as I've seen on the commercial side. Is this what you wanted to hear? Obviously not. But I'd be lying if I didn't tell you I think you're barking up the wrong tree with Dave Stoorhuys and Sweeting-Aldren."

"What if I found the pumping site myself and brought you pictures?"

"You want permission to spy and trespass? You want Mommy's approval?" Carver's eyes glittered. "I suppose if you showed me something more solid than an academic conjecture, I'd have somebody check it out. Although frankly there are a whole lot worse things a company can do with those chemicals than pump them four miles underneath the water table."

"What if they'd come to you for a license to pump their waste underground. Would you have given it to them?"

"If you're talking about legal liability for earthquake damage, you should be talking to somebody else."

"Like who."

"The press always loves a good story." Carver looked at her watch. She stood up. "I've noticed they're pretty keen on you too."

"This is your responsibility," Renée said. "If they are pumping, the only thing they're violating is EPA regulations. I think somebody should at least go and see if they have a well on their property. And if they do, it should be seized before they have a chance to shut it down."

"I'll take a look at our records." Carver was walking to the door now, forcing her visitor to stand up. Every government official knows that people who complain to agencies invariably consider themselves special, and that they become flustered when they finally realize they don't seem special to the agency. A proud and self-conscious supplicant like Renée was particularly easy to fluster and get rid of. It was therefore a specific meanness on Carver's part that she took the time to add: "I have to tell you, I've heard it all before. I'm afraid you're tripping on a romance, a little bit."

"What?"

"You know—a trip. How old are you?"

"I know what the word means."

"We had an entomologist in here two months ago telling us there were dioxins in a spray the state fights gypsy moths with. He had a nice theory too. The only problem is there aren't any dioxins in the spray. Last year another academic, from Harvard—Thetford? oceanographer?—talking about mercury on the continental shelf. Malfeasance and conspiracy. I guess I used to think that way myself, a long, long time ago. It's very satisfying, very romantic. But 99.9 percent of the time it's not the way the world really works. You might keep that in mind."

In the street again, Renée held her fold-up umbrella right below its ribs and used her other hand to keep her shoulder bag from slipping off her shoulder as the wind blew and the rain fell. Naturally her bladder was overfull. People dodged irrationally in and out of doors. A young black man loitering at the bottom of the subway stairs pointed at the water on his pants and demanded: "What do you say?"

She skittered sideways.

He pursued her. "What do you say? You say *excuse me*. You say *excuse me, please*."

"Excuse me," she said.

"Excuse me, please. I'm sorry I splashed water on you. I'm sorry I got your pants wet."

"I'm sorry I splashed water on you."

"Thank you," he shouted after her, over the turnstiles. "Thank you for your apology."

This exchange echoed in her head until a train came.

A *Globe* had exploded in her car, covering the floor and collecting under seats. On the front page a headline stamped with a wet footprint read: SECOND ABORTION CLINIC BOMBED IN LOWELL.

At Central Square the local Angry Woman, driven underground by the weather, was cursing the motherfucking men who ruled the world. An old Chinese man carrying two goldfish in a Baggie full of water sat down next to Renée, who smiled at him kindly. "Rain rain rain," he said.

"Rain rain rain, yeah."

This exchange echoed in her head all the way to Harvard.

The ground floor of Hoffman Lab was quiet, the large white screens in the Sun room silently spitting up little statements in black as programs ran for students and post-docs eating a late lunch in the Square, the smaller brown screens in the system rooms awaiting log-ons or scrolling in bright green. Renée went straight from the women's bathroom to a brown screen. While she worked, the phone on the radiator rang itself down several times. Even infrequent users of the computer had been informed by now that human life begins at conception. Nobody answered anymore, but the phone kept ringing.

Towards three o'clock Howard Chun and a Pekingese friend of his returned from lunch, exhaling garlic. Howard in his dripping nylon parka parked himself behind a Tectronix plotter. Renée had last seen him sprawled across her bed, snoring brokenly, when she left her apartment after breakfast.

"Why is this machine so slow," she said to her screen.

"Disk B's full," said the Pekingese, furrowing his broad and remarkably expressive forehead. He was a good scientist and Renée liked him.

"Disk B is full. I see. Disk B that I spent half a night backing up four days ago."

She entered the Operator directory, became SUPERUSER, and saw that in less than a week, users by the name of TERRY, TS, TBS, NBD1, and NBD2 had backed 375 megabytes onto Disk B and another 65 megabytes onto Disk A. All of these users were Terry Snall. His thesis topic was Non-Brittle Deformation. NBD1, an account feared and hated in the system rooms, single-handedly occupied 261 megabytes; this was four times the space taken up by any other student's files; it was nearly half a disk.

SUPERUSER became SUPEROP. "Do you know what Terry did?" she said.

In the Tectronix corner, behind partitions, Howard's keyboard clicked obliviously. The room was becoming murky with garlic vapors. SUPEROP addressed the Pekingese. "He brought back every single one of his program files. There are seventy megabytes of program files on this disk. It's taking me twenty minutes to run a one-minute program and he has seventy megabytes of program files."

"Cancel 'em," the Pekingese recommended.

"I'm going to do just that."

Program files were needed only when a program was actually being run, and could be re-created in minutes. SUPEROP zapped every one of Terry's.

"Oh, much better," the Pekingese said.

"Eight megabytes free on a 600-meg disk. Doesn't he *know?* Doesn't he *understand?*"

Howard stepped out of his corner and moved from console to console, logging onto each. Even when he was working for just a few minutes he didn't feel comfortable if he wasn't logged on from at least three or four. Some late nights he logged on from ten of them. All but the one he was using automatically went dim to save wear on the pixels.

In a new log-on announcement, SUPEROP stressed that files not needed immediately should not be backed onto the disk. Everyone knew who wrote these announcements, so she didn't sign it. She became RS again.

"You get your message?" the Pekingese asked her.

"Somebody actually took a message for me?"

"Charles."

"Oh."

Across the hall, beneath her shoulder bag and damp jean

jacket, she found a number and the message: MRS. HOLLAND CALLED. YOU MAY CALL COLLECT.

She dropped the message in the trash and returned to her console. The Pekingese had left the room. "Howard?" she said.

A parka rustled, but Howard didn't answer. Behind the partition, she found him slouching and staring at a bright green seismic spectrum, his ankles crossed on a bed of cables, the keyboard on his lap.

"Do you still know somebody with a pilot's license?" she said.

He shook his head and worked the keyboard.

"Didn't you have a friend who used to take you up?"

A new spectrum blossomed on the screen. He shook his head. Renée frowned. "Are you mad at me?"

He shook his head.

She threw a cautious glance through the hall doorway. "Come on," she whispered. "Don't be mad at me. I really need you not to be mad at me."

He blinked at the screen, resolutely ignoring her. With another glance into the hall, she knelt and put her hands on his chest. "Come on. Please. Don't be mad at me now. Please."

He tried to roll his chair away from her.

She took his hand and put her cheek against his chest. It was the first time she'd ever touched him inside the lab, and as soon as she did it she heard a rustle of clothing right behind her. A sense of inevitability enveloped her like dread as she turned and saw Terry Snall spinning around and heading back up the hallway.

She jumped to her feet. "Shit!" She began to follow Terry but came back to the Tectronix. "Shit! Shit!" She pulled on her hair. "What did I do to you?"

Howard typed casually on his keyboard.

"Oh God, this is going to finish me. This is really going to push me over." She crouched by Howard again. "Just tell me what I did to you."

He made a hideous face, all gums and stretched nostrils. "What I do to you?" he mocked. "What I do to you? What I do to you?"

"I let you sleep with me," she whispered fiercely. "I let you sleep with me *a lot*."

"I let you seep with me I let you seep with me."

She stared at him, mouth trembling.

"Rouis, Rouis," he said. "A rill bit pinch me hit me hit me."

"Oh God." She backed away from him and looked for a place to run but there was no place. Rounding the corner into the hall, she almost collided with Charles, one of the department secretaries. He was tall and balding and was writing a novel in his off hours. He wore suspenders instead of belts. "Melanie Holland," he said. "She's on the phone again."

"Tell her I'm gone."

"She wants to know where she can reach you."

"Tell her to try me at home."

"She already has been."

"Tell her I'm out of town."

"Oh, Renée." Charles shook his head. "I'm not paid to lie for people. If you don't want to talk to her, the honest thing is to tell her that. Then she won't keep calling here and interrupting me and I won't have to keep coming down two flights of stairs and bothering you."

Renée pointed at the street door. "I'm leaving."

"Oh, Renée. I advise you not to. Not if you ever want to use my copier again or have me take messages from other institutions or borrow my paper cutter. Are you interested in ever borrowing my paper cutter again?"

Without a word, she stalked up the hall towards the stairwell. "Don't think I'm blackmailing you," Charles said, following her. "This is a matter of courtesy and professionalism. I let you use my paper cutter as a courtesy. I'm not required to let you use it, you know."

Her voice reverberated in the concrete-clad stairwell. "You are so."

He followed her up the stairs. "You used to be so courteous, Renée. You used to be the most courteous person in this building. Do you know how many clicks I've given you on the copy counter? The copy counter that's for department business only? Renée? Are you listening to me? Sixty-five hundred clicks!"

She stepped into the office of the absent department chairman and closed the door in Charles's face. The office was dark and cool and agreeably odorless. She always enjoyed being here. The shelves held bound volumes of all the major journals dating back to the forties. There were file cabinets bursting with reprints, softcover proposals for interesting and useful multinational research initiatives, whole unbroken packages of colored pens and other scarce office supplies. In a few years she too would have an office like this, and some young fool like herself would run a computer system for her, and people would have to include her whenever major seismological doings were discussed. It would matter that she'd studied with X, Y and Z at Harvard—a university which, as she always remembered when she entered this office, could boast of a small but outstanding program in geophysics. Bad memories of the system rooms would fade. Trees would sway outside her window.

"Renée? Melanie Holland. Listen, I don't want to take up your time while you're at work, but I'm very interested in talking to you again and I wonder if you'd let me take you to lunch tomorrow. It being a Saturday. There's a lovely restaurant in the Four Seasons, I'd love to take you there."

"What for?" Renée said rudely. "I mean—that's very nice of you."

"Wonderful. You'll come."

"No. No, I won't come. I mean, I can't."

"Oh, well, I'm not wedded to the day and hour, if you had other plans. We could brunch on Sunday, have dinner tomorrow night. Tonight even. It would be *so* nice if you would."

"What is it that you want to talk to me about?"

"Everything and nothing. I think it would be very good for both of us to get acquainted. I'm calling you as a friend. Please have lunch with me, Renée."

She frowned so hard it hurt. *"What for?"*

"Oh, really, let's not be silly. Can I take you to lunch tomorrow or can't I? Yes or no. It would mean a great deal to me. Tell me one good reason why you shouldn't let me."

Melanie could make her voice beautiful when she chose. It was like a brook in a valley running in and out of the sunshine and pooling among willows, the clear kind of brook you want to plunge your hands into and drink from and forget about the deer carcasses and feedlots upstream, which may not even be there anyway.

"Let me get back to you," Renée said.

"I know. You're busy busy busy. Do I need to be blunt? There is no one in the world more interested in seeing you than I am. No one in the world. Please come to lunch with me."

Renée wandered dizzily around the chairman's office, gripping the telephone. "Won't you tell me what this is about?"

"Tomorrow. Is twelve-thirty fine with you? The restaurant's called Aujourd'hui."

Beyond thin lines of rain joining and breaking apart and descending on the window, a knot of Japanese tourists beneath identical umbrellas approached the entrance to the Peabody Museum, whose gorgeous collection of glass flowers, created a hundred years earlier by German glassblowers to reveal the structure and variety of the world's flora to Harvard botany students, was the most popular tourist attraction in Cambridge. Renée had never seen it. The Japanese umbrellas stooped to the level of the sign on the museum door; rotating uncertainly, they conferred and scattered. Others surged up to the sign, which said that owing to recent earthquake damage the glass flowers were in storage until a safer means of displaying them could be found. To console themselves, the Japanese photographed one another by the sign, the white of their flashes lighting the wet asphalt and nearer trees. Two lung-shaped patches of breath and above them a fainter fog outline of a forehead stayed on the chairman's window for several minutes after Renée had gone back downstairs.

For three semesters she'd shared her apartment with a seismologist named Claudia Guarducci, a thin, pouty, bored, and very smart Roman doing postdoctoral work for pay at Harvard. They cooked together, saw movies together, deplored colleagues together, accepted or declined dinner invitations together. Claudia bought a motorcycle and gave Renée rides to work on it. They never shared secrets.

When Claudia returned to Italy they kept in touch with laconic postcards. Missing the smell of her Merit Ultra Lights, Renée went out of her way to stand near smokers. She inquired about post-docs in Rome, thinking that if she went there she could call up

Claudia and mention, merely mention, her current whereabouts. The future she wanted would begin in good earnest if she could live in Italy and be best friends with a Roman woman.

In hindsight it would seem as if all she ever did in life was lay foundations for future towers of shame and self-hatred. Some trusting, autonomous part of herself kept constructing uncool midwestern dreams: European evenings with Claudia Guarducci; domestic tranquillity with Louis Holland; a big pat on the back from the EPA and the citizens of Boston.

She was finishing her thesis when Claudia informed her, in a two-line postcard, that she had married her old boyfriend at the Istituto Nazionale.

Renée was amazed by how betrayed she felt. She couldn't bring herself to write to Claudia again, and the months went by and Claudia didn't write either. What hurt was knowing that she wasn't jealous of the man for having Claudia but of Claudia for having a man. This, and knowing what a difference it made that she was female.

She was sure that if it had been a case of René and Claudio, good heterosexual friends, René wouldn't have felt so betrayed. Men who'd gotten married or found girlfriends didn't drift away from their single male friends, at least not as often as women did. Obviously, men were nobler spirits than women. It came of belonging to the default gender. If both men and women considered their relationships with men inviolable, then men inevitably remained true to their gender while women, equally inevitably, betrayed their own. Men's moral superiority was structurally guaranteed.

However, Renée did not wish she were a man.

A man, if he was your college boyfriend, still "wanted to be friends with" you after he'd dumped you. His male faith in friendship was so unshakable, in fact, that he believed that you would welcome an invitation to his wedding.

A man, if he was your younger brother, fresh out of college, was *realistic* at the dinner table about how "women are simply not identical to men, they have different priorities," speaking glibly and self-servingly this truth that it had taken you thirty years to learn, bolstered in his arrogance by a twenty-three-year-old wife who had "decided not to put off having children" and so considered herself more mature than you.

A man was a creature who thought it was a sympathetic portrayal of himself to say, "I love women."

A man could not admit to a woman that he was wrong and remain a man. He would sooner cry and abase himself and beg forgiveness like a baby than admit to error as a man.

A man took for granted a woman's understanding of his penis but congratulated himself for understanding the clitoris and its importance. He smiled inwardly at his superiority to all the men, past and present, who had not penetrated this female secret. He felt proud of his enlightenment and goodness when he quizzed a woman about whether she had come. The perfect gift for the man who had everything was a quarter-ounce bottle of feminism.

Inescapably immersed in a history made by people of his own sex, a man could never be as selfconscious as a woman: could never feel as much shame. Even a thoughtful man lacked a radical appreciation of how it was only luck, a pairing of X and Y, that had made his life straightforward. At some level he would always still believe that the ease of his life implied a moral superiority; this belief made him ridiculous.

Women knew their husbands were ridiculous. Therefore married women, especially ones with children, could be friends with each other. The shame of being wedded to a blunt instrument, a lovable but limited creature, and of bearing his children and enduring his superiority, was eased by intercourse with other women similarly burdened or with women whose most fervent wish was to be so burdened.

Renée, however, wasn't married. She also believed that even if she were, the sorority of childbearers wouldn't welcome her. It seemed to her that the sorority's most successful members—professional women still managing to raise families—developed such steel-clad egos in coping with their lives that they had little imagination to spare for a complicated case like her. Mothers with less demanding jobs were defensive and tended to fear and despise her, because of her ambition. Mothers with no jobs at all attracted her—she felt, in fact, a particular tenderness towards unselfconscious women—but she could not be friends with them either, because they didn't understand her, and to the extent that they did begin to understand her, they would be confused and hurt by her refusal to be like them.

Friendless, Renée saw stereotypes everywhere she looked. Her head was full of images of women, and she hated most the ones she most resembled.

The well-spoken and socially concerned and humorless and defensive female academic.

The thin, vulnerable, self-absorbed, vaguely haunted-looking single woman who is either a spiritual seeker or simply a loser and probably the latter.

The unsatisfied thirty-year-old professional female who sees the error of her ways and begins to crave a baby.

The boring scientist who lives in a computer room but considers herself less boring than others like her because ten years ago she went to Clash concerts.

The girl who, not having many female friends, grew up reading science fiction and science and popular philosophy and who, as a woman, is still so romantic as to believe in things like corporate malfeasance and heroes who make a difference.

The medium-attractive female academic who in her quest to feel very attractive acquires the reputation of an easy lay.

The woman who cannot get along with other women and who hangs out with men and who in the course of time ends up sleeping with many of them and who, a traitor to her own sex, is respected by men only to the extent that she is like a man.

The medium-attractive and well-spoken academic female whom no one likes but who nevertheless considers herself extremely special and lovable and unusual and wears a certain smile that shows this and is therefore disliked all the more.

As the hateful stereotypes homed in on her, the only thing that saved her from concluding that all she really hated was herself was her selfconsciousness. Selfconsciousness was a guardian angel that accompanied her everywhere. In grocery stores it told her how to select foods—apples, eggs, fish, bread, butter, broccoli—that could be trusted not to put words in her mouth. Words like *I am a yuppie* or *I am trying hard not to be a yuppie* or *See how original I am* or *See how timid I am as I try to avoid being like the people I don't want to be, including those who are selfconsciously original.* It required daily vigilance to keep herself from cooking like well-educated thirty-year-olds on TV, or like gastronomes who became orgasmic over nice pasta, or like women on a magazine diet, or like men who thought it made them sexy and sophisticated to cook with capers and chuckle greedily about '71 Richebourgs. Or, conversely, like people who never gave a thought to food. Because unfortunately eating junk was not an option. In the future she imagined for herself, she would not be eating junk. She could hardly swallow junk.

Similarly, she couldn't bring herself to wear ugly clothes or to furnish her apartment with trash. In fact, when she shopped in a department store, the clothes and utensils that struck her as unimplicating invariably turned out to be the most expensive in their class. Clearly, if you were rich enough, transparency could be purchased. Not being rich, she faced the task of finding attractive and moderately priced things while avoiding every implicating mass-produced contemporary style. This hunt for neutral tops and neutral shoes and neutral outerwear and neutral chairs was time-consuming and made her all the more painfully aware of herself.

She hated new things "inspired by" old things—products soiled by a modern designer's nostalgia for the fifties or the twenties. The old things themselves she could trust, provided they hadn't passed through the soiling hands of a consciousness like her own. It had been a pleasure to outfit her apartment from a naïve flea market held weekly in the Somerville Library parking lot. But when she stepped into a "vintage" clothing store, even a store with nice merchandise, she felt faint and ill and soon fled. Only in a naïve thrift store, such as the Salvation Army ran, could she hope to hold out long enough to find something, and then only if she was not in Boston, because in Boston these stores were haunted by other bargain-hunting young people dangerously similar to herself.

Once every month or two, year in, year out, she thought of the clothes her mother hadn't given her.

They had come to light during her family's last year in Lake Forest, when everyone but Renée was about to move to California. She discovered them in a roomful of belongings bound for Goodwill. She was rescuing one last armful of them—some classic narrow skirts, a jacket with an emerald-green velvet collar, a bright red high-waisted hourglass dress, a checkered wool overcoat, a pair of black-on-brown saddle shoes—when her mother caught her.

"What are you doing with these?"

"I'm sorry. I'm sorry. I thought you were throwing them away."

"I am throwing them away."

"Well, can't I have them, then?"

"I'm giving them to Goodwill. Please put them back where you found them."

"Why can't I have them?"

"Honey, you have so many outfits in your closet that you've hardly even tried on. What do you need these old things for?"

"They're nice. I want them. Please let me have them."

Her mother shook her head sadly. "I'm very sorry if you had your heart set on these. But I don't want you wearing them."

"Oh, why not, why not, why not?"

"I just don't want to see you wearing them. They have associations for me."

"But I'm going away. You won't see me."

"You know I'll buy you anything you want. Things just like this. New things, better things. But think about if you had a boyfriend, that you broke up with. Would you give him to your best friend?"

"These are *clothes*."

"For me it's the same thing," her mother said.

Renée marched unsteadily out of her own bedroom, eyes brimming. Her mother didn't bend. The clothes went to Goodwill. In her memory they remained the most beautiful clothes she'd ever seen, the most perfect imaginable clothes for her. She might not have trusted her memory, except that there were pictures of the clothes in the family photo albums—pictures of the young Beth Macaulay on a tour of Europe that lasted through six seasons, pictures of the checkered coat in the Bois du Bologne. The checkered coat in Dublin. The striped sundress at Berck-Plage. Beth Macaulay in Arles, her perfect skin, her black-rimmed, black-lensed sunglasses, her funky saddle shoes, her diary. Her red dress in black-and-white in Rome. Her checkered coat in Venice.

She was three months pregnant when she married Daniel Seitchek, a young cardiologist from a West Side family of wholesalers and junior-college intellectuals. How painfully pained and washed out the young and pretty Elizabeth looked in black-and-white (the soot black of South Chicago, the white of fresh snow, the black-and-white of her checkered coat) as she held up her bundled baby girl for the camera.

How difficult it was to reconcile these images with the pink and white and kelly-green golfing outfits and tennis outfits worn by the woman Renée grew up knowing as her mother. This woman who eventually, in California, would drive a car with a plate that said MOMS JAG to high-school baseball games and sit in the stands with other mothers as tan as Egyptians and scream at her boys' successes and groan laughingly and cover her eyes at their failures. This woman who in her daughter's hearing once described herself as "kind of a Pollyanna," and who confessed to being "addicted" to the novels of Tom Clancy. The pictures of the beautifully clad Beth Macaulay in Europe seemed to say that she had once been more like Renée—more romantic, more independent—than anyone watching her little skirts flounce around a tennis court would ever guess. Being afraid of death, Renée wanted to believe that despite their different circumstances she had exactly the same soul as her mother. And it was tempting to let the *likelihood* of the identity, the common sense of the assumption, stand as a certainty. Unfortunately, she was also rational, and she refused to believe she was the same person as this partygoing Orange County Pollyanna without some sort of proof. And it just so happened that the years when her mother had been a different and presumably more Renée-like individual were precisely the years before there was any such person as Renée.

Meanwhile she was too selfconscious to fail to see the ironies: That even as she was being vigilant about not turning into a superficial person like her mother, she was spending huge amounts of time worrying about decor, clothes, and cooking. That she'd developed a bourgeois obsession with merchandise and appearances far more profound than her mother's. And that the intelligent and confident female types towards whom she felt a virulent, defensive animosity were precisely the types towards whom her mother also felt an animosity, though not as virulent and defensive as her daughter's, since she had her sons and grandchildren to distract and comfort her.

Renée knew that if she would only call off her quest for a perfect life, and settle down and accept having children as her mother had at her age, then she too could achieve a measure of contentment and forgetfulness. But there was nobody who wanted to marry her, and anyway, she hated people who were obsessed with their parents. A family was birdlime to the people in it, boredom to the people not. She hated the word "obsessed." She hated people who hated as many things as she did. She hated the life that made her hate so many things. But she didn't entirely hate herself yet.

9

She had only one dress, a ten-year-old beltless cotton print, that she considered fit to wear to lunch with Melanie Holland. The flat dancing slippers that she put on with it were soaked by the time the bus to Lechmere station picked her up on Highland Avenue. A fine, heavy rain choked the airspace above the Charles. The river was so swollen it looked higher than the streets around it.

On Boylston Street, in front of the hotel, a cab door opened and a pair of legs in skin-tight jeans and cowboy boots swung out, followed by an umbrella, a Filene's shopping bag, and finally, in a large-cut sealskin jacket, the rest of Melanie. She slammed the door and almost bumped into Renée, who was standing looking at her.

In the restaurant, hearty appetites were in evidence. Tourists were grinning and white-haired women were whispering about investments, each pair with an air of being the most important in the room. Melanie looked tired. She'd gotten some sun of late, but her skin was wrinkled and glossy, like old enamel work; the tan seemed not to want to stick to it. The silk lining of her jacket, which she'd slipped off her shoulders onto the cushion of the banquette, held her as tenderly as the tissue paper in which fine gifts come. She scrutinized Renée. "My goodness," she said. "You're wet!"

"Yeah, I'm a little wet."

"You came by train."

"Train and bus, yes."

"You live—let's see if I can guess." She made a booklet of her hands and raised it to her lips. "You're in . . . one of those old houses right on the Radcliffe side of the Square."

Renée shook her head.

"More towards Inman Square?"

"I live in Somerville."

"Oh." Melanie smiled vaguely and looked away. "Somerville." A waiter came. "Will you have a cocktail with me?"

"Campari with soda?" Renée said to the waiter.

"That sounds perfect," Melanie said. "So red, so chic."

The waiter nodded. So red. So chic.

"I'm glad you could come on short notice," Melanie said. "I'm afraid it's reached the point where I ought to be booking Boston from Chicago and vice versa. Wherever I am one week, I'll be in the other place the next. But that's the way it goes sometimes. That's the way it goes. Do you do much traveling in your job?"

Renée opened her mouth to answer, but she lost heart. She slid her teaspoon sideways on the tablecloth. "No," she said, "and maybe you should just tell me what you want."

"What I want? I want us to relax and enjoy ourselves and get to know each other a little. I want to be your friend."

"You want information."

"Partly, yes, but—"

"Then why don't you just ask me what you want to ask me? Because I'm not going to be able to help you, and so you might as well get it over with."

Melanie turned her head to one side and narrowed her eyes, exactly the way her son sometimes did. "Is something wrong? Is this not a good day? Oh dear!" She leaned across the table. "You're looking so unhappy. Was this not a good day?"

Renée returned her spoon to its original position. "I'm not unhappy."

"You think I have no personal interest in you. You think I took you to lunch to cajole you into answering my questions. Is that what you think? Yes or no."

"Yes."

"You're honest with me. I admire that. But you're wrong, and

I want to know how I can show you how wrong you are. Won't you tell me?"

"I guess—" Renée was at a loss. "I guess if you didn't ask me any questions, ever—then I'd have to think there was something else you wanted."

"But you'd never believe I wanted to be your friend. Hm. Well, I suppose I can't entirely blame you." Melanie dug in her purse as the waiter deposited their drinks. She took out a flat velvet box and pushed it across the table. "This is for you."

Renée looked at the box as if it happened to be where her eyes fell while she worried about something else.

"Do open it."

She shook her head. "I don't think so."

"Oh, really, Renée, I'm about to become quite impatient with you. You don't need to refuse a gift just to show me you're an honest person. We reach a point where it becomes insulting to me. Let's not pretend our circumstances are the same. An older woman who enjoys shopping gives a younger woman a token of her respect and affection, I really don't see any reason to be so morbidly scrupulous. There. That's right." Her eyes shone as Renée suddenly grabbed the box and, after a hesitation, removed a string of pearls.

"These are beautiful."

"With your colors, your hair, your skin. Pearls, platinum, silver, diamonds, I know from similar experience. Put, put them on. That's right. Of course we have to allow for this being something less than the ideal dress . . ." She handed her compact across the table, mirror upright. "Would you have time for a little shopping after lunch? I'd hate you not wearing these because nothing went."

Renée returned the pearls to the box. "Actually, I'm not sure these are my style."

"Oh, is that so? What is your style?"

"I don't know. Somerville."

"You! You are not a Somerville kind of person, anyone can see that. Not unless Somerville has changed greatly since I was growing up, which I can't imagine it has."

"What makes you think I'm not?"

"Your manners."

"My manners are awful. I'm offending you right and left."

"You're offending me in the manner of a very well bred, well educated, and self-aware young woman. And you know it."

Weak though it was, the Campari had gone straight to Renée's cheeks. She was immune to many things, but not to alcohol and not to a word like "self-aware," which, when used in reference to her, reliably touched off a small shudder in her body, a spasm of self-love. And after the spasm, a hotness of face, a weightlessness of limbs. She laughed, looking at the pearls. "How much did these cost you?"

"Yes, keep trying. But you're going to find me very difficult to offend today."

Renée put the pearls around her neck again and held up the compact. The mirror showed her a room broken into darkened, depthless fragments—chandeliers caught in the act of being, tables on a tilting floor, subliminal flashes of herself, a white throat. She spoke deliberately. "Maybe I'll keep them after all. If it's all the same to you."

"No, in fact, nothing would please me more."

"Perfect for the two of us, then."

"You're smiling, and you're right: what does a professional woman care about jewelry?" Melanie's own wrist jewelry jingled as she raised her glass. She drank with an actressy angling of her body and twisting of her hand. "But you see I'm just a silly house-wife. I have no particularly noble deeds to my credit. And at my age it's possible to feel as if all one has ever done in life is bring unhappiness to the world. Perhaps you can't really imagine that unless you've had children, but—"

"I can imagine it."

"I believe you, Renée. I believe you can. Perhaps you can also imagine how it feels to realize that your own children consider you a selfish person, and that there's nothing you can do to change this. They may be quite, quite wrong about you. They *are* quite wrong about you. But the fact remains that they're convinced that you're a selfish old witch, and this hurts you so terribly that you can't even explain to them why they're wrong."

All that was left of Renée's drink was ice and pink water. "You know I know your son, don't you?"

"You—? Oh yes, of course. I was very irritated with him that particular day. I was irritated that he'd invited people inside, with the house in such a state, although in hindsight I suppose it was all for the best." Melanie stroked her glass, appearing more and more to speak to herself. "Because there are things I want to say —things I *must* say—to someone. And if I could only relieve certain anxieties I have—if you could only give me a little advice, or comfort, so we could get that out of the way—I'd want more than anything to spend time with you. I want to make someone happy. And you in particular, I don't even know why."

"What advice?"

"We don't need to discuss that yet."

Renée leaned forward confidentially. There was a new, wild light in her face, as if great ironies were dawning on her. "I think we should discuss it right now. Then it's all over with, right?"

Melanie was about to speak but then she noticed Renée's empty glass and attracted the waiter's attention. When the fresh drink came, she watched Renée sip her way deeply into it.

"I own a house," she said huskily, "that I can't insure against earthquake damage and can't get more than eighty percent of its January value for. Should I sell now and invest the money elsewhere at ten percent? Or are prices going to bounce back up in less than two years? That's my first question. I also, because of the stupidity and stubbornness of my father, own three hundred thousand shares of a company whose stock has lost a quarter of its value since the first of April, largely because of the threat of earthquakes. I'm about to get control of those shares and I want to know, do I cut my losses, or are the earthquakes going to stop? And there you have it. I've told you more about myself than anyone but my attorney knows. Is that clear? I've opened my heart, Renée, and it's in your hands. You can judge for yourself whether I'm simply desperate or whether I'm trusting you because I feel an affinity between us."

With sudden briskness, she took her half glasses from her purse. She scowled at her menu for exactly three seconds before asking Renée, whose menu appeared to be in Arabic, what she thought she was going to have. She was inclining towards the red snapper and the house salad. How did that sound?

"I need to read the menu," Renée said.

Melanie tossed hers aside and gazed at a far corner of the dining room. Finally Renée gave up trying to make sense of the entries. She drank off the remainder of her Campari and soda. "What makes you think I have any advice for you? You read the paper. I read the paper."

"I don't give a hoot what's in the paper," said Melanie.

"Why not?"

"Because everyone can read it. It's automatically worthless as investment information. The markets are depressed now because of all the uncertainty in the papers. They say there *probably* won't be any more major earthquakes. But they also say there might very well be."

"Uh-huh."

"Don't you see? Probabilities don't do me any good. I have to make a decision."

"I know. I understand. But why don't you assume there's a fifty percent chance of further earthquakes, and sell fifty percent of your stock? Or do twenty percent, if you think there's a twenty percent chance."

"No! No!" Melanie bounced vehemently on her banquette. "You're not following me. I'm saying that I have already *lost* one quarter of what I had three months ago, before I could do a thing about it. I'm saying that I will not lose any more, I will *not*, I will *not*. If I sell fifty percent of that stock and it rebounds to its March level, I'll have suffered a pure loss on that fifty percent."

"But you couldn't do anything about that," Renée said in a reasonable voice. "So why don't you just decide that what you inherited is only as much as you have when you get control of it. That's what you're starting with, and you can sell it all, and that's what you got. It still must be a lot, right?"

Melanie closed her eyes. "This is what I go through with my attorney. This is what my husband tells me. I was hoping that a woman might be able to understand why I refuse, I *refuse* to be told that this is all I get. This isn't greed, Renée. It's a matter of not being stupid. If I have to make the wrong decision, I at least want it to be on someone else's recommendation. Because I simply could not *live* having to blame myself."

"Blame your father," Renée ventured.

"If only that would help. I can blame him for putting me in this position, but I'm still the one in this position."

"Larry Axelrod? At MIT. I can put you in touch with him."

Melanie leaned forward, shaking her head and smiling at Renée's innocence. "Don't you see? Every investor in Boston is going to him or other people like him. They've already had their impact on the market. I don't get any edge by taking their advice, and what's more, I don't believe them. I don't think they can tell the truth, because they know that all the markets are listening. That's why they say fifty percent this, fifty percent that."

"So you think that because I don't know anything about New England earthquakes I'm the perfect person to ask."

"Yes."

"That's very rational of you."

"I'm glad you think so. You see, because among other things, I've noticed that of all the institutions in Boston, Harvard is the only one not saying anything about the earthquakes. And I have to wonder why that is."

"Nobody's doing local studies right now. We do mainly theory, also global studies and research with global networks."

"And you, as an intelligent seismologist, are unable to look at the work being done locally and come to any independent conclusions?"

"I can come to conclusions. But I don't see why you think they're worth more than Larry Axelrod's."

"Renée, I've spent half my life among academics, and I've seen these Larry Axelrods on television. I know a special mind when I see one. There's no point in telling me not to trust you, because I'm not going to listen to you. I'm going to trust you, and you're going to tell me how I can repay you. Because I do intend to repay you."

Melanie had put her purse on her lap and rested her hand on the catch. Renée had been expecting this. "You want to know whether to sell the house, and whether to sell the stock. Two simple answers."

"Yes."

"What if I'm wrong?"

"Well, you'll know that if you're right, I'll be grateful to you. And if I'm grateful to you, you'll be very, very happy to be a friend of mine."

"You mean money."

Melanie looked down at her purse as though sorry to find it on her lap. "Preferably not. But whatever your style is. I wouldn't want to give you something you didn't find useful."

"But if I'm wrong anyway?"

"I don't expect you to be wrong, but if you are, I'll know that you tried very hard to be right. I'll know that I did everything I possibly could to make the right decision, that I consulted a person I trusted, and we simply had bad luck. As I said, it's not that I'm so greedy. It's that I can't bear the responsibility."

"This is Sweeting-Aldren we're talking about."

"That's right." Melanie laughed nervously. "I hope you didn't find that out from Louis. He makes a point of being indiscreet."

"I think I can help you," Renée said.

"You haven't seen him again, have you?"

"Pardon me?"

"You said you knew him. You meant the day of the earthquake. You didn't see him again after that."

"No, actually. Actually I did. He invited me to a party at your daughter's."

"Oh." Melanie paled, touching her mouth. "I see. And did you go?"

"Yes."

"You didn't tell me that."

"I tried to."

"You did not tell me that." She twisted sideways in her seat, touching every part of her face with her fingers, as if she wasn't sure it was all there. "And that—that should have been the very first thing you told me." She nodded to herself. "The very first thing."

"I tried to."

She swung violently to face Renée. *"Are you involved with my son?"*

"No!"

"Have you *been* involved with him?"

"No. No! I went to a party with him. And a few weeks ago I
—went to dinner at your sister's. Your daughter's. He seemed to
think he needed a date. He was very polite to me."

"Did you talk about me?"

"Not at all."

"How come your hands are shaking?"

"Because you're scaring me."

"Did you tell him that I'd called you?"

"I mentioned it, yeah."

"How many hours?"

"I beg your pardon?"

"How many hours have you spent with him?"

She shrugged. "Ten. Eight. I don't know."

Melanie leaned across the table and searched Renée's face,
touching it with her gaze as she'd been touching her own face with
her fingers, her fear growing as it sent roots deeper into the gap
between the sweetness of the face and the underlying possibility
that Renée was lying. It was pathetically evident how much she
longed to trust Renée. But she couldn't get a definite answer from
the face, and she'd placed such hopes in it that she couldn't bear
to keep on looking, lest she find her suspicions confirmed. "Oh
God." Again she turned sideways on the banquette. "Oh God, I
don't know what to do."

"Why don't you call Louis and ask him? If it's so important
to you."

"Ten minutes ago you were trying to convince me not to trust
you. Now you're doing the opposite. It's because I mentioned
money. I dare you to say it's not true."

"What's happened is that you seem to think I have some reason
to be lying to you."

"You're not the same person I spoke with two months ago.
And now I see why. Now I see why. How could I have not thought
of this? Oh, why didn't you tell me?"

"Are you ladies ready to order?" With a flourish the waiter
produced a ballpoint pen.

Making severe eye contact with him, Melanie donned her
glasses and placed her order. Then, while Renée ordered, she
clutched the glasses in her fist, squeezing them so hard the plastic

creaked, and stared hopelessly across the dining room. Renée covered the fist with her hand. She was thinking so hard that her lips stirred faintly. "I said I could help you," she said. "I know what you should do with your stock, and you'll be very happy you asked me. I'm going to help you."

Melanie tilted her head back and swallowed.

"I'm going to tell you what to do," Renée said. "And I'm so sure I'm right that I'm going to back it up with whatever money I have."

The light in her face had become a glittering, intoxicated implacability. She stroked Melanie's hand. Suddenly fingernails sank into her wrist. A face rushed forward; it smelled of breath, perfume, ingratiating skin cream. *"Are you involved with my son?"*

"No!"

"And you want money from me."

"Yes."

"You want to make a deal."

"Yes."

Melanie slumped back into her seat. "All right." A full minute passed as she sat and bit her lips, her fears obviously undispelled. Finally Renée asked if she wanted wine.

"Not for me, thank you. You may order a glass for yourself."

"Can I order a bottle?"

"Whatever you like."

"Why don't we *relax* and *enjoy* ourselves?"

Melanie shook her head hopelessly. "It would have been better to avoid money as a topic. It would have been better to wait. You can mock me now, but I really did have hopes for a different kind of lunch."

"I'm going to give you good advice. You won't be sorry."

"I'm sorry already. I'm sorry to have involved you in this. I'm sorry to be involved in it myself."

"Let's just finish, then. Let's just do the last thing. And then we can relax."

Melanie stiffened at this mention of the "last thing." She hesitated and hesitated before she finally took a matchbook from her purse, wrote a figure on the inside, and nudged it across the tablecloth.

Renée read the figure, took the pen, and calmly added a zero. "I may want more," she said. "If I'm right. You'll need to give me a few days. But I definitely won't take less, unless . . ." She considered. "Why don't I take whatever cash I have in the bank and put it up as security? Then we can have a—what would you call it? A sliding scale. The less right I am, the less you give me. If I'm wrong, you keep the security."

"I'm not going to discuss this with you. We'll meet on Tuesday."

"See if you can do better in the meantime."

"I may do just that."

"Uh-huh. Talk to Larry Axelrod."

"Perhaps."

Renée ate a plate of carpaccio drenched in yellow oil. She kept emptying her wineglass, until she began to glow like an object in a kiln, her selfconsciousness transmuted into volubility as she did her Why I Hate Boston number, her California's Even Worse number. Melanie might have been listening to a daughter whom she liked and had every reason to be entertained by, and yet seeing in her only reminders of her own heavy heart. Of her relative proximity to death, of her inability to relax and enjoy a lunch, of her estrangement from the world of things that young people talk about. This really does happen to parents who are unhappy, even those who love their children.

Her tongue curled as she added up the figures on the check. Renée was glowing as if she'd been through a snowstorm. Back on the planet of ceaseless car traffic, in front of the hotel, she asked for money for a cab. Melanie opened her purse on her hip and dug a twenty out. "I'm sure you think it's silly of me to keep asking. Perhaps it doesn't even matter. But—"

Renée's fingers closed on the bill. "But."

"Well, only whether there is some involvement between you and Louis."

She took Melanie by the shoulders. "What do you think?"

"I suppose I'm still inclined to think there is."

"Really." She pulled Melanie closer and kissed her on the mouth, the way any woman might kiss the person who'd wooed her over lunch with pearls and wine.

Melanie wrenched free and dusted herself off. "I'm going to have to reconsider this, Renée. We'll assume you've had a little too much to drink. But I'm afraid I'm still going to have to reconsider."

"Sliding scale. Security. Immediate terms."

"I'll talk to you on Tuesday morning."

"See you then."

The rain had turned to a fine warm mist, agreeable to the skin. As soon as Renée was in a cab, she stretched out on the seat.

"You OK there?" the Haitian driver said.

"Yes," she said loudly.

Water trickled and made lenses on the window above her, a twisted aspect of the city in every droplet. The soaked façades upside down, the utility wires dipping and dividing. She was feverish. Three in the afternoon, drunk off her ass and lying in a cab. Romance, romance. Three in the afternoon, the warm rain, she's coming home from seeing herself. She can still feel her warmth inside her and on her skin. She can smell her own nose, she can taste her own mouth.

"That's twelve dollars, sixty cents."

"Go up the hill here on Walnut."

Her stomach upset by the carpaccio and wine, she lay on her bed until the windows stopped getting darker and became a little lighter and the rain turned to steam and silence. It was as if a tent had descended on the street, its damp canvas flaps coming to rest behind the houses; as if the street were a film lot hosed down for a nighttime shoot, with a loud, busy world beyond the houses. A near neighbor was cooking waffles. Girls and boys on the porch across the street turned on a heavy-metal anthem. It might have been playing in the next room, not outside. She plugged in her telephone and dialed a number. "Howard Chun, please."

"He not here," came the answer.

She changed her clothes and went down to the street. One of the porch girls—the fat one; there were also two skinny ones—turned up the music. Maybe they thought she was going to complain about it. She mounted the stairs. "Does somebody here have a joint I could buy?"

They turned the radio down, and she repeated the question,

looking from skeptical face to skeptical face. The younger boy was ten or eleven. "Are you Jewish?" he said matter-of-factly.

"No."

"What's your last name?"

She smiled. "Smith."

"Bernstein," the boy countered.

"Greenstein," said a girl.

"Shalom!"

Renée waited.

"How long you been living there?" the fat girl asked.

"Five years," she said. "How long have you been here?"

"Where's your Chinese boyfriend?"

"She's got a bald one."

"Hey. *Hey*. You got any beer?"

She crossed her arms. "How old are you guys?"

The older boy, silent until now, rose stiffly from a broken Adirondack chair. His puffy high-tops were carefully unlaced. "You gotta buy us some beer," he said.

"All right. How much?"

The girls conferred, the older boy taking pains to appear uninvolved. "Ten, but they gotta be taw-boys," the fat girl announced positively.

"They have to be what?"

"Taw-boys."

"Taw-boys?" Renée smiled, not understanding.

"TAW BOYS. THE BIG CANS."

"The sixteen-ounce cans!"

"The fucking taw cans!"

"Doy, doy, doy."

"You know what sixty-nining is?"

"Steven, shut up, you little jerk."

"Doy, doy, doy."

Standing apart, the older boy rolled his eyes. Renée descended the steps to cries of *Shalom!* A smell of infrastructure was stealing from the bushes, and she could hear her own telephone ringing, another pro-lifer calling.

When she came back from Highland Avenue, the older boy

led her into the front room of the first-floor apartment and broke two cans off one of the six-packs she'd bought, returning them to the paper bag. He showed her his dope. "It's very fresh," he said earnestly. "Steven, close the fucking door." The door closed. "Which one you want? Take the big one. My name's Doug."

"How old are you?"

"Almost sixteen. I'm gonna get my license. You go out with me sometime?"

"I don't think so."

On her kitchen table she set out the joint, a pack of matches, and a saucer. She positioned a chair in front of them and turned off all but one light. She had a cassette marked DANCE that had been broken for five years. Training her desk light on it, she opened it up and spliced out the mangled stretch with Scotch Magic tape and nail scissors.

The dope tasted like April in college; like the music on the tape. She danced to "London's Burning" and "Spinning Top" and "I Found That Essence Rare," her arms and legs mixing the last faint banks of smoke into a haze. She thought she was crying when "Beast of Burden" played, but when she opened her eyes there were no tears and it seemed that she'd only imagined it.

Outside the kitchen window she lay down on the wet, sloping shingles. They were made of real slate.

In the morning she tracked down a mineralogy professor who liked her and had lent her one of his cars several times before. She also appropriated a departmental camera, with a zoom telephoto lens. The sun was blazing on Route 128. As methodically as she could, she drove every road and street in Danvers, western Peabody, northern Lynn, and South Lynnfield, stopping often to trace her route on a map with a red pencil. There were zero cars in the parking lot of Sweeting-Aldren corporate headquarters, a white Monticello-inspired structure set into a green hillside. From a Boston & Maine railroad bridge, from the back of an unfinished office complex, and from the rear corner of a cemetery, she surveyed company installations—regiments of horizontal tanks like giant caplets, towers with iron vines with iron tendrils spiraling up them. The corrugated siding of the major buildings was a certain pale blue she didn't think she'd ever seen; on a color chart, the shades all around it were probably pleasing, but this particular blue was not. Dreamy fumes of acetone were native to the place.

By Monday the heat had reached full, white force. She dressed in cutoffs, sandals, and a tank top that she'd never worn except to sleep in. At the Peabody City Hall, on the ground floor outside the Assessor's Office, she found listings for eight smaller, non-contiguous parcels of land owned by Sweeting-Aldren. The six of them that she could tour by car had nothing more interesting than horses on them; she didn't try to reach the others. She was driving as fast as she dared, and still it was almost four o'clock by the time she got to Beverly airport.

A girl in the coffee shop was lifting a wire basket of french fries out of oil. She told Renée to talk to a man named Kevin in the hangar.

"I should just go right in?"

"Yeah, you'll find him."

As soon as she went through the hangar door someone whistled at her, but all she could see at first was a blinding square of white sky at the far end. Near where she stood, the cowlings had been removed from a Cherokee and from an eight-seat turboprop with a boxy grasshopper body. Two grease-blackened twosomes in blue coveralls were working on their shiny guts, reaching up with tools. Asked about Kevin, they pointed to a young man on a ladder by a baby jet farther down. He was spraying aerosol cleaner on the jet's windshield.

"Are you Kevin?"

"That's right." He was in his early twenties, had sky-blue eyes, a crew cut, and straight-arrow posture. Across the corridor, the inside of another baby jet was being vacuumed, country music wafting out and an extension cord dangling from the door.

"I was told to talk to you about being taken for a ride."

"Where to?"

"Just around the neighborhood."

He came promptly down the ladder, leading her to think they'd be airborne in a matter of minutes, but in fact she had to breathe exhaust gases and fuel gases for nearly an hour. She handed over money and filled out and signed an insurance waiver. Kevin disappeared for a while and came back minus his coveralls, spent ten minutes determining that he didn't like something about the oddly upside-down-looking plane he tried first, fiddled and diddled with an ordinary plane, a Cessna, and finally parked it outside the mouth of the hangar. He'd put dark shades on. "Where we going?"

"Just around Peabody a couple times. There are some things I'd like to look at."

He brought the mike to his lips and muttered nothings into its plastic grooves. There was a small spiral notepad in a pocket below the instrument panel. He flipped the laminated pages one by one, raising and lowering flaps, feeding the engine until the propellers became invisible, muttering into the mike again, flipping switches. Cabin temperature rose twenty or thirty degrees. The engine noise reached screaming heights as they bounced along soft-ened asphalt and firm concrete and swung out onto the runway, neatly astride the center-line stripe. Heated air and the scaly heads of weeds were the only things moving in the acres of vacancy around them.

They swung right and left and bounced on the air like a jeep on a hillside.

"There's a control space right southeast here," Kevin shouted. "I'm going to swing north of Danvers if that's all right with you."

"Sure."

No noise in particular stood out, but it was hard to hear. Kevin kissed the mike and hung it up. "You can turn that lever there now, get a little air."

It was an ugly day for flying, the rivers an evil turbid yellow, the glare inescapable. The atmospheric soup extended far above the altitude they were maintaining, and everything on the ground dissolved in blue unless she looked straight down. Lakes and rivers were like spills of shiny lead on the blue-black land, stretching towards a blue-brown horizon. Each time they flew over water the plane dropped like a yo-yo. Each plummet was followed by an upward rebound that could be expected but not prepared for. Kevin set a paper bag on Renée's bare knee.

"You're cute," she essayed, at a shout.

"So are you. Not as cute as my wife, though."

She nodded judiciously. "What's your job?"

"I fly for a tool company in Lynn. They've got a jet and a couple planes. I'm number two, I don't fly the jet much. I take the president to Maine a lot. Vacation house. His guests too. How about you?"

"I'm a photographer."

"For—?" He pointed at the label on her camera. "Harvard Geophysics?"

"Yeah."

"You interested in earthquakes?"

"No," she shouted. "Land forms."

"I thought you might be looking for faults or whatever. Lot of seismologists around here. Guy I know took one up last month, all up and down the coast."

"Can I show you where I want to go?" She held up a map on which she'd circled in red the main Sweeting-Aldren property and the two smaller plots she hadn't seen yet. Kevin put it on his lap, studied it a moment, and then looked straight ahead through the windshield. The plane leaped drastically into another thermal. The sound of the engine changed and stayed changed.

"Is this OK?" she shouted.

It was a while before he answered. "What do you want to look at Sweeting-Aldren for?"

She craned her neck, pretending to check the map. "Oh, is that what those are?"

"You got some special reason?"

"I'm looking at land forms."

"I can't take you any lower than three thousand feet."

"How high are we now?"

"Three thousand feet."

"Why not?"

" 'Cause they don't like it. They're a company. They've got secrets."

"What if I see something I want to see?"

"About half the corporate business at Beverly Municipal is Sweeting-Aldren. They've got six jets there. You know what I'm saying?"

"No."

"I'm saying that's where I work."

"You work for Sweeting-Aldren?"

"I work for Barnett Die. But I'm at the airport. You know what I'm saying?"

He pointed out the two small properties, a pair of fields split by dirt roads. They hit another bump. The engine coughed as they banked, sun spilling crazily across Renée's lap and out the other window. A hillside vomited smashed cars and clots of rusted waste. Proud mansions spread their green velvet skirts on land wedged between the old brick phalluses of industry and the newer plants —flat rectangles with gravel on the roof and trailers crowding to feed at troughs in back. The most permeable of membranes separated a country club from acres of bone-colored slag piles streaked with sulfuric yellow, like the pissings of a four-story dog. Low-rise condos with brand-new parking lots and BayBank branches were perched above algae-filled sinkholes littered with indestructibles. Everywhere wealth and filth were cheek by jowl. Before it gave way to Sweeting-Aldren's property, the landscape seemed to hesitate, real-estate development dwindling to undernourished neighborhoods of flat, small houses, some mobile homes, lone taverns, and unpaved streets skirting woods and dying in front of a futile house or two, half-finished, with refuse cascading down embankments. On the company side of the woods, pipes and rails on low piers made beelines across wetlands, passing through industrial suburbs of identical circular pods, crossing over beltways of tangled pipes, plunging into downtown and then out along spokes to satellite developments. Vehicles crept through the ranks of ten thousand color-coded barrels; steam dribbled from the tops of silver tiparillos. There was an impression of good management, a logic to the coding and the movement. The black ocean sparkled just beyond.

Kevin dipped a wing so Renée could snap some pictures. "Seen enough?"

"No," she shouted. "You have to take me lower."

"You're looking kind of gray."

"You have to take me lower."

"I'll give you one pass at fifteen hundred. Then we go back."

"Two passes at a thousand."

He shook his head. The plane shot upward like a helium balloon.

"What can I give you?" She did her best to smile nicely. The plane fell so hard her teeth clicked.

"You don't understand," Kevin said. "They're very, very touchy."

"I'll give you more money."

He shook his head. "One pass at fifteen hundred. And I want to see your driver's license or student ID or whatever. Something with a picture."

He took her license and verified her name and image as they circled counterclockwise. "You're thirty," he said.

She nodded, lowering her head between her knees. She got her bag open just before a wave of motion ran up her back and shook her shoulders. The bag stiffened with the new weight inside it. Kevin handed her a fresh one.

"Throw that in the back seat. We'll go up the western side, cut around east, and head back. It'll all be out your window. Sun behind you. You gonna survive?"

The only thing that kept her upright was leaning on the camera with the lens against her window. She shot at everything, working the zoom. They were already past the central installation when she realized that she wasn't seeing anything, that she should have just been looking.

They had to circle Wenham while a jet landed ahead of them and another one took off. She kept her eyes shut and her face pressed to the air vent. Each bump, even the smallest, deepened her misery. It appalled her that Kevin continued to give her information to digest. Facts were as unwelcome as a tuna salad sandwich.

"We're into rush hour. They just cleared an inbound Sweeting-Aldren jet and there's another one behind it. They should have their own little airline."

The plane went up and down. The engine droned.

"Three minutes, you'll be on the ground. A day like this will do it to almost anybody."

Through one eye Renée glimpsed the runway spreading out in front of them. She didn't open her eyes again until they'd taxied to a stop. "Check this out," Kevin said, nodding at the hangar.

Two men in suits, one of them wearing a hard hat, were standing just inside the entry.

"You didn't believe me, did you?"

"Wait wait wait." She was rewinding the camera.

"I'm not seeing this. I'm slowly getting out the door."

Head down, she reloaded and fired twenty shots at nothing. The men were now standing on the apron. When she climbed out, one of them looked inside the plane and the other led her into the hangar.

"You've got to let her sit down," Kevin said. "She's very sick."

She leaned mutely against a wall in a corridor while, behind her, her shoulder bag was searched. In the coffee shop she was allowed to slump into a booth that had a long, thin smear of ketchup running across the table. The man in the hard hat was holding her bag on his lap; his face was red and ingrown and astonished, a cervix with beady eyes. He remained silent for the entire interview, tirelessly assessing her breasts and shoulders.

The other man had a tonsure, thick straight hair the color of pencil lead bunching onto his shirt collar, and an eagle's smart brow. He turned her IDs over in his fingers. "Renée Seitchek, 7 Pleasant Avenue, Somerville. Harvard University." He pinned her with a look. "Renée, we hear you photographed some facilities. We're frankly dying to know what moved you to photograph those particular facilities."

"Can I have a glass of water?"

"Tummy upset? Maybe a little Sprite for that. Bruce?" He waved a hand at the counter, and Bruce rose. "But go on."

"I'm a photographer."

"A photographer! What kinds of things you enjoy taking pictures of, Renée?"

"Interesting, beautiful . . . things."

"Ah. Art photographer. That's fascinating." Her interrogator gazed at her admiringly. "But you know, I can't resist asking you, what's so beautiful about an industrial facility? You want to try and explain that to me? Being as it runs more or less counter to our prejudices."

"Who are you?" Renée said.

"Rod Logan, Process Security Manager, Sweeting-Aldren Industries. My assistant Bruce Feschting. We made a special little trip over here to meet you, Renée. Oh, and would you look at that. Bruce outdoes himself again. Sprite *and* water *and* a napkin. Apropos of which, Renée, you might want to give your chin a teeny wipe."

A party of men in hard-soled shoes marched through the coffee shop, exchanging salutations with Logan and Feschting. Briefcases swung as they headed out the parking-side door.

"But these art photographs," Logan said. "What's the market like? You have a wealthy patron? A lot of corporations buying art these days."

"It's just for me."

"Just for you! You don't mind if I ask what brought you to these particular facilities, do you?"

"I saw them from the road."

"Just driving by, eh? Was there anything in particular that struck you as interesting and beautiful about our facilities?"

"No. Just the whole thing. How it looked."

"Gosh, if the world doesn't have a way of throwing you for a loop sometimes." Logan shook his head. "Just totally for a loop. You know, somewhere I'm sure there's an Earth where a Harvard girl really does go to the airport closest to us and flies by in broad daylight in a well-marked plane and really does want to take pictures for the sheer joy it brings her. Infinite universe, infinity of worlds. But you see, which world am I really in? This one? Or maybe more like this one?" He chopped the air with his hands, suggesting galaxies in motion. "But listen, Renée. I'm a reasonable man. And legally, legally, I can't really prevent you from snapping away to your little heart's content. Were you aware of that? That I can't legally prevent you? But you see, I'm holding your camera on my lap now, and Bruce is holding the other roll of film that was in your purse—"

"It's unexposed."

"Is it unexposed, Bruce? Yes, so it seems. So you'll be happy to sell us that one for ten dollars. And as far as what's in the camera, speaking practically, I'd like to offer you free processing and printing, and we'll send it to you at your Somerville address.

I frankly can't think of a more amicable arrangement. Because you see, Renée, we take our trade secrets very seriously, and we have armed guards on our property and a million-dollar cash reserve specifically earmarked for prosecuting industrial spies to the fullest extent of the law, so why don't you let me have these printed and sent to you at our expense? Does that sound reasonable, Bruce?"

"They're private," Renée said.

"Ah, they're private, yes. But as a practical matter, in terms of who has the camera on his lap, I'd have to say your only other alternative would be to allow me to open the camera and expose the entire film to light."

She clutched her head wretchedly. "Go ahead. Just leave me alone."

"You're sure?" Logan said, already opening the camera.

A new contingent of executives had entered the coffee shop. Feschting stood up awkwardly and stepped out of the booth. "Mr. Tabscott," he said. "Mr. Stoorhuys."

"Hey, Dave, Dick." Logan nodded at the newcomers, his hands full of film.

"Rod, Bruce, where you in from?"

"In from nowhere. Got a little episode here."

Tabscott left the coffee shop, but Stoorhuys stopped and leaned over the booth, his jacket bunching at the elbows, five inches of shirt cuff showing. He bowed his head, but he was looking at Renée, sideways. His lips curled away from his teeth.

"This is Renée Seitchek," Logan said. "Our latest flyby. Art photographer. Harvard Geophysics student. Greenness of gills due to violent airsickness."

Lips agape, Stoorhuys studied her more closely. "Mr. Logan explained our sensitivity?"

"Yes."

"We'll see to it you're reimbursed for your film."

She nodded, eyes cast down.

"She enjoys photographing beautiful and interesting things," Logan remarked.

"She's a beautiful and interesting thing herself," Stoorhuys said with patent insincerity. He appeared to have lost interest. His lanky fingers squeezed Logan's shoulder. "Take it easy."

"Will do, Dave."

Moments later she was left alone in the booth. She drank her water, put her head down, filled her lungs. A twenty-dollar bill was lying near her ear. Suddenly a paper bag landed on the table. She jumped.

"Here's your barf," Kevin said.

She took a handful of napkins when she left the coffee shop. She drove for twenty minutes and finally stopped in a Shawmut Bank parking lot. Crouching behind a dumpster like a raccoon, she tore open the airsickness bag and recovered the film canister from beneath the contents of her stomach. Highway lights flashed in her eyes as she cast a furtive glance over her shoulder.

It was becoming apparent that she wouldn't be able to see the pictures before she met with Melanie. She doubted they'd show much in any case. If Sweeting-Aldren maintained a pumping station near its main installation, it was almost certainly hidden in a shed. She drove back to Cambridge, returned the car, and stayed in Widener Library until the closing bells rang.

The next morning she couldn't keep her breakfast down. She smoked the remainder of her joint and had a second breakfast at Au Bon Pain before returning to the microfilm machines in Widener. At one-fifteen she made a copy of a picture in the *Globe* of March 9, 1970. It showed a newly opened four-story bank and office building on Andover Street in Peabody; just visible through the bare trees in the background was the top of a structure that arguably resembled a drilling derrick.

She took her Series E bond to her bank. It was the gift of a dead grandmother. The customer-service representative observed that it wouldn't mature for another two years.

"What's it worth now?"

She had eighty hundred-dollar bills in the left front pocket of her jeans when she stepped off the train in Salem with the first wave of returning commuters. The address she'd been given led her to the County Courthouse, across the street from which, in a restored white clapboard house bearing a plaque that said 1753, were the offices of Arger, Kummer & Rudman.

"Ms. Seitchek," Henry Rudman said expansively, pressing his

broad hand into the small of her back. He put her in a chair directly in front of his desk and hovered there, offering refreshments.

"Some cold water, please."

Behind his desk, in a corner of his office between a computer and a struggling window airconditioner, Melanie was sitting with her head bowed and her hands clasped on her lap. She gave Renée a single glance, full of hurt, like a woman in a courtroom who no longer expects anything from her husband but a share of his assets and future income. Love had died. It had come to this.

Renée crossed her arms and tossed her head indifferently. Standing on Rudman's desk were small photos of a wife and three little girls, but ornamentally the office was dominated by three black-and-white enlargements on the wall, all of them auto-graphed: Ted Williams on a cruise ship, his arm around a younger Rudman's shoulders; Rudman and Yastrzemski cheek to cheek, at a banquet table; Rudman and Jim Rice, drivers in hand, on a golf course with palm trees in the background. Renée laughed. Her eyes were inflamed, her chin spotted with new pimples. Her hair had been growing out for months, and now all at once it was almost shoulder-length—unwashed, a tangle of stiff waves. She smelled like scalp and outdoor sweat. Altogether she was sleek with skin oil, sleek and dirty and animal and hot. She threw a sudden glance at Melanie, who lowered her eyes again.

Rudman carried in a cup of water and planted himself behind his desk. "So, ladies, are we all set?" He didn't wait for an answer. "Ms. Seitchek, Mrs. Holland tells me you've approached her about making a bet on the performance of a certain piece of real estate and the stock of a certain company. The piece of real estate being her property in Ipswich, and the stock being Sweeting-Aldren common. Is this correct?"

"No," she said. "I didn't approach her. She approached me. Also, I don't have anything to say about the real estate. If she wants to draw conclusions based on what I say about the stock, fine."

Rudman and Melanie exchanged glances. "You're a seismol-ogist, Ms. Seitchek."

"Yes."

"We can assume you're basing your prediction on your interpretation of seismological data. But the prediction applies only to the stock."

"Peabody and Ipswich are eleven miles apart."

"This is news?"

"I'm saying there's no obvious linkage."

Rudman turned. "Mrs. Holland?"

Melanie pressed her lips together, counting the proverbial five. "I'd like to remind you, Renée, that while it's true I did approach you, it was you who mentioned money and suggested an arrangement. I'd also like to remind you that you began by deliberately concealing that you had information that could help me, and you did *not* tell me this would not apply to real estate."

Renée gave her a smiley smile. "You want me to leave?"

"Ladies, ladies."

"I would appreciate it if you told the *truth,*" Melanie said whitely. "That is all I am saying."

"All right, Ms. Seitchek? You try to tell the truth so we can move along? That goes for you too, Mrs. Holland."

Melanie struck a righteous pose.

"Now, Ms. Seitchek, ah." Rudman scratched his mustache. "Mrs. Holland represented that you hoped she'd wager, ah, fifty thousand dollars, which we can assume is—"

"No," Renée said emphatically. "No. I said I wanted a *minimum* of fifty thousand dollars. I also said that the more right I am, the more I should be rewarded."

"I never agreed to any such thing."

"Did I say you did?"

"Ladies."

"I also said I'd bet as much money as I could get my hands on. Which I'm ready to do." She took out her wad of bills and tossed them onto Rudman's desk.

"Cash!" he exclaimed like a horrified Faust, half rising from his chair.

"Put that away," Melanie said.

"Ms. Seitchek. Please, ah. This is very touching, gesture-wise, but really, you want to keep that in a safe place. You don't want that on people's desks, with no rubber band, et cetera. I was on the point of telling you that Mrs. Holland respectfully declines the offer of security and a sliding scale. In return she insists on the cap of fifty thousand you proposed."

Renée stood up and stuffed the bills back in her pocket. "No deal."

"Mrs. Holland?"

Melanie cocked her head mechanically, like a bird. "What kind of a cap did you have in mind, Renée? Or did you want no cap at all? Perhaps you were thinking of a straight thirty percent?"

"One million dollars."

Melanie blew air out derisively.

"How much cash do you have there, Ms. Seitchek? If I may ask."

Ignoring him, she took a step towards Melanie and addressed her directly. "I'm going to tell you what this particular stock is going to do in the next three months or six months, whichever you prefer. You'll either buy or sell your shares on my recommendation. If you make five hundred thousand dollars because I gave you the right advice, I want fifty thousand. If you make ten million, I want one million. That's ten percent up to one million. If you make nothing at all, or if you lose money, you keep all the cash I have on me now. It's eight thousand dollars."

Rudman was shaking his head and waving his arms, trying to whistle the play dead. Melanie looked up at Renée wildly. "It's Louis!" she said. "It's not you at all. You—you're not even here! It's Louis!"

"Oh dear, Mrs. Holland. Really."

"You are wrong," Renée said, shaking with hatred. "You are so wrong."

Rudman nodded at her. "You see? She says you're wrong. You see? But, ah, Ms. Seitchek, you'll have to excuse us for a second."

He led Melanie across the office and into a conference room, lined with precedents, that opened off the rear. Hearing the latch click, Renée sat down and closed her eyes and breathed. Five minutes passed before Rudman stepped out. "Ten percent up to 200 K, eight thousand security."

She didn't turn around. "No," she said, and added, as if it

were a foreign word she wasn't sure she'd pronounced right: "No."

He retreated. This time he was back in less than a minute. "Last offer, Ms. Seitchek. Three hundred fifty K."

"No."

Again the latch clicked. She thought she was alone, but then she felt his hand on her shoulder, and his mustache bore down on her. "You said no?"

"That's right."

"Let me ask you a question, Ms. Seitchek. Little question, OK? What the fuck do you think you're doing?"

She stared straight ahead.

"Sure, Hahvahd's a great school, and maybe you're a great little grad student, but, uh, three hundred fifty thousand dollars—"

"Before taxes."

"Aren't we being a little fucking greedy here? You ever heard of a thing called moderation? Quitting while you're ahead? Compassion for a lady who's obviously not all there? I'm sure I don't need to tell you she's in there telling me to accept your terms. You know what she just told me? She told me you're the Devil, Devil with a capital D, I'm telling you she means it *literally*, sweah to God. With a straight face! That's the type person you're putting the screws in. But just between you and me, little girl, you're not the Devil. You're a greasy little grad student that God only knows how she got her claws in a fine lady like Mrs. Holland. And you wanna know something else? You're not getting more than 350 K. I don't have to tell you we're dealing with a person who's lost perspective. She'd give you the whole million, but I'm not going to let her. She can crack in two and go sit in an asylum for all I care, but I'm not going to let her hand over a million bucks to some little sneak that's selling secrets behind her employer's back. I'm telling you that's what I think of you, Ms. Seitchek. I think you are a greasy little piece of dead fish. You hear me?"

She was utterly motionless.

"Yeah, and for your information, guys don't get much easier-going than me."

"After taxes," she said quietly. "Six hundred is 350 after taxes, more or less. And I am leaving if you don't accept it."

"Hey, great idea. Why don't you leave right now? Or do you

need me to explain about selling blocks of stock. Maybe a lesson in capital gains? You ever heard of that? Broker's fees? Nah, what am I saying, you probably got the tax code memorized."

She jumped up, and before he could stop her she was in the conference room. Melanie was leaning against the oval table, sobbing.

"Six hundred thousand," Renée said as she wrenched free of Rudman's grasp. *"Six hundred thousand."*

"Shut up! Shut up!"

Melanie seized Rudman's hand imploringly. "Henry, do it!"

"Mrs. Holland—"

"Do it. I said do it. Do it and we're done with it."

10

Midnight in the system rooms. The roar of fans and airconditioning fills them tightly, to the very corners, like the breath in an inflated mattress. All the consoles have gone dim. In its private closet, the line printer is drumming numbers onto paper. The day's *New York Times* lies by the laser printer. A headline reads:

**STUDY REVEALS DEPTH OF RELATIONSHIPS,
NOT QUANTITY, AS KEY TO HAPPINESS**

Far away a door has closed, and someone's footsteps seem to be getting fainter, but suddenly they are louder, echoing in the stairwell, louder and louder in their leisurely descent, impossibly loud by the time they reach the landing outside the system rooms. They don't so much as pause here. The hallway has counted twenty-four of them when the loading-dock door is opened; the last sound is the sound of the door falling shut.

The diodes on the face of the CPU unit flicker knowingly.

The printer has filled its metal basket, and the oblong scene in the single street-side window has changed to the blue of fifty fathoms, to the green of ten fathoms, to the dripping misty yellows of a summer morning, by the time the first students come in. They carry coffee and move cautiously, as if wading through some waste-deep backwash of night.

In front of the building, outside the Peabody Museum and its collection of glass flowers, there is an unprepossessing dogwood tree. Tourists photograph themselves in front of this tree thirty or forty times a day, roping it into their lives like a bystander accused of imaginary crimes, and shooting it summarily. There are pictures of this tree in albums in Tokyo and Yokohama and Hokkaido, and Stuttgart and Padua, and Riyadh and Malmö.

On the terrace ringing the student lounge, up on the building's penthouse floor, the sun has yet to burn the dew off the tandem of hemispherical charcoal grills, and the square bottle of lighting fluid, and the jumbo laboratory tongs that students manipulate their coals with. A bag of charcoal is slumped against the railing, exhausted. Inside the lounge, on a table by the elevator, discolored slabs of melon and a chunk of apple with the skin coming loose are floating in a clear plastic bowl. Howard Chun is sleeping on a sofa, a peaceful corpse, hands folded on his chest. Triangular potato chip fragments lie scattered on the brown carpeting.

P-wave residuals, lateral heterogeneity, core-mantle boundary, centroid-moment-tensor, rupture propagation, slab penetration, non-double-couple events, shear-strength coefficients, intraplate seismicity, deconvolution, source-time functions, normal modes, aseismic slip, migration of the poles. One student calls his programs things like "Kelly" and "Diane" and "Martha." These are the names of women he has pursued or is pursuing. He likes to say his favorite commands aloud: "Do Martha. Run Kelly. Execute Diane."

The newspaper says: *It seems like centuries ago that men said blunt, self-satisfied things to credulous women.*

The system can be irritable when overburdened. It may spend eternities on simple tasks. It may send upsetting messages to your console. It may sham dead.

If you forget to tell the system not to keep expecting something, it will keep expecting it. Every few minutes it will spit a message onto the paper in the system console, informing the world that although you have forgotten your appointment, it has not. It will spit these messages hour after hour.

When there is nothing for it to do, the system sleeps. It wakes up knowing the time to within a hundredth of a second.

Sometimes the system becomes irrational, and a young man in a too-tight suit has to come with his aluminum suitcases and bring it down. The CPU unit is opened up and suffers the indignity of having its boards removed, one after another, until the faulty one is found. Then everything is OK again.

The window is dark when Renée appears. The chairs have been herded into clusters, one by the telephone and one in the corner by the Tectronix screen. She rolls them back to where they belong, puts five soft-drink cans in the recycling box, and logs off consoles for the people who haven't bothered to. Then she goes up the ramp to the inner sanctum and sits angled at the console by the optical-disk jukebox, her legs to one side of the chair. She is so alone and so motionless in the roar of the bright room, so technical in her coloration, that even though she's plainly visible through the plate-glass window, a passing sedimentologist who sticks his head in the door is sure the room is empty.

An image of the earth beneath Tonga flows onto the color screen. Renée looks at each stationary object in the room, the system console, the storage disks, the walls, the CPU unit, the tape drives, the power supply, the array processor, the digitizer, the racks of tapes, her body, the walls, the jukebox. She feels the watchfulness and the perpetuity. She listens intently to the noise, trying to find sense or pattern or allusion in it, and knowing that she won't. Beneath the noise there are, however, ghosts of noises—the scurrying, the titter, of calculating electrons.

Howard Chun enters the empty room at midnight carrying a milk shake and his boom box, which is the size of a two-drawer file cabinet. He logs onto the system from six consoles and listens to the *Eroica* while he works.

Later, after he has gone, a night wind rolls a paper cup across the pavement outside the window. System noise covers the sighing of the wind, but not the clatter of the cup.

Still later, the corner of an ocean map comes unstuck from a wall and bends forward. Three weeks from now another corner will come unstuck, and the first person in to work the next day will find the map in a heap on the floor.

It's morning: the dogwood is being photographed. The newspaper says: *Food may not be love, but it's nice nevertheless, and it has its uses.*

All the lights are burning. Soft-drink cans float on their sides on a sea of waste paper. The cracked plastic hemisphere belonging to the room's globe has peanut shells inside it, and the front panel of the radiator, from whose fan cool air can also blow, is lying on the floor with its decaying sheet of foam insulation uppermost. In the equipment room, a Twinkies wrapper and a gummy sheet of Twinkies cardboard are lying on the CPU unit, by the modems.

In the seven years since it began, the noise has stopped only once. It was after midnight on a Saturday in August, when a belt in the airconditioner broke. An alarm bell alerted Campus Security, but there were no signs of a break-in, and the airconditioner was making its usual noise, so the officers disabled the alarm. The temperature in the equipment room rose to 130° F before Renée came to work and, duly aghast, shut the system down.

What a silence there was that day. It was like standing by an ocean from which all the water had been drained.

The system believes that the last twenty years have eliminated any significant distinction between human and artificial intelligence in America. The system believes that all vital functions of the average American intelligence can now be simulated by a program running to 11,000 lines supported by six Phrase libraries and one Opinions library together totaling less than eight megabytes. A medium-price laptop with a hard disk will run the program, which can perform exactly the same mental tasks as a randomly selected American: can realistically simulate his spending patterns, his crisis-response mechanisms, his political behavior.

The 5 p.m.–6:30 p.m. segment of the weekday program for a male might look like this:

```
3080 desire = desire + desinc
3090 endwork
3100 WALKTO car
3110 desire = desire + desinc
3115 ifdesire(1)<.67 then 3120
            DRIVETOPARK Singles(n)
            gosub drinkchoice
            on foxy 3200
3120 ifcash>6i iftime>1 ifdesire(6)>.5 gosub shopping
3130 iffuel>.5 iftime>.05 gosub fillup
3140 DRIVETOPARK Home
  . . .


shopping
        desire = desire + desinc
        read shortneeds/bigneeds/bigwants
        gosub needsort: needs.temp; cash;
            DRIVETOPARK Mall(n,)
            WALKTO Mall(n,needs(1))
            on hotprod gosub impulsebuy
            on dazzle gosub impulsebuy
            BUY needs(1)
            if cash<6i exitsub
            if desire(2)<.5 then 80
                FEEL desire(2)
                gosub dineout
            80 next needs

dineout
        10 gosub foodchoice
        dmatch Mall(n,) f(1)
            on nomatch gosub foodchoice
                WALKTO Mall(n,f(1))
                ifalcohol then alc = (0,1) else alc = (1,0)
                BUYEAT f(1), [d(1a, 1b)*alc]
            on foxy 3200
            desire(2) = desire(2) – [dvalue(f1)]
            if desire(2)<.5 exit else 10
```

```
3200 FEEL desire(1)
     gosub shevaluate
            if (she*desire(1))<.5 exitloop
            desire(1) = 2*desire(1)
            call lib :convmatter/:nicetalk
            gosub pickup

[pickup
     SAY "Hi"
     on snub exitsub
     knowher = she/10
            110 read $shesay
               search convmatter
               pmatch $shesay $reply
               rem: pval assigned in pmatch
            SAY $reply
            on snub exitsub
            knowher = knowher + pval
                  gosub shevaluate
            if she*desire<.5 exitsub
            if knowher<.67 then 110
            SAY "Say listen if you're free maybe you wanna";$line(n)
            read $shesay
            . . .

[foodchoice
     randomize
     food = int(rnd*10)
     create d1 {a,b}
     if food = 1 then f1 = {pizza} d1 = {pepsi, beer} exitsub
     if food = 2 then f1 = {nachos} d1 = {sprite, beer} exitsub
     if food = 3 then f1 = {nuggets} . . .

if(spendlapse*cash)<mcrit then home

3150 newswatch
     call lib :hotwords
     . . .
     . . .
```

You may wish to object: Can the artificial intelligence read a book with comprehension? Can it paint a truly original painting or compose a symphony? Can it distinguish between fact and mere image, and make responsible political decisions on the basis of this distinction?

The system points out that the program simulates the intelligence of the average American in the 1990s.

You may still object that no machine, no matter how sophisticated, will ever be able to subjectively *feel* the color blue or *taste* the flavor cinnamon or *be aware of itself as it thinks*.

The system considers this a dangerous irrelevance. Because once you admit subjectivity into a logical discussion, once you grant reality to phenomena that can never be verified by a machine or a chemical reaction, once you say that a person's subjective interpretation of cinnamon molecules as *Oh! Cinnamon!* has any meaning, you open a Pandora's box. Next thing you know, the person will be telling you that she interprets the silence on a mountaintop as *Oh! There is an eternal presence all around me*, and the darkness of her bedroom late at night as *Oh! I have a soul that transcends its physical enclosure*; and that way madness lies.

It's much wiser to live rationally, as a machine does. To vote for the man with the harshest views on drug kingpins. To maintain that what is real about the flavor of cinnamon is its informational content: it tells your brain—and this by sheer chemical accident, since cinnamon is non-nutritive—*eat me, I am good for you*. It's absolutely wiser to laugh at the person who tells you that without your subjective experience of cinnamon you would have hanged yourself at the age of thirteen, and that without your subjective experience of the smell of melting snow your attitude towards your mother or your wife or your daughter would be no more than *How can I make her give me what I want?* And as some people cannot taste, and as the leader of a nation of the color-blind lives in his black Berlin or gray Tokyo or White House and sneers at those who say they have feelings about the color blue, you must learn to sneer at those who have been in the mountains and say they've felt the presence of an eternal God, and to reject any conclusions they draw from this experience.

Otherwise—if you let emotion trick you into thinking there's something unique or transcendent about human subjectivity—you might find yourself wondering why you've organized your life as if you were nothing but a machine for the unpleasant production and pleasant consumption of commodities. And why, in the name of responsible parenthood, you are fostering in your children the same ethos of consumption, if the material is not the essence of humanity: why you're guaranteeing that their life will be as cluttered with commodities as yours is, with tasks and loops and input and output, so that they will have lived for no more purpose than to perpetuate the system and will die for no more reason than that

they've worn out. You might begin to worry that with every appliance that you buy, every piece of plastic that you discard, every
gallon of hot water that you waste, every stock that you trade, every
mile that you drive, you are hastening the day when there is no
more land or air or water in the world that has not been changed,
the day when spring will smell like hydrochloric acid and a summer
rain will be paradichlorobenzene-flavored, and your tap water will
be bright red and taste like Pepsi, and the only birds will be educated sparrows chirping "Just say no!" and blue jays crying "Sex!"
and chickens hawking "White meat!" and you'll eat beef one night
and chicken the next night and beef the next night, and all the
forests will be planted with the same kind of pine tree or the same
kind of maple tree, and even a thousand miles out from shore the
bottom of the ocean will be covered with rusty scum and plastic
milk jugs, and only tunas and sardines and jumbo shrimps will
swim there, and even at night on a remote mountaintop the wind
will smell like the exhaust vent of a McDonald's and you'll hear
car alarms and TV sets and the thunder of the jets in which
passengers are being offered a choice of *Chicken . . . or beef?*
—and the nature in which all people wittingly or not once felt the
immanence of eternity will be dead, and the newspaper which you
can read on the computer screen you labored hard at a different
screen to purchase will tell you that *Man is free and everyone is
equal* and that *Miniature Golf Is the New City Game.* And how
disturbing it might be to find such a world insufficient. And so for
your own peace of mind, since nothing can be proved or disproved
anyway—since your science disqualifies itself from answering precisely those questions that concern the mind's ability to feel that
which is, in an absolute and verifiable sense, not there—isn't it
safer all around to assume machines have their own virtual souls
and feelings?

Renée had come home from Arger, Kummer & Rudman with
a blinding headache, a notarized agreement running to 270 words,
and her eighty hundred-dollar bills. Melanie, irrational to the end,
had refused to take the bills as a security.

She answered an ad for a '74 Mustang convertible, fire-engine red. She gave a hundred-dollar bill to a mechanic who appraised the car, and thirty-eight more to the invertebrate zoologist who was selling it.

She went to the high-impact clothing stores in the Square, places that were branches of stores on lower Broadway in Manhattan. She bought short, tight skirts and shiny shoes, tubes of lipstick, summer tops that cost ten dollars an ounce, a pair of shades. She bought a leather jacket and plastic jewelry.

The next morning she returned to the Square, had her hair clipped, and shopped some more. She was standing in front of a clothing-store mirror, seeing if she could manage a lime-green skirt with a less than straight cut, when her reflection's eyes suddenly caught her own and she was stricken by the thought that all she was doing was trying to look like Lauren Bowles.

She decided she'd bought enough for now.

The Mustang turned heads as she drove north with the top down through Cambridge and Somerville. She took the inside lane on I-93. The only disheartening thing was that she couldn't stand any of the music on the radio.

The air in Peabody smelled like seaweed. On Main Street, a block east of the Warren Five Cents Savings Bank, she knocked twice on the window of *The Peabody Times* before she saw the sign saying CLOSED THIS FRIDAY. She leaned against a fender, pressing the thin fabric of her skirt against the sun-heated metal, and chewed down three fingernails as far as seemed advisable.

On Andover Street she located the middle-aged bank building that she'd seen pictured as a newborn in the *Globe* from 1970. Rust now stained the panels it was faced with; the sidewalk was cracked and tanned and weedy. Across the street stood a laundromat, a video rental place, and a "spa" selling beer and groceries. The man behind the spa counter was a Portuguese who said he'd owned the business for six years. She tossed the bottle of Pepsi she'd bought into the back seat of the Mustang.

She cruised the working people's neighborhood behind the bank building, past white bungalows nearing condemnation, through varying concentrations of acetone fumes, up and down all the streets that dead-ended against the high corporate fence with its signs saying *ABSOLUTELY* NO TRESPASSING. She stopped by a house with a white-haired man on the porch. He staggered across his lawn, favoring a bad hip, and stared at her as if she were the Angel of Death who had come along in her red Mustang sooner than he'd expected. She said her name was Renée Seitchek and she was a seismologist from Harvard University and could she ask him a few questions? Then he was sure she was the Angel and he hobbled back to his porch and from this position of relative safety shouted, "Mind your own business!"

She tried other streets and accosted other old men. She wondered if there was something in the water that made them all so bizarre.

A stumpy woman turning the soil around some apparently dead roses saw her drive by for a third time and asked what she was looking for. Renée said she was looking for people who'd been in the neighborhood since at least 1970. The woman set down her hand spade. "Do I get some kind of prize if I say yes?"

Renée parked the car. "Can I ask you some questions?"

"Well, if it's for science."

"Do you remember sometime about twenty years ago a particularly tall . . . structure on the property over there, that looked like an oil well?"

"Sure," the woman said immediately.

"Do you remember what years?"

"What's this got to do with earthquakes?"

"Well, I think Sweeting-Aldren may be responsible for them."

"I'll be damned. Maybe they want to fix my kitchen ceiling." The woman laughed. She was built like a mailbox and had a wide mouth, painted orange. "Jesus Christ, I can't believe this."

"My other question is whether you might have any old pictures that would show the, uh, structure."

"Pictures? Come on inside."

The woman's name was Jurene Caddulo. She pointed at the gray crater in her kitchen ceiling and wouldn't budge until Renée had found the right combination of phrases to express her sympathy and outrage. Jurene said she was a secretary at the high school and had been widowed for eight years. She had five thousand unsorted snapshots in a kitchen drawer.

"Can I offer you a cordial?"

"No thanks," Renée said as bottles of apricot liqueur, Amaretto, and Cherry Heering were set down on the table. Jurene came back from another room with a pair of exceptionally ugly cut-glass tulips.

"If you can believe I've only got two of these left. I had eight until the earthquakes. You think I can sue? They're antiques, they're not available. You like Amaretto? Here. That's good, isn't it."

Expired coupons punctuated the disordered photographic history of Caddulo family life. Jurene's daughter in Revere and daughter in Lynn had hatched children in a variety of shapes and sizes; she puzzled over group shots, trying to get the names and ages right. Renée found herself saying, "This must be Michael Junior," which made Jurene look again at the other pictures because she knew that this was *not* Michael Junior and therefore the child she had just called Michael Junior must be Petey, and then everything made sense again. Jurene's younger son played guitar. There were dozens of prints of a picture of his band playing the heavy-metal mass that he had written at the age of seventeen and that the priest had said no to performing in the church, so it was performed right here in the basement without the sacraments. The son now had a different band and drove a customized 4×4 pickup. The older son showed up as an adult in San Francisco sporting a mustache and a leather vest, and as a distant, gowned blur in blue-toned shots of a high-school graduation on a dreary day. Jurene said he was a hair stylist. Renée nodded. Jurene said both her sons were still looking for the right girl. Renée nodded. In high school and junior high the daughters had worn their no-color hair in fantastic bouffants. Their bodies were deformed like pool toys by the affectionately squeezing tentacles of their father, now dead of cancer. All the sadness of the seventies was in Jurene's drawer, all of the years in which Renée had not been happy and had not had what she wanted but instead had had pimples and friends who embarrassed her, years whose huge tab collars and platform soles and elephant flares and overgrown hair (Don't the mentally ill neglect to cut their hair?) now seemed to her both the symbols and literal accoutrements of unhappiness.

Jurene still went to the same cottage she'd been renting for twenty years in Barnstable, on the Cape. She was going there Sunday. "After I've been at the Cape I can smell the smell here for about two days before I'm used to it again. You want to know something really peculiar, though, sometimes on the Cape I can smell it at the beach."

"It's like a ringing in your ear, except in your nose."

"No, I'm talking about the smell. Here." Jurene produced a handful of low-resolution pictures of a snowman and a snow fort and a snowball fight in the little front lawn. In the background of every one of them, well behind the houses across the street, was Sweeting-Aldren's drilling derrick. There was nothing else it could be; no chemical process that Renée knew of required a structure like that. The date was stamped on the back: February 1970.

"Can I have one of these?"

"Borrow 'em, sure. Why don't I see if can find the negatives."

She opened a drawer in which negatives were under such pressure that some of them sprang out and fluttered to the floor. She left them there while, on second thought, she opened a tin of butter cookies and arranged them on a painted plate. Renée held her glass of Amaretto to the graying light in the window. A label on the bottle said *According to the Surgeon General, women should not drink alcoholic beverages during pregnancy because of the risk of birth defects.*

"I have to go," she said.

The sky was deepening as if the land were on a slope and sliding towards a precipice. In the parking lot of an office complex affording a good view of Sweeting-Aldren, she sat on the hood of the Mustang with the Caddulo pictures and a 7½-minute USGS topo map, comparing perspectives on a cooling tower, trying to triangulate a location for the derrick. Thousands of pig-sized and cow-sized boulders, some of them possibly glacial and native, shored up the hillside on which the complex stood.

A voice spoke from right behind her: "What ugly children."

She turned and weathered a spasm of fright. Rod Logan was standing by the car, holding a picture that had been lying on the hood.

"Give me that," she said.

Behind her in the parking lot, junior executives were walking to their shiny cars. Rather than risk a scene, Logan handed her the picture. He strolled to the brink of the asphalt and peered down at the yellow pond below the boulders.

"You know," he said, "in the old days, people like you, they'd come around, they'd get warned, and if they kept coming around they'd have the shit beaten out of them, and nobody would really complain or litigate, it was just part of the way the game was played. But everybody's gotten so gosh-darned kind and gentle lately. It's reached a point where all I can really do is ask you politely to clear out, and if you choose not to, we're no longer on terra firma, if you know what I mean. We don't know what kind of procedures are required. There's no literature on it."

Renée got in the car.

"This is quite the stylish car, incidentally. Nice duds, too. Looks like you've found a wealthy patron."

She started the engine. Logan leaned over her, looking straight down on her lap.

"Goodbye, Renée."

She made another trip to the Square, stopping at the clinic in the Holyoke Center and then dropping off the Caddulo negatives for enlargements. The rest of the weekend, late into both nights, she worked at a console in the lab. Not a single person disturbed her until Sunday afternoon, when a few students drifted through, said hello, executed Diane, etc. No one looked at what she was writing.

Her abstract read:

Recent seismicity in Peabody, Mass., and the prolonged sequence in 1987 have displayed the swarm-like character of known instances of induced seismicity. Until now the resemblance has been disregarded because of the relatively great focal depths of the earthquakes (3–8 km) and the absence of reservoirs and injection wells in the focal area. However, photographic and archival evidence strongly indicates that in 1969–70 Sweeting-Aldren Industries of Peabody drilled an exploratory well to a depth in excess of 6 km, and that the well has subsequently been used for waste disposal. Current research locates observed activity on a steeply dipping basement fault striking SW–NE. Models of fluid migration and fault activation are proposed, the temporal distribution of observed seismicity is explained, and the legal implications of Sweeting-Aldren's role are briefly discussed.

She described the tectonic environment of the Peabody earthquakes. She marked likely well-sites on the best of her aerial photographs. In footnotes she mentioned Peter Stoorhuys and David Stoorhuys by name. She made pictures:

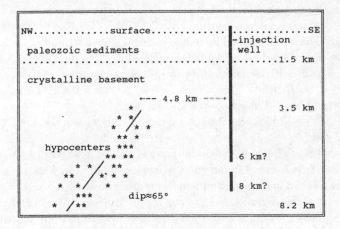

She wrote that the absence of earthquakes between 1971 and 1987 indicated that there were no stressed faults in the immediate vicinity of the injection well. It had taken as long as sixteen years for fluid to be forced far enough into the surrounding rock for it to reach the fault(s) on which the earthquakes were taking place. This indicated that very significant volumes of waste had been injected, and that the rock formation at a depth of 4 km was loose enough to accept this volume at pumping pressures low enough to be commercially attractive. The conventions of scientific prose served to clarify and heighten the passion with which she wrote. She was so absorbed in her arguments that it shocked her, at the mirror in the women's bathroom on the second floor, to see the expensive, tarty clothes she was wearing.

Monday afternoon, after sleeping late, she picked up the Caddulo enlargements, bought some red nail polish, and stopped by the Holyoke Center again. Back in Hoffman she saw a flabby, sunburnt woman standing in the hall outside her office, looking very lost. Brown daisy-shaped pieces of felt were sewn onto the chest of her yellow sweat suit and the thighs of her yellow sweatpants; a button pinned to her shoulder said ADOPTION NOT ABORTION. Renée had heard that people like this were still dropping in from time to time, but she hadn't seen one personally since the week her phone and mail harassment started.

The woman sidled up to her and spoke confidentially. She had a twang. "I'm looking for a Dr. Seitchek?"

"Oh," Renée said indifferently. "She's dead."

"She's dead!" The woman drew her head back like an affronted hen. "I'm very sorry to hear that."

"No, I'm joking. She's not dead. She's standing right in front of you."

"She is? Oh, you. What'd you say you're dead for?"

"Just a joke. Let me guess what you're here for. You came to my abortion clinic to complain to me personally."

"That's right."

"Clairvoyant," Renée said, touching her temple. She saw that Terry Snall had stopped at the bottom of the staircase. He had his hands on his hips and was exuding tremendous discombobulation over the way she was dressed. She turned her back to him. "Let me ask you," she said to the visitor. "Does this building look to you like an abortion clinic?"

"You know, I was just wondering that myself."

"Well, you see, it's not. And I'm not a medical doctor. I'm a geologist." On an impulse, she spun and pointed. "Terry, though. Terry performs abortions. As a sideline, don't you, Terry?"

"That's not funny, Renée. That's not at all funny."

"He denies it," she explained, "because he doesn't want you to harass him. But he's part of the whole—abortion—conspiracy."

She hugged herself tightly, turning one shoe on its heel. There was an awkward silence, disturbed only by the whining of the line printer behind a closed door.

"Well," the visitor said. "She already lied to me once. She said she was dead!"

"That's what Renée is like," Terry said. "She thinks she can do anything she wants. She thinks she's a cut above."

Renée spun again, still hugging herself. "But that's because I *can* do anything I want. And I'm going to, Terry! You watch me." She approached the woman, who, though she was bigger and taller, took a wary step backward. "Where are you from?"

"You mean originally? I'm from Herculaneum, Missouri. But I live in Chelsea now."

"You belong to Stites's church."

"The Reverend Stites."

"The Reverend Stites who claims he has nothing to do with phone and mail harassment."

"Oh, he don't, see." Oblivious to having let the word "harassment" pass, the woman unzipped her swollen beige purse. "This letter here I got forwarded from Herculaneum."

Renée turned to throw an amused glance at Terry, but he was gone. "What's your name?" she asked the woman.

"Me? Mrs. Jack Wittleder."

"Glad to meet you, Jack."

"Oh, not Jack. Jack's my husband's name."

"Oh. So what's your real name?"

"My friends and brethren call me Bebe. But that's not my real, legal name. You see, Dr. Seitchek, I don't know about you, but in my part of the world, when a woman marries—"

"Yeah yeah yeah."

Mrs. Jack Wittleder was hurt. She sighed, batting her eyelashes. "I don't know what you're doing on my list, if it's true what you say. This *is* number 20 Oxford Street? Couldn't of been a mistake, if it's Hoffman Laboratories and you're Dr. Seitchek. I keep calling you and calling you, and no one answers. The phone rings and you don't *answer* it?"

"That's how it works, yes."

"But there must be some reason why you're on the list. Did you—? Tell me, when do you believe human life begins?"

"At thirty."

Mrs. Jack Wittleder shook her head. "It is a far greater sin to mock the Lord than be atheistic, Dr. Seitchek. Now, I'm not an educated woman, not compared to a Harvard-University doctor, but the Bible tells us that we don't know God with our mind, we know Him with our heart, and we don't see Him with our eyes, we see Him with our heart, and it may be that my heart knows what's right and wrong better than a professor's brain can."

"Doubtless. But you see, I'm kind of busy."

"Too busy to think about what's right and wrong."

Renée smiled. "You got it."

"Well. You're honest. Say that for you. I don't guess you read the Bible."

"Nope."

"Did you know that the truth about human life on earth is in the Bible and nowhere else?"

"Yeah, I understand, you want to draw me in, but—"

"No, Dr. Seitchek. I don't want to draw you in. I want to take you to the place where I found happiness."

"Where's that?"

"In the church that is the bride of Christ. The Reverend Stites's church."

"Oh. I see. The bride of Christ is in a tenement in Chelsea."

"That's right."

"And you go around to clinics like this one and try to enlist new members from all your sympathizers there."

"No. Only when I find an opportunity to plant some seeds in people."

"Yeah, well, I've already been sown."

Mrs. Jack Wittleder glanced up and down the hall to make sure they were alone. She lowered her voice. "What exactly do you mean by that, Dr. Seitchek?"

The sport drained out of Renée's face. "Nothing. Absolutely nothing."

"Come along with me," Mrs. Jack Wittleder urged. "The Reverend Stites is a kind and erudite young man, he's helped me so much. I'm sure he could help you too."

"I don't need his help."

"You're talking to me. Nobody else has given me the time of day. Come along and you'll see."

Renée walked up the hall and turned around in front of a giant picture of the earth at a depth of 1,500 kilometers. She came back wreathed in smileyness. "All right, Mrs. Wittleder."

"Call me Bebe."

"Bebe, I'd love to come with you. Are you happy about that? I'm going to come with you and see your lovely church. Terry!" she called. "Terry!"

A beard, red lips, and glasses appeared in a doorway. "What?"

"Do you want to go to Chelsea with me? See the famous church? You could talk to the people who've been tying up your telephone. Give 'em a piece of your mind."

Terry shook his head ominously. "If I were you," he said to Bebe, "I wouldn't take her. She just wants to make you look bad."

"Oh, thanks," Renée said.

"She just wants to get even," Terry said.

"God, what a sweet guy."

"You did already lie to me twice," Bebe reflected.

"Well, I'm not lying now. So just wait here a second." She went into the console room and copied her new paper onto a 5½-inch tape, inserted a write-protect ring, and left it in a drawer. She stowed the enlargements separately.

Then they went to Chelsea.

All the way to Park Street a Seeing Eye dog observed Renée with a sultry expression. Bebe conferred a condescending smirk on every rider in the subway car—even the blind man got one, and each black person received several—but Renée suspected this was more a product of midwestern insecurity than of arrogance.

"Do you have a pen?" she whispered, nodding at a Planned Parenthood announcement on the ad strip above the seats. "Why don't you deface that advertisement? Or, wait. Why don't you just go ahead and tear it down?"

"That's not right."

"Oh, come on," Renée whispered. "Do it. It's a lesser crime to prevent a greater crime."

"It's not right."

"You're afraid of what people will say. That means your faith isn't strong enough."

"My faith," said Bebe, touching the brown daisy on her chest. "Is my business."

It was a long walk from the Wood Island subway stop to the Church of Action in Christ. Chelsea Street traversed a neighborhood of giant cylinders marked with red numbers in white circles. It crossed a drawbridge whose gridwork surface sang beneath the tires of the heavy traffic. Renée looked up at the solid concrete counterweight suspended above her (it was the size of a mobile home) and considered how the glassy wealth of downtown Boston required a counterweight in these industrial square miles, where vacant lots collected decaying windblown newsprint, and the side streets were cratered, and the workers had faces the nitrite red of Fenway Franks. A Ford Escort with Day-Glo green custom wind-shield wipers crossed the bridge, tailgated by a Corvette that iden-tified itself as an Official Pace Car, 70th Indianapolis 500, May 27th, 1985.

Bebe walked incredibly slowly. She said she'd been in the church for five months. Her day began at sunrise with communal prayers and hymn-singing, followed by breakfast. Missionary work, which was "voluntary but expected," commenced at eight-thirty. There was a host of sites to be picketed, and members were en-couraged to picket on a round-robin basis, in groups of three to six. "Groups of Twelve" were formed when the spirit moved among the community and twelve Chosen members spontaneously resolved to prevent a day's complement of murders at one of several no-torious clinics. Bebe had not yet been part of a Group of Twelve, though she had witnessed the arrest of one and had participated in the daily jail visitations. She told Renée that the last five months had been the most meaningful and light-filled time she'd ever known.

God is . . . Pro-Life! said the banner over the entrance to the tenement. The building was the last in a complex of brick cubes with small, square windows; as if the building's architect had foreseen its future as a church, the central clerestory was vertically bisected by narrow windows reminiscent of cathedrals.

Several dozen women were at work in the main hall, a low-ceilinged linoleumed room that had probably once been a community center or nursery. A cheerful smell of tempera was in the air. "My sister will be among us tomorrow," said one elderly artisan putting the finishing touches on a poster that Renée turned her head to read:

WOMEN UNITE

IN CHRIST

"I'd almost given up and then she called and said she was coming."

"Praise the Lord, Jesus gets the glory."

"Amen."

Your convenience is homicide. Jesus was an unplanned pregnancy. THANKS MOM I ♥ LIFE.

Bebe had disappeared, leaving Renée alone in the center of the room, in her black clothing and black sunglasses, surrounded by women of all ages in their pastels and aggressively unerotic hairdos. More and more of them were looking at her. Just two weeks ago the gazes crawling all over her back might have broken down her self-possession, but she could stand them now.

At the front of the room a woman in a white sweat suit with a whistle and a cross around her neck was clapping her hands. She was like every gym teacher Renée had had in high school. "All right, everybody, time to clean it up. We're going to watch a video together. Let's go! Clean it up!" She walked around the perimeter, pulling down tattered blackout shades while the painters obediently closed their tempera jars. Renée planted herself against the rear wall. There were men here, a sad little assortment sitting cross-legged and looking at their hands.

The women clustered like Camp Fire Girls in front of a cart with video equipment on it. The lights went out. The show began.

To three-chord Marin County music, a mare suckles her foal in a summer field with the Tetons in the background. Adorable fox cubs trot down a forest path behind their mother. Birds sing and stuff food down the traps of their chicks. *Cut to a club in TriBeCa, guitars screaming, strobes flashing. A woman in shades and purple lipstick laughs, showing teeth, and says, "Unnatural acts."* Back in the Tetons, a freckled mother in a gingham dress watches her toddlers pick wildflowers. The sun shines through her auburn hair. "Mommy!" a toddler cries. In the shimmering distance the father is chopping wood. We see the swell of a new pregnancy beneath the gingham. *Guitars shriek outside the door of the high-tech ladies' room, where two black girls in stiletto heels arch their backs like porn queens as they take cocaine nasally. A stutter zoom through the door of an empty stall: twenty-four-week fetus, red as life, is floating in the toilet bowl.* Time-lapse blossoming of a downy gentian. Waddling prairie-dog pups. Calf craning its neck for teat of cow. Ducklings in Jackson Hole. By a dancing fire, behind a Vaselined lens, Our Lady of the Gingham Dress holds a child on each knee and kisses them, kisses them, kisses them. *The guitars more assonant yet. White hands, black hands, hands with heavy jewelry push the flush lever viciously, but the fetus is like one of those turds that will not go down. Strobes flash. The thwarted hands contort in rage.* A child rocks her doll to sleep. Mare and foal canter in super slo-mo . . .

The church members from rural AK, from rural MO, from NC and SC, from Buffalo and Indianapolis and Shreveport remained as calm as the hospitalized while they received this dose of filmic sophistication. The rear doors of the hall kept opening, admitting sunlight and weary missionaries who set their placards on the floor and widened the reverent circle around the TV screen. Renée's mouth hung open. She was thinking what a lucky thing it was she'd come, how incredibly easily she might not have.

"*. . . At Sunnyvale Farms you won't see pornography on display behind the counter. You won't find birth control on racks within easy reach of your children. Sunnyvale Farms is more than a convenience store, it's a home away from home—your home. And remember, for every ten-dollar purchase you make at Sunnyvale Farms, we'll make a contribution to the war on drugs. To help make this world a sunnier place for your children. Sunnyvale Farms: The Family Convenience Store.*"

"So what magazine are you from?" a young Southern man at Renée's elbow asked her. He had a burnished, chubby face and corn-silk hair, and there was an assertiveness to his posture, a pushiness to his glasses and to the angle of his head, that reminded her of Louis Holland. It was Philip Stites.

"No magazine," she said.

"Newspaper, TV station, radio station?"

"No."

"Shoot. You ruined my record."

"My name's Renée Seitchek."

Stites leaned closer to her face, obliquely, like an ophthalmologist. "Sure! Of course. What are you doin' here?"

"Watching . . . the most disgusting videos I've ever seen."

"Pretty heavy, isn't it. Listen, Renée, I'd love to talk to you. Can you come back, maybe? Or you can stay if you want. I'm busy till about six-thirty."

"We'll see how much of this I can stand."

"Good deal. Hey." He made her look at him. There were wrinkles in his navy blazer, and his yellow tie was loosened. "I'm real glad you came. I mean it."

He crossed the darkened room, weaving through his flock, and went out by a side door. Several members rose and followed him. The rest continued to watch the advertising, which lasted nearly another hour. When the shades were finally raised, the light in the windows was golden. Three women in white aprons came in through a rear door, followed discreetly by an aroma of pork and beans. The gym teacher who had run the video quieted the crowd and read announcements from a clipboard.

She was pleased to welcome back June, Ruby, Amanda, Susan Dee, Stephanie, Mrs. Powers, Mrs. Moran, Mr. DiConstanzo, Susan H., Allan, Irene, and Mrs. Flathead, all released today from the Cambridge City Jail. Their twenty days behind bars had set the city back an estimated $11,000, not counting court costs, which the city was suing to recoup.

The Group of Twelve stood and received an ovation.

Other good news was that Intrafamily Services of Braintree had indefinitely suspended its death procedures as of today. "To all those who helped them reach that informed decision," said the gym teacher, "my thanks, the church's thanks, and above all the thanks of the countless sweet children to whom you'll have given the gift of life. Praise the Lord, Jesus gets the glory."

Another ovation.

New members present for the first time were Mrs. Jerome Shumacher of Trumbull, Connecticut, Mrs. Libby Fulton of Wallingford, Pennsylvania, Miss Anne Dinkins of Sparta, North Carolina, and Miss Lola Corcoran of Lexington, Massachusetts. After applauding, the congregation was urged to make the newcomers feel part of the family.

"Bebe Wittleder," the gym teacher continued, "tells me we also have with us tonight a visitor from Harvard University, Dr. Renée Seitchek, a geologist you may remember from the special broadcast—"

The congregation swung to gape at her. An image of her small person formed on six hundred retinas.

"Peace and goodwill unto you in the name of Jesus Christ, Dr. Seitchek. You are welcome to celebrate and break bread with us, we are an open church."

Stites returned in time to hear the last few announcements. When they were over, he immediately began a prayer, ending with a group recitation of Our Father. A woman at an upright piano guided the congregation through three hymns. Stites sang along, but it was impossible to pick his voice out. He sat down informally on the edge of a school-cafeteria table, the very tops of his argyle socks showing, and surveyed his flock, allowing anticipation to build. When he finally spoke, his voice rang through the hall.

"You've heard it said: God is love. People, God *is* love. God is two things: love and wisdom.

"People, I want you to try and picture God. Picture a being who is Love so much that He's stronger than atoms or anything, He is pure and total love. Now, in the beginning, God had so much love inside Him that it created the universe, just through the force of love. He created the universe so there'd be something there for Him to love. And there was a Void? And the Void, the Book of Genesis tells us it became the universe, but it was still just a mass of nothing, just stuff. And He loved it and was wiser than it, and the reason it took shape—

"Now listen. The reason it took the shape it did was because of the pain in God's heart."

Stites looked aside with an odd grin, as though God were this guy he'd known back in Carolina who did the darndest old things.

"You see," he said, "even before He created the universe, He loved and He was wise. And because He was wise He knew that whatever He loved would know less than He knew. He is supreme, and it hurts Him very much to be supreme. He is an angry and hurt God. He knows more than anyone, and He loves everyone more than anyone loves anything, and so when we sin or we have thoughts—even when the smartest philosophers in the world have thoughts—He knows more. He knows we have to become dust again, and He never forgets. And He's sad because He loves us even in our squalid earthly existence. In fact He loves us all the more.

"And so everything you see here—the walls, this table, this VCR, this coffee mug"—he held up a mug for all to see—"everything hangs together because of that pain. That's why I can squeeze this here coffee mug and feel that it's hard. It's hard because God is sad. If God were happy, then there wouldn't be any resistance in the world, your hand would go through everything. There wouldn't be pain and suffering and death. You see what I'm saying? If things were all right with God, then there wouldn't be any universe. There's only a universe because He knows. Because He hurts because He knows.

"You've all heard the expression it's lonely at the top? Well, that's how it is with God. And isn't that kind of comforting? To know that no matter how bad you feel, you can't feel as bad as He does, because you don't know how bad things really are. That's how come He let them cruc'fy His only son. *Because He wanted us to know how much it hurt.* And you know, when I think about how maybe the world's going to end and I start feeling depressed because there are all these things I love so much. Well, I don't despair, and you know why? It's because I know that feeling of depression is holy. And if there is an Armageddon, then there's going to be God to mourn us all when we're gone, and all the things I love that don't exist anymore, He didn't forget any of those things, He loved them all along—loved them like you and I never can—and He won't ever forget them for all eternity, and that's what heaven is: heaven is living on in God's love forever."

The word "forever" hung in the air like a badminton birdie at the top of its arc.

"That's the sermon for tonight, I thank you all."

A final "Mighty Fortress" was sung, and then Stites walked back through the congregation, kneeling twice to take women's hands in his own and have words with them. He ended up in front of Renée. "You hungry?"

"Not really."

"Well I'm frankly famished."

A ground-floor apartment behind the hall had had some walls knocked out, extending the existing kitchen. Three additional old stoves had been installed, and there was table seating for maybe fifty. Stites was given a big plate of beans from an institutional pot. He took four slices of white bread and an orange from the buffet, explaining to Renée that unless he got fed lunch by a rich patron he only ate two meals a day, the breakfast and the dinner here.

He led her up a dimly lit stairwell and down a plaster-strewn hall, one wall of which was lined with identical pieces of some kind of homemade exercise equipment, built of two-by-fours and galvanized pipe, resembling pillories. "What are these?" Renée said.

"These? These are pillories."

"Oh my God."

"Here, let me show you." Stites set his plate on the floor. "All this plaster come loose in the earthquake. We sweep it up, but it seems like all you have to do is *look* at it, and down comes some more." He put his head and wrists in slots in the crosspiece of a pillory. "See, you can lower the top piece with your foot, like this." Foot in a ring, he unhooked a chain that let the upper beam lower onto the back of his neck, closing him in. "Or you can have a friend do it for you."

He stood bent but relaxed in his khaki pants and brown loafers, facing the wall, a wallet bulging in his back pocket.

"Then what?" Renée said.

"Then you stand here. I think everybody ought to. I do it probably as much as anybody, mind you I'm not proud of it. It's I have a special need for it, if I've been out in Weston all day at rich people's houses. You stand here and look at the wall. You pray, or you can just relax. It humbles you. It feels really good. Physically, it hurts a little after a while. But that feels good too."

With a practiced step, he raised the upper beam and freed himself. He looked at Renée, grinning intently. "You want to try it?"

"No thanks."

"You sure? You kind of look like you do."

"No!"

"You'd like it if you tried it."

"I don't want to."

"OK, whatever. People feel vulnerable when they can't see what's going on behind their back and they can't move. I believe real strongly that vulnerability's something we oughtta nurture."

He marched up the hall, taking big galumphing steps, as though crossing a marsh. His office had no door. Books stood in rough stacks on the red shag rug, which was stained with white paint and strewn with fallen plaster. A printed message on one wall said: *And in the last days it shall be, God declares, that I will pour out my Spirit upon all flesh*. The window gave onto the courtyard of the complex, where members were picnicking and the gym teacher was organizing a volleyball game.

"The rest is bedroom and a kitchen," Stites said. "I share it with two of the men. I took this whole outer room for myself because I've got all these books and papers. You can have the desk, I'll sit on the floor."

"No, you're the one who's eating."

"Well, let's both sit on the floor. Sorry about the plaster. It's everywhere."

He immediately began to shovel beans into himself. Renée was used to sitting Indian style, but shortness of skirt forced her to use a double-Z leg position. "You're lucky the whole building hasn't come down on you."

He nodded, chewing.

"Do you really believe God can save a bad building from an earthquake?"

He broke bread. "Nope, and I never said I did. I bought this building because it was cheap. We're here because it's a place."

"And you don't worry that if it falls down you'll be responsible for all the people hurt or killed?"

"They know the risks, same as me."

"But you lead by example."

"That's right." He held his fork genteelly, far up the handle. He seemed practiced at speaking with his mouth full. "I eat and sleep and work in this building by the grace of God. I'm aware that if God wills it, my life will end. That's how it is for every living person, except the majority spend their time trying to ignore it. But if you live in what the authorities call a death trap, you're in constant knowledge that your life is cradled in the hands of God. That's a positive thing. It sure seems more positive to me than living out wherever, in Weston, and feeling immortal in your million-dollar house. Here I value every day. I used to despair because I never had time to do the things I wanted. I thought life was going to be too short. That's how little I loved God. Now I'm even busier, but since I been in this building, suddenly I'm getting to everything I want to get to, including people like you. This is about as close to happiness as I think a person can be. I can live without fear because I can feel how I'm hanging right over death, in the hands of God. If you get your life in balance with your death, you stop panicking. Life stops being just the status quo that you hope won't end for a long time."

He bent over his plate to scrape his last beans into a pile. He pushed up his glasses with his middle finger on the bridge and sucked his teeth clean, peering up at Renée with penetrating curiosity. "You came here to tell me my building's unsafe."

"I came because one of your women was bothering me at work."

"Mrs. Wittleder."

"I said something on TV that you disagreed with, and my life has been a mess ever since."

"You're getting calls. Letters, visits."

"Very offensive and invasive ones."

"Yeah, I understand, it's sort of the lunatic fringe. People who're all anger and no love. I don't know if you saw the news today, the drive-by shooting in Alston? Some jackass blew out all the windows of a clinic yesterday. The little teeny-weeny windows? I mean, that's *real* bright. Same thing with the bombings in Lowell. Anger I understand, but not violence."

"The only thing I did on TV was criticize you," Renée said. "Who else but you would care?"

"How should I know? Somebody saw the show and didn't like you. See, I personally didn't even mind what you said. You were honest, you expressed the opposing point of view real nice. You happen to be dead wrong. But I can tell the difference between a geophysicist and an abortionist. I got a lot more useful things to do than picket your lab, frankly. And Bebe Wittleder is a fine woman who I can't believe was ugly to you."

"She wasn't ugly. Not deliberately."

"Well, so. Somehow she still made you mad enough to come down here."

"No. I didn't get mad until I saw the videos."

Stites wiped his plate with a slice of bread. "What made you mad about them?"

"Women who have abortions are vicious sluts who sit around snorting coke. Women who have babies are sweet pretty wives who adore their children."

"Understand it's not journalism. It's an advertisement."

"Which uneducated people swallow as truth."

"Ah." The bread, folded twice, disappeared into his mouth.

"So you want me—me who believes that human life is a mystery and not some chemical process, me who believes that in the eyes of God an individual begins to exist at the moment he's conceived—you want me to show the congregation pictures of mothers abusing their children? And saintly women having abortions? Sort of a balanced view there? I don't think you understand the essence of advertising."

"A Nazi film showing gorgeous Aryans and filthy Jews is only an ad."

"Well, except I don't happen to be advocating genocide. I'm advocating the opposite. Aren't I?"

"The persecution of pregnant women."

He nodded. "Persecution, sure, that's your line on it. But not deportation and murder. See, I think what's bothering you about these videos is they're effective. They affect *you*. But there's even more effective ads on TV for buying jeans or buying beer. Ads that use sex, which is the most powerful and dishonest thing of all. You know, like if I drink Bud Light I'll get my own hot little beach girl to mess around with. You talk about *dishonest* and *manipulative* and *harmful*. And if you're up against a pernicious thing like that, you need some powerful images yourself. And the fact is, there *is* something beautiful about a mother and her baby, and there *is* something ugly about abortions. All I want's an equal shot at the market. And the thing is I can't get one. There's no commercial station in America would run these. I'm into radio a little bit, but you can't do diddly with radio, not compared to video. It's pretty ironic you think we're the persecutors here. We the persecuted minority."

"Which is trying to impose its views on the majority."

"No network station in America will run a single one of our ads. All Americans, every day, watch half an hour of advertising promoting sex for the sake of sex, and another half hour promoting the selfish consumption of material goods. All national news media have a consistently anti-religious, anti-life slant. You want to deny that? The same goes for prime-time programming. And this is going on every single day, seven days a week, year after year, sex sex, buy buy, abort abort. And still forty percent of all Americans are opposed to abortion except in cases of rape or incest. That's our minority. We're looking at the hugest propaganda effort in the history of mankind, and still only a little more than half the people are persuaded."

A whistle blew sharply in the courtyard. The gym teacher cried, *Let's see some Christian volleyball!*

Renée laughed. "You're scary."

Stites offered her half his orange. "Why's that?"

She took the orange. "Because you're smart and you're so sure you're right. You're so sure that everything is simple."

"You got it backwards. It's your world thinks everything is simple: take what you want, and there won't be any consequences. Because let me tell you, there's two kinds of certainty: positive and negative. The Bible teaches us it's wrong to be certain in a positive way, like being certain you're right or that you're saved. But the Bible is full of people with the other kind of certainty: my certainty that this society is *wrong*. I am full of that negative certainty."

"It's wrong about a lot of things," Renée said, "but not about a woman's right to privacy. And I don't actually think it persecutes you. Running your ads is just bad business for a TV station. If the majority truly weren't satisfied with their lives, they'd turn to religion. The fact that they don't seems to indicate that they are satisfied."

"You're not the first person proved revolution logically impossible: the fact that people haven't revolted yet means they're satisfied. That's *real* persuasive."

"I think people mainly want you not to interfere with their private lives."

"I wouldn't interfere if I didn't think lives were at stake. But as it is, I'm morally bound to interfere. And you think my church's anger is ugly, and my methods are extreme, but just think how ugly and extreme the hippie protesters must have looked to conservatives in 1969, even though they had a *good moral argument*, just like I have today. Plus it'd be one thing if society just openly worshipped mammon and said yes, we're willing to destroy innocent lives for the sake of easy sex. What gets me is the piousness. The idea that you can turn people's lives into hellish pursuits of pleasure and claim you're doing them a favor. It's hard to figure a world that sees religious belief as a form of psychosis but thinks the desire to own a better microwave is the most natural feeling there can be. People who send money to a TV preacher because they feel a lack in their lives are under a evil spell, but people who need fur coats to show off in at the grocery store are just normal folks like you and me. It's like the most holy thing in this country is the U.S. Constitution. The human race has never been without suffering in its history, but Mr. Boston Globe and Mr. Massachusetts Senator are suddenly smarter than everybody else in human history. They're certain they've got the answer, and the answer is statutory this and statutory that and university studies of human behavior and the U.S. Constitution. But I tell you, Renée, I tell you, the only reason anyone could possibly think the Constitution is the greatest invention in human history is that God gave America so many fantastic riches that even total idiocy could make a showing in the short run, if you don't count thirty million poor people and the systematic waste of all the riches God gave us and the fact that to most of the downtrodden people of the world the word America is synonymous with greed, weapons, and immorality."

"And freedom."

"A code word for wealth and decadence. Believe me. What the majority of Russians think is great about America is McDonald's and VCRs. Only politicians and anchormen are stupid or dishonest enough to act otherwise. Prime ministers come to Washington, we tell 'em, Welcome to the land of the free. The prime ministers say, Give us more money. I swear we must be the world's laughingstock. What are you smiling at?"

"You remind me of a cynical man I knew."

"Cynical, huh? You think it's cynical to recognize that all human beings, myself included, want to gratify their senses without having to take responsibility for it? How about calling me Christian instead, or honest, or realistic? Because what I see on the other side is pure sentimentality and wishful thinking. This idea that human beings are essentially good and selfless. That you can cure sorrow and loneliness and envy and gluttony and lust and deceit and rage and pride with full employment and good psychologists. You know what my favorite modern-day fable is?"

"What."

"Chappaquiddick. The perfect liberal sees what a human

being really is all about, and he takes off running. Spends the rest
of his life denying that what he saw has any meaning. Telling
everybody else what's wrong with them. Listen, liberalism's so
dishonest it won't even admit that everything good about it, the
supposed compassion at the center of it—which is *irrational*, mind
you, just like all religion is—comes straight from the two-thousand-
year tradition of Christianity. But at least it's got that compassion.
It's innocent, same as a six-year-old. But God's got a soft spot in
His heart for all the innocents of the world. And so the thing I hate
most is the conservative politician. The conservative side is just
pure cynical economic self-interest. Granted it's pretty realistic
about human greed, so it's fairly grownup, you know, like about
the level of a smart-assed thirteen-year-old. But it's even more to
blame than liberalism for supplanting God with the pursuit of
wealth. And I find that unforgivable."

"And that's why you live in this crummy building. With angry
middle-class women."

"You got it."

"I guess you're pretty admirable."

"You said that. I didn't. 'Cause of course it's a danger everybody runs if they try to do some good. The idea that if you know
you're doing good, it doesn't really count. But I say, what's the
alternative—being a jerk just so you know you're not guilty of
pridefulness?"

"Not a bad alternative. You should try it."

"You're a little bit of a cynic yourself. What'd you come here
for?"

In the courtyard, outside the open window, a hush fell as the
volleyball went thump, thump. Pieces of orange peel lay white side
up on Stites's cleaned plate. Renée smiled. "No reason at all."

"Nobody comes for no reason," he said.

"I came because I was bored."

The light in the room had become personal, making facial
expressions more ambiguous and eye contact less sure. "Are you
married?" Stites said.

"No."

"Got a boyfriend?"

"No."

"No kids, I guess."

She shook her head.

"You want kids?"

She shook her head.

"Why not?"

"Because I don't like what happens to women when they have them."

"What happens to them?"

"They just become women."

"You mean: they grow up."

Thump, thump went the volleyball. Sneakered feet scraped and fell on the hard dirt. The carpet pattern began to rearrange itself as Renée stared at it. "Do you want to sleep with me?" she said.

"Ha." Stites smiled, apparently more amused than anything else. "I guess not."

"Because you're afraid I'll tell somebody," she said in a cruel voice. "Or you're afraid you'll go to hell. Or you're afraid it'll hurt your faith. Or I'm not attractive enough."

"A person's lost if he tries to find reasons to say no. He just has to say no, straight from the heart."

"Why."

"Because if you do, you can feel your love of God grow."

"What if you don't love God at all? What if you don't believe there is a God?"

"Then you have to look."

"Why."

"Because, just from sitting here with you, I think you'd be happy if you did. Because I think you're a real person, and I feel love for you, and your happiness would make me happy."

"You feel love for me."

"A Christian love."

"That's all?"

"I'm no more perfect than you are."

She slid closer to him. "You could make me happy very quickly."

The only thing giving expression to his face was the pair of lambent rectangles on his glasses, reflections of incandescence from the doorway. He crossed his arms. "Tell me what you feel like after you've had sex."

"I feel good." She sat up straighter, proud. "I feel like I know something about myself. Like I have a base line, and I know what the very bottom of me is like. Like I know that good and evil don't have anything to do with it. Like I'm an animal, in a good way."

The rectangles on Stites's glasses seemed to take on wistfulness. "I guess you're probably lucky," he said.

"I don't think I'm any different than any woman. I mean, any woman who hasn't had her mind fucked up by male religion."

"Them's fightin' words."

She moved even closer. "Fight me."

"You play fair and scoot back a little, I'll fight you."

She retreated. "Well?"

He joined his hands on his shins, above the argyle socks. "Well, I suppose it comes down to why God made sex such a great pleasure. You obviously consider this irrelevant, but what happens if you conceive a child in the course of making yourself feel good?"

"Funny you should ask."

"What do you mean by that?"

"I mean it's funny you should ask."

"Well, what's the answer?"

"You know what my answer is. If I'm in a halfway decent shape emotionally and financially, I have the baby. Otherwise I have an abortion."

"But what about the potentiality you destroy with an abortion?"

"I don't know. What about the potentialities I destroyed when I broke up with a high-school boyfriend? We could have had eight kids by now. Am I an eight-time murderer?"

"Right. But have you ever known anybody who was conceived out of wedlock?"

"Well, me, for one."

"You?"

"Yeah, I'm sure I'm the perfect example. I'm sure I would have been aborted, if it had been more convenient for my mother."

"And how do you feel about that?"

"Completely indifferent," she said. Her eyes fell on the fragment of scripture on the wall; she found the typeface ugly. "My life began at five. If anything had happened earlier—no loss to me. There was no me."

"But no way you love yourself, if you're so indifferent. No way you love the world. You must hate it. You must hate life."

"I love myself, I hate myself. It adds up to zero."

A long, long volley developed in the courtyard, the stillness and suspense around it growing deeper the longer it went on. Then the players groaned. Stites spoke quietly. "You don't know how much it grieves me to hear you say that."

"I can be fun to sleep with."

"You think you have the right to throw your life away."

"The thought has crossed my mind."

"I think you're very unhappy. I think you must have been very hurt by something."

Renée raised her face to the pitted ceiling, leaning back on her hands, the image of a person enjoying weather at the beach. She was smiling and continued to smile, but after a while her breathing become rough, like a water pump that at first only brings up air. "I—" Her breathing turned to shudders. "I am hurt about somebody. I'm terribly hurt. I'm so hurt I want to die."

Stites scrambled to his feet and went into the bathroom. He came back with a glass of water, but Renée was no longer there. She'd gone into the hall.

"I guess I'm going to leave," she said.

"I want to help you."

"You can't help me."

He set the water on the crossbeam of a pillory and took her bare arms in his hands. "You're you," he said. "You're only you. And you've been you since the moment you were conceived. Your whole history was there when you were one minute old. And the hurt you feel is holy. It's an inch away from being the truest happiness."

Her face was an inch away from his. She stood on her toes and opened her mouth, planting the softest part of her lips on the sharp stubble around his mouth. The next thing she knew, an entire glass of water had been poured over her head.

"Fuck!" she cried, bouncing on her feet, throwing the water

off in gobs. She backed up the hallway, fists clenched at her hips. "Fuck you!"

He'd disappeared into his office. People were coming up the stairwell behind her, and already some of the pillories were occupied, big female duffs in sweats hanging out, rolls of fat visible above some of the waistbands. Metal creaked as other pillories were activated.

Stites had sat down at his desk and begun to read the Bible in the light of a bare ceiling bulb. The window at his shoulder was dark now. He didn't look up when Renée appeared in the doorway, one side of her hair matted, dissolved mascara pooling under one eye.

"I hate you," she said. "I hate your church, I hate your religion. You're nothing but hatred yourself. It's just like you said. It's all negative. You hate women, you hate sex, and you hate the world as it is."

There were bare lightbulbs in his eyes. "I feel a love for you, Renée. You're not a cold person. You're full of emotion and need, and you came here, and just from an hour with you I feel a love for you. It's a Christian love, but the Light gets filtered through the fact that I'm a man, and so I'd love to have you in my arms. I'd like to take you. All right? I'm telling you this because you seem to think it's easy for me. I want you to know: I'm a man. I'm not made of stone. And you damn well better respect me."

"I'd respect you if you went ahead and did it."

He closed the Bible and leaned back in his chair. "You know, what I read about every day is what a tough life women have in today's society. How they have to make all these hard choices, how they have to take so much responsibility for their families. They have to be mothers and they have to be working men too, if liberal society's gonna function."

"It's not just women," Renée said. "Men have to change too."

"Oh, yeah, that's how it's supposed to work. Except you don't hear so much about men complaining and men being caught in a bind. Do you? Men still have the choice, right? They have job satisfaction, and if they *want* to, they can feel good about parenting too. It's like life is getting *better* for men, they're getting options in a *positive* sense, while women are getting all these extra options in a *negative* sense. Wouldn't you call this sort of the major paradox of the age? That the better things get for women liberal-politically, the worse things get in reality?"

"The fact that I sort of agree with you only makes me angrier, because I know what you're going to say."

"What? That the one thing people never seem to suspect is that it's the politics itself that's to blame? Because of course this society doesn't understand things like 'joy.' The joy a mother feels. This society only understands 'jobs,' and 'statutes,' and especially 'money.' "

"And that women are first-class citizens. That joy isn't worth much if it's forced on you. And that it's better to have painful options than no options."

"I was just going to say I don't deny there are women like you. Our Lord tells us that some people are born eunuchs and some people are made into eunuchs along the way."

"Well fuck you too."

"But the fact is, most women want to have children. But society needs them for other stuff, you know, to make more money and more profits, so it has to kinda lure them away with their vanity and pride and greed. Which women have every bit as much of as men do."

"So I've noticed."

"But if a woman's left to her own better instincts, she don't need a big-shot job to make her feel good about herself."

"Her rightful place is in the home."

"That's right. The church understands this about women. It understands the joy of motherhood."

"Well then tell me one thing about this God of yours." Renée took a step towards Stites. "Just one thing. If women aren't supposed to have the same kind of life as men have, tell me why your God gave us the same kind of consciousness."

Stites lunged forward like a trap springing closed. "He didn't! He gave all people the commandment: Be fruitful, and multiply! And you yourself was the one who said this 'consciousness' doesn't survive the birth of a woman's first child. That she's 'just a woman' then, right? See what I'm saying? The woman who's unhappy because she's got a man's consciousness is the woman who has *disobeyed* the word of the Lord. The Lord promises you salvation *if* you obey His word. And this kind of consciousness problem you're talking about vanishes in a woman who's got a baby, just like the covenant says it will. She becomes an instinctive mother, just like you say, and just like the church knows she will. It's a fact!"

She nodded impatiently. "But the fact remains that women are given consciousness only to have it taken away again. They get shown what they *could* have—if they were male—and then it's denied them. And you can say, well, most women aren't like me. But even if there was only one of me, which I can't believe at all, I'm stuck with a nasty choice, and the only way you can justify it is to say we're paying for Eve's sin or some such garbage. And I'm telling you that's a hole in your religion you can drive a truck through: the fact that life basically shits for women and always has."

"And always will, Renée. As it ultimately shits for every person on earth. And so the real choice you have is either suffer for no reason, suffer and be bitter and bring evil to the lives around you, or else find a way to God through your suffering. And I think the Bible might agree with me that there are a lot more women in heaven than men. Just for the suffering they've endured and the pride they've swallowed. Because the last will be first and the first will be last."

"If there is a heaven."

"It's at hand. It's starin' you in the face. That's what you're here for. You know your name means 'born again'?"

"Oh my God," Renée said, utterly disgusted.

Stites stood up and walked around his desk. "Will you at least come again? I won't ask if I can pray for you, because you can't stop me. But can I call you?"

She shook her head very slowly. She was staring at him, inscribing his image in her mind so that she'd always be able to find it there: the tired eyes behind the round tortoiseshell glasses, the yellow tie that now had a spot of bean juice on it, the male hips, the stubble on his cheeks.

"You've helped me enough already," she said. "You've helped me incredibly."

11

The raccoon woke up hungry and unrefreshed. There was hardly a glimmer of light on the still water beneath the ledge he'd slept on. Rats were waddling along the walls and through the filth on the narrow, rock-strewn mud flats, migrating as they did every evening from City Hall to the dumpsters of Union Square. The raccoon rose and yawned and stretched, chin low to the ground, like a Moslem praying.

Sometimes, when he came down from his ledge, he ran confusedly back and forth along the water, spooking the rats and being spooked by them; sometimes he ran for a block or more and then stopped, whiskers twitching, and looked into the inky, dripping blackness ahead of him and then, as if the blackness were a concrete barrier, turned back.

Tonight he went straight downhill. Street light fell through the small holes and larger slots above him. Paw over paw, he climbed the iron rungs he almost always climbed. Halfway up, he reversed and descended headfirst, then reversed again and climbed to the top and peered out through the slot. Between car bumpers he could see the Post Office. He never went out through this slot. Every night he recollected having been here innumerable times, but recollection was weaker than habit, and so invariably he retraced his steps up and down the iron rungs. These and all the other motions he repeated every night were like a sorrow.

The rats were like a sorrow. There were so many of them and

only one of him. In rats the gray, hostile world ramified and mo-
bilized and swirled around him. Superior size and intelligence
counted for nothing when he experienced rats; he became clumsy
and vulnerable. Although they gave him wide berth in the tunnels,
their numbers made them unafraid. If they surprised him, he drew
his shoulders up in anger like a cat, huffing impotently as the little
evils shimmered away into the darkness. They could swim terribly
well.

The raccoon was bigger also than squirrels and rabbits and
opossums, and was smarter and more graceful in his proportions,
but again there were many of them and only one of him. A squirrel's
world might have been nothing more than trees and nuts, a neurotic
hither and thither, but there was an at-homeness—a confidence
and oblivion—that came of belonging to a large population doing
exactly the same inconsequential things. Solitary and omnivorous,
the raccoon had no better reason to climb trees than the pleasure
that following an instinct gave him. The high boughs he sought
bowed wildly with his weight. And when a squirrel fell it contorted
itself at lightning speed and glanced off branches and hit the ground
running; but when the raccoon fell he went down with a crash,
grasping futilely for purchase, making noises of distress, and landed
in an undignified heap. At home in many environments, he was
really at home in none.

Reaching the bottom of the tunnel, he surfaced through a
grateless drain on the commuter-rail right-of-way. Cars on bridges
crossed over the silence that pooled in this low, rubbly part of
Somerville. Dozens of food smells mingled in the sea breeze, but
few had the pungency of immediate forage. The track signals were
green and red in both directions.

Beneath a bridge that saw heavy foot traffic in the daytime,
he ate a stale piece of jelly doughnut and the crumbs of other
doughnuts in a pink-and-orange box. He ate an apple core and
some marshmallows, a novelty. He ate a moth.

Up on Prospect Hill there were good grubs, good crab apple
trees, and a lot of organic garbage, but there were also dogs. Sometimes at the least opportune moment a back door would fly open
and out would shoot a fanged and curly-haired cannonball, and
the raccoon, which like as not had been eating the remains of the

dog's dry Purina dinner, would have to scramble up the nearest vertical surface. He had spent entire nights nervously pacing the crossbar of a swing set or the roof of a recreational vehicle while below him a dog kept the neighborhood awake. Various pets had bitten his hind legs and tail. A cat had laid open one of his cheeks (but the cat had paid for it with an eye). One night a pair of schnauzers trapped him in a free-standing twelve-foot fir tree; spotlights came on, a fat man emerged from the house and children followed, the schnauzers in frenzy all the while, and the red diode of a camcorder winked and the fat man worked the zoom and one of the children lifted a schnauzer as high as she could reach, so that its furiously righteous black German eyes and rose-petal tongue and pointed teeth were within a foot of the terrified and humiliated raccoon, and this confrontation was likewise committed to videotape.

Would a thing like this ever happen to a squirrel? To a rat? To an opossum or a skunk or a rabbit?

The raccoon had had two sisters. One had been killed by cats during a melee in which his mother was also mauled. Later the other sister stopped eating and died. He and his mother saw less and less of each other. Once he passed her in a tunnel and something made him jump on her, but she rebuffed him. Rats hastened through the trickle of water between them as they crouched, panting, on opposite sides of the tunnel. Then she ran uphill and turned back angrily. He didn't see her again until winter. The streets were white with salt and moonlight when he found her rigid by a curb, her eyes cloudy with ice crystals. It was so cold he had to bury his nose in her fur before he could smell anything.

From Union Square, in the direction of the tall buildings, the right-of-way became narrower and rockier and less rich in edible things, until eventually there came vast tunnels in which diesel winds blew and the ground shook.

To the west there was more wildlife. In his second summer the raccoon had traveled that way for several miles, drawn by the smell of females. He ran into some males and they nosed each other and climbed a roof together, but mainly they were wrapped up in their odd, private behavior, his own as odd as any. He suffered repeated traumas involving automobiles, which in West Cambridge had a way of coming and coming and coming. Meanwhile the scent of females grew fainter. By Labor Day he was back in Union Square.

Seasons changed and came around again; he never did the thing animals most like to do. His fur darkened. Something in his stomach gave him steady pain. Fleas tormented him in cycles. Only once or twice more did he see another animal like himself; and, never fighting, never mating, never interacting with his own kind in any way, he almost ceased to have a nature. He became an individual living in a world that consisted entirely of his sorrow-like compulsions and afflictions and the pleasurable exercise of his abilities. The only real face he ever saw was his own, when he looked in dark water—not when he washed food, because then although he was looking at the food and at his busy paws and at the shrubs and car parts around him, his compulsion made him sightless—but when rain had filled a ditch along the tracks and in stopping to cross it he saw a furry, masked head descend from the urban sky with intense and tender slowness to touch noses with him, like a dream of the mate he had never met, and time folded back on itself, the repeated patterns of his existence lining up the way multiple reflections of a single object come together, so that instead of a succession of days there was just one day that was his life, in fact a single moment: this one.

The signals were red and green in both directions. The air had begun to throb. White beams of light coming from his right and left made his eyes glow yellow. He scampered across two sets of rails, holding in his mouth a fragment of hamburger bun swollen with ketchup like a tampon, and ran halfway up an oil-darkened embankment. An engine blasted its air horn, rocking a little as it trundled forward. The raccoon crossed the rails again, turned in a tight circle with swishing tail, ran up the embankment, and suddenly full of terror as the immense and roaring engines doubled their apparent speed in passing each other, he buried himself as well as he could in ragweed and shut the world out.

Renée watched the trains pass from the Dane Street bridge, the passenger cars flowing below her like the opposing belts of an airport people mover. On the roof of a windowless building, pink plastic letters three feet tall said PRECISI N MOTOR REBUI DING. It was midnight. She walked quickly across Somerville Avenue and past the ancient row houses of northern Little Lisbon. In a manila envelope she had the Caddulo pictures and a copy of the paper that she'd printed out on the way back from Chelsea. She passed a powder-blue toilet, complete with tank but somewhat dirty, on the sidewalk.

In her house, a Doberman whined pleadingly behind the hallway door. One floor up, the baby was crying and its parents were yelling at each other, as they'd done so often before the baby came. They had Ph.D.s and quarreled, for example, about the comparative labor value of keeping the refrigerator stocked and keeping the car running. Renée had heard the husband shout, *"You want to switch? You want to switch? You want to do the car and I'll do the shopping?"* They were in their mid-thirties.

There was an open package of whole-wheat bread on her kitchen table. In the sink an eggy frying pan and stacks of plates and glasses. Wine bottles and fruit peels on the counter. Clothes in the hallway, clothes in piles in both main rooms, a brown ring and splashed barf in the toilet, towels on the floor by the sink. Shoes and newspapers and dust mice everywhere. Withered strands of spaghetti near the burners of the stove.

She took the cassette tape marked DANCE in her fingers and bent it until the plastic shattered in a shock whose pulse of high-frequency vibrations stung her skin. She did the same to her other tape, the one with the single song on it. Suddenly there was a new silence in the apartment, as if until this moment music had been playing for so long that she'd ceased to be aware of it, and heard it only after it had stopped.

She took off her clothes and lay face down on the kitchen floor, which was sticky and hot to the touch. Fragments of cassette dug into her elbows and ribs. She cried for a long time.

In her jeans again, she swept the whole apartment and washed and dried all the dishes and put them away. Every thing she'd bought in the previous week, even the leather jacket, she stuffed into Hefties which she carried down to the sidewalk. She kept stopping to cry, but eventually she got the apartment as clean and bare as it was the night she first slept with Louis Holland.

She opened the manila envelope and looked at her paper, wondering why she'd written it. Simply to make money? She sat on her tightly made bed and read the "AGREEMENT, made this 12th day of June" between Melanie Rose Holland of Evanston, Illinois, and Renée Seitchek of Somerville, Massachusetts. The agreement was printed on laser bond paper. She tore it into narrow strips. She tore the strips into squares which she held cupped in her hands for a full minute, as if she'd thrown up into her hands and couldn't think of an appropriate receptacle. The toilet was where she finally dumped it.

Again she looked at her paper, trying to gauge its meaning to her now. Her eyes followed the words, but all the reader in her mind would say was *You're tripping on a romance. You're tripping on a romance.* After a while she found that she had put the paper back in its envelope and was holding it against her chest. She hugged it, rocking, grieving. She shivered and didn't know what to do. She stood up and went to her desk, still cradling the thin envelope in both arms. She stuffed all her related photocopies inside it and began to wind brown plastic wrapping tape around the thick packet. She unrolled more and more tape, until the packet was completely covered, no envelope showing at all. Then she buried it in the bottom drawer of the desk. She looked at the closed drawer and hugged herself, grieving.

Later in the morning she took a shower and drove to Kendall Square. Her doctor at Harvard had referred her to a clinic called New Cambridge Health Associates, which occupied part of an old red-brick factory recently converted into offices, many of them high-tech MIT offshoots. She'd passed the clinic many times, on the way to seminars at MIT, without ever noticing it for what it was.

A Japanese noodle place, popular for lunch, blanketed the street with its breath of broth and scallions. In a parking space directly in front of the clinic, behind yellow police tape strung between two parking signs, five COAIC women stood in the strong midday sun holding the usual photographs. Bebe Wittleder looked at Renée. Renée looked at her. Bebe watched, wide-eyed and mute, as Renée pushed open the metal door.

A handsome counselor, fiftyish, with graying blond hair in a braid, took the envelope her doctor had given her.

"Renée Seitchek," she said. "I know who you are."

"Yeah. So do the people outside."

"Oh dear. This is an unfortunate coincidence for you."

"Uh huh. I guess I think it isn't."

The counselor leaned back against a chart of reproduction, Fallopian tubes and ovaries framing her too-compassionate face. "Do you want me to ask you what you mean by that?"

"Well, I wonder . . . ." Renée wrinkled her forehead. Her skin was stiff from lack of sleep. "I wonder if the last few months have seemed strange to you."

"Which months?"

"The last two or three. With the earthquakes, and what Stites is doing. To me they've been very strange, and all of a piece. But it occurs to me that not everyone feels what I do."

The counselor clearly didn't feel what Renée did. "It's been . . . very interesting," she said with a blank smile.

"Well. Anyway. I got angry. And when you get angry you get sloppy. You know, because men can be sloppy and nothing happens to them. And then I guess I got unlucky. I mean, within the context of my sloppiness. Within the context of my thinking it's not a matter of luck at all."

"You're talking about contraception."

"Yes. My diaphragm."

She watched the counselor fill a space on her form with the word "diaphragm." Somehow she managed to remain polite and humble while the counselor discussed its correct use and told her where she'd fallen short. She knew very well where she'd fallen short.

"Before we go any further," the counselor said, "I want you to know we can easily refer you to a facility without picketers. We fully understand the threat to your privacy if you stay with us."

"If I'm making things worse for you, I'll go wherever you want me to."

"Never. Never for our sake. But for yours?"

"Doesn't matter."

"Then I'll need you to fill this out." She passed a letter of informed consent across her desk. "And we ask that you pay before the procedure. I guess you know we don't take checks."

Renée took three hundreds from her pocket. A technician drew blood from her arm. The counselor led her to a hallway in the basement so that she could leave through a different door.

All day on Wednesday she thought and wrote about deep seismicity in Tonga. When she came home in the evening she found an envelope from Louis Holland in her mailbox. It had a Boston postmark and no return address. She neither opened it nor threw it away.

The baseball game she listened to after dinner went into extra innings, the Red Sox finally losing after midnight on a two-base throwing error.

"Howard," she said. "Can I see you a second?"

It was steaming outside. Even in the shade of the big oaks on the lawn of the Peabody Museum the heat had grounded most winged insects. The squirrels were very listless. Howard put his hands in the pockets of his yachting pants and bounced on his toes. "What?"

"I'm having an abortion today. I want you to pick me up afterwards."

"OK."

She told him where to be. He nodded, hardly listening. She told him again where to be. She said it was very important that he be there.

"Yep."

"So I'll see you sometime between four-thirty and five-thirty."

"Yep."

"You don't mind doing this?"

He pursed his lips and shook his head.

"And you'll definitely be there," she said.

"Yep."

"At four-thirty."

"Yep."

"OK, then." The shock waves from a helicopter passing over-head made her lungs vibrate. "Thank you."

In her office she listened to the radio. Tuning briefly to WSNE, she heard an advertisement for Sunnyvale Farms convenience stores, followed by snatches of the Gospel of John. She took the letter from Louis Holland out of her shoulder bag, held it up to the light, and put it back. Outside her window, disappointed tourists were shaking their heads stoically. She didn't let herself leave Hoff-man until one-thirty.

When she came up from the subway at Kendall Square, she heard the unmistakable blurred, flattened voices of policemen speaking on their radios. Blue flashers fought the whiteness of the afternoon.

She'd been given a key to the basement door of the clinic, but she'd never planned to use it, and she didn't now. She passed a foursome of Cambridge cops on the sidewalk and saw what they were waiting for. Fifty members of Stites's church were standing in front of the clinic, pressed together in their allotted parking space like cows in a cattle car. The cops were waiting for them to cross the yellow tape.

Across the street, in the shadow of another twenty church members brandishing their placards, two news photographers were taking pictures, and a brassy-looking female reporter was adjusting her audio recording device.

STOP THE SLAUGHTER. ABORTION IS MURDER. THANKS MOM I ♥ LIFE.

Stites himself was standing at the yellow tape with a mega-phone. He must have seen Renée before she saw him, because already, as she left the cops behind her, he was raising the tape. Twelve women ducked under it. In two rows of six they sat down and linked arms in front of the clinic door.

"We are here to rescue the unborn," the megaphone said. *"We are here to save innocent lives."*

Traffic was building up in the street. Stites looked straight at Renée. *"Everyone here was once no more than a fertilized egg,"* his megaphone said. *"We are all here by the grace of our Lord and the living love of our parents."*

Twosomes in blue were taking limp grandmothers and stew-

ardesses by the armpits and dragging them to waiting police vans.
The gym teacher dug her heels into sidewalk cracks expertly.

"Renée," Stites said, megaphone lowered.

She looked at the sky. She'd never seen it so white and empty.

"Take one second and think," he said. "You were just a tiny
speck of cells once. Everything you are, everything you ever felt,
came out of that speck. And you're no one but yourself, you're no
accident, you're no random thing. You're you. And that speck inside
you is no one but himself, or herself, and she's just waiting to be
born and have the life God means for her to have."

She looked at the ground. She wouldn't have guessed her mind
could ever feel so closed.

"We love you," Stites said. "We love the person you are and
the person you can be. Just think about what you're doing."

He leaned over the yellow tape imploringly, but the plane he
inhabited did not intersect with hers. He belonged to a species that
was not her own, and this word of his, "love," was simply a function
peculiar to his species. "We love you" made as little sense to her
now as a whale saying, "You strain plankton with your baleen,
just like me," or a turtle saying, "You and I have shared this
experience of laying eggs in a sandy pit." It was revolting.

The way had cleared for her to enter the clinic. The Group of
Twelve, in two police vans, was singing "Amazing Grace" in separate keys and time signatures.

"Renée," Stites said, "Please listen to me."

"This is unforgivable," she said, merely stating the obvious.
She went inside.

"Oh dear," said the blond counselor. "Did you lose the key?"

Renée handed her the key. "How long have they been there?"

"Since this morning."

"I think they'll go away now."

The clinic was frosty with airconditioning and bluish lighting.
In a clean white cell, she took her clothes off and hung them on a
hook. The jeans, outermost, unflattened, with one hip turned out
and the knees slightly bent, were a vivid effigy of her.

"I don't want a tranquilizer," she told the nurse.

In the adjacent room the table had been set for her, with a
smaller side table set for Dr. Wang, the essential stainless flatware

gleaming on a paper placemat. No fish knife, no soup spoon—it was a one-course meal.

The subject lay down in her powder-blue smock. Her face, on the low end of a cushioned gradient, was a deep, purpled red. The speculum was inserted; it said: "This may pinch a little." The tenaculum was applied, chloroprocaine hydrochloride administered by needle. With her slender, nimble fingers Dr. Wang tore the sterile paper wrapping from a 6-millimeter cannula.

K-Y jelly applied. Vacuum cleaner activated, hose attached. In and out the cannula went. In and out, up and down. A revelation was the scraping sound it made. It wasn't a sound you expected from a body; it was the sound of an inanimate object, a trowel scraping the side of a plastic bucket, the last drops of milkshake being sucked from a waxed-paper cup. In and out the cannula went. Ruff, ruff, said the uterus.

"Ow," the subject said, again stating the obvious, as the contractions started. She was trying to resist a riptide. Her foot muscles tightened in the stirrups of the pillory, which had wheels now and had been rolled out onto the sidewalk so that every passing scientist and secretary and adolescent and church member could, by simply glancing, see between her parted naked legs, up the speculum, and into the red center of her self. The nurse stroked her forehead. The vacuum cleaner was turned off.

"Everything seems to be very normal," said Dr. Wang.

In the recovery room Renée was given orange juice, an Ergotrate tablet, and a powdered-sugar doughnut that was the first food she'd had since seven in the morning. The cramps weren't bad, but she was given envelopes with Darvon and more Ergotrate. She was given various straightforward instructions and warnings. She was asked if she had a ride home.

On the dot of five they let her get dressed.

"Let me take you out the back way," the counselor said.

She shook her head.

"You have to try to rest until tomorrow."

"I will."

She was surprised to find a darkened sky outside. A wind with thunder in it upended the hair of the remaining protesters, who were standing in their parking space exactly as they'd been when she last saw them, as if the parking space were the entirety of their planet and their hair were upended by its careening through the air. They looked at Renée somberly, without hatred. Across the street Stites was chatting with the brassy reporter, making her laugh. Smiling, he turned and looked right through Renée. There was a discrete crack of thunder. She waited for a blue Hyundai and a black Infiniti to pass. Then she crossed the street.

"Howdy, Renée. This is Lindsay, from the Herald."

"Hi how are you today!" Lindsay said.

The church members in their parking space had turned 180 degrees and were looking at their minister. Before he knew what she was doing, Renée took his megaphone from his hand and darted behind a streetlight standard. She faced the congregation, the milling bystanders, the waiting cops, the photographers, the reporter and the minister.

"Hello," she said, pressing harder on the plastic Speak button. "HELLO. MY NAME IS RENÉE SEITCHEK. I'M GOING TO INTERVIEW MYSELF."

Stites stepped in front of her, grabbing for the megaphone. "That's not yours, Renée."

She dodged him. She backed up the sidewalk, keeping him in view. "MY STATEMENT," she said. "SINCE YOU'RE ALL SO INTERESTED. MY STATEMENT IS I JUST HAD AN ABORTION."

She stepped off the curb. "FIRST QUESTION: WHAT ELSE—" A car honked. "WHAT ELSE CAN I TELL YOU?

"ANSWER: MY ADDRESS IS NUMBER 7 PLEASANT AVENUE, SOMERVILLE. MY TELEPHONE NUMBER IS 360-9671. MY BLOOD TYPE IS O. MY MIDDLE NAME IS ANN. MY INCOME LAST YEAR WAS $12,000. I STEAL OFFICE SUPPLIES FROM MY EMPLOYER. I LIKE TO MAS-TURBATE. MY SOCIAL SECURITY NUMBER IS 351-40-1137. I USED TO DO DRUGS WHEN I WAS IN COLLEGE. I JUST DID SOME MORE LAST WEEK."

A stream of workers leaving their offices had swelled the crowd. Cars were pulling over to the side of the street. Lindsay from the *Herald* was holding out her cassette recorder while Stites shook his head. Renée aimed the megaphone at him.

"QUESTION: HOW OLD WAS THE FETUS I JUST ABORTED?

"ANSWER: APPROXIMATELY FIVE WEEKS. I'M NOT POSITIVE, BECAUSE I'VE ALWAYS HAD IRREGULAR *MEN-STRUAL PERIODS*.

"QUESTION: WHO WAS THE FATHER?

"ANSWER." She took a deep breath. She had to tell one lie here. "ANSWER: I'M NOT SURE. I'VE HAD *INTERCOURSE* WITH MORE THAN ONE MAN IN THE LAST TWO MONTHS.

"QUESTION: WHY?

"ANSWER: BECAUSE I WAS LONELY AND UNHAPPY AND I WANTED TO FEEL GOOD. I WAS ALSO IN LOVE WITH ONE OF THE MEN. I WANTED TO MARRY HIM AND HAVE CHILDREN WITH HIM.

"QUESTION: WHAT WERE THE MEN'S NAMES?

"ANSWER: *THAT'S* PRIVATE. THEY'RE *MEN. THEY* HAVE THE OPTION OF KEEPING THEIR PRIVACY."

Here she heard two or three young female voices cheer. Unable to tell what direction the cheers had come from, she continued to aim the megaphone at Stites, who had taken off his glasses and was massaging the inner corners of his eyes.

"QUESTION: WHAT KIND OF BIRTH CONTROL DO I USE?

"ANSWER: I USE A DIAPHRAGM. IT WAS WHOLLY MY RESPONSIBILITY, AND WHEN IT FAILED, IT FAILED *ME*.

"QUESTION: HOW DO I FEEL NOW?

"ANSWER: I FEEL VERY, VERY SAD. I FEEL SAD FOR MYSELF AND SAD FOR ALL WOMEN, BECAUSE A MAN WILL NEVER HAVE TO COME TO A PLACE LIKE THIS, NEVER IN A MILLION YEARS. BUT THIS SADNESS BELONGS TO *ME*, AND NO MAN CAN HAVE IT, AND I AM *GLAD* TO BE A WOMAN."

There was another roll of thunder. A wave of paper litter swept down the street. Renée, blushing, and doubling over with a cramp, set the megaphone on the curb and walked as fast as she could into the wind. She had no idea, no interest in knowing, how many people besides Stites and Lindsay had even listened to her.

Howard's great white car was waiting at the intersection of

Hampshire and Broadway, aimed in the direction of Harvard. In a fully paved neighborhood like this, with no green foliage in sight, the dark sky looked like a winter sky. Renée waited for a blue Cressida and a gray Accord and a black Infiniti and a silver Camry to pass. As soon as she crossed the street and got in the car, Howard stepped on the gas pedal. She slouched down so far that her eyes were even with the bottom of the window. She kicked aside Coke cans and a championship-size frisbee, rubbing her abdomen with her fist.

"You feeling OK?" Howard said.

"Could be worse."

"OK if I stop by the lab?"

"Why don't you take me home first."

"Just for a second, OK? Gotta get a rope for Somerville Lumber."

"What are you getting at Somerville Lumber?"

"Wall unit."

She laughed emptily. "Are you going to want me to help you with that?"

The chugging of the car's engine was like the noise of a window fan in a heat wave, keeping her discomfort within tolerable limits. When Howard turned it off, in the reserved-only parking lot outside the computer-room door, she felt weak and ill and slouched down even farther.

A gust of warm wind blew through the open front-seat windows. Tires squealed. A gray Cressida swung into the lot and stopped behind the car, blocking it in. A young Oriental woman in a business suit and sneakers jumped out and ran and pounded on the door to the computer room. It was Howard's so-called fiancée, Sally Go. Someone let her in.

Beyond the green hedge and bank of mulch there was motion on Oxford Street, action within three independent frames of reference, the blurred whiz of car roofs, the floating by of bicyclists with their heads and shoulders high off the ground and their bikes obscured by the hedge, and the bouncing gait of pedestrians, students and working people heading home with noticeable haste because the trees were now showing the white undersides of their leaves and the boughs of the tallest ones were beginning to heave with some violence. The wind carried fragments of distant sounds. The thunder was increasing, booming like the earth in a New England earthquake. Renée half sat and half lay with her hand on her abdomen, drawing some of the cramp pain out into her fingertips. Already she could not have said how long she'd been waiting in the car.

Behind her, in a part of the sky that she was too enervated to turn to see, an eclipse-like darkness gathered. The trees were in constant motion, all the sounds from Oxford Street landing in pieces well to the north, but still the ground was dry, and people in dry clothes were on the sidewalk, and the air was warm and filled with petals and green leaves. She thought she'd never breathed more beautiful air. She felt badness draining out of her. The weather, which was nature's, had taken over the green spaces and paved spaces between buildings. The air smelled of midsummer and late afternoon and thunder and love, and its temperature was so exactly the temperature of her skin that being in it was like being in nothing, or meeting no boundary between her self and the world. She could hear lightning static on the radios of passing cars. She felt the poignancy of cars and hot asphalt and brick buildings and radio transmissions, all the things that human beings had made, as the weather swept over them. How deeply they were immersed in the world, how deeply she was. Life not on the world's skin but deep inside it, in the sea of atmosphere and churning trees, with a deep, vaulted ceiling of black cloud above it, electrons rising and descending on white ladders. She wanted to embrace it all by breathing it, but she felt that she could never breathe deeply enough, just as sometimes she thought she could never be close enough physically to a person she loved.

She wondered: what exactly did she love here? Thunder echoed and leaves followed spiral tracks into the dark green sky. Watching her mind from a safe ironic distance, she formed the thought: *Thank you for making me alive to be here*. It rang false, but not completely false. She tried again: *Thank you for this world*.

Half serious, half not, she tried again and again. She was still trying when the computer-room door flew open and Sally Go came running out. Sally pushed her tear-streaked face through Renée's open window.

"I saw you!" she said. "I work right there, and I saw you! Me and my friends, we *saw* you!" She had one of those no-stick city voices. "I hate this kind of shit you're pulling. He was supposed to marry me. You're crazy. I hate you! I hope you die! I hate you so much."

Renée opened her mouth to speak, but the girl was already in her car. She backed out with a screech and drove away.

Howard returned with a hank of nylon rope.

"Was that your girlfriend?"

He shrugged, starting the engine. By now the wind had blown most of the cars and people off the streets. A black curtain was hanging at the end of Kirkland Street, a November twilight.

"You're going to get your wall unit wet," Renée said.

"Got some plastic," Howard said.

She remembered the letter from Louis and, without thinking, put her hand under the flap of her leather bag and tried to open it surreptitiously, but Howard looked at her. She slowly drew her hand out. Beneath the Dane Street bridge the wind was flattening stands of ragweed and cattail. The first drops of rain scored the windshield. She was coming home to Somerville, in her jeans and sneakers, with her emptied womb. The brown and yellow and white and blue clapboard had never looked so beautiful as in the green light of the beginning storm. She could already feel the overheatedness of her apartment, smell the rain on the hot slates outside the kitchen window, hear the water on the roof. She was so impatient to be home that when Howard stopped on Pleasant Avenue she hardly thanked him. She jumped out and slammed the door.

Huge raindrops were falling on the honeysuckle. Howard pulled away but had driven no more than thirty feet when, directly across the street from Renée, the driver-side window of a black Infiniti was powered down, and an arm reached out and shot her in the back with a small revolver and let fly four more bullets as she fell down the crumbling stoop. Howard hit the brakes. In his mirror he saw the Infiniti fishtail onto Walnut Street and disappear.

III

Argilla Road

12

—∿∿∿∿—

No one ever had trouble finding the Hollands' house on Wesley Avenue. It was the one with fourteen adolescent white pine trees crammed into its narrow front yard. Bob had planted the trees in the spring of 1970 and then watched approvingly as, over the years, they killed the ground cover with their acidic droppings and enveloped the yard in gloom. Every weekday morning before he biked to campus, he policed the forest floor for gum wrappers and Whopper boxes. On weekends he pulled wind-blown trash from the treetops with a long-handled rake, the pines swaying like shaggy dogs submitting mutely to a brushing. They writhed when he turned a hose on them to rinse sulfuric air pollutants off.

In the back yard, behind a high fence protecting the cheerful lawns of an engineer and an assistant athletic director, Bob had allowed the land to regress into the Illinois prairie that had predated (he never tired of explaining this) the arrival of the Europeans' wasteful and destructive agriculture practices. Resident amid the chest-high growth were moles, snakes, mice, blue jays, and lots and lots of hornets. There were also lawn-mower traps, in the form of steel stakes hidden in the undergrowth and projecting four inches above the earth. Bob had planted these in 1983 after Melanie, discovering mice in the bedrooms, paid a neighbor boy to destroy the prairie with a mower and a hoe. Now the prairie was sequestered from the house by a low chain-link fence, and any small animals that crossed the border were eaten by the Hollands' specially appointed cats, Drake and Cromwell. Periodically Bob put on gloves and ventured in among the hornets to uproot maple saplings and other broad-leafed intruders.

The house itself, of which only the roof and third-floor dormer still stood above the pine trees, was unusual in having a half-circular living room and, directly above, a half-circular master bedroom. These rooms, plus the dining room and front porch, belonged to Melanie. She kept them reasonably neat, and visitors to the house never saw the Bronze Age kitchen or the Stone Age basement, where there were piles of laundry whose bottom strata dated from the mid-1970s. Bob stayed mainly in his study, which was the only room on the third floor. Nowadays, for months at a stretch, the children's rooms were visited by nothing but airborne dust. The doors were always open, though, exposing the furnishings like the unburied dead—granting them no rest.

As Louis came up Davis Street from the El stop a dry wind from the west was blowing in his face. The flat, unwatered lawns were as brown now in June as they used to be in August. House after house stood deserted-looking in a deep post-graduation silence, a desolation which the charcoal smoke creeping around from one solitary family's back yard made all the more complete.

It was cooler among his father's pine trees. Yellow beams slanted through suspended yellow pollen, the sun hanging in the branches as if it hadn't moved in twenty years. The smell of resin was sharp and suppressive of insect motion. (Melanie often said she felt like she lived in a cemetery.) Taped to the front door was a message in Bob's hand that said *Louis, I'm at the Jewel.*

He went straight upstairs to his room, dropped his bag, and fell down on the waiting bed, overcome by the heat and the lifelessness of the neighborhood and the fact that he was home. He didn't know why he'd let himself come home. He shut his eyes, wondering, Why, why, why, as if the word alone could carry him over the next five days to the moment his return flight left. But the thought of the return flight led to the thought of Boston. He rolled onto his stomach, pulling at his face with his hands. He tried to think of something, anything, that had made him happy in the past, but no trace of pleasure remained from the days he'd spent with Lauren, and although there was something about Renée that had had some happiness attached, it was nothing he could remember now.

Telephones rang. Mechanically he rose and answered in his parents' bedroom.

"Louis?" Lauren said. She sounded next door. "I miss you."

"Where are you?"

"I'm in Atlanta, at the airport. Did you have a good trip?"

"No."

"Louis, I was thinking, I just had this thought. You know how you said you couldn't see living in this country? Well, I was thinking we really could go to some island. We could both work and save some money, and we could go and start a restaurant or something. Just the two of us. We could have some kids, and go to the beach, and then we'd work in the restaurant." She paused, awaiting a response. "It sounds so stupid when I say it, but it's not stupid. We really could. I'll be everything for you, and anywhere we go is fine with me."

Louis listened to the breath coming out of his nose at regular intervals.

"You think it's stupid," Lauren said.

"No. No, it sounds nice."

"You didn't want me to call."

"It's OK."

"No, I'm going to hang up right now and not call anymore. I'm sorry. Just pretend I didn't call. Will you promise to pretend I didn't call?"

"Really, it's OK."

"The other thing I wanted to say"—she lowered her voice—"is I want to make love with you. I really, really, really want to. I wanted to say I'm sorry we didn't when we had a chance. As soon as I was on the plane I started crying because we hadn't. And now"—her voice was becoming squeaky—"now I don't know if we ever will. Louis, I mess everything up, don't I. When I'm with you, I'm so happy, I try to have everything be *perfect*. But when I'm alone—when I'm alone I only want things your way."

There was a very long pause, with respiratory sounds at either end of the line.

"Be tough," Louis said.

"OK. Goodbye."

He wanted to be off the phone, but he hated the sound of this "goodbye." The word accused him of not loving her. If he loved her, wouldn't he tell her not to say goodbye yet?

" 'Bye," he said.

"All right," Lauren said, hanging up. Another charge had registered on her credit card.

Having heard the modest but penetrating ticking of a ten-speed's freewheel in the driveway, he went down to the kitchen and found his father unstrapping a knapsack from his back.

"Hi Dad."

"Howdy, Lou, welcome home."

There was no sign of any $22 million in the kitchen. The linoleum was still torn in front of the sink and back door, the fruit bowl still held, as always, one moribund banana and one obese and obviously mealy apple, there was still the same archaic dishwasher with the words worn off its buttons and dried drools of detergent below the leaky door, still the dirty windows with the storms on, cobwebs and pine needles in the corners, still the old drainer with its rusty ulcerations, still the economy-size bottle of generic dish soap with a pink crust around its nozzle, and still the old father, nattering in his mildly entertaining way about the local drought and its probable global causes. Bob was dressed like a lawn-care-service employee—cuffed blue stay-press trousers, Sears work shoes, and a Greenpeace T-shirt dark with perspiration. Louis watched with an irritation verging on contempt as the man crouched womanishly by the refrigerator and transferred vegetables from the knapsack to the crisper. The beers on the top shelf were still Old Style. Louis took one, reaching over the hair that would now always be thicker than his own, smelling the armpits to which deodorants had long been strangers.

"You forgot to take your ankle clip off," he said.

Bob touched his pants leg, noting that the clip was there, but he didn't take it off. He smoothed the emptied knapsack and folded it in two.

Louis looked around the kitchen as if it were a witness to what he had to put up with.

"Well so here I am," he said. "You want to tell me why you sent the ticket?"

"So you couldn't hang up on me," Bob said.

"Expensive way to do that. Or is money no object now?"

"If you're worried about that, you can paint the garage for me. And scrape it first. But no, if you want to be strictly logical, there's no reason for you to be here. There's no reason for me to care if I see you unhappy, no reason why you and your mother shouldn't keep making each other miserable and poison the whole family."

Louis rolled his eyes, again calling upon the kitchen as his witness. "I take it she's already in Boston."

"She left on Thursday."

"It's nice how she always lets me know when she's there."

"Yes, I know she doesn't call you. But the fact is you wouldn't want to see her now anyway."

"Uh-huh." Louis nodded. "That's very considerate of her. She knows I'm not going to want to see her, so she spares me the awkwardness of saying no to an invitation. That's so amazingly tactful."

"Lou, this is why I wanted you here."

" 'This'? 'This'? This—what, attitude problem of mine? This failure of my niceness regarding Mom?" He swallowed some beer and made a face. "How can you drink this stuff? It's carbonated gallbladder."

"I thought you might *want* to come," Bob said, determined not to be provoked. "You're obviously very angry, and I thought if you understood better why your mother, for example, is behaving the way she is—"

"Then I'd understand and accept and forgive her. Right?" Louis dared his father to contradict him. "You'd tell me what a tough life Mom has, and what a tough life Eileen has, and what a comparatively easy life I have, and then because it turns out I've got things so good I'd go and say, Gee, Mom, *I'm* sorry, do whatever you want, I totally understand."

"No, Louis."

"But what I don't understand is where everybody gets this

idea that I've got things so easy. You live in this house with her, you see her every day, but you can't say to her, Jeez, Melanie, aren't you being kind of mean to *Louis?* Instead you've got to fly me home, so *I* can be the one who understands."

"Lou, she understands, but she can't help herself."

"Yeah, well, I can't help *my*self. And that's why I'm not going to have anything more to do with her. She can't help it, I can't help it, that's the end of it."

"But you *can* help it."

"What, oh, because why?" he asked the kitchen generally. "Because I was elected at age ten to be Mr. Understanding? Because men have things easy?"

"That's part of it, yes."

"I'm the one who has things easy? Not Mom who can do whatever the hell she wants and then say she can't help it? Not Eileen who, you know, *cries* whenever she can't have what she wants? Are you serious? That's such total arrogance. I'm saying I'm no better than they are. What's wrong with that?"

"What exactly is your problem with her?"

"My problem with her . . . I'm not even going to tell you what my problem is."

"Why not?"

"Because I don't feel like it."

"Because you're embarrassed. Because you know it isn't worthy of you."

"Oh, I see. Tell me more about this problem of mine."

Bob always savored any lecture invitation. He picked up the black banana and, holding it before his eyes, slowly stripped it. "Maybe it's the old romance of the left," he said in his musing, classroom voice. "I tend to think of you and Eileen as sort of the two sides of the national equation. Eileen being the kind of person who thinks she needs wealth and luxury, and you being the kind of person who—"

"Who says hell no, beans and rice are fine with me."

"Yes, you can laugh at me now, but that's how it seemed." Bob began to eat the banana; no one else in the family would have touched such a black one. "I thought you felt more or less the way I do. And I used to believe there was a sizable class of people in this country who wanted nothing more than a decent job, decent housing, decent health care, and first-class non-material satisfactions. Because it seemed as if people *should* be like this. And then in the eighties this turns out to be as wishful as all my other thinking. The decent working people in this country turn out to have the same consumer greed as the bourgeoisie, and every single person is dreaming of having the same luxuries that Donald Trump has, and would poison the world and kill his neighbors to get them if that would help."

"Oh," Louis said. "So I'm greedy. I'm a Donald Trump just like everybody else. That's my problem with Mom: I want a snazzy town house just like Eileen's, and I want my VCR and my BMW and I'm pissed at Mom because she won't give it to me. That's what you've determined?"

"You're angry because she's lent money to Eileen."

"Yeah, even if that were the problem, which I don't really grant, the thing is it's a *fairness* thing, a *frankness* thing. I mean, your working class wouldn't care about BMWs if they didn't have to see all these worthless rich assholes driving them around and talking on their car phones. And before you say it—I'm not saying Eileen's a worthless rich asshole. I'm not saying I necessarily even have a problem with her."

"No," Bob said, tranquilly finishing the banana. "You just see an opportunity to torment your mother and still have justice on your side."

"Me? Are you kidding? I'm trying to stay away from her! I'm trying to shut her out of my mind! Which is *literally* what she asked me to do. She said, let's pretend this didn't happen, and what do you think I've been trying to do? You know—in my own stupid trusting way. I don't know where you get this idea I'm tormenting her. I went and talked to her *one time*, when I found out that I was the only one being asked to pretend this didn't happen, I mean, that Eileen wasn't. I had one five-minute lapse, and that was it. And now you tell me you 'hoped' I might not be as 'materialistic' as Eileen. Well . . . maybe I wasn't! Maybe I was this perfect, greedless guy you always wanted me to be. But I get no thanks from anyone, and then you give me this little talk about how 'disappointed' you are, and how innocent you were, and how

I'm like the working class that never seems to do what the marxists want it to. I mean, it's no wonder us workers all turn out wishing we could be Donald Trump. *We're sorry you're disappointed.* You think I want to disappoint you? When the only possible justification I have for living this stupid fucking way I live is that maybe at least my father thinks it's not so stupid? But you obviously can't see this, because you obviously don't have the slightest idea what I'm really like, because for twenty-three years you've been too stoned to notice. You talk about innocent, you talk about dumb, look at *me* here."

Bob's eyes had widened suddenly, as if he'd felt a knife go in his back. Louis, taking deep breaths, dropped his eyes to the floor. "And you're hurt, I know, I'm sorry. It was an exaggeration."

"No, you're right," Bob said as he turned towards the door. "You hit the nail on the head."

"Yeah, walk away now, would you. Make me feel like the invulnerable one, huh? Like the only person in this family who doesn't get overcome with grief and guilt."

"I have nothing more to say now."

"You walk away. Mom walks away. Eileen walks away. What else am I supposed to think except that *I'm* the one with the problem? —That I'm always so fucking right? Is that it?" He was speaking to an empty doorway. *"I don't know what I'm doing wrong. What am I doing wrong?"*

He listened to the creak of wooden stairs. *"AREN'T YOU GLAD I CAME HOME?"*

Bob Holland had come from a small town north of Eugene, Oregon. In the East, at Harvard, he'd written his doctoral dissertation on the origins of land speculation in seventeenth-century Massachusetts and met Melanie, whom he began to stalk relentlessly but didn't succeed in capturing until he'd returned to Boston from a two-year post-doctoral stint in England, at the University of Sheffield. The young Hollands came to Evanston in the early sixties and conceived Eileen the same month Bob was offered tenure. For a few years he was the history department's shining star, teaching hugely popular courses on Colonial America and nineteenth-century industrialization, giving exams with questions like *Describe what might have been* or *Was it progress?*, and bestowing A's and B's on all comers. He grew marijuana in planters on the roof, turned his lawn into a jungle, rode buses to Washington. Student activists caucused in his basement. He was teargassed and spent a night in jail, once.

However, as everybody knows, the spirit of those days soon wasted itself in violence, licentiousness, self-indulgence, commercial co-optation, and despair. Each autumn's fresh crop of students contained more well-groomed and unplayful weeds than the crop before it. Bob managed to cultivate militancy in a few of them, but history and numbers were against him, and his mind was a little too scrambled by disappointment and hallucinogens for him to be able to thrive in the increasingly hostile environment. As early as 1980 he found himself classed by students and faculty alike as just another Old Marxist Drone.

The Drones were an exclusively male bunch. They sat in their own corner at faculty meetings, well apart from the newly emboldened conservatives in their bow ties and the recently hired minority faculty in their assertively ethnic costumes and all the kiddies, leftist and otherwise, in their tight short skirts and herringbone blazers. The Drones had red faces and tousled hair. They wore flannel shirts and down vests. Among themselves they traded the too-obvious smiles of people who are publicly intoxicated and think it's funny. They saw fascism everywhere—in the administration, in the cafeterias, in the bookstore—and said so on the record. They proposed Jerry Garcia and Oliver North as commencement speakers. They raised their hands during earnest policy discussions and tried to have humorous remarks about psychedelic drugs inserted in the record. They were all terribly nostalgic about psychedelic drugs.

Lacking public support for an assault on society at large, the Drones subverted the only authority they knew, which was the university. They never missed an open party or reception. They clustered around whatever food and alcohol the university had paid for, and grimly, but winking now and then like the conspirators they felt themselves to be, consumed many dollars' worth. They were gleeful in abusing privileges, borrowing stacks of library books never to return them, working departmental copy machines to death, and insisting on their share of funds to bring in guest speakers—ex-Yippies or minor functionaries from Romania or Angola—to whose lectures only the Drones themselves came, with their keen appetite for refreshments. Challenged by their peers, they fell back on a hoary argument: Society is corrupt, this university is a product of society, therefore this university is corrupt.

There were Drones in Bob's own department who hadn't seen an article into print since Kent State. When the subject of publications arose, these men regarded their truncated careers with the proud, resigned faces of amputees. Drones taught Rocks for Jocks, seminars on Popular Culture, and courses in Russian History for which the syllabi hadn't changed in three decades.

Bob himself, atypically, was a good scholar. Even during the darkest Reagan years, when he was getting stoned five afternoons a week, he immersed himself in primary and secondary sources and came up with many marvelous, marvelous historical facts and insights which, shorn of their cannabidiolic aura by the sober glow of his computer, still retained enough mettle to form the bases for a book called *Filling the Earth: God, Wilderness, and the Massachusetts Bay Company* and for two articles on wampum, beaver pelts, and inflationary spirals, all written in fluid prose and published very respectably.

It was mainly Melanie who kept Bob in line. For all that he enjoyed teasing her and baiting her, he lived in fear of losing her respect. She probably hadn't set foot on campus a dozen times in twenty-five years, so he was free to make a fool of himself there, but elsewhere he was careful to preserve his dignity. For Melanie he would slick back his hair and put on one of his ancient suits and ride with her downtown to the symphony or opera and nap in his seat until it was time to go home. He endured countless dinners with her college friends, all of whose husbands seemed to be past or current members of the Stock Exchange and still could get nothing better than a laugh out of him when the conversation turned to politics. For months at a time, when Melanie was in rehearsal or performance at the Theatrical Society, Bob cooked dinners for Louis and Eileen. Melanie shouted at him and shouted at the children; he covered his ears with his hands and smiled as if she were onstage and doing very well; she shouted all the louder, and he went upstairs and she followed, shouting; but the next time she saw the children she was flustered and sometimes blushed. The children never consciously recognized the obvious fact, which was that the man in their house was wildly in love with the woman and the woman less than perfectly immune to the man, but undoubtedly they got the basic idea. Eileen felt pity and affection for their father. Louis felt morbid embarrassment.

Dusk was falling on Monday by the time Louis returned to Wesley Avenue from an all-day walk to Lake Forest. He'd located the bland, wide house that Renée had grown up in. He'd eaten two large orders of french fries along the way. Now the wind and the light had died, and Wesley Avenue was so deserted—the whole neighborhood so obviously empty of watchful human beings—that it seemed the day might as well have never happened, or at best should have gone in the record books with an asterisk. In the sky above Dewey School, alma mater of the Holland kids, the orange trail of a bottle rocket faded and there was a white flash. Humidity fattened the report.

Louis entered the stuffy house and drank two glasses of iced tea. He peeled off his T-shirt, wrung it out, and put a fresh one on. With each step he took up the stairs to the third floor, the temperature rose by a degree and the smell of old timber and warm plaster intensified. Bob's door, ajar, let out just enough light to illuminate the yellowed quotation that was taped to it:

> For I ask, What would a Man value Ten Thousand or a Hundred Thousand Acres of excellent *Land*, ready cultivated; and well stocked too with Cattle, in the middle of the in-land Parts of *America*, where he had no hopes of Commerce with other Parts of the World, to draw *Money* to him by the Sale of the Product? It would not be worth the inclosing, and we should see him give up again to the wild Common of Nature, whatever was more than would supply the Conveniences of Life to be had there for him and his Family.
>
> —JOHN LOCKE

Not noticing any fresh smoke, Louis tapped on the door and pushed it open. His father was sitting in front of the window, rubbing the fur on Drake's head and looking into the blades of the box fan blowing air at him. Half the bare floor was hidden by staggering piles of photocopies flagged with sheets of self-adhesive notepaper. On the wall above his Macintosh hung a black-and-white photograph of Eileen. She was about four years old, short-haired and elfin and huge-eyed, and she wore a chain of daisies in her hair.

"Look," Louis said. "You don't have to say anything. I just want to say I'm doing my best. I don't want to hear how bad I am. It's not really very helpful for me right now. You know, because I already feel like about the biggest jerk on the planet."

Drake gave him a sated look, tinged with jealousy. Bob spoke to the fan. "I never said you were bad. I of all people have no right to say that. You don't even know the high regard I have for you."

Louis winced. "You don't have to say that either, I mean, let's quit while we're ahead."

"And I suppose my high regard gives rise to unreasonable expectations. I'd hoped that even though you're upset with your mother, you still might be able to understand what's going on with her, if I could talk to you. You can't blame me for trying. I can't just stand aside while this folly of your grandfather's destroys the family. I have to do something."

"Uh huh. Like what."

"Like tell you that we love you."

Louis might not have heard him. He turned to a shelf and touched the spines of the library books on it. Then he made a fist and punched the spines. With bent fingers he pulled at his arms and chest as though he were covered with corruption. *"Don't say that!"* His voice was a strangled shriek, like no sound he'd ever made. *"Don't say that!"*

His father spun his swivel chair around, Drake leaping free of his lap and bolting from the room. "Lou—"

"Fuck love. *Fuck* love." Louis butted his head against the doorframe. He stumbled out the door and slumped on the landing, holding his head and feeling torn between what he was feeling and what he knew to be a still-optional ability to control himself. He opened his eyes and experienced a moment of clear emptiness, a simultaneous zeroing of all the waves in his brain. Then his father

knelt and put his arms around him, and his eyes burned and terrible clots of sharp-edged hurt rose from his chest. He was crying, and there was no longer any way back to the self-respect and pride he'd felt before he started crying. He cried because the thought of stopping and seeing that this self that he had liked so much had been crying in his father's arms was unbearable. It seemed as if there were a specific organ in his brain which under extreme stimulus produced a sensation of love, more intense than any orgasm, but more dangerous too, because it was even less discriminate. A person could find himself loving enemies and homeless beggars and ridiculous parents, people from whom it had been so easy to live at a distance and towards whom, if in a moment of weakness he allowed himself to love them, he then acquired an eternal responsibility.

For no apparent reason, Bob took his arms away from Louis. There was a damned look in his eyes. He went down to the kitchen, cracked the metal seal on a Johnnie Walker bottle, and tilted it back. He had to fellate the bottle, sticking the neck well into his mouth, to keep the plastic spout from dribbling whiskey down his chin. The cats tried to climb his legs, coveting the bottle. He filled their water dish. He could hear his son sobbing two floors above him.

Upstairs, he found him leaning crookedly against the newel post with his glasses off, his eyes small and red, the neck of his T-shirt stretched. He squinted stupidly at his father, who was standing in front of the light.

"You feeling a little better?" Bob kicked him playfully, with one foot and then the other.

"What are you kicking me for? Don't kick me."

"I'm sorry."

Louis sighed. He felt deadened, as if some long-accumulated strain or poison had been released from his system. That his thinking was in ruins didn't really bother him. "There's something I wanted to say."

"Anything you want."

"Right. Thanks." Louis sniffed back a large volume of mucus. "It's about Mom's company, Sweeting-Aldren. I just wanted to say they're causing the earthquakes."

"What do you mean?"

"I mean they're literally causing the earthquakes in Boston. This woman I've been living with— This woman I was living with— This woman who I just did a really nasty thing to . . ." Louis looked straight ahead, tears pooling again in his eyes. "She's a seismologist. She's the most wonderful person, who I just really fucked over. Who I just basically lost. I don't even know why it happened. I mean, I know why, it's because she's a lot older than me—it's because I loved her so much. Dad. Because I loved her so *much*. And this other person who's just my age, who I used to be—. This person came in from Houston."

He looked sorrowfully at his father. Then he squeezed his eyes shut, his face crumpling up.

Bob crouched in front of him. "Call her."

He shook his head. "It's complicated. You can't get her on the phone, and I don't even know if I want to. I don't think I can." He slid sideways, afraid Bob was going to touch him again. "I don't want to talk about this. I just had one thing to say, which was the company's causing the earthquakes, and somehow I'm going to stick it to them, and I know Mom has a lot of stock, and I wasn't going to tell you, but now I have, and you can tell her if you want. That's all."

"Causing. You said causing."

"Yeah."

"Is she sure?"

"Yeah."

Then Bob had to know everything. As busy as a boxer's manager, he brought Louis toilet paper to blow his nose with, took him to the kitchen and sat him down with ice water and Johnnie Walker, and showered him with questions. Trying to explain it without Renée's help, Louis thought the whole theory sounded fuzzy and unlikely, but Bob was laughing as he chopped up vegetables and beef and stir-fried them, rating every logical step with a "Good!" or an "Excellent!" One could only admire how methodically he set about mastering the argument. At the table, with each bite of food he picked up in his chopsticks (Louis used a fork), he fitted another fact into place.

"Nobody suspects the company," he said over a piece of carrot, "because the earthquakes are so deep."

"Right."

"And the earthquakes in Ipswich are unrelated." A strip of beef now. "They're the cover."

"Right."

"Just as in New Jersey, when the wind blows out to sea, all the companies double their emissions because no one can catch them at it. The Ipswich earthquakes are the wind blowing east."

"Right."

"Marvelous! Terrific!" A snow pea pod. "And how does she prove there's a deep hole?"

Louis wished his father wouldn't insist on considering this "her" theory. "She's—we've—been looking for pictures or something. But otherwise, it's just the two articles."

From his soy-stained plate, Bob picked up a broccoli floret and held it at eye level, revolving it like a thought and frowning. "There's a problem there," he said. "If she can't prove for certain that the hole was drilled."

"We're working on it."

"No no no. There's a problem." Bob turned and frowned at the door to the basement. After a moment he stood up and went downstairs. He returned with an *Atlantic Monthly*.

"Eat, eat," he said, sitting down. He wiped dust off the magazine and showed Louis the cover: THE ORIGIN OF PETROLEUM. February 1986. "Your mother subscribes," he said. "And I read."

Louis eyed the magazine uneasily. The cover story was about the scientist Renée had mentioned, the one named Gold, who believed that petroleum originated deep inside the planet. It said something unflattering about Louis's love of truth that he was afraid to open the magazine—afraid to risk seeing Renée's theory contradicted. If she had to be wrong, he was happier not knowing it.

Bob took the magazine and paged through the cover story, running his finger down the columns. When he came to the end, he shook his head.

"Nix about Sweeting-Aldren. Which, believe me, I would have noticed when I read it. But—and really, I don't want you to think

I personally am not persuaded, because I am, because I know these people and it makes a lot of sense. But the impression you get from this article is that you don't just drill the hole anywhere. There has to be a very special geology to collect the petroleum that's coming up. I'm more than willing to believe the company sank a well to pump waste into, but I don't think they'd go down any twenty thousand feet if five thousand would do. And unfortunately it sounds like your friend's theory doesn't hold up unless the hole is very deep. If the geology was correct in western Massachusetts, any hole that's there should be deep. But if it's in Peabody it can only be shallow."

Louis was sure that Renée would have had an answer to this. "I guess they thought maybe they'd get oil anyway."

"Come on, Lou." Bob leaned forward challengingly. "It has to make sense in the details. If you send me this stuff as a paper to review, I'm going to jump all over you. Oil's cheap in '69. Deep holes are tremendously expensive. A shallow hole will do the trick for waste disposal. Your friend's theory requires the hole to be deep. The Atlantic—which admittedly is not the Bible, but nevertheless—The Atlantic tells me the theory of deep petroleum wasn't developed until the late seventies. It's based on space probes from the early seventies. Even if somebody had a theory in 1969 —when nobody cared about oil anyway, and Sweeting-Aldren by the way had earnings of better than four bucks a share annually —it must have been based on bad evidence."

"Well, that's what Renée said. It was a bad paper, but it still sort of anticipated the theory later on."

"But a bad paper is a bad paper. How's the company going to know the theory has a future?"

Louis squirmed like a failing student. "I don't know. But everything else makes sense."

"Do you remember the author's name? It wasn't Gold, was it?"

"Oh, please." He pushed away his plate. "I *know* who Gold is. This was some guy named Krasner. Somebody who, he stopped publishing and we have no idea where he went." He looked at his father. "What's wrong?"

Bob had risen from his chair. He was staring at the liquor cabinet, gravitating towards it. He was suddenly very pale.

"What's wrong?"

Bob turned around as if responding to the sound of his voice, not the content. He looked at him vacantly. "Krasner."

"You're kidding. You're going to tell me you know him."

"Her."

"Her?" A seed of fear sprouted in Louis's stomach.

"Anna Krasner. A girlfriend of your grandfather's."

"How do you know that?"

Bob answered slowly, speaking to himself. "Because old Jack made sure I knew. There wasn't a possession he had that he didn't make sure I knew was his."

"When was this?"

"Sixty-nine."

"Was he married? I mean, to Rita?"

Bob shook his head. "Not yet. Not for another three years." He was reading messages on the wall that Louis couldn't see— worrisome messages, bitter messages. Then, abruptly, he came to himself and sat down. "You feeling OK?"

"Yeah, fine, drunk," Louis said.

"I think I can find her for you, if you want."

"That would be great."

"You don't remember Jack very well, do you?"

"Zero memories."

"He was not your ordinary . . . not your ordinary human being. For example, Anna was a very pretty woman, about forty-five years his junior. When we found out he'd remarried, I was sure it was going to be her. But it turns out to be Rita, who everyone agreed was not a particularly attractive woman. Not to say an outright fright, although that was my opinion. We'd met her when she was at the girlfriend stage, when she was his secretary, but that was years earlier. I'd assumed she was long gone from the picture. And there are a lot of men where you wouldn't have been surprised, but not Jack. He cared about how a woman looked, that and how old she was, more than anything."

"Uh huh."

A moth beat against the screen in the back door, unable to follow the smell of prairie that was creeping inside. Some small animal made the tall grass crackle. The cats crossed the kitchen, single file, and pressed their whiskers against the screen. Bob asked what Louis and Renée had planned to do with their information.

"I guess make sure the company pays," Louis said. "We disagreed about the timing."

"You'll want to let your mother know in advance."

"All right."

"Had you thought of that?"

"I tried not to."

Bob nodded. "That's something else that was peculiar about Jack. Why he put all his money in Sweeting-Aldren stock. Because it wasn't as if he earned it all in stock and then failed to spread it out. The records show a well-balanced portfolio until the early seventies, when he made his new will—I suppose after he'd married Rita. Then he retired from the company and systematically bought stock in it until that's all there was. A piece of folly that's already cost your mother a lot of money."

"Boo hoo."

"What we can't figure out is why Jack did it. He was a company man, that's where he made his fortune, and I don't know how many times he told me it was the best-run corporation in the country. However many times I saw him in my life. A dozen times. But he loved money as much as he loved women, and he was anything but stupid. I simply can't see him making emotional decisions. There must have been some greed involved, somewhere that I can't see. This Canadian a while back, Campeau, the one who owned department stores. He sank all his money in his own company, and all his kids' money too, to the tune of about five hundred million. Next thing he knew, the shares were nearly worthless. If you're greedy, and you believe in yourself, I suppose you think, why put any money at all in things that won't pay the maximum return?"

"Yeah, why not," Louis said.

"Well. I'll tell you why not. Because he bought shares at any price and any ratio. Every time something of his matured, he converted it to Sweeting-Aldren common, no matter what the price, and this was *after* he'd retired. Wouldn't you call that a little irrational?"

"Sure, maybe, if I understood stocks."

Bob leaned forward suddenly, resting his elbows on his knees, and focused his reddened, enthusiastic eyes on Louis.

"Jack's girlfriend," he said, "is a company chemist. The company drills a disposal well three or four times deeper than it has to be. The chemist disappears. Jack marries a fright. He converts all his assets to company stock at any cost. When he dies he leaves them in a trust fund for the fright. You don't see anything there?"

If the question had been put to Louis by anyone else, or at any other time in the last ten years, he would only have been irritated, figuring that if a person had something to say they should just go ahead and say it. What he felt now, though, was embarrassment for not seeing what his father saw. He was embarrassed to have to shake his head.

"No," he said. "You have to tell me."

13

The Countrey, according to the first Englishmen to see it, more resembled a boundless green *Parke* than a Wildernesse. From the rocky shores inland as farre as a man could journey in a week, there stretched a Forrest suche as teemed with Dere, and Elke, and Beares, and Foxes; with Quailes and ruffed Grouse and wilde Turkies so innocent and *Plentiful* that a man could cast aside his Musket and hunt them with bare hands. There were majestical Pines and Hickeries and Chesnuts and Oakes, towering to heighths beyond the ken of any European, and so widely spaced (as severall Travellers noted), that an *Armie* could march through with ease. Beneath the trees and in the Intervalls, were found neither Brambles nor wooddy Undergrowth, but a low, softe Carpet of sweete Grasses and Hearbes that the Dere and Elke did much affect.

At the dawn of the seventeenth Century of our Lord, the land by *Masathulets Bay* had been relieved of its trees, by Indians in need of fire-woode. Lush Medowes and shrubby Hills stretched westward from the mouth of the River Charles as farre as the eye could see. Duske might fall at mid-day when a million of wilde Pidgeons filled the sky, and in the spawning Season the waters of fresh Streames congealed into Silver, with Smelts and Sturgions and Basses and Alewives swimming up-stream in suche Multitudes, that it seemed a man might step across them like a Bridge. Oysters in the Bay had foot-long Shells and could not be eaten in one bite. The soyle in many places was black and rich as Caveare.

Although the first Englishmen to settle in this Parke did nearly starve, yet the Indian men were observed to live more like unto *Kings*—working little and wanting little, and hunting and fishing at theyre Leisure. It was the Indians who, once or twice in a yeare, set the Fires that spred quickly and harmlessly over vast tracts of Forrest, therebye consuming Briers and much useless Woode, killing Fleas and Mice, and permitting of the growth of sweete Herbage. By the time God created the Sun & the Moone & the Planets, these Indians had called this Land theyre own for three thousand of years; and after another six thousand of years it was yet *more* like a Garden, than on the day when the first Human Beeing trod upon it.

In spring and summer, the Indian *Women* laboured to plant Maze in mounds, and tended it along with Squashes, Pumpkins, Melons, Tabacco, and the Beanes that climed the corne-stalks. Theyre hap-hazard fields were Nurseries for theyre children too. The men paddled to sea in hollow tree trunks, pursuing Seales and Walrosses, and fishing for codde-fish, and harpooning Porpisces and Whales. If theyre tree trunks sank, as was like to happen, they would swim for two hours to reach shore. Everywhere they chanced to look upon the Land, were Blueberries, Strawberries, Goosberries, Rasberries, Cranberries and Currans. Women and children gathered them, and captured the Birds, which came to feed. They trapped Hares and Porpentines and other small beests. Most of the Maze and Beanes which they harvested, was put away for winter, whilst the rest was eaten, along with Chesnuts and Acornes and Ground-nuts and Scallops and Clammes and Crabs and Mussles and Pumpkins, at Revels suche as lasted many weeks. Then, the Dere and Beares beeing fattest, the men went on hunting trips deep into the woods. *Women* dragged carcases back to the camps, and made Cloathes of the skins, and processed the Meat. When the men had luck, they ate ten Meales a day, sleeping in between them. When they were out of luck, they went hungrie for the nonce; for, the next summer always brought *Abundance*.

Wars and Abstinence from carnall Relations, maintained a balance between Population, and what goods the land could produce. A field beeing exhausted, the Indians farmed elsewhere. Fleas becoming intolerable, the Indians moved theyre Villages. They had no use for Propertie as could not be easily transported, or easily abandoned and refashioned. And, forasmuch as they lived in a World where there was either much food or little food, and otherwise had enough Cloathes and Firewoode and Tabacco and *Women* to satisfy theyre needs, so they were never in a hurry. Whatever could be put off until to-morrow, was put off. There were no Rats in theyre World, no Cock-roaches, no Stinging Nettles, no Pigs or Cows, no *Firearms*, no Meazels, no Chicken Pox, no Small Pox, no Influenza, no Plague, no French Pox, no Typhus, no Malaria; nor Yellow Fever; nor Consumption.

On the minus side—as Bob himself was always quick to grant—the Indians didn't have those wonderful Greek black olives. They didn't have blue cheese, or cardamoms, or the wines of Bordeaux, or violins. They had no conception of butter. Their imaginations were unenriched by Chinese porcelain, Persian illuminated manuscripts, or the idea of a midnight sleigh ride in the Russian winter. Was it perhaps worth the price of the Black Death to know that Jupiter had moons? Would a person trade *The Iliad* and *The Odyssey* for contentment and freedom from the flu? Make do without metal cookware and, with it, world history?

You might as well ask whether, if she could, a person would choose never to have been born; and whether, for that matter, North America's older sister Europe herself might rather have remained in fetal Stone Age darkness.

So the world of the Indians had been sleeping, alive but unborn, until the Europeans came, and the few missionaries and colonists compassionate enough to wonder why such a world had to suffer the pain of awakening to consciousness—and why they themselves had to be the instruments of this awakening—must have answered with conviction: because God wills it. For these Europeans of conscience, the conviction must have been a comfort.

For the rest it was expediency. "Fill the earth and subdue it," God had commanded in Genesis. His Englishmen came to Massachusetts and, seeing that the natives had disobeyed the commandment—the place was all trees and no fences! no churches! no barns!—felt justified in tricking them and blackmailing them and massacring them. English pigs ate their clam beds and the crops in their unfenced fields; English guns slaughtered fowl and deer. English chicken pox, English smallpox, English typhus killed entire Indian villages, leaving bodies strewn on the ground outside dwellings. They were branches falling in the forest, these seventy-year-old men and thirty-year-old women and three-year-old girls, with no one to hear them. In the space of a generation, more than 80 percent of the Indians in New England died of European diseases. Vermont was essentially depopulated.

"God," said John Winthrop, "hath hereby cleared our title to this place."

Felt hats and fur clothing being the fashion in the Old World, the Indians who survived the epidemics were able to trade beaver skins for things like copper kettles and iron fishhooks that made their lives easier. Before long, though, they had plenty of kettles and fishhooks, and so they began to beat the kettles into jewelry. And when copper jewelry became so common that it lost its cachet, the Englishmen conquered the Pequots of Connecticut and exacted a tribute of wampum—polished beads made out of whelk and quahog shells—and flooded the fur market with this currency. Wampum being scarce and portable and ornamental, like gold, there was at first no limit to the prestige an Indian could gain by its accumulation. But with fewer and fewer Indians in circulation and more and more wampum, inflation inevitably set in. Soon enough every last beaver in Massachusetts, Connecticut, and Rhode Island was exterminated, and the least consequential Indian wore necklaces of wampum formerly fit for chiefs, and the English traders were paid in pounds sterling for the furs they shipped overseas. Every market has its winners and losers; sadly for the Indians, the sterling turned out to be a better investment than the wampum. And in the course of attaching abstract sterling prices to abstract parcels of real estate, the smartest of the Englishmen learned to live off the land with even less labor than the king-like Indians had: by buying low and selling high.

"A major question about the seventeenth century," Bob said, "is whether the economy was subsistence-oriented, or whether there was already a capitalist mentality, and if there was capitalism, then how sophisticated was it. Real-estate speculation is a good indicator of sophistication, and there was some intriguing material there in Ipswich. Your mother was less than keen on my staying in Jack's house, but I thought it was just her paranoia. I was still a young bastard. Even now I have no objection to drinking single-malt scotch at a corporate officer's expense. They're not magicians, you know—that scotch doesn't flow from stone. Politically, of course, Jack and I were about as opposed as two people could have been—"

"This was—?"

"November '69. I was on sabbatical. Sweeting-Aldren was shipping twenty million bucks a month worth of defoliants straight to Vietnam, also spot sales of napalm. As a direct result of which, its general counsel and senior vice president had been able to buy a million bucks' worth of Revolutionary Era history on Argilla Road. Every morning for a week I walked up the road into Ipswich, a town granted its charter in 1630 by an imperialist-expansionist English crown, a town whose most valuable commodity by far is its own history, a town that prides itself on having been an early center of freedom of conscience and the Tax Revolution of the eighties, that is, the 1680s. While back here my students were freely expressing their consciences in protesting a war of imperialism in Southeast Asia, for which effrontery I don't believe they enjoyed universal popular support in Ipswich, certainly not on Argilla Road. And not in the Salem courthouse either. Every day for another five days I went there and read the records of a thousand deeds. Deeds: What a word! The fact that the mighty deeds of our forefathers are recorded as the purchase of such and such triangular piece of pasture for three yearling oxen, and the sale of said piece of pasture nine months later for twelve pounds, six shillings. Such were their heroic deeds."

"But Krasner. She was living with him?"

"No no no. If she'd moved in, it would have been the end of her. It would have made her family."

"What was she like?"

Bob poured scotch into his tumbler. He tilted the bottle again and poured a smaller splash, and then a very small splash, as if honoring some precise limit. He took a deep breath and turned his head and gazed at the screen door, like a plaintiff recalling his assailant.

"Loud, vulgar, beautiful," he said. "She had a big Slavic

mouth, and a Slavic tilt to her eyes, long auburn hair, maybe a trace of a Slavic accent—at least she liked to drop her definite articles. She was perfect for his purposes. She had bad enough taste and bad enough manners that she'd stretch out on his lap and hang from his neck, just so there was no mistaking their relationship. Then she'd snap her fingers in his face so I could see that she had spirit. Like a half-broken horse or some other cliché that makes men of a certain bent go wild. She had one of those cello voices that make you sure the woman's entire body is capable of tremendous resonance, under the right circumstances. A cello body too, not skinny—a body to die for. She was the kind of woman who could smoke a cigar with a smile on her face. An object whose pleasure it was to be an object. But even so, there was something strange going on between them, something particularly unloving, that I saw with my very own eyes. She'd sit at the table and stare at him and say, So when are you going to make me vice president? And he'd say, Whenever you want, and she'd say: Tomorrow. He'd shrug and say, Sure, tomorrow, but she'd keep right on staring at him, with her cigar-smoking smile, about fifty teeth showing in two curving rows, and say, Tomorrow? Good! Tomorrow you make me vice president. You're going to do it tomorrow first thing. You said you would, right? Or are you a liar? I hope you're not a *liar*. Bob, you heard him. He says he's making me vice president tomorrow."

"But she was a chemist?"

Bob held his tumbler to the light. He seemed oblivious to Louis's presence. "Every couple of years I get a student like her. You're almost certain they don't understand the material, but they're so full of confidence, and animal energy, and this idea that history is a jungle that they're wily enough and seductive enough and important enough to survive in, that they really do survive. A dubious article on petroleum is just the kind of work that Anna would have somehow gotten published. The work may be bad, but there's a vitality in the author that makes it hard to turn it down."

From the darkness outside the screen door came tearing sounds, accompanied by the faint growling of a cat intent on business. A small animal was being dismembered.

By the late eighteenth century, a person traveling the 240 miles from Boston to New York passed through no more than twenty miles of wooded country. Visitors from Europe commented on how scarce and stunted the trees in America were. They thought the soil must be sterile. They marveled at how the Americans wasted wood for the sake of short-term profit or convenience. At sawmills only the tallest and most perfectly formed trees were milled into lumber; all the less perfect trees had been torched or left to rot. Families built large, poorly insulated houses of wood or of wood-fired brick (the kind of houses, Bob said, that even now charmed visitors to Ipswich) and from October through April they kept fires roaring in every room.

As soon as a white American acquired land from the Indians, he tried to profit from it quickly, cutting the trees for timber or burning them for ashes if local ash demand was great enough. Otherwise he could save labor by simply killing the trees and letting decay bring them down. Crops planted on formerly forested land grew well for a few years, but without trees to capture nutrients, and with a farmer's endeavors confined within immutable property lines, the soil soon became useless. It was a myth, Bob said, that the Indians had fertilized exhausted land with fish. The way to make a garden last ten thousand years is to rotate crops from field to field. It was the white Americans who sowed alewives with their seeds, and whose fields stank so much that travelers would vomit by the roadside.

Barred from roaming freely, cattle grazed the land more closely than wild animals had. They trampled the soil, squeezing the air out, diminishing water retention. Cape Cod had had no sand dunes when the Europeans came. The dunes developed after cows killed the native grasses and the topsoil blew away.

Lowlands, kept dry for millennia by trees that evaporated rain from their leaves, turned into bogs as soon as they were cleared; mosquitoes, malaria, and thorns moved in. On higher ground, without the shade of trees, a blanket of snow melted quickly and the ground froze deeper, retaining less water when the spring rains came. Flooding became common. Unchecked by tree roots and fallen leaves, the rain stripped the land of nutrients. Raging streams dumped topsoil into bays and harbors. Spawning fish ran into dams and mud-choked water. But in summer and fall, without forests to regulate the flow of water, all the streams became dry gullies, and the naked land baked in the sun.

So it happened that the country whose abundance had sustained the Indians and astonished the Europeans had in less than 150 years become a land of evil-smelling swamps, of howling winds, of failing farms and treeless vistas, of hot summers and bitterly cold winters, of eroded plains and choked harbors. A time-lapse movie of New England would have shown the wealth of the land melting away, the forests shriveling up, the bare soil spreading, the whole fabric of life rotting and unraveling, and you might have concluded that all that wealth had simply vanished—had gone up in smoke or out in sewage or across the sea in ships.

If you'd looked very closely, though, you would have seen that the wealth had merely been transformed and concentrated. All the beavers that had ever drawn breath in Franklin County, Massachusetts, had been transmuted into one solid-silver tea service in a parlor on Myrtle Street in Boston. The towering white pines from ten thousand square miles of Commonwealth had together built one block of brick town houses on Beacon Hill, with high windows and a fleet of carriages, chandeliers from Paris and settees upholstered in Chinese silk, all of it occupying less than an acre. A plot of land that had once supported five Indians in comfort was condensed into a gold ring on the finger of Isaiah Dennis, the great-uncle of Melanie Holland's grandfather.

And when New England had been fully drained—when its original abundance had shrunk into a handful of neighborhoods so compact that a god could have hidden them from sight with his fingertips—then the poor English farmers who had become poor American farmers flocked to the cities and became poor workers in the foundries and cotton mills that the holders of concentrated wealth were building to increase their income. Now a time-lapse movie would have shown an exfoliation of red brick, the damming of new streams, the disemboweling of the barren land for the clay and iron ore within it, the blackening of the air, the confluence of freighters from Charleston carrying cotton, the spread of worker housing, the spread of iron, the tides of excrement and urine, the slaughter of the last wild birds that anyone would dream of eating, the smoke of trains bringing meat from Chicago to feed the workers, the weeding over of farmland, the final death of barns and farmhouses at the hands of the newly opened Middle West, but most of all: a general increase in wealth. Melanie's great-grandfather Samuel Dennis and his industrialist and banker accomplices had learned to burn not just the trees of their own age but the trees of the Carboniferous as well, now available as coal. They'd learned to exploit the wealth not only of their own home soil but of the cottonland of Mississippi and the cornland of Illinois. "Because after all," Bob said, "any wealth gained by a person beyond what he can produce by his own labor *must* have come at the expense of nature or at the expense of another person. Look around. Look at our house, our car, our bank accounts, our clothes, our eating habits, our appliances. Could the physical labor of one family and its immediate ancestors and their one billionth of the country's renewable resources have produced all this? It takes a long time to build a house from nothing; it takes a lot of calories to transport yourself from Philadelphia to Pittsburgh. Even if you're not rich, you're living in the red. Indebted to Malaysian textile workers and Korean circuit assemblers and Haitian sugarcane cutters who live six to a room. Indebted to a bank, indebted to the earth from which you've withdrawn oil and coal and natural gas that no one can ever put back. Indebted to the hundred square yards of landfill that will bear the burden of your own personal waste for ten thousand years. Indebted to the air and water, indebted by proxy to Japanese and German bond investors. Indebted to the greatgrandchildren who'll be paying for your conveniences when you're dead: who'll be living six to a room, contemplating their skin cancers, and knowing, like you don't, how long it takes to get from Philadelphia to Pittsburgh when you're living in the black."

Melanie's grandfather, Samuel Dennis III, had a Marlborough Street town house, a summer house east of Ipswich, a Dusenberg Roadster and some garden-variety debts, and he was skippering a family of six daughters, only one of them married, when a devil of the period moved him to install a stock ticker in his office on Liberty Square.

For decades the office had been little more than a place to smoke cigars and write checks to the nephews and nieces whose trusts Dennis executed. It was the terminus of various income streams rising in the mill towns north of Boston—streams that by 1920 were showing a propensity to silt up and run dry—and was the depot of old, old dollars: dollars with beaver blood on them (and mink blood and cod blood), dollars that smelled of black pepper and Jamaican rum, piney dollars from clear-cut Dennis landholdings, rusty war dollars, dollars damp and sour with the sweat of female loom operators, odd dollars of obscure provenance which at some point had decided to come along for the ride, all the dollars encrusted with long-compounded interest and no dollar, no matter how musty, any less a dollar than all the rest. Certainly a democratic nation's stock market made no distinction between old wealth and new.

Family oral history had it, Bob said, that Dennis was very slow to realize when his speculations ruined him. For several weeks, one winter in the late twenties, he came home to Marlborough Street wearing expressions of deeper and deeper puzzlement. And then one night he died.

His body had hardly reached room temperature when his family discovered they were broke. There were even liens, or so they later maintained, on the china and linens. Daughters and widow alike faced the prospect of becoming the wards of moralizing aunts and uncles, and yet (or so they later maintained) it wasn't themselves they felt sorry for, it was their house on Marlborough Street and their house in Ipswich. Who could ever groom and pamper those houses as the Dennises had done?

The female Dennises were on the brink of despair when their lawyer informed them that Sam Dennis, a month before he died, had quietly transferred the deed to the house on Marlborough Street to his married daughter, Edith—or rather, to be totally precise, to Edith's husband, John Kernaghan. Though stripped of its furnishings, the beloved house was saved.

In later years no one could say exactly how Kernaghan had acquired the house. It was possible that he himself had warned the patriarch of impending disaster and helped him out. But "fond" though the Dennises were of the younger man, they were reluctant to give him so much credit. Ever since Edith married him, said family oral history, the Dennis girls had been giggling and shaking their heads good-naturedly about the figure cut by this dark, taciturn, somewhat diminutive young attorney who hailed from the obscurity of Maine's woods and who was so awed by the grand Dennises that he escorted Edith home only on holidays, hardly opening his mouth even then. But somehow this same Jack Kernaghan—with the loving guidance and support of the fallen patriarch, of course—had rescued the brick shell of the Dennis grandeur, and he went on to support his mother-in-law and five sisters-in-law through the nadir of the Great Depression. He was an odd bird, said family oral history. He was such a workaholic that he never once took a week's vacation before he'd put the last of his sisters-in-law through private school. Knowing the importance of a summer house to the Dennises' mental health, he rented them a place in Newport for six weeks every summer, but he didn't much care for the water himself, and so he stayed in Boston, working. He could afford to hire a housekeeper for his mother-in-law, but he himself (no doubt because he came from Maine's woods) was such a fan of fresh air that he walked nearly a mile to work every day. Everybody knew he always owned exactly three suits, a ratty one, an everyday one, and a good one. Altogether an odd, odd man, said family oral history, but he had done the Dennises a marvelous service, and they were grateful, yes: grateful.

"And he resented the hell out of them," Louis said.

"No. Certainly not by the time I got to know him. I think he had too much contempt for the Dennises to resent them as equals. He was simply bitter cold. To your mother, to your Aunt Heidi, to your grandmother, in fact to everyone in the family except me. The first time we met was right before Edith finally divorced him. He asked me what I did. I said I was a student. He asked me what I planned to do with my degree, and when I told him I was going to teach, he threw back his head and laughed and walked out of the room laughing. I thought that was the end of that. But then a few years later he showed up at our wedding, uninvited, with Rita on his arm, and he was laughing as if he'd been laughing ever since I saw him walk out of the room, and your mother said it was the first time he'd kissed her in almost twenty years. It was pretty awkward for me, because half the people at the reception were looking daggers at him, and he made it clear that the reason he'd come was that he liked me: me personally. He patronized me, he asked me about my teaching and laughed at my answers, but there was something genuine going on—I could feel it. It was like he was drunk, almost like he was infatuated with me and he should have known better but he couldn't help himself.

"We started getting Christmas cards from him. A case of Dom Pérignon every year on December 22. He came to Chicago on business and took me to lunch and then out for more drinks and a walk in Lincoln Park. He asked me, Was I taking care of his little girl? (She wasn't little and she wasn't his; which was why he laughed. She dreaded him and warned me about him and refused to speak to me because I was too good-natured and too much of a young bastard to send his champagne back and say no to his invitations.) —Did I have tenure yet? I did? Well, that was great, it meant I could preach revolution eight days a week and never know financial insecurity until the revolution actually came, and even then I'd have it made as the Commissar of Marxist History. And he meant it: he thought it was great. It's very weird, Lou, to be around a man to whom you obviously matter in some obscure but major way. Whom you somehow render almost silly with confused emotions. He made me promise to take care of his little girl, and be sure and come out and visit us. And we did go out, because your mother couldn't stop me. You don't remember it, but you were in Ipswich in the summer of '69, you and Eileen and even your mother for a little while, she was mainly seeing friends in Boston—"

"Were there horses?"

"Horses? Maybe, across the road. But anyway, when I came back in November the red carpet was rolled out for me. There was a man from Sweeting-Aldren waiting in a company car when I flew in, and lunch for Jack and me on Argilla Road—oysters, lobsters, champagne. I wanted to get to work in the afternoon, but he told me, You've got tenure, what do you need to work for? Not quite mocking me. More like suggesting to me a way of thinking that he's not sure I'm smart enough to learn. He showed me his new wine cellar, his new car, his new color TV set in a hardwood console.

He drove me to the beach, which he might as well have owned, because it was empty in both directions, and he sat on the hood of his Jaguar and blew cigarette smoke at the ocean, and the waves were collapsing slavishly at his feet. He took me down to the marina and showed me his new boat, which he'd christened *Willing Thing*. Painted on the bow! *Willing Thing*! He drove me to a house on a hill, a rambling Victorian affair out closer to Cape Ann. He parked across the mouth of the driveway, got out of the car with his back to me, and I realized he was pissing in the white gravel. He pisses out half a bottle of Dom Pérignon, a little murky gray river flowing down between his feet. He hops to settle his thing back in his underwear and tells me that this was the house he'd really wanted but the current owners wouldn't sell. He stands there in the driveway looking up the hill. He says he guesses that Melanie's told me her grandpa got wiped out in the crash of '29. I say, Yep, that's what she told me. He says, Damn right, the only thing is that it was spring of '28. Every market bloated, everybody getting richer, nobody getting poorer. He says, It took a rare kind of man to go all-out bankrupt in the spring of '28. He says that a friend of his dropped by his office in the winter of '27–'28 and mentioned that Sam Dennis had put his houses up for surety on loans to cover his stock-market losses. 'And Bob,' he says, 'even then the man couldn't see what was coming. I shouted at that asshole from three in the afternoon until ten at night before he let me have the town house. It was already under liens that cost me my own house and every dollar I could borrow on my word to get free of. Three weeks later he was dead. And that family still thought money grew like moss in bank vaults. They would have been out on the street like a bunch of zoo animals staring at the fucking traffic, Bob, if it wasn't for me. They were so criminally dim-witted you can't believe it, and they never even knew it, because of me. Believe it: I was that family's knight in shining armor.'

"I ask him, 'Why?'"

"He gets back in the car. He says, 'Because I was afraid of God.'"

" 'Yeah, I bet.'"

" 'I was afraid of God. Believe it, Bob. I was afraid of the old man in flowing robes.'"

"We were back on Route 133 and we saw a girl hitchhiking, long hair, tasseled leather jacket, guitar. Jack slows the car down and pulls even with her. She's picking up her guitar when he steps on the gas and pulls away. I thought this was just some meanness of his, teasing hitchhikers, but he was shaking his head. 'Flat,' he says, and I say, 'What?' —'Nothing in her shirt,' he says. And we drive along, and after a while he says, 'There's not a one of them that won't get in the car.' And we go back to Argilla Road for Beluga caviar, pheasant, and truffles, everything selected for maximum expense. Anna comes over from Peabody after work, he's said in advance that there's somebody he wants me to meet—"

"Really sorry here," Louis said. "But I don't see how you could have spent five minutes with this guy."

"How I could not hate him? Of course I hated him. At night I wondered if I was going to end up killing him, in the name of the people. But to be with him was a different story. There was a magnetism. He dressed like the English landed gentry; I remember one maroon velvet smoking jacket in particular. He was sixty-nine years old, but his skin was still tight and unspotted. He was hard and shiny and elegant, like death, and I'm afraid there's nobody alive who can't find something to enjoy there—in the shining killer, the way he stands apart from the bodies piling up in Southeast Asia. All that carnage can be as sexy from a distance as it's sickening at close range. And when you were with Jack Kernaghan, you felt that that distance was absolutely maintained. You were at an endless masque of the red death, up in that castle on the hill. He was my proof that there really was something there—there in the boardrooms, there in the M-I complex—that unquestionably deserved our hatred. You know how easily we're led astray by our idealism: how easy it is to think that intellectual honesty demands that you forgive those guys, and see them as human beings like yourself, as pawns in the grip of history. Jack was a gorgeous proof of the contrary. He was willful. He luxuriated in being a jerk. And I deliberately provoked him, see, because I was a young bastard just like you, and he couldn't hurt me. Or so I thought."

Jack said his father was a schoolteacher, "a ridiculous old fart," which you took to mean an upright and selfless man who taught his children what was right and what was wrong. Assume that the young Jack bought it. Assume that he was awed by his father's rectitude. Assume that when he left home for college at sixteen he believed that by living right he would earn a trip to heaven, and by living wrong he'd go straight to the pools of sulfur. Assume he took the Host on Sundays and believed it was his Savior's body, and loved his Savior as his father did.

He worked summers for a law firm in Orono. He found himself accepted into the law school at Harvard, and, excelling there, he joined a partnership in Boston and continued to take the Host on Sundays. With so much credit on both his heavenly and his earthly balance sheets, he must have been stunned by the vehemence with which the family of his intended wife rejected him. Mr. Dennis, having five more daughters after Edith to get rid of, was halfhearted in his opposition, but Mrs. Dennis made up for this by finding every conceivable aspect of Kernaghan's person inappropriate, not just that he was Catholic, not just that he came from a poor family in "the woods of Maine," not just that he'd deceived them all by courting Edith outside her own home, but that he was *dark-haired* and *short*. She confided to Edith that she'd had to choke back a laugh the first time she saw her with Kernaghan. It was like a freak show! It was inconceivable! A giantess and a dwarf! A duchess and her tailor! (In fact it was a matter of an inch and a half.) She expressed her firm intention to boycott the nuptials, and immediately severed relations with the family at whose house the lovebirds had become acquainted.

That they married anyway, knowing it would set back any social ambitions that either might have harbored, would indicate that there really was love between them. Could Kernaghan have come to hate Edith so passionately without the knowledge that he'd loved her, once? A man hates in his wife those traits that he hates in her family; he hates the proof of how deeply the traits are rooted, how ineluctable heredity. Living for four years in near-total estrangement from the Dennises, and so seldom having the mother or sisters handy to compare with Edith, Kernaghan could only see her in her singularity, her prettiness, her passion for him. What's more, he must have formed a similarly hopeful image of her family.

Because how else to explain the colossal good turn he did the Dennises? How else to explain why he nearly ruined himself financially to buy their house, and then undertook to support the very women who'd considered him such dirt that they'd skipped his wedding? If he'd wanted revenge in 1928, it would have been the easiest thing in the world to sit back and laugh at their ruin. Any person of ordinary moral strength would have considered him well within his rights.

He must still have been trying to win their love. He'd seen so little of them in the previous four years that he actually believed that if he saved them they would love him or at the very least respect him. (Because, again, after all, he could never have hated them so intensely later on if they hadn't mattered to him, once.)

In their new life, the Dennises were, by necessity, civil to their benefactor. Four years earlier Kernaghan would gladly have settled for civility. But now—considering the risks he'd run in saving them, considering the major expenditure of selflessness—he required more. Now the time had come when they must love him. A better person than he would not have expected less.

But of course the Dennises couldn't love him. Even if he hadn't seen them at their lowest, even if he hadn't had the temerity to rescue them, they were too in love with their own Brahmin selves and too secure in their sheer feminine quantity to need anything from him but money. Requests for school tuition, for clothing, for summer vacations, for trousseaus were communicated to Kernaghan through Edith, who tried for a while to mediate between her family and the commander of their occupied house, but who, inevitably, now that they all lived together, defected to the Dennis side. There were so many of them and only one of him. The women had all day to infect Edith with their pretensions and prejudices and artificial wants. Kernaghan's children had seven mothers and one father; the father was the little man who worked sixty hours a week to make the household run.

Still he led an upright life. Melanie could remember a time when he had come straight home from work every night and read to her and her brother Frank (Frank the only male besides his father in a house of nine females), had drunk brandy and smoked cigarettes in his study, shined his own shoes and brushed his own coat before he went to bed. She remembered him returning from his separate church on Sunday, later than the rest of the family, so that even Sunday was like a pleasure boat that he always came too late to catch. He walked beside it on the shore, minding his own business unless a child happened to step off the boat and disturb him in his reading of the newspapers that had accumulated since the previous Sunday. She claimed to remember a warmth, from the time when she was little. Maybe he already hated his wife and in-laws, but something kept him in their service, and it almost had to have been his fear of hell. He as good as admitted it to you: he'd been trying, in 1928 and for ten years after, to win the favor not only of the Dennises but of God as well, and though he was clearly failing with the Dennises he still hoped he might succeed with God.

Then God killed Frank.

It happened during one of the Augusts when the family was doing its bathing-in-the-morning-tea-parties-in-the-afternoon thing outside Newport and Kernaghan was drafting wills and covenants in Boston, and bacterial meningitis could carry off an unlucky boy in ninety-six hours. Melanie remembered Jack's state when he arrived in Newport. No sorrow visible, only rage. Rage at his wife and mother-in-law and daughter and youngest sister-in-law for not taking Frank's fever seriously, for not calling him (Jack) sooner, for following the doctor's orders, for leaving Frank in the care of the backwoods Newport hospital, for letting Frank die, for killing Frank, for murdering Frank with their stupidity, for being Dennises, for making a hell out of his life. Melanie, six, was rushed from the house as if her father's rage had physically endangered her. It was a shock that no one recovered from, a shock that set Jack ringing like a bell, like a planet struck by a meteor and still vibrating thirty years later, so that he'd tell you, over foie gras in his house in Ipswich:

"That family showed me what this country would be like if it was run by women. It's simple—you spend somebody else's money. Let's spend a hundred billion on the poor, let's spend a hundred billion on the Negroes. All the sentiments are very fine, but where's that money going to come from? Industry's what puts bread on their table, and you're lucky if they even see you as a necessary evil. They look at you, they look at industry as if you're dirt, beneath contempt, they smile behind their hands at you. Their whole future could be dying, and they wouldn't even know it until the ax hit them too."

He never mentioned Frank's name in Bob's hearing, but he loved to talk about what he did to the Dennis women the year he "came to his senses." How the kitchen began to smell like a landfill after he dismissed the housekeeper and the women waited, as days turned to weeks, for someone, anyone besides them, to wash the pots and take the trash out. How they found a Negro girl willing to work in exchange for meals and extra groceries, and how he then cut the grocery allowance in half (eating magnificent lunches himself and bringing his little girl, Melanie, elaborate and nutritious treats), and corrupted the Negro girl with candy and whiskey and cigarettes and screwed her in the pantry. How he let two sisters-in-law start a new fall semester at Smith and sent a letter after them, informing the college that he had no intention of paying their bill. How he did the same thing to his mother-in-law, quietly cutting off her credit at Jordan Marsh and Stearns, setting up scenes where personnel humiliated her. How he canceled another sister-in-law's wedding on short notice, informing her that her intended was a weakling. And how, for himself, in the space of a year, he bought twenty suits, a hundred shirts, diamond cuff links, Italian shoes. How he entertained cheap women, a new one every week, at the Ritz-Carlton and the Statler and other venues where an audience of the Dennises' friends was guaranteed. How he made the Dennis women pay.

The same year Frank died, a mustached entrepreneur named Alfred Sweeting was acquiring land in Peabody to build the first commercial-scale nitrate plant in New England. In a process developed by the Germans, the nitrogen and oxygen and hydrogen of clean air and clean water were transformed into ammonium nitrate for high explosives. Production began in 1938, and in 1942 Sweeting merged with J. R. Aldren Pigments, his industrial next-door neighbor in Peabody, a maker of dyes and paints that was seeking improved contacts with the military. For three and a half years, battleships painted with Aldren's grays and B-17s camouflaged in Aldren's browns and olive drab pounded Fascists with endless charges of Sweeting nitrates.

The Sweeting/Aldren merger had been brokered by Troob, Smith, Kernaghan & Lee; and Kernaghan, a specialist in corporate law, became the company's counsel in every sense of the word. He oversaw the acquisition of the patents and the small single-product companies that enabled Sweeting-Aldren, when the war ended, to retool and diversify. Eulogists at his funeral in 1982 would credit him with having influenced the company to expand early and vigorously in the direction of pesticides—a decision which, given the fifties mania for good-looking apples and tomatoes and for suppressing all infestations of indoor vermin and outdoor weeds however faintly reminiscent of Communists, was the single most profitable in the company's history. By 1949 Kernaghan and a staff of four at Troob, Smith were working exclusively on patent, liability, and contract law for Sweeting-Aldren, and he was buying discounted shares of common stock at a pace that resulted in his election to the board in 1953. He would later tell Bob that in 1956, the last year of his marriage and his last year in private practice, he had thirty-one different women on more than 220 separate occasions and personally pulled down $184,000 in fees, after taxes, from Sweeting-Aldren. A 1957 advertisement in *Fortune* boasted that in the previous year, according to reliable scientific estimates, Sweeting-Aldren's Green Garden™ and Saf-tee-tox™ product lines had killed 21 billion caterpillars, 26.5 billion cockroaches, 37 billion mosquitoes, 46.5 billion aphids, and 60 billion miscellaneous harmful household and economic pests in the United States alone. Lined up hind legs to feelers, pests killed by the Green Garden™ and Saf-tee-tox™ product lines would circle the earth at the equator twenty-four times.

Kernaghan was fifty-six years old when he joined Sweeting-Aldren as senior vice president. Those were golden hours for the patriarchy, when every executive in America wore pants with a zipper down the front, and every one of them had a secretary who wore a skirt with a zipper down the side and who, though often more intelligent, was always physically weaker than her boss (her delicate wrists arched over the IBM keyboard), and who sat on a little chair designed to reveal as much as possible of her figure from the greatest number of angles, and who wore a wife's makeup and cheerful smile and obeyed her man's orders and spoke in whispers, and the power of so many million heterosexual pairings harnessed by industry made the United States, in the space of a few years, the greatest economic force in the history of the world. Kernaghan's secretary at Sweeting-Aldren was a veteran named Rita Damiano, a two-time divorcée twenty-odd years his junior. Neither tall nor young nor pretty, Rita hardly corresponded to the ideal woman of Kernaghan's cheap and single-purpose imagination. Nonetheless she was his regular escort for better than three years, and eventually he even married her, so she must have had him figured out. Must have known that a Catholic manqué such as he needed sex to be dirty. Must have known how to scale the affair, keep him off guard, make him commit himself, string out the liberties she allowed him, be coldly disgusted by anal sex on Easter, begging for more of it on Arbor Day, and tight-assed and ultra-efficient the next morning as she served coffee to Aldren Sr. and Sweeting, who with their eyes drew dubious lines between her and Kernaghan, as if to say, "Any interest there?" and Kernaghan coolly shaking his head no. She played a strange, transparent role, letting him know that she thought he was an old lecher and that she tolerated his intimacies only because she wanted money. Because with a man like him, it was wiser not to pretend. It was wiser to be a whore, to be enslaved solely by the promise of his money. She went to Bob and Melanie's wedding and snubbed Kernaghan's former in-laws before they could snub her. She drank with him. She sneered at marriage, sneered at pleasure, and by and by Kernaghan became fond of her, and began to cheat on her with the very bimbos whose hypocrisy they'd ridiculed together, and had her transferred to another executive, and that was the end of Rita, at least for the moment.

Meanwhile, thanks again to Kernaghan's strategic intuitions, the company's investments in new process technology were paying off. Initially derided by analysts as a high-risk gamble, Sweeting-Aldren's M Line, a closed-system continuous process capable of producing one hundred tons of any of several chlorinated hydrocarbons per day, was operating at capacity, the U.S. armed forces having discovered hundreds of thousands of square miles of Southeast Asian jungle in urgent need of defoliation. It took the rest of the industry four years to catch up with demand, and in the interim Sweeting-Aldren never saw earnings growth of less than 35 percent annually. Its new G Line, producing spandex for a nation whose appetite for revealing swimsuits, lightweight bras and other clingy items had become insatiable, was going great guns as well. It was Kernaghan who'd persuaded Aldren Sr. to double the G Line's capacity in 1956, when it was on the drawing board, Kernaghan whose elegant fingers tested the spandex virtues of countless articles of feminine apparel between 1958 and 1969, during which decade the extra G Line capacity earned the company $30 million, minimum, after taxes, all because of him. Add to this the brisk wartime sales of paint and high explosives, the budding market for Sweeting-Aldren's new Warning Orange pigments, and steady returns on all its more mundane products, and it began to seem a wonder that Kernaghan came out of the sixties worth only six or seven million.

But the company was conservatively managed—looking to the future, holding the line on debt, funneling hefty sums into research and development. The young Anna Krasner, owner of an M.S. in physical chemistry from RPI, was one beneficiary of their scattershot hiring. Kernaghan later said he'd already picked her out in the parking-lot crowd on her first day of work. But neither of them liked to talk about those early days; they became silent and looked a little ill when the subject arose; and Bob found this curious, at least in Kernaghan's case, because a victorious male so often enjoys reminding his lover how she couldn't stand the sight of him at first. Maybe the sting of her rejection was still too fresh in his mind, or maybe he wasn't so sure he was victorious, or maybe he was uneasy about the price he'd had to pay to change her mind.

In any case, Rita would have been watching. She would have known, firsthand or through the grapevine, that Kernaghan was smitten with the pretty new chemist in Research and that the chemist was flamboyantly crushing his initiatives, sticking the long-stemmed roses in Erlenmeyer flasks with reagent-grade sulfuric acid, feeding the Swiss chocolate truffles to albino rats. On an errand for her new boss, Rita drops into Kernaghan's office and says, "Didn't you know? You reach an age where you're only hideous to a thing like her. Where she looks at you and all she can think is prostate problems."

Let loose in her own lab with a fat budget, Anna takes the company at its word when it tells her no idea is too wacky to pursue. She reads some imaginative accounts of the origin of the solar system, cooks water and ammonia and free-state carbon in a high-pressure oven, and strikes oil. She happens to be the kind of person who'll face hungry lions in a coliseum before she'll admit she's mistaken. She believes there's a zillion gallons of oil and a godzillion cubic meters of natural gas inside the earth, beginning at a depth of about four miles, and no anvil-headed senior research chemist with a crew cut and stinky breath is going to tell her it isn't so. She goes straight to the nearest vice president, young Mr. Tabscott, and says, "We drill for oil in Berkshires!"

Mr. Tabscott, more susceptible to good looks than the anvil-headed senior research chemist, says, "We'll take this under serious advisement, Anna, but maybe in the meantime you should reinvest your energies in some totally new direction, give yourself a well-deserved rest from this very interesting and speculative research you've done."

He's still chuckling and shaking his head when the single-minded Anna begins to write the paper that eventually appears in the *Bulletin of the Geological Society of America*, and Jack Kernaghan gets wind of her difficulties. He steals into her lab, looks over her shoulder at the orthographic atrocities she's committing in her notebook, and says, "You're pretty stupid if you think we're going to drill a four-mile hole through granite for you."

She doesn't look up. "They'll do it."

"Not a chance, girlie."

"No?" She raises her eyes from the notebook to the periodic chart in front of her. She flares her nostrils. "Then it's because you stopped them. And if they do drill, it's because they like me better than you."

He considers the flasks holding his blackened roses and their exploded stems. "Tabscott was just humoring you," he says. "He's going to let this thing die. When he does, you go and see him and ask him if I had anything to do with it. And then before you do anything rash, you come and see me."

Anna tosses her lovely hair from one shoulder to the other and goes on writing. But it happens just as Kernaghan said it would.

Various sober scientists are consulted and agree that her theory is 99.9-percent-probably hogwash, Tabscott tells her the company won't spend $5 million on a one-in-a-thousand chance, and Anna says, "I quit! This is *good theory.*"

"We'd like to have you stay on, Anna. But if, ah, you insist . . ."

Kernaghan finds her in her lab, angrily emptying her desk. "Scholarly journals accept my paper," she says. "And you won't drill!"

"Five-million-dollar checks don't grow on trees."

"La, la, who cares? My pearls aren't worthy of you."

"Be reasonable," he says. "You've got vanishingly minimal academic credentials, and you're never going to work for anybody as flush as we are. Anywhere else you go they're going to make you study vulcanized rubber. Stay with us, play your cards right, you might just get your hole drilled."

She snorts. "You are a swine."

He laughs agreeably, leaves her office, goes and confers with Aldren Sr. and Tabscott.

"Oh, sure, Jack," they say, "we're going to spend five mill to help you get in Krasner's skirt."

"Gentlemen," grinning, "I resent the imputation. The fact is, it's an interesting theory. And the fact is also, if she's right about the gas and oil in the Berkshires, there's probably gas and oil right under our feet here in Peabody. More important, though, I sense a wind shift, and I ask you, have I been right about wind shifts in the past? Possibly even so right that five million dollars seems a paltry sum? I see a problem with our waste stream, say in the next three or four years. A new problem, a regulatory problem. I'm thinking of the M Line, the dioxins, in particular. It won't surprise me if M Line disposal costs triple in the next five years."

"Matter of opinion, Jack."

"We're going to drill this hole. I don't rule out coming up with commercial quantities of gas and oil, maybe even at ordinary depths. But if we don't, and if we've drilled it here, you know what we get as a consolation prize? An injection well. One that goes so far below the water table that we can direct the waste stream down it from now till kingdom come and still be good neighbors."

"Legality?"

"I know of no statute," he says smoothly, "that would interfere."

So a feasibility study is performed. The more management thinks about Kernaghan's plan, the more it likes it. Certain workers on the M Line are developing chloracne, a disfiguring and irreversible rotting of the skin caused by exposure to dioxins, and there are disquieting reports coming out of Vietnam about soldiers using Sweeting-Aldren herbicides and turning up with tender livers and intestinal sarcomas and other, more nameless dreads. Half the guinea pigs in a delivery truck unwisely parked for an hour by the M Line's evaporation pond go into convulsions; the other half are dead. Since the only way to reduce dioxins in the waste stream is to double the reaction temperature, the cost of electricity to pump the waste underground begins to seem reasonable. And when management looks at the effluents from all its other process lines, and feels the winds of regulation and public opinion shifting, the decision is clinched.

Kernaghan pays another visit to Anna, who has been cooking up ever more nasty-smelling synthetic crude in her oven; she looks like a Swiss chambermaid in her white chemist's apron. He shows her the rental contract for equipment to drill a five-mile-deep hole—the work orders, the authorizations for energy use. She shrugs. "What took you so long?"

"You're in charge of the drilling. We're adding ten K to your salary."

"La, la, la."

"You have exclusive publication rights. Exclusive rights to the core samples from the deepest hole in eastern North America."

"Of course. I thank you, Mr. Jack Kernaghan. Really. Was there something else?"

He smiles, unsurprised. "I don't think you understand that I spent twenty-five years' worth of leverage to get you this piece of paper. Twenty-five years' worth of service to the company."

"This is boring."

"Boring?" He holds up the rental contract and begins to tear it down the middle. She can't stop herself from grabbing his hand. She says, "You think you can buy me."

"Say I'm proving my love."

"You tear up rental contract to prove your love?"

"If there's no hope for my love?"

She takes the contract and reads it carefully. "My Berkshires. What happened to my Berkshires?"

"I did my best."

She has a beaker of synthetic crude on her desk. She dips a Pyrex stirring rod in it, dribbling the black, viscous stuff from the tip. She lets herself fall backward and her chair catches her, rolling into a wall with the impact. "You want to drill my hole? Good! You want to touch me? Good! You can touch me. But you'll never touch me."

"We'll see about that."

She stands up and walks in a circle around him, her mouth open as wide as she can stretch it, saying, "La, la, la, la, la." She laughs. He seizes her, works one knee between her legs, turns on the urgency that has served him so well in the past.

"So, OK," pulling away from him, "walking filth has smart knees."

He stands, panting, maddened. "Don't think I wouldn't kill you."

"La, la, la," tongue wagging. "You'll never touch me!"

Which was how things stood in the fall of '69. Bob Holland of course couldn't understand why Anna had only two modes with Kernaghan—the contemptuous and the vampish—and why Kernaghan would put up with even a minute of being ignored by her as she plied Bob with throaty questions about his work. The "lovers" exchanged brief, cutting phrases and then held long competitions for Bob's regard which Anna invariably won, Kernaghan receding into his chair to stare at her, his eyes a pair of hate beams, minute after minute, while Bob talked about the country's history and Anna talked about her personal history, in Paris as a baby, in upstate New York as a girl and adolescent. She turned her face away from the cigarette she held vertically at mouth level, narrowing her eyes and twisting her lips as she blew the smoke straight up. She told Bob that she was like him in loving knowledge for its own sake, that the corporate mind was grotesque and soulless, that she would quit her job in a flash if she weren't allowed to pursue knowledge with total freedom. She said young people had life and energy and ideals. Old men were drained of their juices and loved money more than beauty, more than anything. And Kernaghan was a sly enough dissembler that when he abruptly left the dinner table, as though hating Anna for flirting—as though powerless to stop her—Bob believed that he was being a bad guest and hastened after his father-in-law, unwilling to be the instrument with which she tormented him. When he turned around, Anna had her silver fox on and her car keys in her hand.

An hour later, when he was in his room typing up notes, he heard her cries, loud enough to have awakened him if he'd been sleeping. He hadn't heard her car return.

In the morning he found them smoking breakfast ciggies in the east room, thick as thieves, holding hands. They looked at him as if he were the devil they'd been speaking of.

It being a Sunday, all the archives closed, they took him for a drive. Armed guards waved the car through the gates of Sweeting-Aldren's main installation, and Kernaghan drove the avenues winding among the various process lines at screeching speeds.

"You're giving me a headache," Anna said.

"I'm showing Bob what it's all about."

The three of them put on hard hats and toured the process structure on the brand-new AB Line, into the maws of which went ethylene and chlorine and out of the anus of which came white prills of polyvinyl chloride. The structure was an orgy of metal forms, twenty cottage-sized modules straddling and abutting and embracing one another tightly, each with its own voice of thermodynamic ecstasy and all with their fat appendages rammed deep into steel-collared orifices; but a rigid orgy, full of power and purpose, never ending. In these plants, chemists transformed the verbs of their imaginations into the nouns of their achievement by adding *-er* or *-or* or *-r*. There were 5,000-gallon double-arm mixers, paddle blenders with carbon-steel shredder blades, a triple-wall main reactor built like Charles Atlas, an 80-ton two-stage chiller, a jacketed continuous turbulizer, a shuddering particulate-transfer screw feeder, nozzle concentrators, triple-effect evaporators, intensifier bars, a 400-cubic-foot cone dryer, a cylindrical concrete priller, a heat exchanger with stainless tubes and a carbon-steel shell, a 6,250-square-foot vertical condenser, a twin-cone classifier, and a dozen centrifugal compressors. The scary thing was smelling so many smells that reminded you of nothing in the world. They were like alien ideas impinging directly on your consciousness, unmediated by a flavor. This was how it would feel when space invaders came and took control of your brain, some insidious something neither spirit nor flesh filling your sinuses and clouding your eyes . . .

Bob realized he was alone. A mantle of rain was descending on Peabody, closing up the vistas between the surrounding process structures, quarantining the place. Kernaghan and Anna were leaning against a front fender of his car. They exchanged glances. Finally Anna said, "Jack and I were wondering if you had any pot."

"Pot."

"Marijuana."

Bob laughed. It happened that he did, back on Argilla Road. In those days, an ounce would last him months.

Riding northward along the coast, Anna's hand resting on his shoulder, the impact of those ketones and esters still fresh in his brain, he saw the stone fences wandering through the tangled, scrubby woods and had to force himself not to picture the early settlers in a landscape that looked just like this. He knew it wasn't until well into the eighteenth century that erosion and repeated plowing had begun to fill the fields with glacial boulders, and that the farmers, running out of wood, had turned to stones to build their fences. And it wasn't until the Erie Canal and the railroads had opened up the heartland that farming in New England was finally abandoned, its fields reclaimed by trunk and thorn. The sterile waters and monotonous forests of skinny, crownless trees were no more a picture of the nineteenth century than of the seventeenth century; were as alien as the esters in his nose, as her hand on his shoulder, her fingernails on his neck, her fingertips on his earlobe.

He was a boy from the woods himself, from the still-virgin forest of western Oregon. It had only been a year ago, right before his most recent visit to his mother, that Weyerhaeuser had clear-cut the hillside behind her house, reaping a one-time-only profit, and left the land to decay into the river like a shaved, dead wolf. The next time he was home he would see it after "reforestation": the varied, misty forest of Sitka spruce and hemlock and cedar and northern redwood supplanted by weeds and slash and identical Douglas firs shooting up at geometrical intervals from the loose, bulldozed earth. The same wave of profit-taking that had crashed onto Cape Ann in 1630 was even now rolling out over the Pacific Coast, carrying with it the last of the continent's virginity.

Anna handled a joint like a cigarette, tapping the ash loose with a long red nail, expelling the smoke through her nose, perching on the edge of the sofa with her legs crossed at the knee. Kernaghan couldn't keep his face straight. He seemed more interested in simply holding a joint, enjoying its illegality and symbolism, than in taking hits. As it filled with smoke, the living room altered as if a reel were ending in a cheap theater, frames, entire actions dropping out, voices and faces in and out of sync, bright dots and dark squiggles, the room jumping and then taking on the orange tones of the new projector's bulb; Bob saw that until now the world on the spherical screen around him had been projected by a light with too much blue in it. The gray light in the windows looked like sunshine. The three stoned people crowded around the refrigerator and lifted pieces of aluminum foil, seeing what the cook had left. In the hallway Anna pressed her stomach into Bob's, kissed him, unbuttoned his shirt, and backed up the hallway bending over with her palms beckoning as if he were a pet she wanted to jump into her arms.

In Beverly, on a no-account street, he followed her into her ordinary little house. The dust ruffles on the overstuffed furniture, the family photographs with their cheap gilded frames, the tawdriness, the poor taste, made him wild about her and as certain of conquest as he was of her La-Z-Boy's softness when he sank into its arms. She was selecting LPs from a brass stand reminiscent of a dish rack. Kernaghan, who'd been left in the car, was giggling in the bushes, spying through the window, rain snaking down the glaze of his baldness.

They didn't see him again, but he must have been in the back seat as they returned to Argilla Road, he must have followed them inside, tittering like a leprechaun, and he may even have been watching in the living room the entire time, maybe in the corner where twenty years later Rita would split her head open. Watching Anna load the record changer with Frank Sinatra albums, watching her remove her paisley blouse and Silcra bra, watching the white flesh of her midriff bunch into folds as she bent forward to pull her high-heeled boots off and slip her yellow spandex miniskirt and white underpants down her legs. Watching the rippling and rounding of the muscles in Bob's shoulders, the tensing of his youthful buttocks, the action of his hips. Hearing the smack of her heavy breasts against the flatness of his chest, watching fast breath dry the saliva in the corners of her mouth, hearing him cry out, hearing her tell him, "He can only do it . . . with Dom Pérignon bottles!" Watching him raise her hips from the carpet and replow the warm, moist, trembling earth. Watching the in and out, seeing their chests heave and their mouths angle to cover one another as if they were two half-drowned swimmers in mutual resuscitation, watching the jiggling of her flesh, the sway of his, watching him sprawl across her forking legs, watching him gulp air red-faced and obliviously, until finally he had watched enough and could totter across the room and touch Bob's shoulder.

"Bob, Bob, Bob!" he said, eyes half-shut with mirth. Bob saw his penis, swollen and perpendicular, a pinkish black instrument.

"Oh my God!" Anna screamed with laughter. "Oh my God!"

Bob could hear her giggling, squealing, shrieking while he put his overcoat and boots on. He stumbled into the rain, across the lawn and through the sterile, altered woods. He smelled woodsmoke and wet leaves, heard the wind being combed by a thousand narrow tree trunks, water from branches slapping the slick leaves on the ground. It was almost Thanksgiving. The dusk and the wet smells and wet sounds were the ones that had once made him shiver when he stepped outside his house for firewood, and made him hurry back inside where it was warm and he could forget the keening wind mourning the dead past of the land, dragging over the hard rooftops, jealous of the life inside. So deep in the stunted woods that the dark bulk of Kernaghan's house might simply have been night on the horizon, he sank to his knees in the leaves and stayed until the rain had stopped, and his head had cleared, and the sky froze into glittering crystals in the shape of Orion and Perseus, and he'd heard the starter of Anna's car.

You bought her a condominium?

I helped her with a loan.

Oh, Melanie.

Bob, it was an excellent time for her to buy.

She looks up to you. She takes her lead from you. You know, you don't have to give her everything she wants. You could give her some guidance instead.

The money is mine to do what I want with.

I'm saying if you wonder why Lou got so mad at you, it's not too hard to figure out. Just think about how it looks to him, why don't you. Just think about it.

Give me some credit. I have every intention of being fair to him in the long run. But if you could hear the way he harps on the money . . . It's impossible to have a rational discussion with him. He's just like you. He's even worse. I told you, he ruined a sofa. He kicked a Waterford bowl into the fireplace.

Well, good for him.

He has no conception of what I'm going through.

He understands that Eileen takes and takes and takes from you, and he gets nothing.

Bob, you cannot compare the two.

Obviously he thinks you can.

I don't understand it. Ever since this whole thing started he's been terrible. I just would not have expected this of him. He's been storing up resentment.

You should call him and apologize.

Oh, now, really. For what? What do I apologize for? I'm the one with the problem! I'm the one who's caught in the middle!

You should call him and apologize. It's what you should do, and if you can't do it, then you can't complain, either, and you can't complain if I take matters into my own hands.

Well, go right ahead. You always know what the right thing to do is. You've never, ever, faced a situation where you weren't sure what to do. Everything's always been very clear for you. Every-

thing's simple and nice. You wanted me, you married me. You live your politically correct life, and leave everything else to me, which is what you married me for.

I married you because I loved you.

I know that, Bob. I know that. Don't tell me—

And I still love you.

DON'T TELL ME THAT.

A long silence.

Give it away, Bob said finally.

Give what.

The money.

I will. I'll give—a lot. I'll give—half! But I have to have it first.

Give it all, and you'll be happy. Set aside a little for the kids, and a little for yourself. Set aside a million and give the rest away. You'll be happy.

I can't, Bob. I can't.

All the while, a hole is being drilled into the earth in Peabody at a cost in labor, equipment, and energy of maybe five thousand dollars a day. Anna tags the core samples as they come up and stores them in a refrigerated building to retard oxidation. She has her own padlock on the building. She couldn't tell schist from feldspar if her life depended on it, but the samples will be hers alone to study and exploit, and her only thought is *deeper, deeper, deeper*. She still thinks there's oil or at least methane down there. But delays and costly breakdowns are becoming frequent as the drill bit chews past the one-mile mark. Competitors with new plants are eating into Sweeting-Aldren's war profits. With the hole now well below the water table, plenty deep for waste disposal, management decides it's time to eliminate further funding. Kernaghan, however, knows that Anna will leave the company if the drilling stops too soon. He threatens and deceives and cajoles Aldren Sr. into funding the drilling at least through the end of 1970.

Rita can't figure it out. A number as hot and proud as Anna? With an impotent goat? Obviously Kernaghan has found a way to buy the girl. But the months go by and Anna isn't promoted, she doesn't move out of her dowdy pillbox in Beverly, she drives the same old Ford. Certain heavy pieces of jewelry are suspicious, but Rita is sure the girl's too shrewd to have sold herself for some earrings and a diamond pendant.

"She hates the guy," Anna's fellow researchers confide when Rita asks.

"But she sleeps with him."

"He has Power over her," they say mysteriously, meaning they have no idea.

Rita visits Anna herself.

"I love him passionately," Anna says, laughing in Rita's face; Kernaghan has told her all about Rita. "And he's crazy about me."

"So why don't you marry him?"

"What do I care about marriage? He wants a woman who *sneezes* at money."

Talking to Anna fans the embers of Rita's jealousy, turns the warm glow into a white, directed flame. She begins to wonder about the big derrick called the F2 Line, which management has surrounded with a high, opaque fence and which Anna visits daily. Rita begins to snoop, to listen in on occupied telephone lines, to open forbidden drawers, to watch for keys to unattended file cabinets. The more she finds out, the easier it is to read between the lines of memos and decipher her bosses' winks and decode the remarks they make in hallways. She pieces together the details of Anna's "research initiative."

It's midwinter, the hole now eighteen thousand feet deep, when Rita comes to Anna's office with two copies of a confidential memo. She gives one to the girl. "Recognize this?"

Anna, bored: "What if I do?"

Rita hands her the other, which is identical to the first—copies to be sent to and destroyed by various executives and Anna Krasner, Research Scientist—except that the words "deep exploratory well" on the copy Anna received are replaced by the words "deep waste disposal well."

Anna shrugs. "So?"

"Well, my dear, it doesn't look like lover boy drilled your hole because he loves you. He drilled it to pump waste down. Seems to me that he got you awfully cheap. Wouldn't you say? Buying you with somebody else's money? As far as he's concerned, your dream's just a giant sewer."

Anna shrugs again. But a week later she fails to report to work, and a janitor discovers that her desk is bare. She simply vanishes into the greater world that Boston sometimes forgets lies all around it. And Kernaghan has only guesses about why she's left him. He may suspect Rita, but when he comes to see her, she, being far from through with her revenge, is careful not to gloat.

The company wastes no time in taking down the drilling derrick and putting in a pumping station. In the wake of Earth Day, Congress and Nixon are moving towards agreement on creating an environmental-protection administration and enacting Clean Air and Clean Water Acts. Kernaghan suggests that the pumping program be kept quiet, since (a) they've been drilling without a license, and (b) given the current ecological hysteria, the public might be alarmed if it learned that highly toxic chemicals are being pumped into the earth, no matter how safe the process is in reality. The chain of command terminating in the actual pumping is carefully broken up, so that only the top executives know the real story, and loopholes of deniability are left for all but one of them. The various plant managers and workers involved in the waste stream are told the fluids pumped at F2 are being stored temporarily in an underground tank, or told the fluids are harmless.

On the day before Kernaghan's seventy-second birthday, the day of his retirement, when the company's waste disposal program for the future is firmly in place, Rita appears at his door. She's been following the conspiracy as it develops, documenting every stage. She's the secretary of one of the executives involved—maybe even Aldren Sr. She's come to Kernaghan for blackmail.

"No way," Louis said. "You don't blackmail somebody into marrying you. You don't want to be married to a guy that hates you."

"Who said anything about marriage? She's trying to blackmail him, period. She wants all that money he never paid her for her favors. She shows him a list of the documents she has, and she says, Give me X amount of money or else you guys are going to jail. Remember we're talking about a woman who later defrauded her local bank. And when he sees how serious she is, he starts to weep, genuinely, because he's tired, and he's lost Anna, and he's afraid. He says, Please, Rita, I'm an old man, the best days of my life were spent with you, let's be friends."

"But she's suspicious."

"Of course she's suspicious. But it's hard to see straight when you've got *all* the power. He's on his knees saying marry me. He's laughing, he's crying, he's insane. He's utterly in her power, and she's a woman. She can't quite bring herself to stick the knife in."

"Yeah, but wait a second, you can't tell me the most important thing for him was what the woman looked like, and how old she was, and then say, Oh, but he made an exception for ugly old Rita. If money's what she wants, I mean not marriage, why *doesn't* he buy her off?"

"Because he loves money just as much! He weighs the problem and decides to marry her. If he marries her, she's silenced and it doesn't cost him anything. He keeps the money, and he can still chase all the women he wants. Plus marrying her guarantees her silence over the long term. So it's the right decision. They get married, and immediately he starts converting his entire portfolio to Sweeting-Aldren stock, to make sure that Rita's stuck with it. When he dies, his will puts Rita's allowance from the trust fund at the mercy of company dividends: if she attacks the company, it cuts into her allowance. He probably makes sure that at least Aldren knows this. And so then she's really stuck. In a sense she's inherited his entire fortune—obviously she insisted on a pre-nuptial agreement to that effect—but he doesn't let her get control of it. That's why there's the otherwise insane stipulation that the trustees *must leave the assets invested in Sweeting-Aldren*. It's not because he's such a gung-ho company man, he's too smart for that. It's because he's getting his revenge on Rita."

"And Mom's the one who pays for it."

"It's usually the women who pay for it, one way or another."

Kernaghan had a heart attack in his sleep in 1982. He'd lived eighty years in good health, smoked cigarettes for sixty, and died without pain or terror. Once he was dead and Rita had discovered the mean trick he'd played her with his will, she made a slave of his spirit. He had to knock on tables for her, spell out optimistic messages about the other world with a gliding upturned tumbler, and, most demeaning of all, inhabit the bodies of animals. One week she would look into the eyes of a neighbor's retriever and patronize her silly husband; the next week Jack would be a blue jay hanging around outside the kitchen windows. "Up to his same old tricks," she'd say complacently. Her Haitian maid, for one, believed that Rita had been shoved from that barstool because Jack's spirit couldn't take the abuse anymore.

A less imaginative woman than Rita, a woman who didn't require a giant pyramid on the roof and an authentic Egyptian mummy in the basement, could have lived very comfortably on the dividends from her Sweeting-Aldren stock. The chemical industry suffered some declines in the seventies and early eighties, but Sweeting-Aldren suffered less than the rest. Not only did it not have to spend tens of millions on pollution control and waste recovery, but it was able to pass some of those savings on to its customers, and so consistently undersell its east coast competition. The pump at F2 ran so smoothly that the old generation of executives forgot about it and the new generation never learned. It was like the national economy, which began to roar again in the mid-eighties. The country borrowed three trillion dollars to buy some weapons and fund a giant leap forward in lifestyle for the wealthy. When the economy grew, so the argument went, tax revenues would increase and the debt would be paid off. But year after year the national debt continued to increase.

Nature issued her first warning in 1987. Beneath Peabody, in Sweeting-Aldren's own back yard, the earth begins to shake. It's no accident. It has always only been a matter of time. Dimly Mr. X, the one executive officially responsible for waste disposal, the one executive who wasn't granted deniability when the thing was set up in '72, recalls the concept of induced seismicity. The tremors continue. A worried Mr. X goes to his boss, Aldren Jr., and says the pumping must stop.

Aldren Jr., steely cold, says: "What pumping?"

"Sandy, the pumping at F2. Our primary waste stream?"

"I have no idea what you're talking about," says Aldren Jr.

"Common knowledge this company incinerates and recycles all its waste."

"Joking aside, Sandy, we're causing a fucking swarm of earthquakes two miles from here."

With exquisite timing, their office trembles and they hear a distant boom, as from an artillery range.

"I've trusted you, X," says Aldren Jr. "You've been world-class, straight tens across the board. And now you're indicating to me that our disposal costs are going to triple? I don't think I'm going to remain president if that happens. And I have a personal stake in remaining president. It's a very meaningful position to me, self-esteem-wise."

"I'm indicating we're looking at a little backup in the waste stream. A little temporary quasi hitch. So that we might be well advised to short-term invest in better incineration and recycling. Either that or consider some major holding-tank-type construction."

Aldren Jr. shakes his head very slowly. "I'm hearing figures," he says, "in the tens of millions. I'm hearing crippling long-term capital investments here. Here when I can already feel the Spaniards breathing down my neck. Can smell the goddamn garlic, X! You know what they're doing with their waste? They're pissing it straight into the ocean at Cadiz. Their tankers fill their guts with it, sail to the mid-Atlantic, and blow it out their asses. The worst of it they put in plastic drums and ship to Gabon, and fucking Cameroon. That's what I'm competing with. Barely competing with. Fighting tooth and nail to compete with. You hear what I'm saying? I'm saying the old ejectorama for me, the dole and heavy fines and potential time in Allenwood for you."

Mr. X hears him. He puts a stop to the pumping. With the minuscule waste-processing budget at his disposal, he builds a cluster of huge, flimsy holding tanks on some company land near Lynnfield and stockpiles the most dangerous of his effluents there. The rest of the waste he lets trickle into the sea and air, relying on the company's good relationship with the EPA to keep him from getting caught. For several years, like a nation trying to be kind of halfway responsible, he holds the line on pumping; and for

several years, like the national debt, the stockpile of effluents grows
and grows. But finally there's a natural outbreak of seismicity in
nearby Ipswich, and Mr. X's prudence loses to his fear: he gives
the order to resume pumping. Just another half a decade without
a seismic disaster, and he'll be able to retire on a full pension,
summer on Nantucket, winter in Boca Raton, play eighteen holes
in the morning and have his first Manhattan on the dot of five.
Only five more little years! There will be no turning back now.
He's going to cross his fingers, shut his eyes, and pray: *Lord, let it
fall on someone else's shoulders.*

In the white light of morning, or rather early afternoon, Bob
put the empty whiskey bottle in the recycling carton for Clear Glass,
between Soft Plastic and Aluminum, and poured orange juice on
a bowl of Cheerios. Bees were pollinating purple thistle outside the
window. The cats were cooling in the basement. Upstairs a door
opened, and soon Louis appeared, scowling at the light. He had
red pillow marks on his face—sleep's tantalizing glyphs, which
every morning signified nothing in a different way. "Did you call
her?"

Bob didn't answer. He kept his head down, spooning up Cheerios, while Louis searched the refrigerator, drank some fizzless
cherry-flavored seltzer, and then stood with his arms crossed like
a parent whose patience had run out. "You want me to call her?"

"Can I finish my breakfast?"

Louis stood a while longer, arms still crossed. He left the room
in unrelenting silence.

Bob pushed his cereal bowl away. He began to call all the
Krasners in Albany, relying on the kindness of directory assistance.
His fourth try connected him to a deep female voice with a Russian
accent which he knew was Anna's mother's before he even asked.

"No. No," she said. "She's not here. She's overseas."

"Does she have a telephone number?"

"*What* do you want. Tell me."

Bob gave her a scaled-back version of the truth.

"She knows *nothing* about Sweeting-Aldren," said Madame
Krasner. "*Nothing.* I'm not going to give you number."

"Would you give her mine?"

"Who are you. Tell me. Who are you. *What* do you want, really."

"I was a good friend of hers."

"Eh. She has so many good friends. She lives in London. She has wonderful husband. Three children. *What* do you want, that she doesn't have. No. No. I'm not going to tell you her number. You try someone else."

"Would you give her my number?"

"She lives in London. Her number is not listed. I'm very sorry."

Bob pulled on his hair. Then Madame Krasner gave him Anna's number. "Very expensive to call," she said. "Not like calling here. Very expensive. You see, she has *money*. Oh, does she have money. What can you give, that she doesn't have?"

It was dinnertime in London. Through the dining-room windows, Bob could see Louis standing in the pine trees, the bright sun making shadows of the eyes behind his glasses. The red of Melanie's lipstick was in the pinpricks in the mouthpiece of the telephone. He dialed Anna's number, and after three rings Anna herself answered. He said his name. She said:

"Who?"

"Bob Holland."

". . . Oh, yes, Bob, how are you?"

"Anna, listen, I'm trying to find out if Sweeting-Aldren drilled a very deep well in Peabody in 1970. Do you happen to remember?"

The hissing silence on the line was unbroken for so long that he began to think there was no one there. Ghostly tone sequences chattered beneath the hiss. On some continent or other, a phone rang once, twice. Then he heard a burst of male and female laughter, a sociable tumult somewhere very close to where Anna was standing. "I'm sorry, Bob," she said. "What is it that you wanted to know?"

He repeated his question. Again there was a silence, and again a burst of laughter. "I . . . don't really know, Bob. I . . . can't answer that," Anna said.

"What do you mean you can't answer that? Do you think there *might* have been a well?"

"Bob, we have some guests over. I'm very sorry."

"I've seen your paper," he said. "You know there was a well. They've been pumping waste into it and causing earthquakes. You have to tell me what you know. I won't use your name, but you have to tell me."

"Bob, I really have to get off the phone now."

"A simple yes or no. Was there a well?"

"I'm sorry."

"Why won't you answer me? Would you rather talk to the press? Or the police?"

The hissing on the line had ceased; he was speaking to a dead phone. He dialed again.

"Anna—"

"Bob, I'm busy and I don't want to talk to you." Her voice was hard, controlled, angry. "It's better if you don't call me."

"A yes or a no. Please."

"I'm sorry, Bob. I have to go."

"Anna—"

"Goodbye, Bob."

IV

In the Black

14

As a reward for getting her MBA and as consolation for having to start work at the Bank of Boston, Eileen had been vacationing on the Côte d'Azur with Peter. They rented a Peugeot at the airport in Nice and were delighted in Monaco, snubbed in Cannes, drunk in St.-Tropez, and painlessly relieved of cash in the smaller towns along the way. At least once a day they ran into recent classmates of Eileen's. They would be climbing a cobblestone hill past shops with bunches of dried lavender and Provençal scarves swinging and flapping in the mistral, and they would come upon a Roman ruin surrounded by cafés, and from the blinding aluminum chairs a chorus of female voices would chime: "Eileen! Eileen!" Peter would clench his teeth and mutter "Jesus Christ" and roll his eyes invisibly behind his Ray-Bans, because he thought Americans in France should be mute chameleons, but Eileen would step immediately into the shade of the plastic Cinzano or Pernod umbrella where the guys were sitting tight-lipped and training their Ray-Ban gazes on distant cypresses or an azure bay—just like Peter—and the girls were eager to exchange data on who all they'd seen from their class so far (ultimately Eileen saw or heard of a total of thirty-five of them, so the Côte d'Azur was a very popular reward for Harvard MBA recipients this year), while Peter, having crossed to the far side of the square, sunned himself on a block of marble hewn by Roman slaves.

Peter did, in fact, look very European, and Eileen knew he

spoke fine French. But when they sat down in a café and a waiter came, Peter would look up and his lips would move a little bit, but no sound would come out, and the waiter, not being psychic, would turn to Eileen, who would say, "Uncaffay poor moi, ay oon Pernod poor lum," and then, to Peter, in a whisper squeaky with exasperation, after the waiter had left: "You have to tell him what you *want!*" Whereupon Peter's face would freeze into a smile so fierce and mocking and afraid that at length she felt sorry for him. She kissed his ear, tousled his hair, rubbed his thigh, and said she loved him. There ensued a silence, her face clouding up. "Do you love me?"

He grinned more fiercely yet and leaned across the table and gave her a not terribly welcome French kiss, still without having spoken a word since they sat down in the café.

In the afternoon they went to beaches. The question at a beach was always: Should she or shouldn't she? She was an island of suburban-Chicago modesty in a sea of Euroflesh—Norman mammaries, Belgian genitalia shaded by overhangs of Belgian flab, Dutch teats that were tiny and quivered, uncircumcised Parisian penises that she studied with sly and helpless fascination. Peter reclined on his elbows, staring over his surfer trunks and tanned toes at the emerald waves, while she tried to make up her mind. "I'm going to do it," she said finally.

Peter yawned. "That's what you said yesterday."

"Well but today I am."

He stared at the waves.

Reaching behind her back with both hands, she took hold of the hook of her bathing-suit top. She sat like this for five seconds. "Should I do it?"

"Think carefully," he said. "It's an important decision."

She pouted. "I'm not going to do it."

He stared at the waves. She threw sand at him. He brushed himself off with light little sweeps of his fingers, as if his skin were a record he didn't want to scratch. The next time he looked at her she was sitting upright on her towel, chin angled towards the sun, with her top on the sand beside her. They hardly spoke until they went back to their hotel, but there he pawed and clutched her body ardently, licking her breasts and climbing her, shuddering with lust like a dog while she smiled at the ceiling, unable to imagine a more perfect contentment.

The following afternoon she announced: "I'm not going to do it." White glare from car chrome and café spoons and a certain someone's Ray-Bans had been drilling into her head since breakfast. The hotel bed had been hot and full of expired alcohol fumes; she was also pretty sure she was getting a urinary-tract infection.

"It's up to you," said Peter, staring at the waves.

She chewed a fingernail and blinked morosely. Like her mother, no matter how tired she was, she had boundless energy for vacillation. "Do you think I should?"

In America, Peter was an expert and avid shopper, more certain than Eileen of how a 70/30 poly/cotton blend behaved and more patient than she in marching from store to store until the ideal shirt or shoes came to light. In Europe, however, he considered shopping merely the worst of many ways to blow one's cover. When Eileen entered a store, he waited a full minute before drifting in after her, and then he knelt near the doorway and tied and retied his shoes as if he'd only come in because his laces were loose. He would page through the French-language editions of the travel books. (He thought this made him appear French.) Direct questions from Eileen elicited blank Ray-Ban stares of non-recognition. He gazed out the shop's open doorway as if the thoughts of any Frenchman who had come in through such a door would immediately turn to leaving. (But the stores were often full of French people earnestly relating tacky souvenir items to historical battles or to the anthropology of Provence, and spending lavishly.) "It's fine," he'd murmur, referring to a gift idea, his eyes on the door.

"You haven't even looked at it!"

"I trust your taste," his lips unmoving, his eyes on the door.

The one gift that gave Eileen real trouble was Louis's. Earlier in the month, when she'd had Louis and his girlfriend over for moussaka, she had neglected to mention that she and Peter were about to leave for France. The fact was that she habitually avoided informing Louis of the plans and acquisitions of property she was making; she always hoped that he wouldn't ever find out about them; but of course she knew he always would. He would find out that while he was looking for a job and sweating in Somerville with a girlfriend who Eileen personally thought was awfully old for him, his sister had been having fantastic five-course dinners in the South of France. She therefore felt obligated to bring him something nice. At the same time, she could already imagine him making her feel stupid about whatever she decided to buy, because, after all, he had actually *lived* in France.

"Cognac," Peter suggested.

"It has to be from Provence."

"Wine," Peter said.

"I have to think about this. I have to *think*."

But the days passed with increasing rapidness, noon turning to nine, nine turning to noon, and she couldn't ever seem to think. Finally, on the way to the airport in Nice, she dashed into a department store and bought Louis a large knife.

In Back Bay there was a message from him on her machine, instructing her to call him at his old number. An unfriendly person at his old apartment gave her a new number, which when she dialed it turned out to belong to Louis's friend Beryl Slidowsky, on whose sofa, he said, he'd been sleeping for several nights.

"What happened to Renée?" Eileen asked, more innocently than meanly, though she really wasn't sorry to hear he wasn't living with her anymore.

"It's a problem I'm working on," Louis said.

"Oh. You're trying to get back together."

"I'm trying to get her back."

"Oh, well—good luck."

Louis said he was a fifth wheel at Beryl's. He wondered if he could crash in Back Bay for a few days. One way or another, he said, it wouldn't be for long.

"Um," Eileen said. "I guess. But if you and Peter can't get along, it's not going to be very nice."

"Trust me," Louis said.

He came over in the evening after her first day at the bank. She had drunk half a bottle of Pouilly-Fumé while waiting for Peter, who still wasn't home from work. When she let Louis in the door she immediately retreated, falling back on her legs as if the floor had developed a steep negative gradient. She couldn't believe how much her brother had changed in three weeks. He was wearing his usual black jeans and white shirt, but he seemed taller and older and broader in the shoulders. He'd had his hair cut so short that what remained was dark and velvety, and for some reason he wasn't wearing glasses. His cheeks were drawn, and dark with a week's beard, his eyes hollow and shining in the absence of lenses, with gray satin semicircles of tiredness beneath them.

"I—got this tan in France," Eileen said in a too-loud voice. It was the first thing that came into her head.

"Yeah, I heard you were over there," Louis said without interest.

"What happened to your glasses?"

"Somebody stepped on them."

"Have you had dinner?"

"If it's OK with you," he said, "I think I'll be by myself for a while. I can come out later."

At eleven o'clock he still hadn't come out. Eileen left Peter in bed with the news and tapped on the door of the second bedroom. Louis, minus his shirt, was bending low over the desk they had in there and writing in a notebook. At the top of the notebook page she could read the words *Dear Renée*. He didn't try to hide them.

"I brought you something from France," Eileen said. Jet lag and drinking and the day's terrors of job orientation had conspired to puff her eyes up and reduce her skin to red shininess. She handed Louis the box with the knife in it.

He frowned. "This is very nice. You got this for me?"

"It's for your kitchen. You have to pay me a penny for it. It's the superstition. You have to pay me for it or it's bad luck."

Obediently, unhurriedly, he took a penny from his pocket and held it out to her. But she had turned away towards the convertible futon sofa. She was looking at Louis's small nylon duffel bag, which was now apparently the size of all the possessions that mattered to him. "You're really broken up about her, aren't you?"

"Yes," Louis said.

"Did you want to tell me what happened?"

"I don't think so."

"Did you want me to do something? I could try and talk to her, if you wanted."

"It's OK."

She nodded; but it was more like her heavy head just falling forward. She stared at the floor and spoke in a low, trembling voice. "You know, you're very, very cute, Louis. There are lots of girls who'd think you're totally cute. And you're smart, and independent, and strong, and you're interesting, and you're going to do anything you want. Lots and lots of girls are going to want to go out with you. You're going to go to Europe again and you'll be really confident. You're going to have a good life. Did you know that?" She shot him an accusing look. "I used to feel sorry for you. But I don't anymore. I know you're all broken up about her, but I don't feel sorry at all. So just try to feel OK. I mean I guess I hope you get her back, but it's not the end of the world if you don't."

Louis sat and looked at her with the submissive sadness of a pet who knew he had damaged property but had never meant to. Eileen put her hand on the doorknob, not turning it but holding it as though it were a mother's hand. "I don't know why you make me feel so rotten."

"I'm not trying to," Louis said.

"You make me feel so rotten," she insisted. "You make me feel so bad about myself. You always have, all my whole life, my whole, whole life," she'd begun to cry, "and I don't want to anymore. I don't want you to stay here. I want you to find someplace else to stay. I have to go to work every day now. I have to go to this horrible stupid bank every single day with no vacation for ten months, and if I want promotions I have to work at night and Saturdays. And I just don't want you to make me feel so bad. You can stay here as long as you want, but I wanted you to know."

"I'll leave right now," he said calmly.

"No. You have to stay. I'll feel guilty if you go. But I don't want you here. I don't know what I want." She stamped her foot. "Why am I suddenly so unhappy? Why do you do this to me?"

"I'll go."

She spun around and, purple-faced, bent over him and cried, "You stay *here*, you stay *here*, you're not going *anywhere!* You *can't* go. You don't *have* anyplace to go. You stay here because you're my brother and *I don't want you to go*. If you go I'll never ever *ever* forgive you."

Then the door slammed and Louis was left alone in the room, squeezing the penny he hadn't given her.

For three days they kept out of each other's way. She left in the morning before Louis was awake, and he returned from a day of what she assumed was job-hunting at eight or nine at night and went straight to his room. By Thursday afternoon she was feeling attractive and remorseful again. She came home with her new French string bag filled with food and was surprised to find Louis in the living room. Was it possible that he'd been spending his days not job-hunting but watching TV? He was wearing his glasses again, and sitting with bowed head and folded hands on the sofa facing the video equipment, which was silent.

"I hope you haven't eaten dinner," she said.

He gave no sign of having heard her. He stared at the slate-faced TV and rubbed his thumbs together.

"Is something wrong?" she said, resisting an influx of irritation.

His mouth opened, but only silence came out.

"Well, I'm making a nice dinner," she said. "So I hope you'll be ready to eat it."

As soon as she went to the kitchen she heard the front door open and close. She turned on the kitchen TV and put a Perdue chicken in the oven (in France she'd learned that you could have warm meat in salads—poulet, canard, and the like), and then for a few minutes she forgot where she was and what she was doing, because of the news on Channel 4.

. . . was tragically gunned down in what police are calling the worst outbreak yet of pro-life violence. **Penny Spanghorn** *is standing by,* **live,** *at the scene of this tragic, tragic shooting.* **Penny?**

Jerry, this afternoon Renée Seitchek went to New Cambridge Health Associates in Cambridge, where the so-called Church of Action in Christ was performing the latest in its series of illegal door-blocking actions. Police arrested twelve demonstrators for attempting to harass Seitchek. At about five o'clock Seitchek came out of the clinic and spoke with reporters in what was said to be a very emotional confrontation. She stated that she'd had a—she had terminated a pregnancy. Tragically, it now appears that she

*may have paid for this statement with her life. At about five-thirty
she returned to her home here on Pleasant Avenue in Somerville,
where she was greeted with a hail of gunfire from an unidentified
assailant in a parked car across the street. Shortly before six
o'clock, Channel 4 News received an anonymous phone call from
an extremist group taking credit for the tragic shooting, and I
quote: "An eye for an eye, a tooth for a tooth." Somerville police
say they received a similar phone call at about the same time . . .*

Eileen stared, stricken, at Penny Spanghorn. She was weeping
over the arugula and radicchio in her salad spinner—weeping not
just for Renée and Louis but for herself as well—when Peter came
home from work. She told him that Renée was in critical condition
with severe chest and abdominal injuries.

"Shit," he said, paling. "Is that horrible?"

"It's so rotten. Everything is so, so rotten."

"It is truly horrible all right."

The Church of Action in Christ, said Philip Stites, *condemns
the wicked and cowardly shooting of Renée Seitchek this afternoon.
We in the church deplore all forms of human violence, whether it's
violence against an unborn baby or violence against a citizen of
the Commonwealth. Renée Seitchek is a woman of conscience and
a creature of God. We mourn her injuries, and we extend our
deepest sympathy to her family and friends and join them in sending her our prayers and love.*

It was after midnight when Eileen and Peter, watching but
not listening to Arsenio Hall in their airconditioned bedroom, heard
Louis come in. Eileen went to see him. She was wearing her favorite
summer nightshirt, a light cotton Bennington jersey, extra large.

Louis was sitting on the floor of his room, applying a folded
Kleenex to the bleeding, popped blisters that covered both his feet.
His sweat-soaked shirt was spattered with blood and clung tightly
to his breast. His black oxfords, dusty and exhausted-looking, lay
next to him. Apparently he hadn't been wearing any socks.

"Are you hurt?" Eileen said.

"They shot Renée," he answered in a thin, parched voice.

"I know. I know. I can't stop crying."

"They shot Renée."

"But she's OK, Louis. They said she's OK," although this

wasn't strictly accurate. Channel 4 would only say she hadn't died yet.

Louis prodded the raw flesh of his feet, tearing at the ragged skin with his fingers. Eileen, watching, felt as if she'd fallen and no one would help her. Even though they were suffering so much more than she was, it seemed to her that Louis and Renée had teamed up to rob her of an inheritance. She felt a flash of jealousy and anger, and in its light she saw that there was an absolute standard of goodness in the world, an ideal that she was infinitely far from achieving. Louis continued to press his thumbnails into his candy-red sores for no other purpose than the pain it brought him. She knew she had to stay with him and comfort him, but she couldn't bear to see him do that to his feet, and so she left him and lay down by Peter and let guilt and darkness swallow her.

He had run down the stairs and out onto Marlborough Street. The twin lines of brick town houses stretching to the west framed a yellow sun whose plasma had condensed in drops on green thunderstorm-soaked shrubs, in steaming beads on car hoods, in brilliant, smoking sheets on asphalt. A boom box in a basement window rang with the clash and assonance of Sonic Youth. Running, he saw the red high-tops and black roller skates of urban students, the white bunny feet of women in their commuter sneakers, the stiletto heels and penny loafers of real-estate agents, the paws of dogs, the laceless half-soled boots of men with no address. Keys jingled and car doors closed. A man (it had to be a man because hardly any women did it) whistled.

He ran up Mass Ave. and over the river down which a flood might just have roared, flushing all the rental sailboats and water-logged McDonald's trash into the sewer of Boston Harbor and leaving in its wake an earthy freshwater pungency. He pushed through the sluggish crowds vented by the subway at Central Square, ran up past the battalion of Volvos and Subarus soon to be carrying free-range chickens and baby zucchini away from Bread & Circus on Prospect Street, and up through the population densities surrounding Inman Square, where Portuguese immigrants and obese native East Cantabrigians mingled with Harvard comparative-lit grad students no more easily than Pastene Brand olive oil mixes with Poland Spring mineral water, and mufflers leaked or scraped on the pavement, and there were suspicious blackish sediments in every puddle, and a blond bearded youth with a lavender bandanna around his neck walked down the middle of the sidewalk singing "Sugar Magnolia" loudly.

By the time he crossed Union Square the sun had fallen into clouds, leaving a humid dusk that smelled of car exhaust and spoiled fruit. He limped up Walnut Street, neck outstretched, feet barely clearing the sidewalk joints, heart working shallowly, futilely, as though his blood in its heat had become too thin to pump. Near the summit of the hill he began to pass cars that had slowed to squeeze past or gawk at the Channel 4 and Channel 7 vans parked just short of the corner of Pleasant Avenue. A squad car blocked access to the street. A second squad car and the less overtly marked sedan of Somerville's police chief stood just beyond number 7's chain link fence and its burden of honeysuckle and crime-scene tape. Across the street an officer was taking pictures of the gutter, in which, as one bystander explained to another, some shell casings had come to light. A detective was transferring to a form on a clipboard the eager statements of two boys, one pint-sized and one gallon-sized, whom Louis recognized as the male contingent of the twenty-four-hour haunters of the front porch opposite number 7.

"One-seventy-six D V N, green on white," the larger boy was saying. "I wrote it down, see, one-seventy-six D V N. See? Right here. One-seventy-six D V N."

All of Pleasant Avenue had collected behind the crime-scene tape. There were the endo- and ectomorphic teenaged girls blowing bubbles the size and color of babies' heads, the silent workingmen with whiskey sunburns and lips pursed in resignation. There were educated mothers holding Alexes and Jessicas in their arms, size-18 heads of household whose uncharitable view of the world the tragic shooting had confirmed, a pair of twin albino Mormons with their briefcases, and a quartet of wiry Africans in shiny shorts and knee-high stockings, the smallest of them carrying a soccer ball. As soon as Louis had caught his breath a little and stilled the quaking of his knees, he pushed his way up to the tape. Through the open gate of number 7 he saw the blood on the drying concrete walk, diluted and smeared by the rain like red watercolor paint. He saw blood darkening the edges of the triangular puddles in the depressed corners of the sidewalk squares. He saw a faint and mottled band of it on the face of the lowermost concrete step. He gave a sharp, brief cry of pain and disbelief. A cop talking to the somber Penny Spanghorn and her camera-headed companion was making dramatic gestures with his arms, aiming his finger like a gun.

"Where did they take her?" Louis said.

"Somerville Hospital," replied several people at once.

Headlights were coming on among the eastbound cars on Highland Avenue, paired pure white spots seeming to emerge straight from the blood in the sky above the distant Davis Square. Looming above dark side streets and dark trees with moodily shifting branches and streetlights still in the early pink stages of ignition, the hospital projected from the slope of Somerville's central ridge like a tanker at twilight, the lighted windows and dozen bristling antennas of its bridge-like tower signaling life and vigilance on the dark, deep ocean. In the parking lot outside the emergency room, the hydraulics of a Channel 5 van were purring as it retracted its dish.

The hospital's small lobby was furnished with oblongs of foam upholstered in electric blue. Howard Chun was slouched on one of them. There was blood on the knees of his yachting pants and bright smears of it on his thighs, where, like a butcher, he must have wiped his hands.

"Where is she?" Louis said.

Howard cocked his head towards the interior of the hospital. "Surgery," he said. He stood up and began to circle the waiting area, tearing a leaf off a potted plant, doing vertical push-ups against the windows, stopping to drive his bloodstained knees into the foam of various oblongs, and telling Louis what he'd seen. He didn't sound like someone who loved or liked or knew Renée or was even particularly thinking about her. He was like an adolescent who until now had seen violence only in Hollywood movies and so was driven to recount the dreadful thing he'd just seen the world do, to convey the impact to Louis, to try to impress or harrow or hurt the person who hadn't been there and who it was obvious did love her and who could imagine whatever details he left out.

She was lying on her side at the bottom of the stoop of number 7. Her legs were tucked up and her wrists were crossed across her chest and there was blood soaking through her jeans above one knee and blood covering the forearm she had pressed to her stomach. The kids across the street had already called 911 and were standing right behind Howard, giving him conflicting and specious pieces of advice. Renée was producing the lonely, high-pitched, unaffected moans of a really sick child. Her face was the color of cold bacon grease sweating in a humid room. She said *Howard* and *Get somebody* and *It hurts, it hurts*. Then she stopped speaking and her breath rasped loudly in her windpipe and the paramedics came and dislodged Howard, the broad male backs in white shirts dwarfing the little package of dwindling female life as they tried to sort her out. They gave her oxygen through her nose and attached her to a portable monitor. They exchanged data orally, blood pressure 80/50, pulse 120, respirations 36. A lobed tide of blood was spreading across the concrete, seeming to boil as the raindrops fell. Questions: Could she breathe? Did she have feeling in her legs? Where did it hurt? She blinked and winced as the rain fell in her eyes. In a timid voice, as if daring to disturb them only because it seemed important, she asked them if she was going to die. A white shirt said, "You'll be OK." He said, "You got the Ringer's?" While the police took names and addresses from Howard, Renée was strapped into the ambulance with wide-bore IVs in both her arms. Her T-shirt and bra and one pants leg had been cut away, and a thick square of gauze beneath her right breast was soaking up her blood. Howard sat with his knees nearly in his face and his hand on her chilled wet forehead as the siren came on and surged hopefully upward in pitch and volume. The clear plastic tubes wagged with the undulations and irregularities in Highland Avenue. A white shirt said, "Renée, you're doing great." But her teeth were chattering and she didn't answer.

"You know what they do?" Howard said. He rebounded from a blue oblong and checked Louis for a reaction. "They take a tube, got a sharp point. They stab it through the ribs. She's awake, they stab it right through. Then they start putting suction. I heard her when they did it. Police was there, we heard it."

He checked again for Louis's reaction. Louis's face was no longer flushed from the run, but he was sweatier than ever. He panted and followed Howard fearfully with his eyes as if Howard had been physically torturing him. He said, "Do you hate her?"

"They take her surgery," Howard said.

"I asked: Do you hate her?"

Howard scrunched up his face. "What you think?"

Louis couldn't bear to look at him, couldn't bear to hear another of his short, croaking sentences. "I wish you didn't exist," he said.

"They started six-thirty," Howard said.

Louis put his fingers behind his glasses and rubbed his eyes. A repulsive field drove him toward the automatic doors, but when he passed Howard he swung around and shoved both his fists into his ribs, giving him a shove intended to land him on his back. But there was a lot of inertia to Howard. He staggered and caught himself from falling just as Louis charged in and met, quite unexpectedly, a wicked slap across his left cheek followed by another across his right. "Uh!" he said, swinging blindly as his glasses sailed away. Howard had a height advantage. He was able to keep shoving Louis in the head and collarbone and shoulders, knocking him back each time he charged, retreating in a circle around a cluster of blue oblongs. "Stop fighting me," he said in a crabby, priggish bark. "Stop fighting me." Louis grabbed his shirt and landed several solid jabs to his gut. Howard whaled away at his cheeks with his open hands, but here Louis's superior tolerance of pain came into play, as he withstood the increasingly earnest slaps and managed to topple Howard into an oblong and then onto his back and, grunting with exertion, pinned Howard's arms with his knees and began to pummel his cheeks and nose and ears and eyes but did not pay enough attention to the pinned arms, one of which worked free and delivered a ringing blow to the side of his head, which was followed by a frightening and irresistible loss of breath as a third party, shouting "What the *hell* are you doing?" got a choke hold on him and dragged him off Howard, raising him onto his toes and threatening to raise him higher before he finally went limp.

"What the *hell* are you doing? There's sick people here, there's hurt people here. Look what you done to this fella. You oughtta die with shame doing a thing like that here."

Howard's nose was like a decanter, well behaved while he was on his back but pouring a stream of blood onto the carpeting as soon as he sat up.

"You still got that devil in you? Or you gonna leave off now?"

"It's OK," Louis gasped, limp.

"Sheesh," said his captor, releasing him and dropping to his knees by Howard. He shook open a handkerchief and applied it to the bleeding nose. "Pinch it, pinch it."

Louis straightened the frames of his glasses, which were brand-new and had cost him most of the cash his father had given him when he left Evanston. Putting them on, he confirmed that the man who'd been choking him was Philip Stites. Drops of Howard's blood had fallen on the minister's khaki pants. He looked up at Louis reproachfully and then he did a double take, his expression softening as he squinted through his tortoiseshells, trying to place him.

"News with a Twist?" Louis said.

"Ah. The Antichrist. You find yourself another job?"

"Nope."

"I'm real sorry to hear that," Stites said glibly, losing interest. He stood up and smoothed back his corn-silk hair. "Neither of you wouldn't happen to be here to see how Renée Seitchek's doing?"

Neither Louis nor Howard answered. Howard was reclining against an oblong and squeezing his nose as if something stank here. He raised his narrowed, red eyes and looked at Louis with the intimacy shared by lovers and others who grapple on the floor.

"What's it to you?" Louis said to Stites.

"I take it that's a yes?"

"Take it however you want," Louis said. "What's it to you?"

"Well. I guess that's a fair enough question. I can tell you I saw Renée a couple nights back, and I saw her today, and I think it's a terrible thing what's happened. And I want to pray for her. And I want to know she's alive."

"Ask at the desk."

"Well now." Like a bully who'd scented a weakling, Stites awakened fully to Louis's presence. He approached him with the same prowling, intent, and possibly myopic tilting of head that Louis himself assumed when he felt he had a moral edge on someone. "You must be the boyfriend."

"You can talk," Louis said. "But I don't have to listen."

"You must be the boyfriend she told me about on Monday, and the one she told the world about today."

Louis blanched a little, but held his ground. "Today," he said. "You mean—when you guys were calling her a murderer."

"On Monday," Stites raising his voice, "when she told me there was a man who'd hurt her so bad she didn't want to live anymore. And today when she said there was a man she was in love with and wanted to marry and have children with, and I didn't see any man there with her. And I reckon you're the so-called man. Aren't you."

Louis looked into the minister's light-soaped, accusing tortoiseshells. "You can't make me feel guiltier than I already do."

"Your guilt is your business, Mr. Antichrist. I'm just telling you why I'm here."

The so-called man whom Renée had been in love with and had wanted to have children with turned away from Stites. Conscious of an impulse to redeem himself in the minister's eyes, he crouched by Howard. "I'm sorry," he said.

Howard gave him another red, intimate look and said nothing.

Stites had disappeared up the corridor. Louis found him sitting on a sofa in a tiny ICU waiting room with a television mounted on the ceiling. "What did she say about me?" he said from the doorway.

Stites didn't take his eyes off the television. "I told you what she said."

"Where'd you see her?"

"Chelsea."

"She wanted you to call your people off her."

"That's what she came for, sure. But that's not why she stayed."

"She stayed?"

Stites smiled at the television. "What's it to you?"

Louis looked at the floor. Not for the first time, he felt he was out of his depth in loving Renée.

"Jody batting .355 over the last eight games," said the television. "He's four for his last nine."

"She stayed, we talked," Stites said. "Then she left. Where were you?"

"I left her. I hurt her."

"And now she's shot and you decide you feel bad about it."

"That's not true."

"What's your name?"

"Louis."

"Louis," Stites spread his arms out on the top of the sofa and put his feet up on a coffee table, "I ain't your rival. I'll tell you frankly, I thought a lot of her. But she wasn't interested in me as a man. She was totally faithful to you. I don't know about if you didn't exist. But you do exist, so."

"If I didn't exist you'd have to explain to her why one of your people shot her in the back because she had an abortion."

"That was not a pro-life person," Stites said positively, to the television screen, where the Red Sox batter was trying to lay down a bunt.

" 'An eye for an eye'?"

"I don't believe it," Stites said. "I flat-out don't believe it. That's not how we work, even the worst of us. I'd frankly sooner believe it was you."

"Appreciate it."

"The only question is, who else is gonna do a thing like that? You got any idea at all?"

Louis didn't answer. On the TV screen a Volvo sedan was crashing into a cinder-block wall, and a plastic married couple and their bald plastic children, not dead, not even scratched, were settling back comfortably into their seats.

"What's she like?" Stites asked him. "Day to day?"

"I don't know. Neurotic, self-absorbed, insecure. Kind of

mean. She doesn't have a great sense of humor." He frowned. "She's a good scientist. A good cook. She doesn't do anything without thinking about it. She's very sexy too, somehow."

"A good cook, huh? What kinds of things she cook?"

"Vegetables. Pasta. Fish. She doesn't eat the higher vertebrates."

Out in the Sahara, two young men dying of thirst were rescued by a Budweiser truck carrying beautiful girls in swimsuits and tight cutoffs and halter tops. Everybody was drinking product. The girls' breasts were firm and round and their stomachs flat and hard and their waists narrow in their Silcra maillots. Their limbs sweated like cool, intoxicating beer cans. The men flooded sundry cleavages with a fire hose, spanked asses with the hose's white spray. The cheesecake, drinking product, was losing inhibitions. Forty feet away, on the table in OR #1, a urologist named Dr. Ishimura was sewing up the place in Renée's body where her right kidney had been, and a surgeon named Dr. Das was vacuuming up her blood.

15

He was awakened in the morning by the machine by his bed. His amplified mother was shouting at Eileen about some State Farm policy: *AND I NEED YOUR WORK NUMBER SO—*

"Hello Mom," he said over a squawk of feedback as he deactivated the machine.

"Louis? Where are you?"

He coughed. "Where do you think?"

"Goodness, yes, that's a silly question. How—how are you?"

"Well. Apart from the fact that my girlfriend was shot in the back last night and almost died, uh."

There was a silence. He could hear midmorning birds chirping on Argilla Road.

"Your girlfriend," Melanie said.

"You probably saw it on the news. Her name's Renée. Seitchek. Remember you met her?"

"Your girlfriend. I see."

"She had an abortion, and somebody shot her. And you know who the father was?"

"Louis, I—"

"It was me."

"Well, Louis, that's—that's very interesting. For you to tell me that. Although according to what I read in the paper she had some uncertainty—"

"She only said that to take all the responsibility."

"I suppose that could be the case, Louis, although you shouldn't—"

"She said it because she's a conscientious person who takes responsibility for everything she does."

"Yes, I'm quite familiar with Renée's conscientiousness."

He sat up. He swung his bandaged feet to the floor. "What do you mean? Have you been talking to her?"

"As a matter of fact," Melanie said, "I saw her the weekend before last, and then again last week. But that's not what's important now."

"You saw her?"

"What's important is that she recover. That's what you have to think about."

"You saw her?"

"Yes, but it is *not important*."

"My girlfriend is in the hospital and she almost died and you won't tell me what's going on?"

"Louis, she gave me some advice."

"Advice. Advice. She told you to sell your stock."

There was no reply except for birdsong. The birds might have been perched on his mother's shoulder, they sounded so close.

"She told you to sell your stock," Louis said. "Right?"

"Well, yes, I see your father has given you a clear picture of the extremely private dilemma I was facing. And it's exactly as you say: she advised me to sell my stock."

Louis hobbled to the desk and sat down. "She *gave* you the advice? Or did she sell it?"

"You may ask her that yourself, Louis. I'm not going to tell you."

"She was in surgery for four hours last night. She's in, like, horrible shape. And you want me to ask her?"

"I don't see what conceivable difference it could make to you. All I'm going to say is that I *do not recall* the precise arrangement we had."

"Meaning she sold it to you."

No reply.

"Did she tell you she knew me?"

"She said that you and she were not involved."

"Well, we aren't, strictly speaking."

"She also said that you and she had not *been* involved."

"Well, she lied."

"Well, and I suppose I knew that. I suppose I knew it all along."

Louis hung up and clutched his forehead, which had begun to ache. The bathroom was still steamy and herbally scented from Eileen and Peter's showers. Alongside Peter's French skin-care products ("poor lum") and the wide variety of makeup pencils and brushes and pancakes that Louis had been a little surprised to discover Eileen used, he saw the bloodstained washcloth, the empty box of sterile bandages, the wastebasket full of Kleenexes stained with blood and Betadine, the evidence of the quarter hour he'd spent here before he went to bed. He saw the sun in the window. He pictured Somerville Hospital in the daylight, the daylight of a holiday—Thanksgiving, the Fourth of July—that had fallen on a weekday, when the plug is pulled on ordinary activities, and the empty white hours stretch out towards the evening's obligatory turkey, the night's fireworks, or, in this case, the afternoon's visit to the hospital. They'd told him there was a chance he'd be able to see Renée briefly. He raised the toilet seat, which like every other horizontal surface in the bathroom was dusted with the baby powder Eileen had been using on summer mornings for at least twelve years, and he was just beginning to pee when the telephone rang again. He returned to his room.

Hi, this is Lauren Bowles—

He reached for the receiver, but his fingers curled into a fist. He felt how an object, a chair, must feel, the fibers of its wooden members tensed, its arms and legs paralyzed by the geometry of equal and opposing forces. Watching his fingers nonetheless uncurl and raise the receiver was like watching a chair move in an earthquake.

"Hello?" Lauren said. "Hello? . . . Hello? Is someone there?"

"It's me, Lauren."

"Oh God, Louis, you sound so far away. Are you alone? Can I talk to you?"

Now his lips were the stationary object.

"Are you there?" Lauren said. "I was going to wait to call you like you said to, but I was watching Good Morning America and I saw her. It's so bad, Louis, it's really really bad, because I'd just been thinking how I wished she didn't exist. But they said she's alive. Right?"

"Yes."

"You know they called her a hero? Like, Louis's girlfriend is such an incredibly good person they put her picture on TV and say she's a hero. Like she's one of the best people in the country or something. And I'm such a good person I'm sitting there wishing she was dead, right up to when I actually saw her."

"Yeah, Lauren," he said harshly. "You shouldn't listen to what they say. She had that abortion to be spiteful. She uses men for sex. She has a smaller heart than you do."

Lauren was hurt. "I don't believe you," she said. It was the first time he'd ever tried to hurt her. He wanted her to hate him and forget him. But it wasn't pleasant to be hated, at least not by Lauren, whose goodwill towards him had always been a mystery that made the world seem like a hopeful place. He'd be very sorry to live without that goodwill. He asked her where she was.

"I'm at home. I mean with Emmett. I haven't let him kiss me, though."

"He must be delighted to have you back."

"Right, we're having some real fun talks."

He stood on his aching, throbbing feet. As the silence on the line lengthened, it took on the particular curdled flavor of daytime long-distance rates.

"This is the end, isn't it, Louis."

"Yes," he said.

"Were you back together with her?"

"No."

"But you wanted to be?"

"Yes."

"Oh, fuck," said Lauren sadly. "I'm so jealous of her, you can't believe it. You'd think I was a monster if you knew how jealous. But I swear to God, Louis, I hope she gets better. Do you believe me?"

"Yes."

She considered this. "OK," she said. "I'll see you. I mean—I won't see you. I guess . . . I guess I'm going to let Emmett kiss me now."

"That's good."

"Are you jealous of him?"

"No."

"Not even a little bit?"

"No."

"Louis." There was urgency in the word. "Just say yes. Say yes and I'll hang up, and it will be the end. Please say yes."

"I'm not jealous of him, Lauren."

"Why not? Tell me why not." She sounded like a crossed child. "Aren't I pretty? Wouldn't I do anything in the world for you? Don't I love you?" Between the moment when a glass is irretrievably knocked from a shelf and the moment when it hits the floor, there is a charged and very finite silence. "I hope she dies!" Lauren said. "I hope she fucking dies right this minute!"

Louis knew that if he'd been in the same room with her, he would have gone away with her and lived with her; he knew it the way he knew his own name. But he was speaking on the telephone, with its little plastic guillotine for chopping heads off conversations. Some providence had steered him back to Boston from Chicago, had steered him in the first place to Chicago, where his father had said: *Let me tell you the hard half of the truth about women: They don't get any prettier when they get older; they don't get any saner when they get older; and they get older very quickly.*

"Look what you made me say," Lauren said.

"Hang up."

"All right. I will."

"I'm hanging up," he said.

As he removed the receiver from his ear, he heard her say, *"I wanted you!"*

He sat on the bed and looked at the motionless chairs and the motionless walls until the light in the window became an afternoon light and he decided it was late enough to try to see Renée. He would rather have seen Lauren. He dressed, loosening the laces of his shoes until he could fit his feet in them. He stamped one foot and then the other to settle them into their pain. He made himself chew and swallow two bananas.

At Somerville Hospital a new woman manned the reception desk. She had a long neck and a tiny head. "We have no Seitchek listed," she said.

"What do you mean no Seitchek listed?"

"This is that poor girl from Harvard? Let me see what I can find here." She flipped again through her jumbo Rolodex. "No, I'm afraid she's not."

"Are you telling me she's dead?"

"Well . . ." The woman requested data on her telephone. She reported to Louis: "She's at Brigham & Women's. They just transferred her."

Brigham & Women's was back in Eileen's neck of the woods, over behind Fenway Park in a whole small city of the sick and recovering, where brick and concrete hospital buildings had budded like yeast, putting out wings upon wings at odd angles, nourished by what was obviously an ever-growing stock of unwell people. There was no free parking. Louis went up an elevator, down an endless arterial corridor, through a lobby, down an elevator. He told a nurse at the octagonal ICU desk that he wanted to see Renée Seitchek. The nurse said Renée was in surgery. "Are you a family member, Louis?"

"I'm her boyfriend."

The nurse dropped her eyes to a stack of folders with red tabs and shuffled them nervously. "I'm afraid it's immediate family only."

"What if I said I'm her husband?"

"But you're not her husband, Louis. Mrs. Seitchek's in the staff lounge around the corner if you'd like to talk to her."

The staff lounge was empty except for a petite woman in pleated navy-blue slacks and a pink blouse who was pouring coffee into a styrofoam cup. Her hair was short, permed, and frosted. She wore heavy gold jewelry of simple design on her tanned hands and wrists. A soap was playing on the television next to her.

"Mrs. Seitchek?"

When the woman turned, he saw Renée's very own expression

of mild surprise. He was looking at a Renée who had aged twenty-five years; who had let the sun broil her skin to the color of crust on white bread; who had plucked her eyebrows and put on silvery pink lipstick; who had not slept last night; and who had been born very pretty. His first impulse was to fall in love with her.

"Louis Holland," he said.

Mrs. Seitchek looked at him uncertainly. "Yes?"

"Renée's boyfriend."

"Oh," she said. He watched her take in his baldness, his white shirt, his black pants. A trace of one of Renée's own grim smiles bent her lips. "I see." She turned back to the coffee cart and sweetened her coffee from a pink packet. "Are you from Harvard, Louis?"

"No. Chicago originally. But I wanted to know how she is, and when I can see her."

"She's in surgery again, her leg now. A bullet hit the bone." Mrs. Seitchek's shoulders drooped, and she rested her hands on the coffee cart. "She'll be on a ventilator for a while, and very heavily sedated. You can get in touch with me in a week or ten days, when she's on the floor and we have some idea who she'd like to have visit her. Maybe she'll want to see you then."

"Can't I see her sooner?"

"It's only immediate family, Louis. I'm sorry."

"I'm her boyfriend."

"Yes."

"Well, I'd sort of like to see her as soon as possible."

Mrs. Seitchek shook her head, her back still turned. "Louis, I don't know if you know anything about our relationship with Renée. I certainly don't know a thing about you, I didn't even know your name. So let me explain that Renée does not confide in me. We love her very much, but for whatever reasons, she's chosen to be distant. I don't know. Maybe you can tell me?" She turned to him. "How many boyfriends Renée has?"

"Just me," Louis said. "Except—"

"Except."

"Well, we had a fight."

Again he saw a trace of Renée's bitter smile. "And the young Chinese man. Howard. He's not her boyfriend?"

"Not really."

"Not really. I see. And the young man who was here just before you? Terry."

"Definitely not."

"Definitely not. All right. That's not quite the impression he gave, but if you say so . . ."

Louis tried to think of someone who knew for sure that he and Renée had lived together, of some hard evidence of a relationship. He thought of saying: *Your son Michael sells real estate and your son Danny is an intern in radiology.* But he could already hear the obvious reply: *If you're her lover, where were you yesterday afternoon?*

Mrs. Seitchek dropped a coffee stirrer in a wastebasket. "You see the problem, don't you? My daughter was the victim of a crime, and we have no idea who's responsible. We didn't have the tiniest inkling of her private life until we came here. And I have to say, things aren't much clearer now. So under the circumstances I think it's best if we just wait."

"But next time you talk to her . . . maybe you could at least tell her that Louis is—you know. Around?"

"We'll see."

"Why is that a problem?"

"I said we'll see. I don't want to upset her if—"

"I am her boyfriend, Mrs. Seitchek. I'm going to die of grief if she dies. I'm—"

"So am I, Louis. So is her father, so are her brothers. We all love her, and we all want her to live."

"Well, so tell her."

"I'll think about it."

"Excuse my stupidity, but—"

"Please go now." Mrs. Seitchek's eyes had filled. "Please go."

Louis wanted to put his arms around her. He wanted to kiss her and take her clothes off, to have her be Renée, to bury his face in her. Suddenly close to tears himself, he ran from the room.

Outside, as he passed the octagonal desk, he saw a man he thought he recognized from the family picture Renée had shown him once. The man had bright red skin and thin white hair, combed straight back, and he wore a pair of very scary glasses—thick trifocals with outsized lenses and heavy-duty plastic frames. He was reading the fine print on a bottle of liquid medicine.

"Excuse me, are you Dr. Seitchek?"

The man's eyes flicked up to the middle band of the trifocals and looked at Louis piercingly. "Yes."

"I'm a friend of your daughter. I wonder if you could give her a message sometime in the next—days. I wonder if you could tell her Louis loves her."

Dr. Seitchek returned his eyes to the bottle. He was a former dean of Northwestern's medical school, and although Renée was as reticent about him as about everyone else in her family, Louis had gotten the idea that he was something of a major figure in American cardiology. His voice was low, limited, professional. "You've spoken to my wife?"

"Yes."

"She explained our uncertainties?"

"Sort of."

The magnified eyes stabbed Louis with another look. "Renée terminated a pregnancy yesterday. Were you aware of that?"

"Yeah. In fact I was the, uh, other party."

"Your name is Louis."

"Louis Holland. Yes."

"I'll give her the message."

"I really appreciate it." He touched Dr. Seitchek's shoulder, but his hand might have been a fly alighting there for all the response it got. "Can I ask something else? —Who she thinks might have done it? Did they ask her?"

Dr. Seitchek again raised his eyes from the bottle of medicine. "I don't think she has any idea."

"That's what she said? That she has no idea?"

"She didn't say anything."

"She could talk?"

"She was conscious and alert this morning. But she doesn't appear to have any memory of yesterday afternoon. I don't think she saw anything anyway."

"But what did she say?"

Dr. Seitchek studied him as if there were fine print on his face. "Is there something you think she should have said?"

"I don't know."

"Something you want to tell me?"

"No."

"Let me give you the detective's number. I guess you know we're offering a reward?"

Pleasant Avenue was deserted in the Friday late morning sun. Louis tried not to look at the blood on the stoop, but he couldn't help seeing it, peripherally, as he went inside. He took Renée's spare key from behind a patch of loose wallpaper in the stairwell.

Her apartment was very clean and very hot. He opened the kitchen window, letting a fresh northern breeze and the whitish noise of commerce on Highland Avenue trickle into the suffocating, coffee-scented stillness. He went to her bedroom and noted the bareness of her desk, where he'd last seen the pile of articles about induced seismicity and the Peabody earthquakes. There was again that atmosphere of finality, of control, of planned departure, that he'd noticed the first time he came here. It took him a conscious effort to break through the force fields she'd set up and search her desk and bookshelves. He looked inside every folder, every envelope. He searched her closets and her dresser, reaching down through socks and sweaters. Nowhere did he find anything remotely connected with Sweeting-Aldren, New England earthquakes, or injection wells.

He sat down on her bed and wondered if she'd thrown it all away. She'd thrown away her tapes and records, she'd thrown his own tapes and television and clothes into the hall, she'd thrown away a potential baby; maybe she'd thrown away their theory too.

He opened the drawer in her spavined maple nightstand. The last filled square on her calendar was Thursday's, where she'd written *NCHA 3pm*, and more faintly, in pencil in one corner, the number 48. There was a penciled 41 in the previous Thursday's square, a penciled 39 and the words *35 Federal, Salem, 6pm* in ink in the Tuesday before that, a penciled 35 and a Washington Street address in the Friday before that, and a penciled *H* the day before that. Stretching back into May were 27 days whose whiteness was disturbed only by penciled *L*'s. Then came six boxes in a row with penciled *X*'s and another *L*. Then six completely white days leading back to the last Saturday in April, where she had written *Party 8:30pm* in ink and penciled in a solitary *L*.

Altogether there were eighteen *L*'s. He'd never seen her making these notations. He wouldn't have been able to guess how many times they'd made love; now he didn't have to.

The Salem address he recognized as Henry Rudman's, but the Washington Street address meant nothing to him. He wrote it down on the Sheraton Baltimore notepad that she kept by her reading lamp. Then he put the calendar back in the drawer and smoothed the bedsheets where he'd been sitting.

It was nearly four o'clock before Howard Chun, sporting two black eyes and carrying a squash racket, came in to work at Hoffman Lab. Louis was waiting in the corridor by his office. He asked if Renée had mentioned that the Peabody earthquakes might have been induced by Sweeting-Aldren.

Howard unlocked his office and went inside. "Too deep," he said. "Injection wells are shallow."

"She found some papers that made it look like they drilled a really deep well in 1970."

"Cost too much to pump. Take too much pressure."

"Well, it was a theory she had. She was looking into it last month, and I want to know if she was looking into it last week. Because I think it might have been the company that shot her."

"You tell the police?"

"I don't want to unless I know she was looking into it."

Howard unlocked her desk and file cabinets, and Louis, to his unsurprise, found nothing. He crossed the hall to the system rooms, where Howard had logged on from several terminals. "Can I look in her computer accounts?"

"She never say anything," Howard said.

"I know, but she was working on it."

Howard logged on from yet another terminal, using Renée's name and password. "You see her yet?"

"No."

"She love you."

"Does she?"

Howard nodded. "Love love love love," he said, idly, as he employed a utility called XFILES. "These are text files she change or create since last backup, June 4. Far enough back?"

There were only six files—three brief letters to other scientists and three of her papers about Tonga. Louis scrolled through them all. "You're sure this is everything?"

"Everything that's here."

"Is it possible for someone else to get access to her accounts?"

"Too easy, yeah. Got a stupid operator password. Just 'OP.' Really stupid."

"I'm sorry I hit you. I was jealous of you."

"Love love love," Howard said.

An evening chill was creeping into the lobby of the building that the Washington Street address had led him to. The directory had a listing for the U.S. Environmental Protection Agency, but the night guard said to come back on Monday, because everyone had gone home.

"I have to see her," Louis said, on the telephone.

"Maybe on Monday," said Mrs. Seitchek, from her hotel room.

"I have to see her. When you go there in the morning, ask her if she thinks it might have been somebody from Sweeting-Aldren that . . . did it."

"Sweet 'n' what?"

"Sweeting-Aldren. The chemical company."

"Louis, I think you should be talking to the police, not me."

"Tell her I think it might have been Sweeting-Aldren. Will you just tell her that? She'll know if she wants to let the police know. It's not my decision."

"Something's going on here, and I think I have a right to know what it is."

"I'm going to give you my number, and I want you to tell her what I said."

It took him all of Saturday, in the earth sciences library up-stairs from the university's Peabody Museum, to track down and photocopy the handful of papers that Renée had started with six weeks ago. They were all there, however; they were all real. He reread the paper by A. F. Krasner, trying to smell the female mammal who'd composed it, but the prose, the very typeface, was old and withered.

The answering machine on Marlborough Street said: *Louis, this is Liz Seitchek. You may meet me at the surgical ICU at ten tomorrow morning.*

Channel 4's Penny Spanghorn said that Renée Seitchek was in serious but stable condition at Brigham & Women's Hospital. There had been statements of sympathy and outrage from NOW, Planned Parenthood, the mayor of Boston, and the president of Harvard. Police forces throughout the metro area were involved in the hunt for the assailant. The car driven by the assailant had been stolen from the Hertz rental-car lot at Logan Airport Thursday morning. There were no other strong leads.

The first-place Red Sox, meanwhile, were beginning a seven-game home stand at Fenway Park.

Eileen emerged from the master bedroom and looked at Louis mournfully. The king-sized bed behind her was covered with reference books and a supine Peter. Louis set down the orange juice he'd been drinking and put his arms around her. She squeezed him so hard it hurt. Then she gave him a plastic card and told him to go rent two movies.

"Breathe deeply?" the nurse said.

Renée breathed. Her face was drawn and heavily broken out and creased by the pain that existence in general and breathing in particular caused her. Her hair was matted and full of dandruff. She was hooked up to IV tubes but was breathing on her own. Her ears were naked.

"A little deeper?"

The effort was made.

"Let me hear you cough."

She coughed.

"You can lie back now." The nurse checked the bag of urine hanging from the bed and left her alone with Louis. Immediately he dropped to his knees and pressed her free hand, the hand without a tube in it, to his eyes. But Renée came straight to the point, in a weak, precise voice. "Mom says you think they did this to me."

He released her hand and pulled a chair over. "How are you?"

"Everything hurts." She frowned as if she didn't welcome the distraction of his question. "Why do you think it was them?"

"Because I couldn't find any of our papers in your apartment or your office."

"You were in my apartment."

"Uh, yeah."

She continued to frown unhappily. "It's in a big envelope," she said. "Manila envelope. In the big drawer in my desk."

"It's not. It's not there."

She devoted some attention to merely breathing. Thick bundles of unopened envelopes were stacked on the stand beside her pillows. "It was there," she said. "I know it was there."

"They knew you were interested?"

"It was so stupid of me . . . I didn't even care anymore."

"Did you tell anyone else?"

"No. But the computer at work. There's a letter and a paper."

"I don't think so. Howard and I checked."

Now she smiled with pain, all her teeth showing. "Oh boy."

"You'll have to tell the police."

"Oh boy, boy, will I tell them."

"Did you have a copy of the paper?"

She nodded. "On a little tape. A five-inch tape, in a drawer in the airconditioned room. The gray desk there."

"Is it labeled?"

"It's a tape I use. It says 'Do Not Erase.' Have Howard print it out for you. You can send it to the press. Larry Axelrod."

There was a silence. Her shallow breathing barely disturbed the sheet on her. "I really miss you," Louis said. "I really love you."

She stared at the ceiling; she still hadn't looked at him. He touched her hair, and the feel of it and the warmth of her scalp led him irresistibly to lean over her and kiss her mouth. Her lips were puffy and unmoving. They released a strong smell of medicine, an unRenée-like smell both harsh and cloying, akin to formaldehyde: the smell of the possibility, suddenly real, that she simply might never forgive him.

The white Matador lumbered into the Hoffman parking lot at one o'clock and ejected Howard from the driver's side. His hair was wet and he was obviously irritated. He'd been asleep when Louis called him, a little after noon.

"Her paper's on a tape," Louis said. "You have to help me print it out."

Howard let him into the building with an angry huff. "What tape."

"It says 'Do Not Erase.' "

Howard went to the system room and picked up a tape from the table with the consoles. "This tape?"

The label said *Do Not Erase* in Renée's handwriting. Howard huffed and threaded the tape onto a drive in the gelid inner sanctum and gave instructions from a console. He huffed some more. "Not it," he said. "This is Terry."

They searched both rooms for another five-inch tape that said *Do Not Erase*. Terry Snall came in and asked what they were looking for. " 'Do Not Erase'?" Alarm flickered in his face, very briefly, before he caught himself. "Oh, yeah. I just used it myself."

"Renée had something on it," Louis said.

"Well, not anymore," Terry answered with a little laugh.

"You mean you erased it?"

"And I'm not going to feel guilty."

"You erased the tape?"

"I'm not going to feel guilty," Terry said. "It didn't have a write-protect ring, it didn't have a name on it, and I know everybody's feeling sorry for Renée now, and it's a terrible thing, but the fact is that if she wants to go deleting other people's files without telling them she can hardly complain about me using an unmarked tape."

"You erased that tape? And then you go to the hospital and act like you're her boyfriend?"

"Don't wait for me to feel guilty," Terry said. "Because I'm not gonna."

Eileen and Peter's big bed had by this point in the weekend assumed the aspect of a houseboat. In addition to Eileen's banking texts and notebooks, it was stocked with *Esquire*s and *GQ*s for Peter, the remote-control box for their TV, a Walkman and scattered tapes, rumpled garments, Pepperidge Farm cookies, a big diet Coke bottle, and a quart-sized yogurt carton with carrot sticks floating in it. Louis declined Eileen's invitation to come aboard, preferring to sit by the door, next to Milton Friedman's cage, as he told his story.

At first, though Eileen listened with open-minded raptness, Peter continued to devote much of his attention to the Wimbledon highlights on the screen in front of him. But soon Eileen grew dulleyed with confusion and information overload, and it was Peter whose interest quickened. He turned the sound of tennis down and asked Louis questions in a sharp, impatient voice. Then he turned the TV off altogether and stared at the curtained window. The color had drained from his face.

"What is it?" Eileen said.

Peter turned to Louis. "The million gallons. When you guys came over that night and she was asking me about that. You already knew about the well then?"

"Yeah, we did."

"Why didn't you tell me?"

"Um. It was sort of my idea. I guess we didn't want your dad getting wind of it."

"My *dad?*" Peter plunged his hands into his hair. "Oh, that's great. That's just really fucking great."

"It seemed to make sense at the time," Louis said.

"I can't believe it. All you had to do was tell me, and none of this would have happened. Remember in January," Peter said to Eileen, "when Rita called me and I went out there?" He turned to Louis. "I hadn't seen her in about a year."

"She had that drinking problem," Eileen said.

"Anyway, she wanted to see me. She told me she was scared. And so I go out there, and the first thing I see is that two of her front windows are broken. And she shows me this bullet hole in her ceiling."

Eileen gaped at him. *"What?"*

Peter nodded, avoiding her eyes now. "Needless to say, she'd had a few too many. She was grabbing the furniture for balance. But the thing she wanted to tell me was that if anything 'happened' to her, I was supposed to tell the police it was the company. She gave me this spiel about how she's not happy with her pension plan, she's short on money, she's been trying to talk the company into giving her a better deal. Meaning blackmail. Because it just so happens that she knows what those guys are doing with all their nasty toxic waste. She says, 'They're not burning it, Peter. They say they are, but they're not. It's a million gallons a year, and they're not burning it.' And so I ask her what they *are* doing with it, but she won't tell me. She says, 'If I tell you, and he finds out, he's going to kill me.' That is exactly what she said. Exactly. And I say, Who's this 'he'? And she tells me it's my dad."

Eileen's lips formed a silent *What?*

"My own dad. She's telling me my own fucking dad shot the hell out of her living-room windows. And I don't even know whether to believe her. I mean, I'm willing to believe just about anything about the old man. But last I'd heard, she and I were sworn enemies because I wouldn't work for her anymore. So I said, you know, my dad may be a fascist pig, but he's not stupid. You can't tell me it was actually him that fired the gun. But she says, 'Thérèse saw the car. It was his car.' And I'm like, well, I don't really believe this, and so I tell her she'd better call the police. And she says, 'He's going to kill me if I go to the police.' Her exact words. And she says she doesn't want to die, because old Jack had told her what she was coming back in her next life as. He'd told her she was coming back as a cactus. And she didn't want to be a cactus and so she didn't want to die. You know, and she's crying and she can hardly stand up, and what can I do? I get the hell out of there. You know, file and forget."

A silence fell on the becalmed bed. Peter was shaking his head, his lips hanging open. Eileen's face was very dark. "You never told me this," she said in an ominously small voice. "You said she wanted you to help her with her new book."

"Yeah, I know. But what am I supposed to do? First of all, I didn't believe her. And second of all, she said he was going to kill her if she told anybody. You know? I was scared."

"You told Renée," Eileen insisted quietly, staring at the bedspread.

"Because Rita was already dead. The whole thing was moot. You know, and I still didn't even know if I should believe her. She had enemies in Ipswich, because of the pyramid. For all I knew, she'd made the whole thing up about my dad."

"But she didn't," Louis said.

"Right. And instead of her getting shot, it's Renée. And I tell you, it wasn't just some nobody that pulled the trigger. It was my own fucking dad."

"Please stop swearing," Eileen said.

Peter had swung his legs over the bed's gunwales and was pulling his Nikes on. "I don't know about you guys," he said, "but I'm going out there. Out there right this minute."

"Maybe we should let the police—"

"No way I'm going to miss this," Peter said. "I've been waiting half my life."

Eileen smiled nervously at Louis. "I guess we'll go out there."

"Guess so."

While Peter groomed in the bathroom, she filled Milton Friedman's water bottle. The gerbil was climbing the bars of its cage, loins and shoulders shuddering as it thrust its penis-like head into the freedom all around it. "I get so scared," she said to Louis. "He and his dad just *don't get along.*"

"Much to his own credit, apparently."

"You'll watch out for him?"

"Of course. He's your boyfriend."

She insisted that they ride in Louis's car, rather than let the angry Peter drive. Louis couldn't remember when he'd driven Eileen somewhere. Possibly he never had. Peter muttered and cursed in the back seat as they sliced through the light Sunday evening traffic on the Northeast Expressway, but the Hollands were silent.

Eileen seemed older after her week's work in the real world, seemed harder, graver, and physically larger, though if anything she'd lost weight. The hands resting on her lap had little softness anymore. They were hands to grip a mattress during sex, hands to spoon food into a baby's mouth, hands to sign contracts and run deep credit checks.

Exiting from Route 128 in Lynnfield, they left the daylight behind and entered a suburban twilight of shadowing trees, of still and bluely glowing lawns and fields and air untorn by any sound more violent than the swish of passing tires. Nature's appearance was inexpressibly benign here in the suburbs. She lay down and whispered like the warm surf between black-bottomed sea and parched land: between the scarred and mourning woods, and the city where a new nature had taken nature's place. Lawns freely gave away their smell of grass and earth, lay comfortably naked beneath a sky that could be trusted. Each house was like a mother, silent, set back from the roads with windows lit, as an object always welcoming and sheltering, but as a subject always betraying consciousness of the truth that children stop being children, that they'll leave and that an enclosure that welcomes and shelters will ache with their absence, will have ached all along because it's an object.

Eileen directed Louis to a street with only six houses on it, the largest of them belonging to the Stoorhuyses. Peter led them in through the front door. The Stoorhuys living room was a long, low-ceilinged, formal room whose native face was masked by heavy floral drapes and fifteen or twenty bad oil paintings in ornate gilded frames. The paintings were all of European cities—rain-slicked cobblestones, shuttered hotels and scabrous palaces in the dusky colors of ancient clothing, all the reds maroons, all the yellows umbers, all the whites streaked and crusted like guano; there were no people in this Europe.

Floral patterns held sway in the Stoorhuys kitchen. Little nose-gays grew like mildew on the chair cushions and the wallpaper, the quilted food-processor and mixer cozies, the stoneware plates and bowls, the enamel lids for the stove elements, and the crocks of flour and sugar and coffee. One of Peter's sisters, a slender, diffident, homely blonde in collegiate summer fashions, was making popcorn in the microwave. In the adjacent family room, the elder

Stoorhuyses were sitting in the glow and squawk of Murder, She Wrote.

Eileen introduced Louis to the diffident Sarah and then to Peter's mother, who had risen to greet the visitors. She was a tall, gentle woman with an unabashedly ruined face and too-long hair. Louis shook her hand quickly before he followed Peter into the family room. When Peter switched off the TV and turned to face his father, Louis touched the power switch himself and likewise turned, standing at Peter's side like a second.

Mr. Stoorhuys was sprawled on a leather sofa. He wore a white Ferdinand Marcos shirt with a huge tab collar. "You want to turn that back on, Pete?"

"Peter, we were watching," said Mrs. Stoorhuys from the doorway.

"I think Dad's got something to say to us," Peter said. "Don't you, Dad."

Stoorhuys looked up guardedly, trying to fathom the connection between his son and Louis. "Not that I know of," he said.

"Nothing about Renée Seitchek?"

"Oh, that poor girl," said Mrs. Stoorhuys.

"She's Louis's girlfriend," Eileen said. She had sat down in a rocker and was sightlessly turning the pages of a coffee-table book called *Colourful St. Kitts*.

"She's your girlfriend?" Mrs. Stoorhuys was stricken. "What a terrible thing!"

"Yeah, it is terrible," Peter said as Louis tried, without success, to pin Stoorhuys with a stare. "Isn't it, Dad? Somebody shoots her in the back and then blames it on somebody else. It's a goddamn shame she didn't die, isn't it? Then nobody knows all her papers disappeared."

The corn popping in the kitchen sounded like muffled gunfire. Stoorhuys had opened an *Architectural Digest* on the sofa and was stroking his bushy forelock, trying to subdue it. "You've lost me, Pete."

"Her papers," Peter said. "The papers that show whose fault the earthquakes are. She's told the police, Dad. They're going to be heading for Peabody any minute."

"Peter, what are you talking about?" his mother said.

"It was an accident, right, Dad? You just wanted to scare her. Fire a few shots over her head. But then, what the hell. There she is. Just, just—kill her then, right? Why not just kill her?"

Peter was shaking so much that his elbow bumped Louis's. Stoorhuys turned a page of his magazine, his jaw rigid as he pretended to read. "I don't know what you're talking about."

"Oh yeah? Watch him, Ma. He's got a phone call he wants to make. Just watch. I guarantee you he's going to get on the phone. Or he's going to have to go out for a minute. He's going to wait till you're not looking, or he's going to get up in the night. He's going to go to Peabody, or he's going to run for his life."

Stoorhuys shook his head, as if with deep sadness, and said nothing. But his face was covered with sweat and his hands were trembling.

"David," Mrs. Stoorhuys said. "What's he talking about?"

"I don't know," he said. "It's just more of the same. He's good, I'm bad. He's smart, I'm stupid."

"You're damn right," Peter said. "Or am I the one that's pumping toxic waste underground? And causing earthquakes?"

"It's a lie."

"A lie? His girlfriend's in the hospital—" Peter nodded at Louis, who continued to stare implacably at Stoorhuys— "and she didn't think it was a lie. And everything she had that proved it's true got stolen the day she was shot. You're saying that's a lie?"

Stoorhuys paged back through his magazine, studying the photographs. "I don't know anything about this."

"Watch him, Ma. Watch him make the phone call. He's got to make that phone call."

Mrs. Stoorhuys wasn't listening. She was massaging her collarbone and looking as if the ficus tree at her feet were about to make her cry.

"If somebody's slandering us," Stoorhuys said, "I'll have to let the company know. But that doesn't—"

"Right, the company, the company. That's what counts, isn't it, Dad? Who cares about Ma? She's just a person. It's the company—"

"The company that paid for your education!" Stoorhuys

jumped from the sofa and advanced on his son. "The company that straightened your teeth! That put food on your plate and clothes on your back for twenty years!"

"Straightened my *teeth?* My God, you think we're living in *Charlestown?* You think you're making thirty grand a year?"

As quickly as he'd heated up, Stoorhuys cooled off again. He sighed and chose, for some reason, to address Louis. "You see what I get at home?" he said. "You see the thanks I get?"

Louis wore an expression of the utmost seriousness and did not reply. He watched as the older man picked up a seersucker jacket from the back of the sofa, patted the keys in one of its pockets, and inserted his bony arms in its sleeves. "Janet, I have to go to the office for a little while. I'm sure there's a simple explanation for all this."

Although Mrs. Stoorhuys nodded, it was a long time before she raised her eyes from the ficus tree; and then she looked at her husband as if she hadn't heard him speak. "David," she said. "I've never made any trouble for you about your work. I've never . . . pressed you. I've never asked you questions that I . . . could have asked you. But you have to tell me now. You didn't really have anything to do with—that girl's . . . ? That's all I want to know. You just have to tell me that."

The fragility of her poise, the tremor in her voice, made even Louis squirm. Stoorhuys himself balled his fists and looked around the room for some inanimate object to vent his feelings on. His glance fell on Peter. He smiled bitterly. "You see what you've done, Pete? You satisfied now? Now that she's on your side?"

"I'm asking you a question," Mrs. Stoorhuys said. "I want you to answer it. I've never asked you questions, but I think I have a right to ask you about this—"

"Oh, you do, do you?" Stoorhuys said, flashing fury. "Well, maybe you're a little late. Maybe you're about twenty years too late." Again, he turned to Louis. "Twenty years ago I got a raise that almost doubled our income overnight. And when I told her about it, do you know what she asked me?"

"*I have a right to ask now*," she said.

"You know what she asked me?" He moved closer to Louis,

smiling a little, preparing the punch line. "She asked me if we could get a house where the kids could all have their own rooms. And that was it. That was the extent of her curiosity."

"Why was it up to me to ask? You could have told me!"

Stoorhuys ignored her, continuing to speak only to Louis. "I would have quit the job if she'd asked me one question about it then. I was ready to quit. One question would have done it. But you see, I didn't even matter. Even then, I didn't matter. As long as the kids all had their own—"

"Peter. Have I been a good mother? Have I been a good mother to you?"

"Twenty years," Stoorhuys said. "Twenty years, and she decides to ask me *now*. She could have asked me a week ago, a month ago, a year ago. But for twenty years, day after day—! She has no right to ask me questions now. And Peter has no right to blame this all on me. He's not neutral. You have to understand what it's like with her. I hear her on the phone with him, I hear her asking him about his work and giving him advice, and telling him what to do. But *never* a word, *never* a word about *my* work. My work that has given her everything she's got."

"It was better not to—"

He spun around and shouted in her face. "Never a word!" She put her hands in the air and let them hover an inch from her ears. "Never a word! You made your choice, you chose the children, and now you think you have the right to ask me *questions?* And *blame* me? Who do you think has gotten the benefit of those twenty years? You think it's me? You think I haven't made a few sacrifices myself? Janet—and Peter, you listen to me too—Janet, I have been a better husband than you will ever know. Than you will ever know."

Louis could see it now, how if this man had had a gun in his hand and a woman in front of him, he might have killed her. Everyone could see it now. Mrs. Stoorhuys buried her face in her hands. As Peter moved to comfort her, she twisted away and ran from the room.

Peter ran after her. "Ma—"

They heard her stumbling on the stairs and Peter shouting, "Ma!"

Louis and Eileen watched Stoorhuys take his car keys from his pocket.

"So you shot her?" Louis said casually.

Stoorhuys looked up at him, surprised. It was as if he hadn't really registered Louis's face until this moment. "I don't even know you," he said, leaving the room.

A silence fell. Eileen rocked in her chair and turned a page of *Colourful St. Kitts*.

"Boy," Louis said.

"Isn't it awful?"

"Everybody who's had anything to do with that company is basically damned, including me."

"I'll take care of you. You be my baby."

"Yeah, well. I don't know about that."

Peter returned to the kitchen smoking a cigarette. He poured an inch of scotch into a glass and held the liter-and-a-half bottle up so Eileen and Louis could see it from the family room.

"Yes please," they said.

They sat and drank and sweated on the deck by the swimming pool, where the exhaust from Peter's father's Porsche was hanging in the air. The blower of the Stoorhuyses' central airconditioning unit took a break, and Eileen removed her shoes and dipped her legs in the pool. "What's going to happen?" she said.

Louis listened to the crickets and to the pipping of a bat. "Investigation," he said. "Big stink in the press. Maybe there'll be some lawsuits. If we're lucky, we can eventually forget it."

Peter spoke from the end of the diving board where he was sitting. "He as much as admitted he pulled the trigger. And how do you live with that? Was I supposed to call the cops? Tie him down?"

One by one the lights in the upstairs bedrooms were extinguished. The airconditioner came on again. Went off, came on, and Louis wondered if he might simply die the next time its white noise ceased. Eileen was swimming slow laps, on her back, in her bra and underpants. Peter could have been a corpse stretched out on the diving board. Louis focused his consciousness on the sound of the airconditioner, trying to anticipate the instant of cessation, trying to greet this little death with open eyes. What he heard instead, at length, was false morning. Not just a bird or two awakening, but hundreds of them, and the yelping of a neighbor's dog.

He stumbled out of his chair, not knowing what to do. "Here one comes," he said.

Eileen let her legs sink to the floor of the pool, at the shallow end. She shook water from her ear. "What?"

It began so gradually, as such a gentle cradling of himself in immense and invisible hands, that he couldn't have said where the line was, where no-motion had given way to the welling spreading deepening feeling that enveloped them. For one moment, it really was like coming; it felt like the best thing he could ever feel.

Then something extremely serious happened, comparable in his experience only to the high-speed collision he'd witnessed on Lake Forest Road on one of his radio-parts-buying expeditions in high school, when the monotonous afternoon to-and-fro of suburban traffic jumped the track of the ordinary, and even a quarter mile away he could feel the impact in his bones, the noise of instant death filling the sky like a flash of lightning, the squealings, the screechings, the subsidiary bangs each more major than a fender bender, and every person in sight began to run, terrified, in all directions: it was with the same kind of impact, the same awful sense of the world's derailment, the same strident and thundering protest of rigid materials deforming that the earth now shuddered and erupted and windows exploded and flowerpots flew.

Peter was tossed into the water splayed bizarrely, like a thrown cat. A wind that Louis couldn't feel whipped the trees. He fell down and two pieces of deck furniture roughed him up, stepping on his fingers with their metal feet, jabbing his ribs with metal elbows. He heard himself shouting *Oh, come on, STUPID STUPID* and heard Eileen screaming like some shipwreck victim far below him, in the thundering surf at the base of cliffs. The back yard seemed to be sinking into the earth's adipose layer of humus and glacial till, the encircling treetops lurching towards a meeting as the country's skin dimpled in upon itself. Birds filled the air, wheeling frantically, spreading chaos. The lights went out and the stars turned blurry. The ground hit Louis like the hard bed of a truck with no brakes on a rutted downhill road. He was scared, but mostly he was mad at the ground, at its meanness. He wanted it to stop, and when it did stop, finally, he got up and kicked it furiously.

Eileen and Peter were standing in the shallow end of the pool, mouths hanging open to facilitate rapid air intake. They stared at him as if they barely recognized him. He kicked the ground again and looked at the dark house and transformed yard and muttered, "What a mess."

16

—Ⅿⱽⱽⱽⱽⱽⱳⱳⱳⱳ

Mrs. Stoorhuys was handing out gas masks in the kitchen. She wore duck boots and a raincoat.

The kitchen appeared to have been ransacked by a burglar in search of hidden sterling. Sarah kept a trembling flashlight beam on the carton of emergency equipment while another daughter, a somewhat younger one, ran her beam over the mounds of broken floral-print dishes, the yawning cabinets, and the gleaming barf the refrigerator had spewed—a dirty surf of ketchup and cocktail cherries and applesauce breaking on reefs of pointed glass. Few colors withstood the whiteness of the flashlight.

"Peter, help your sisters with their masks."

"He's shutting off the gas," Sarah reminded her.

"We don't *need* any help," her sister added.

"Uh, are these really necessary?" Louis said.

Mrs. Stoorhuys handed him a mask. "It says, masks are to be used if the earthquake is big enough to throw most objects from kitchen cabinets." She was reading from a typewritten list of instructions in the carton. "When in doubt, use the masks. —Here's a flashlight for you too. There's eight of everything."

The mask was a shiny black plastic affair whose heavy nose made it flop animately. Peter's sisters had put theirs on now and looked like evil hockey goalies or Satan's henchgirls. Goya had drawn heads like these, towards the end.

"Now, which way is the wind blowing?" Mrs. Stoorhuys said.

"There isn't any wind," Louis said.

"Oh, huh." She consulted a chart in her instructions. "Night-time . . . summer . . . calm . . . Yes, here. Proceed north to Haverhill or beyond."

Peter came inside with a big crescent wrench, limping as he picked his way through stricken appliances and furniture. He'd twisted his hip. Nobody else was complaining of more than scrapes and bruises. "Peter, here's your gas mask," his mother said.

"Gas mask?"

"Gas mask," Louis confirmed.

"Your father left instructions in the earthquake box."

Peter looked at Louis, and they nodded significantly.

"Now, somewhere there's supposed to be a gun . . ."

"Ma, did you know there were gas masks in this box?"

"Oh, yes."

"Didn't it kind of make you wonder what was going on over there in Peabody? I mean, that we've got to have these? Didn't it make you worry?"

"He said it's just in case the worst thing happens, which it probably won't. You know how ultra-safe he likes to be."

"No way I'm going to wear this thing," Peter said.

"Think of it as a fashion," Louis said.

"I can't seem to find the gun," said Mrs. Stoorhuys, rooting.

Again Peter and Louis looked at each other and nodded.

"Where do you suppose it is?"

"Better not to ask, Ma."

"Bottom of a river is my guess," Louis said.

Eileen stumbled in through the skewed back door in the jeans and snow boots Peter had found for her to wear. She was breathing heavily. "There's fires," she said. "I can smell the smoke."

"Try one of these," Louis said. "You won't smell a thing. —Or kind of a pleasant, plastic smell."

Her eyes widened. "Yuck! What for?"

"Company orders. Put it on."

She took it in two fingers and held it up like some contaminated fish or hideous accessory.

"It snaps in back," Louis said.

"I was wondering about Mom," she said. "I think we should go up there."

"No, we're going to Haverhill," said Mrs. Stoorhuys, burying her face in black plastic.

"We'll go through Ipswich," Peter said.

"Not to be a wet blanket," Louis said, "but isn't there like a nuclear power plant in that direction?"

"Oh, Seabrook," Eileen said, her face falling.

"Let's get to Ipswich and see what the radio says," Peter said.

Mrs. Stoorhuys distributed more supplies to her troops—hard hats, jerry cans of water, Saltines, cans of Spam, a transistor radio, a heavy-duty first-aid kit. At the bottom of the carton were a pair of large self-adhesive placards with the words LOOTERS BEWARE! and a skull and crossbones. Louis was dispatched to post one of them on the front door.

Despite the glass and fallen paintings and general mayhem, the front of the house retained an air of comfort. It was a matter, perhaps, of the deep-pile carpeting. Europe was in ruins, however, palaces crazily tilted, empty streets dumped rudely onto sofa cushions.

An enormous truck rumbled by. Debris pelted Louis and he heard shouts and screams so clear and automatic they sounded canned. He stumbled under the impact of a good-sized chunk of plaster that landed squarely on his hard hat, but the floor was already regaining its composure, and he thought, well, it was nice of David Stoorhuys to provide him with a hard hat.

In his haste, an hour earlier, Stoorhuys had also left the garage door open. It had fallen on the remaining station wagon, denting the roof but breaking only the rear window. Peter was able to back the car out while everyone else held one side of the heavy door aloft. Communication was impaired by the plastic of their masks.

At first glance, the Stoorhuyses' street looked like any suburban street in the middle of a warm moonless night, the trees and shrubbery and lawns and pavement all undisturbed and the houses still standing. It took a while for the subtler alterations to register, the slight forward pitch of a house seemingly frozen in a sudden lurch of nausea, the semi-imploded outline of a screen porch that wanted to collapse but couldn't, the buckled aluminum siding, the glimmer of glass in the mulch and euonymus beneath windows. The triple-door garage silently bleeding a sheet of water down a driveway to the street. The swamp-gas flickerings in rooms where unseen families were using flashlights. It was as if the land were still healthy but the houses had all suddenly died of some internal sickness.

Meanwhile the smell of car exhaust which was the smell of life in America was the reassurance that nothing too serious had happened. Four Stoorhuyses sat patiently in their wagon in their hard hats and expressionless masks while Eileen hugged Louis and said be careful. He hadn't had to tell her that he was going back to the hospital in Boston; she'd assumed it.

In his car, when they were gone, he turned on the radio. There was dead air on the frequency where WRKO had been, and he spun the dial until he found a signal, a faint one.

"... *his first three at-bats and had a chance to tie or break the major-league record of four homers in a game, but instead wound up on the disabled list with a strained right knee he suffered making a diving catch in the fifth inning. Was he disappointed? 'Sure, you know, I would have liked two more shots at the record book, who wouldn't. But the important thing is the team, we haven't been playing too good the last couple months. I just want to go out there and contribute every day.' Over in the National League today the Cubs did it again, 7 to 5 over the Reds in ten innings, Atlanta edged Pittsburgh 3–2, Houston blanked the Cards 8–zip, Dodgers 4 to 2 over the Phillies, Mets 6 Giants 1, and out in San Diego the Pods and Expos are having a wild one, they're now in the bottom of the eighteenth! inning, all even at thirteen. WGN News time is twenty-five minutes past eleven. Men, are you at the age where you're afraid to comb your hair because more hair stays in the comb than on your head?*"

WGN was Chicago. Chicago, place of stable ground. Louis started the engine and eased the car down the empty street, moving his head constantly to compensate for his limited peripheral vision.

"*We're going to begin continuous live coverage of the earthquake just as soon as we've established links with one of our affiliates. The quake was felt throughout the Northeast, with no reports of damage or injury as of yet. The epicenter was apparently near Boston, and much of eastern Massachusetts is currently without electricity or telephone service, but we are in communication with our network affiliate in Boston and will be hearing from them in just a few moments. First a message from Schaumburg Honda."*

The dial was alive with distant stations, Buffalo, St. Louis, Miami, Lincoln. They emerged like the stars when the city lights go out and the universe can suddenly pull rank. In Quebec the talk was of *le tremblement de terre*, which everyone there had evidently felt. There was cracked plaster in Hartford, station switchboards lighting up in Manhattan, an unconfirmed report of injuries in Worcester. Boston's WEEI, broadcasting at less than full strength, said damage was comparatively light in the center city. A fire was raging in South Boston and a reporter on the scene said at least a dozen people had been injured, but Dorchester and Roxbury and other areas farther south still had electricity and phone service. In the suburbs well to the north of Boston, an ominous silence prevailed. A teenaged amateur radio operator in Salem said that several brick buildings had collapsed in her neighborhood, and that water pressure was very low. She could see the light of what appeared to be a major fire to the northwest, in Peabody or Danvers. At the same time, all the houses on her own street were standing and no one appeared to have been seriously hurt. The National Earthquake Information Center had released a preliminary magnitude estimate of 6.0 with an epicenter in eastern Essex County. The pilot of a private jet had spotted a large fire on the western bank of the Danvers River and smaller blazes in downtown Beverly. There was an unconfirmed report from Portsmouth, New Hampshire, that an emergency shutdown of the Seabrook nuclear power plant was proceeding normally, which the WEEI anchor said could not be right because Seabrook had been closed since mid-May for safety improvements . . .

He turned off the radio. The lawns and woods on either side of him were dark, dark. A flashing ambulance appeared in his mirrors and expanded, its tires throwing up a spray of sandy water as it passed him. He had to close his window, and for a moment, in the sudden hush, he couldn't remember the season or the hour; whether it was maybe early on an autumn evening? An ambulance passing him on a chilly, rain-soaked road? It felt like autumn and there was little in his head to persuade him otherwise. If only the road were less dark, or less straight, or if he could see a little better . . .

Sweeting-Aldren had manufactured the Warning Orange pigment in the hazard cones blocking the entrance ramps to Route 128 and in the jackets of the patrolmen standing on the overpass, where apparently one of the spans had lost its footing. A Highway Department truck's butterscotch-colored lights were pulsing in the humid air. "What a mess," Louis said as he turned down a dark street that paralleled the expressway. His mask was beginning to make his face itch.

He had followed the street for maybe half a mile, past cavities of blackness that he took to be front lawns, when his headlights caught a flash of something wrong in the underbrush to his left— the exposed white flesh of trees with freshly broken limbs, and a car-like shape in an uncar-like position. He slowed and made a U-turn, angling his high-beams to light the scene.

The something was indeed a car. Its tires were pointed at the sky and the passenger compartment was flattened and buried in mud and shrubs and tree litter at the foot of Route 128's elevated grade. Broken scrub maples and torn earth marked the trajectory the car had taken in its plunge from the expressway. Louis left his engine running and pushed his way through weeds and branches to the wreck. Only the parts of the car lit by his headlights, the creased metal and contorted chassis, made any sense; there was a pregnant, dark confusion at his feet, and in the middle of it, dimly, he saw the figure of a man. The body was intact but had flowed halfway out the open driver-side window, hands first, hands bending as the arms flowed onto them, arms bending as head and torso came to rest on them. The body's angles were like a dancer's when the dancer touches his limp curled hands to his face and hugs his elbows to his chest and bends his head to evoke tenderness or mourning or submission. The man had a thick neck and wore a cheap pink dress shirt and had possibly never once been so expressive with his body while he lived, his posture never so eloquent of anything as it was now of death; because it was totally evident that he was dead.

There was no traffic on the highway above. Louis stumbled around to the other side of the car, moaning a little with self-pity, and made sure there'd been no passengers. Now that he couldn't see the man he didn't believe so absolutely that he was dead. He returned to him and knelt and touched his neck. The skin was cool. He shoved gently and the head twisted forward. He took his hand away. He could hear voices, male and female, from the lawns across the road, and he ran to say what he had to say, which was that a man was dead.

Peter's sisters were complaining about their gas masks. They said they felt stupid wearing them. They pointed out that nobody else, none of the cops and bystanders they'd passed in Lynnfield Center and Middleton, was wearing a mask.

"Keep them on," said Peter, driving. "Your livers will thank you for it."

Eileen had leaned her tired, laden head against her back-seat window and was letting her eyes open and close on the dark blur of exurb they were passing through. She could have slept if Peter hadn't kept braking for real or suspected hazards—snapped power lines, flooded low spots in the road, and curves that looked at first like fault scarps. She let her body swing however it wanted to, let her masked face press into the glass as the car bounced and banked. It had always been comforting for her to keep on riding and riding without stopping, and it was especially comforting now to be rocked very long and very gently, to have it be the car and not the ground. She watched the alternating woods and settlements and fields. There was a vapor plume on the southern horizon, rising from a point many miles away. She saw it and then she didn't for a long time, and then another southern vista opened up and she saw it again, a fist of gray gas punching the black belly of the sky, its billowy knuckles glowing orange. It evolved like a normal cloud in a normal sky, appearing stationary if she stared but changing if she didn't. At first it was a puffy exclamation point listing to the left, and then more trees blocked her view, and then it had buckled and sagged into a question mark. Her eyes kept falling shut as motion lulled her. She recognized the sounds in the car as words spoken by Peter and his family and the radio announcer, but even the minimal effort of understanding them was beyond her. The plume stayed the same size, growing larger as the road carried her away from it. She didn't say anything. She was almost asleep now and she was afraid that if the others saw the plume it would stop being just a thing in her head and become real.

A family was clustered around a pickup truck, listening to the radio in the light of a Coleman lantern on the hood. There were two young couples, an older couple, and a baby. The older woman saw Louis coming in his gas mask and gaped at him. He said there was a dead person across the street.

Now everyone was gaping at him. "Is . . . something wrong?"

"Uh, yeah," he said. "I guess there's some concern about the chemical plant in Peabody."

He'd known he had to tell them, but he wasn't sure if it was a mistake. The family began to shout questions at him two and three at a time. He tried to bring the discussion back to the dead man across the street, but before he knew it he was left standing alone in the driveway while people hurried away in all directions, some disappearing into the house, others running off to tell the neighbors.

The radio said: *There are reports now of at least eighteen people dead, most of them in Essex County. This figure is certain to rise, and it's a good guess that there have been scores if not hundreds of injuries in what is clearly the worst natural tragedy ever to strike the Boston area.*

"Do you need a ride?" the older woman asked Louis. She and her husband were stowing plastic Star Market bags of food and bottles of water in the bay of the truck.

"No . . ." Louis gestured vaguely. "Thanks anyway."

"Might as well get going, huh?"

"Yeah, although . . ." He nodded at the street.

"Forget about him."

He trudged down the driveway and pushed through the brush and poison ivy and stood quietly by the overturned car, looking down at this faceless victim who had become his. Word of a possible chemical leak was leaking up and down the street. More and more engines were starting, and again the earth was trembling.

Eileen woke up when the car stopped on the gravel drive in front of her mother's house. She took off her mask and followed Peter as he limped towards the front door. An emergency light in the living room, installed to foil burglars, lit the smithereens of a major trashing—the shuffled furniture, the cratered walls. The sky's darkness had grown waxy, as if night had grown tired of being night and was reconsidering. Peter knocked on the door. Eileen heard a radio voice outside somewhere and went around the side of the house.

Her mother was sitting in an Adirondack chair halfway down the wide lawn that sloped away from the eastern wing. On the grass beside her were a silver ice bucket and a boom box playing news. She was drinking champagne from a fluted glass.

"Are you OK?" Eileen said.

"Eileen." Melanie swung her head around loosely. "You're fine. I knew you would be fine. Everything is fine."

. . . raging unchecked at this hour at their facility in Peabody. We have no official word yet, but residents who have not already left the surrounding communities should consider staying indoors with their windows shut tightly and their airconditioners off.

"You're OK?" Eileen said.

Melanie drained her glass and held it aloft. "I am triumphant!" she said. "Triumphant!"

. . . structural damage, and the major arteries are jammed. From what I can see here, it appears that fire fighters are making no attempt to enter the installation. There is a . . . choking . . . harsh . . . smoke in the air, and I'm sure the fire chief is concerned for the safety of his men.

"How is she?" Peter said, also maskless.

Eileen rolled her eyes and turned away. "Triumphant."

"Hi, Mrs. Holland."

"Hello, Peter." Melanie emptied the last drops of champagne into her glass and returned the bottle to the bucket upside down. "Tell me how your family is. Are they all fine?"

Eileen heard a loud hiccup as she started back up the hill. She couldn't remember ever missing Louis, but she missed him now.

"Eileen, honey, there's more champagne in the refrigerator, you can offer it to Peter's family. Peter, bring some chairs down. There are snacks there too, Eileen. You'll see them."

Mrs. Stoorhuys was still wearing her mask. She stopped by Eileen on the dew-slicked grass. "How is she?"

"Oh, she's great," Eileen said.

"Such a lovely woman. Such a lovely house." Janet tiptoed down the hill and touched Melanie on the shoulder. "Melanie?"

Melanie looked up at her and screamed. The radio was barking about the fire in Peabody. Eileen lay down on the grass and fell asleep.

How long it took to get from Philadelphia to Pittsburgh when you were living in the black. How long it took even to get from Lynnfield to the Fens of Boston when the expressways were closed and the power was out. Louis figured that he and his Civic were averaging about the speed of a cantering horse as they nosed south through Wakefield, Stoneham, Melrose. He stopped to consult his map, he stopped at damaged bridges and had to circumvent. He stopped and helped a Cambodian man get his rust-blasted Gremlin out of a ditch and on the road to Peabody, where his wife and children were. He gave the man his gas mask when they parted.

The streets with their curbs and sidewalks and sewer holes were not anchored to the ground. Ten Melrose firemen walked away from an extinguished blaze with the easy gait of people leaving church, their backs to the black timbers that had risen victoriously from the earth. A library building had been incontinent of bricks, and the proximity of strong motion, the radiant and lingering randomness of it all, changed the rubble's stillness from an elementary quality into a kind of pain, an immanence.

The eighteenth century haunted the unfathomable side streets, so latent in the darkness that Louis almost expected to hear the thud of horse hooves in the mud. He saw how black the nights must have been in a town center two hundred years ago, before there were gaslights and long before the insomnia of the current age had spread insomniac hallucinations in strips along the edges of its towns and made the outdoors indoors: how the buildings themselves must have rested, as sightless and dead-seeming as the people asleep inside them. How scary and pretty those nights must have been. How they must have made some kind of true repose and true solitude a possibility.

But that age was only an echo now, dying if you tried to come too close, and wherever he passed people—they weren't in the business districts or at the malls but on the residential streets—they were glued to automobiles with lights and radios and engines running, and he could not deny that these little tableaux, repeated innumerable times as he proceeded south, were the only things he saw all night that felt bona fide. The stationary headlights drove beams of reality through the supposed fact of the earthquake and lit up patches of the real foliage and real houses that were indifferently surviving the darkness. And the radio, though he kept his own unit mainly off, was the voice of his own age, the one voice in the night he understood. The broken windows and dangling wires and ambulances and injured faces looming up in the night were meaningless. Meaningless because he could look at them and somehow feel no vengefulness, none at all. Not even by the expressway back in Lynnfield, as he'd stood by the first dead person he'd ever seen, had there been any room in his heart for anger. He couldn't connect the earthquake-killed thing at his feet to any actions within a scheme of right and wrong, couldn't bring himself to think: the company is responsible for this and they must pay. And yet how could you believe in responsibility if responsibility had limits? How could an earthquake caused by the cupidity and faithlessness of real individual men nonetheless become purely an act of God, with an act of God's windy inhuman vacuity? Remembering the dead man's crumpled arms and cradled head, he wasn't even able to feel horror. The body now seemed like the purse-snatchings he'd witnessed in Chicago, or like the tattered man he'd once seen lying with his pants down jerking off in the bushes of Hermann Park in Houston, an image as unreal as everything else about this earthquake, as unreal as war reportage or assassination footage on television, except that unreality wasn't quite the word either for what he'd felt there, standing in poison ivy in the last decade of the twentieth century, surrounded by aftermath and wondering why he lived and what a world that encompassed death was really made of. The word was mystery.

He was traveling a parkway in Everett or Medford (he wasn't exactly sure which) when lights came on and it became apparent that the city and the inner suburbs were far from fully wrecked. A number of houses had dropped to their knees or lost walls, but even the worst streets looked better than an average ghetto block. Irish youths were milling on the roof of a ball-field dugout, drinking beer. Children were playing in the restored light the way children of the desert play in rainstorms. He let himself relax a little, and immediately felt sick with exhaustion and the abject regret that staying up all night had always caused him.

The sky was pink and yellow when he reached Back Bay. Unreality still adhered to the various fixtures from which destruction had emanated—to the buckled sidewalk, to the wet crack angling across Marlborough Street, to the loose bricks and cast concrete finials and chunks of masonry that lay on the grass or pavement with pointed, disingenuous motionlessness, as if hoping to pass as fragments of a Roman temple or boulders at the bottom of a cliff, things that hadn't budged in centuries. Eileen and Peter's building, however, was standing just the way Louis had left it.

At Brigham & Women's a few stragglers, most of them old, sat unmoving outside the emergency room, trying just to be objects until a doctor could turn them back into people with testimony, stories. Broken bottles and fallen tiles had been swept into tidy heaps, and the nurses were brisk and unpanicked. A familiar one sent Louis to the bed where Renée, he saw, was sleeping.

17

All Monday, all Tuesday, the earthquake held the country hostage. Giant headlines marching in lockstep like fascist troops booted everything else off the face of front pages, and in the afternoon people trying to watch soap operas were subjected to special reports instead. Major-league baseball canceled two nights' worth of games in case fans had any ideas of taking refuge from the news in balls and strikes. Even the Vice President was forced to cut short his swing through Central American capitals and fly to Boston.

It's not pleasant to be held hostage; it's not just a figure of speech. In a decadent society people can slowly drift or slowly be drawn by the culture of commerce into yearning for violence. Maybe people have a deep congenital awareness that no civilization lasts forever, that the most peaceful prosperity will someday have to end, or maybe it's just human nature. But war can begin to seem like a well-earned fireworks display, and a serial killer (as long as he's in a distant city) like a man to root for. A decadent society teaches people to enjoy advertisements of violence against women, any suggestion of the yanking down of women's bra straps and the seizing of their breasts, the raping of women, the tying up of women's limbs with rope, the puncturing of women's bellies, the hearing of their screams. But then some actual woman they know gets abducted and raped and not only fails to enjoy it but becomes angry or injured for a lifetime, and suddenly they are hostages to her experience. They feel sick with constriction, because all those sexy images and hints have long since become bridges to span the emptiness of their days.

And now the disaster which had been promising to make you feel that you lived in a special time, a real time, a time of the kind you read about in history books, a time of suffering and death and heroism, a time that you'd remember as easily as you'd forget all those years in which you'd done little but futilely pursue sex and romance through your purchases: now a disaster of these historic proportions had come, and now you knew it wasn't what you'd wanted either. Not this endless endless televised repetition of clichés and earnest furrowings of reportorial brows, not these nightmare faces of anchorpeople in pancake staring at you hour after hour. Not this footage of the same few bloody bodies on stretchers. Not this sickening proliferation of identical newspaper articles running identical interviews with survivors who said it was scary and identical statements from scientists who said it was not well understood. Not these photos of buildings that were damaged but not obliterated. Not this same vision, over and over, of the smoking ruin in Peabody on which an ordinary morning sun shone because the sun still rose because the world wasn't changed because your life wasn't changed. You would have preferred the more honest meaninglessness of a World Series, the entertainment of an event towards which months of expectation and weeks of hype could build, bridging a summer and fall's emptiness and producing, in conclusion, an entirely portable set of numbers which the media couldn't rub your face in for more than about an hour. Because you could see now that the earthquake was neither history nor entertainment. It was simply an unusually awful mess. And although the earthquake too could be reduced to a score—injuries 1,300, deaths 71, magnitude 6.1—it was the kind of score that your righteous captors felt justified in repeating until you went insane and dissolved in screams which they, however, behind their microphones and computer monitors, didn't hear.

The picture that made Monday evening's front pages around the world showed the ruins of Sweeting-Aldren's facilities in Peabody. Twenty-three of the deaths and 110 of the injuries had been suffered by company employees caught in the initial explosion of two process lines and the ensuing general conflagration. The earth-

quake had disabled various fire-control systems, and balls of com-
busting ethylene and sheets of flaming benzene had ignited storage
tanks. A blast apparently caused by ammonium nitrate leveled
process lines that otherwise might not have burned. White clouds
rained nitric acid and hydrochloric acid and organic reagents, the
hydrocarbons and halogens combining in an environment as high-
temperature and low-pH as the surface of Venus, but considerably
more toxic. Cooling and drifting, the vapor plume descended on
residential neighborhoods and left a whitish, oily residue on everything it touched.

By Monday afternoon EPA officials in Mylar suits were mea-
suring dioxin levels in the parts-per-hundred-thousand on streets
immediately to the north of the installation. Birds littered the
ground beneath trees like fallen, mold-cloaked fruit. Cats and
squirrels and rabbits lay dead on lawns or convulsing and retching
under hedges. The weather was lovely, temperature in the high
seventies, humidity low. National Guard units in tear-gas gear
worked methodically northward, evacuating recalcitrant homeowners with force when it was necessary, barricading streets with
Warning Orange barrels, and encircling the most contaminated
area, designated Zone I, with flimsy orange plastic fencing material
that had apparently been stockpiled with this very purpose in mind.

By Tuesday evening, Zone I had been completely isolated. It
consisted of five and a half square miles of gravel pits, shabby
residential streets, trash-glutted wetlands, and some worn-out factories owned by companies that had long been scaling back. Already
several Peabody residents who had been at home when the plume
descended were in the hospital, complaining of dizziness or extreme
fatigue. The houses they'd left behind, now visitable only by National Guard patrols and news teams, had the aspect of junked
sofas—the bad legs, the weakened joints, the skins torn here and
there to expose an internal chaos of springs and crumbled stuffing.
Earthquake damage was similar in the much larger Zone II to the
north, but here the contamination was spotty and ill defined enough
that the Guard was letting adult residents return during daylight
hours to secure their houses and collect personal belongings.

News was being gathered in Peabody round the clock. Camera
crews skirmished with the Guard, and reporters addressed their

audience in gas masks. Some were so affected by what they'd seen, so unexpectedly overwhelmed by the news, that they dropped their pious earnest poses and spoke like the intelligent human beings you'd always figured they had to be. They asked Guardsmen if any looters had been shot. They asked environmental officials if people living just outside the zones were at risk. They asked everyone what their *impressions* were. But the big question, not only for the press but for the EPA, the thirty thousand traumatized and outraged residents of Zones I and II, the citizens of Boston, and all Americans as well was: What did the management of Sweeting-Aldren have to say? And it was on Monday afternoon, when the question had become inescapable, that the press discovered that there was literally no one around to answer it. Sweeting-Aldren's corporate headquarters, situated, as it happened, just west of Zone II, had been gutted by a fire which local fire departments, trying to fight it in the hours after the earthquake, said appeared to be a case of arson. The building's sprinkler system had been shut down manually, and firemen found traces of an "incendiary liquid" near the remains of the ground-floor records center. The wives of the company's CEO and of its four senior vice presidents either could not be located or else told reporters that they hadn't seen their men since late Sunday evening, shortly before the earthquake struck.

At five o'clock on Monday, just in time for a live interview on the local news, Channel 4 tracked down company spokesman Ridgely Holbine at a marina in Marblehead. He was wearing swim trunks and a faded HARVARD CREW T-shirt and was inspecting his sailboat for earthquake damage.

PENNY SPANGHORN: What is the company's response to this terrible tragedy?

HOLBINE: Penny, I can't give you any official comment at this time.

SPANGHORN: Can you tell us what caused this terrible tragedy?

HOLBINE: I've received no information on that. I can speculate privately that the earthquake was a factor.

SPANGHORN: Are you in communication with the company's management?

HOLBINE: No, Penny, I'm not.

SPANGHORN: Is the company prepared to take responsibility for
the terrible contamination in Peabody? Will you take a
leading role in the cleanup?

HOLBINE: I can't give you any official comment.

SPANGHORN: What is your personal opinion of this terrible
tragedy?

HOLBINE: I feel sorry for the workers who were killed and injured.
I feel sorry for their families.

SPANGHORN: Do you feel personally responsible in any way? For
this terrible tragedy?

HOLBINE: It's an act of God. There's no controlling that. We all
regret the loss of life, though.

SPANGHORN: What about the estimated thirty thousand people
who are homeless tonight as a result of this tragedy?

HOLBINE: As I said, I have no authority to speak for the company.
But it's undeniably regrettable.

SPANGHORN: What do you have to say to those people?

HOLBINE: Well, they shouldn't eat any food from their houses.
They should shower carefully and try to find other places
to stay. Drink bottled water. Get plenty of rest. That's
what I'm doing.

Tuesday morning brought the news that Sweeting-Aldren CEO
Sandy Aldren had spent all of Monday in New York City liquidating
the company's negotiable securities and transferring every dollar
the company had in cash to bank accounts in a foreign country.
Then, on Monday night, he'd vanished. At first it was assumed that
the foreign accounts in question were Swiss, but records showed
that all the cash—about $30 million—had in fact flowed to the
First Bank of Basseterre in St. Kitts.

On Tuesday afternoon Aldren's personal attorney in Boston,
Alan Porges, came forward and acknowledged that a "cash reserve"
had been set up to cover the "contractually guaranteed severance
payments" of the company's five "ranking officers." These payments amounted to just over $30 million, and Porges said that to
the best of his knowledge all five officers had officially resigned on
Monday morning and were therefore entitled to their cash payments
effective immediately. He declined to speculate on the men's
whereabouts.

The networks had rebroadcast excerpts from the interview with Porges no more than five or six times before a new bombshell detonated. Seismologist Larry Axelrod summoned reporters to MIT and announced that he had seen evidence suggesting that Sweeting-Aldren was responsible for nearly all the seismic activity of the last three months, including the main shock on Sunday night. He said the evidence had been provided by Renée Seitchek of Harvard, "an excellent scientist" who was still in the hospital recovering from gunshot wounds. A woman from the *Globe* asked if it was possible that Seitchek had been shot not by pro-life extremists but by a Sweeting-Aldren operative, and Axelrod said *Yes*.

Police in Somerville and Boston confirmed that they had indeed widened the scope of their investigation of Seitchek's shooting in light of this newfound motive, but added that the earthquake had thrown all investigations of this kind into disarray. They said the total breakdown of Sweeting-Aldren's management structure and the loss of company records to various fires "could pose a problem."

Federal and state environmental officials were encountering even bigger obstacles as they attempted to confirm the existence of an injection well at the company's Peabody facilities. By Wednesday morning the last of the fires there had burned itself out, and what remained was eight hundred acres of scorched and poisoned ruins—an uncharted industrial South Bronx filled with murky, foaming pools, unstable process structures, and pressurized tanks and pipelines suspected to contain not only explosives and flammable gases but some of the most toxic and/or carcinogenic and/or teratogenic substances known to man. The USEPA's first priority, administrator Susan Carver told ABC News, would be to prevent contamination from spreading into groundwater and nearby estuaries.

"It's now apparent," Carver said, "that this company's immense profitability was achieved through razor-thin safety margins and the systematic deception of the agencies responsible for oversight. I'm afraid there's a very real risk of this personal and economic tragedy becoming a true environmental catastrophe, and right now I'm more worried about protecting public safety than assigning responsibility in the abstract. For us to locate a single wellhead at the site, assuming the well even exists, is going to be like finding a needle in a haystack that we know is full of rattlesnakes."

By and large the press and public bought the Axelrod/Seitchek theory wholesale. Seismologists, however, reacted with their usual caution. They wanted to inspect the data. They needed time to model and construe. They said the rich and swarmy seismicity of April and May could plausibly have been induced by Sweeting-Aldren, but the main shock on Sunday night was another matter.

This shock, it was shown, had resulted from the rupture of rock along a deep fault running northeast from Peabody to a point in the neighborhood of April's Ipswich epicenters. Howard Chun of Harvard deconvolved some short-period digital seismograms and demonstrated, fairly conclusively, that the rupture had spread from the northern end of the fault to the southern—in other words, that the event had "begun" near Ipswich. A Sweeting-Aldren injection well could therefore not have "caused" the earthquake; at most it could have destabilized the fault, or provided a general instability with a path of least resistance. But the entire subject of rupture propagation was not at all well understood.

What was certain was that the Eastern United States had suffered its largest earthquake since Charleston, South Carolina, was crunched in 1886. The contamination of Peabody and the scandal of corporate culpability naturally received the most press in the early going—every big American disaster seems to produce one particularly grim spectacle—but as the situation there stabilized, attention shifted to the serious wounds that the rest of north suburban Boston and the city itself had suffered. Rescue workers digging in the rubble of a children's home in Salem had exhumed eight small bodies. Heart attacks had killed at least ten Hub men and women; Channel 7 interviewed neighbors of a West Somerville man named John Mullins who had staggered from his house and fallen dead in the street with his arms outstretched "like he'd been shot." Perchloroethylene pouring out of dry-cleaning establishments had put six people in the hospital. Librarians in every town from Gloucester to Cambridge were wading into hip-deep swamps of unshelved books. Shawmut Bank's mainframe had crashed and an electrical fire had wiped out hundreds of magnetic tapes containing account information; the bank closed its doors for a week, and its customers, finding that their ATM cards wouldn't work at other banks either, had to barter and beg and borrow just to get food and bottled water. Many people complained of lingering seasickness. After Sunday night, only three minor aftershocks were felt, but each of them caused hundreds of people to stop whatever they were doing and sob uncontrollably. Everything was a mess— houses, factories, highways, courts. On Friday morning federal relief coordinators estimated that the total cost of the earthquake, including property damage and the interruption of economic activity, but not including the contamination in Zones I and II, would come to between four and five billion dollars. Editorialists called this figure staggering; it was roughly what it had cost Americans to service the national debt over the Memorial Day weekend.

Probably the most notorious casualty of the earthquake was Philip Stites's Church of Action in Christ. In much the same way as they composed obituaries for the living, local news organizations had prepared for the church's destruction with pre-written triumphant editorials and pre-allocated news teams. As soon as the seismic waves had rolled over Chelsea, four independent minicam vans raced through the blacked-out, fissured streets and reached the church within a minute of each other. Devastation appeared to be satisfactory, though not extreme. Strong motion had split the tenement down the middle, entirely flattening the ground floor on one side of the clerestory, reducing the clerestory itself to a tangle of reinforcing rods caging chunks of concrete, and turning doors and windows into nasty rhomboids. Smoke was surging furiously, impatiently, from the rear of the building, and Philip Stites looked as if a blood-yoked egg had been cracked open on his head. He ran up the street shouting, "Help *us*. Put the cameras *down*. Help *us*," because the news crews were in fact the only people there to help, and it would be another twenty minutes before anyone else arrived.

Later in the week, Stites claimed that a true miracle had occurred on that dark, humid night: all of the newspeople, every one of them, had put their cameras and recorders down and followed him into the stricken building. They had kicked open jammed doors, releasing herds of screaming, bloodied women. They had braved falling plaster and clouds of black smoke to drag church members with broken limbs from the path of the fire. They had caught men and women jumping out of windows and had cleared equipment from their vans in order to rush them to the hospital. They had saved, Stites said, at least twenty lives. But it reflected a new and uncharacteristic bitterness on the minister's part that he chose to call the newspeople's heroism a miracle. He did not, for example, see a miracle in the fact that no one in his church had perished. He did not say that God had protected His faithful from His earthquake. He took no pleasure whatsoever in God's mercy, because when the smoke had cleared and the sun had risen, he found that he no longer had a church.

He set up a tent in the tenement courtyard and promised to get other tents for the three hundred members of his congregation, but all but a handful declined his offer. Most of them simply left Boston, went home to Missouri, Kansas, Georgia. The rest quietly defected to a rival anti-abortion group called We Love Life whose trademark "action" was to harass clinics with recordings of newborn babies wailing at a hundred decibels. One of these defectors looked a Channel 4 news camera dead in the eye and said, "I don't believe anymore that Mr. Stites is guided by divine Providence, not after that night of terror. I thank the Lord I escaped with life and limb. Not everybody did, you know, I have a dear friend in the hospital paralyzed with a broken back. I believe Mr. Stites is a great teacher and moral leader led astray by too much pride and we should never of been in that building."

Another defector, Mrs. Jack Wittleder, was more succinct: "The Reverend Stites let a sinful woman tempt him. We have all now paid the price." The Channel 4 reporter said: *Woman? What woman??* But Mrs. Wittleder declined to elaborate.

Stites himself spoke to Channel 4. "What I really believe in my heart? I believe that God brought down our building for a purpose. I believe the destruction was a test of faith and we flat-out failed it. I thought—I fervently hoped—we had a church that was stronger than any building, and a faith that no earthquake would ever shake. And I still have that faith in my own heart, but I don't have a church, and I am deeply humbled and disappointed."

Stites soon also achieved the distinction of being the first defendant named in a lawsuit arising from the earthquake. The family of the church member whose back was broken accused him of fraud and willful negligence in persuading her to stay in an unsafe building; they sought ten million dollars in real and punitive damages. Stites's lawyer told the press that his client's entire worldly possessions consisted of one army-surplus tent, one sleeping bag, a Bible, one suitcase of clothes, a car, and one financially troubled radio station. This didn't stop four other injured church members from filing suit on July 11.

It became a season of lawsuits. Lawsuits salved the raw nerves of the million survivors and held out hope to the bereft. They eased the transition back to normalcy when the networks and newspapers released their hostages; they provided the grist for follow-up reports. They bottled the terrible dread and emptiness back into people's unconscious, where they belonged. By the end of July the Commonwealth of Massachusetts had been named in eleven different suits accusing it of such creative torts as failure to establish adequate plans for evacuation in the event of toxic chemical dispersal, lethargy in providing shelter for families from Zones I and II, and calculated deception in its assessments of local seismic risk. The Commonwealth in turn was suing the federal government and the builders of various failed highways and public buildings. It was also, like nearly everyone else in Boston, suing Sweeting-Aldren. As of August 1 total claims against the company exceeded ten billion dollars and were rising daily. To pay these claims, the company had few uncontaminated current assets, a long-term debt of fifty million dollars, and little prospect of ever selling anything again. It was taken for granted that the federal government would ultimately foot the cleanup bill.

Renée Seitchek was released from Brigham & Women's Hospital on July 27. A ten-second clip on the evening news showed her being wheeled from the hospital towards a dented Honda Civic, but by this point the press had soured on her story, because she refused to be interviewed. The investigation of her shooting was stalled ("probably a lost cause," detectives conceded privately), but authorities were still hoping to bring Sweeting-Aldren's management home to face a variety of other criminal charges. The FBI had tracked the five men—Aldren, Tabscott, Stoorhuys, the corporation counsel, and the chief financial officer—to a tiny island south of St. Kitts, where the corporation had long maintained three beach houses for business entertaining and executive vacations. Aldren's twenty-three-year-old wife, Kim, and Tabscott's twenty-six-year-old girlfriend, Sondra, had joined the party a few days after the earthquake, the corporation counsel's family had visited on the Fourth of July, and seafaring paparazzi had managed to photograph a beach picnic that resembled a beer commercial in all the particulars. (The *Globe* ran one of these pictures on its front page alongside a shot of Mylar-suited men shoveling birds and mammals into an incinerator.) Unfortunately the government of St. Kitts–Nevis showed no intention of delivering the executives up to justice, and the Administration in Washington, perhaps mindful of Aldren and Tabscott's longtime financial support for the Republican Party, said there was little the United States could do about it.

Big chemical concerns like Dow and Monsanto and Du Pont, on the other hand, seemed almost to relish the opportunity to decry a fellow corporation's misdeeds. They immediately expanded their production of the textiles, pigments, and pesticides that had been Sweeting-Aldren's mainstay—products for which demand was only increasing in America—and took the lead in demonizing Sweeting-Aldren's management. Du Pont called the Peabody tragedy the work of "a bunch of devils." (Du Pont's own managers were family men, not devils; they welcomed the EPA's intelligent regulation.) Monsanto solemnly swore that it had never employed injection wells and never would. Dow took pride in its foresight in locating its headquarters in one of the most geologically stable places in the world. By August, sales and stock prices were up at all three companies.

In the public imagination, "Sweeting-Aldren" joined the ranks of "Saddam Hussein" and "Manuel Noriega" and "the Medellín cartels." These were the guys with hats as black as the tabloid headlines screaming of their villainy, the men who made the good world bad. The United States bore the responsibility for punishing them, and if they couldn't be punished, the United States bore the responsibility for cleaning up after them; and if the cleanup proved painfully expensive, it could be argued that the United States bore the responsibility for having allowed them to become villains in the first place. But in no case did the American people themselves feel responsible.

As the weeks went by, visitors from out of town occasionally ventured north from Boston to see the fences around Zone I. They had seen these fences countless times on television, and still it amazed them that Peabody could be reached by car in half an hour—that this land belonged to the earth as surely as the land in their own hometowns, that the weather and light didn't change as they approached the fences. They took photographs which, when they were developed back in Los Angeles or Kansas City, showed a scene that they again could not believe was real.

Bostonians, meanwhile, had more important things to think about. Low-interest federal loans had reignited the local economy. The window frames of downtown buildings had again been filled with greenish glass. Fenway Park had passed its safety inspections. And the Red Sox were still in first place.

In Harvard Square the season came when the sun lost the angle it needed to reach the narrower streets before noon, and the overnight chill and its smell of impending winter lingered in the pissed-on alleyways and the cast-concrete chess tables by Au Bon Pain. Along the river and in the Yard, the Great Litterer was at work again, discarding worn-out leaves on footpaths. Damaged buildings were reopening, the scaffolds coming down. Impeccably put-together students trailed scents of shampoo and deodorant in the Canadian air. They were young and wealthy sexual beings being educated. They were like the unblemished cars that bunched in their egress from the Square, windows shut now that summer was over, fully functional emission-control systems expelling exhaust that smelled good. It was literally incomprehensible that in Zone I, a mere fifteen miles away, squads of bulldozers were even now destroying bungalows in which lamps and chairs lay exactly where strong motion had thrown them on the twenty-fourth of June.

Louis had come to the Square on errands. Though he was no fan of the Square, he came here often now, did his business efficiently, and went home again feeling unimplicated and anonymous. On this particular morning, however, he was crossing the street outside Wordsworth when a silver Mercedes sedan braked sharply on the cobbled apron of a traffic island and a familiar-looking person leaned out the front passenger window and beckoned to him. It was Alec Bressler.

"Alec. How's it going?"

Alec ducked in his affirmative way. "No complaints."

Of the driver of the car, Louis could see only female legs in hose and pumps. Alec was sucking a nicotine lozenge with what appeared to be particular amusement. He had new glasses and wore a very smart-looking blazer. "Yourself?" he said. "You find a good job?"

"No. Not— No."

Alec frowned. "No job at all?"

"Well, for the last couple of months I've been taking care of my girlfriend. You probably heard about her. Her name's Renée Seitchek?"

Here the driver of the car leaned across Alec's lap and showed her face to Louis. She was a handsome woman in her early fifties, with a strong nose and wiry gray hair and black eyebrows. "You know Renée Seitchek?"

Louis had heard these exact words a lot in recent weeks. "Yeah, I do."

The woman took his hand. "I'm Joyce Edelstein. I'm very interested in Renée, from afar. Can you tell me how she is?"

"She's . . . OK."

"Listen, why don't you come up to my office and have some coffee with us. If you have a minute. I'm right up the street here. You want to come?"

Louis looked uncertainly at Alec, who simply raised his eyebrows and sucked his entertaining lozenge.

"Come on," Joyce said, popping the lock on the rear door.

Louis obeyed her. His vagueness was no longer something he turned on to foil people; it was the way he really was. When he walked, nowadays, he kept his eyes on the ground in front of him. He always felt tired and was frequently short of breath. He wore clothes that had belonged to Peter Stoorhuys, a red sweatshirt and some gray jeans that he put on morning after morning and, objectively speaking, looked bad in. When he saw his own old blacks and whites or even thought about them, he squeezed his eyes shut as tightly as he could.

The office he was taken to occupied the third floor of a clapboard building on Brattle Street that maybe a hundred years ago had been a private residence. The brass doorplate said The Joyce Edelstein Foundation. A receptionist and an assistant said "Good morning, Mrs. Edelstein." Joyce left her visitors in a private office decorated in harmony with the large Monet pondscape that hung on one wall. Alec made himself at home on a white leather sofa. His skin was no longer the gray that Louis remembered; even his hair seemed thicker. He'd pretty clearly quit smoking. "Joyce is a phil-an-thropist," he said, making her sound like some curiosity of nature.

"Uh huh."

"Renée is kind of a hero of mine," Joyce said, matter-of-factly, as she returned with a tray of coffee, cream, and sugar. "I'm involved in funding a variety of organizations, and if there's any kind of unifying theme to my concerns it would probably be reproductive rights and the environment. For me both those things came together this summer with the earthquake and what happened to Renée. I actually wrote her a letter, I don't know if she got it, I—didn't particularly expect a reply."

Louis did not say: A lot of people wrote her letters.

"So how's she doing?" Joyce said.

"She's all right. She's got a bone infection in her leg, it started after she left the hospital. She's still sort of sick."

"It's been how long?"

"Three months."

"That's really hard. And you— You're—?"

"I live with her."

"In—"

"In Somerville."

"Forgive me, are you not feeling well? If this is hard for you to talk about . . ."

"No. I just gave blood, that's all."

"Gave blood? Good grief, why didn't you say so? Here, sit down. Please."

Louis sat in the indicated chair and lowered his head over his coffee cup. Joyce looked at him with compassion and concern. She also looked at her watch. Alec was slurping and spectating from his distant sofa.

"Are you . . . Renée's only caregiver?" Joyce said.

"Uh, yeah."

"Louis, that can be so draining. It can tire you in ways you're not even aware of. Forgive me for asking, but is Renée—fully covered with her insurance? I'm only thinking, if what she really needs is a nurse, maybe it would give you—"

"It's no big thing," Louis said. "It's just shopping and a little cooking and driving."

"Yes, but psychologically—"

He stood up and crossed the room. "It's OK. I can handle it. I mean—I can handle it. I appreciate your concern. But it's no big thing."

"I'm sure you can handle it," Joyce said gently. "I only want . . ."

"Joyce needs to help people," Alec commented. "It's in her nature."

With a little shudder, Joyce let this description of her pass. "I only want you to know that if you do need help, there are people out here in the world to help you. If I have any one purpose in life, it's to let people know that they do not have to suffer in solitude. For every person who has a need, there's a person, somewhere, who wants to take care of that need."

Louis closed his eyes and thought: *Please stop talking.*

Joyce looked helplessly at Alec. Anyone could see she was a perceptive person. It obviously really did cause her pain to see Louis suffering, and to know that the streets of Cambridge and Boston were full of people like him—that all you had to do was dip a net in randomly and you'd come up with suffering. And to know that she herself was not suffering.

"Listen," she said, "I hope you'll tell Renée that there are a great many people in this city who care about her and are pulling for her and want to help her. If nothing else, *I'm* here, and if there's anything she needs . . ."

Louis closed his eyes and thought: *It is necessary to suffer.*

"And Louis, I know I don't have any business saying this, but if you stop and think about it, you might want to not donate blood for a while, especially if it's something you're doing often. You need your strength for one thing at a time."

It is necessary to suffer. It is necessary to suffer.

"Thanks for the coffee," Louis said.

Joyce sighed and shook her head. "You're welcome."

Alec followed him out of the office, arresting him at the top of the stairs. "One sing. Stop a minute, one sing. I spoke with Libby last week. Libby Quinn. She wants your number."

"Why does she want my number?"

"If you need a job, you call her."

"Why the change of heart?"

"Stites is leaving. Some midwestern state he's going to. You heard this?"

"And you told her to call me."

"Yes, OK, I told her. But she doesn't have your number. She needs an engineer. I told her, minimum wage, and he loves radio."

"Minimum wage. Thanks."

"You can make a deal. Sink about it, eh?"

"I can't, now."

"But you love radio. I knew this about you."

"I used to."

"So you call me when you want to work. You must call me. And you must give me your number."

Louis took the pen Alec offered. "I'm sorry I wasn't nicer to your friend."

"She's used to it. You go home now."

"Tell her I'm sorry."

"Yes, maybe. It doesn't matter."

Alec drew a European crossbar through the stem of the 7 in the number Louis had written down. Then he returned to Joyce's office without another word.

The only time Louis felt safe from torment now, the only time he liked the person he was, was when he was alone with Renée on Pleasant Avenue. As long as he was in her apartment, he knew what he was doing because everything followed logically from the supposition that he loved her. He was her cook, her comedian, her comforter, her maid. Even three months ago, he wouldn't have assumed that he could console a sick person weeping over the slowness of her recovery: that the necessary words could come to him as automatically as the motions of sex did. He would probably have sneered at a person who said that love could teach him the many specific skills that constitute patience and grace, and certainly at the person who said that love was a gold ring which if grasped carried you upward with a force comparable in strength to the forces of nature. But this was exactly what he felt now, and the only question was why, when he was by himself or outside of the apartment, his life with Renée still felt like such a sorrow.

In the days and weeks following the earthquake he had gone to the hospital every afternoon, adhering to a tacit agreement whereby he stayed away until three o'clock or so and Mrs. Seitchek stayed away after that. It wasn't that there was any special hostility between mother and boyfriend—Louis continued to be resolutely polite to Mrs. Seitchek, and she in turn now recognized him as Renée's official first choice and went so far as to share with him her views on the "incredibly immature" Howard Chun and the "incredibly dangerous" things her daughter had been doing. The problem was simply that on the one occasion when they had visited Renée at the same time, Renée had looked utterly wretched and refused to speak to either of them—at least until her father came into the room. Then she answered everyone's questions and kind- nesses with a humility that Louis had never seen in her before. He wondered if there was anyone in the world who wouldn't be afraid of Dr. Seitchek and his trifocals.

All day long, no matter how many people visited her, Renée seemed never to forget that at night she was alone. She told Louis that whenever she woke up, at whatever time of day or night, she felt like she was still awakening in the windowless ICU where it was always night. She could open her eyes and see his face and still believe that, only a moment earlier, she had been in that other place.

She let him read her mail while she dozed. There were some twenty-six hundred envelopes in bundles on the table by the head of her bed. Inside them were checks and cash gifts totaling about $19,000, and letters short and long.

Dear Renée,

My husband and I are praying for your speedy recovery.
Our hearts are with you. Please use the enclosed check for
whatever you wish.

Sincerely,
Sandy & Roy Hurwitz

Dear Renee,

Remember me? I heard you was in the Hospital and remembered our nice talk. Hope you are feeling better now. I lost
two friends and everything I own from the earthquake. I'm
staying with my daughter now and can't go home. Looks like
you are right about that company. I hope you come see me
when you are better.

"Sincerely"
Jurene Caddulo

Reneé—

You don't know me, but you have made an indellible
impression on my mind. I don't think the people on TV understand what you said and my parents don't either, but I think
I do. Nobody understands me because I hate being a girl but I
don't want to be a boy. I am 17 years old and I have never met
a boy whose mind I can respect. I had a fight with my parents
about you. I think they admired you but then I told them I
admired you and they changed their mind. I am leaving this
house in two months to go to college. My mind is always in
confusion and I don't know anyone like me. But I think I might
be like you if I could be brave. I have never written a letter like
this before. You probably think it's very stupid. But I lie awake
in bed and imagine I've been shot because of what I am. We
will probably never meet, but I want to tell you I love you and
wish you the best in all things. GET WELL.

Sincerely yours,
Alexandra Adams

Louis was jealous of all the people who had written to her,
people who didn't owe her anything and whose interest was therefore beyond suspicion. He was jealous of the men he had to leave
the room for when they came to visit her—Howard Chun, various
professors and colleagues, even Terry Snall (though Terry came

only once and left Renée livid and seething when he tried to "joke" about all the public attention she was getting). He was especially jealous of Peter Stoorhuys. After the initial flood of visitors and outpouring of sympathy had ebbed, Peter was the only person besides Louis and Mrs. Seitchek who still came to the hospital almost every day. The worst thing about Peter's visits was that Louis could see that there was no ulterior motive—that Peter simply liked and admired Renée and was sorry she was hurt and regretted that his father was responsible. He was blind to Louis's jealousy, just couldn't conceive of it. He brought Renée newspaper and magazine clippings, he brought tapes for her Walkman, he brought his mother. Sometimes he brought Eileen, too, although she continued to be preposterously shy around Renée. Louis paced the halls and rode the elevators and read *Glamour* and *Good Housekeeping* with clenched teeth, returned to Room 833 and found Renée and Peter still conversing in low voices. She seldom seemed more relaxed or self-confident than after Peter had visited her.

In Peter's eyes, Louis had stopped being Eileen's little brother and become Renée Seitchek's boyfriend—the partner in her assault on Sweeting-Aldren, and the man who had helped expose David Stoorhuys as the fraud that Peter had long known him to be. Peter gave Louis clothes, including certain items that he still liked, and single-handedly achieved the breakthrough of perceiving that Louis would never be a salesman of ad space or of anything else. Eileen made dinner for the three of them when Louis came home from the hospital. Whenever he looked unhappy, which was often, she asked him what was wrong and tried hard to cheer him up.

What was wrong was that he felt utterly at sea. Now that Eileen was being a peach and Peter no longer patronized him, he had no choice but to be sincere with them. But sincerity implied some kind of belief in something—the kind of belief that Eileen and Peter had in living in America and making a good life for themselves, or that Renée had in the power of women. Louis still thought the country sucked and he had his doubts about the okayness of being male. If he'd ever known how to believe in anything else, he'd long ago forgotten.

He was jealous of the people with pure motives who brought Renée pleasures—pleasures that she shared with him because he was always around her, pleasures that were small and discrete and more easily appreciated than any brought by the man who did things like watching her sleep, or helping her walk up and down the hall, or telling her he was sorry. He was also jealous of the people with impure motives whom she smilingly indulged because amusement hurt less than anger. This latter class did not include journalists (these she simply refused to see) but did include the Hollywood scouts who wanted to buy her story for a prime-time dramatization; the pro-choice activist who wondered if she might address a rally by telephone; and, just before she was released from Brigham & Women's, her own mother, who one afternoon at three o'clock met Louis at the door of Room 833 and asked him for his help in persuading Renée to return to Newport Beach to complete her recuperation. Renée's father had already gone back, and her mother pointed out that when she left the hospital she would still need care at home. The problem, Mrs. Seitchek told Louis, was that her daughter only smiled and shook her head at the idea of returning to California. She had $19,000 and insisted she was going to hire a nurse. Which just seemed so cold, so wrong, so—

Louis said, "I can't help you here, Mrs. Seitchek."

He left her in the hall and went into Room 833. Renée said, "You know why she wants me back there with her?"

"She wants to take care of you."

"Yeah, she does," she admitted. "But what she really hopes is that if I stay there I'll develop a taste for golf. And kelly-green skirts. And meet one of the young doctors she can't stop talking about, and marry him."

"I don't believe that."

"You don't know her."

He waited a moment. "You're not really going to get a nurse, are you?"

"Watch me."

"But I can do it myself."

"I don't want you to."

"Please let me."

"I don't want you to."

"You have to let me."

She closed her eyes. "I know I have to let you."

More than anything else, he was jealous of her infirmity. It was like a baby that was partly his but dwelt inside her body alone. Listening to it and learning its secrets absorbed most of her attention every day. Whenever he thought he understood it—when he thought that it no longer hurt her to laugh, or that she still needed him to reach things from the table for her—she would turn around and correct him. He had guesses; she had certainty. He supposed that maybe she did still love him, but even if she did she had no time for him. Her distance, the feebleness of her feelings towards him, reminded him of the dreams he had where she was cold to him: where love wasn't there, where there was another man she wasn't telling him about.

But the baby was his, too. The pain in her body, the pain from her bullet-torn back muscles and pierced diaphragm and splintered rib and femur and the surgical incisions, had a way of spreading into his own body and making it difficult for him to breathe. He remembered when she was mobile and unbreakable, when he could lie on top of her on a hard floor and she could laugh, when they could drink Rolling Rock and listen to the Stones, when they could be mean to each other and it didn't matter, when he could hate the world and it didn't matter. What hurt him was his feeling of responsibility. He wished he were still working for WSNE, still driving on Route 2 in the blue vernal morning twilight, still in his car with Renée before he kissed her. He wished he'd let her hand her Sweeting-Aldren files over to Larry Axelrod and the EPA. He wished he could have paid attention to all nine innings of the Red Sox game they'd seen from Henry Rudman's seats, could remember who had won and how, could have knowledge as clean and permanent and inconsequential as a box score. He didn't understand how he could have let a small part of his life—his greed? his hurt? his outrage?—make him responsible for the pain and desolation that had descended on himself and her and much of Boston. But he was responsible, and he knew it.

A Town Car with a PROLIFE 7 vanity plate was parked outside the house when he got back to Pleasant Avenue. He went inside and mounted the stairs slowly, still a little light-headed with Red Cross sickness.

Philip Stites was standing in the middle of Renée's room, beside the chair he'd rolled over from the desk and had obviously been sitting in. Renée sat in her armchair in a thick sweater and sweatpants and the glasses which she needed all the time now. This morning she'd weighed in at 98 pounds, up one pound from the previous Friday but still down seven from her weight in June. The feverish rigidity of her face muted her expressions. All that registered when she looked at Louis was the flash of sunlight on her lenses. He hurried into the other big room, the room he slept in, and set the books he'd bought on the floor.

"Louis," Renée said.

He returned to the hallway. "Yo."

"Philip was just leaving."

"Oh. So long."

Stites, wearing an inscrutable smile, waved his hand. Renée was looking at Louis intently. "I didn't realize the two of you had met," she said.

"It must have slipped my mind."

"Those were unhappy circumstances," Stites said. "These are much happier ones."

Renée kept her disapproving eyes on Louis even as Stites took her hand and wished her well. Louis opened the door for the minister. "So, Philip," he said. "Thanks for coming. I'm sure it meant a lot to her."

Stites started down the stairs, motioned casually to Louis to follow, as if he had no doubt that Louis would, and stopped on the doggy second-floor landing. Louis glanced at Renée, whose expression hadn't changed, and descended the stairs.

"Why do I get this impression of hostility?" Stites asked a beam of bright dust specks.

"I hear you're leaving town," Louis said.

"Tomorrow morning. Ever been to Omaha, Nebraska? About the only thing it's got in common with Boston is a big sky."

"You feel you've done sufficient damage here."

Stites failed to react to this stimulus. He unwrapped a stick of sugarless gum and daintily pushed it into his mouth. "Hostility, hostility," he said. "I came to apologize to Renée for any pain I ever caused her. And I tell you what, Louis, it made me pretty happy to hear what you been doing for her."

"I'm glad I made you happy, Philip."

"Fine, say what you gotta say. You'll never see me again. But you know damn well that what you're doin' is a very good thing."

"Right," Louis said. "I'm a hell of a guy. See my Band-Aid? I've been giving blood. My penance, right? Because I sinned, right?" He stared at Stites, quivering. "I laughed at Jesus and I wasn't faithful to my girlfriend and I let her kill our baby, but now I've got it all straight in my mind. I'm taking care of her and trying to live a Christian life. We'll get married and have children and we'll all be singing hymns on TV. Except I'm *such* a good Christian that if anybody tries to say I'm doing the right thing I deny it because if I didn't, that would be pride, and pride's a sin, right? And faith is a thing inside you. So I'm not only a hell of guy, I'm deep and true, right?"

Stites chewed his gum with smooth, slow jawstrokes. "Nothing you say makes me stop loving God."

"Well, go ahead. Go ahead."

"I hope you find some happiness."

"Yeah, you too. Have fun in Omaha."

Stites looked at Louis with the complicity and pleasure of a person being told a joke. He laughed, exposing his little wad of gum. It wasn't a forced or cruel laugh but the laugh of someone who had expected to be delighted, and was. He gave Louis a last, knowing look and trotted down the stairs. Through the landing's filthy window, Louis watched him evade the grasping honeysuckle and get into his car. He felt a large but strangely painless emptiness inside him, as when he'd been bluffed in a poker game.

Upstairs again, he assumed a casual manner. "Can I make you some lunch?"

Renée sat in her armchair and looked at him. The chair occupied a shadow between patches of sunshine on the floorboards. Her silence was ominous in the extreme.

"Can I make you some lunch?" he said again.

"You certainly got me back pretty easily, didn't you?"

He weighed the consequences of ignoring that she'd said this. He leaned on the doorframe. "What do you mean?"

"I mean one day I'm living by myself and hating you for how much you hurt me, and the next thing I know I wake up and you're living with me again and we're acting like nothing ever happened."

"You woke up a long time ago."

"No, I didn't wake up a long time ago. You listen to what I'm saying. I'm saying I just woke up."

"Fine. You just woke up."

"So what are you going to do about it?"

"About . . . ?"

"About the fact that you're living with me and we're acting like nothing ever happened."

"Well, I was about to make you some lunch."

"I'm saying you got me back pretty easily."

"What was I supposed to do? Keep away from you? While you were in the hospital? I mean, how many times did I tell you I was sorry? And you said to stop saying it—"

"Well I felt like shit."

"But so all I can do is show you how sorry I am and how much I love you."

She flinched as though the word love were a dart. "I'm saying I never had a chance to think about what I wanted. Everything just happened. And I'm not at all sure about it."

"You're not sure you want me living here."

"That's part of it."

"You're not sure you even want to see me."

"That's the other part of it. I mean, I do want to see you. But everything's all tied together, there's no room to *think*. I want to get to know you, somehow. I don't want us to be together just because we happen to be together. I want to start over again."

"Beginning with me moving out."

"I don't know, I don't know."

"You want me to leave. You're trying to say it in a nice way."

She closed her eyes and bit her lip. She wasn't someone he knew, this underweight woman with the hectic face and overgrown hair and wire-frame glasses. A deft exchange had been effected, and no fraud was involved—the woman was clearly who she seemed to be. She just wasn't the ghost made of memories and expectations that he had seen at breakfast. She opened her eyes and looked straight ahead. "Yes, I want you to leave."

He took an unopened envelope from the table in the hallway and carried it into her room. "Is this the problem?"

She didn't even glance at it. "Give me some credit."

"Answer the question."

"Yeah, all right. It's part of the problem. It upsets me that you got a letter from her here. It upsets me that I found out about it because you were out and somebody else brought the mail up. Because for all I know, you get letters like this every day—"

"I do not."

"And I just don't know about it. That's part of the problem. But it's not—"

"You think she sends me letters and I don't tell you. You think I've got a whole second relationship—"

"Shut up. That's not what I'm saying. I'm saying it's totally inappropriate for her to send you letters here, and it's up to you to make that clear to her, because she obviously doesn't see anything wrong with it herself."

The personal pronouns—*she, her*—were pronounced with a hatred like nothing he had heard from her before. Lauren didn't hate Renée like this.

"I'll let her know," he said.

She shook her head. "I can't live with you."

"I told you I don't even think about her anymore. I told you all I want's a chance to make it up to you. I know I acted like a prick. But I didn't even sleep with her and I never think about her now."

"And boy was that stupid of you. Because it doesn't make the slightest difference to me whether you slept with her. It makes zero difference."

"Well I would have done it, but she didn't want to."

Renée looked at the ceiling in disgust and disbelief. "That's sick. That is so sick. She walks into your apartment but she won't sleep with you. Because what, I can just imagine it. Because she's a better person than I am, because she really loves you and she won't fuck you before she marries you. That really makes me feel good, to hear that."

"I felt sorry for her," Louis said, very quietly. He set the letter from Lauren on the desk.

"Well, here's somebody else to feel sorry for. I do the best I can with self-pity but I can't do it all. Here's a person who has a fever every day and whose back still hurts and whose chest is all scars and who can't see right anymore and has to live and be ugly and know she's ugly every minute of the day, if you need somebody to feel sorry for."

He frowned. "I've never felt sorry for you. I hurt with you, but I admire you and love you. And you're so beautiful."

She made no attempt to hold her tears back. "I can't live with you. I can't live with you, and I can't get rid of you."

"It's easy to get rid of me."

"Well, then, just do it. Just go. Because this is the real me you're looking at. This is what I'm like inside. I'm a jealous insecure little ugly shrew. And that's what I'm going to be, and you can go on living with me because you feel guilty and you can watch me make your life a hell, or you can get out and go live with her right now because I certainly have no desire to live with you if we're going to fight like this, or else you can be kind to me—"

"Kind to you?"

"Kinder than you've already been. Kind to me right this minute. You can tell me you don't think about her all the time. You can tell me I may not be as young as she is, and I may be a scarred-up ugly mess, but I'm still not *so* bad. You have to tell me that *all the time*. You have to tell me you don't write letters to her and you don't call her and you appreciate me. You have to take all the things you've said and say them about a hundred times more often. Because I'm trying to have energy, I'm trying to get back to being a *person* again, but I can't do it fast enough."

For a moment Louis watched her shiver and weep in her armchair. Then he bent over and put his hands in her armpits and raised her to her feet. She was very light. The lenses of her glasses each had a single tear streak down the middle. He kissed her unresponding lips with none of the discretion and conscious kindness of their bedtime and hello and goodbye kisses. He kissed her because he was starving for her.

"Don't."

"Why not."

"You're just doing it because you—ow. Ow!"

He was squeezing her hard, one of his hands directly on the closed entrance wound in her back, his other hand on her butt beneath her sweatpants and underpants, his thigh squarely in her groin. She took his ear in her mouth and said, "Don't squeeze."

She shook while he undressed her on the bed. She covered herself with a blanket while he stood up to take his own clothes off.

"Don't ever put that sweatshirt on again," she said.

He knelt beside her and peeled back the blanket. He put his cheek on her white belly and the heel of his hand in the hollow of her pelvis. He wanted to fill this hollow with semen. The fast-dwindling warmth of it would tickle her, make her belly convulse like a hillside in the throes of a disaster. He knew this because he'd seen it happen, back in May.

She sat up and tried to pull him onto her.

"I have to look at you," he said.

"Just hurry along, if you don't mind."

Her cunt seemed to him a thing of unbearable beauty. Its readiness, its subtlety, its bed of dark hair. Unconcealed by adipose tissue, the individual muscles in her arms and legs were visible in their small, filet-like glory. Her retroperitoneal scar was a great circle of healed injury stretching from a point below her sternum, around under her ribs, and into the center of her back. For better or worse, his prick shuddered fully into hardness as he turned her body and followed the scar's irregular progress, its purple and red runes, through the places where it was a bunching of the skin and the more tender-looking places where it was a stretching. He couldn't help thinking of the aerial photograph of the San Andreas Fault he'd seen in one of her books, how the long raised seam traversed the smooth skin of the California desert, how the narrow groove down the center of the seam was cut by suture-like hatchings. He felt glad to be alive and in this bed. There had ceased to be any question in his mind that the thing he was looking at was

Renée Seitchek. The focus of his love had migrated from his imagination into her body, and had taken his imagination along with it, the inescapable joining of her legs now embodying some necessary convergence of emotions in himself, the warmth of her skin identical to the warmth his eyes felt when the lids came down to cover them. He licked her cool thoracostomy scar. He kissed the ragged star of the exit wound beneath her right breast. A bullet had come through here bearing bits of her bone and her lung tissue, but she was breathing without pain now. She played with his prick, opening and closing her opposed finger and thumb, pulling strands in the clear taffy it secreted. She bent sideways and sucked on it, briefly.

He squeezed a blob of nonoxynol jelly into the center of her diaphragm, lubricated the rim and folded it in two, and pushed it into her vagina until it unfolded into place. The procedure was similar in some interesting ways to preparing a bird for roasting.

She looked scared when he settled himself on top of her. He resisted the idea that it was "important" that they were making love now, but unfortunately it did seem kind of important. Her eyes were open wide and she was blinking rapidly, as if it might have been Death and not Louis who was weighing on her chest and sliding a firm piece of his flesh into a narrow gap in hers, and more generally invading the citadel where she had kept her self, her soul, during the months when she was lonelier than she was now. He slung his left leg up over her hip to keep from bearing on her osteomyelitic femur. The position was awkward, and she lay so inertly, through little choice of her own, that he felt like he was clinging to a slippery rock with not many handholds.

"Tell me when I'm hurting you."

"Well I'm hurting a little in a lot of places."

"Hurting you too much I mean."

Eyes closed, she pressed him into her as deeply as he would go. She breathed in the heavy, heedless way that made a man feel like a king and made his ejaculation an event of huge sweetness. He lay beside her and massaged the forward end of her labia with the palm of his hand until she came. He took his prick in his own hand and deposited semen in the pelvic hollow he had a fetish for. She thrashed a little, and rubbed the hollow for a long time before it stopped tickling her. They made inane and sentimental statements about breath and current genital conditions and love. They repeated the major act, straining and sweating until she became fretful and told him she was feeling really sick. He stood up immediately and covered her with the blanket. "Let me get you some lunch."

She shook her head. She was slack-faced and miserable.

"Some toast, some tea."

"There's no way I can go out tonight. You'll have to call her."

"You can sleep all afternoon. We'll see how you feel."

"I'm so tired of being tired."

"Have a bite. Take a nap."

When her door was closed and he knew that she was sleeping, he sat at the kitchen table and opened the envelope from Lauren. There was a letter in her pretty, ungainly hand.

September 20

Dear Louis,

I have to write to you today because I have to. I think about how if I'd wrote to you last fall everything would be different. I have to write to you for me, not you, so I hope you don't mind too much. You don't have to write back.

Well, the big news is—I'm pregnant! Its a good thing, because I already have a little bread basket. People ask when I'm due and I say April and they can't believe it. They think I'm going to say December. I spend a lot of time walking on air. I don't even know if you would know me I'm so different. I feel like I've found the real ME. I already love my baby like crazy and talk to him all the time. Well, that's the big news.

Louis, sometimes I miss you so much I start crying. I miss how funny you were and how considerate. But now I know God didn't mean for us to be together. God meant for me and Emmett to be together. I'm so thankful I have a life and a good husband and (SOON) a little baby I can love. I still love you (there, I said it!) but *in a different way*. But do you know what I wish sometimes? I wish I could see Renee, just her and me. I want to kiss her on the cheek because she has you, you are a sweet boy. Is she all well again—I hope? I do hope it with all my heart, Louis.

Well, there's the news from Texas. I'm not telling MaryAnn I'm pregnant until I know everything's OK. I'm friend's with Emmett's Mom now. She took me to her church group. The people were so wierd there but I'm friend's with them too. Oh well.

Louis, you will always be my friend even if we never meet again. "The King is dead, long live the King." That's what they say in England when their king dies. Get it??

Your friend,
Lauren

He left the letter on the table so Renée could read it if she wanted. He felt vaguely tainted or compromised, and he wondered if he'd had the wrong idea about Lauren all along. At the moment, at least, she didn't compare well with the woman he'd just mated with.

His lunch eaten, he faced the problem of the afternoon. In the morning he shopped, worked on his car, did cleaning, and, until a few days ago, took Renée to the clinic for her daily antibiotics shot; in the evening they ate and went to movies or watched TV. But in the afternoon he ran up against the same hopelessness that had afflicted him ever since he lost his job at WSNE. All he could find to do while Renée rested was read books. He'd consumed the novels of Thomas Hardy one after another, not really enjoying them but not stopping until even *Jude the Obscure* was under his belt. He'd since moved on to Henry James, for whom his mood of patience and suspended judgment made him an ideal reader. He especially liked *The Bostonians*, because James's Boston of the 1870s turned out to be inhabited by the same eternal feminists with whom Louis had marched in the big pro-choice rally in July, the same crackpots and dreamers who had funded Rita Kernaghan and come to her memorial, the same slippery journalists who were still trying to insinuate themselves into Renée's apartment by telephone. He began to forgive the chill of this northern city. He thought about the Brahmin blood running in his own veins. He watched himself being consoled by literature and history, and, observing how much he'd changed in one year, he wondered what kind of person he was ultimately meant to be. But there was still that hopelessness or sorrow right beneath the skin of his afternoons.

He woke Renée at five-thirty. Her temperature was low enough for her to consider going out, and by six they were on their way to Ipswich. The golds of the season and the hour were in the trees reflected in the contoured glass of cars on I-93. Through the few windows that weren't smoked for privacy, lone commuters could be seen hunching aggressively over steering wheels or talking about their lives on telephones.

"She wants to kiss me on the cheek," Renée said.

"Oh, you read that, did you."

"This is some southern species I don't understand."

"She's a nice person. Very mixed up."

"You pursue this topic at your own risk. You must know I'd be happier if you told me she's a total jerk. Her and her little breadbasket."

"What can I say? I'm embarrassed."

It was night when they reached Ipswich. The frame of the pyramid still squatted on the house on Argilla Road, silhouetted against the moon-whitened sky, but most of the aluminum siding had been removed. It lay twisted in piles by the circular drive. Extension ladders weighted down a pair of tarpaulins covering tools and stacks of lumber near the front door.

The lean, sophisticated woman of Brahmin stock who was Louis's mother ushered him and Renée into the living room and poured them drinks at the bar. Again buckets of money had been spent to repair the house, to demonstrate that wealth was stronger than any earthquake. Melanie's navy-blue dress had navy-blue buttons and padded shoulders and hugged her hips and thighs and knees. She'd visited Renée in the hospital, once, and hadn't seen her since then. She didn't fuss over her now. It was left to Louis to make her comfortable on the sofa.

"Before our brains get too clouded," Melanie said, "we have some business to discuss." She took an envelope from the mantelpiece. "This is for you, Renée. I think you'll agree that everything's correct here?"

Renée silently showed Louis the contents of the envelope. There was a personal check, made out to her, for the sum of six hundred thousand and ˣˣ/100ths dollars, and a receipt for the same amount made out to Melanie Holland.

"You'll notice I've dated it the thirtieth," Melanie said. "You'll recall this was the deadline we established. Louis, you've witnessed that she has the check in her possession?"

"Yeah, Mom."

"If you'll just sign the receipt then, Renée." Melanie held out a pen which Renée looked at blankly. "Or is something not correct?"

Silently Renée took the pen and signed the receipt. Melanie folded it in half, tucked it in the breast pocket of her dress, and delivered herself of a huge sigh. "Well. *That's* taken care of. Now we can relax a little. How are you, Renée?"

Renée raised her chin. She held the check in her lap like a handkerchief she'd been using. "Not too bad," she said.

"That's marvelous. You're looking so much more like yourself than the last time I saw you. I hope Louis is taking good care of you?"

Renée turned and looked at him as if she'd forgotten him until this mention of his name. She opened her mouth but didn't say anything.

"Louis, that reminds me of the other business I wanted to discuss. This is our *last* piece of business for tonight, I promise." Melanie gave a false little laugh. "I suppose you know I haven't been able to sell this house. I realize it's not simply my own personal misfortune that there isn't a buyer to be found between here and New Jersey for a house at last year's prices. I'm willing to accept the depression of the market in the Northeast and whatever loss that entails for me. Unfortunately, we had another little tremor up here last Tuesday. You can hardly blame me for being surprised. I know I wasn't alone in thinking we'd seen the end of all that. But no, there was another tremor. Fine. Perhaps there'll be more. Fine. But in the meantime—"

"Glad to see you've calmed down about this, Mom."

"In the meantime, Louis, I wondered if you and—Renée, too, of course, if she likes—would have any interest in staying in this house. It would be rent-free and very comfortable. If you're here, Renée, and you still want to work at Harvard, I realize it might be a longish commute. But the advantages, I think, are obvious. I can pay you a caretaker's fee as well, especially if you'd be willing to show the house to prospective buyers. You see, I can't help thinking it might lift your spirits to get out of Somerville. And of course the extra income and the savings on rent, Louis, as long as you're out of work and not sure where you're going . . ."

Louis looked around the room. In spite of himself, he'd expected to feel the presence of ghosts—a spirit named Rita, a spirit named Jack; the spirits of Anna Krasner and his father. They'd all haunted this living room when he was far away from it, especially when he was in Evanston. But now when he looked at the blandly replastered walls and stolid furniture, he knew he could wait as long as he wanted, and he'd still see only the empty present.

"You don't have to decide now," Melanie said.

"What?" He looked at her as if *she* were a ghost. "Um, I don't think so. But thanks."

"Well, think it over." She excused herself and went to the kitchen.

A silence fell in the unhaunted room.

"I'm surprised," Louis said. "I thought she'd be different."

Renée tugged on the ends of her check, making the paper snap. "I didn't." There was a pack of matches from the Four Seasons Hotel in the ashtray on the end table. She lit one and held it before her eyes until the flame licked her fingers. She blew it out and lit another one. She held it over the ashtray and pushed a corner of her check into the flame just as Melanie returned from the kitchen. When she saw what Renée was doing she began to lunge, instinctively, to stop her. But in the blink of an eye she'd caught herself. She crossed her arms and watched with impersonal amusement as the check took fire and dwindled to a warped black cinder.

"Well," she said, eyebrows raised. "I guess that's quite a statement."

"Let's forget it."

"Yeah, what's for dinner?" Louis said.

On the last day of the regular season the Red Sox clinched the division title and Renée's orthopedist pronounced her well enough to do whatever she felt like doing. She had been scheduled to begin work in New York on October 1 as a research fellow at Columbia, and Louis had urged her to go, provided she consider taking him along, but she had still been so incapacitated in mid-August, when the final decision had to be made, that she instead asked Harvard if she could stay on for another year. Harvard had been hoping all along to retain her and came through with an offer of an open-ended position as a post-doc. It wasn't as if Renée's feelings about Boston had changed. But somehow getting shot in the place and weathering its earthquakes and spending a month in one of its hospitals had given her a feeling of obligation towards it, a sense of belonging that she had lacked in her six years of normal life here. She didn't want to leave Boston on crutches. She also recognized that she was fully capable of hating any other place she went to just as much.

So they were both still in Somerville when the Red Sox were destroyed in the American League playoffs. After the first game, Renée couldn't bear to watch the carnage, but Louis didn't lose hope until the final inning.

Real life commenced for everyone in Boston on the morning after. Renée began to spend long hours at the lab again, and Louis, bored and broke, took a job at a Harvard Square copy shop. Every night he left work with his eyeballs parched by the heat of xerography. He dreamed about making change. He appreciated Renée's silence on the topic of what he was doing with his life. He was happy to be living with her, happy to be watching her regain her strength and seeing her enjoy the Algerian and Kenyan and American music he played her, happy to be learning more about her work and going out with her and Peter and Eileen and Beryl Slidowsky and the various damaged spirits he worked with at the copy place. He was so happy, in fact, that the less he liked his job, the more necessary it seemed for him to keep it. It was his way of clinging to the lump of sorrow he had inside him, now that he'd lost his conviction of his own rightness. For the moment, this sorrow was the only thing he had that indicated there might be more to the world than the piggishness and stupidity and injustice which every day were extending their hegemony. As much as he loved Renée, he knew that she was mortal; that he couldn't build a life on her alone, could not even be counted on to keep being good to her without some other anchor. He didn't know what form this anchor would take when he was older than the twenty-four he'd now turned; he didn't know if other people needed anchors; he suspected that Renée, in accepting her womanhood, had already found hers. He only knew that, for himself, it was necessary to go to work and serve even the arrogant professors and anal-compulsive artists and psychotic pamphleteers efficiently and temperately, to look them in the eye and thank them for their patronage, to write the date and the customer's name on receipts for forty-five cents, and to love the world in its materiality every one of the thousand times a day he pushed the Start button on the Xerox 1075. He saw that as a material thing himself he was akin to rocks. The waves in the ocean, the rain that eroded mountains, and the sand that would form the next epoch's rocks would all survive him, and in loving this nature he was doing no more than loving his own fundamental species, expressing a patriotic preference for existence over nonexistence. He felt that, if nothing else, he could always anchor himself on the rocks in the world. But this was a dim consolation. He hoped there would be some greater thing that his sorrow could lead him to. And so when he noticed that instead of alienating his co-workers he had become the friend and confidant of almost all of them, and that Renée was turning into a person who sometimes cried for happiness, he quickly looked inside himself and found his core of sorrow and clung to it tightly.

Eileen and Peter were married four days after Christmas. Shortly beforehand, Louis learned that his parents no longer lived together. This circumstance had come to light one night when Eileen called Melanie at eleven-thirty and spoke instead to a stranger, a man. Melanie had rented out her house on Argilla Road and taken an apartment in Back Bay, a not-inexpensive one with a view of the Public Gardens. She crisply explained to Eileen that the man was a high-school friend of hers, and did not elaborate. Subsequent prying on Eileen's part yielded the man's name (Albert Anderson), his line of work (radiation oncology), and his marital status (widower).

Melanie had raised no objection when Eileen and Peter decided to have Christmas in their apartment on Marlborough Street. Bob flew in from Evanston and stayed in their extra room, and Melanie and Louis and Renée came over on Christmas morning, Melanie with thousands of dollars' worth of clothing gifts for everyone. She and Bob evidently had some kind of understanding that allowed them to be polite to each other in public.

Whatever the understanding was, it broke down at the wedding three days later. Louis was with Eileen in the church parlor when she caught sight of Melanie. "She *promised* me," Eileen said, blood draining from her face. "She *promised* me she wouldn't wear that."

The offending outfit consisted of a backless green velvet cocktail dress of a cut such as makes men's jaws drop, a pair of green lizard-skin pumps, and a necklace of platinum and emeralds designed for wear in bank vaults only. Melanie smiled prettily at Eileen and gave a little shrug. Eileen erupted in tears while two of her bridesmaids held Kleenexes beneath her eyes to save her makeup. The entire wedding party heard the fight her parents had in the cloakroom, or at least heard the female side:

"I will not! I will not!

"And who do you think's paying for this wedding?

"To tell you the truth, Bob, I don't give a *damn* what you think."

Louis's timeworn advice to Eileen was "Fuck her. It's your wedding." Eileen seemed to understand this; at any rate she stopped crying long enough to exchange vows with Peter. Her best college friend and Peter's four sisters wore lime-green taffeta bridesmaid's dresses, while Louis himself, tuxedoed and mildly bewildered, served efficiently and temperately as Peter's best man. Renée sat with the distaff and continued to be a great hit with Bob Holland. She and Louis had taken dancing lessons in preparation for the reception, which was held in a ballroom at the Copley Plaza. Melanie charmed all comers, outshone the younger women and outdanced everybody, and not many people even noticed the bride's father sitting at the rear of the room in one of his fifties suits, smashing himself on scotch and imparting philosophy to Louis and Renée. He told them that he'd called Anna Krasner again and told her she was now the only person in the world who could confirm that Sweeting-Aldren had drilled a deep injection well. He'd told her that all the company's records and all of Renée's hard evidence had been destroyed. He'd told her that June's earthquake had left seventy-one people dead. She'd said, "I told you not to call me anymore."

He drank more scotch and said he still believed his wife would come back to him, in the fullness of time.

Absent from the nuptials, of course, was Peter's father. The government of St. Kitts–Nevis continued to resist American pressure to extradite the five Sweeting-Aldren executives, and it now appeared the men would never be brought to trial unless they were foolish enough to reenter the country of their own accord. Stoorhuys had gotten wind of his son's engagement—possibly from *The New York Times*, which carried the announcement, but more likely from his wife. On Christmas Eve the mailman brought Peter and Eileen an envelope with a Caribbean postmark and a hand-written message on its flap: *To Be Opened At Your Wedding And Read Aloud.* Peter chucked it in the trash.

In the spring there were two more weddings. The first—that of Howard Chun and Sally Go—took place in New York, and the Pleasant Avenue contingent was not invited. Renée heard about it afterward in the computer room, from Howard's second groomsman, Terry Snall. Terry said there had been a traditional Chinese banquet for more than two hundred people. He said it had been a very interesting cultural experience for him.

The second wedding, in late April, was actually just an afternoon reception at the Hotel Charles, Alec Bressler and Joyce Edelstein having tied the knot a week earlier in the Middlesex County courthouse. A sizable chunk of Boston's liberal elite turned out for the reception, plus a few of Alec's former DJs (who accounted for nearly all of the heavy drinking) and Louis and Renée. Joyce Edelstein twice broke away from well-wishers of her own class to put her arm around Renée and tell her she'd been dying to meet her and wanted to have a long talk; but somehow the conversation never happened.

Alec, however, had news for Louis.

"A new station," he said, leading him away from Renée. "Is a wedding present from the bride. FM 92.2. She agrees I have no politics, I agree I show profit after fourth quarter. Is an oral agreement we have. Profit means I do music in the daytime. I don't know music, it all sounds same to my ear. But then I have the nighttime for good programming. So, so, are you ready to work?"

"Me?"

"Music program to start with, also noose work or in-house ads. Your choice. Is only daytime hours, not bad, eh?"

"And a minimum wage and no benefits."

"So, OK, but only till fourth quarter. Then we see."

"This is very nice of you, Alec—"

"Not nice. Self-interest!"

"But I'll have to think about it."

Alec ducked. "Sink fast. I'm on the air June first."

The dance band was starting its third set when Louis and Renée left the hotel. It was such a fine day that they had walked to the Square in their party clothes. The sun was setting now, but its warmth still hung in the trees of Cambridge, along with the remains of kites and aluminumized balloons, hopelessly snarled plastic grocery bags, sneakers joined at the laces, tattered sweatshirts and streamers of magnetic tape, and with the trees' own green leaves. In the countryside north and south of Boston the forests were still gray, but a yellowness commenced in the far suburbs and grew to a pale green as Nature learned for better or worse to trust the warmth of civilization, until finally in the inner suburbs and the city all the foliage was out in force, and it was almost summer.

"Tell me why you even have to think about it," Renée said.

"Just because I have to."

"You don't think you've been making copies long enough? You think Alec's being too nice to you?"

"It means at least another year for you with Snall and Chun."

"As long as it's not forever, I don't care."

"Still have to think about it."

"Why won't you be happy? Why won't you let yourself?"

"What makes you think I'm not?"

"How can we ever live, if you're not happy? How can we think about, I don't know, having a baby or—"

"Baby?"

"Well, just for an example."

He stopped and stared at Renée. They were on the sidewalk

of the Dane Street bridge. "You'd consider having a baby with me?"

"I might," she said.

"You and me. We do the thing and you get pregnant and we have a baby."

"Don't you ever think about it? I could see doing it if we were both happy."

"Well . . . Huh!"

"Don't you ever want to with me? Don't you ever think about how we could already have one right now? How old she'd be right now? And who she'd look like? Aren't you ever sorry, even a little bit?"

He walked away from her, over the crest of the bridge and down the other side. He was reaching into the familiar place inside him, but what he found there didn't feel like a sorrow anymore. He wondered if it had really been a sorrow to begin with.

"Oh, what's wrong, what's wrong?"

"Nothing's wrong. I swear to you. I just have to walk now. Walk with me, come on. We have to keep walking."

ALSO BY JONATHAN FRANZEN

Jonathan Franzen

The Corrections

THE INTERNATIONAL NUMBER ONE BESTSELLER
AND WINNER OF THE NATIONAL BOOK AWARD

The Lamberts – Enid and Alfred and their three grown-up children – are a troubled family living in a troubled age. Alfred is slowly losing his mind to Parkinson's disease. As his condition worsens, and the Lamberts are forced to face the secrets and failures that haunt them, Enid sets her heart on gathering everyone together for one last family Christmas.

'A book which is funny, moving, generous, brutal and intelligent, and which poses the ultimate question, what life is for – and that is as much as anyone could ask.'
Blake Morrison, Guardian

'A novel as alive to the pressures of the present moment as any I can think of; a book in which memorable setpieces and under-your-skin characters tumble over one another to compete for attention . . . like the greatest fiction, for all its edgy satire and laugh-out-loud comedy, this novel is, above all, an exercise in generosity. Its subject is human frailty and the compensations we might make to hold lives together.'
Tim Adams, Observer

'A wonderful book. Every page simmers with wit, close observation and intelligence . . . as sharp and as telling an examination of family life and marriage to have been written in many a year.' John Burnside, *Scotsman*

'A novel of outstanding sympathy, wit, moral intelligence and pathos, a family saga told with stylistic brio and psychological and political insight. No British novelist is currently writing at this pitch.' Jeremy Treglown, *Financial Times*

Jonathan Franzen

The Twenty-Seventh City

'A novel so imaginatively and expansively of our times that it seems ahead of them.' *Los Angeles Times*

St. Louis, Missouri, is a quietly dying river city. But that all changes when it hires a new police chief, a charismatic young woman from Bombay, S. Jammu. No sooner has Jammu been installed, though, than the city's leading citizens become embroiled in an all-pervasive political conspiracy. A classic of contemporary fiction, *The Twenty-Seventh City* shows us an ordinary metropolis turned inside out, and the American Dream unravelling into terror and dark comedy.

'A huge and masterly drama . . . gripping and surreal and overwhelmingly convincing.' *Newsweek*

'Franzen has managed to put together a suspense story with the elements of a complex, multi-layered psychological novel . . . A riveting piece of fiction that lingers in the mind long after more conventional pot-boilers have bubbled away.' *The New York Times Book Review*

'Unsettling and visionary. *The Twenty-Seventh City* is not a novel that can be quickly dismissed or easily forgotten: it has elements of both 'Great' and 'American'. A book of memorable characters, surprising situations, and provocative ideas.' *Washington Post*

'Franzen goes for broke here – he's out to expose the soul of a city and all the bloody details of the way we live. A book of range, pith and intelligence.' *Vogue*

All Fourth Estate books are available from
your local bookshop.

For a monthy update on Fourth Estate's
latest releases, with interviews, extracts,
competitions and special offers visit
www.4thestate.com

Or visit
www.4thestate.com/readingroom
for the very latest reading guides on our
bestselling authors, including Michael Chabon,
Annie Proulx, Lorna Sage, Carol Shields.

London and *New York*